OMINOUS

K.V. ROSE

BOOK I

Copyright © 2021 by K V Rose

All rights reserved.

This is a work of fiction. Names, characters, places, and incidents either are the product of the author's imagination or are used fictitiously. Any resemblance to actual persons, living or dead, events, or locales is entirely coincidental.

No part of this book may be reproduced in any form or by any electronic or mechanical means, including information storage and retrieval systems, without written permission from the author, except for the use of brief quotations in a book review.

For more information, please contact authorkvrose@outlook.com

Cover design © Ashes & Vellichor (Ashlee O'Brien)

Edited by: Amy Briggs

*To anyone who has ever wanted to be forgiven.
To my favourite regret.
And to CJR. We've been through hell and back,
haven't we?*

PLAYLIST

Check out the playlist on Spotify. I literally cannot write without music, so those things mean a lot to me. If I wasn't a writer, I'd be a groupie.

AUTHOR'S NOTE

If you're looking for a reason, **there isn't one.**

I'm not really sure I'd call this a *romance*. I don't know exactly what genre it fits in. There are romantic elements, maybe. There's a bit of mystery, kind of. But mostly, this is a deep dive into lust, mental illness, and all those shadowy thoughts many of us are afraid to say out loud.

It's not a mental health handbook. This isn't told with a clinical eye. I tried my best to inject my own battle with mental illness into this book (in fictional ways), and everyone's experience will not be the same. Most mental health issues exist on a spectrum, and what's true for me or my characters may not be true for you.

It's certainly not a relationship guide. Many of you will read this after *Ecstasy* (which I highly recommend), and it isn't that book, either. Hell, you might find this boring, if you've read my other works. It might make no sense to you at all, and possibly, you'll hate it. But it's a story close to my heart, it's a passion project, and whatever your take, I appreciate you taking the time to read it.

Proceed with caution. If it is a romance, *it's a dark one.* I hope you enjoy.

PROLOGUE

Eden

Before

"YOU UNDERSTAND I would never do anything to hurt you, right, baby girl?"

I lift my head, my eyes locking on his dark green ones. I see the circle of black around his iris, shards of emerald glistening from the lights surrounding the pool. His icy fingers are splayed along my jaw, his thumb brushing over my mouth, and I don't realize the significance of this moment until he points it out.

"I think it's the first time you haven't flinched when I've touched you, Eden." There's a roughness to his words, like he's swallowing down an emotion.

My teeth start to chatter, and he smiles. His eyes rake down my body, clad in his sweatpants, the drawstring pulled tight. A hoodie, Trafalgar wrestling. Black, the letters are etched in an aqua blue. On the back, at the hem, is our motto just below a dragonfly.

Tempus edax rerum. Time devours all things.

Everything he owns overshadows me, and I used to worry

he would eclipse me entirely. I'd disappear behind him, and he wouldn't be able to find me. Or worse, he couldn't care enough to look.

Now, I'm the sole object of his affection, and I. Am. *Terrified.*

But soon enough, it will be over. And that is the best and worst thing about being so close to Eli Addison.

Time devours all things.

He glances past me, toward the sliding glass door of his back porch. Does he know his dad is coming? Eli hates when he leaves, but he really can't stand when he stays, either.

"Remember what we talked about that first night?" Eli asks, shifting his gaze back to me as he squats down at my feet, dropping his hand to my thigh. The sky is dark overhead, and I recall walking from the library after we first met, side-by-side. I remember thinking I had found someone who sees me.

I remember thinking I should run far, far away.

I was petrified. I think, on some level, he was too.

Our entire lives were about to change. *Would I take it back?*

He squeezes my leg, hard, as if dragging me back from inside my head. He's tried to work on that for quite a long time.

I'm on one of the patio chairs, and it swivels, my green Vans slipping against the bottom rung. I can turn easily, my fingers clenched tight around the cold armrests. North Carolina's Decembers shouldn't be this cold, but before the clouds set in, I watched little flakes of snow drift toward the pool, the cover still retracted this late in the season.

Glancing past Eli, I see the blue-green surface illuminated by underwater lights.

We spent a lot of time in there.

He would duck under, again and again, while I timed him holding his breath.

I tried it once, too.

The first time he invited me to his house, and he showed

me his favorite hobby, I was scared. For the very first time, something he did truly unnerved me.

Maybe that was all the start of the end.

"I won't die, Eden."

Bringing me back to this moment, another lifetime it feels like, he asks, "I think you might've been happy then. But you've just been low, haven't you?"

It's true. I have. I nod once, thinking of when I was high. When I could fly, and when we were both in the clouds.

Slowly, he turns away from me, staring at the glittering ink of the pool. I think this boy belongs in the water. If he ever does die, if he ever goes back on his word, it just might be the water that kills him.

His hand tightens again on my thigh, like he's holding on. Like I'm a lifeline.

But the problem is, I never signed up to be that for anyone, let alone Eli. Or maybe, at some point along the way I did, but now I understand, I'm so, so ill-equipped to handle just what it means.

I watch his jaw jump.

I wonder if I could convince him we'll get through this.

But inside my head, away from my heart, I know it isn't true. The proof is in the past few weeks.

Shattered glass. A psychotic laugh. The fight in Latin.

I feel a sick guilt at admitting I'm glad someone else saw.

Because Eli is unwell, and I am coming undone.

Maybe that's not quite right either. Because maybe, after everything we've been through, maybe after all of this… maybe everyone is wrong.

Maybe I do mean something to him, despite it all.

After

He woke something in me. I hadn't been asleep, really, but I had never dreamt either. He helped me do just that, and it was beautiful.

Until, somehow, the exhilaration made me queasy. The adrenaline spikes wore down my nerves. I took so many of my pills, not to hurt myself, but to help my heart. I was worried it wouldn't survive it. Him. *They were both the same thing.*

I was dreaming, and it was all a fucking nightmare.

"And empty words are evil."
- Homer, The Odyssey

Act 1

1

Eden

I ROUND THE AISLE, looking for Chaucer, when I see *him*.

The same boy from my Latin class. The one who sits in the front row, and has for three weeks, since the middle of August when we started at Trafalgar. Or rather, I started, and he's probably always been here, the way students and teachers alike seem to fawn over him.

Hair of onyx and ink, thick with the slightest wave hanging in his eyes.

He wears a choker around his throat, two inches wide, a strip of leather.

And right now, nearing nine o'clock at night, he's not in uniform. White sweats, white T-shirt, white, high-top Chucks. It would look stupid on anyone else, but it doesn't on him. Broad shoulders, taller than most of the students here, he's got a swimmer's build; lean, green veins snaking up his hands, over his wrists and forearms, to his biceps. I know he doesn't swim though. I've seen the wrestling hoodie on over his white dress shirt enough times to figure out his sport.

It's strange because he doesn't seem so… aggressive.

In the same vein, right now in this moment, a pale orange glow overhead illuminates him in softness, tuning down his features. But physically, his edges are sharp, and the lighting is a façade, just like the smile he wears in class.

There's something off about it, like it's rehearsed.

I turn my back to him, resigning myself to wait until he's meandered out of the aisle. In the meantime, I can scrawl out ideas about my British Lit essay, then checkout the book and go home, hoping Sebastian has finished his nightly routine in the bathroom so I can have a bath and relax.

I head toward the circular table tucked away at the far end of the cavernous library behind a section of Greek classics when I hear someone clear their throat.

I stiffen. My pulse picks up speed. It was a throat-clearing with a purpose. Meant to draw attention.

Dragging my gaze around the empty seats, the main aisle of polished marble, lined with sleek, dark shelves, and sculpted clay statues on the endcaps, I realize the sound was directed toward me. No one else is in here.

Slowly and with a dry mouth I turn around.

The boy has a book in his hand, splayed wide, and I refuse to think about how much attention I've spent focused on those hands in the early morning hours of Latin before everyone takes their seats. They're big, his fingers are long, but not too thick.

At night, when I'm alone under my covers, I've imagined his fingers inside of me, instead of my own. I devour porn and lately, I've imagined him devouring me.

I feel my heart racing, paranoid he could impossibly read my mind.

His lips are tilted upward into a small smile, and it's really the first thing anyone notices about him from this distance. Not his black hair, or his tall frame, not even the biceps beneath the sleeves of his shirt, how his clothes seem to fit *just right;* it's his mouth.

"Hi," he says. The first word he's ever spoken to me. I

wonder if he knows I sit three rows back in first period. Does he have any idea we have a class together? As many cumulative minutes as I've spent watching his ringed fingers curl around a pen, doodling in the margins of his notebook things I can't quite see, I'm hoping the answer is no.

He takes a few steps toward me, standing at the outer edge of the aisle and he snaps the book closed in his hand as he moves, slipping his other into his pocket.

"I'm sorry," he starts, not meaning it. "Were you leaving?" His voice is quiet. Even in class, in spirited discussions about the subjunctive, vowel changes, the *real* meaning of texts like the *Vulgate*—allegory or literal? Are you a Christian or a hellbound Atheist?—his volume is always low. Initially, I thought he was shy.

He's not.

I also thought he was born in another country, grew up there too. His words are *almost* accented. It's hard to explain the musical lilt to his voice, but it is certainly not Southern, the common dialect spread throughout Raleigh.

I quickly gathered the pitch of his voice isn't from any sort of timidity on his part, the way he garners adoration which he greets with charm wherever he goes. I personally think his voice is a way to draw people in so they step closer to him. It's almost as if I can hear it in his head, even right now, when he's trying to convince me to stay for whatever reason.

Come closer, he says. *I don't bite.*

My face heats the longer I don't answer him, a nervous habit, and sweat blooms beneath my arms. It's a curse to feel inwardly assertive, but every external tick of the trait I don't check off.

Still, I refuse to fiddle with my clothing. I resist the urge to pull at my cropped, black sweater or run my sweaty palms down the smooth faux leather of my high-waisted leggings. Besides, this outfit looks good on me. It shows off my ass and the smallest part of my waist. It's why I changed into it from Trafalgar's uniform after class.

My nerves, however, aren't settled with my own confidence.

While his clothes aren't more formal, I've quickly learned that doesn't mean much here. It's something I can't explain. A general refined and well-kept air I don't possess. As good as I want to feel in clothes like these, he could radiate an on-top-of-the-world confidence in a tarp.

I clench my hands into fists as I glance at the chipped black and silver of my nails and want to bury them into the flesh of my palms. I was in a hurry this morning from Sebastian taking up too much time in the bathroom and couldn't repaint them. Then there's a bandage wrapped just below the cuticle of my middle finger. Paper cut, on my sigil notebook.

But *this* boy lacks the dirty edges that come with Section 8 apartments, from my not-so-distant past. I assume he's got a mansion, no grants or need-based financial aid.

I don't hold it against him. We don't choose who we're born to, but I have always been afflicted with the desire for *more*.

"Soon," I tell him in answer to his question. Sweat pricks at the base of my neck as these thoughts race in my head. My hair is braided in a crown on my head, courtesy of my new neighbor, done last night while Mom was working.

Even still, up off my neck, it's so thick and heavy I feel dampness gather at the strands just above my spine. *Why am I always so hot?*

My pulse thuds too fast in my chest as this boy's eyes roam over my face, the polite smile still pulling at his mouth. I have tachycardia when I stand up too fast, and sometimes when I'm anxious, or nervous. A result of something minorly wrong with the valves in my heart, or maybe part of my anxiety. It's nothing currently life-threatening. I have beta blockers to slow my pulse if I need them, and interestingly, they're banned in archery, shooting, golf, and an entire list of sports I care nothing about. Swimming is the only thing I enjoy. It calms my nerves, but now we've moved from Wilmington, and I don't have access to the ocean.

I feel sweat slick beneath the dozens of black bands along my wrist, similar to the ones I earned as a kid when Mom put me in swim lessons. Only now, they've got nothing to do with swimming.

He doesn't know any of that.

I take a deep breath, slowly straightening, tipping my chin up to meet this boy's gaze.

He takes another step closer, the book held by his side, and I notice the way his shirt, starkly clean, is rumpled just above the waistband of his pants, a tiny sliver still tucked into them. Enough for me to see the outline of his abs, and something darker, too. A birthmark, maybe? A tattoo?

We wear uniforms during school hours, and I've never seen more than his arms and the strong column of his throat.

"How soon?" he asks me, tilting his head, his smile still affixed to his swollen lips.

Why are you talking to me? "I'm not sure."

"Well, do you mind if I sit with you?" he asks, indicating the cluster of tables by the back wall made of white bricks. I catch the gleam of rings on his fingers, silver and matte black, and I follow the gesture he makes with his hand, the one holding the book. The chandeliers hanging from the high ceilings cast everything in that orange glow, and almost nothing is its true color. Even the white wall looks muted, nicer somehow than it does when light streams in from the floor-to-ceiling windows on the side walls in daylight hours.

The pounding of my pulse grows louder in my ears.

"No," I tell him, because it's polite and he can sit where he wants. I'll be leaving soon regardless. Then, not wanting to endure the awkwardness that might come from him walking beside me the entire way to the tables, I turn my back to him—which feels dangerous somehow—and head to the table alone.

My stuff is scattered over it anyhow, so I reason with myself I'll have to clear it, which is a perfectly normal thing to do, even as my anxious brain screams at me I've just made a fool of myself by walking off without him.

I push the fear aside and pluck up three green highlighters, a green pen, and shove my notebook in front of one seat, instead of the two it was flipped horizontally between. Quickly sweeping off *Elements of Style*, *The Kybalion*, and my romance-filled Kindle from the table, I hide them in my bag. Yanking the checkered black and blue backpack from the padded wooden seat, I drop it to the floor. My hands are shaky, nervousness flowing through me, and I'm grateful I can finally sit, skirting around the table and dropping down as slowly and as gracefully as I can. Even so, my movements feel too big, my body too hot, and my thighs splay against the seat cushion, so I scoot myself up closer to the table, setting down my pens, all but one, for something to do with my hands.

I am five foot two, and yet I've always felt as if I take up too much space. Like, maybe if I was just a little more sophisticated, a little more polite, the world wouldn't mind me so much. But some days, my brain can be my worst enemy, and I don't think I'll ever be any of those things.

For a second, I think the boy hasn't followed at all. I heard nothing behind me, save for my own pulse in my ears, and I didn't once look up. Now, with no other choice, I do, and I almost flinch to see him standing across from me, the book still in his hand, his other curled around the back of the chair he's standing behind, veins stark against his tanned skin.

I crush my fingers around my pen, resting my wrist on the table and crossing one leg over the other, the faux leather of my pants swishing together with the contact.

"Don't worry," I say, glancing at him, then away, nerves tumbling in my veins. "I won't bite." *Hard*, anyway. My pulse skips a beat, and I'm pleased with my own bravado. "You can sit."

He runs his tongue over the underside of his teeth with interest as he stares at me, like he knows what I'm thinking. What I didn't say.

"I'm Eli, by the way." His voice is low and extremely polite.

"Yes, I know." *Everyone knows who you are, don't they?*

He holds my gaze, and I wonder if he's waiting for my name in return. I should give it, but I don't. The dark emerald of his eyes, the thickness of his lashes, flashbacks to fantasies I've had watching him in class…

Heat flares in my body. I drop my gaze. I need to check the time because my curfew is ten and I do really need to get the book I was looking for and—

Gracefully, every movement eloquent, he pulls back the chair and sits down, bending at the waist just slightly before he makes contact with the seat. I don't know how someone can make every move of theirs so fluid and ethereal. It seems a little unfair.

"Studying for our exam tomorrow?" he asks me, hand still on top of his book, the other in his lap. He curves a single, dark brow the same way only one side of his mouth tips into a smile.

I'm so busy staring at the unevenness of it, the way he's feigning politeness, it takes me a few, long seconds to process his question.

The heat in my body grows hotter. Sweltering. Trafalgar is a relatively cool campus inside. The library even colder. Sometimes I bring a hoodie, but tonight I left it in my locker and I'm grateful I did. If I'd had it on, I would currently combust.

"Exam?" We only have Latin together, and unless I've completely forgotten—

"Oh, sorry." Eli lowers his gaze to the table for a second, shaking his head. "I… I should've told you from the start. You're new to Ms. Romano's classes, right?" He peers at me from under long, thick lashes, like he's genuinely confirming and slightly embarrassed we're not on the same page.

Confusion brings me out of my nervous state. My grip relaxes a little on the pen and I'm no longer concerned I'm going to break it in half. "Yeah… and she didn't mention an exam." I would've remembered if she had. I need to ace every test here.

Eli sits up straighter, sighing as he does, like an apology in advance for what he's going to say. "She gives one every third week. Unannounced."

I pored over the syllabus for each course, and nothing about surprise tests were there.

Then again, I was only able to transfer my senior year because we moved from Wilmington, so maybe I'm the only one who doesn't know, and she just forgot about me.

"Relocation for employment," the admission's advisor jotted down with a swift, momentary glare at my mom that seemed to demand, *why couldn't you wait one more year for her to finish?*

We didn't discuss what happened at Shoreside High. I didn't have to disclose it. *It was only a suspension.*

Besides, I never asked Mom to wait. Reece got a new job at his brother's tech firm, able to take on Mom's share of the bills until she relocated her cleaning business too, and I was fine with leaving, after what happened at my old school.

Reece's brother mentioned Trafalgar, his Raleigh-based IT company hires some of the donors, and I applied with his reference.

My closest friend from Shoreside, Amanda, I've kept up with through texts, but they've died off, fewer and fewer every week. After what happened… I don't really want any reminders of the day I lost my mind.

The only thing I'm attached to is my dreams. Even those, some days, start to slip from my grasp.

"It's not too in-depth," Eli continues, and I can tell from his tone he's trying to soothe my nerves. It must show in my face how much these grades matter to me. I'm waiting until the cut-off to send in college applications solely so I can have straight As from Trafalgar and my AP classes lit up like a shiny beacon on my transcript, burying the shadows of my past school record. "Ten questions, max." His gaze searches mine as his fingers curl over the edge of the book he brought with him from the aisle. One of his rings is a skull. *How edgy.* "The way you read out loud in class…" Another lopsided smile graces his lips. "You're going to nail it."

My sarcastic thoughts aside, I feel lightheaded with his words. *When I read out loud in class…* It's my least favorite part of Latin, reading aloud. A dead language, I don't know why we even need to pronounce any of it, but Ms. Romano ensures we each have a turn every day we're in her class to speak it. I never knew Eli paid any attention when I read. I've never once seen him turn to look at me stumbling over the text.

I took Latin my freshman year of high school, back in Wilmington at Shoreside. A fluke, bizarre course only offered once, I was fascinated with it. It's how I managed to get into *this* Latin class, but my skills are poor. In fact, it's the course I study for most.

"What?" I blurt out, knowing now he's, for some reason, manipulating his way into my good graces with his compliment. A small laugh escapes my lips, and he tilts his chin up, his smile even wider. "I suck at reading out loud." The exam slips from my thoughts completely as Eli's dark green eyes, circled with a thin line of black, light up. I feel strangely proud of myself, like I'm the reason for his newfound pep.

Then I'm promptly annoyed I'm allowing myself to be sucked in.

"No," he tells me, dropping his gaze, those lashes *fluttering.* "You don't." He lifts his eyes then, and there's something disarming about his expression. Like he's nervous paying me a compliment. If this is an act, he's an excellent artist.

I grip my pen tighter again, overcome with a need to be distracted so I don't have to keep looking at him. It feels a little like looking at a lie. "Thanks," I mutter, ducking down to swipe my phone from the side pocket of my backpack at my feet. I straighten but keep my eyes down, checking out the time.

Nine thirty, which means I have fifteen minutes left here. If I come home late, I'm grounded. Doesn't mean much when I have few friends and fewer opportunities to socialize, but I don't like disappointing Mom. I've already done too much to her heart.

"I mean it, Eden."

It's the first time Eli's said my name, at least to me. I freeze, unable to avoid looking at his face any longer. As always, my gaze snags on his mouth. His lips are ridiculously full, pale pink, such a good color contrasted with his olive skin. I remember I shouldn't stare at his mouth, though, and of course my body flushes hot all over again. I guess I shouldn't be shocked he knows my name, considering he's confessed to listening to me read aloud in class, but it just all feels strange. Why has he never talked to me before? But I *am* always the last one to leave, mainly so *no one* speaks to me, and in the hallway, I have earbuds in my ears. I guess I'm unapproachable, and I like it that way. It keeps me out of trouble.

But how long has he been watching me? I shift a little in my seat.

I've studied you too, I want to tell him, but I clamp my mouth shut so I don't say all the things I'm thinking. *You have nice hands. Do you know everyone is drawn to you? Has it always been this way?*

Come closer, he might say.

Tell me when to stop, I want to respond.

I look at my phone again, flat on the table. "I have to go." I start gathering up my stuff, trying to force out a little poise, but I'm clumsy from my nerves, every movement awkward, nothing like the grace with which Eli slipped into that chair with. I close my notebook, nothing written in it about my Brit Lit essay at all, even though it's the entire reason I stayed late tonight. I got caught up in the bully romance I'm reading on my Kindle, until I decided I should work on Chaucer after all.

So much for that.

I drop my pens in the top section of my backpack, tugging the zippers of both compartments closed. I grab the bag, stand up so fast I knock my chair over, and hastily turn, red-faced, to right it, my hands shaky. I pluck up my phone, gripping it tight enough my hand aches, worried I'll drop it if I don't, and I'm thinking of walking out of here without saying goodbye because this entire show of me packing up my stuff has gone horribly.

Two thumbs down, Eden.

But just as my pulse thumps so hard against my ribcage I think I may need a beta blocker tonight to sleep, Eli stands, and his shadow casts over the table and me, as he says, "Oh, yeah."

Then he slides the book he's been carrying around my way, a gentle gesture, even as it reaches me.

For the first time, I read the title, at the same time he says it out loud.

"The Canterbury Tales."

A tingle of something runs down my spine. Nervousness? Unease? I can't place it, but Eli isn't even looking at me anymore. His gesture was casual, like it didn't matter. As if it was pure coincidence as he pulls his own phone from his pocket, and I see nothing on his screen but the time, and a solid black background. I might find it odd no one has texted him, called, no social notifications for a boy so adored, save for the fact I'm still stuck on the book.

We only have Latin together. He isn't in my English class, but this is the book I was originally looking for of Chaucer's. The one I completely surrendered because my nerves were shot by being the focus of this boy. I told my Brit Lit teacher just today the topic of my essay. *But Eli is not in there.*

Gingerly, I reach for the book, my mind on high alert. *Something is off about you, Eli Addison.*

Blinking, I grab the thick volume, full of scholarly notes and dissections, and I tuck it under my arm, phone in my other hand.

When I look up, his back is to me.

I see the muscles along his shoulders flex through his T-shirt as he glances over his shoulder, and his expression is almost daring me to ask how he knew.

Come on, he says. *Play with me.*

But maybe I'm misreading him, because when he speaks, it's not an encouragement to pick apart his motives, his actions with this book he shouldn't know I needed. "Did you park in the senior lot?" He doesn't even wait for me to answer, and I wonder if he already knows that too. "I'll walk with you."

I didn't park there.

I don't say it, because on some level, I'm worried he already knows. So, wanting to one-up him at this bizarre game, I simply answer, "Okay."

2

Eden

WE EXIT through one of the many side doors of the castle. It looms behind us, and I spare a glance at it. When I'm this close, I have to crane my neck back to see every gray turret, every windowpane glowing with moonlight.

The monstrosity of it, up close, overwhelms me. Even tucked away inside, there's this distant but unshakeable feeling it's whispering to me when I'm in its old hallways, the library I just left, or the athletic facility over eight thousand square feet, the one I've only seen on my tour.

You don't belong. Don't belong. Don't belong.

Eli doesn't look back at all. To him, it's probably inconsequential, this pale black, stone-washed building resembling a structure built hundreds of years before, even though it's relatively new. Eli could walk away from castles much grander without ever looking back. He is who these places were made for, so he could desert them at the earliest opportunity, only to move on and conquer something far greater.

We jog down the steps on the cement walkway, then more steps, the ground sloping gently down, the darkness of the night obscuring the green, rolling lawn. The most impressive view of Trafalgar is at the back, with well-maintained gardens, fountains, and the ability to see just how far this building stretches from the east to the west. But we pass a fountain now too, the only one out front, ironically placed by the library instead of the main entrance with its glossy red doors, towering high above me every morning, a poster of a missing girl I never met, Winslet Landers, taped to each door, blowing in every breeze, tattered edges curling in on themselves. I know Winslet wasn't taken from campus. I did a search of her name when I first saw it. She disappeared from her own home.

The fountain out front is a gargoyle with pointed ears, a scowl, and wings kept tight to his body, like he isn't quite ready to fly.

I can't relate. If I had wings, I would be long gone.

When we finally take the last step down, the music of the softly twinkling water at our backs, Eli breaks the quiet between us, his tone light, as if we haven't spent the past few minutes in a tense silence.

Maybe it was only tense for me.

"How are you liking it so far?" He glances my way without breaking his stride, the walkway seeming to stretch on for miles to the senior lot. Then, beyond that is the paved driveway leading to the high iron gates, always open as far as I can tell, with a guardhouse just past it.

"Trafalgar, I mean?" Eli clarifies with another regal clearing of his throat.

I blink in the dark, lampposts every few feet the only light. They're the same dull orange as the lights in the library, casting everything in a soft glow. I stare at the cars in the distance, not many of them, but every single one a luxury vehicle. Porsches, BMWs, Mercedes, I don't know what Eli drives. I've never actually seen him leave.

With that thought, I realize he doesn't have a bag over his shoulder, and I wonder if he takes any books home. Does he do his homework? Does he care at all, or is he content to let money pave the way for him, dollar bills like a golden highway to any future he chooses?

One day I'll have the same. *A gilded life.* The difference, I suppose, is I'll earn it. Maybe it'll feel better for me. Or, perhaps, it won't matter at all. Luxury is luxury, and poor is... *poor.*

"I like it," I say, meaning it mostly. If I keep staring ahead, ignore the feel of his eyes coming to me every so often, and the way he has to look *down* at me, because he is nearly a foot taller than I am, I can speak easier.

"No," Eli says, and he stops walking, his tone lower than I've heard it yet.

I stop, too, but I don't face him, even though his eyes on my body feel like a physical weight.

"How do you *really* like it?" He stresses each word, but there's slightly more emphasis on the "really."

With his pressing, I think of Sebastian, what I don't want to be. I think of him losing his job, just last week, the one he only held a month, since our move. I imagine the things I've taped to my wall. A printout of the Minoan goddess. A quote from *The Odyssey*—*out of sight, out of mind.* A postcard from Bloor College, nestled in the mountains, my attainable dream school.

I want to tell Eli it doesn't matter how much I *like* it. People like me don't get to pick and choose what we *like* and *don't.* We take what we can get. I want to tell him I want to be something, at the same time I'm terrified of leaving the bubble I've always known.

I think of Shoreside. The suggestion of therapy from the school nurse. How Mom would have given up anything to pay for it, but I refused. It seemed like a luxury, and we can't really afford those.

Even so, I want to tell him I'm feeling apathetic. It is a constant vice I cannot shake. I just can't help but wonder sometimes... *what's the point of anything at all?* My mind plays out every next move, each new goal, and the steps I need to get where I want to go, and yet I feel I'm missing things along the way. Joy, euphoria, the feeling of being alive, they're fleeting and sporadic for me. Do we just plan and search and wish until we grow old and perish?

I say none of it.

But I do take a breath, and turn to face him, only to find his entire body is already angled toward me. There is hardly any room between us, and I don't know how that happened, but my eyes crawl up from our shoes, a foot apart—white Chucks, black boots—to his legs, the shirt still tucked ever-so-slightly into the waistband of his pants, the dark shape—tattoo, birthmark?—beneath the white material leaving my head spinning, to his throat, with the choker of solid black leather around it, then his jawline, straight nose, tipped slightly upward, almost feminine.

Finally, I rest on his eyes.

Although "rest" isn't right. His eyes are full of intensity even his casual posture, hands in pockets, slightly parted lips, can't conceal. In his charade, it's the look in his eyes which ruins his acting. He's not relaxed. Maybe more than me, but not really. He's *tense*.

It helps me feel as if he's not quite so high above me.

I give him a better truth than my first answer to his question. "I like this school." I run my tongue over my lips, and I watch as his eyes track the movement. "But I have no expectation of falling in *love* with it. It's a steppingstone." My chest flushes hot with the word "love," and I'm glad my shirt covers me even as a breeze dances on my exposed low belly.

He doesn't laugh, or smile, or mock me. Holding my gaze, he only says, "Because you don't belong here, do you?"

Cold runs down my spine, prickles along my scalp as I stare up at him. "What does that even mean?" I should never have entertained this conversation. He wants to mess with me for whatever reason. Maybe see if he can get into the poor girl's pants. But the answer is no. I could've told him from the start. My fantasies stay inside my head. I never trust myself to let them out. Not anymore.

He sighs, like he didn't expect me to understand, and his shoulders drop just slightly. It's the most basic change in his posture, but it's the first time he looks *less than*. He steps closer, but looks up, away from me, and if he hadn't, I would have had to back away. Put more space between us.

Instead, I'm staring at the elegance of his throat. The way the choker lies flat with his skin but doesn't pinch. It fits tightly enough I know he feels it, always a constant pressure, but it won't leave an indentation. I wouldn't be able to slip my little finger between the leather and his neck though. Not without hurting him.

The idea is mildly appealing.

"I can tell," he says quietly, almost as if to himself. "Every day you walk into class, there's something in your face. Like… you're not quite sure what you're doing here. Like no one will ever come close to understanding your thoughts, your brain, and you hold yourself so apart, you don't even want them to, do you?" He still doesn't look at me.

I take a deep breath, catching the scent of the beach. *He smells like the ocean,* and I am *intimately* familiar with the fragrance. But this—deep, intense conversation with a stranger —it's foreign to me. I feel as if my brain may be tricking me again.

"How long did it take you to rehearse that?" I counter, lifting a brow.

He slowly smiles, dropping his gaze, almost to affect a bashful look. It's complete when he peeks up at me through his lashes, a dimple flashing below his cheekbone. "Tell me I'm wrong." His words are barely more than a whisper. He's good, with his deep sentiments, but it feels like it's part of his act, and I'm the willing thespian, getting sucked into his play.

"Of course I don't belong," I say with a touch of annoyance. "I'm not like… *you.*"

I'm thinking of stepping away when he lowers his eyes to me, intently focused on mine, pinning me to the spot, I couldn't get away if I tried.

"You're not at all, are you?" He practically whispers the words.

I pull my bottom lip between my teeth, biting hard for a second. But I can't hold back. "What is that supposed to mean?"

He smiles and it flusters me more. "I know you're here with scholarships and," he gestures vaguely like money is trivial, before slipping his hand back into his pocket, "financial aid."

I freeze, my fingers squeezing the phone in my hand, the book in the other. I glance down at my shirt, wondering if my clothes gave me away, their lack of polish, the years of wear. And I'm only here because Reece's brother has connections; he helped me get a leg up. But I don't really belong, do I?

"Shit, sorry," Eli cuts through my ringing ears, the mortification at being found out. "It's not..." He trails off, cupping the back of his neck with his hand, his bicep flexing, and I see a tattoo there with script I can't read before he drops his hand.

The corners of his mouth turn down in something which isn't quite a frown. More like he's puzzled as he looks over my head, like he's searching for the right words.

"It's not your clothes," he finally says, looking at me again. His eyes drop over my body.

I hold my breath, waiting for him to tell me what it *is*, if not my outfit.

"I saw your files." He doesn't look remorseful over the words, even as cold floods my body, the distant feel of arousal at his admiration draining away. *How? When?* "On accident." He doesn't hurry along, the way someone truly embarrassed about seeing something they shouldn't would. This is where his charade breaks down, and I don't know if it's intentional or not. "You had just left, I think, the first day of classes, and I was in Ms. Corbin's office, going over some paperwork."

What kind of paperwork could you possibly need? Don't your parents just cash checks without missing the weight from their balance, and you move along?

I don't say anything though. I let him keep going, because

this requires some sort of explanation if he wants to keep up his cover.

"Your files were there, on the corner of her desk. Then you were in Latin, and Ms. Romano called your name, and I put it all together—"

"Why didn't you say anything to me before now?" I feel unnerved. *Found out.* I hold his gaze this time, and he doesn't blather on about my files or not *belonging.*

"You're in your own world, aren't you?" His tone is almost accusing, this reason for how I *look* like I don't belong. It's like he's flinging charges my way, ready to hold me accountable for operating on a different plane than everyone else.

My stomach drops. Maybe not everyone else. *Maybe him.*

He leans down, almost imperceptibly. Not too close but close enough I feel my heart racing all over again, adrenaline flooding my body, a stiffness in my limbs.

Don't touch me.

It echoes in my head, at the same time another contradictory thought bounces around.

Touch me, so I can see if I hate the way you feel like I do everyone else.

"It looked like a nice world," he continues, and I can smell his breath. It isn't mint, like I thought it might be. He seems like the kind of guy who's polished enough to have a stick of gum in his pocket at all times. But his breath is sweet. Cotton candy. It's ridiculous.

"I didn't want to ruin it."

Lines from a poem. Words he can't possibly mean. Where did he find them? What does he want from me?

He straightens, and the moment of tension in my veins is snapped too soon. He even takes a step back, letting me breathe deeper, and nods his head toward the parking lot. *He is very good at this.* "Do you need a ride?"

I blink, disoriented at all the things he knows. All the things he shouldn't.

I have a car, a ten-year-old Sentra Mom put her Christmas

cleaning bonuses together for. I hold out on the hope that is one thing he does *not* know, because it would be too much. It would take observation to the level of stalking. I need to stay away from those things, for my own good. Away from... *obsessions.*

Either way, what I *don't* have is a parking spot.

A single one is an additional thousand dollars, on top of tuition and books and uniforms. The grants and aid wouldn't cover it. It was stretched too tight as it was, like hide over a too-big drum, the circumference too wide, my dreams tumbled inside, and Mom is too proud to ask her brother-in-law for more than he's given us.

I realize I'm staring at Eli's mouth again when I shake my head and look at my phone screen. I need to leave. It takes fifteen comfortable minutes for me to get home from here, and I have exactly that many. We aren't even at the parking lot yet and Sebastian isn't on his way. *Shit.*

I unlock my phone and start typing out a text to Sebastian, all one-handed, *The Canterbury Tales* in my other.

I've got *Can you* typed out on my screen when Eli clears his throat. Again.

I pause, my thumb hovering over the keyboard as I lift and narrow my eyes on his.

"I don't mind." He says this as if it's all I need. The permission I'd been waiting for. Like if he doesn't mind, nothing else matters. Another slip in his mask.

An emotion aside from embarrassment wells up inside me. *Hostility.* "Well, I do." I snap the words out and I don't really mean to, but he's thrown me off balance. Knocked me sideways. I can barely stay upright with his hurricane. "I don't know you, and my parents wouldn't want a stranger to take me home." The last part is a lie because I would tell them it was only a friend.

Still, I hold his gaze in a challenge. I expect him to cut me down for being rude.

But he doesn't bite back.

"Ride with me, Eden." He turns away from me, angling himself toward the parking lot. *Come closer. I don't bite.* "I'll just wait here for someone to pick you up otherwise, and that would be a waste of both of our time."

"That's your problem." I drop my gaze to my phone again. "I don't need a—"

I sense him turn back to stare at me. Lifting my eyes slowly, they lock with his. "I get it. You don't *need* a ride." He smiles, the dark green of his irises morphing to something more like emeralds. "Indulge me, just this once?"

"I think you're probably *indulged* every day of your life." But I don't keep typing out my message to my brother.

His smile widens. "Maybe," he agrees. "But not by you."

HIS HAND IS ON THE SHIFTER, ALL FOUR BLACKED-OUT windows of the matte black G35 cracked to let the warm summer air in. My dream car is Italian, something Sebastian pointed out to me in a magazine one day, but I find it a relief Eli drives this instead of one of the many BMWs or Mercedes in the lot.

I clutch my bag close to my chest, arms wrapped around it, and I try not to stare at the way his veins ridge against his olive skin. How his palm covers the entire shifter knob, his fingers curled over it. The skill with which he doesn't miss a gear, no danger of stalling out as he drives.

Glycerine by Bush is loud through the speakers, and it might seem rude to some people, the volume turned up enough to drown out any hope of a conversation, but it is exactly what I want. And I love this song.

He glances my way, dash lights glowing across his cheekbones and the straight ridge of his nose. A smile curls his mouth, and I don't want to return it out of some misplaced spite—*you have everything I want, including me in your passenger seat. I've given in, and now I'm not sure how I could climb out*—but I can't help it. I try to bite back my own grin, but it's impossible. He might be deceptively charming, but there's no denying the allure.

And just as he looks at the road again, his lips hitch higher, and mine mirror the movement. I'm kind of annoyed with myself by how easily he won me over.

But only for tonight. Just this once.
And yet… who am I kidding?

I'm in a car with a boy I have stared at for nearly three weeks of class, thinking he never even glanced at me. Never once saw me out of the corner of his eye. Heard me speak up in class.

Turns out, he knows my name *and* my financial status—and he's going to find out more, unfortunately, when he follows the directions I gave him when we first got into the car.

More than those shallow facts, he knows the way I feel alien in my own brain.

Dangerous. A guy like this could make me falter. Return me to where I was, that moment I barely remember when I got suspended, then had to live out the rest of the semester with my head down while everyone whispered around me.

But I push it aside, getting ahead of myself as I usually do. I focus on the now. The drive. The upcoming drop off. *Real things. Not fantasies.*

I contemplated having him leave me at the gas station half a mile from my house. I wanted to protect something of my dignity, because seeing my dusty road through his eyes—watching the LED headlights illuminate Mom's pale green van, Reece's battered truck, Sebastian's Mazda 6 with a busted taillight, and my old, turtle-like Sentra, all crowded together on the cloud of dirt that serves as the driveway to the trailer—seemed like too much.

But he would know I was hiding something. Worse, he'd understand I was self-conscious.

I'd rather pretend I'm proud of my home. Or, at the very least, unaffected by it.

When he makes the final turn onto Castle Lane—the irony is not lost on me—then pulls into the driveway of the first trailer on the left, his car bumping over the uneven ground and spackling of rocks Reece intended to use to make a proper driveway, he doesn't pretend to love my place.

He doesn't remark on the gray siding, the screen door I know sticks; he doesn't even try to spin the yard into something worthy. And it *does* have a decent yard around back. Hardly any grass grows in the front, but there's a lot in the rear, and beyond it, forest stretches on for miles. I've lost myself in there some afternoons, and it's my favorite part of this place.

But instead of any of that, edged out at the end of the driveway by the rest of my family's vehicles, he says after turning down the volume, with some sort of wonder in his words, "Wow. You have a lot of cars."

And even though it could be a way to make me feel less shitty about what I don't have and what he probably does, I survey the driveway. Four sets of wheels.

I guess we do.

Still, I only make a noncommittal noise in the back of my throat as I undo my seatbelt, savoring the swift zip of it across my body before it lodges firmly in place somewhere near my head.

"Thanks for the ride." I glance at the clock in the car. He must have driven fast, and I either didn't realize or didn't care, because I have three minutes to spare. I reach for the silvery cool handle of his door, grateful it opens on the first tug without some complicated child lock shit, and I swing one foot to the ground, the car very, very low.

"I can take you home any day." He sounds almost hopeful.

I keep staring at the trailer, the single light on in the living room I'm to flick off when I get in. Mom will be trying to wait up for me to ensure I'm safe, and I feel a little guilty, knowing after cleaning three houses probably the size of Eli's, she's got to be exhausted.

"It's okay," I tell him, trying to keep my tone even. I think he has wrestling practice, preseason workouts or something; I've heard him talking about it in the hallways. And besides, I don't stay after every day, and some nights I work at the gym. Not many during the school week, but occasionally. He probably doesn't know about that job. Or jobs in general.

I know I'm judging him, but I can't seem to stop because I feel like there should be some catch to being offered his kindness. Like he's going to demand a blowjob the next time I see him or something. It's not as if I haven't fantasized about it, but I'm not giving head for rides home. I don't suppose I'd be very good at it, anyway, considering I've never done it before. *No ride for you today, that was sloppy.*

I almost laugh at myself, but instead I put another foot out, scooting to the edge of the leather seat, the scent, alongside his smell of the sea, invading his clean car.

"No, really." There's something like impatience lining his words. "If you need a ride, anytime, just... well, you'll see me around, right?"

I look at him over my shoulder. "I don't know. You pretended I didn't exist for nearly a month."

His hand is still on the gearshift, his other around the bottom of his steering wheel. But at my words, he looks perplexed. "I thought I told you why. You're unapproachable." His eyes glance over my entire body, and I think I might melt his seats, as hot as I am. "But tomorrow, I promise, I'm doing it anyway. Approaching you." His cheekbones lift with his smile. "Have a good night, Eden."

I let myself drink him in two seconds longer than I should. Then I'm out of the car. I'm slinging my bag over one shoulder, slamming his door closed with my free hand, a little harder than I intend to, when a searing, bright and violent pain lances up my middle finger.

"*Fuck!*" The word rips from my mouth, low and hushed as I snatch my finger from the door I just closed it in. My backpack slips from my shoulder and to the dirt as spots pop in front of my eyes, and I'm clutching two fingers in my opposite hand, squeezing tightly to stop the flow of blood and therefore, the pain.

It tapers off almost immediately, a dull throb underneath the Band-Aid I already have wrapped around my papercut. I don't know if my pain tolerance is high, or if I'm going to lose the tip of this finger because I'm squeezing it so hard, but my breathing evens out in a few seconds.

Until.

Until I realize Eli is right beside me, his car dinging to let him know he left his driver's side door open, little lights glowing inside.

"Let me see," he says, reaching for my hand, and I don't want to let go of it, the way I'm suffocating my own circulation, and I don't really want him to touch me, but he does it anyway.

His skin is cold, and I flinch with the feel of it as he pulls my hand, tucked close to my body, toward him.

"Really," I try to fight him by stiffening my muscles, "it's fine."

His eyes come to mine in our tug-of-war with my hand, staring up at me through his long lashes. Amusement ticks at the corner of his mouth. "Then let me see," he says again, his words flat.

After several seconds in our standoff, I release my grip on the wound, slapping my palm over the side of his car to keep myself steady, right above the door jamb that just tried to break my finger.

My body locks up, knees stiff so they don't tremble, and it feels as if there's sandpaper over my flesh, with both of his hands cupping mine. He has calluses along his fingertips and the edges of his palms, but it isn't what makes my skin crawl. I don't know what it is, about being casually touched, but I don't like it. Not at all.

Or maybe I do know. Maybe I just don't like to think about it.

I try to breathe in through my nose, out through my

mouth, staving off the impending panic attack which will be far worse than slamming my finger in the door.

Gently, as if he's caring for a wounded bunny instead of a very tense girl, he coaxes my knuckles out, to straighten, and he runs his thumb very carefully over the underside of my middle finger, pausing at the Band-Aid, frayed at the edges. I imagine even his medical supplies are far superior to mine and I clench my teeth, my pulse erratic.

I just want to run to my front door.

But I can't move.

He continues running his thumb over the sticky soft feel of the covering, then his eyes lift once more to mine. I can feel my heartbeat in my finger, but I can feel it everywhere, so I'm not sure it really means anything.

"You're bleeding." His words are little more than a whisper.

"Good thing I've got a Band-Aid," I say through a locked jaw.

He shakes his head, huffing a sigh of a laugh. It's enough to make me wonder what the full thing sounds like. But that thought is obliterated as he brings my fingers up, toward his mouth.

My lips part, just like his do, and fire courses through me, telling me to pull away. To snatch my hand back and fucking run.

Don't let him get this close.

It's bleating in my brain, firing on all cylinders. I can't even hear the dinging of his car anymore. The hairs on the back of my neck raise and all I want to do is get away.

But before he does what I thought he was going to do, he stops, my fingertips inches from his mouth.

He looks down at me through his lashes, and he says, "I think this means something, you know." And without elaborating, he slowly lowers my hand, releases it, and swipes up my bag, slinging it on his shoulder. Casually, as if nothing just happened, as if I'm not trembling everywhere, he turns toward my tiny porch, the three steps leading up to the door, content to ignore the ding of his car. "I'll walk you up," he says, not even looking back.

IN THE DARKNESS, I CLOSE MY EYES AND SINK DOWN UNDER THE water, holding my breath as I go. A single candle flickers on the counter, a mere foot from the bathtub, but down here, shower curtain pulled closed and eyelids blocking out any light, I can't see it.

Down here, everything is calm.

The faucet is off, the water is boiling, my fingertips graze the bottom of the tub.

In my head, I see Eli's dark green eyes.

Come closer. Come closer. Come closer.

A shiver of fear slips under my spine, my nipples tighten into sharp points, and I think, perhaps, I should come up.

Just a little longer. I can be unafraid.

Sebastian is home, one wall away. If I need anything, I know I can go to him.

Eli's mouth over mine. His fingers wrapped tight around my throat.

My hand drifts over my low belly, desire coiling inside. Then I think I hear something. The picking of a lock. A man's footsteps inside the small bathroom.

I shoot up to the surface, gasping for air as I twist around to the ledge of the tub, snatching back the curtain.

I blink in the flickering candlelight. Shadows dance along the wall.

The door is closed.

No one is there.

AFTER I DRAIN THE WATER, BLOW OUT THE CANDLE, TOWEL OFF and pull on my pajama shorts and top, brush my teeth, and wash my face all while avoiding looking into the mirror, I open the bathroom door.

And clamp a hand over my mouth to stop the scream from bubbling up my throat. A strangled gasp comes through instead when I see a shadowy figure in the hallway.

"Jesus, it's just me."

My chest is heaving, my phone clutched tight in my hand, I slide my palm away from my mouth, down to my throat as I try to breathe, try to see.

Slowly, in the dim glow from the light of his bedroom, his features come to light. Shaggy blond hair, light eyes, a lip ring, T-shirt and gym shorts over his short, bony frame. Sebastian is only a few inches taller than I am.

My breathing evens out, but my heart still races.

"Maybe don't take baths in the dark?" His tone is condescending. I can smell cigarette smoke and maybe something stronger on him. "I gotta pee."

"Yeah, sorry," I manage to say, edging around him toward my bedroom. When my shoulder brushes his, he speaks again.

"Who dropped you off?"

I freeze, staring into the shadows of the hallway, Mom and Reece long asleep. "A friend," I manage to say.

Sebastian is quiet as we stand shoulder-to-shoulder. Then he says, his voice low, "Don't let them distract you." And he walks into the bathroom without another word.

3

Eli

I WATCH her mom hug her in the mint green minivan she always arrives to school in. Even from here, I can see the thick, ugly scar along the back of her mom's arm. I wonder where it came from; if Eden saw her get it. With the thought, I feel the ache in my shoulders, along my solar plexus.

Partly from wrestling, partly from Dad.

I shake the thought as I watch Eden. One of the few students at Trafalgar to be carpooled, and I think she knows it, the way she closes the door quickly and trots off without a glance back, her slender fingers wrapped around the straps of her bag, the dozens of black bands on her wrist slipping down her arm.

Beside me, Dominic nudges my knee with his, the two of us sitting together on one of the stone tables in the courtyard, the September sun blocked by thick, gray clouds. "There she is." Lust is thick in his words. Smoke curls from between his teeth, his wrist resting on his knee, cigarette dangling from his fingers, the scent of nicotine heavy between us.

"You're a pig," Luna snaps from behind me. I hear Janelle,

beside her, sigh heavily. A few people call out to us on their way up the stone steps to the double red doors at the entrance, both propped open, missing posters for Winslet Landers curling at the edges, taped to both doors.

Dom waves back to our so-called friends, mainly people on the swim team, for him, and wrestling, for me. "Baby, I'm not interested," he responds coolly to Luna, dropping his hand and elbowing me with a grin. "But *Eli* is."

I glance at him, his dull blue eyes glassy from what he smoked before he drove to school. He takes a drag from his cigarette, and I imagine putting the cherry out on his pale temple. He asked if I'd seen the "weird new girl," told me about the way she pronounced *"The Canterbury Tales"* in class yesterday. *"I want her lips wrapped around my dick while she tries to say it three times fast."*

I let him know she's in my first period. Latin.

I shouldn't have said anything. That one sentence alone tipped him off. *"You wanna fuck her, don't you? You never notice anyone, man."*

He's wrong, but Dominic is wrong about a lot in life.

Luna reaches between us, jerking Dominic's black tie and yanking him toward her as he twists around, a smile on his lips. "I only share you with Eli," she says, and I can see her knuckles blanch white with her grip, but I keep my eyes on Eden. *"No one else."*

"I really think you both need to see a therapist," Janelle says lightly, and I know she's talking about Dom and Luna, because she's aware I *do* see a therapist.

Luna laughs, a loud, sharp sound as she releases her sometimes-boyfriend and Eden heads up the cobblestone walkway, closer to us, her dark hair coiled into braids on top of her head. I want to take all the pins out, tangle my fingers in her long strands. Looking at her is like looking at sin.

"I don't trust anyone that much," Luna declares.

I arch a brow, unseen by my friends. *If she only knew all the secrets that keep Dominic up in the night.* But I don't say anything because I have secrets of my own.

And as Eden walks by, her hips swaying, the fabric of her uniform pants pulled tight around her round ass, I still keep quiet. She's either oblivious to me sitting here with my friends, or she's pretending to be because she's nervous. I think I know the answer when I see the corner of her cherry red lips pull into a slight smile, her platform boots clomping up the three steps perpendicular to the table I'm sitting on.

Don't worry, baby girl. I'll chase you.

Eden

I approach the open doors of Trafalgar and feel the A/C from inside wafting toward me. The perspiration coating nearly every inch of my skin is thankful for it. It's overcast, but *hot.* With Eli's and his friends' eyes on me back there in the courtyard, I feel even hotter.

As I've done every morning since I've started, I look at the poster for Winslet Landers. Her photo is in black and white. Long blonde hair, smiling, wearing the uniform of Trafalgar, but the edge of the paper is rolled up, over the top half of her face.

Goosebumps erupt on my arms. The urge to look over my shoulder is strong, like someone could be stalking me. Like I could be Winslet.

Like Eli isn't harmless.

Then again, I've always been a little paranoid. My imagination can be... damaging.

I realize I've been staring at the missing poster too long when someone jostles me, and I move my feet, entering the foyer and trying to breathe as I focus on the interior of Castle Hall.

It's never too thick and crowded here, even at the start of school. There's a lot of movement, a flurry of laughter, finding friends, slamming lockers, shoes squeaking along polished wooden floors, but it's not like my public school. There, thirty students in a classroom weren't against code, and it took half an hour to move through the masses in the commons. Despite the crowd, I was anything but invisible at Shoreside in the end. People I'd been friends with my whole life whispered behind my back.

I could feel their eyes on me like living things, no matter how far I used to pull my hood over my head. Now, I don't hide as much. I'm just *sharper*, so nothing can touch me.

And here I can breathe, and I do, inhaling the dusty, transport-you-back-in-time castle scent, the musk of bricks and boys spritzed with cologne, the cleaner used on the floors. I move through the common area, four white columns of brick staking out the points of the crossroads in the hallway. There are so many blue-green and black plaid skirts in here, I'm very aware of my thighs touching in my black pants.

After stopping by the bathroom to check my reflection in the mirror, I duck into room 242, forcing myself not to search every chair for Eli. Most of the seats already full, I head to the back, replaying the various conjugations of "to bury" in my head over and over to prepare myself for the quiz he warned me about.

I drop my bag down, take a seat slowly, and pull out my dark blue pen, matching notebook, and our red textbook before I lift my head, the students chatting around me a nice distraction from straining to hear a distinct voice.

When I look up, determined to plant my eyes on Ms. Romano, to not let them jump around and find a black-haired boy with a pretty nose, I immediately lose.

Three rows up, my gaze taking in the tie around his neck, just below the choker, Eli is turned around in his seat, his eyes on mine. He's smiling at me, even as a girl to his left calls out his name, her head propped on the arm on her desk, and annoyance in her tone as she says, "Eli," for the fourth time and pops her gum.

He lifts his hand in a wave to me, moving his fingers as he does. It takes me a second, but finally I feel compelled to wave back. His gaze drops to my hand, and I glance down at my freshly painted matte black nails. Then, I see what it is he's looking at.

The damn Band-Aid.

This is what makes me blush, because of course it does.

I raise my eyes, and he winks at me, then turns to the girl beside him, who doesn't spare me so much as a blink.

I sit up a little straighter, aware a few heads swivel my way, having seen our interaction as Ms. Romano clears her throat at the front of the room.

Even as I duck my head, my teeth dent my bottom lip to bite back my smile. I have to fight the urge the entire way through the seven question pop quiz, lecture, and reading two paragraphs out loud.

As I flip the page in our textbook to finish the last sentence, I risk a peek at the front row.

Eli has his head propped on his hand, elbow on the desk, his body twisted toward me, sleeves of his white dress shirt rolled up over his forearms, a smile on his lips.

I catch sight of a green vein, one arm draped over the back of his chair.

Somehow, even as my pulse quickens, I don't stammer across the words I looked away from.

I take my time leaving. Everything is in slow motion, from the way I pick up my pen to the long seconds it takes to zip up my backpack.

The only thing moving fast is my pulse.

Don't wait for me, don't wait for me, don't wait for me.

I saddle my bag on my shoulder, shake down the black

rubber bracelets on my wrist, ensuring the three letters nestled among my veins are covered, but despite how I take deep breaths and drag out the time, I don't need to scan the room to know he's waiting. I can feel his presence, and a second later, a question piercing the air confirms it.

"Is there something I can help you with, Eli?" Ms. Romano sounds vaguely disinterested, but her voice is a touch lower than usual. She's used to my dawdling. She's not accustomed to… whatever is happening right now with Eli.

I find him staring at me, bag on his shoulders, arms folded over his chest as he half-sits on his desk. "No, Ms. Romano, I'm good."

Shit.

Out of the corner of my eye, I see our Latin teacher shuffling papers, gazing at me above the rim of her reading glasses.

Her eyes flicker to Eli.

Then back to me.

"May I speak to you for a minute, Eden?"

Surprise bolts through me, and I start to wonder if, despite my studying, I failed the pop quiz. I glance at Eli, but he only smiles, and doesn't move.

I slowly approach Ms. Romano's desk, sweat dripping down my back with nerves. She keeps her eyes on the papers she's shuffling, her red-tipped nails catching my eye, her straight, dark A-line bob hiding the severity of the angle of her jaw.

"Your quiz," she says, her voice betraying nothing.

I squeeze the straps of my bag tighter. If she tells me right here, right now, with Eli watching, I failed, I might flip this desk over between us.

Slowly, her light brown eyes lift to mine, and she stops fucking with the papers. "You aced it."

Relief is warm in my veins, and I take a breath, for the first time since I'd been standing here, I realize.

A slow smile curves Ms. Romano's thin lips. "What colleges are you applying to?"

I bite the inside of my cheek, aware Eli is listening. "Bloor," I say, my voice a little hoarse. "I want to major in Classics."

She arches a perfectly manicured brow, lifting her chin, her hair falling away from her face. It feels as if she's searching for something. I'm worried she won't find it.

But then she says, "And so you will." She waves one hand, dropping her eyes back to her papers. "You may go."

I can't stop the wide smile on my face with her words. I feel a little dazed, but I manage to keep myself together as I turn to face Eli.

The smile on my face is almost reflected on his. A little more subdued, but it's there.

I try not to get sucked in.

"What's your next class?" he asks, straightening when I pass by, saying nothing about his tip last night, helping me with the damn quiz. And together, like maybe it's normal, maybe we've done this before, maybe we'll do it again, we both head to the door, my elbow touching his wrist, just slightly as we walk out.

I put more space between us, trying to breathe a little easier.

I swear I feel Ms. Romano's eyes on us, and I can't help but to wonder what she thinks of him.

With his question as we walk toward the commons, I imagine the book I needed splayed in his palm last night.

"Guess." It's easier for me to play with Eli when I don't look at him, so I keep staring straight ahead. Unfortunately, that gives me the viewpoint of all the people who are brave enough to stare right at him. And call out to him. And furrow their brows at me. Or check me out.

I keep my expression bland and resist the urge to itch my scalp as sweat makes me want to rip out my braids. *You're putting me under a microscope, and I don't want to be dissected.*

Eli's elbow grazes my shoulder, his hands loose by his sides while mine are damp around my backpack straps.

I move away again. He doesn't comment on it.

"An Introduction to Ancient Greece and Rome." Eli's guess makes me bristle. I don't have that course next.

But I have it for third period. Slowly, I turn to face him as we come to a silently agreed upon stop in the commons, by a bank of lockers.

I have to lift my chin up to see his dark eyes, no flecks of emerald there at the moment, maybe because there are no windows in this part of Castle Hall. It's a little dreary, ideal for holding secrets.

His smile is easy, but there's something to the press of his lips. Daring me to call him out.

"Do you know my schedule?" I manage to keep my tone hard, despite the fast beat of my pulse.

For the first time around him, I feel more than anxious when he answers. His voice is even, low. *"What do you think?"*

It takes an effort to hide the shiver skating its way down my spine.

Is something wrong with Eli? Chaucer, my car, reading my files, staying in the shadows even though he claims to have listened to me every day I read aloud in Latin? Now, this very, very specific course. What's next?

What other secrets of mine are left?

I drop my left hand from my backpack strap, shaking it out slightly, making sure the bracelets cover my wrist.

Too many.

"I think you're stalking me." The thud of my pulse beckons my retort along, lacking any amusement.

Eli doesn't smile or speak or brush it off. He just keeps staring at me. His lack of a denial, of a defense, causes the shiver to work its way back up, wrap around my shoulder blades, and creep over my neck, brushing my throat.

And if I am? He seems to be challenging me to walk away. To tell him he's crossed a line. The tension between us pulls tighter.

"I'm not interested in stalkers," I manage to say.

He tilts his head like he's studying me. "And what are you interested in?"

But before I can answer, I hear a vaguely familiar voice call out, "You comin' next Friday, Eli?"

Slowly, with reluctance, Eli turns his head. I focus on the fullness of his lips, even as his words echo in my brain. *"What do you think?"* A premonition.

I realize Eli hasn't answered the question, and I haven't torn my eyes from him in order to find the source of the voice. But when I hear a brash laugh, I look up. There's a very tall, very blond guy smiling down on me. He looks like he was spit out of a prep school catalog, save for the way he's bleached his hair white.

His crystal blue eyes, trained on me, are boring, like the still surface of a bland lake you might find in a family friendly magazine between an ad for tampons and cheap perfume.

He's got on the black blazer of our uniform, wearing the same black shirt I am, our pants both black, mine rolled up over my boots, a sneak peek of my Slytherin socks showing. He's in white boat shoes, and I resist the urge to roll my eyes at his entire ensemble. It's like he's trying to be edgy with his bleached hair and pierced ears, but everything else about him reeks of conformity.

"Hey," he says, drawing out the word, his voice deep and full of rich, white, spoiled dickhead, complete with a head nod. "I'm Dominic, we have English together?" His mouth is smiling but his eyes are full of a darker amusement as he brazenly looks me up and down.

Irritation burns through my chest, both with his stare and the fact I didn't realize we had a class together.

It must show on my face.

"Ouch." He shakes his head, laughing a little as he runs a hand over his jaw, causing his blazer sleeve to be pulled taut and reveal the blue veins along his wrist. For the first time, I notice black smudges beneath his eyes. They're faint, closer to violet, I guess, but definitely there. Like he's sick or tired or maybe both.

Something in those circles reminds me of Sebastian and I feel the slightest bit softer toward him at the exact same time I decide I don't want to be his friend. *Especially* if he's friends with Eli.

He taps the back of his hand to Eli's chest, and we're both looking at Eli now.

Eli's expression reflects nothing. And he says… nothing.

Dominic gives a little laugh. "Come on, you should invite *her.*" He turns to look at me. "Edith, is it?" I can tell in the sarcastic curl of his mouth, he knows my name exactly and he wants me to correct him.

I don't give him anything at all.

Eli turns his gaze to me. I should just go to class, but they both have me trapped against the locker bank. Gripping the straps of my bag, I say, ignoring Dominic as I lift my chin, "I have to go to class."

Eli's lips tip upward. "Do you?"

I raise my brows. "Um. Yeah. Pretty sure."

Beside me, Dominic snorts.

The hallways are growing emptier, and I'm struck by the fact, if this keeps dragging out, Dominic and I could be walking to English together. Probably alone. I want to remove myself from this unwilling trio now.

"Move," I tell Eli, ignoring the way his eyes light up with amusement at my command. "I need to go."

"Hear that?" Dominic grins, smoothing down his tie. "She wants to get away from you, man. Come on, I'll walk you to class, Edith."

I narrow my eyes at Dominic. *"Eden."*

He feigns shock, like he isn't used to anyone smarting off to him, then an easy grin breaks out over his face. "My deepest apologies," he says, one hand over his heart.

I roll my eyes, toss Eli a wry smile, and pivot to the right, darting around them, turning my back to both of them to head to English.

I hear Dominic laugh again, then Eli's cold voice.

"Dom."

I don't stop, but I slow down slightly, to the point I hope no one notices I have.

Dominic doesn't say anything, and I hold my breath to hear Eli's next words. They're not meant for me.

"I saw your sister last night."

It's the first time Eli has sounded like a teenage boy. Like he just told a "your mom" joke. I want to laugh, but I cover my mouth with my fingers, holding it back. I know he probably *didn't* see Dominic's sister last night, unless he went to their house very late, and I guess he could have but I don't want to think about that and—

There's a jarring *crash* at my back, and there's no point in playing it cool anymore. My heart gallops in my chest and I spin around, dropping my hand from my mouth.

Dominic is pinning Eli to the bank of dark blue lockers, the collar of Eli's shirt fisted in Dominic's hands. His jaw is set, his pale face blushing furiously red.

Eli is smiling, his hands loose by his sides, not bothering to defend himself. The halls are empty now, and I'm the only witness.

"You can't take a joke?" Eli asks the question almost sweetly. For some reason, it causes my skin to crawl. Then a second later, he brings his arms up, underneath Dominic's, breaking his hold as he snakes his hands beside Dominic's inner biceps and squeezes. I blink, and Eli has spun them both around, Dominic's back and head colliding with the lockers now, far louder than the first rattle.

I can practically see the breath leave Dominic's lungs with the impact, and Eli has hold of his forearms, bending his elbows back painfully as he keeps him against the lockers. He leans in close, having to tilt his head down to get his brow to

Dominic's, their noses lined up, their chests brushing due to the angle of Eli's grip.

It looks almost intimate.

I take a step forward, unsure what to do or say.

Eli must notice my movement.

He turns his head slightly, which only angles his mouth so close to Dominic's I swear they're touching. His gaze finds mine, a lock of hair over his brow. His lips are parted, turned up in a dark smile.

Do you want to play with me? I can almost hear his voice saying those words in my head. *I can do far worse than this.*

I don't know what he sees in my face, but a second passes, and another, my stomach tightening the more he breathes over Dominic's lips, and finally, *finally*, he releases him.

Dominic slumps against the lockers, and even though it wasn't a real fight, his arms fall by his side. But the exhale he shudders out isn't dissimilar from mine. I don't even know why I was holding my breath. What did I *think* was going to happen?

Eli straightens, appearing as if *nothing at all* happened between him asking me what I thought, and Dominic's interruption. I realize somewhere in the middle of all this, the bell rang, but it was secondary to Eli's lips next to Dominic's.

"Tell Mr. Baston you were in the bathroom," he calls to me as Dominic looks toward me, then Eli, never moving, still catching his breath. "He'll excuse you." Then he turns his back to me without another word, adjusting his dark gray, leather backpack, going *past* our shared Latin class.

I don't stay alone with Dominic in the hallway.

And when I slip into my seat in the front of my next class, I mutter to Mr. Baston I had to pee, and he looks a little shocked at my brashness, but ultimately nods and says nothing about my lateness.

4

Eli

I SLIDE OFF MY TIE, grazing the choker around my neck with my knuckles as I do. Sturdy leather, when I take it off at night—*if* I take it off at night—my skin can breathe.

Slamming my locker shut, I shift my bag on my shoulder and head toward the commons, threading through students, ignoring the clap on my shoulder, head nods, someone from the team calling out my name.

I see Eden at the farthest bank of lockers, her dark hair again piled high in braids on her head, and even Dominic's eyes cutting to mine in my periphery can't stop me from getting to her. Friday, it's been three days since he shoved me against the lockers. *I hope he got the fucking point.*

As usual, when Eden sees me, she pretends she doesn't. But I can tell she's a liar, in the way the slender column of her throat rolls, her lips press tight together, and she's shaking those bracelets down her wrists so the rubber bands float just over the top of her hand.

School dismissed two minutes ago, and I walked out of Intro to Law early just to get here in time. My last class of the day is on the second floor of Castle Hall, and Eden's history course is five feet from where we stand now, on the first floor.

She closes her locker door after tipping Chaucer back into her checkered backpack, then zips up the bag, threads her arms through the straps, tucks a few stray locks of hair behind both ears, showing off all of her piercings, before she finally turns and meets my gaze.

I like the fact she doesn't feign surprise. Maybe it's not even she pretends she doesn't see me. Maybe she simply doesn't feel like she's got to acknowledge me.

I kinda like that. It's a little bitchy. She's been like this all week, no matter how many times I've approached her.

"I've gotta go." Her voice always sounds slightly hoarse, like she needs to clear her throat. It does things to my dick.

Not giving a damn about my dick, *or me*, by the looks of it, she glances past me, tilting her body to the side a little as she does, trying to see something out the bay of windows behind me. She's a lot shorter than I am so she doesn't see much, I know that.

I like our height difference.

Her body is compact. Not tiny despite her height, she's got thick thighs that touch in her school uniform, a fat ass, and a smaller upper body. Including her little fucking neck.

"Someone picking you up?" The sounds of lockers slamming, people whistling, a few guys laughing and a teacher telling someone to, *"Watch it!"* echo in the hall behind us as everyone gets ready to head out for the weekend. There's a football game, and Dominic's family has a vigil tomorrow night, so it doesn't conflict. He'll probably throw a fucking party afterward like he does every weekend. His question about the one next weekend—when his parents will be away—in front of Eden on Tuesday was a way to get under my skin. But his parties are frequent, not exactly special. You ask a dozen people here what their weekend plans are, you can find a dozen different answers. Heading to the coast to hop on a yacht, political networking, Ivy League campus tours, sports, drugs.

And Eden, who is…

"Yeah, I have to work." Probably won't hear that answer from anyone else here. The way she says it, as if daring me to ask why she needs a job, I know she's very aware of the fact.

She brings her gaze back to me, and not for the first time, I can't stop staring at her eyes. Shards of blue, green, and brown, they don't meld together nicely. Jagged edges, I could extract each piece out and the other two colors I left would remain untouched.

"Work?" I repeat. "Until when?"

Her brows pull together, a shade darker than her hair which catches the light from a row of windows on the opposite wall. Chestnut and soot, it's impossible to describe the shade exactly, particularly in those braids roped on her head. But I've seen her with it undone, and it hangs to just above her waist, curled at the ends.

When she wears the uniform white dress shirt, the buttons up to her throat but the fit showing the slight curve of her tits, her hair spilling over and past them, it's really, really fucking hard to think about dead languages and verb conjugations in class. *And she sits behind me. And never wears the plaid fucking skirt.*

I grit my teeth to stop from groaning out loud, just imagining it in my head.

"Why do you need to know?" she asks in answer to my question about work.

I want to know so much more than that.

But she looks slightly annoyed, her cherry red lips tugging downward.

Her bottom lip is the plumpest, but she has this white scar above her top one, right beside her Cupid's bow. It's tiny, from far away, impossible to see. But this close to her, looking down at her, it's in my line of sight, and I want to kiss her, just to scrape my teeth over it.

I pull my phone from my pocket, ignoring her question. I

unlock the empty screen, open up a new contact, leave the name blank, and turn the phone around to her.

She looks down through heavy, dark lashes, the slightest crease in her forehead as she does. I take in the profile of her face from this angle. A strong nose, wide lips, lifted, round cheekbones. She's almost a contradiction in some ways, prominent features with delicate touches. She's small but not skinny. Wide eyes, thick brows, the slightest of curves to her ears.

A little strange to look at.

I think that's why everyone can't seem to stop.

She glances up at me, almost like she's furious, and I think she's going to say something about me having no right to ask for her number like this, which we both know is a lie, or else walk off without saying a word which seems to be her preferred exit.

But instead, she snatches the phone from me, and her thumbs fly over the keyboard while I watch the rubber bracelets around her wrist slide further toward her inner forearm. I see a faint tan line, a jumble of pale circles in her otherwise summery skin.

"Here," she mutters, thrusting the phone back toward me. She's marching past me before I can say anything else, even though an invitation for this weekend is on the tip of my tongue as I watch her blush. But I lose the words because I'm staring not at her number, which she surprisingly gave me, but at her name in my phone.

Eden Rain, and beside that, a knife emoji.

I bite my tongue to hold in my smile and turn around, watching her hips sway as she walks with her head held high through the crowd. She's full of surprises, and she seems so much more confident when she's not close to me. *Do I make you nervous?*

Just as she rounds the corner for the front entrance, she looks over her shoulder, and I swear to God she winks at me.

Okay, baby girl. Do that to my face.

"Were you at Luna's last night?"

Sweat drips down my back as I twist out of my cousin Jasper's cradle. He releases me because he knows I'd get out anyway, and we roll away from each other on the mat. All around us, those who showed up for pre-season practice are sparring, and Coach Pensky is talking to his wife, Annie, at the front of the wrestling room. She's got an armful of black robes with huge, silver pins dangling from them. To represent each pin we get, but probably a pain in the ass to wash. Still, Mr. and Ms. Pensky are from New Jersey, the high school wrestling capital of the country, and they're married to the sport. Both short and slim and with New Jersey accents and raised voices, they're arguing now about who-knows-what.

Someone bumps into me, and I look over my shoulder with a frown, only to find Josh Holland stammering apologies.

I almost choked him out one day, I guess that's why he seems so nervous now, sweat dampening his blond hair over his eyes.

I ignore him and turn back to Jasper, who's fucking with the waistband of his gym shorts. None of us are in singlets for practice.

Jasper is carefully avoiding my gaze, and I know he has a crush on Janelle. She was just leaving when I got to Luna's, and he must've heard I went there last night. He doesn't want me to *corrupt* Janelle before he gets a chance to fuck her.

I think the corruption is the fun part. Besides, Janelle knows too much what I'm like. She'd never sleep with me.

"No," I lie easily enough because it's better that way.

Jasper picks his head up, running a hand through his sweaty, black hair. He frowns, and I get the distinct feeling he doesn't believe me. But I know he won't question me.

We didn't see much of each other growing up. Dad wanted to hide me away, and Uncle Edison wanted to protect his son from his brother's own. It's a miracle he lets me work at his body shop. Still, Jasper's been at Trafalgar with me the past three years. Addison secrets stay hidden, but some things even Dad can't conceal.

Jasper drops his hand to his thigh and curls his fingers into a fist, then spreads them, the bones in his wrist working as he repeats the motion. He looks down through thick lashes, sweat dripping from the tip of his nose. "Dom was talking about the new girl."

I run my tongue over my teeth, fingers splayed on my thighs as I stare at Jasper, willing him to look up. But he doesn't. "Oh yeah?"

Jasper nods once. "At lunch, said he was thinking of going to the library because she hides out there. Said he wanted her to come to the party next weekend when his parents are out of town." He snorts. "I mean, Luna wasn't around, or he wouldn't have said shit, you know?" He glances up at me.

Yeah, well Luna was sucking my dick last night so it's not like she's got much room to… talk.

I bring my thoughts back to Eden. I know she eats lunch in the library. It's not unusual. We can leave campus, and a lot of people don't stay in the cafeteria. They disperse all kinds of places. Theater kids on stage, art kids in the studio, athletes in this building.

But I've never interrupted her.

I really like to watch her when she doesn't know I am. People are more themselves without an audience.

"Did he say anything else?" I ask my cousin quietly, watching his throat bob as he swallows. I wonder what he's thinking about. Is he remembering his dad breaking the news about the first time I went away? Did he give him all the gory details? Or is he thinking about when Mom left, and what I did in the aftermath? Uncle Edison has never chastised me. He's never been afraid of me, either. But I know him and his wife, Maria, want their son safe above all else. What do they tell Jasper, so he keeps loving me, but his guard stays up around me, too?

Jasper blows out a breath, then lifts his big brown eyes to mine. "No," he answers me. "If you take her to the party… just watch her. She seems like a nice girl, and you know how he is, with drugs and shit."

It's why Jasper won't go. I offer my cousin a smile, because I'm not so sure I can get Eden there either. But I know exactly how Dom is. And he doesn't want Eden. He just wants to make sure if I have her, I share her. Because that's how he wants everything between us. Except his darkest secret. *He wants me to keep that, doesn't he?*

"You ready to go again?" I ask, letting it go as I stand. I stretch my arms behind my back, loop my fingers and pop my shoulder. I drop my hands and crouch into a sparring stance.

Slowly, Jasper pushes to his feet too and nods. His eyes linger on my face a second longer than they should. He saw me this morning, walking Eden from class.

It's why he told me any of this. I think he thinks it's like some kind of bro code. I make a note to throw him a bone with Janelle at some point. We're not close. We never will be. But I'll take the loyalty for a little longer.

Regardless, I still get him in a quick pin. It's mindless, really. We're hovering around the same weight class, but I don't have to think about going for a sweep, dragging his feet out from under him as my shoulder connects with his solar plexus. It's over faster than it should be considering my head isn't in the game. Then again, maybe that's why it's so fast. Maybe this is the flow state Dad's business gurus like to talk about.

Either way, even after five consecutive takedowns and pins of five different wrestlers on Trafalgar's team, I'm still on edge after I shower, catch a fresh *Trafalgar Dragons* tee from Ms. Pensky in the hallway as she grins at me, and pull it over my head, grabbing my duffel bag and heading toward the parking lot. Our mascot is a dragonfly. Someone, probably a man, didn't think it looked too good on our athletic gear, so they shortened it. Guess what's on the back in blue?

A dragonfly. Personally, I feel it makes us look stupid, like we don't know the difference between a very real insect and a very mythical creature, but I didn't make those decisions.

I grab my phone from my sweats, the warm feel of the mid-September sun heating up my bare arms and the back of my neck as I stare at my screen and see Luna has texted me several times.

Her: You didn't say anything, did you??!

I roll my eyes, and I don't bother texting back as I dial her, holding the phone to my ear and heading to my car, double parked behind the gym.

She answers on the first ring. "What the *fuck*, Eli?" Her words aren't angry so much as panicked.

I press the button on my key fob, unlock the doors to the G35, open up the trunk, and toss my shit inside. Then I close it and slip into the driver's seat, shutting the door softly after I'm in. Once I start the car, my phone connects to Bluetooth, and I throw it into the passenger seat, the scent of coconut enveloping me in here. It's from one of the air freshener bags Mom used to make. They're full of essential oils and some organic beads or some shit, I don't know, but she had a whole stock of them put away in the attic. One week straight when I was a kid, it was her nightly project. I don't even think she slept.

I wonder if she intentionally made them smell like… *me*.

I grit my teeth as I put the car in gear and start to drive off, lifting my fingers from the wheel as a few of the guys wave at me, and Dominic, coming out from swim practice, offers me his middle finger.

I smile at him, and drive around the castle of the school, glancing up at the gray turrets stretched out into the darkening sky.

"I've sent you like, five texts—"

"Seven," I correct Luna under my breath, but I know she hears me because she starts going off.

"Yeah, because last night you sneak into my bedroom and

today you act like I don't fucking exist so you can go after that weird fucking—"

"What do you really want, Luna?" I downshift as I coast to the red light leading out of school, past the gates. But after waiting several seconds while Luna sighs loudly on the phone, I see there's no traffic in either direction. Biting my tongue and glancing in my rear view—no one behind me—I curl my fingers around the shifter and shoot through the red light, changing gears smoothly as a smile graces my lips and Luna keeps talking through the speakers of my car.

"Did you tell him?" Her voice is quieter now, her swallow audible through the line. Luna has a lot of friends, won from fear. Her and Janelle both play lacrosse, and while they're friendly, they couldn't be more different.

Janelle knows exactly who I am, and she won't let me get too close because of it.

Luna thinks because she's known me for years now, she owns a piece of me, despite the fact this week her and Dom are "on."

She's constantly disappointed when she realizes… it's never going to be true. She doesn't like to lose things. It's what drew me to her in the first place, back in middle school.

I know she knows I didn't tell him; she just wants to ensure I'm still thinking about her.

I rarely ever am. "Why would I do that?" I ask her as I shift gears, feeling my adrenaline spike as my speed does. I feel free like this. *Alive.* I wonder what makes Eden feel alive.

In my head, I see her downcast eyes, the way she'd look up at me in Latin as if she didn't know I had ever noticed her. How could I not? It's like… it's like she called out to me without saying a word. I don't believe in fate. Life doesn't care enough to be anything more than random. But something about her, it fits with something in me. I don't think she'd care about my secrets. I don't think she'd judge me for any of the terrible things I've ever done. Even the ones Luna and Dom don't know about. *Even the ones they do.*

Maybe it's just a fantasy inside my head, but I think I can make it true.

"I don't know, Eli, because you like to… fuck shit up." I can picture Luna shaking her head, raking a hand through her bright auburn hair as she sits in her white Mercedes, tapping manicured nails against the steering wheel. "Dom is pretty vulnerable right now and I know you said some petty shit to him on Tuesday in the hall. Just… don't ruin this."

I smile to myself. "You mean don't tell him we're getting each other off every night he's at home having a breakdown?"

Luna groans. "Eli, I'm serious!"

I smile to myself. "Good talk." I end the call with the buttons on my steering wheel, biting the inside of my cheek as I turn up Landon Tewers, glancing at my GPS to ensure I'm headed the right way.

5

Eden

I STACK white towels up on the counter, the steady whir of treadmills and ellipticals playing beneath *Higher* by Creed, a constant on the gym owner, Scott's, playlist. He said I could make my own, connect it to the wireless speakers in the gym, but I don't think the patrons would appreciate my taste in music. Sometimes, I don't even appreciate it. It just depresses me.

A collection of thousands of songs, most about drugs, suicide, psychopaths, alongside a few more socially acceptable ones mixed with Russian and Greek hip-hop, it's not something I show off often. A secret tucked into my pocket most days.

When I'm done with the towels, my hands are dry and I reach for the lotion in my backpack, on the floor behind the counter and the old, unreliable computer we use to let people scan in with their key cards.

The scent of coconut and pineapple reaches my nose as I slather the contents of the small bottle of yellow lotion on my hands, and I think of Eli. It's been several hours he's had my number now, and he hasn't texted me. My cheeks flush, even though no one can see me.

"Have a good night, Eden!" A woman's cheerful voice reaches me where I'm crouched down on the thin carpet of the check-in area, and I drop my lotion in the side compartment of my checkered bag and straighten so fast my head spins.

But I catch sight of Carol as the door chimes with her exit. She's a regular for our evening Pilates class, and I offer her a smile. "'Night, Carol." Her wrinkled face stretches into a grin of her own and she pushes out the door, water bottle and her own fluffy, pink towel clutched in her hand, a bob of white hair disappearing into the darkening night of the plaza Fit4Ever is located at.

I wiggle the mouse on the old computer, glancing at the red-lighted scanner facing the glass doors. Tracking my eyes back to the screen, over the data, I see we've got seven people in here right now, a drop from the fourteen who had been in just minutes ago for Pilates.

Looking over my shoulder, I spot the rows of cardio machines, where most people currently trudge along with phones or paperbacks in hand. Behind them are the weight machines, then free weights, with mirrors lining the entire L-shaped corner, men with beer bellies but impressive biceps doing curls and staring in the mirror.

One of the guys, in a white muscle tank and short shorts, sees me watching and grins. It doesn't feel the same as Carol's smile, but I return it all the same. His name is Fred or Frank or something and he often lets his eyes linger a little longer than I feel comfortable with. He comes in a few times during my shifts for different types of workouts and to bake in the tanning beds. I swear he just spends his entire life here.

I shift my gaze from him and find the cut-out door frame that, if you take a left, leads to the tanning beds in the back, none of them currently in use. To the right are change rooms, no showers, and right at my back is the group activity room, with an actual door which is now cracked open. It's like a dance room, with mirrors making up one wall, and currently, I see Patty, the Italian Pilates teacher, stretching, her mass of dark, curly hair draped over her knee as she does.

A chime for the door Carol just walked out of sounds and I turn back around, plastering on my customer-service smile.

Immediately, it falters at the figure gliding through the door, and the sweat I'd staved off for two hours now due to the impressive A/C blowing through this place returns with a vengeance.

Eli. Fucking. Addison.

Before I can think the better of it, I look down at my loose, black tank top, *Not Famous Yet* printed across the front—I cut the sides so it shows off my ribcage—and my black, ripped yoga pants, my favorite gym attire, a gift from Mom when I first started here and had only a few pairs of loose, ratty joggers in the way of gym clothes. I never worked out to be *seen* before, but here, it's my entire job.

I've got green Vans on my feet, black socks pulled up high, and my hair still in braids. I look more or less the same as I did at school I guess, minus the uniform and the boots, but if I had known Eli would show up at my work…

"What the hell?" I hiss each word with vicious annoyance.

Eli's mouth curves upward as he approaches the counter, scanning the place quickly, almost dismissively. I try to view it through his eyes. Pale yellow walls, thin, beige carpet. It's nothing impressive, a dollar store next door, trash blowing in the parking lot, a grocery store with gum stuck to the tiles every time I go in to grab a protein bar for dinner.

I look beyond Eli, now leaning against the counter on his elbows, and see his blacked-out Infiniti, out of place among the Chevys and Fords dotting the lot. Sebastian is picking me up since I needed Mom to drive me straight here so I wouldn't be late, so my Sentra is nowhere in sight.

"Excuse me?" Eli replies, tilting his head as he gazes down at me. Even leaning on his elbows, he's still taller than I am.

Regardless, there's an entire counter separating us, and I'm grateful for it.

I grip the edge of it to keep myself steady, noting Eli's damp hair, wavier than usual. The black choker around his neck over his black T-shirt, *Trafalgar Dragons* printed on the front which must be some inside wrestling joke I don't get because our mascot is a dragonfly. Gray joggers, I can't see his shoes from here, but I imagine the white Chucks he was wearing Monday night in the library.

I take a breath, and beyond the scent of the gym—bleach, sweat, and laundry detergent from the stacked white towels a foot from me at the end of the counter—I can smell him. Clean, soap, the beach. It's better than the lotion I used, which is now making my fingers slippery against the counter as they clam up.

"What, exactly, are you doing here?" *Why did you never text me?*

In the background, I hear the clank of weights. A grunt, probably unnecessary, and the hum of the Pilates teacher softly drifting from the cracked door of the dance room. I try to hold onto the familiar, Eli's presence completely throwing me off.

He grins, showing white teeth. "Am I not allowed in?" *Why would I text you when I could just stalk you?*

I shake my head, feeling warmth spread down my chest. "You don't have a membership here."

Eli eyes the scanner at his elbow as if he's profoundly interested in becoming intimately acquainted with it. "Not yet," he agrees, slowly dragging his gaze back to me, curving a single brow in an expression that's almost innocent. "But maybe in a second, if you're offering."

"I'm not." I glance at the camera above the glass door, aimed at the counter. For my sake, not for the company's, Scott told me. To keep records of customers, not employees. *I can't murder Eli right here and now, so I'm not sure that's really true.* Folding my arms over my chest like some sort of protection from his charm, I hold his eyes for long seconds. He's still smiling, but his irises look darker, and I don't know what he's thinking, but he has to know coming to *my work* after our conversation in the hallway about my schedule on Tuesday, is over the top.

"Oh?" he finally asks, a single word, quiet like he always is, yet it somehow rings louder, above anything else happening in this gym right now, and there is a *lot* of noise here. It's one thing I don't like about it. Too many sensations make it hard for me to focus.

But hooked into Eli's attention, like a fish at the end of a line, it all fades away, my heart thumping wildly in my chest. I think of the pills in my bag, wishing I could down one to still my pulse. To gain outward control over my nerves.

"You don't need a gym membership." Surely, he has one in his house? It seems like a rich kid requirement, at least based on the clientele *here*.

Eli rakes his fingers through his damp hair, tousling it forward so the dark strands hang in his eyes, but I can still see them very clearly when he straightens, tapping his fingers against the counter. "I don't need a lot of things, Eden."

Something that could be butterflies erupt in my stomach, and I'm not sure why. It wasn't as if those words were a compliment.

"But there are quite a few things I *want.*"

The butterflies swirl around, a tornado of mixed emotions in my gut. My throat feels dry, and I think of the water bottle, half empty, on the counter behind me, but I don't reach for it. "You want to be a member of *this* gym?" I hitch a thumb over my shoulder and Eli follows the movement with his eyes. Another clang, the speeding up of a treadmill as someone starts to jog.

This place isn't half-bad, and it's affordable. But I've seen F. M. Fink's Hall at Trafalgar. Eli probably has access to the gym there anytime he wants it, being a wrestler.

His biceps flex as he keeps drumming his fingers on the counter, looking back at me. "Sure. Can I get a discount? Since I know you?"

"You don't know me." *But I want you to.* The thought is unavoidable.

In his eyes, I swear I see the same thing reflected, just more aggressive. *But I will.*

"What about since I helped you ace the quiz Tuesday morning?"

I don't even blink. It's true, he did, but… *I don't trust you.*

He concedes when I don't respond, shrugging. "Sign me up." He pulls his wallet from the pocket of his sweats without looking away from me, thumbing free a black card and pushing it forward on the lip of the counter, so it's half-hanging over the edge, ready to drop beside the keyboard of the company computer.

I reach for it instinctively, my customer service training kicking in. The card is heavier than a normal credit card, and I almost say something about it, but instead I just glance at his name etched in raised silver.

Eli Adonis Addison.

My heart thumps faster.

Adonis.

A mortal, lover of Aphrodite.

In the sliding drawer beneath the counter, I fumble for the paperwork he has to complete—name, age, sign a waiver, a contract for the money to be taken from his bank account every month—keeping the card clenched tight in my other hand and pushing Greek mythology from my mind.

I slide the paperwork his way, pluck up a pen without a cap from the wire cupholder beside the computer and give it to him, then open up the software I have to use to manually put in his card info.

"There's a one-time, fifty-dollar application fee, but you won't be charged the first thirty dollars until the end of the month—"

"The first thirty?" He says nothing about the application fee. If he had, just one thing, I could have waived it. He might be the first person I *haven't* waived it for in the month I've been working here. Scott will be happy.

I glance at Eli's grip on the pen, which always looks strange to me.

He's left-handed.

Imagining holding a pen that way, I could never replicate the small, tidy loop of his handwriting.

"Yes. It's thirty dollars a month, you can cancel with a two-month notice—"

"I want to pay ahead."

I'm typing in the numbers of his credit card, laid against the cash register below the computer stand. I finish the numbers, then look up at him. "What?"

"I want to pay ahead." He repeats the words slower, causing me to blush harder, the heat uncomfortable in my cheeks, like a sunburn.

"Okay." It's not unheard of, but I think I've done it twice, both for people who lived near this gym and were unlikely to move anytime soon. I guess Eli *could* live in this tiny pocket of Raleigh's outskirts, but it's not close to Trafalgar. Twenty-minute drive, maybe eighteen if he's behind the wheel. "For how long?"

He goes back to filling out the form. "Are you staying here until graduation?"

Probably through the summer. I'm going to Bloor. *I'm definitely going to Bloor.* But I don't see how it'll be possible to move before term starts next fall, and part of me is terrified to leave my family. *What if something happens again? What if I lose my mind and no one is there to find it?*

But I want something bigger.

I want to be someone bigger.

The gravity of Eli's question, beneath the noise of my own quiet ambition, suddenly sinks into my bones.

"You should sign a contract for a gym membership because you like the gym, not because you like an employee."

He doesn't even look up. "Fuck it, I'll pay through August.

I assume I'll be in college then, although who's to know?" He drops the pen, like a mic drop, then pushes the paper toward me, letting it curl over the edge.

I keep my eyes on the computer screen as I mentally do the math in my head. Eleven months at thirty dollars. "You're sure?" I ask without looking at him.

"Hit me."

I don't mean to, but I smile at those words and I'm not even sure why. Then I charge his card, for the application fee and the pleasure of seeing me for the next year.

When I'm done, his receipt in his pocket, card back in his wallet, gripped loosely in his hand, I expect him to leave. I'm positive he had wrestling practice today, and I imagine it's pretty brutal. He's in impressive shape, and with the veins straining beneath his hands, even more prominent than usual, he has to be tired, right?

But he doesn't leave. Instead, he says, "When are you off?" at the same time Fred or Frank rounds the counter, his back to the door as he spins to face us both and Eli pivots, one arm still on the counter. I glance at the computer screen and see his check-in.

Fred. His name is *Fred.*

"You all good, Eden?" he asks, a blender cup in his massive hand, sweat dripping down his sun-lined face. He spares a single glare in Eli's direction.

"Great," I say, plastering on my customer-service smile.

Fred returns it, the glare gone as he focuses on my face. "I'll be back later for the beds." He jerks his chin, indicating the tanning booths in the back of the gym.

I nod, keeping my smile. The door chimes, Fred shoots one more glare to Eli, then walks out, and we both see the way his shirt is dampened down his spine from sweat.

"He loves me," Eli mutters under his breath. "Anyway, what time do you get off?"

I glance at the time on the computer. It's six now. "Two hours."

"Great." He pushes off the counter, walks by the computer, swipes a towel from the stack I folded, and saunters toward the weights, leaving me staring after him.

Near close, I head to the back of the gym with a towel and spray bottle in hand to clean up the tanning beds. I refuse to look at Eli, still here and by the weights, in conversation with a woman I know is training for a physique competition. I roll my eyes at his charm but lift my chin and breathe a little easier when I disappear down the hall to the tanning beds.

It's quiet back here, the three rooms vacant, and I duck into the first two for a couple of minutes max, swiping at the glass over the bulbs, discarding sticker wrappers of different shapes people can put on their skin for the tan to go around it, like a strange, reverse tattoo. One is the outline of a Playboy bunny, and I smile a little as I toss it into the trash. If I had a sticker with innuendo, it'd probably be whips and chains or hands around a throat or something, at least based on my porn preferences.

My face grows hot, and I shake my head, rolling my eyes at myself.

I head to the last room, not bothering to flick on the lights because there's enough to see by from the hallway. It smells like every stereotypical beach scent ever bottled in here, and the bed is still warm when I wipe my cloth over it, bending down so I can reach the far side. My shirt rises up, exposing my low back, cool air drifting along my skin. I can see the gleam of some kind of oil in a tiny spot at the top curve of the bed, and I'm irrationally annoyed I have to scrub at it harder after I spray the bottle to get it cleaned off. Oils aren't supposed to be used in these beds.

My mind drifts to homework and calling Sebastian to pick me up and hoping he's sober when he answers, to what I'm going to eat for dinner.

Then just as the oil gives way on the glass and I'm almost done, *I feel something graze my lower back.*

I jump, banging my head on the top lid of the tanning bed, stars popping in my eyes. I spin around, holding out the spray bottle and pulling the trigger when I see a looming figure. I hear a puff of diluted chemicals and water spritz into the air at the same time I open my mouth to scream but it comes out as a strangled shriek.

The bottle is pulled from my hand, dropped to the floor, then there's a thud and the door is slammed closed, the light from the hall gone, extinguishing me in darkness.

I back up, but the bed hits my back, and all I've got fisted in my hand is the cleaning towel.

My heart stutters inside my chest. I'm drawing in a deep breath, ready to scream again, terror ice in my veins, when a familiar voice breaks through the darkness.

"What the hell was in that?"

My chest heaves, skin tingling, when the door is pushed open, the person inside with me grunts as they're thwacked with it, and my eyes dart from them, to Eli, looming in the doorway, light spilling into the room.

"I think you blinded me," Fred grunts, his meaty hand slapped over his eye.

"I think you deserve it." Eli's voice is cold as he takes in the dropped spray bottle, me clutching the gym towel, and Fred, who was the last person to use this bed. I know, because I set the timers, but that was half an hour ago.

I'm still catching my breath, but relief swims through me at the sight of Eli, especially when he flicks on the light switch.

When it illuminates the space, I turn my head and find Fred glaring at Eli, one of the former's eyes red and swollen. "What are you even doing back here, dude?"

Eli smiles, but there's nothing nice about it. "I think you should leave."

I find words, finally, and ask, "Why were you in here?" looking in Fred's direction.

He swallows, his thick neck rolling as he looks at me. "I thought I left something," he mutters, glancing around the room. There's a small trash can with the backings of stickers in it, a stack of towels on a ledge screwed into the wall, and a little fan, plugged in but off. Nothing else. "I guess not." He glares at Eli but looks apologetic when he turns to me again. "Sorry, Eden. Didn't mean to scare you," he mutters. He shuffles toward the door, and Eli turns only enough to let him walk by, but he doesn't move from the doorway.

Fred is thick, but Eli is taller, and when he passes by, Eli says, so quietly I barely hear him, "Don't follow her again."

Fred stiffens, his hands curled into fists, T-shirt pulled tight over his wide shoulders. But he doesn't say a word as he leaves the room, disappearing down the hall, leaving me alone with Eli.

Eli swoops down to pick up the spray bottle, and carefully hands it to me. I take it without touching his skin, my movements jittery.

He stares down at me, and for a second, I'm reminded of bully romance novels. *Is he going to, like, slam me against the wall?*

But instead... he backs up.

"You have fast reflexes," he says quietly, sounding almost proud of me.

I'm looking everywhere but at him, my fingers clammy around the plastic bottle, but I hear a smile in his words.

I wait for him to admonish me for that sneak attack Fred pulled, but he doesn't. Instead, all he says is, "Do you want a ride home?"

"My brother can pick me up." I clench my fingers in the gym towel, still looking down. *Did Fred touch me on purpose? It was probably an accident, right? What if Eli hadn't come back here?*

Eli huffs the softest laugh. Then he says, "I'll wait 'til you're done. Meet me at the front. Preferably without that bottle." He walks out before I can argue, and with the lingering feel of Fred's fingers on my low back, I don't even want to.

"You're taking me straight home, right?"

He's standing at the driver's side door of his car, my bag in his hand, hanging by his side. He insisted on carrying it out, just like he insisted on opening the passenger door for me.

But I'm still standing outside his car, and I keep one hand on the top of the door, the scent of leather and coconut strong enough to feel like a physical warmth in my chest.

In the lights of the parking lot, I see him roll his eyes. "I did Monday night, didn't I?"

True enough. I glance at the bandage on my middle finger. It's easier than looking at Eli without a shirt on. It's around his shoulders, like a towel, and his body is covered in sweat, which makes me feel a little less alone with the sheen of it on my forehead, even though only one of us was working out. He only slipped his shirt off—one handed, curving his back, in that hot way boys do—after we'd walked out into the night. I clear my throat before I speak again. "But Monday night, I didn't know you knew my entire schedule, and where I worked. I also didn't know you were planning on stopping by my place of work, spending over three hundred dollars on a membership so you'd have an excuse to stalk me harder and get me alone in your car again, instead of just… I don't know, texting me?"

He bites his lip, his cheeks lifting with a half-smile. "Stalk you harder, huh?" His tone is suggestive, and I feel every inch of the suggestion in my core. He glances at the gym. "Looks like you've got a few stalkers."

My stomach flips with the reminder. *Fucking Fred.*

Resting his forearm on the roof of the car, Eli looks toward the grocery store of the strip mall. "You upset I didn't text you?"

I don't give that question an answer. I'm afraid it's painfully obvious and I feel kind of stupid for making it so. I mean, he showed up here instead. "How did you know where I work?"

"People talk."

I stare at his side profile but I refuse to give that non-response a retort.

"Tell me you don't like it." His voice is low, like it was in the hallway Tuesday morning when he asked, *"What do you think?"*

"Like what?" I want him to say it. *Stalking.* At the very least, I want to hear what *he* calls it.

He still doesn't look at me, but he runs his tongue over his top lip, and I wonder if he can taste his own sweat. "Feeling wanted."

I blink in the night, warm air too hot on my skin. My stomach tightens, butterflies and tornado gone, something like humiliation there instead. "I don't need *you* to feel wanted."

He turns his head toward me, expression blank. "You missed the point, didn't you?"

"What's the point? That *you* want me?" I cross my arms over my chest. "Is your stalking supposed to make me feel special? I can promise you Fred's doesn't."

He looks amused with my retort. "Good thing I'm not *Fred."*

Before I can say anything to that, behind him, I think I see a shadow over the door of the gym.

I startle, dropping my arms, widening my eyes.

Slowly, he turns to face the door too, noticing my attention is off of him. I blink. It's gone. There's no shadow, just the yellow light above the door of the gym, lights on inside.

Nothing is there.

My face heats as Eli looks toward me again, tilting his head, like he's waiting for an explanation of what I was so spooked by.

I don't have one.

"I'm going to take you straight home," he promises after a moment, then ducks down into his car.

It's only after we're both buckled in and he's pushing his arms through his shirt, all of the muscles along his body flexing with the movement, that I see the bruises.

Along his chest, just above his abs.

They're not terrible, faded really, but something about them makes me squirm in my seat. Even still, I don't ask.

Probably wrestling.

The easiest explanation is often the simplest, I repeat it in my head, a phrase from Reece about conspiracy theories Sebastian believes in. *Vaccines have trackers, man.* I don't think Seb *really* believes it, but when he's high, his logic is fucked.

Pushing my brother from mind, I brush my thumb over the rubber bracelets on my wrist and think about telling the story of those three letters beneath them to someone.

Sometimes the explanation is not simple at all.

AFTER A QUICK DRIVE WITH ONLY MUSIC BETWEEN US, ELI pulls onto the dirt driveway, every car here but Sebastian's, he says, "Who drives the Mazda?"

I shouldn't be surprised he memorized all of my family's vehicles, but it still jars me, and maybe not in the way it should. There is something odd about his behavior. It *is* borderline stalking. But his observation is truly impressive.

"My brother."

"Older?" Eli's hand is on the shifter, and as usual, I can't look away from it as he stares out the windshield. The same usual light is on in the living room, and down at the far end of the trailer, I see the flickering of Mom and Reece's TV through their closed blinds.

"Yes. Twenty-one."

Maybe he hears something in the way I say it, or maybe it's because I haven't reached for the door handle yet, but I feel him looking at me when he asks, "Are you two close?"

The answer is automatic. "Yes." We're as close as two people like us can be, I think. I'm closer to Sebastian than I am to anyone else in my life except for Mom. Amanda always felt like… a placeholder.

Eli makes a noise like a hum, and I wonder if he's going to

ask more about my brother, but instead he changes topics completely. "Do you work tomorrow?"

I feel his eyes on me as I shake my head. "No."

"I have a thing," he says.

I rest my head against his seat as I turn to face him. "Okay?"

"A pre-season tournament. Wrestling. It's at Trafalgar."

I roll my eyes. "You should probably get some rest."

"Do you not like taking hints or do you just enjoy me cutting myself open for you?" He smiles with the question, but there's still an edge to the morbid words.

"I enjoy honesty." Even as I say it, butterflies tumble in my stomach.

He doesn't say anything for a moment, and I get the distinct feeling I'm going to regret those words. "Honesty?" His eyes flick over my body, and I press my thighs together, hugging my bag to my chest, feeling the fabric on my ribcage where the slits of my shirt are, grateful he can't see much of me. "You want me to be *honest?*"

"This sounds like a trap."

"Answer the question."

"It's better than lying."

"Not for everyone." He furrows his brow, staring at me. "But for people like us, it's a relief, isn't it?"

People like us. I don't know what that means, and I don't want to ask. It feels too much like he knows things he shouldn't.

He lets it go, like he didn't expect an answer. *"Honestly."* He smirks as he says the word, and I want to get out of the car, but I don't dare move, like I'm under scrutiny while he gives me what I asked for. "You fascinate me. I should've spoken to you on the first day of class, but you did not look like a girl who wanted to be spoken to." *He's not wrong.* "And *honestly,"* that word again, "I want you to come to my wrestling tournament because it would make it far less boring, and maybe you'd watch me win all fucking day and you'd be equally as fascinated with me as I am with you. Or, at least, *closer."*

Closer.

My mouth goes dry. I don't say anything about his spiel. I just clear my throat and ask, "Isn't your family going to be there?"

I don't want to meet his family. I don't want to meet *anyone's* family, but especially not his. He might be okay with the trailer we're parked in front of right now. The fact I won't be going off to Harvard or Yale or Brown—Bloor is decent and affordable, but it certainly isn't Ivy League—but I don't think his parents would feel the same and besides, we're not even friends, are we? Meeting his parents would just be unnecessary and awkward and what if they saw my scars and what if…

"My dad is away for work." He genuinely doesn't seem to care, but I can't help poking at it.

"Does he usually miss your matches?"

He smiles, and I don't know why, but he answers, "No."

But you didn't mention your mom. Maybe too much honesty for tonight, so I don't press. "This is a lame date." I'm surprised at my own gall.

He laughs. It sounds *real,* and I feel proud I made him do it. His white teeth flash and he sighs, resting his head back against his seat as he looks up at the headliner. "I don't know why you're being like this. We both know I'm going to kiss you soon."

My mouth drops open. I'm grateful he isn't looking at me as heat flushes up my neck, into my cheeks. I squeeze my bag tighter as my pulse drums too fast inside my chest. "You're absolutely not." Even as I say the words, my eyes drop to his mouth. His lips are just so full, it really, really isn't fair.

They curve upward, and I stare at the column of his throat, the vein along his neck, his Adam's apple, the stark ridge of his clavicle, and—

"I am, Eden." He whispers the words, but still doesn't look at me, and somehow, it makes this all the more… intense. Slowly though, he turns his head to stare right at me. "Please come tomorrow. It's only for the best of the best." He laughs a little, like he knows how arrogant those words sound. "I mean, really, you should be honored I'm inviting you."

"Shut up." I roll my eyes at his teasing, shaking my head. "I don't know." A different response than my original. I've never been to a wrestling match, but if I don't go, I'll... what? Spend all day in my room, studying and reading and hoping Sebastian wakes up before noon so maybe we can get lunch together? Text Amanda just so I don't feel like a complete loser?

A lapse of quiet. Then, "I'll pick you up tomorrow morning." He says it like law. Like it's simple. *Settled.*

I don't want to give in so easily. "I'll have to see if I can—"

"You can. But find out if you *want* to." He glances at his phone in the center console before he opens his door. "I'll text you tonight. Don't ghost me."

I HEAR SEBASTIAN HEAVING IN THE BATHROOM THAT SEPARATES our rooms. Staring at the ceiling fan on high overhead, covers pulled up to my chin, arms framing my head, bent at the elbow on my pillow, I think about going to check on him.

Sirens wail outside, probably down the street, but my entire family is in here and it's such a common occurrence, I don't much care.

As the toilet flushes, though, I can't help but think... *maybe we need help too.*

I hear water running in the sink.

A second later, rushing footsteps, the bathroom fan flips on, the house shakes as Sebastian sinks to his knees, more heaving, and the sound of something emptying into the toilet.

Check on him. You're not going to sleep anyway.

It's true. I'm not. A few minutes ago, reading the newly discovered *Brothers Poem* by Sappho on my phone, it was after two in the morning.

No texts from Eli.

I don't have his number, and while I found his profiles on social media, they're locked up tight. I deleted all my accounts after I was suspended at Shoreside, so I couldn't request to see more.

It doesn't matter.

I think about grabbing my phone again. Amanda texted me earlier tonight, asking about my weekend plans, but I haven't responded. Right now, though, I need a distraction and—

Sebastian flushes the toilet again. *What the fuck is he even doing?*

I sigh, throwing off my covers, the soundtrack of sirens still wailing in the distance, beneath the hum of my overhead fan and the bathroom one.

I unlock my door, tiptoe into the dark hall. There are blinds directly in front of me, covering the window here. I step close, pushing down one with my index finger, staring out at Castle Lane, looking for the source of the sirens.

I see nothing but darkness.

Letting the blind pop back into place, I turn toward the bathroom door, an orange glow beneath the crack at the bottom.

Softly, I rap my knuckles against it. "Seb?" I whisper, not wanting our parents to wake. "Are you okay?"

There's nothing. Just the steady purr of the fan.

I close my eyes, pressing my temple to the door. *What are you doing with your life?*

But then I hear footsteps. I open my eyes, step back.

The door is jerked open, and the scent of marijuana and alcohol drifting from his body is dizzying. He stares out at me with bloodshot eyes, flipping the fan off, but leaving the dim light on. He sniffs, runs the back of his hand over his nose, then drops it to his hip. His wrists are so bony. "What's up?"

I wrap my arms around myself, taking another retreat back. "I just wanted to see if you're good."

He blinks, his light blue eyes going to the floor as he rests his forearm against the door jamb, hanging his head. "Great," he lies, his voice crackly.

I swallow the lump in my throat. The protests, too. In the quiet, the sirens are louder. "Wonder what's going on," I mutter, dropping my gaze, searching for something to say. I can never quite get this right with him.

There's a pause. A silence. Then, "What do you mean?"

Shifting from foot to foot, the thin carpet creaking beneath me, I say, "The police. Or ambulance, or whatever. I wonder what's going on." It's not unusual. Not for this trailer park, and not for our old apartment. It's just conversation. Just meaningless words because I can't find the correct ones.

Just like I never told him about his friend, all those years ago in our apartment. Supposedly, he knows, but now I'm older, I'm not so sure. Another lie I let my mind believe. That he knew and didn't care. That it wasn't a big deal.

I feel Seb staring at me. Perplexed, I lift my gaze to his.

He's frowning, his light brows knitted together, hair hanging in his eyes.

For a second, I'm confused. Then I stand up straighter, my body very, very cold. I swallow, hard, tilting my head. "You don't... you don't hear them?"

"You should get some sleep, huh?" Seb's words are too soft. Full of pity.

The hairs on the back of my neck stand on end. I don't trust myself, in my own skin. "Yeah," I say, forcing myself to speak. "Yeah, goodnight." Then I dart into my room, closing and locking the door behind me, although I'm not sure it's a good idea. Sometimes, I don't know if I should be alone with myself.

But I still hear them. *The sirens are real.* Unable to let it go, I wait until Sebastian's door is closed. Then, my pulse pounding too loud in my ears, I tiptoe back into the hall.

They're louder, here. The sirens.

With a shaky finger, I pull down the blind again, holding my breath.

At first, I see nothing but darkness. Nothing but night.

My stomach sinks, then I sweep my gaze to the right, further down Castle Lane.

Blue lights. *Right there.* Cop cars parked at the end of the street, in front of the last trailer, which on my last walk I saw was empty. Probably squatters.

But the cops, the lights… they're real, aren't they?

I release the blind, turning to stare at Seb's door. No light slips through the crack underneath it.

I scurry back into my room, slowly closing and locking my door, not feeling any better than I did before.

I dive into bed, yanking the covers over my head. *A distraction. I need a distraction.*

I try to breathe evenly.

I imagine Eli. Dark green eyes, circled with black.

I clutch the faded silver of my sheets tighter, pressing my knees together, curling them up to my chest so I'm in a ball. Heat rises in my blood, and I think about him without his shirt on. His clavicle, his olive skin, dark hair, *Adonis.*

I'm chewing the inside of my cheek, stretching one leg out and angling onto my back again, my hand drifting from my sheets to my stomach, just under my sleep shirt, when my phone buzzes underneath my pillow.

My heart pumps hard.

I blink open my eyes as I reach for my phone, holding it over my head and dimming down the brightness, squinting against the screen.

An unknown, local number.

I widen my thighs, bringing one foot to the inside of my knee as I read his text.

Him: I'll be there at eight.

Two emotions war within me, strange thoughts and I don't know which one to cling to. Irritation he didn't offer an excuse or an apology for waiting until this late to text me, and a dizzying sort of awe he didn't.

I consider not texting him back as I save his number into my phone.

But before I have to make a decision, he's typing again.

I smile, waiting, holding the phone over my head under the sheets.

Him: Then I'll take you on a real date.

I roll my eyes, and another text comes through, my phone pulsing in my hand as it does.

Him: Bring your checkered bag. Put some clothes in it for a sleepover. Tell your parents you aren't coming home.

Another laugh bubbles through my fingers, but even so, even thinking of all of this as a joke, I decide to indulge him. Talking to Eli is better than worrying over my brother. Over *myself.*

Me: And where, exactly, should I tell my parents I'll be?

His response is immediate and imagining him lying on his back like I am, one arm slung over his brow in his mansion-esque room, a fan tousling his hair, no shirt on, those bruises on his abs… it makes me feel feverish.

Him: Ah, you are awake.

My cheeks ache with my smile.

Him: You tell them you're safe with me.

Him: It's a lie, of course.

Him: Because when I get you alone, I'm going to eat you alive.

My pulse is flying, and I have to swipe my covers down over my head, letting the cool air rush over me, my unbraided hair fanned out on my pillow.

Him: JK.

It takes me a minute to regulate my breath, and I push one hand under the covers, my fingers coming to the waistband of my oversized sleep shorts. My core is hot, and my fingers are cold. The sensation causes me to shiver, and I text him back with one hand, feeling far braver with miles between us, our only connection this phone.

Me: You're not kidding.

Don't be kidding.

Him: I'm not kidding.

I shift my hand lower, goosebumps rising along my skin. I don't know what to say. So many things in my head, Eli's skin, his voice, his nearness, how clean his car is, how he smells so good. The gym membership, the sweat slick on his body, even being so close to him in the stupid tanning room, where he followed Fred, to check on… *me.*

Him: What are you doing, Eden?

The fact he typed out my name makes me want him more. I glide my fingers over my pubic bone, chewing the inside of my cheek, and my face flushes hot when I answer him.

Me: What do you think?

I dip my middle finger over the short hair between my thighs, but I don't go lower as I wait, holding my breath, my heart pumping so fast it hurts in my chest.

Him: You're wrapped up safe and sound in your bed, because you're a good girl, huh?

My heart skips a beat, and I imagine him whispering those words in my ear, his fingers drifting along my skin. **Me: Is that what you think?**

Him: Stay the night with me and let me find out.

Me: I don't know you. You could be dangerous. My face grows hot as I send off the text, knowing I'm playing with fire. *An act, an act, an act.* What happens when he wants to cash in on all this foreplay?

Him: I think you'd like that.

I bite my bottom lip, thinking of the scars on my wrist. **Me: I'm an angel.**

His replies come fast. **Him: A beautiful one.**

I feel a little dizzy. **Me: A really, really good one.**

Him: Yeah. I bet you are.

Him: But would you ever be bad? For me?

Him: Who am I kidding. Of course you would, just because I asked.

I imagine his smirk in my head. I touch myself, feeling how wet I am, my stomach muscles jumping with the relief of my finger circling my swollen clit, everything slippery and hot.

Him: Answer me. You're not asleep.

There's something in his demand, in the accuracy of his accusation, it makes me want to please him. I feel like putty, eager to give in, so different from the ways I know I'd shy away if he was here. I push my finger lower, parting my lips, then lower still, into me. My walls tighten around myself. The rough feel of the Band-Aid inside of me only heightens the pleasure.

It takes me a long time to type out the message as my breath hitches while I finger myself, but he doesn't interrupt my typing, and I know he sees it.

Me: I'm not asleep.

Him: You're coming to watch me tomorrow.

Lust numbs my mind as I clench around my finger, then drag it out of my tight hole, up the slickness of my pussy, circling my clit again, biting my lip.

You can give in. He isn't actually here. You don't have to go.

Me: I'm coming to watch you tomorrow.

Please him.

Him: I like when you listen.

Does he know what I'm doing? He can't. The only touch he's given me is when I slammed my finger in his door. But there's been so much in his eyes, and his nearness.

Slow down, slow down, slow down. I could stop texting him now. I could give this up. *But this is safe. I'm safe here.*

Me: I like when I listen too.

Words I shouldn't say, I'm digging myself into a hole.

I gasp, arching my neck, so close, my core muscles tightening, and all I'm doing is texting with him, and he doesn't even know. *He doesn't know.*

Him: To me.
Me: To you.

It feels like a mistake, even as I give in. I just don't care. I need one more text. Something filthy. I need… I need…

Him: I want you to listen to me all day tomorrow, do you understand?

This is stupid. This is a hormone-laden mistake. A decision born from the brink of an orgasm. I keep circling myself, pulling my bottom lip between my teeth, wanting him here. His hands all over me. His body pressing mine into the mattress, uncaring I don't like it, I don't want it, and feeling skin on mine makes me feel sick and…

Me: I understand, Eli.
Him: Fuck.

Yeah. *Fuck.*

I'm so close. I suck in a breath, my chest swelling, my stomach tightening. I sit halfway up, using my core muscles, pushing my middle finger inside of me, using my thumb to get me there, closer, *closer.*

Give me something else. Something more.

Me: Yeah…
Him: I'm going to be all over you.
Me: Please.
Him: But I want you to beg me before I am.

And there it is.

I'm coming undone without his physical presence, his words enough to unravel me. In this moment, as my eyes are forced closed and I circle my fingers tight around my phone, I'd definitely beg him to touch me, even if I might hate when it actually happened. The orgasm crests, and I can feel myself tighten around my finger, my body lurching up off the mattress.

Spots pop in front of my eyes, thoughts of Eli in every brain cell, consuming me as I come, and when I finally drift back down, breathing hard, my wrist cramping, my phone still in my free hand, my other wet, I don't feel any regret.

I slide my fingers up my belly, resting my palm over my

chest and feeling the nerve-wracking thunder of my own pulse as I blink open heavy eyes, staring at his newest text.

I didn't even feel the vibration in my hand, thanks to the one ripping through my body.

Him: Don't fall asleep without telling me goodnight.

I smile at the words, no less hot now than when I was coming. In the morning, maybe I'll be mortified with his demands. Maybe I won't go to the tournament or see him at all. Maybe I'll pretend this didn't happen.

But tonight...

Me: Goodnight, Eli.

My eyes are heavy, finally drifting closed, but I force them open when he sends another text.

Him: Good girl. Goodnight, Eden. I'll see you in the morning.

We'll see.

6

Eli

"WHERE WERE YOU LAST NIGHT?" Dad's greeting, full of bite. He doesn't look at me as he comes sweeping into the kitchen, adjusting his tie like it needs it, fiddling with his cufflinks.

I keep staring down at my coffee, the newspaper beside it, soft gray pages turned over to the classifieds. Cars. I pick up the blue, ballpoint pen on the island and trace a thick circle around an older model Supra.

I hear the suction give on the fridge as the door is pulled open. I don't need to glance over to know Dad is grabbing his orange juice. Me and Mom never drank the stuff. Sometimes though, when he's not around… I do. Straight from the fucking bottle.

"We were supposed to watch that movie." He continues talking, losing the edge in his tone, and I marvel over the fact he has none of the Southern drawl his brother, my Uncle Edison, has. Jasper speaks just like his dad. I guess my accent is a careful mix of my parents'.

Dad swipes a glass from the cabinet after he closes the

fridge, sets down his cup on the gleaming white marble counters, by the sink, and starts pouring his juice. His back is to me, and I doodle in the margins of the newsprint, a car of my own making. Nothing that should actually ever exist. Something out of *The Flintstones*, maybe, powered by feet.

"I ended up getting stuck on *How to Get Away with Murder.*" Dad caps the juice and drinks from his glass, gazing out at the windows over the sink, giving half a view of our sprawling gardens. Bushes and flowers and a fire pit we don't take care of. He hires people for it.

He hires people for everything.

He's probably giving his secretary a raise this weekend for accompanying him on his business flight to Dallas, then fucking him in her hotel room later. Maybe not ethical, but shockingly, lawyers and ethics don't always come hand-in-hand. Hence the show he referenced.

I grip my pen a little harder, working on the second tire of my car, sloped dome roof, only two wheels visible because I'm not an artist.

In my head, I see Eden's fingers holding her pen. I watch her chew her nails when she thinks no one is looking. I wonder if she can draw. She can probably do anything.

"I'm sorry I can't make it today." There's genuine remorse in Dad's words and I hate the way the pity pricks at my skin. I preferred his angry tone.

I shift on the bar stool at the sprawling white island.

So much white in this house, I spare a glance to the burnished, textured tile of the floors just to scrub the color from my brain for a second.

My phone pulses beside my coffee mug, face down, I know who it is, but I don't reach for it. I just set my right elbow on it, feeling the vibration on my skin.

"Make sure you're not tiring yourself out." He finishes his orange juice, rinses the glass in the sink, then opens up the dishwasher, finds it's full of clean dishes, and instead of emptying it, he sets his glass carefully on the counter before he puts away the container of juice. He's still staring at the closed fridge when he speaks again. "Season hasn't even started, you know?"

I chew the inside of my cheek, wondering just how long I can sit here in silence before he snaps. As the quiet between us stretches on, only broken by the distant hum of the pool pump at my back through the triple set of glass doors that lead to the patio, I go to work on the grill of my car.

He still hasn't turned around. That means he's really, really trying.

I bite back my smile and color in the windows, tinted black. Definitely illegal.

A soft sigh, which means he isn't going to explode. Not yet. "Luna's mother sent me an email."

I freeze, teeth clenched together as I grip my pen so hard, I'm surprised it doesn't snap. No longer coloring in my windows, I don't lift my eyes as I wait for him to speak again, knowing he will. He's trying to bait me, but he doesn't have enough patience to do it properly.

Even Mom's was bigger than his, sometimes. But he doesn't snap like she did when she lost her temper. He tries to hold it in, but I can usually see his chest swell with the effort it takes to swallow it down. His back still to me, with a single glance, I can't see much but the rigid set of his broad shoulders beneath his suit, his hands clenched into fists at his side.

No wedding band.

He wore it for years after she left, there's still a pale circle of skin set against the tan of the rest of his fingers.

"You're going to the vigil tonight?" He phrases it as a question, but I don't answer him. "It's at Dom's?"

"I didn't see her walk out."

"You slept in the living room, how the fuck could you not?"

"I know things have been rough between the three of you, but you need to stick together, you know? And if Dominic is headed to Columbia, and Luna is applying there too, I think it's a good idea for the three of you to—"

"How many friends from high school did you drag with you to Duke?"

I see him turn to face me, but I still don't look up. "Regardless, even if you go your separate ways, you only have until graduation and—"

"I'm not going to change my mind about school."

"Even if you don't, being there for Dom will make you feel a little better—"

"I don't feel bad." *I never did.* Not once. Maybe I should have. If I were like everyone else, I would have felt *something* after what happened to Dominic's sister. But the whole thing about being me is I don't feel things I should.

I thought Montford might have educated Dad on that.

But as usual, with mention of my lack of remorse, his temper starts to spike. Like if he gets angry enough, rages enough, he'll burn away my truth.

"Have you even tried?" His voice is louder, and I imagine on those rare occasions he sees the inside of a courtroom—when he's been unable to mitigate or mediate—this is the voice he uses. Clear and ringing, meant to squash any opposing viewpoints. "Have you ever once listened to Dom?"

I hate how he uses his nickname in a show of familiarity. Yes, we went to the same middle school, too. Private, a few blocks down from Trafalgar, same place we met Luna. *Dom* should understand, just like Dad, how things work for me. But they like to think I'm on their side, don't they? That for them, I can change just enough. Fold and conform and be what they need.

"Have the two of you ever talked it out?"

I set down my pen as my phone vibrates again beneath my elbow and I turn my head slowly to look at my dad.

His eyes are a shade darker than mine, muddied with gold. His hair is impressively thick, warmer in tone than my own. More brown-black than pure black like mine and Mom's. The streaks of silver aren't visible from here, but I've noticed them. And right now, he's got a line between his brows, furrowed as they are. Clean-shaven, his face is smooth, and he's as tall as I am. Still in good shape, he has a personal trainer for that.

I've felt his blows.

He can throw a punch.

But even with his physicality, and his fucking J.D., and his accolades, and his quick rise to partner when I was a kid, the way he shut Mom up with luxury and things and control, he cannot begin to fathom the first thing about his only child.

"Have we *talked* about it." I repeat the words, not as a question, but maybe so he can *listen* and realize how fucking stupid they sound.

But he doesn't because Dad never listens. Not to the doctors, not psychiatrists, not even to Mom, the supposed love of his life. The one he wore a golden band around his fucking finger for while he put them inside a multitude of women over the years after she left.

My only saving grace was he never pretended they would stick around.

If another woman had tried to be my mother, it's possible I would have killed her.

"Yeah. It's what two people do when they have a disagreement, Eli." He looks upward, at the recessed lights overhead, shadows of clouds from outside passing over the lean cut of his jaw. I look a lot like him, and a lot like Mom. I'm the perfect blend of the two of them.

Unfortunately, it wasn't just in physical makeup.

"We're fine." It's not true. Since I was away, things have spiraled for Dominic. But we're still friends. What the fuck more does Dad want?

"The vigil, just… consider it, okay?"

I won't. "You got it, Dad." The idea of standing around holding a lit candle with Luna, Dominic, and their respective parents makes me want to shatter the glass at my back with the chair legs of my stool.

Dad senses my sarcasm. At least he can pick up on that.

His hazel eyes come to mine again, a muscle in his jaw

jumping. "I don't understand you." Probably the most honest, raw thing he's ever said to me.

I curve a brow in surprise, my fingers shaking just slightly against the soft newsprint. Warmth spreads in my chest, and I can't hide the fact I'm fucking *pleased* he admitted it.

"I know."

He runs his tongue over his teeth, keeping his lips closed.

I sweep one foot over the cool tile of the floors. I can feel the grout even beneath my sock. I need to change. I have to pack shit for the tournament. There will be food and freshly laundered singlets thanks to Ms. Pensky, and all the Trafalgar Dragons T-shirts I could want, but I like multiple pairs of sweatpants, boxers, my own snacks, headphones. I'm going to bring Eden back here tonight. I'm going to fuck her while Dominic holds his *vigil*. I think about letting Dad know about Eden. He'd like her, smart and driven as she is.

He'd probably try to warn her away from me. Might make this all the more fun.

For a moment, Dad and I just stare at one another. He has a flight to catch, I have an unusual girl to pick up, but in these long seconds, it kind of falls away, taking a backseat to our loathing of one another.

"I know you didn't do anything," Dad says, his words gentle. "But it would be really nice if the Landers knew you didn't too. If they saw you supporting their son."

I smile at him. "Fuck them." I think maybe tonight, after the tournament, I'll stop by and burn down their fucking house and let them know if I had wanted to do something horrible to their daughter, *they would've known I did it.*

Dad's eyes soften. "Eli, you don't get it."

I hate those words. I fucking *hate* them. Because I get it, more than most people. I can observe things without attachment, unlike Dad, unlike the Landers, Dominic, Luna, even Janelle. I can see things without skewed loyalties clouding my vision. The Landers needed someone to blame. I was there but forensics cleared me. None of it matters. They still think I saw something. *Did* something.

My blood grows hot, but I try to reign it in. I try to keep fucking calm. I count in my head. I think about the reward, like Montford taught me. But what is the reward? Dad leaves and we don't fight? We get through a morning without blowing up at each other?

Doesn't seem like a fucking reward to me. Not at all.

"Fuck you, too," I tell him, pointing my index finger in his direction, newspaper floating to the floor, every page coming apart, scattering around the tiles as I get to my feet. "It's *you* who doesn't get it." My pulse is racing, and I can feel my blood pressure spiking. "Fuck you, Dad. You're the reason I'm like this, you know? Why they don't believe me. *You're the reason I'm fucking like this!*" I scream the last word, swiping my hand over the counter, the ceramic mug of coffee hitting the floor and shattering at the exact same time Dad takes a step toward me, the muscles in his shoulders stiff.

His eyes find the splintered mug, white shards glittering from the rising sun poking through the clouds, pouring in through the back doors behind me.

Dark coffee threads through the mess, snaking in rivulets and settling into the grout of the floor.

"All these therapies and medications and fucking time off of work and flights and specialists and you still don't know the first thing about *respect*, Eli." He whispers each word as he stares at the mug, but I'm surprised he hasn't come closer. Maybe he plans to fuck his secretary in the car to the airport. He doesn't want to get *dirty*.

I shrug one shoulder in a lazy gesture even as my mind and heart race, excitement coursing through me. "Sorry to cut into your life, *Dad*. I never asked for help. If you'd have turned a blind eye like Mom did, you could've made perfect attendance at the fucking firm—"

Before I can finish the sentence, he's coming toward me. A snarl leaves his lips as he gets in my face. I'm as tall as he is, and I'm in better shape. Dad is far removed from his wrestling years.

"Do you remember why I had to shell out all of this money for you? Do you remember the things you said to your mother? And you were *killing* animals, Eli. You cannot *torture* things and your... your family and expect me to just... just pretend you're not..." Spit flies from his lips as he averts his eyes, looking over my shoulder and holding up his hands, searching for the word, desperate to hurt me but scared to sink the knife in. He's mad, and he probably hates me right now, but he still can't say it, can he?

"I'm not what, Dad?" I whisper the words as I step closer and his gaze snaps to mine again, his nostrils flaring. I can feel the heat and rage coming from his skin. See the sweat down his neck, the vein near bursting beneath the surface above his white collar. "I'm not... *what?*"

But he still doesn't say it. He shakes his head, pressing his lips together for a second. "I'm not doing this with you." He starts to turn but I dart my hand out, unable to stop myself. My fingers dig into the soft, expensive fabric of his suit jacket and he stills, his muscles stiff beneath my grip. "Eli. Let go of me."

I smile at him. My adrenaline is through the roof and all I want to do is smash his fucking head against the glass door at our side. I don't even know why. I have no clue where these impulses come from. But I want to hurt him.

And I want him to hurt me back.

"No."

He grabs my wrist to get my hand off of him, but I tighten my grip.

"You're pathetic, you know that?" I keep my smile as I say the words. "I've heard you talk about it. To the doctors and especially the nurse you were fucking up in Idaho. I know how you really feel, Dad." I step even closer, our chests nearly touching. "Just fucking say it."

"Eli. Let. *Go.*"

I don't, and I keep quiet, holding his gaze.

He narrows his eyes. I know he's close. He's about to snap. *I just have to wait for it.*

"Eli! Get your fucking hands off of me!" He yanks at my wrist again, but I just grab his upper arm with my other hand, and then he screams in frustration. It's a loud, broken sound, followed by him shoving me against the glass at my back. My head thuds against it, and I laugh, trying to keep him off even as he yanks me away from the door by his grip on my arms just to slam me back again. This time hurts worse, a roaring in my ears as I drop my hand from his jacket to cock my fist back. I curl my fingers and shove him away with my palm at the same time I land a blow to his throat.

He gags, coughing as his face turns red, but he doesn't even miss a beat. I guess he still has wrestling reflexes after all. His fist hits my gut and I curl over, the wind knocked out of me. He doesn't stop. He hits me again, and again, and again, the last time in my chest, my head thudding with the door once more in time with the violent motion. My hands come to my knees as he backs up, his palms held up toward me like he's surrendering. I try to catch my breath as I close my eyes, sinking down to the floor, my wrists on my knees, hands clenched into fists. The pain is deep, but bearable. It just knocked the fucking air out of my lungs.

"I don't want to do this with you," he says, and I smile, eyes still closed as I try to breathe, my adrenaline fading, a little of my impulses curbed. "I can't fucking do this with you anymore." Then he turns and I hear him stalk off. A few moments later, the side door slams shut so hard his glass rattles on the counter by the sink.

I open my eyes in time to watch it fall and shatter.

The sound pierces through the pain and I start to breathe normally again.

The need in my head to fuck something up is momentarily sated.

Staring at the two broken cups in this house, I think of Eden. I think of telling her about this morning, casually. My eyes catch on the newspaper, the classified section damp with coffee, smudging the tiny black print.

What would she say, I wonder?

I prop my elbows on my knees and drop my head into my hands, then smack my palms against my face. Once. Twice. Three times, harder.

I don't think she'd say anything.

I think she'd just get it.

I think *she* would understand.

7

Eden

"WHAT AM I supposed to do here?" Trafalgar's turrets are half-hidden by low-hanging clouds, and heat lightning spikes through them. It's a strange mix of cool and warm today, the windows down on Eli's car, and little hairs stand up on the back of my arms despite the fact they're covered.

A sheer, black long sleeve shirt pushed into my faux leather pants. The shirt is buttoned to the top, but I wore a lime green sports bra underneath, for a pop of color, and a silver necklace with an ouroboros pendant is around my neck. Now, glancing at all the pricy, shiny cars in the parking lot, I'm starting to regret that act of brazenness. I knew I wouldn't have to wear my uniform, since it's not school hours, but I guess I didn't think through being under the eyes of wealthy Trafalgar parents.

I pull down the visor in the passenger seat for something to do with my hands, waiting for Eli's response, and tilt my head to each side, checking my hair. It's in a big, tortoiseshell clip affixed to the back of my head, my long bangs hanging down around my face. I tuck them behind my ear and twist my cartilage piercing, wincing as I do. One day, it won't hurt. I've had it for nearly a year now, so maybe I should give it up, but I like the way it looks.

Eli turns down the music, "What Do You Gotta Lose?" by Islander. It's in my collection of liked songs, but I don't tell him as much. Our ride has been quiet, as they all are. I like we don't have to break the silence. It's comfortable, and after dealing with Reece's probing questions this morning, Mom shaking her head and getting up abruptly to leave the table while Sebastian barely looked up from his cereal, deep purple shadows under his eyes, I didn't really want to talk.

"You're going to watch a boy you hardly know roll around with other boys in a singlet all day?" Reece rolls his eyes and leans back in his chair, the wood creaking beneath him as he does. He spears a piece of thick, burnt sausage at the end of his fork. It looks remarkably like his fingers. *"Sounds like he's really got you brainwashed."*

He's right, maybe, because when I woke up to Eli's texts to tell me I wasn't getting out of this, I darted out of bed and put this outfit together without once trying to turn him down again. *Shit.*

"Watch me," Eli answers my question.

I close the visor with a snap as I turn to face him, his seatbelt off, mine still across my chest.

He looks good in a white T-shirt, black sweats. I wonder how many pairs he owns. On his feet are white Chucks, and I imagine his closet, row after row of the same pair, waiting for him to choose them. I could be making it all up in my head, but I wouldn't be surprised. They're just so blindingly *white.*

And for whatever reason, staring at his shoes, I'm hit with the memory of last night, my fingers in my sleep shorts as I waited with bated breath for Eli's texts. Even imagining them in my head now, his words, my blood pricks with heat, and as lightning flecks the sky, it's like I can feel it in my chest, too.

Averting my gaze, I turn to look out my half-lowered window, watching other students enter F. M. Fink's athletic building. It's quiet out, parents and students far enough away I can't hear any conversation, and the music is still playing inside the car, but I wish it was a little louder to drown out the sound of my own pulse in my head.

I think of our texts this morning.

Him: Good morning. I hope you slept well because you're going to be up a while. Can't take this back, I'm leaving to pick you up soon.

Me: I'll nap in the bleachers.

Him: Not a fucking chance.

Me: …

Me: If you don't win every match, I'm going home.

It took him so long to reply to the last message, I wondered if I had actually upset him. But I don't know why I thought such a thing, now beside him in his car. He seems completely serene.

"What if watching you becomes boring?" I smile as I ask the question, but I don't look at him. Between us, though, I feel the tension amplified. Worse than it was before, and for me, it was always bad. But after last night, it's like I can't stop thinking of how I wanted to *give in* to him. I'm a little more collected now, not quite ready to fall to my knees, but no less enamored. In fact, my infatuation has broken new ground. He's just so *pretty*, his physicality makes it hard not to think of whispered things. Stuff I've watched in porn. My hands on his body. My mouth all over him, even as I don't let him touch me.

Or maybe… maybe I think of other things. His palm pressing into my chest, forcing me down, his fingers digging into my jaw, *making* me look at him, *endure* him—

"Do you think that's even a remote possibility?" *And his fucking voice.*

I dig my lime green nails into my palms. I'm still wearing the same Band-Aid I was last night. I have the sudden urge to tell him what I did, but I clamp those words down, swallowing them like the lump in my throat. "Everyone can become boring."

A second later, I hear the leather of his seat shift, and I sense him before he speaks.

Right next to me, his breath, like candy, skates over the side of my mouth, even as he doesn't touch me. A shiver slides down my spine, and I'm holding all the air in my lungs, dizzy with his nearness.

"What do you feel right now?"

Paralyzed. Alive. Nervous. Scared. Very much not *bored.*

Back up, Eli.

"Tired." I almost choke on the lie, and I don't dare turn my head toward his. If I did, our lips would touch.

"Look at me."

No. I can't say it. I just shake my head, a fraction of an inch, not wanting to bring our mouths closer together, because in my head I hear him telling me he's going to kiss me soon.

He says nothing, and I almost wish he'd make me do it. Listen to him.

Grab me. Force me. Don't let me get away with this. It all rings alongside of *don't touch me, don't touch me, don't touch me.*

The anticipation slithers under my skin, my pulse ballooning comically loud in my ears, I'd be surprised if he couldn't hear it.

But a long second later, he pulls away, and I don't know if I exhale with relief or disappointment. I sink back into my seat, closing my eyes, but still not able to face him.

"Boring things are easy to look at." He starts to roll the windows up in his car, and I almost wish he wouldn't. Like I need the fresh air to get enough oxygen into my lungs. "It's why people reread books, spend hours watching the same show they've already seen a dozen times, listen to a song they heard over and over on the radio when they were a kid." He finishes with the windows and turns the engine off, plunging us into silence. "It's comfortable. Meaningless. *Boring.*" There's a slice of anger stabbing through the last word. "When you can look at me without blushing, or flinching, or wanting to grab me, wanting *me* to grab *you,* then we'll have a problem."

I take a deep breath, open my eyes. "I don't want you to grab me," I tell him, mostly truthfully, ignoring his commentary on *boring*.

I can feel his eyes on me, drifting over my skin like a living thing. "Yeah? What *do* you want?"

I run my tongue over the sharp points of my top teeth, staring at the storm surrounding the castle. *I don't know. Help me decide.* Instead of that, all I say is, "You'll figure it out."

He answers by getting out of the car.

Wrestling is fascinating.

Similar to the MMA I've seen sporadically with Sebastian, I'm always shocked how such stagnant positions can expend so much effort. Eli, in a black singlet, and his opponent, in red, are head-to-head, their fingers wrapped around one another's biceps in a strange sort of hug, and they don't seem to be actually moving. Even still, I can see their flexed muscles, squared shoulders, the tension in their inaction.

Trafalgar's wrestling coach, standing beside the desk chair placed at the edge of the mat, has his arms crossed, a bundle of papers clenched in one hand, the other under his chin. He's wearing glasses, a small man in good shape, he hasn't once looked away from Eli.

The other coach is doing something similar on the opposite end of the square mat, but he isn't silent like Trafalgar's.

"Let's *do something*, Erling!" His face is pink and he's probably a decade older than Eli's coach.

Despite my determination to appear unaffected by anything that happened in this enormous, gleaming gymnasium, I'm leaned over my knees, black, chunky boots tapping up and down on the dark blue bleacher seat below me, thankfully empty. My arms are crossed, my eyes locked in on Eli's triceps, and I imagine I might look like I have a stomachache, because that's exactly what so many parents scattered beside and behind me appear to have. Some of them weren't content to stay up on the bleachers near me though, with the A/C fanning over the back of my neck, rattling the soft, loose fabric of my sheer shirt.

Those parents are dotted around the gleaming, tan floors of the gym, on every square inch not covered by thick black mats with white circles. Eli's dad may not have come, but it hasn't stopped his teammates' parents from cheering him on, calling out his name specifically, every so often for reasons sometimes obvious to me and sometimes not.

This is his second match.

His first ended quickly, in the first period with a takedown that led to a pin, Eli draped over the guy's upper body like he was using him as a pillow. It was fast, and almost lazy.

Now, though, the ref brings his fists together, knuckles bumping, saying "stalling." It seems to be a warning, because they break apart, the red headed guy shaking his head as they do, adjusting the strap of his red singlet. Sweat gleams along his ropey muscles, and I watch Eli's chest heave, but he's smiling, which seems a little out of place. Then again… it's Eli. He enjoys a challenge, I think.

I don't move from my crouched over position, rocking back and forth, and when they come together again, the ref circling them, a whistle in his mouth like he's on guard to correct them once more for doing nothing, I almost leap to my feet in outrage.

The guy gets Eli on his back in seconds. A sweep of his feet, hugging him close as he causes him to fall.

I think it's over.

The ref is on his hands and knees, making a sweeping motion with one hand, like he's counting something, and Eli's coach narrows his eyes, but while the other guy's coach is screaming, Trafalgar's says nothing. It seems like it's coming to an end, and I feel a sense of dread in my chest. Like it isn't *fair*. Like I want to drag the guy off of Eli.

As if he needs saving.

But regardless, saving or not, the match has to be over, and I exhale, sitting up straighter, dropping my feet to the shiny center of the bleachers, unwilling to watch Eli lose as I turn my head to the buzzard. Second period, forty-five seconds left.

Six minutes total. Three two-minute periods. Eli told me as much when we walked into the gym together. He shoved a bundle of dollar bills in my hand before he disappeared into the locker rooms, and at first, I was offended, until he laughed and told me it was for snacks, from the vending machine. Organic animal crackers and sparkling water, I think of getting something after this. Or maybe now, while Eli loses.

But I hear someone yelling.

Multiple people. I think it must mean the match has officially been called, but as I drag my gaze to Eli, I see his hips lifted into the air, the inside of his elbow around the back of his opponent's head, his other arm beneath his stomach. Eli throws his arms up, tossing the guy off and twisting his body, knee crashing down to the mat as his upper body comes over his opponent's, gaining the dominant position.

His coach still says nothing, but now *he's* smiling.

The referee sweeps his hand two times, in slow motion, then he blows the whistle, and it's done. *Eli won.*

After they're on their feet, when the ref holds up Eli's hand by his wrist, his eyes find mine, his cheeks pink. He lifts a brow, as if to say, *did you really think I was going to lose?*

"WHAT DO YOU THINK?" HE PULLS BACK FROM THE WATER fountain, releasing it, then swiping at his bottom lip with the back of his hand. His singlet is pulled off of both shoulders, his heaving chest exposed, sweat lining every inch of defined muscle.

My phone slips from the side pouch of my bag, hanging off of one arm, and before I can tell him what I think about watching him wrestle, in this musky back hallway, he bends down to retrieve my phone after it clatters on the tile floor.

The words I try to form die in my mouth.

The tight spandex of his black singlet falls lower as he grabs my phone. In the moment before he straightens, I see it completely.

A fresh bruise, still red with edges of darkening purple. The size of a large apple. His skin is tan with an olive complexion, but the red of the bruise is so stark, it wouldn't matter his skin tone. There's no mistaking it.

And what I just saw on the mat... even when his opponent took him down, there was no fist to his chest. Just his body over Eli's. It wouldn't form a bruise. And before that, the earlier match, Eli had the upper hand from start to finish.

He offers me the phone as he stands to his full height, looking down on me.

I try to wipe the shock off of my face, but I must do a poor job of it because I know he sees something in my expression. His brows pull together, phone still offered in my direction, but it's not the focal point.

I close my mouth and try to ignore the feelings flooding through me. Curiosity, concern, *anger*.

Who touched him like that?

I take my phone from his hand, my fingers grazing his own, but I don't let them linger as I avert my eyes on pretense of fiddling with my bag, putting the phone away.

"That bad, huh?" There's a lightness to his words, so out of place with the heaviness in my chest, like someone just pulled a rug out from underneath me and I'm trying not to fall, my heart racing hard.

"I..." My tongue feels thick in my mouth. I finally drop my hands from my bag, hefting it onto my shoulders as I look up, searching his eyes for something. *Anything*, like I might read an explanation there, or he might offer it, as if he could read my mind.

I never asked why it took him so long to text me last night.

It didn't feel like my business. But now I'm wondering where he was. Did he get into a fight? Was he with someone else?

My own fantasies of Eli pinning me down like those boys on the mats, digging his fingers into my skin, wrapping them around my throat, hurting me, *bruising me*... Does he dream of the same thing? Or is it no longer a dream for him?

Feelings of inexperience, inadequacy, stupidity, they all converge on me at once until I want to run. I glance at the double glass doors leading out to the back parking lot of the athletic center.

Eli must see my look because he steps closer and pivots, blocking my view of the dark gray skies beyond the exit.

"Eden."

I blink a few times before I look up. "It's great," I say, but I don't believe my own words. Truthfully, it *is* great, but the distraction of blooming red and violet on his chest is making it very hard to think about watching his athletic prowess.

He hooks one arm at a time into his singlet, pulling the straps up on his broad shoulders. My eyes come to his throat, a strip of pale skin where his choker lay this morning. I wonder if it's against regulations, or he just doesn't want to give someone the chance to hurt him with it.

Hurt him. I dig my nails into my palms.

"Don't lie to me." His words come out even, but they feel like a warning.

I think of our conversation about honesty. But it's just a bruise. I get them often enough. Perks of being clumsy.

I roll my shoulders back, lifting my chin, standing taller.

I'll ask him about it later.

He has two more matches. *No more than five in a single day.* He told me he wanted more than the four. Just one more, to max it out.

Four seems like so many now I know what the sport entails. Even in a stalemate, he's expending so much energy. And the bruise on his chest, it has to hurt when his opponents collide with him, right?

I realize I don't like it. Thinking about him getting hurt. It stuns me, my own feelings, but I don't show it. I school my features to neutrality, like I've seen him do dozens of times. Like *I* do.

"No, really." I loop a strand of hair behind my ear and resist the urge to put my nails into my mouth and bite, ripping off a piece with my teeth. "Two down, two to go. You think you're going to walk out of here undefeated?"

He doesn't smile even though I force myself to fake one. His dark green eyes are roving over mine, a sheen of sweat beneath his lower lash line, beautiful like highlighter on his skin. "Will you stop bullshitting me if I do?" This time, after he asks the question, he smiles.

It makes it much more sinister.

"I'm not bullshitting you." The annoyance in my tone is real. I don't want to throw his head for a loop by telling him I saw something he's probably trying to hide. Or is he? I don't know, but it seems like Eli *Adonis* Addison would not like anyone knowing he isn't invincible.

Later. I'll ask him later.

I hear a stark clap of hands, and we both turn, although I'm the only one who flinches. A few feet from us, the slim coach with small glasses still has his palms together as he nods toward Eli.

"Let's go, Stunner." His dark eyes flicker to me, but he says nothing, then turns on his heel and starts calling out other wrestlers in his charge, posted up along the hallway with water bottles in hand.

Stunner. It makes me smile a little.

"For every win I get, Eden Rain, you're giving me an answer to any question I want to ask." Eli takes a step back, untying the drawstring of the gym shorts he has on over his singlet, eyes still holding mine. "An *honest* answer." He looks proud of himself for that one. "Now get your fine ass back in here." He jerks his head to the entrance of the gym, double doors propped open.

"Excuse me?" I feign outrage because the lust bubbling in my core with his command pisses me off.

He smiles at me, like he knows as he walks backward toward the gym. "Don't act like you don't like it." His eyes rake over my body, which grows warm from his gaze. "Walk in with me. Too many dads out there checking you out."

My skin crawls and automatically, I hurry to walk next to him. The moment he laughs, I know I just lost this game too.

8

Eden

"GET IT OVER WITH." I know he's savoring all four of his wins. Three pins and the final match by points, I think he would've had the pin if he hadn't been so tired. Even though I knew it would add another question to the tally, I still couldn't stop from standing in the bleachers, and while I didn't clap like the Trafalgar parents around me, my smile made him reflect one back to me as the ref held up his arm, *again*.

I waited while he showered, the aftermath of the tournament no less busy than the duration of it. People mopping down mats, rolling them up, chairs carried back to classrooms, wrappers picked up from around the edges of the gym. I felt I should do something, but no one asked me to help out, and the boys from both the home and away teams seemed to have it under control.

I watched Eli interact with his teammates. His coach seems to quietly adore him, the coach's wife too, with glasses just like her husband's. She hugged Eli close, and he towered over her, giving her a squeeze back. Not for the first time, I thought about his mom.

His teammates seem to regard him with awe, and he's the quietest in the group, but he's the clear leader by the way everyone pivots toward him after a match, at the end of the tournament, before they got on the mat, anything at all, it's like they're looking at him to decide which step they should take next. Asking silent permission. *Submission.*

What would it feel like, I wondered more than once, to take control of someone like Eli? Does he ever let it happen?

Now, behind the wheel of his car, smelling like soap and the sea, his hair damp from the shower he had in the locker room while I read Chaucer from my backpack, he's smiling like a cat, the faintest dimple showing in his cheek.

The day has gotten grayer, and as he pulls through the high iron gates of Trafalgar, I see a crack of lightning fork violently down from the sky, the boom of thunder seconds later. I think of Mom at the trailer, Sebastian on the road, and I slip my phone from my back pocket, waiting for Eli to ask the first of his four questions.

Mom: Are you still going to your friend's house?
Me: Yeah, is it raining there?

Eli turns up the music at the same time he increases the speed on his windshield wipers, cool air from the vents clearing the smoggy glass when he turns right at the light outside of the school.

Mom: A little. We're keeping an eye on tornado warnings. Be careful. What time will you be home?

I bite my lip, bouncing my knee as I glance at Eli. He'd told me to stay the night with him, but I can't do that. *It was a joke, anyway.* Besides, tomorrow I have to work, and I shouldn't be considering a sleepover.

Before I text Mom back, there's a loud ringing through his speakers. I jump with the sound, and Eli glances at his dashboard. I see his eyes narrow, but surprising me, he answers the call.

"Hey." His tone is dull and subdued.

My heart feels like it's going to fly out of my chest, and I don't even know why.

"How did it go?" The voice through the speakers is cheerful. Deep and male and attractive.

Eli's grip tightens on the shifter. "Great." His tone is clipped.

I frown, dropping my eyes to my phone screen, which has gone dim.

The person on the other line laughs, but it sounds a little tired. "Just great?"

Eli takes his time replying as he drives. Thunder booms outside of the confines of his luxury vehicle. "Yep."

Why are you being so rude? I don't even know who it is, but he's older, I think, maybe… it's his dad? My pulse decides to hammer harder against my ribcage.

The man clears his throat. "You're headed to the vigil, right?"

I blink down at my phone, my limbs stiffening. *Vigil?*

Eli gives a sexy, disrespectful half-laugh, half-scoff. "Sure." It doesn't sound like he's telling the truth.

"Dominic will really appreciate it, you know. His family too."

Eli says nothing to this. I peek at him from my side of the car, and I see his full lips are pressed tight together.

"Well, call me if you need me, okay?"

"Yep."

"Love you, son."

Shit, it is his dad.

"Bye." Eli ends the call, and music fills the interior of the car again.

I look back down at my phone, questions spinning in my mind. I read Mom's text again, about what time I'll be home. She's let me go to sleepovers with Amanda, hang out late, encouraged me to, even, to get out of my own head.

But that was all before what happened at Shoreside. Besides, Eli's got a *vigil* to attend. I didn't see that coming.

Me: How late can I stay out? I ask it, even knowing I might have to be dropped off earlier. Because... *vigil.* I think of the purpose of one. It comes from a Latin word we learned just last week. *Vigilia. Wakefulness.* To keep watch. *For whom?*

Her: You have work tomorrow, how about 11?

I exhale a little, like I thought she might actually say I should stay over, and I wanted an excuse not to.

Me: Okay, thanks.

"You done over there?"

I look up as I click off my phone screen, flipping it to rest on my thigh, my palm over the bright green case on the back where I clack my lime green nails.

"What was that about?"

"I think it's my turn to ask questions." His voice has a teasing edge, but he doesn't look at me.

I glance at the road, having no idea where we're going. This is a nice part of Raleigh, with wide, freshly paved streets, yards like estates and houses more like mansions set far back off the road. "A vigil?" I press. "Who is it for?"

"An old friend."

I squirm a little in my seat. "An old friend?"

"That's what I said."

I narrow my eyes at him, and watch as he glances at me, smirking a little. "A *close* friend?"

He sighs, shaking his head as he leans back in his seat. "A girl I used to fuck."

My blood runs cold with his bluntness. I feel a little shaky and I grip my phone so hard, my palm starts to sweat. "A girl you used to... I think you should elaborate."

"I don't think I should."

My stomach flips. "Where are you taking me?"

He huffs the smallest laugh. "Are you nervous, Eden?"

I don't really know the answer to that, so I just blurt out, "Is she dead?"

He shrugs. "I don't know."

"What?" My nerves raise my voice an octave as I sit up

straighter in his seat. "What's the vigil for? Tell me now."

"It's for a friend of mine who went missing. A long time ago. Could be dead, could be alive." He says it all so blasé, like he doesn't care either way. Then he just changes the subject. "I'm really tired, you know. Pretty sore, too. I'd really like a massage, but—"

"I'm not giving you a massage." The offense in my tone is only partly real as I glance at the lines of his biceps and squeeze my thighs together. What would it feel like, to touch his skin?

"*But* since I don't think I could talk you into that, can we start now?" He continues speaking like I didn't interrupt him, but he's smiling again, eyes on the road.

I drop the vigil. He gave me an answer. Maybe I don't want to know more. There are things I don't speak of, and ignorance truly can be bliss.

"You have a question?" I counter, seeing Eli rubbing his thumb over his chin before he drops his hand back to the shifter. I'm glad the A/C is blasting to keep the windshield clear from fog. It helps keep my sweating at bay.

"How do you think I see you?"

I tip my head, catching his eye as I ball my free hand into a fist, my bag on the floorboard at my feet. I kick it, just a little, shifting it onto its side. "Really? That's your question?" I don't know what I expected. My favorite song, worst memory, maybe how I see *him*. But how *does* he see me? I'm not sure how to answer, mainly because I have no idea. I could be a project, a challenge, something to poke and prod because he's bored.

Blue gum flashes between his teeth as he brings his eyes back to the road. "Yes." He sounds very smug, like he knows it's a difficult thing to answer. "That's my question."

I lean my head against the leather seat, staring at the rain splattering the windshield, oddly enough going *up* instead of down, almost as if it's dispersing away from the glass and out of his line of sight. Like it's easier to see through. Vaguely, I recall Sebastian putting something on my windshield before, he claimed it would repel rain. It was two years ago, when I first started driving and he wasn't so… messed up. Maybe he was then, too. He just hid it better.

I wonder if Eli applied the repellent himself or if someone did it for him.

"I don't know." As I say the words, I know they're a cop out, but trying to imagine how he views me makes me feel uncomfortable, which is probably why he asked. "Obviously you don't think I'm *boring* yet, or I wouldn't be in the car with you right now."

"Okay, so that's how I *don't* see you…" He trails off and I want to smack the grin off of his face when our eyes briefly connect, more thunder rumbling outside, rain coming down in sheets. The wind feels as if it might blow the car off the road, but Eli seems to have no problem managing it. He isn't egotistical about it, either, the way he keeps a low speed, plenty of space between him and the bright red brake lights in front of us.

"Now get your fine ass back in here." Those words I pretended to loathe echo in my head.

I feel myself growing warmer, but I still speak, clearing my throat before I do. "You think I'm attractive." I can't say any other word. "Hot" or "sexy" or "cute" would sound juvenile and Eli seems to be anything but that. My palms are sweaty, but if I just focus on the back-and-forth track of the windshield wipers, I can get this question over with. "Shy." I think of how he commented on my blushing. Then other voices seem to intrude, voices that aren't his. "Maybe naïve. Socially inept." I can't seem to stop spilling out negative, self-deprecating adjectives, all from my own brain. "A hermit. Clumsy. Not very good at makeup." I laugh, but I loathe myself for it. "I sweat too much. Lame, because I just spent an entire day watching you wrestle, and I don't even know you." I don't want him to stop me, and he doesn't. He's silent, music playing beneath the roar of the storm, but I can't make out the words, and I don't care. It's like now I've started, I can't really stop. "You probably think I'm easy to manipulate and that's why you're doing it, and maybe I'm just some pet project, a mouse to play with until you get bored and squish me between your fingers." The image plays in my head, and I feel sick. Not physically. Just, of myself. Like if I could get out of this car and go back to my room and do my homework and keep myself small and—

"Are you done?"

His voice is jarring, the coldness of his tone bringing me back to right now, here, in this moment at a blurry stoplight.

I turn my head to see him staring right back at me, expression blank.

"Yes." I whisper the word, disgusted with myself.

The light changes to green, and I see it out of the corner of my eye, our gazes still locked, but he doesn't move. Not at first. Then, slowly, the muscles in his forearms twitch, then jump, and he's shifting gears, driving through the intersection as he turns his head away from me.

"What's the darkest thought you've ever had?"

I don't know if I'm gutted he didn't say anything about my answer to his first question, or giddy with relief. The feeling is hard to parse, the way it's a physical ache in my stomach. I leave it in the past and when I speak again, it's with a false note of *I'm fine*.

"The darkest thought I've ever had about someone else, or…" *Myself,* is what I don't say. I think I want to counter his question with a question, so I feel more in control.

His fingers tighten almost imperceptibly on the wheel, but I see the way his knuckles blanch. For some reason, it's like I've won something, and I have no idea what it is.

"Yourself." It sounds as if he's unsure. As if he really hadn't thought about it and would've liked me to answer both. I wonder if he'll waste his next question on asking me about my worst thoughts on other people.

But I'm a little distracted with the worst thought I've ever had about myself, beneath the way I tore me down just moments ago. I have a more morbid thought, one I know will distract him from all of my own insecurities I just vomited up for him to dissect.

Still, I'm reluctant to share it. I want to go with something easier to stomach. To deflect, I say, "You tell me first."

He smiles. "That's not how this game is going to go."

"It is if you want an answer."

"God, you are fucking stubborn." It sounds kind of like a compliment, the way he says it. But before I can respond, he keeps talking. "I won't tell you the worst, but I'll give you something better. Something I did when I was a kid."

I'm eager for the insight because I can't imagine Eli as a child. I assume he's eighteen, based on the script tattoo on his arm I still haven't been able to read, and I briefly wonder if I'm older than him. I turned eighteen September seventh, earlier this month. But it seems like we've skipped right past ages and into something far more intense.

Eli glances at me. His grip loosens then tightens on the wheel, and I stare at his rings while he speaks. "I almost drowned my neighbor."

I'm not sure what I expected to hear, but if he was trying to throw me off, he succeeded. My mind is kind of blank, and I blink a few times, like clearing my vision will give me room to dissect his words. All I can come up with is a strangled sort of, *"Excuse me?"*

He lifts one shoulder up in a lazy shrug, eyes back on the road. "I was a bad kid." He says it without any emotion. "It was a long time ago. It was a birthday party. I just… pushed him." He glances my way once. "He's okay, though. He was in diapers. I think they helped buoyed him a second so his mom could save him. So, come on. Tell me your worst thought about yourself, I promise I won't judge you."

In diapers. Jesus Christ. I think of asking all kinds of things about the incident, but I know he won't answer me.

It takes me a minute to speak, but suddenly, my morbid answer doesn't seem so… terrible. Or, perhaps, it simply seems like he'd understand. I clear my throat again, and I stare straight ahead, at the storm, as I speak. "My parents watched a lot of crime shows when I was growing up." I lump Reece in with my parents, so I don't have to explain they're divorced, and I don't have to field a question about my dad. There's not much to say about him, and I like to say as little as possible where he's concerned. "I kind of became obsessed with *CSI*." I never missed an episode, and I was never scared. Not once. Not until I got older, anyway, and Sebastian's friend *happened*. Before that, I imagined being a crime scene investigator. I fantasized about it all the time. Got on forums and message boards from the family computer as a kid, pretending to be older and smarter than I was, skirting around adults playing amateur detective about local, small town crimes.

I take a breath as we make a turn into a subdivision. The worst thought about myself has nothing to do with an abandoned dream job.

Focusing on the here, the now, giving myself a moment, I take in the neighborhood. The homes are enormous, and for a second, shrinking into Eli's passenger seat, I forget about the question and my answer. Spaced far apart, built high up on hills, every driveway angled upward, these really are mansions. Stone and brick, gray and brown and red, minimum three-car garages attached to each one.

Can Eli see I don't belong here?

I turn my head to find him staring at me as the wind picks up, knocking the rain sideways, even with the repellant I think Eli has on his car. "Go on."

I want to ask where we are, but I don't. Best to get this over with. We'll be halfway done.

"Anyway, I always thought the reenactments of the murders were fascinating." I stare out my window, taking in the sheer enormity of the homes. Trees dot the landscape, forests in the backyards, the road winding up and up and up. "I was kind of obsessed with the mind of a violent criminal. But it was never them I empathized with. Instead…" I trail off, my mind frantic for a lie.

I can't say this out loud.

Eli is quiet. More mansions, circular driveways, stone columns. *What the hell have I started?* My mind blanks out on any alternative, any way I could spin this into something else.

"I meant it. I swear I won't judge you." Eli's words are hushed, spoken softly. I wouldn't believe him; except I think I hear something underneath his statement. Something darker. Hidden. *Play in the shadows with me.*

I squeeze my eyes shut tight, still facing away from him. *What if we never come back into the light?*

I take a deep breath and a risk as I open my eyes. "I always wondered what it would be like, having sex with a man who killed me at the end of it." I hurry over the last sentence, and I don't dare look at Eli. I can't.

Is this too dark for you? My heart seems to stutter violently in my chest.

Seconds tick past.

Eli says nothing.

Jesus.

Even my eyes feel hot, and I force myself to keep my shoulders back as I wait. If I curl in on myself, hunch over and retreat, *he might not believe me.* Some people enjoy flaunting their depravity, talking loudly about the underside of humanity. I saw it in the forums, too. I think, though, the most twisted among us speak in whispers.

Still, I can't help but wonder if I've misjudged him. Is he going to turn around right here, right now, take me back home? Will he tell everyone he knows at Trafalgar how insane I am? Did I mistake our connection, thinking it was something deeper than it is? We don't *really* know each other. This could be just like at Shoreside. Just like with *Nic.*

The thoughts come too fast. I should've known better. I gave him a weakness to exploit.

This was a mistake.

I'm about to twist in my seat and tell him I can get a ride

home when he finally breaks the silence, still coasting through the wooded, magical subdivision.

"How would he kill you?"

I blink a few times, relaxing the vise grip I have on my phone, unsure if I've heard him correctly with all the blood thumping around in my brain. But I play the words back in my head. *"How would he kill you?"*

Relief spreads through my limbs along with a healthy dose of fear as we drive in the middle of the storm. I can barely speak, my throat so dry, but I manage to ask, "Is that your third question?"

Eli sighs, a sound of surrender. "Fuck." The word is flustered. I think of last night, when he texted me just that, and a flush of warmth spans from my thighs upward, to my core. "I guess." He hates it, giving up another question to join his second, but he really wants to know.

The fact he wants it so much, it makes it easier to just say it, out loud, the fucked-up fantasy in my head. *Don't run now.*

"He'd press his hand over my mouth, my nose… as he, you know… while we're having sex." I have to clear my throat, and my voice is hoarse as I keep going, but I don't stop. "I'd… suffocate, I guess."

Eli's words sound rough, like he's having a hard time speaking, too. "Is that all? It's just… like that, in your head?"

It's never so simple inside my head. "Maybe he…" I trail off, sure I'm about to go too far now.

"Tell me. I want to know."

My entire body grows incredibly hot. I cough a little, for something to do with my mouth that isn't spouting off all of these insane truths that should be locked away. "Maybe he'd have to… hit me. Or punch me, so I… stop fighting—"

"You're trying to get away? Defend yourself?"

I give him these questions, because I can't think clearly about limits when we're prying into the darkest recesses of my brain. "It's only human nature."

"He punches you." Eli says it slowly, like he's clarifying. Like he really wants this all to play out inside his mind, too.

"Yes." My word is whispered, barely a breath.

"Do you like it? Does it hurt? Is it the pain you enjoy?"

So many questions, so many lines, but my mind is racing and my heart, too; I don't keep track. "Yes. To all of it. Yes."

"So, he's keeping you pinned down while he assaults you and stops you from breathing?"

I think of what I wanted last night. Eli all over me. The ways I wonder how it would feel. "He'd use his body weight to keep me still. Yeah." I still don't look at him, even as he turns left, into a driveway. Up and up, then Eli spins his car around, and we're reversing, until the world grows dark.

He reaches for something attached to his visor, and a garage door comes down, trapping us inside.

I finally face him, sure he can't see the extent of my nervousness in the darkness.

Suddenly, no longer in motion, I don't want to talk about what I just said. I silently hope he'll let it go like the first answer I gave him.

"Is this your house?" I glance at the two spaces beside him. This place is nothing like a garage I've ever been inside. It's clean. There's not much beyond a black Tesla, a green and yellow riding mower, and what looks like tires and car tools on a built-in shelving system behind Eli's car.

He has one hand still clenched tight around the wheel, the other holding onto the shifter in a grip that looks painful, fingers digging in with such force I see the way his hand is turning red, veins straining against his skin.

His eyes gleam from the lights of his dashboard. "Ghost" by Halsey is playing from his speakers, and my thoughts snag on my own surprise. I didn't expect it would be a song he'd listen to, but it's playing from his phone's connection.

I realize his jaw is clenched as he stares at me, and I suddenly don't know what to do with my hands, my mouth, or where I should look or if I should get out or...

"If I don't turn my car off, we're going to die in here. I have one more question and you better answer it fucking fast, or they'll find us just like this." He jerks his chin, indicating the interior of his car.

"No," I correct him, unwavering, ignoring his theatrical threat. "You asked two more questions after your third. I gave you a bonus." A few actually, that I couldn't count, and I only mean to tease him, but my tone is all wrong, not light, and neither of us smile.

He presses his lips together and doesn't look away from me. For once, I don't look away either.

The song loops again, and I didn't realize he had it on repeat. I don't know if *he* realized it.

As the chorus comes on, I glance in the side view mirror.

I see exhaust fumes in the glow of his red taillights.

"Eli." I could reach for the door handle. It opens easily. I know that from the first night he gave me a ride. It would take nothing for me to get out, to walk through the door which I assume leads into his house, or else out the door on my side of the garage, which probably opens up to the yard.

I'm not trapped in here.

But I don't move.

It's probably my imagination, but I'm suddenly overcome with a wave of exhaustion, and even my pulse, always frantic like a hummingbird, drops to something far slower.

"Are you scared to die?" The same quality of *restraint* is in his words when he asks the question anyway, ignoring my protest completely.

I take a deep breath, tearing my gaze away from the red-tinted smoke curling up behind his car.

Meeting his eye, I reach across the center console, and I see it, the moment before I get to what I'm after. His lips part, his breath hitches, and he thinks I'm going to touch him.

It was anticipation in his eyes.

Maybe a little fear. I imagine grabbing his throat, twisting the choker, the leather cutting into his skin. A rush fills my veins. My nerves seem to subside.

But I simply press the button on his car, killing the engine.

The purr and the music drops, wrapping us in silence.

Still close to him, the console digging into my ribs, my face inches from his, I repeat, "You already used all of your questions." I start to lean back in my seat, retracting my hand, when he grabs my wrist.

A shudder runs through me, his fingers cold on my hot skin.

I freeze, and now it's my turn to be afraid.

"All those things you think I think about you?"

I clench my teeth with his reference to the first question. I don't want to ever speak of it again. I liked how he didn't comment on it, and I don't want him to start now. But he doesn't give me a choice.

He closes the space between us, leaning down so we're eye level.

I want to pull back. I want to yank my arm from his grip, but I don't think I could, and I don't even try.

"Only the first one was true."

Then he releases me as suddenly as he grabbed me, straightening in his seat and opening his door after he swipes his phone and his keys from the console.

"Are you scared to die?"

For a moment, the question echoing in my head, I can't move, my limbs heavy and my mind numb. But he comes around to my side and opens my door, offering me his hand.

It's what I need to think again.

I don't take his offer, but I get out of the car, his arm still braced on the door, bringing us close to one another. I have to look up at him, a smirk on his face, but I don't feel intimidated.

"Fuck."

"How would he kill you?"

"Only the first one was true."

He didn't judge me. And before I can stop myself, when I

know I should just leave it alone, I say, "If you didn't know, I think you're attractive too."

He stares at me a moment longer. Then his smile pulls wider, becomes more genuine, and he drops his hand, stepping back, shaking his head with the smallest laugh.

He might've been asking the questions, but I feel like, in this moment, I won the game.

9

Eli

SHE LOOKS down when she reaches the kitchen island, her fingertips gliding softly over the marble. Neither of us speak. I didn't tell her where we were going but I'm sure she's figured out I live here, despite the lack of personal touches in the areas of the house she's seen thus far.

As I watch her, I think of Dad and I this morning. Our fight, the shattered glass.

I wonder what she'd think. I want to tell her, but it'll sound as if I'm looking for pity, and I don't want her pity.

I just want her to *hear* me, like I heard her in the car. All the things she might not have said in the confession about getting fucked and hurt and… *Fuck.*

I wonder if she's a virgin, if all these things are fantasies she'd actually hate, because there is a huge gap between what we think we want and when push comes to shove, what we *really* want. I wouldn't care either way, but she's jumpy when I touch her. Paranoid, almost, no matter the cool front she puts on.

I press my knuckles to my mouth to stop from moving,

speaking, interrupting this moment when she peeks into my life and decides what to think of it all.

She pauses, drifting her slender fingers on the countertops, frowning as she watches where her green nails touch the marble, as if she's concerned her touch will cause it all to crumble to dust.

Moving on, she drops her hand by her side and stares out the three glass doors to the back patio. In my head, I hear Dad slamming my skull against the middle one. I imagine what Eden would say, if she could see it replaying in my mind on a loop.

Would it scare you? The ways I want love?

She doesn't look back, but her narrow shoulders stiffen, and I glance at the peak of her neck above the collar of her sheer, silk shirt. The thick roots of her hair, pulled up into her clip. In all black, with those black leather leggings clinging to the round curves of her ass, her thick, black boots, but there's something delicate about her, even in the ways she seems to say, *you can't scare me, Eli.*

You have no idea, baby girl.

I smile to myself and follow her gaze, seeing the onslaught of rain over the pool, gray pelting against brightest blue. The umbrellas dotted around the mosaic tiles, a waterfall spilling into the hot tub set above pool level, separated by green plants draped over the edges of dark stones.

Another fire pit curved against the burnished tile, built-in bench of seats. And that's just the pool.

Even the wind doesn't move the chairs, and the umbrellas are closed, near the sheltered bar and glass walls of the rectangular pool house.

Eden's red lips are pressed together, and she stares with cool detachment. *I'm not impressed.* She says it without words.

My body feels hot, and there're only a few feet between us, but somehow, it feels like too much, when I want her like this.

"Nice pool." She says the words flatly, folding her arms

across her chest and glancing at me, arching one thick brow. "What're we doing tonight?"

I smile at her forced disinterest. I didn't tell her we were stopping by, worried she'd refuse to get in the car with me, or inwardly panic the entire drive, too caught up in her own head to focus on my questions. She puts on a cool front.

It's a lie.

"You like my pool?" I counter, still smiling.

As I ask the question, I imagine her in it.

It's September. We have at least until November to swim. By Halloween there's usually too much of a chill to do so comfortably, but the pool is heated, so we can stretch it out. Dad doesn't care either way, but I do.

I want every minute I can get in it.

The hot tub is always available, and I can sit on the bottom of it, but it's not enough. They say you can drown in a teaspoon of water, but why die in the shallow?

If water ends me, I want it to be an ocean. Something far *bigger* than me. Something that deserves to kill me. Hot tubs, pools, lakes, none of those are good enough.

I think of my hand over Eden's nose. Her mouth. My body moving above hers. Wild eyes, scratch marks down my arms as she fights me, just like she said she would.

Are you sure?

Is it what you really want?

You know you can't take these kinds of things back.

I know you're not as tough as you try to look. Be soft with me.

The teaspoon of water doesn't deserve my mortality. Suffocation, even if I was fucking her at the same time, wouldn't deserve Eden's. Besides, we're the type of people to live forever, even if we don't want to. Maybe *because* we don't want to. I think God enjoys orchestrating a little suffering.

"It's… pretty." Eden shrugs, and with the movement, my gaze drifts over her shoulders again, down her slender arms, made smaller by the black of her top. The lime green of her bra. She's a fucking tease despite her buttoned collar, and I like knowing she doesn't seem to care. She isn't looking to please anyone at all, she just likes what she likes.

I drop my gaze to her ass, not small at all. If anything, *bigger* because of the leather of her pants, the high waist.

She turns fully then, stepping slowly toward me, and I flick my eyes upward to meet hers, a jarring mix of blue and green and brown, I don't think I'll ever get them out of my head, no matter where we go from here.

With me. Wherever we go, come with me. It's crazy to think these things, and yet I can't stop.

"Pretty?" I counter.

She rolls her eyes. "Your dad…" She clears her throat and I wonder if she's thinking of my mom. Any other parents she might think I have. "He's not going to be here, right?"

I kind of want to make her squirm, drag out the answer. But instead, as if I'm compelled, as if I couldn't deny her if I tried, I just tell her the truth. "No." I wonder what she'd think of my dad. I can tell she's nervous to meet him, she started bouncing her leg with his voice through my car speakers. Does she not want any kind of permanence? Is she worried she won't be enough for him? She'll fail to impress him? What kind of man does she imagine raised someone like me?

I see relief in the set of her shoulders, even though she tries to keep her expression blank.

Smiling, I nod my head toward the hallway which leads to the foyer which leads to the dining room, which leads… who fucking cares. "Come on, I'll show you the rest of the house."

Thunder rumbles outside, and the rain hasn't let up. I wonder if it will in time for me to take her to eat or something. My low-profile tires aren't great in rain, but it's the risk that makes the reward. Driving too fast, taking a turn over the speed limit, slipping and sliding on wet pavement, it does something to me. Maybe it'll do something to her, too.

As she follows, I lead the way through the foyer, the massive double doors in the entranceway. Thinking of her meeting

Dad, the memory of the last time Mom was in this house echoes in my head.

Mom and Eden are both very hard to outwardly impress. I wonder what they'd think of each other.

I discard the thought, the memory too, because like many things, it doesn't matter.

Eden and I come to a stop just before the formal dining room.

She walks past me, and the scent of her—dreamy, in a strange way, soft, like violets—envelopes me, like it did in the car. I could smell her sweat, too, and while it was musky as sweat is, to me, it smelled *good*. My nostrils flare as she stops, just in front of me, and I catch the scent of something else. Maybe peaches? Her shampoo?

I want to reach for the clip in her hair and let it all spill down her back.

I don't move.

I just cross my arms and lean against the doorway as she gazes at the silver table in the living room. Pleated gray chairs, a chandelier of varying shades in the same color hanging overhead, emitting a soft golden glow. Gray tile, curtains, a dresser with a mirror over it that stretches to the ceiling so if you sit in my dad's seat, you can watch yourself chew steak or pass the potatoes.

I don't remember the last time we had a meal in here. The silver and white warped bowl in the center of the table is collecting dust, the housekeeper not bothering, flitting through a place for ghosts.

"This is…" Eden trails off and I eye the clip again, keeping her mass of dark hair held up. I want to wind my fingers in the length of it and pull. I want to know how seriously she takes the fantasy she told me about in my car.

I want to know how far we could go.

"A lot," I finish for her.

She shakes her head, almost like she wants to laugh as she spins around to face me. With my gaze, I trace the loose fit of her shirt, the ouroboros on the silver pendant around her neck as I resist the desire to grace my fingers over my choker, back on after the tournament. Her shirt would rip easily. The choker would take more work.

My dick swells, thinking about it. Her fighting me.

Glancing over her shoulder, toward the curtains pulled closed at her back, seeing a sliver of darkening gray sky, I ask, "Do you want to come upstairs with me?" I gesture down, toward my clothes. "I need to change."

She arches a brow, disdain, but even in the low lighting, I can see her summer tan turn pink. "Why? Where are we going?" She tries to mask her nerves, but she sounds uneasy.

I kind of like it, throwing her off. I don't have any definite plans for us, but I wore this between matches and I want something without my sweat on it.

I smile at her, then turn and head upstairs without a word. I know she won't follow me. There's a softness to her, wrapped in a sharp edge. She agreed to come watch me wrestle all damn day, and she got nothing out of it. She didn't even look at her phone. She paid attention. I saw her eyes too, when she caught sight of my bruises at school.

She tries to hide her kindness in barbed wire.

But when I reach the top of the stairs, one hand on the bannister, I glance over my shoulder to see her staring right up at me.

I'll cut that fucking wire.

Eden

"Tell me about the vigil. About the girl." I race up the steps of the playground, humidity thick in the air from the sluggish storm. It still hasn't passed, and rain pattered on Eli's windshield as we went through a drive-thru for food before we came here. He's got the brown bag in his lap, sitting on the border of the mulched area of the park, so dark here I can only see his shadow in the night.

He pulls sweet potato fries from the bag as I stand at the top of the slide, looking down at him.

"I'm currently holding a fast-food vigil. Come join me as we pray over these fries." He pops them into his mouth, and I know he must be starving after today, but he chews slowly, with his mouth closed, and he didn't eat in his car at all, so I took the hint and didn't either.

My stomach grumbles, and I realize I don't know the last time I had anything. Sometimes I just… forget.

I grab the sticky plastic of the awning over the slide, laughing a little and lifting my chin, craning my neck back as I stare up at the moon, a tiny crescent in the sky. As I watch, a mass of dark clouds drifts over it, eclipsing the light.

"Is this what you always do?" I keep my head tilted up. "Deflect?"

He's quiet a moment, and I hear the very distant rumble of thunder. When we pulled into the parking lot, down a paved path not far from the playground, it was nine-thirty. We spent time sitting at the pool after he changed, when I told him I had to be home tonight. He didn't like it, his eyes narrowed before he rolled them, but he didn't bitch about my parents because of it.

I can tell though, he's not used to not getting his way. His mask slips then, like a spoiled brat.

Now, he still doesn't answer me.

I concede, looking down and blinking at him in the night. Trees surround us, the temperatures warmer than this morning, and my pants are stuck to my skin, clinging tightly as I sweat from simply being around him. He hasn't brought up our question game again, and I'm hoping he never does. I still can't believe I just blurted all that out to him.

But he fucking liked it. I take solace in that fact.

"Kind of like how you always hide?" His voice is low, despite the fact we're several feet apart.

"Hide?" I bristle with the truth of his question. "I don't hide."

"Yeah? You eat lunch in the library, you make minimal effort to engage with people who try to engage with you, and you wear all this bad bitch shit to scare people away."

My temper spikes and I flex my fingers against the plastic, wanting to zip down this slide and wring his neck. "Bad bitch shit? I wear a school uniform—"

"With boots you could snap my neck under."

"Are we criticizing my wardrobe choices now? You've got a skull ring on your finger. What're you trying to do there, Edgelord?"

For a second, he's silent. My heart thumps fast with annoyance and my retort. Obviously, he likes my bad bitch shit, or he wouldn't be stalking me. But I feel like he's calling me out on it and using my clothing choices to point out daddy issues or something.

He breaks the silence with a laugh. It's soft and low, but despite my irritation, I'm smiling at the sound. "Come here," he says, like he's conceding.

I'm still smiling, but I'm still annoyed, too. "Not until you say you're sorry."

He's quiet, and I can't make out his facial expression in the darkness, but it's like I can feel his eyes on me. Then he sighs, loudly, and says, "I fantasize about you stepping on my neck with those boots. If you think anything I've seen you in doesn't make me hard, you're wrong, baby girl."

My stomach flips. My boot does, too, and I almost fall and crash down the slide, but I grip the awning tighter, righting myself as my heart races.

Well, okay then.

"Come eat with me." He reaches into the bag again. "And stop hiding. I don't want this veggie burger to go to waste."

I roll my eyes. "Have you ever tried one?"

He looks up as I lower myself onto the slide and zip down it, landing with my boots thudding in the mulch.

My eyes meet his in the dark as he pulls something from the bag and holds it up. "Yeah," he says. "I just did."

I lift my brows, surprised. None of my guy friends would ever try "fake meat shit."

But then I realize that means he's eating my food. I stand up fast, feeling a little dizzy as I do, and I close the space between us, snatching the burger from his hand before he can finish it off.

It isn't until he drops me off at home after another quiet ride with music the only break in our companionable silence, I realize he completely threw me off track about the vigil. When I text him about it, he simply says he didn't feel comfortable going, because he doesn't know her anymore.

I roll onto my back, accepting that answer, and we text through the night until I fall asleep with a stupid smile on my face.

10

Eden

AMANDA: **Mom said you met a boy. Tell me.**
Me: Our moms are still gossiping about us?
Amanda: Shut up and send me a photo.

I smile, my cheeks hurting, but I don't have a photo and I don't think I'd want to send one anyway. Like I want to keep Eli a secret, for a few reasons. I don't think Manda judges me for what happened, but then again… *how could she not?*

I glance at Sebastian, smoking a cigarette by the window in my room. He's typing on his phone too, and I think he's on something, the way his pupils are pinpricks and he's in such a good mood. He's been cracking jokes since I got home from my shift at work today. Reece and Mom didn't notice or turned a blind eye to the fact he's high. They just like when he's in a good mood.

I tell Manda I'll send her a photo as soon as I have one, then I flip onto my side in my bed, reading a book on my phone. A modern-day retelling of Hades and Persephone. Only the blue lava lamp I've had since I was a kid gives me and Seb any light.

"School went okay this week?"

Lowering the phone, I meet my brother's gaze as he turns to blow smoke from the window. I think of Ms. Romano giving me extra readings after class. Telling me she'd write a recommendation if I need one and continue to do well in Latin. She knows one of the chairs in the Classics department at Bloor.

It's like the goal is attainable. Not just a pipe dream.

"Yeah, really good, actually."

Sebastian smirks. "Is it because of that boy you watched roll around with sweaty dudes all day yesterday?"

I roll my eyes. "Those jokes from you and Reece are old. Get out of my room if you want to talk shit."

He pulls from the cigarette, exhales and huffs a laugh. "Chill."

My phone buzzes in my hand and I look down and open the message.

Eli: I miss you.

I think my heart skips a beat. A smile pulls at my mouth.

Me: Yeah?

"Eli, right?"

I dart my gaze to Seb. "How do you know that?" I guess my family has been talking about me behind my back.

He gestures toward the poster on my wall of Artemis, in black and white, it's laminated. A gift from him earlier this month for my birthday, alongside the Fallen Angel painting Mom gave me a couple of years ago. Not Greek, and yet one of my favorite pieces of art.

I know it's the former Sebastian is pointing to, though. Especially as he says, "Goddess of the hunt. You're not prey, Eden."

Something like guilt lodges in my stomach as my phone vibrates in my hand, but Sebastian is still staring like he has more to say.

"Just slow down. Take it easy, all right? You're so close to your dream school." He turns from me, leans over and lifts up my window screen to throw out his cigarette before he drops it again. He's still staring at the woods when he keeps talking. "Don't stay here for anything."

I open my mouth with a comeback. Something about him doing exactly that, spiraling through this path I can't even see down. But he looks at me as he stands from his squatting position, and asks, "What's his last name?"

I arch a brow, surprised. "Why do you need to know?" I snap back.

"He's taking my sister home and making her watch him *wrestle* all damn day—"

"He did not *make me!*" I keep my voice down so our parents don't hear, but I don't lose the edge in my words. "Just get the hell out of my room."

Seb softens his tone and asks again, "What's his last name, E? Is it Addison?"

My pulse jumps and I know he can read the surprise on my face.

He rubs his thumb over his chin as he shakes his head. "Yeah. He knew the missing girl. Winslet?" He drops his hand. "Rumor is they fucked around."

Winslet. The vigil. *Was it for* her?

"How do you know—"

"People talk. Be careful." He steps closer to my bed, and the scent of cigarettes engulfs me as he stares down at me. "Don't make this like last time."

I hold my breath, my pulse rapid in my head. I need to take one of my beta blockers. It's the only way I'm going to sleep.

"This is different." I can't keep the defensiveness out of my tone.

Sebastian's eyes search mine. I wonder if he's thinking about his friend. What he'd say if he knew what really happened that night. Or maybe he's thinking of Nic, and how fucked up I am. Then he just sighs and says, "Look, I trust you, I just don't trust *him.*"

I nod like I understand, but I think, really, *I* might be the untrustworthy one.

He flips his hand in a dismissive gesture and says, "Goodnight, E."

"'Night."

He walks out, closing the door softly behind him.

Only then do I read Eli's text.

Him: I can't stop fantasizing about you in the bleachers. In my car. The things you said…

I close my eyes tight. I think of Sebastian. Artemis. A hunter. But on the wall above my bed is another printout.

Aphrodite.

I open my eyes.

Me: Did you like them?

His response is immediate.

Him: I want to say something, but I'm worried I'll scare you.

I think of Sebastian again. Winslet. The missing girl.

The vigil.

And still, as I lie back on my bed, inching my fingers under the waistband of my shorts, I respond.

Me: Scare me.

Eli

Her: Scare me.

I close my eyes and bite my lip. Inside my head, I see Eden's flushing cheeks. Her zipping down the slide. In the stands at my tournament. I hear Dom talking shit about wanting her to suck his dick.

I look at my phone again.

Me: Let's play a game.
Her: I'm terrified.

I roll my eyes at how big of a smartass she is, but I know I'm being confusing. I'm already obsessed with her, and yet… most people need things slower.

Me: Questions. Yes or no, or one word answers. We'll take turns. What's your favorite color?

Her: I'm so scared I'm shaking.
Me: Be careful before you fall asleep tonight. I might climb through your window and give you a reason to shake. Answer my question.
Her: Green. Yours?
Me: Blue.

I like green, too. I like it a lot. Probably more now because she loves it. But blue is the ocean. Blue is an escape.

Me: Have you ever done something illegal?

There's a pause. I smile, rolling onto my back, imagining her biting her bottom lip. Shaking her foot or her leg, maybe she's not even sitting down. I see her eyes, those swollen, red lips. Her fingers wrapped tight around her phone.

I bring my hand down, running my palm over my erection.

Her: Yes. Have you? Aside from your "almost" drowning?

I laugh a little because I don't think she believes me on that. Now, she's stealing all my questions, but I don't care. I'm imagining her answer and kicking myself for making this a one word game. I try to back up, although her adherence to game rules is firm and fascinating. Like in my car over the weekend, after the tournament.

Me: What did you do?
Her: Answer the question.
Me: Yes.
Her: You tell me what you did. I'll consider telling you.

I smile and roll my eyes, glancing up at the ceiling. Blue lights along the edge. What should I tell her? So many things, I don't want to scare her. She has ambition. I can tell in the way she studies. Answers in class. Does her fucking homework. The grades she had at Shoreside I saw on her records. She was recommended, I saw that, too, but her GPA is better than mine, and mine is damn good.

Me: I drove without a license.

It's an oversimplification. I was thirteen, and it ended horribly. But on its most basic level, the words are true.

Her: Wow. So edgy. Very hardcore.

Me: By all means, tell me about your homicide, Eden.

Her: I took a knife to school.

I flick my gaze up to her knife emoji, my body growing hot.

Me: Bad, bad girl.

She takes a few minutes to reply, and I imagine her hand down her pants. Her fingers inside of her, her eyes fluttered closed as she thinks of me.

Her: You like bad girls, don't you, Eli?

I shove down my shorts, wrapping my fingers around my cock as I stroke myself. I want a photo. I want to see her naked. But I don't want to mess this up.

Me: I like you.

Her: An angel, remember?

It's just like her to avoid my confession entirely.

Me: Be a devil for me.

Dominic texts me as I stroke myself and I see the message at the top of my screen.

Him: Thanks for coming to the vigil. I didn't come, and we both know it.

Him: I don't want her knowing shit she shouldn't, all right?

I know he knows I was with her, but there is no part of me that cares about Dominic's empty threats and his fucking warnings. Besides, Eden's text comes in, and I don't even bother to reply to him.

Her: How bad do you want me to be?

I want to ask her how bad she's been, if everything she puts on is a front. But the answer she gave me in my car yesterday… there's something shaded dark in her brain. It doesn't mean that she has any experience whatsoever though. It could all be a façade. I wanted to tell her about… snuff films. I wanted to tell her about all the ways I've fantasized about *her* fantasy. I want to tell her I'm not as good as I seem. I'm a liar. I'm a cheater. I'd have watched that boy drown and not felt a fucking thing.

I want to tell her the worst thing I've ever done, and it wasn't even illegal.

I don't, because I'm not fucking stupid.

Me: How bad have you been? I run my thumb over the bead of precum on the tip of my dick, biting my lip as I watch her typing. I can't tell when she's acting, but I know she's far bolder through texts, about sexual things. She's shy when I get too close. I want to ask if she's a virgin, but I don't want her to think I care about the answer. I'm just... curious.

Her: What exactly are you asking?

She doesn't keep up the sexting, and I think I know why. Squeezing my dick with one hand, I type with the other, and I just decide to get it out of the way.

Me: How many people have you slept with?

I stare at my phone as I stroke myself, but she isn't typing.

Minutes go by. I get myself off imagining her crawling into my lap in my car, cradling my face in her hands. Hitting her head against the car window. Hearing her cries against my ear.

Being the only one who has ever fucked her.

But I never find out if it could be true.

She doesn't text me back.

11

Eden

"WHAT DO YOU THINK ABOUT THIS?" Mom holds up a dark red tank top across the aisle from me, with black laces through the middle, like a backwards corset, it goes all the way to the collar.

I love it and I know she sees it in my smile. After work today, we came here together to her favorite thrift store, needing to get Reece more dress shirts for work. He hates shopping so I got her to myself. Good thing, because Eli wants us to hang out Friday night, and he wants to take me to a party. I'm not sure, but I think I should ask to stay the night.

It's Thursday, so I need to ask… today.

I've been good about not staying out except for work, and I've tiptoed around Reece to stay on his good side this week. I know Mom might be reluctant to let me go after what happened at Shoreside, but I'm eighteen. She can't lock me away forever.

I just need her in a good mood before I drop the question.

I slowly hold up the hanger looped around my finger with a

green, Taking Back Sunday T-shirt on it. "But can I have both?" I flash what I hope is a winning smile.

She rolls her eyes, laughing as she sets the burgundy tank in the cart already filled with plaid shirts for my stepdad. I have my own money from work, but she never lets me pay when she takes me shopping. I don't let myself take it for granted.

"Yeah, yeah." She acts like it's a hassle, but she's still smiling. I think she enjoys these moments when we're together. I think after Shoreside, she thought maybe she didn't know me at all. But when we're alone like this, I get to be her innocent daughter again.

Innocent. I think about Eli's text I ignored. He didn't ask again, and when he texted me Monday morning, he pretended I didn't ghost him about it.

"Thanks, Mom," I say, doing a little victory dance in the aisle. Then I glance forlornly at the rows of clothes I haven't gone through yet. I'm on the green aisle, this entire place organized by color. I haven't even gotten to the black aisle yet, which is my favorite.

But I don't complain as I head around the aisle to drop the band tee into Mom's cart.

She starts pushing it to the outer aisles, heading for the register. "There're a few necklaces you might like at the counter there." She nods her head up ahead, a glass display case just before checkout.

My eyes widen as I meet hers. "Mom, you got nothing for yourself." I shake my head, arms crossed. I'm in thrifted jeans Mom helped me destroy last year on the kitchen floor of the apartment. Reece bitched about ruining perfectly good clothes, but Mom ignored him. She's not really into clothes, but she indulges me.

She gives me a small smile, her brown eyes adoring as she looks at me. It makes me feel a little guilty, knowing I'm probably going to lie to her about where I'm going this weekend.

But I'm dying to be alone with him once more. I feel kind of crazy, the way I can't stop thinking about him. We text constantly, he's walked me to my classes this week, it's like a drug, having his attention. I don't trust him, but it doesn't seem to matter. I *like* him.

"Nothing here fits me," Mom says, wrinkling her nose and glancing around the spacious store. I doubt she even looked. "Besides, Reece got a bonus, and I'm having him take Seb next weekend, so have at it before your brother does."

I laugh, imagining Reece and Sebastian shopping together. They can barely stand to be in the same room as each other.

"Thank you, thank you, thank you." I spin around, heading to the glass top counter, and I spy a few shelves of books along the walls behind it. Turning to Mom, walking backward, I point at the shelves, raising my shoulders in question.

She rolls her eyes as she waits in line to check out but just says, "Hurry."

And I do.

"Tell me about this boy," Mom says on the drive home.

I tear my eyes from my phone, where I was just reading *this boy's* texts.

"Um. What do you want to know?"

Mom fiddles with the radio, eyes still on the road. She stops on the Christian radio station, and I have to bite back my groan as she hums to the music until she gets to a stoplight. I hide my discontent, though. She would faint if she knew I was reading *magic* books.

"When do I get to meet him?"

Oh, God. *Never.* "It's not that serious, Mom." I look back down at Eli's text.

Him: I'm coming to kidnap you.

Not serious at all.

"Danica said Amanda was complaining you haven't been texting her much."

I grit my teeth at the reference to Amanda's mom.

"But your nose is always in your phone. And you spent all day Saturday watching him wrestle, and didn't let him come inside to meet us." She glances at me. "Tell me about him."

I squirm in my seat, clicking my phone screen off and tapping my nails against it. I don't want to tell her too much. She'll look him up if she gets his name, and I like to keep my relationships all in separate boxes. It stresses me out, people I know mingling.

"He's a wrestler," I deadpan.

Mom accelerates, the light green. "Okay, smart ass." She laughs after she says it and I do, too, texting Eli back.

Me: Too serious, too fast.

I don't mean a word of it.

"What's his parents do? What does he like? Why do you like him?"

"Mom, Mom, chill out." I shake my head, my face heating with her questions. "He's hot, I don't know. And funny, I guess." I ignore her question about his parents because I don't have the answer. "He's got a nice car."

Mom snorts. "Be careful with those kinds of boys."

Eli: Don't play with my heart, baby girl.

Baby girl. I grow hotter by the second, sweat forming under my arms. "He's not like… that. He's nice."

Mom laughs. "You're not nice, so I'm not sure how that's going to work out for this poor boy."

I smile to myself as I look up at her. "It'll work out perfectly."

She frowns, her brows pulling together. My smile falters, and I wonder if she's thinking of Nic. "Just take things slow, okay, Eden?" She keeps her eyes on the road.

The sting of shame burns under my skin with her admonishment. Eli texts me again and I drop my eyes to the message.

My heart skips a beat as a photo comes through.

He's got his hand tucked behind his head, and I think he's lying on a wrestling mat, the material soft and blue beneath him. He has his tongue between his teeth, sweat on his brow, just over his dark green eyes, the circle of black intensifying his expression.

But it's the tattoo I study as I squeeze my thighs together. The one I couldn't read before. It's three words, and as Mom keeps talking in the passenger seat, something about the neighbors needing her help with a seasonal clean, I can't stop staring at it.

My heart squeezes, reading the three words.

All for nothing.

12

Eden

SEB: **Call me if you need me but need me before midnight.**

I roll my eyes and shove my phone into the pocket of my denim jacket, ripped to shreds with an inverted cross on the back.

Eli backs into an unmarked spot outside of an enormous stone and brick home, his windshield wipers on high speed as thunder cracks over the sky, storms forecasted for this weekend. I scan the paved lot, seeing a row of luxury vehicles beside ours, and this house has a four-car garage attached to the main home, ahead and to the right, lined with a high, steel fence and the glimmering blue of an in-ground pool complete with a pool house, like Eli's house.

I don't think that's where the party is though.

There's a fire exit stairwell on a detached building that's tall, skinny, made of stone and gray siding. At the top there's a door, and through the onslaught of rain, I see people hanging over the black railings, plastic cups in hand, a bright, red light casting everyone in an eerie glow.

I told my mom I'd be staying the night with "Janelle" after her party. Eli gave me the idea when I brought it up to him yesterday after shopping. Janelle is a friend of his, he told me. Mom was surprised, but I think she wants me to get out a little more with girls, and she's never caught me in a lie yet, I guess, so she let it go.

"This is Janelle's house?" I ask, the purr of Eli's engine almost drowned out by the storm, but not quite.

I like how his car sounds. I like how it smells. I like everything about this moment, except, maybe, for the nerves twisting in my gut. But even then, some part of me is eager to see more of his life. The friends I've caught only glimpses of as he disentangles from them at Trafalgar in the halls, to walk with me.

Eli twists in his seat to look at me, seatbelt still on.

I hold his gaze, and notice out of the corner of my eye, his ringed hand tightens and loosens around the bottom of the steering wheel. It takes an effort not to stare at his veins. Not to crawl across this console and climb onto his fucking lap.

Chill, chill, chill.

I think of Sebastian's and Mom's warnings. But this is different. This isn't like that. *This time, he wants me too.*

"It's Dom's," Eli answers me, his tone betraying nothing. I can't tell if he's happy to be here, with me, at his friend's house, or… not. "Remember what I told you? The night before the tournament?"

I pull my brows together, confused. My mind races through all of our texts. Every night, I get off to his filthy words. I still don't know if he has any idea. "You told me a lot." I keep my tone neutral, but the words come fast.

He lifts his lips in a half-smile. "I told you to listen to me."

My heart thrums fast in my chest.

"Do it tonight, okay?"

I narrow my eyes. "Who are you? *Daddy?*"

He smiles fully, turning away from me, giving me a good view of his side profile. "Let's go, Eden."

. . .

Music with heavy bass blares from somewhere above us as we make our way up the exposed metal stairs. Eli reaches for me when the chunky soles of my boots slip on a step. His cool fingers circle my wrist, over the top of the rubber bracelets lining my arm.

I flinch. A reflex.

Then I tighten my grip on the slippery railing, my head held high even against the rain. There are Trafalgar students by the awning of the door, laughing and drinking, and while no one has ever made fun of me outright at my new school, I want to pretend I belong here tonight. Affecting confidence I don't feel is something I taught myself to do last spring, when whispers and stares lingered everywhere I went.

I keep my head lifted high.

Until I turn to stare at Eli's fingers looped around my wrist like they belong there. Like one of my bracelets. A protection charm not to save *me*, but my secrets.

He pauses, one of his own black leather boots, laced in light gray, on the step above me.

Looking over his shoulder, he stares down at where we're joined.

His eyes lift to mine. *You're mine.*

I tilt my head. *Show me.*

A second passes. Rain dots along my temple, over the burgundy shirt Mom bought me that I'm wearing, laced up to my throat. A shiver courses down my spine at the look in Eli's eyes, darkened with an emotion I can't name, his hair growing damp in the storm.

Then, without a word, he releases me, and I can breathe again. Still, he waits until I'm beside him on the stairs to keep going, even as people call his name from the exposed balcony.

A few seconds later, and we're under the awning, but there're so many people smoking out here, we're still getting soaked, despite Eli's offer to grab a hoodie from his trunk, which I refused.

I knew I'd never give it back, and some people don't like their things stolen.

Mercifully, the door is hauled open for us by a kid with a vape in his mouth and a beer in his hand, grinning despite all of it, and we step into the dark, red-lit room.

The music is as thunderous as the storm outside, "Save Me" by Hippie Sabotage. I'm a little surprised Dom has such good taste in music.

Eli is instantly swallowed up into the masses of people here, covered in expensive perfume and strong cologne, almost all of them with drinks in hand. The sharp tang of marijuana hangs heavy in the air alongside the fruity scent of vapes. I take in a large living space, shadows dancing along the red tinted walls, hardwood floors slippery from rain, long sectionals, people sitting and passing joints on short, poufy chairs. There's a small kitchen with a fridge and drinks littered on the counter space, everything open plan, nothing like I've lived in.

Wherever I look, there's alcohol and clouds of smoke and bodies pressed close together.

I shuffle over so I'm not right in the way of the door, and I press myself against a wall of exposed brick. I'm watching Eli greet people with a smile, letting people clap him on the shoulder, a few girls hugging him, and he wraps one arm around them, but his eyes drift over to mine when he does, and for now, I let it be enough. I vaguely recognize some of these people, and while I've become friendly with a few students at Trafalgar, I'm not close with anyone.

Still, I put on a smile, too, and a few people smile back, nodding at me with cups in their hands.

And after a few moments, Eli still making his way across the vast room to talk to people, someone speaks directly into my ear at my side, causing me to jump.

"Hello, *Eden*."

I spin around, heart racing as I put my back to Eli, tipping my head up to meet Dominic's blue gaze. He's got a smirk on his face, a black polo beneath a zipped-up navy jacket, tan pants, dark gray slip-on sneakers. He looks like he just left a track meet, but I think it's supposed to be *style*.

Dropping my gaze, I see he's offering me a red plastic cup, full of something dark.

"I'm good," I tell him, in reference to the drink, apprehension tightening in my chest. I don't like to feel out of control of myself. It's hard enough to take charge of my brain when I'm sober, and when I start drinking, it's kind of hard to stop.

He brings the cup to his lips, taking a drink as he keeps his eyes on me. "You go to many parties, back at your old school?" His gaze sweeps over my body, and the hairs on the back of my neck stand on end. But at the same time, I'm grateful to have someone to talk to.

I bring my fingers to my necklaces, the ones Mom bought me yesterday. I have a choker, silver with an inverted cross, a slightly longer necklace that says *Poison* in Gothic letters, and my ouroboros just below that. They're all cheap metals, but I coated them in clear nail polish last night to keep them from tarnishing.

Dominic's lake-blue gaze drops to my chest, and I grip my Poison necklace tighter.

"A few," I say, in answer to his question. "You host many?"

He nods, taking another drink before he lowers the cup to his side, lifting his gaze to mine. "Either me, or…" He grins, flashing white teeth as he looks past me. *"Him."*

I turn to follow his gaze, over the throng of boat shoe-wearing mini frat boys trying to talk their way into the pants of girls with perfectly arched brows.

Past them all, I catch sight of Eli, close to the dark corridor that leads off from the living room.

Facing one of those girls.

"Who is that?" I ask, keeping my tone neutral. I've seen her at school, but we don't have any classes together. Shoulder-length auburn hair, everything about her kind of pixie-like, a little ethereal, like a drunken, sexy fairy. She has a bottle of vodka dangling from her fingers, half-empty, and I'm not entirely sure it wasn't her alone who finished the other half, based on the way she's leaning against the wall like it's the only thing to hold her up.

"Luna." Dom pronounces her name slowly, with the slightest edge of disdain.

The song changes and someone turns it up, "PRBLMS" by 6LACK, as my heart races. I consider the fact I may need the prescription pills in my purse, back in Eli's car. I place a hand flat over my chest, one arm crossed to grip my opposite elbow.

Eli smiles down at Luna, and she straightens from the wall, stepping closer to him, tipping the bottle back, little space between them.

"See how she looks at him?" Dominic's words are in my ear. I feel his breath on my skin.

I want to elbow him in the chest, but I grab my choker tight, my fingers growing clammy.

"It's the same look you have." Dom's mouth is closer. "He does that to people, you know."

My stomach tightens. Eli's smile curves higher as Luna says something to him, tipping her head back and laughing as she does.

But then something happens, catching his attention, and he slowly turns his head, his eyes finding mine through the crowd of people and clouds of smoke.

His smile slips, but he doesn't outright grimace.

The hairs on the back of my neck stand on end, the way he holds violence quietly inside of him.

I like it. Inside my head, I think of Eli breaking Dominic's jaw along the railing outside before he throws him over to the parking lot, all while keeping a smile on his face. I think of him doing it *for me.*

But then another girl separates herself from the crowd, one I've seen walking with Eli at Trafalgar, but he's never introduced me to any of his friends. She's tall, wearing white, dreads piled high on her head, and she's got a cup in hand she offers Eli, almost like a distraction.

He can see over her, and I watch as he shakes his head, not taking the drink, just like he doesn't take his eyes off me.

"That's Janelle," Dom says in my ear. *The girl I'm supposed to be staying the night with.* "Now, one of those girls is my girlfriend."

I widen my eyes, a little surprised because, well, in looks at least, they're leagues above him.

"Guess which one."

I frown, observing them both. Janelle sips from her cup, keeping a little distance between herself and Eli. Luna, though, she's cozied up next to him, her shoulder brushing his arm.

My stomach burns and I know I have no right to be jealous, but I am.

"Janelle," I guess, my voice hoarse.

He laughs, and his breath skates over my ear. "You'd think, huh?" There's something of annoyance in his tone.

I turn to look at him, frowning.

He shrugs, forcing his gaze away from *his girlfriend,* Luna, all over Eli. "The three of us have all slept together." He takes a drink, glancing into his cup as he does. "I guess it's not the worst thing I've seen her do."

"Why the fuck would you tell me that?" Anger forces the words out as my head spins with that news, something I'd rather he had kept to himself. Inadequacy floods through me, naivety. I mean, it's not like I thought Eli was a virgin, but threesomes already…

Dom shrugs, nothing apologetic in his gaze as it finds mine. "You should know what you're walking into."

I glare at him a second, then reach for the cup in his hand. He releases it, smirking down at me. Then he pulls a cigarette from behind his ear, offering it to me.

I shake my head, taking a long drink, letting the alcohol burn down my throat.

"How are you liking Trafalgar?" he asks, tucking the cigarette back, something a little caustic in his tone. His question mirrors Eli's, from the first night we met, and yet I have no desire to confide anything in him. I just want to use him in this moment because Eli is pissing me off. Maybe irrationally. I have no claim on him. I know that. But we've been texting and talking for two weeks, and… *God, I'm stupid.* That doesn't actually *mean* anything now, does it? *Why do I always jump the gun on these things?*

Still, I think of everything I told him. About the… murder fantasy. *Fuck.* My face heats, and I ignore Dominic's question as he watches me with amusement, his eyes bright. I tip back the cup again, but before I can take another sip, a hand reaches around me and pulls it from my fingers.

Eli's voice is in my ear, his other hand around the back of my neck as I startle.

"You want a drink?" he asks, his voice cold, condescending, because I clearly *had* a drink until he took it.

I don't speak, shutting my eyes for only a second as a chill runs down my spine, relief tangled up tight with lust.

"I'll make you one."

I take a deep breath, trying not to snap back, annoyance flaring in my chest.

He flexes his fingertips against the bones of my neck, his other arm still curved around me, drink in hand. "By the way." His lips linger over my skin, and I shiver, despite the way I try to hold onto hot anger. "You're sexy as hell when you're jealous."

He straightens away from me, but doesn't let go, pulling me into his chest, and I can sense his eyes are on Dominic, the way Dom stares right back at him, smiling a little.

Without another word, Eli steers me around, dropping the drink I had at Dominic's feet as he does. It splashes up on Dom's pants, the cup rolling over to the door, and I hear a few people booing and jeering, some laughing, too, but despite the mess on his floor, Dominic only smiles.

"Don't take drinks from him," Eli says, still gripping the back of my neck.

I try to duck out of his grasp as we move through the throng of people, toward the kitchen island full of cups and bottles. He flexes his fingers, tightening his hold, and I turn to glare up at him right as we find a spot by the fridge not squeezed between other people.

"That was rude. Let go of me."

His eyes are focused on mine, fingertips kneading my flesh, over my necklaces, and it kind of feels good, but I just can't think when he's touching me. After a moment, though, he drops his hand, but he doesn't back up. "Are you mad?"

I cross my arms, feeling childish. "Why didn't you introduce me to anyone?" I shake my head, glancing at the crowd of bodies dancing and making out and laughing and getting high together. Luna, Janelle, he didn't bring me together with either of them, he just... left me by the door.

He lifts a brow, slipping his hands into his black pants. Glancing around the room, it takes him a second to bring his focus back to me. "Honestly?"

I bristle with the word, and I know I'm practically pouting over here, and I can see the amusement in his lips, pulling upward, but he doesn't make fun of me for it.

He just says, "I don't really want anyone else to know you."

I narrow my eyes, but I don't know what to say to that. He glances at my chest, and I'm completely covered, the way my shirt comes to my throat, but I'm unprepared when he steps closer, and I step back until my spine hits a countertop, and his thighs touch my waist.

He lifts his left hand, slowly brings his finger to the collar of my shirt, just skating over my skin. My muscles jump, but I don't tell him to stop.

"I like you wear things like this. Covered and shit."

"Of course you do." I roll my eyes, trying not to let him see how his touch affects me. "You're a player, but you want a sweet little innocent v—" I almost say the word, but I choke on it at the last second and replace it with something that doesn't hit quite so close to home. "Angel, huh?"

His brows lift, his lips tipping up. His fingertip glides over my skin, calluses rough over the very tip of my collarbone. "I'm not a player." He keeps touching me, and I hate and love it. "I'm sorry I didn't introduce you to anyone." He glances down between us, and he seems sincere, but sometimes I think he's just that good at acting. Pressing his palm flat to my chest, his thumb brushing over the curve of my covered breast, he leans down close, his temple on mine. "I will, okay? Just have a drink with me?"

I swallow hard, and I know he can feel it under his hand. All I can manage back is a childish, *"Fine."*

He's still smiling, but his movements are fast as he grabs one of the laces of my shirt, wrapping it around his fist and yanking me toward him.

My heart is galloping in my chest, my hands limp by my side.

"You forget your manners, baby?" His breath is on my lips.

I blink, my mouth open, but before I can respond, he unwinds the lace from his hand and steps back, smirking. "Don't look so scared. It kinda turns me on." He jerks his chin, half turning away from me as my body floods with heat. "Come on. I'll get you a drink."

THREE DRINKS IN AND I CAN'T HOLD IT ANYMORE.

I have to pee, and I've seen people walking to and from the hallway by the living room after short intervals, so I'm sure the bathroom is just there.

Eli is at my side, a joint between his fingers, the sweet scent of marijuana thick in the air, it seems smoking outside isn't a rule at Dominic's place. There's a guy with us named Baca, and he keeps darting glances my way to include me in the conversation about a future match with a school I've never heard of.

Eli pins his eyes to Baca, and I wonder what he thinks of Baca's attempts to ensure I don't feel alienated. I haven't spoken to Luna or Janelle, and the latter seems to have left altogether. Luna is in the thick of things, knocking back shots and keeping her eyes on Eli more than I like.

Dominic has disappeared, and I don't really care. The crowd has only grown denser, people shouting to be heard over the music, which has also increased in volume. It's a lot, but the vodka and orange soda in my system, a drink Eli made me, is making it easier to cope. *So much for not drinking.*

Warmth bubbles in my chest as I spare a glance at Eli, a cup in one hand, the joint in another, his focus intense as he talks through something about pins and cradles and technicalities with Baca. He's *into* this sport. His brows are pulled together, he gestures with every other word, vodka soda sloshing dangerously close to the lip of his full cup, the lit end of his joint getting a little too close to Baca's eye. Baca backs up one step, like he's aware, but he doesn't break eye contact with Eli.

I take the opportunity to find a bathroom.

No one has spoken to me that Eli hasn't introduced me to, aside from Dominic, but through him, he's made good on his word, and I've met a few people, although Baca is the one who's stuck around the longest.

I squeeze my fingers around the cup in my hand, feeling the plastic flex. I decide I'm done for the night.

I reach for the phone in my back pocket as I stalk to the closest open door, not bothering to dismiss myself. But I think I can feel Eli's eyes on me as I duck inside the room, leaving my drink on a decorative dresser outside of it.

I look down at my phone.

Mom: Are you having a good time?

The smallest twinge of guilt pulls in my gut, thinking about shopping with her yesterday. Mom trusts me, but she was a teenager once upon a time. She cheated on Dad before I was born, and she told me that story when I started high school, as a warning if I ever get caught up in one boy to remember there are a billion more on the planet.

Since Mom's advice, I've never seen cheating as the horror most of my peers have. Then again, I've never met a boy like Eli. It might be a little harder to keep her intended lesson in mind as the school year moves forward, but now is not the time to think about it.

Me: Yeah, probably headed to bed soon. It's not very late, and I'm sure she suspects I'm lying, but I don't want to have to text her more tonight in case the alcohol catches up with me, so it's best to end our communication now. **Love you, goodnight.**

Her response comes a second later.

Her: Call me if you need me. I love you, sleep well.

I pocket my phone, looking up. And immediately… I start to backtrack. There's a glow coming from what I think is the bathroom, but it's spilling over someone's bedroom. A king-sized bed, nightstands framing it, a TV mounted on the wall.

I'm stepping backward, intending to retreat and find a different bathroom because the pressure on my bladder is painful, when I notice the photo on the nightstand directly across from me.

It's in a frame, bathroom light glinting over the glass.

Instead of going backward, I take a step forward, blinking.

A girl with long blonde hair. Smiling in front of a lake. One I recognize from when we drove down the long, private driveway. It curves around the main part of the house, but in the storm, I didn't even think to twist around and see how close it was.

But this girl…

I've seen her before. This very photo.

I bring my nails to my mouth absentmindedly as I stare at her, chewing on one, a nasty habit when I'm stressed or nervous. I forget about the music from down the hall, the people, even Eli, in this brief moment of time.

Until I hear a voice from the right, the far corner of the room. "Do you know who she is?"

I flinch, dropping my hand and spinning around as I suck

in a breath. In the darkness, just beyond the pool of light from the bathroom behind me, I see a figure, bleached blond hair. And I recognize his voice. "This is your room?" I counter his question with a question.

He turns his head toward the photo, the entire room between us, I can't see his expression. "Hers is down the hall." His voice is low, almost contemplative. I hear him sniff. The sound is strangely familiar, but it takes several seconds for me to place it as one Sebastian makes alone in his own room sometimes before he goes out.

A shiver tiptoes down my spine.

"Who is she?" I whisper the words, glancing at the photo again, but not wanting to take my eyes off of Dominic. Excitement and nerves both build inside of me. "To you?"

I know the answer before he turns to face me again, and says the words slowly, with something like amusement. "My sister."

I swallow the knot in my throat. The vigil... it was definitely hers. I thought so, with Sebastian's words, but now I know. And Eli skipped it. To hang out with me at a playground.

Dominic sighs, as if it's nothing, then walks slowly toward me, the bathroom light spilling across his features, over his placid blue eyes, rimmed in red now. He dips his hand into the pocket of his pants and pulls out a baggie, shaking it as he stares at me.

"Do you want to enjoy a real Trafalgar party?" Just like that, he changes the subject.

But I'm still stuck on it. "I'm sorry that... she's missing."

He rolls his eyes. "You and everyone else," he mutters under his breath.

I feel out of my depth, but in my head, I hear Eli's words from the first day Dominic spoke to me. *"I saw your sister last night."*

My stomach flips.

"I'm sure it's hard," I keep going because I'm uncomfortable. "And I didn't know, you know, Eli dated her."

Dominic freezes. He narrows his eyes as he stares at me. "Why the fuck would you say something like that?"

My mouth goes dry. His entire demeanor has changed. I shake my head, unsure what to say.

After a tense moment, Dom clenches the baggie in his hand. "Huh? Why would you say that?" He steps toward me.

I glance at his hand, crushing the baggie in his palm, blue veins ridged under his skin. I should speak, or defend myself, but I don't know why he's losing his shit right now.

"They didn't fucking date," he says when I don't respond, but he hasn't given me room to breathe. He steps even closer. I can smell his cologne, the heady scent of marijuana, alcohol on his breath as he leans down in my face. "I just want to know why you think—"

"I assumed—"

"Hey, do me a favor, and back the fuck up off my girl." Eli's voice slices through my words and the tension between me and Dom, and surprising me, Dom straightens as if on command, and it's like permission for me to step backward.

"I have to fucking pee," I say the words through clenched teeth and turn my back to Dominic, glancing at Eli in the doorway. I walk quickly to the bathroom and close and lock the door behind me.

I don't hear anything beyond the door, but at least I can breathe, away from Dom's weird ass reaction to me assuming Eli dated his sister. But of course he didn't *date* her. I mean, does Eli even date? Is it, like, a thing he doesn't do?

Reaching for the waistband of my pants, I blink, and it's only here, between the white and black walls with the light above the polished mirror over the sink, I realize I am beyond buzzed.

Everything seems to spin a little as I take a breath, and in the relative quiet of the bathroom, I can hear the frantic beat of my pulse. The palpitations become worse when I drink, my heart looping like a butterfly, unsteady, rising and falling.

I close my eyes a second, still standing, my fingers paused at the top of my pants.

Fuck.

I shouldn't have drank so much, but I had little to contribute to the conversations with people I barely knew, very aware of Eli at my side every second that ticked by. After he interrupted me with Dom, he didn't leave me alone again. Drinking was something to do with my hands, my mouth, an excuse not to speak. I didn't watch carefully how much Eli poured into my cup, and the vodka wasn't sealed. Nor was the soda, and I don't think anyone would spike the drinks making the rounds to *everyone*, but I know about Jim Jones.

People with too much power, trip.

And these people feel unpredictable, somehow. Maybe it's the photo of Winslet. Learning she's Dominic's sister. Figuring out something is off with the three of them; Dom, Winslet, and Eli.

I'm hot and sweaty, a wave overcoming me all at once.

I stagger a step back, shaking my head, trying to push the anxiety away. My cardiologist, the expensive one I couldn't drag out seeing because the ER referred me to him after my first panic attack, noting my pulse was well above even panic levels, said the condition with the valves in my heart correlates to anxiety, but they're not quite sure which is the cause, and which is the effect.

Deep breaths.

It really does help, despite how simple it seems. Breathing, apparently, is vital to life.

In. Out. In. *Out.*

I'm fine. You're fine, Eden. Just. Fucking. Fine.

I get my shit together enough to use the bathroom, wash my hands, and lick my knuckle and wipe away the excess liner under my eyes.

Then I unlock the bathroom door.

I'm not sure what I'm hoping to find when I walk out, but it isn't Eli, sitting on the bed, and Dominic, making lines on the dresser across from it.

Both of them turn to look at me.

Eli has his feet on the floor, knees spread, hands dangling between his lap. There's the softest smile on his face, more of a smirk than anything, and Dominic is pushing a black card into his wallet, retrieving a hundred-dollar bill, then opening a dresser drawer and tossing the wallet inside. He doesn't look away from me as he does it.

"Wanna line?" His back is to Eli, several feet between them.

I glance at Eli, but he says nothing. It seems their tension has been severed.

For the first time, I focus on the cocaine. Nerves jumble inside of me. It's just a little coke to them, but… aside from Sebastian, I've never really been around many drugs. Manda got high more than a few times at a couple of parties, and I smoked here and there, but it always made me feel funny. I had a panic attack once, and Manda spent the entire night rubbing my back.

I glance at the photo on the nightstand, but I'm not saying anything more about that.

"It's good shit," Dom adds, excitement in his words.

Eli's voice cuts through my racing thoughts. "Have you ever done coke, Eden?" His tone is neutral, but there's the softest curl of a threat threaded through his words. I'm not sure why.

I shake my head. "No."

"It's my birthday," Dominic says, and I raise my brows, surprised. "Get high with me." His eyes search mine, and I have no idea why no one told me it was his damn birthday. I should've brought a card or a gift or *something*.

"Happy birthday?"

Eli smiles, but Dom just laughs and mutters, "Thanks."

I clear my throat, glancing at the lines. "How long does it last?"

Dom smirks at me. "Not long," he says, looking at Eli, then back to me. "It's a short-lived high."

There's silence between the three of us. I'm not sure what I'm waiting for. I definitely shouldn't do this, but it almost feels like an opportunity to show off or something. To act as if I'm not out of my depth, being at Eli's side.

I don't look at him.

Dangerous, baby girl.

Aren't you, too?

Seconds tick by. Then Eli asks, "Are you scared?"

Dominic straightens, and I lock eyes with the boy I came here with.

"A little." I don't lie, but I feel myself blushing, like maybe I should have. "But it's his birthday." I look up at Dominic, smiling. "I'll try it."

Surprising me, Dom turns to Eli, like he's waiting for a verdict.

And with his eyes still on me, Eli says, "You heard her. *Let her try it.*"

※

"LUST" BY SAINt JHN PLAYS LOUDLY FROM ELI'S PHONE ON the nightstand beside the photo of Winslet, the music rivaling the noise of the party outside of the closed bedroom door.

I glance at Eli sitting on the edge of the bed, hands in his pockets, a water bottle between his thighs. He's studying me, and I feel a little shaky with his eyes on me as Dom taps out coke on the gleaming surface of the dresser across from the bed. It looks different than in the movies. Not so fine and powdery.

"This is for you," Dominic tells me, excitement laced through his words.

I tear my gaze from Eli, catching my own reflection in the

floor-to-ceiling mirror beside the dresser. Behind me, Eli hasn't taken his eyes off of me, and I see his lips part the second before he speaks, and I'm staring at the two, fat white lines as Dominic offers me the rolled-up hundred.

"No." Eli's tone is soft, barely audible over the music.

Dominic lifts his head up, the money between his index and middle finger, tapping on the dresser softly.

I grip the edges of it, pressing my fingertips into the sleek wood, feeling a rush of something hot ping through me, looking at the powder. The forbidden, so close to my fingers.

"Give that to me." Another rush with Eli's words, this time spreading through my chest, lacing its way down to my core.

Dom sighs, but I see out of the corner of my eye he tosses the baggie.

I look up, meeting Eli's gaze. "Come here, baby girl."

Baby girl.

My stomach swoops. I feel a little unsteady on my feet. Beside me, Dominic leans down, his elbow brushing my forearm.

"Let her watch me," he whispers, eyes searching mine as he looks up because now, he's kneeling. "She needs to know what to do." The blue of his irises seems to darken. "Don't you, E?"

I nod once, breaking eye contact with Eli.

Dominic dips his head, and using the hundred, he sniffs up both lines, quick, with ease, no break between either. My heart thunders like the storm outside whose boom shakes this room every so often. Then Dom drops the tightly rolled bill, licks his finger, runs it over the line of off-white, flaky dust. He stands, turning to face me.

"Open your mouth."

He's so close, I can smell his cologne. Something aquatic. I can see how flawless his pale skin is. Smooth, with curved cheekbones. His pulse throbs just above the collar of jacket.

His coke-covered finger is between us.

Eli says nothing. I don't look at him as I part my lips, my tongue just over the edge of my bottom teeth.

Dom steps closer.

My pulse quickens.

"You have a nice mouth," he says, his eyes dropping to my tongue. Another step, and we're almost toe-to-toe. I sway a little on my feet.

"Are you gonna do something about it, or just stand there staring?" The words have bite, but I smile, too. I tuck my hands into the back pockets of my leather pants, fingertips brushing against my ass as I cock my head, staring up at Dominic's darkening expression.

"Tell me you want it." His voice drops to a low whisper, even as he shifts from one foot to the other, like he can't quite stay still. "Just like that. *I. Want. It, Dominic.*" He says the words for me to repeat.

That's never going to happen.

I shake my head, so close I could count each of his long, dark lashes. "How about you tell me?" I smile as his own falters. *"Please suck the coke off my finger, Eden."* I give him a string of words to recite, too, very aware of Eli's gaze, like a brand. It makes me feel like showing off, and the alcohol gives me liquid courage.

Dom must feel Eli watching too, because he glances over to the bed.

I don't dare look.

Dom swallows, turning back to me. He takes a breath, and I see his finger tremble. "Please suck the *goddamn* coke off of my *fucking* finger, Eden."

I grab his wrist then, feeling his roaring pulse beneath my fingertips, and I part my lips, pulling his hand toward me, intent on Eli seeing everything. How I can be surprising. Spontaneous. Isn't that what we wants? Something exciting?

But before I can lick the remnants of a line off Dom's skin, Eli speaks.

"Don't."

It's one single word, delivered with deliberate coldness.

I squeeze the bones of Dom's wrist. I see him wince, and it feels good.

"Let him go." Eli keeps the same frigid tone. "And *come. Here.*" He doesn't raise his voice. I can't imagine Eli screaming. His anger is colder, his temper scarier because of it.

But it's not fear that causes me to obey as I stare into Dom's eyes.

It's *want*.

I release Dominic, who groans, and I step back, putting distance between us as I slowly turn to face Eli, his knees still wide, the water bottle now beside his hip, the coke between his fingers, resting on his thigh, his other hand, too, splayed wide.

I hear Dom sucking his own finger, pulling it out of his mouth with a *pop*.

Lifting my chin, holding eye contact with Eli, I saunter toward him, until I'm standing between his knees, still staring into dark green eyes, unable to read his calm expression.

He shakes the baggie, and I drop my gaze.

"No," he says quietly. "Look at *me.*"

I bite my bottom lip, feeling my cheeks heat. But I look at *him*.

Behind me, Dominic is quietly laughing. I don't care. *Let him watch.*

Eli brings one hand up, curling his fingers into a loose fist, his thumb wrapped around his forefinger. Then he brings the baggie to his teeth, pulling apart the seal, staring at me as he does.

My entire body is warm, my breathing labored, but I keep my mouth closed, inhaling through my nose, exhaling the same way. The party grows louder with the torrential rains outside, slanting against the curtained windows, but the bass beats from speakers somewhere out there still thump, beneath the sound of Eli's own music, on the nightstand, still SAINt JHN, a different song.

With one hand, he taps scaly powder onto the hollow

between his thumb and index finger. Not once does he look away.

I stay still, refusing to squirm under his gaze. At my back, Dominic is drinking water, judging by the crinkling plastic.

Eli lowers the hand holding the baggie, presses the seal together, then tosses the rest on the bed. He brings his hand to my hip, fingers splayed wide, wrapping around to the curve of my ass.

My heart jumps to my throat.

He pulls me closer, and I go willingly, until my knees hit the edge of the bed. Our height difference is so drastic, we're almost, stupidly, eye to eye.

He drifts his hand up, to the small of my back, underneath my shirt, his cold fingers pressing into my spine.

I suck in a shallow breath.

"Here," he says, offering his hand to me with a smirk. "Blow it off of me."

I swallow, my mouth dry as I glance at the coke, not in a line, just sprinkled over his skin.

"Hold onto me," he says, glancing at his shoulder, and I see the green veins in his biceps beneath the loose sleeve of his shirt. "And come closer."

I reach for him, clawing onto the hard muscles of his upper arm. With my free hand, I tuck a lock of my bangs behind my ear, grazing my piercings, my hair in two braids.

He drifts his fingers over the base of my spine.

A shiver runs through me.

Dominic is silent, no doubt watching.

I like it. Being watched. With the feel of the thrill, I reach for Eli's choker, curling my fingers over the leather, and he doesn't speak. I feel his pulse flutter as I dig my way under the band. It's a tight fit, and I know it hurts him, or, at the very least, is uncomfortable.

But I don't wait as his short nails curve into my back. I dip my head, and giving him one last glance, our eyes locking for a moment, I brush the tip of my nose over the powder.

As my pulse roars like the ocean in my ears, I realize I don't know if I can actually do it like this, holding onto Eli with both hands, with no dollar bill or—

Before I can panic, feeling less confident than I did only a second ago, I hear the floor shift, and I know it's Dominic's body behind mine, his nearness warm.

He says, "I'm just going to help you, okay?"

I open my eyes, looking up at Eli, who's still watching me.

Dom's arms come around my body, but it's Eli who speaks next. "Dom?" His eyes shift upward.

Dom says nothing, but I'm sure he's looking at him.

"Back up."

Dom makes a sound between a sigh and a groan, then steps away.

Eli drops his gaze to me. "Just inhale," he says. "Over my hand. All of it."

I nod once, then, scared I'll lose my nerve if I don't do it quickly, my heart flying out of my chest, I inhale sharply through my nose. Immediately, it burns, thicker than I thought it would be, and I taste something down the back of my throat, but I drag out the inhale.

Sniffing, I raise my head, noticing there's still some flakes on Eli's hand.

He pulls me closer, his lips coming to my ear. "Lick the rest of it off."

I feel warmth in every cell of my body, lust churning through me, and for a split second, I think of Shoreside. Nic. Making a fool of myself.

Then, before I can overthink it, getting caught up in memories in the past, I turn my head and lap my tongue over Eli's hand.

The bitterness, like Aspirin on my tastebuds and dripping down the back of my throat too, intensifies. It's not pleasant, and a numbness sets in around my teeth. I straighten and wipe the back of my hand over my septum.

Just as I go to back away from Eli, wanting to spit or cough or sneeze, his hand comes to the front of my throat.

His hold is gentle, his fingers curled softly.

But I still freeze.

I still swallow beneath his hand, dropping my own, but keeping the one clamped down over his shoulder.

I can feel tension in his body.

I can sense it building in mine, too. There's a warmth between my thighs. I want to push him down on this bed. I want to feel him against me.

He brushes his thumb over my bottom lip, rolling it out as he stares at me, his gaze intense, but there's a surprising softness in his touch.

Do you want to play with me? Do you want to hurt me? Do you want to love me? The questions are sudden inside my head, too fast, too soon, crashing into me in waves. *I feel everything.*

He's cupping my face with one hand, and he slips the other from underneath my shirt, then grabs the bottle of water beside him. He he tips my head up with one finger under my chin.

Then he lowers his mouth to my nose, kissing the tip of it.

Butterflies scream inside my low belly.

"Here," he whispers, dipping his brow to mine, nudging my nose with his own. He presses the cold water bottle to my chest, and with the thin fabric of my shirt, I can feel the icy coolness, my body shivering, my nipples tightening into sharp points. He wraps his arm back around my waist, pulling me forward, and one of his knees is between my thighs. It takes everything inside of me not to grind on him, and I think he knows, the way amusement coats his words when he says, "Drink some water."

Then he slowly slides his hand to the front of my hip, and... *pushes me away from him.* He drops his hand, only offering me the water bottle.

I blink with the loss of his nearness, and take another step back, nearly panting for him. Why did he push me away? Can he see how much I want him? Why doesn't he want me, too?

Dominic is somewhere behind me, but he says nothing.

I glance at the water bottle in Eli's hand.

I don't know why he wants me to drink. I'm not dehydrated. Still buzzed from the three drinks I downed, but I feel *good*. Good enough to grind against his thigh. Kiss his mouth. Bring his hand to my throat.

But he doesn't seem to want that.

Dominic snorts, clearing his nostrils, then his throat with a low cough. The sounds remind me of Sebastian, which makes me feel both uneasy and oddly comfortable, all at once.

A grin stretches my face as my pulse thuds fast with my nerves, but the smile is still pulling at my cheeks, and I see Eli arch a brow as he looks at me, smirking, too.

"Water isn't gonna do shit," Dom says from behind me. "Here, drink this."

I glance over my shoulder, and he's by the mini fridge on the opposite side of the room, grabbing a red sports drink and holding it up. He saunters back to the dresser, sets the drink down, and he must have snatched the baggie from the bed because it's between his fingers now. I was so enraptured with Eli, I didn't even notice. I look back at him, the thief of all my attention, the source of too many feelings.

My throat feels a little tight and I bring my fingers to it, over my necklaces as I gaze at Eli's choker, my pulse flying.

Forgoing the water, because the taste is not fantastic in the back of my throat, I exhale and turn from him and take the few steps to the dresser, grabbing the cold sports drink as Dom sinks to his knees again, blowing another line, then slipping his white-dusted credit card back into the top drawer of his dresser.

I twist off the cap and down a few gulps. It's cold and tastes vaguely of cherries. It helps dull the Aspirin-like residue hung up in my throat.

When I twist on the cap and set the drink down, I lean

back against the dresser, turning to face Eli. "Get back over here," he says, water between his thighs once more.

My body buzzes with adrenaline, but I shake my head, teasing him because he fucking teased me.

Dominic coughs, then snorts, then snorts again. He murmurs something under his breath, like, *"Shit."*

It makes me laugh. "Try some," I tell Eli.

Dominic clears his throat. "Can't," he says, his words excited even as his tone is hoarse. "No more."

I don't know how much I did, but I already want more. The warmth in my chest is growing, and I feel bolder, more alert, more... social. *Sexual.*

"I'm going to eat you alive when I get you alone."

"Eden." Eli's voice is mild. "Come sit in my lap." His chest rises and falls a little faster than usual. His only tell.

Of what?

He doesn't look angry. But I drop my gaze, and the numbness of my face fades to heat as I see how hard he is.

Shit. I thought he didn't want me, but he's just really good at foreplay. I grip the dresser tighter, my fingers sweaty.

Before I can decide what I want to do, the door bursts open, thudding against the wall.

All three of us look toward Luna, bracketed by the red lights from the darkness of the party.

It's only grown louder, and I see a mass of bodies behind Luna, most faced away from us, laughing and drinking and dancing.

She glances at me, Dominic, then her gaze is fixed on Eli.

She steps into the room as Dominic laughs and says, "Hello, Luna."

I bristle, clenching my teeth so hard they hurt, but I don't speak, and I don't move.

Luna strides into the room with elegance, her rose gold boots clicking on the dark hardwoods as she swings the door closed behind her and walks over to the bed like she owns this space.

Like she owns Eli.

She sinks down beside him, palms behind her as she crosses one knee over the other and looks up at Eli beside her.

And he's looking right back.

Something twists in my gut.

"You're not gonna say shit to me?" Dom asks, and he sounds pissed. "It's my birthday, and you're not gonna *say shit to me?*"

His anger feels contagious. Why is she sitting beside Eli if she's dating Dom? But Dom said they all hooked up, didn't he?

Rage sparks under my skin. I try to hold onto the memory of Shoreside. How I lost my shit in that bathroom. How I came out a different person. Alienated.

Lost her fucking mind. Freak. Insane. I don't know why Nic ever fucked around with her anyway. She begged him to take her virginity. Can you be any more pathetic?

Luna flutters her lashes, turning to look at Dom as she arches a perfectly manicured brow. "I tried to *say shit to you* last night, remember?" Her voice is sweet, but I know it's fake. She spares me a single glance. "But you didn't want anything to do with me then." She wrinkles her nose. "Guess when you're lifted, I'm the last girl you wanna spend time with."

Dominic laughs, but it lacks any amusement. "You sound stupid right now. I needed a little space. Can't handle that, huh?"

Eli is watching Luna and Dom, and I grind my teeth together, my back to the dresser as *I* watch *him.*

Until Luna's hand comes to his thigh, white manicured nails contrasting against his black jeans as she claims him in front of me. Her smile turns sharp the longer she stares at Dom. She's beautiful, with creamy skin and a pixie face, everything small. Taller than me, but slender, she radiates fragility.

Eli looks up at me, his expression blank. I feel as if they're both waiting for me to do something.

I glance at Dominic, and his eyes are on Luna's hand on Eli too.

My heart hammers hard in my chest.

Her hand glides higher up his thigh.

My face burns and I feel jittery. I kind of want to break her head against the mirror behind me.

I don't move.

Her slender fingers rise higher and higher. She has a ring on her middle one. Gold, with a large, purple stone.

I want her to choke on it.

Eli is still watching me. *Are you mad?*

I grit my teeth. *Are you blind?*

"I think you're right, Dom." Luna sighs dramatically. "We need space."

White noise is staticky in my head. My breath hitches. I frown, holding Eli's gaze. It seems darker than it was even moments ago. I notice his hair looks like it's dried, but it's messy, raked back from his face, and I like it that way, but I don't want Luna to touch it.

Luna tightens her grip on Eli's thigh, not too far from his cock, bulging in his pants, and I shift my gaze to her. I imagine wrapping my fingers around her neck until she stops moving.

All over me. Hand over my mouth. His body pinning me down. His mouth. Teeth. Bruises. Just like his. Worse.

And before I can say anything, or think clearly, lust and nerves amplified by the drugs in my system, Luna leans in toward Eli, one hand coming to his shoulder as she pushes him back on the bed like I wanted to do, and she kisses him.

On the mouth.

But the nightmare gets worse.

She straddles him, a gap in her jeans around her narrow waist, her ass to me and Dominic, her hands on his chest. The short strands of her hair are in his face, hiding the collision of their lips, but I can hear them making out, even over the music playing from Eli's phone. Luna's head turns one way, then the other, and I hear a groan from deep inside Eli's throat.

The water bottle rolls to the edge of the bed, and as Luna

shifts her hips on top of him, it falls to the floor, rolling to a stop at the tip of my boot.

I can't stop staring at them, Luna's body moving over his, dry fucking him. I think about how hard he was.

The breath leaves my lungs.

Luna moans.

Eli's hands come to her ass, squeezing hard, and I feel as if he hit me.

I look at Dominic. His jaw is clenched, and I wait for him to say something. *To do something.* But no one does.

No one says a word.

I think, somehow, Dom is getting off on watching them.

For a brief second, I consider turning my head and kissing him, just to piss Eli off. But it occurs to me Eli might not get pissed off. He might not care, and I think that would hurt worse.

I can't stay still any longer. I kick the water bottle and watch it hit the bottom metal frame of the bed. It must jostle the mattress because just as I curl my hands into fists, pivoting to turn toward the door, Eli—hands still on Luna's ass—sits up, pulling her into his lap as he does.

I stop breathing.

He tilts his head as Luna rocks her hips, her hands trailing down his arms, then back up, her lips on his neck, her lower back visible beneath the gap in her jeans.

She widens her knees, drawing them closer together, and Eli skims one hand up over the waistband of her pants, fingertips grazing the indention of her spine along her back. She sighs, licking a line up his neck, toward his jaw.

Eli's eyes are locked on mine.

He splays his fingers over her back, his lips parted as he lifts his chin, giving Luna access to his throat, her hands coming around his back, no doubt slipping under the hem of his shirt.

My heart races too fast. My mind spins, hot anger bubbling beneath my skin. I take a deep breath. I glance toward the door. I know I should walk out and slam it.

I should just leave.

But...

"Come here." He mouths the words over Luna's shoulder, running his tongue over his top lip as he watches me.

As Luna starts riding him faster, little breathless whimpers leaving her lips.

"You've been summoned," Dom says, and there's something dark and lustful in his words.

They are all fucked up.

I don't think after that. I give in to what I want.

I cross the room, my boots clunking against the hardwoods. I don't know what I'm going to do until my thighs hit the edge of the bed. I'm reaching past Luna, grabbing Eli's choker at the same time she sucks in a breath, turning to face me, her hands coming to his shoulder to steady herself.

He's still touching her, his breaths rising and falling fast, but when I curl my fingers under the leather band, yanking his face toward me, I know I have all of his attention.

I lean in close to him, my pulse jackrabbiting.

My arm nudges Luna's and I hide my grimace as I stare into the dark green of Eli's irises.

"Fuck." I twist the choker, letting it bite into his skin. *"You."*

He makes a low noise at the back of his throat, something like a groan, but I don't stay to figure out what it means. I release him, stepping back and spinning around, walking toward the door.

Dom calls my name at my back.

I ignore him, slamming the door closed behind me as I head into the darkness of the party.

13

Eli

SHE'S GOT her phone pressed to her ear when I find her by the door, one finger plugging her other ear so she can hear, her back to the party. I see a guy from the swim team come up behind her, a red cup in his hand. He peers around her, and although he's facing away from me so I can't be sure, I'm positive there's a stupid, drunken smile on his face.

I keep my own smile on as I thread my way through the mass of bodies in the living room.

She turns her head to look up at the guy, and I see her eyes narrow.

Slap him. Get the fuck away from him.

She's probably tipsy, and definitely high on coke, and pissed off at me, so I know when she pulls her phone down and tells the guy to "back off"—based on what I can read of her lips—it's not for me. But it still makes me feel pretty damn good, all the same.

The guy shakes his head, but he steps back and turns to find someone else to fuck with. When I pass by him on my way to Eden, I shoulder check him, hard, and keep moving.

She's off her phone and slipping out the door when I reach her, grabbing her by the back of her jacket and spinning her around, pushing her against the brick wall outside, beside the door that slams closed. The scent of marijuana and flavored tobacco linger, but no one is out here, the storm probably a part of the reason why.

Underneath the glowing red light out here, I see her eyes are wild, her anger palpable, irises dilated as she crosses her arms, shrugging out of my grip and knocking her head against the wall, taking a step back into it.

"Who did you call?"

"Fuck you."

I smile at her. "I wanted you to pull her off of my lap." I taste Luna on my lips and rub the back of my hand over my mouth, trying to get her off.

Eden shakes her head, her eyes narrowing. "I'm not like that."

I arch a brow. "You're not?"

Her eyes are beautiful, multicolored slits. "Shut the fuck up, why did you even bring me here?" Her words are fast and angry, and it turns me on.

"Why did you let her do it?"

"I told you." Every syllable is cold and clipped. *"I'm not like that."*

"You could be anything you wanted to be." I think of her nose dipping to the coke on my hand, even as I could feel her nervousness. *You did that. You could fight for me.*

My throat is sore where she jerked the choker against my skin. *Fuck. You.* She looked so hot, her thick, heavy boots coming toward me, the jealousy rolling off of her small frame.

"Anything *you* wanted me to be?" It's a low question, almost a whisper. I can tell, despite her anger, she's glad I'm here, not inside with Luna.

So am I.

My body feels hot, and I lean down, getting into her space, willing her to stay. *Don't back away. Don't run.*

She doesn't.

I can smell her breath, like alcohol and mints, and *her*, soft and sweet, even though I know she isn't either. *But with me, you could be everything.*

"You want me to shut the fuck up?" I ask her, my voice quiet as I bypass her question.

She clenches her jaw, swallowing hard.

"Tell me how mad you are."

She rolls her eyes, then shakes her head, giving me nothing.

I plant one hand on the wall above her, my body so close to hers, it's killing me. "Talk to me, Eden."

"That was fuck boy behavior." Her eyes are narrowed into slits, but there's the slightest smile curving her lips.

"Yeah?"

"Yes." The word comes out through clenched teeth.

"I wish you would've done something about it." I brush my nose against hers.

She stiffens. "I told you, I don't do things like that."

"What if I told you to?"

She looks away, glancing at the metal grates beneath our feet, her arms still crossed over her chest, like a shield. "I don't want to become someone else for your sake."

"If it's still you, is it really someone else?" My heart beats faster in my chest, and I couldn't even say why, if someone asked. My eyes go to her mouth, and she runs her tongue over her cherry-red bottom lip as she peers up at me.

I bite my cheek, stopping a groan. I was physically turned on by Luna. But I wanted Eden mad. She was hurt.

It's almost better.

"I would do it," I tell her truthfully. "I would've broken Dom's neck if he did that to you. Maybe I would've let you touch him, if you asked me to. I would do anything you told me to. I would wear any mask, be anyone, I would—"

"You do that with everyone, Eli. Even with Luna, back there." She falters, but I have to bite my cheek to stop from smiling. *She saw through it.* "You are always wearing a mask.

What I want…" She lifts on her tiptoes, until our mouths are a breath away. "Is for you to take it off."

Nothing she says is wrong. "Do you want to know what I want?"

"Only if it's me." She isn't smiling at all.

"This is the part where I say, *let's get out of here.*"

She licks her lips, letting her eyes roam over my face. Her anger has faded. She wants me as much as I want her. But she drags the decision out, to punish me. Finally, she says, "If you promise me two things."

"Anything." My heart pumping too wild in my chest, my breath labored, I'd do it, too. *Anything but stay here.*

"Don't ever do that to me again. I don't care what you're trying to prove."

I nod once. "I won't."

She seems to believe me, that easily. Or maybe she just doesn't trust anything I say, and this is no different. She meets my gaze again, the smile back on her full lips. "We're going to run in the rain."

"Funny." Nothing is funny in this moment, but it's the only word I can think to say. "I've always wanted to see you soaking wet."

Eden

It's *pouring.*

Lightning strikes overhead, violet and violent, and a second later, thunder rolls loud enough to make me flinch. Everything is a blur of gray and rain and giddiness all around me, and I don't care anymore that Sebastian didn't pick up when I called.

I have to stop running, splashing into a puddle that soaks my pant leg, my breath coming in short, shallow bursts. We're at the side of Dom's house, no one else is out here with us in the darkness, lit only by solar lights dotted throughout the garden lining the paved driveway, and a motion light positioned just over the bottom of the stairs.

I spin around underneath the orange cast of it, my smile an ache on my face as I struggle to breathe.

Eli has his shirt off, clutched tight by his side.

He rakes his hand through onyx, dripping hair plastered over his forehead, smoothed back by his fingers. He lifts his head, gazing up at the clouds above us, the moon long hidden. His arms come to his sides, palms facing me as he rolls his shoulders back.

His chest is heaving, I realize as I step closer, shivering from the cold of the rain, my clothes stuck to my body, the surprising chill of the night.

I trace the bruises over his body with my eyes.

I can't make out the details, but I see the red has darkened, a color with purple undertones, even more jarring than last weekend. And it's not the only wound.

He has three others, the size of… *the size of fists.*

The rain roars in my ear and the hairs on the back of my neck stand on end. Lightning strikes, and I realize I could be its next target, but as I stare at Eli, water dripping off the sharp planes of his face, a smile pulling on his beautiful lips, and those ugly, ugly bruises decorating his body like a glimpse of the darkness inside his head, manifested over his rib cage, I don't care.

If I'm struck, it will only be a literal exhibition of my hazy mind, the goo of warmth in my brain. My face is numb, my mouth still stretched into a smile, and my limbs are heavy, and if I knew better, I'd go home. This messed up, I'd call Seb over and over until he answered. I'm not falling all over the place. I'm not in any danger of throwing up or blacking out.

No. The risk is for something far more lasting.

Eli closes his eyes.

There's a weight pressing against my chest.

I reach for my phone, tucked into the black bra under my shirt. The fabric is stuck to my skin, and I have to work to yank it down enough to give me access to my phone, but I get it, and when I do, I swipe the camera lens with my thumb before I take a picture, the flash off.

I glance at the photo.

He looks even more like a god in it than he does in person. The bruises aren't as visible, only smudges of shadows dotting his abs, you wouldn't know if you… didn't know.

But I know.

I tuck my phone away again, wanting to be here in the moment instead of observing it through a screen. I take a step closer, my boots splashing in the inch of rainwater and grime.

He doesn't move.

His arms held at his sides look like wings.

Adonis. A mortal loved by a goddess.

Icarus. A man fallen.

I can't breathe as I come closer, and he slowly dips his chin, relaxing his arms by his sides. His hair hangs in his eyes, rain slicing over the curve of his cheekbones. The edge of his jaw. The ink of his hair.

"I've never seen anything like you." I have to shout the words, and I wouldn't be able to do it—say them or shout them—if I didn't have a mix of vodka and soda and cocaine in my veins. But I do. So I can. My eyes dip to his bruises.

Slowly, he follows my gaze.

I step closer, until the tips of our shoes touch. My boots and his, black leather, light gray laces.

I reach my fingers to his skin, noting the V of his hips just above the low-cut of his jeans. His abs rise and fall, and I realize, for the first time, I can see his tattoo, the darkness I saw beneath his shirt at the library.

When he left the gym, those quick minutes he was shirtless, I didn't notice.

I was too busy looking at his bruises then, too. Faded, now I notice the old ones, just above the edge of his tattoo. It's a skull, cross bones jutting out over his hipbones; I can't see the entirety of the piece, but I see enough to know that. Thick, black ink, little detail and more straightforward darkness.

I press my index and unnecessarily bandaged middle finger to the biggest bruise, higher up, just under his sternum, with jagged green and blue edges.

Looking up, I see he's staring at the contact of our skin.

"It's okay," he whispers, not touching me, not moving, not looking up. "You can press harder."

A jolt of something like power lights through me, my chest expanding, the humiliation I had felt for a split second in his car, when I confessed the worst thought about myself last weekend, long gone. Miles away, we're on a different plane now. This is the opposite. This is seeing into *his* brain. And understanding… it could be just like mine.

I do as he said, until his body tenses, and I know it's taking effort for him not to back away. My fingertips blanch against his olive skin, the indentation where I'm pressing, it looks angrier, redder, like it was last weekend at the tournament. Rain pelts my exposed wrist, and I'm thankful my rubber bracelets are over my left arm, hanging by my side.

I feel the tension in his body. His skin is slick with the storm, his muscles firm beneath my touch, and I could slip. I could press along every wound. I could make them all ache, all over again.

It occurs to me to ask what happened.

I know I could. But I also know he wouldn't answer me. Not here. Not now.

I let up on the pressure, flattening my entire palm over his skin instead. Even with my splayed fingers, I don't cover the biggest wound completely.

But I can feel his pulse points, steady beneath my hand.

It's jarring, knowing my own heartbeat is erratic, and his is… his is calm.

I look up to find him staring at me, rain slipping off the edge of his upturned nose. He still doesn't touch me, like he knows what I'd do if he did.

"What do you want, Eden?" He continues our conversation

from upstairs like we never stopped talking. "Whatever it is, whoever it is... I can be it. *Anything."*

I let my hand slip down over his skin, loving the feel of every muscle, all the strength in his body. His torso jumps beneath my palm, and I love that, too. Affecting him.

I let my fingers stop at the soaked waistband of his jeans. "I want the truth." I lick my lips, breathing hard. *"Of you."*

14

Eli

HER BODY IS hot against mine. She didn't last long after we came inside, and this time, there were no nerves masked with cool detachment. She simply demanded I take her to her room, by which she meant *my* room, because even though there are two guest rooms in this house, there was zero chance she would sleep with walls between us.

And now, for the first time, despite her answers in my car last weekend, there are no guards up.

The string of lights over my double closet doors are on, the faintest glow of blue, and as rain spatters against the glass of my balcony, thunder and wind still raging outside with flecks of forked blue-violet, I watch her sleep.

She fumbled with her boots. I helped her slip them off. I offered her the checkered bag she left in my car when we went to Dom's. She snatched it clumsily, sauntered to my bathroom, closed and locked the door. Drunk, sleepy, crashing, but not completely out of it.

Even her phone is plugged into the charger she brought, set

on the nightstand beside her, empty save for a matching lamp to my own nightstand.

When she walked out of the bathroom, she was in oversized, gray pajama pants and an enormous white, cropped shirt with the words *Wilmington, NC* scrawled across it in pink. Now, the faded print is hidden, because she's slipped my dark blue covers over her chest. She had started on her side, but quickly rolled over, and she's vulnerable here, her arms bracketing her head on my pillow.

She had her hair down when she walked out of that bathroom too, and I felt a pang of longing I didn't get to take her braids out.

I can smell the mint on her breath now as she sleeps, and I think it's cute, the fact even though she was exhausted and not quite sober, she still made sure to brush her teeth.

I'm propped on my side, elbow bent, head in my hand, my bottom thigh against her body, feeling every inch of heat she radiates as she sleeps. Does she ever get cold?

The ceiling fan spins on high overhead, a thing I did for her because she mumbled something about white noise and getting hot at night.

I watch as the breeze ruffles a strand of hair from her face, still damp from our jog in the rain.

She's beautiful with her guard down. She was beautiful with it up too, but this version of Eden would believe anything I told her. Maybe she wouldn't remember it in the morning, but there would be no questioning looks, no narrowing her eyes, no turning her back on me.

No walking out.

She's softer like this. *I want her like this, only for me.*

I could touch her. Tell her anything I wanted to.

Confess.

My free hand is between us, the fitted sheet heated from her body. An inch, and I'd brush against her ribcage, over her shirt, under the covers.

I force my gaze back up to her face.

Her lashes appear even longer with her eyes closed. I realize they're more straight than curved, which is why I couldn't quite tell just how long they were until now.

No makeup on her face, I assume she washed it off in my bathroom too.

I press my fingertips into my mattress, gritting my teeth. My hands ache, wanting to touch her. I've gotten off to the memory of her inside my head in this bed. More than once. More times than I'd ever say out loud, even before we first spoke in the library.

Over a month now, I've fantasized about Eden.

And here she is, in my bed.

And it was easy.

But I don't think it's because *she's* easy. Not in the sexual way, although that's probably true too, the way she flinches when anyone gets too close. No. She's not easy in a more complicated way. Slipping into her head, touching her heart, those things sometimes don't take much effort with people. At Trafalgar, as we've moved through our grades and gotten older, we want to be wanted. *We want to be loved.*

I don't think Eden is any different, but she doesn't believe she deserves love, and she doesn't trust anyone who thinks otherwise. Low self-esteem doesn't quite cover it.

It's a self-loathing so intense, the idea that anyone could be interested in her, *the real her*, is unfathomable. She throws up a shield in her demeanor, her clothes, her attitude, to keep everyone away.

She is a mess, she's decided, and no one wants a mess. Not a real one. Not an unromanticized version of one.

Flared tempers and tension-filled fights can be appealing. *Dreamy. Passionate.*

Haunted memories, waking up in a cold sweat because they infected your dreams, remembering you have no future because you live with a brain which hates you, imagining someone you love walking out, over and over and over…

Therapists. Medications. Psychiatrists. Studies.

Blood on your hands.
No one wants that.
No one wants the reality of mental illness.
No one wants to be the recipient of one of those disorders with no cure, no treatment, no understanding. Those are the type of things people write angry blog posts about. Self-publish books on how to avoid people just like that.
Just like me.
Five Signs of a Sociopath: Run, Don't Walk.
I curl my fingers into a fist between us, sweeping my gaze over the bow of her lips. I want to kiss her. I want to touch her. I want to *fuck her.*
I want her to want every second of it.
Rolling onto my back, I exhale, reaching my hand down to run my palm over my aching dick. I shift as close to her as I can get, my shoulder bumping her elbow, we're sharing the same pillow.
Even this feels like crossing a line, but it's the least bad thing I could do.

15

Eden

I FORCE a fake smile as I listen to my dad and wonder if I'm looking into my future.

A few days ago, waking up in Eli's bed and panicking for a moment, forgetting most of the night before—then I saw how disarming he was in his sleep, and it soothed something in me—I hadn't been thinking about *this* being in my future. The choppy, irregular visit with my dad that occurs approximately once or twice a year, more if both of us are unlucky.

My fingers are linked together between my knees as I sit on his brown leather couch, saggy from years of use, probably with other families, other bachelors, other lives.

Clave Belle is tall, as is my mom, his ex-wife, Lucy. I know I was stunted from my grandmother, on Dad's side. Named after her too, although like Mom, I kept my maternal grandma's maiden name, like a compromise between my two unwilling parents.

Eden Arella Rain.

Arella Belle shot herself twice in the head with a rifle

before I was born. Before I was even a thought, when my dad was twelve years old.

The family consensus is she could've been bipolar, but mental health wasn't really a *thing* in this part of the state, during that time. I think of the offer for a therapist my mom extended, and I refused.

I feel a little guilty.

"Anyway, I just couldn't support it, so I switched tickets."

Political parties. He's talking about political parties, I remind myself.

I nod politely. I'm not sure what he's not supporting anymore. I tuned out of that part of the conversation. I'm dying to get out of here, but I don't move.

He settles back in his recliner, same color as the couch I'm on across from him in the little living room. It's freezing in here, and I'm thankful. The TV above the mantel of the fireplace—which doesn't work—is on, but muted. I glance at the screen and see a car race.

I think of Eli.

I try very, very hard *not* to think of Eli.

Talking about boys with my dad has never been an issue because we've never really talked about much of anything. When him and Mom split when I was in preschool, he moved here, an hour outside of Raleigh, and very occasionally, he'd jet up in his sports car of the season and whisk me away for an outing on the beach. Mainly, he'd read *Car and Driver* magazines while drinking from little bottles of Mountain Dew, and I'd jump the waves alone, but it was fun, because Mom worked a lot, and we didn't get out to the ocean as much as I'd have liked as a kid.

Now, he rarely leaves his house.

I glance around at the low ceiling, the rickety kitchen table with one single chair where it could fit at least four, the hallway which I know leads to a guest bathroom that always smells faintly of mildew.

The whole house has that smell, actually, but hey, at least

Dad has a new motorcycle parked along the burnt lawn to show all of his neighbors. He was standing beside it like a proud father when I pulled up. Ironic, yes, but when you work at a used car lot, you steal perks where you can, I guess.

"How's writing going?" Dad asks this like I've been working on the next great American novel.

"Well, just trying to get through the semester first." I wonder for a moment if he remembers I go to a fancy new private school. I almost don't want to talk about it, but I see his dull blue eyes light up as recognition sparks.

He says, "That's right, you're at Trafalgar now, huh?" He pronounces it all wrong, but it's endearing. It reminds me of my roots. Where I belong. Which is… *not at Trafalgar.*

I press my knees to the outside of my hands, glancing down at my ripped jeans, platform boots that took all weekend to dry after Dominic's party. Unfortunate, because they're the only black pair of shoes I own, so I had to wear them to school.

I spritzed them with a lavender essential oil concoction Eli thrust into my hands this morning after I told him about my dilemma while he walked me to English.

It's on my faded green dresser back in my room.

"Yep," I tell Dad, slipping into my own Southern accent. I usually try to talk around it, as if it's a ball of bitter candy lolling around my tongue, but here, I suck on it, wincing as I hear myself speaking out loud.

"Anyone giving you any trouble?" Dad schools his features into something resembling concern at the same time he tugs on the hem of his oversized black *Star Wars* shirt, crumbs from the crackers he ate spilling down his chest, landing on his blue jeans.

I glance at the plastic wrapper from his snack, on the TV tray beside the arm of his chair. There's an empty two liter of Mountain Dew holding it down, as if a stray breeze might blow it away. Based on the crumbs and wrappers littering the floor in the kitchen beyond the living room, cracker packages close to the white trash can but not *quite there*, it seems cleanliness is not on Dad's menu.

I repeat his question in my head. Oh, right. People giving me trouble.

A feeling of annoyance settles in my chest.

Would you care if they were? I have to force myself to bite the words back. *Where've you been, Dad? When Mom was scraping money together for a car, and you were sitting on an entire lot of them, where the fuck have you been? Sebastian is in trouble, Reece is the same asshole he always was, and where the fuck have you been?*

He used to ask me about Reece. Wanted to make sure he was "treating me right." I don't think he'd have done anything at all if Reece wasn't.

I stare into his face, still molded into an almost earnest expression of giving a fuck. The line between his brows has deepened, his brown hair is edged with gray, thinning a little at the crown.

His arms used to be lined with muscle, now they're softer, and so is he, generally speaking.

"Nope." I see dark green eyes in my head. I feel an arm draped over my chest. I freeze, staring at an unfamiliar ceiling, the memory on a loop. Then the soothing words that were in my mind, waking up in a bed not mine.

It's just Eli.

It's just Eli.

I see him watch me take my things to his bathroom to get ready for work. He watches me as I lie to Mom too, through texts about Janelle's house, when I'm in his passenger seat, holding two waffles squished together, cashew butter between them and a hint of jam. I protested, but Eli made me compromise because I'd already shrugged off his offer of eggs.

"I'm a vegan."

He smiles, shadows beneath his eyes. "Break the rules for me."

I think about the cocaine, lying to my mom, sleeping in his bed, all as we walk to his car. "What the fuck do you think I've been doing?"

He rolls his eyes, but his smile stays. I eat all of the waffles.

"Met any boys?" Dad coughs as he asks the question, lowering down the foot stool of the recliner by leaning over and grabbing the wooden handle on the side.

I bite my bottom lip, staring at the carpet, thinking of my phone in the passenger seat of my car. Mom said my dad wasn't getting any younger when I complained about his invitation to come over when she picked me up from school. The invites are so sporadic, it feels like I'm bending over backwards to accommodate him.

I'm not, of course. He doesn't live too far out of the way, in a subdivision where most of the lawns are overgrown and no one cares if you park a car on the side of the road for days or weeks at a time.

A lot like the trailer park.

Nothing like Eli's subdivision.

"No," I lie to my dad. I lift my eyes to find him staring down at his chewed fingernails. I'm hit with the realization we share the same bad habit.

He knows about Shoreside. Mom told him. He never talked to me about it, and I'm grateful.

I squeeze my fingers tighter, my chest aching, and I'm not sure why.

We'll always be like this, won't we?

Pretending to connect, keeping everything surface-level? *What was it about me that made you not want to parent? To let it all go?*

I glance at the photos on the wall behind his head, something I've avoided doing since I sat down.

The frame is too small for the space, and it's a collage. I find it hard to believe he did it himself, and I wonder if one of his three sisters helped him put it together. Aunts I never speak to.

There's a photo of me on his lap when I was a baby, with lighter hair. A lot of it, even then, no smile on my face, a Mickey Mouse shirt that hits my chubby thighs.

Beside the photo of me, there's another of a boy.

He's older than me in the picture, but I know he's younger,

currently. Eighteen months younger, Dad tried to hide that secret from me and Mom for a long, long time.

In the wrinkled photo behind the glass of the frame, my half-brother is playing with a toy car, only the side profile of his face visible. A shock of red hair, his lips curved into a smile.

Maybe that's why he lives in this house, and never comes by when I'm here.

He's happy. I was born sad.

Dad *can* parent. He's keeping a teenage boy alive who watches this TV. Sits on this couch. Dad knows how to make it work, somehow. He just… can't do it with me. There were excuses over the years. Split custody between him and his former mistress, she lives not far from here, so Jonah is *closer,* and I spent most of my life at the beach, a full ninety minutes away.

Then there were the times Dad lived in places not suitable for a little girl to visit, in his words. But Jonah, younger, more fragile, it was okay for him.

I swallow the knot laced tight in my throat and stand, wanting to get to my phone in the car.

I'd drive to Eli. I'd meet *his* dad. I just want to see him and get the hell out of here.

A flicker of sadness passes over Dad's face as he stands, too, towering over me.

He bends down to hug me, and I don't have to make an excuse. We don't need to, do we? We'll always be this. Surface. More alike than we probably want to admit, we can't find the words, the ways to connect. Mom invades my bubble. Hugs me when I don't want it. Eli keeps space between us, but he won't let me too far out of his sight.

Dad doesn't know what to do with me, because he doesn't know what to do with himself.

Please don't let me wander, Eli. Don't let me go.

Pathetic thoughts, desperate, the same ones I had at Shoreside. *Fear of abandonment. Perhaps some kind of mania.* Words from the school nurse, a recommendation to my mom to get more help. Help I refused.

I bite my cheek to bring myself back to the present.

Dad's touch is light, and he backs away quickly, because I don't bring my arms around him. I can barely stand the scent of his cologne, despite the fact it's pleasant.

I just feel itchy, and maybe more than my aversion to touch; I feel the heaviness of his pity. *He's sorry, he's sorry, he's sorry.*

I do my best not to run out of the house.

I do my best not to sling gravel as I pull out in my Sentra, the A/C struggling, slowing an already slow engine.

I ignore Dad's wave from the porch. I pretend I don't see it. I'm holding the phone to my ear, waiting for Eli to pick up.

Pick up.

Fucking. Pick. Up.

I turn right, away from my house.

Eli answers. "You called me." He sounds shocked. He sounds *happy*.

Pressure builds behind my eyes, but I say nothing about Dad. Or my feelings. Or any of it. I wouldn't know the words, anyway. "Can I come over?"

There's a pause, and I imagine him frowning, confused. "I'm downtown." He says it slowly.

I don't ask. He doesn't offer an explanation. In my head, I see Luna Nelson on his lap. In my head, I rip her off of him and kick her in the skull.

"But I'll meet you anywhere." He sounds almost desperate, like he knows I'm about to hang up and wants to blurt his offer out quickly before I do.

I drive even faster, speeding through a yellow light. I think Eli would be proud, but I don't tell him. "The library." It's between here and downtown. It won't take him long, and he has to go that way to get home anyway.

"I'll be there." A pause. Then, "Are you okay?"

It's easier to breathe already. I smile as the sun sinks below the horizon, casting the road in shades of purple and gold. "I have questions for you tonight."

There's a heavy sigh on the other end of the line. Then, amusement creeping into his tone. "Under one condition." I don't speak, waiting for him to tell me. "You're coming to swim with me Friday."

I frown, one hand on the wheel, other pressing the phone to my ear. "But you have practice—"

"Teacher workday, Rain. Don't you look at the school calendar?" He uses a voice that isn't his. A mock teacher voice. Nasally.

I can't stop my laughter. I've never heard him mock anyone before, and it's hysterically funny. I can hardly see the road, tears pricking in my eyes, and I never laugh like this. *Jesus.* "Shut up. Fine."

"See you soon." I hear the smile in his words.

"See you—"

"Eden?" The smile is gone.

"Yeah?" My heart skips a beat.

"If you ever tell me to shut up again, I'm going to…"

I'm back in his car. I'm telling him the worst thought about myself. I'm ripping myself open and offering him the dark. I'm giving him permission. "You're going to what?" My breath is shallow, my words cracked. My face hot, even though I know he can't see me.

"I'll slap you."

I squeeze my thighs together, my foot slipping off the gas pedal. I have to pull the phone from my ear and push it against my leg, letting myself breathe, my pulse so erratic, I know I need to reach for one of the little powder blue pills in my purse. I will before I walk in that library, I make a promise to myself.

I need to calm down.

Blazing hot, even with all the A/C vents on me, fresh antifreeze in the car thanks to Sebastian, I bring the phone to my ear again.

"Is that a promise?" My voice is hoarse. I fight back on the desire to clear my throat. *All over me. His hands, all. Fucking. Over. Me.* "You didn't eat me alive, you know. When you had the chance, after the party." My bravery astounds me, but I'm thankful for it.

I hear a scoff. Then, "Next time, don't get wasted and don't do coke. I want you to see everything. I want you to want everything."

I want everything with you.

"And yes. It's a promise. Consider it a keyword, telling me to shut up. Okay?" He doesn't use the teacher voice, but there's something far more demanding in his question.

I don't need to think about my own consent. "Yes."

His voice is haughty, but it's for my benefit. For this game. "Good girl." I want to faint. "Make sure you have good questions. You only get three." Before I can protest, he hangs up.

💀

"What's the worst thought you've ever had about yourself?"

He pauses in reaching for the water bottle between us. An entire liter, he brought it in with him when he sauntered over to my table, and we've been sharing it since he broke the seal. "You're a thief," he says, grabbing the bottle and leaning back in his seat, cocking his head and keeping his eyes on me as he drinks.

I tap my pen against my notebook, the page blank. I was pretending to work on an essay I have to write for An Introduction to Ancient Greece and Rome. Differences between their empires. I couldn't possibly work on it now, because all I'm thinking about is Eli.

"Come up with an original question." His words are taunting.

I stop tapping my blue pen and lift my brows. "No. There

were no rules, except my three-question limit, which seems unfair since you had *five*."

A cocky smile spreads on his face before he takes another drink, and I can't stop staring at the way the black choker around his neck moves when he swallows.

The plastic of the bottle flexes beneath his fingers before he rests the water on his knee, ankle over his opposite thigh. He's dressed in gray pants and a loose, black shirt. I have no idea where he was, and he doesn't tell me. He didn't ask what I'd been doing either, although I'm in my favorite pair of ripped black leggings and a white T-shirt tied at my hip, so he probably assumed I just left the gym. He doesn't pry into why I called him, and I'm happy to keep that secret.

"I did have five," he agrees, one hand on his shin. "Your answers were illuminating." He presses his lips together, furrowing his brow, as if he's thinking, before he adds, "And so was the fact you did blow at the party."

I bristle with the reminder of it, flexing my fingers on my thigh, concealed beneath the dark wooden table. Thinking of how I felt, *high*, it makes me want it back. Even the heart medication in my system can't quelch that desire. "You couldn't take your eyes off me when I did." It's like I'm right back there. I feel his face inches from me, watching me blow coke up my nose from his hand. It was a rush, and I'm not sure it was all from the cocaine. My fingers wrapped around his neck during it felt *good*. So did his knee between my thighs. *But then he pushed me away.*

"I still can't."

His words overwhelm me, but unlike the night we met down here, I force myself to hold his gaze, lifting my chin like I can take his charm without flinching.

Even still, I almost say it, then. *Shut up.* I almost do, but I think of his promise, and it makes me want to blurt it out more, just for a split second.

It's like I can feel him egging me on, his eyes boring into mine even though it's fucking hard to hold the contact.

Say it for me. His whispers echo in my mind.

I swallow the keyword down, clearing my throat as my palm grows sweaty. I should've taken two pills. I do my very best not to let him see how nervous he makes me. "Answer my question."

"Last chance to take it back."

There's something of a threat in those words. I'm not sure if it's because what he's going to say is so awful, or something else. For some reason, I think it's the latter, but it only makes me want to know more. A little bit of mystery, I can't help biting off the entire thing, even if it's going to be bitter as it goes down. "Answer my question," I repeat, never looking away.

He doesn't either. "My worst thought is a lot like yours in the fact it has to do with someone else too. But unlike in *your* version, I'm not the victim."

My stomach flutters and I feel a little breathless, even with my meds, even just sitting in this darkened library. The scent of old books hits me hard as I inhale deeply, trying to relax. If I make a wrong move, I'll ask another question, and I'll waste it. It might be a game, but there are rules. I think if there weren't any between us, we'd go off the rails. A train wreck, nothing would stop us except death.

Relax, Eden. You're getting carried away.

I think he can see my eagerness, the smallest of smirks pulling at the corners of his mouth.

"I'm the murderer, and it isn't anything as easy as strangulation."

I dig my nails into my palm, in the hand I have under the table, my bracelets feeling heavy on my wrist. Every sensation seems amplified as I wait for him to keep going, because he hasn't given me the entire thought. I force myself not to squirm in my seat as my pulse rings loud in my ears, fingers slippery around my pen.

He takes another drink of water, because he is an asshole, and he holds my gaze the entire time he does, drawing it all out, making me wait. "Have you ever watched someone drown?" He asks the question carefully, like he's thought of it before. Practiced the words coming out of his mouth. It strikes me as odd, because Eli seems good at any and everything, what's the use in practice when you embody perfection? His charm seems to know no bounds.

But maybe that's the key. Manipulation comes with preparation.

Besides, I'm not shocked at the manner of death. Perhaps, if he was a different person, it'd be full of gory violence. Blood splattered on walls, dripping down the hallway, a trail for the police, a crime that might initially appear to be one of passion but ultimately forensics and questioning give way to a simpler truth. The perpetrator was a psychopath. They planned every bright red detail.

Blood did not make them queasy and killing came easy.

But Eli… maybe he's too pristine for that sort of chaos. Cold and controlled, he wouldn't slip up.

I realize I haven't answered him as he huffs the smallest laugh. "Is this too much for you?" His voice is sensual, and I exhale, trying to focus on this moment, and not Eli off on an out-of-character bloody crime spree.

I remember he told me he almost drowned someone, but it seems irrelevant. A flippant thing to say to get me to open up. I don't mention it.

"No, I've never watched anyone drown." I swallow, intentionally loosening my grip on my pen. I almost ask it. *Have you?* But I bite my tongue at the last moment, because he already said *almost*. Besides, it's not my second question and he won't rob it from me.

His teeth flash like he knows what I just stopped myself from doing. "Well, my worst thought about myself is I drown someone I love, in a bathtub." He clears his throat, glancing away, and it's the first time I've ever seen him unsure of himself.

It feels like something I shouldn't be witnessing. Like I want to save him from the awkwardness of it. Or maybe it's part of his magnetism.

"Sounds easy to me."

He still stares at the bookshelves behind me, over my head. "Because you haven't seen someone drown. Besides, there'd be a struggle. Blood in the water, from my victim fighting back. Maybe a razor blade against my skin, and maybe I'd be upset enough to return the favor to them, just over their throat, and maybe it would be a straight blade instead of a disposable thing you buy at the store. The water would turn red and after what felt like forever, they'd stop struggling."

I'm panting, and I'm glad he's not looking at me. He'd see the truth in my eyes, how much this stuff turns me on. *So, there is blood after all.* Eli is fascinating, perhaps because he's so unpredictable.

There's a follow-up question bursting to come forth, and unlike the last times I stopped myself, I don't bother now. "Is it sexual?" My cheeks are warm, but I keep going. "Any part of it? Do you… do you rape them or—"

"I don't rape them." He seems angry I even asked as he brings his gaze back to me. "That part, they wanted." It isn't cockiness coating his statement. It's something else, like he *needs* it to be true.

We stare off for a long moment.

Is it me? A question I won't ask.

Who else would it be? An imaginary answer. My wish fulfillment.

"That's two questions." He taps the water bottle against his knee to a silent beat.

I roll my eyes, relaxing a little as the fantasy washes away in my head. "I can count." Before I lose my nerve as he gives me a blank expression, I just press onward. *Excelsior* sounds in my head, learned from Latin, and it gives me the lightness to ask. "Why doesn't your mom live with you?"

The look on his face stings. It's one of disappointment. He cocks his head, staring at me. I wonder if his mom is dead.

"I'm going to give you a chance to take that one back, and trust me, you want to."

I don't trust you. "No."

"Take it back."

I drop my pen and cross my arms. "Answer it."

"Why would you waste your time with this?"

I feel hot shame course through me, like I haven't lived up to the idea of *me* inside his head. It makes me want to walk the question back, retreat, come up with something else a little more clever. Even with my arms over my chest like some sort of defense mechanism, I want to shrink down into my seat. Or just get up and walk away.

But there's a reason he's acting this way, isn't there? He's getting angry with me, for the first time.

"Tell me." I inject coolness into my tone. *We can both play.*

Good luck with that. Even with those phantom words stinging inside my head, he won't make me back down.

He doesn't blink for long moments, but the longer he looks at me, trying to shrink me, the angrier I get, the bolder in knowing this is the question I want the last answer to.

Answer it, Eli, and tell me the truth. I clench my teeth, waiting, thinking it over and over in my head, knowing he could lie and hoping I'll be able to tell. But I think he's very good at it. I think lying is like breathing for him and I'm not sure how many times he's either kept or discarded the truth with me already.

Another second ticks by. Another.

Then he looks away, sitting up straighter, uncrossing his knee and putting both feet on the floor as he releases the water bottle.

"She died." He stands then, turning his back to me. He looks as if he's going to walk off, disappear into an aisle.

I'm careful with my chair, unlike the last time we were in the library together, and I stand too. "Eli."

I see tension nip into his shoulders, but he doesn't look at me and he doesn't speak.

Annoyance rolls through me, and I think of Sebastian. Our parents have bugged him to get another job, but he doesn't even apply. He does whatever he wants, and they let him get away with it.

I thought Eli's dad might have hit him, with those bruises on his body.

But it seems Eli is as spoiled as my brother, and Reece would never lay a hand on Sebastian.

I push thoughts of him aside. "How did she die?" I ask Eli, my voice unwavering.

"Three questions, Eden. You said you could count."

My face is hot, spreading down to my chest, sweat beading on the back of my neck, my hair down for once, heavy and thick, not for the first time, I think of shaving it all off. "You sound like a toddler."

The muscles in his back shift as he looks at me over his shoulder. "What?"

"You sound like a spoiled brat. Don't sulk. I'm sorry your mom died, but I just want to know—"

The look he gives me causes the words to break apart in my mouth, and a new thought weaves itself in my brain, fast, a haphazard sweater of nervous energy.

I almost dismiss the idea immediately, but it takes root and won't leave.

I blurt it out before I can stop myself. "Did you… did you *kill her?*"

He doesn't react. His expression is eerily blank.

My heart overcomes the drugs meant to slow it, and I feel the nervous flutters in my chest. My fingertips graze the table to steady myself.

"Are you nervous?" He glances around the library, quiet and dark, the only librarian is probably on the lower level, where the oldest texts are kept. I'm sure if I screamed, she'd hear me, but would Eli let me draw breath to do it?

I think of our fantasies.

A murderer. A victim.

A smile pulls on his lips as he turns all the way around to face me. "You're thinking those *worst things* might've been better left unsaid, huh?"

I swallow the fear wringing a noose around my throat. "What happened to her? Your mom, what happened?"

"You think it was all just a fantasy?" He enjoys my discomfort.

I laugh dismissively, despite my fear. "You didn't do it." I don't know that for a fact, but I think he's toying with me.

He steps around the table, slow, deliberate movements designed to cause me anxiety, until we're toe-to-toe, and my hands are by my sides because I've turned to face him too. I have to tilt my head up, and he has to lower his, and we don't physically connect, but the hairs on the back of my arms stand on end and it's like he's touching me. I'm not sure how I feel about it.

"You didn't do it." All he has to do is agree.

His eyes search mine for a beat. Then he says, "I think whatever we're doing here is getting out of hand."

It's like he's thrown icy water over my head. A shiver runs through me, cold, then hot all over again. *What?*

He looks down at me through his lashes, his tone condescending. "We don't even know each other, Eden, and you're accusing me of murder." He bends lower, so we're eye level, his eyes darkened, no emerald to be found. "Maybe we should take a step back, huh? This probably isn't good for either of us."

"You fantasize about drowning someone, then you tell me your mom is dead and get angry about it, about to walk off," I stab my hand in the general direction of the bookshelves, my arm trembling from anger and rejection, "and now you think we've gone too far when what's really happening here is you aren't good at communication and—"

"Just over two weeks."

I drop my hand, my knees shaky, and I have to grip the

ledge of the table. He doesn't back up, his hands in his pockets as he stays down on my level.

"We've known each other two weeks."

I know that. *I know that.* I understand, on some biological level, my hormones are out of control and Eli is really, really good looking, and he's smart and he says all the right things, and he's rich, and he has a future I could never be a part of. He drives a fast car, and he does it well, and he tells me all this shit I want to hear. I *know* I'm falling too fast, and it won't ever last, but I don't need it to.

I need until graduation.

I only intended to survive this year. To get good enough grades to go to a good enough school to get far enough away from my limited life so I could pretend to be something I'm not and maybe attend a decent grad school and become a professor and write a book, and maybe it would all be very mediocre, but I wouldn't live in a trailer and I wouldn't lug around cleaning supplies all day only to come home at night to a man who is ugly and ill-tempered like Reece.

I don't believe Eli will be in any of that future. No college, no grad school, no professorship. He belongs in none of my realities, but he's here. Right now. And he makes me feel *something.*

Something scary and alive and irrational, but something more than going through the motions.

Now, he's telling me it was all a very temporary dream.

"Let's just slow down, okay?" He sounds as if he's trying to pacify me. He arches a dark brow, and I hate how it makes him look so *wise*, like he knows what he's talking about. I hate how he smells so good, and how when he's this close, I can't think of any good rebuttal. "We skipped all of the small talk and jumped right into homicide and when you dive into the deep end so fast, you're likely to drown."

I narrow my eyes. "Not if you know how to swim."

This makes him stop in his tracks, and I can tell he wasn't expecting me to say anything. Neither was I if I'm being honest. He straightens, and I catch my breath as he runs his tongue over his teeth and looks up at the ceiling.

"I need to go."

"You're lying."

He sighs, and for the first time, I glance at the circles beneath his eyes as he keeps them trained above me. Dark blue, like a bruise. Like the color probably spattered over his chest right now. I think of the photo of him on my phone, and I have a feeling tonight I'm going to be grateful I took it. "I'm not. I promised my dad I'd be home for dinner."

I shift on my feet, wishing he'd invite me and knowing he won't. "Okay." I'm not going to beg him to stay.

He gives me a smile full of pity before he turns around to gather up his stuff. Mainly, the water bottle we were sharing, and his phone, face down on the table, it hasn't gone off once. "I'll see you tomorrow in class." He looks as if he wants an answer, phone now in hand as he waits.

I hate him walking away. I don't know where that leaves me. Was this all in my head? Like with Nic? All overhyped? Am I naïve? Is he?

There's no more imaginary conversation between us. His body language betrays nothing except for slight impatience that he's still waiting for my response.

I decide not to give him one. Arching a brow in the only dismissal he'll receive, I then drop down into my seat as elegantly as I can, like his movements from two weeks ago in this same library.

I can feel his eyes on me for long moments as I pick up my pen and pretend to ignore him. But he says nothing before he finally walks out, my question about his mom long forgotten.

16

Eli

TEN MINUTES after I leave the library, when I'm joyriding on the highway, I see the cop, and I know he clocks me, but he doesn't bother coming after me. We both know he'd never catch up. Still, I watch in the rear-view mirror for long seconds, eyes off the road as I do, and I don't fucking care about that. Who I hit. If I swerve.
I just don't care.
When the police car disappears from view, I pick up speed, glancing at the speedometer.
I could lose my license for this. I could lose my fucking car.
Dad would get me out of it, because Dad doesn't want anyone to know just how big of a fuck up his son is, does he?
"You missed your appointment." His voice through my speakers, connected to my phone, is full of concern.
I wish he was angry. It would make him easier to deal with. We could argue, I'd hang up, it would make sense. But his pity is stifling, and I turn up the air conditioner in the car, trying to breathe through this fucking conversation now I've had to roll my windows up so I could take his call.

I watch the sun disappear through my windshield, casting the highway in shades of dark blue.

"I know." I was outside of my psychiatrist's door when Eden called. I could've told her it would take me an hour. I could've not answered. I could've done anything, but between seeing a doctor and spending time alone with Eden, the choice was easy.

Dad sighs, and I know he's waiting for me to tell him why I missed, but I think he also knows I won't. Finally, he breaks first. "Every time you don't show, there's a problem."

I tighten my grip on the wheel.

"Montford keeps up with Dr. Langley, and he keeps up with *me*—"

"I'm eighteen. Transfer the file to me. Give them my number."

"The world does not give parents a break when their kids turn eighteen, Eli. It isn't an automatic cut off for anything, and especially not this."

This. Montford. Based states away in Idaho, even so, they'll be persistent in their follow up because they've got permission to communicate with my psychiatrist, and vice versa, and Montford is the only place of its kind in this country. They take this seriously. Not because they care, but because every scientist loves when their hypothesis is backed by results.

I am an experiment.

"They've already emailed twice *and* called three times." There's an edge to Dad's voice.

Just yell at me. Just break. Get it over with. Stop trying to be a good parent, tell me what you really think, Dad. How you really *feel.*

I don't say any of that.

I pass a car without slowing once, glancing in my rear view, and swerving into the right lane, then back over. I'm still speeding. Maybe more than before. I don't know. I don't look. I don't care. "Damn, Dad, patients get sick sometimes, you know? I'm sure I'm not the only person in the world to miss a therapy appointment here or there—"

"Be home for dinner. Seven." He clears his throat, and I glance at the clock on the console. I've got fifteen minutes. "I'll deal with Montford and Dr. Langley. Just get home."

I press harder on the gas.

I wonder if Dad hears the whine of the engine because he says, "Eli. Please be careful."

I inch the needle of the speedometer up a little more, smiling as I do, my steering wheel vibrating beneath my hand. "You got it, Dad."

When he hangs up, I think about calling Eden. Telling her I'm sorry, I shouldn't have overreacted, all those things you're supposed to say when you fuck up. I shouldn't have slipped up so hard and so fucking fast. I should've feigned indifference, but I didn't expect her to ask about *Mom*. I thought maybe it'd be about the fucking vigil, but since she blew Dom's coke up her nose, she doesn't seem to give a fuck about that little secret anymore.

Still, anger aside, I think about giving in because I want to talk to her. Right now. *Right fucking now.*

My throat feels tight, and I reach for my choker, plucking it away from my skin but not pulling it off. I try to breathe, releasing the necklace, rolling down my windows, letting the air rip through my hair, slashing across my face.

I pass four more cars, all on the right side, ducking and weaving without slowing down.

My exit is coming up, and it wouldn't take me long to get to Eden's. I'd miss dinner, Dad would be pissed, but he already is, isn't he? And since I didn't see Dr. Langley, Eric Addison is going to ensure he plays the part of my therapist by poking and prying and demanding to know why I bailed. He doesn't trust me. He doesn't believe me either, about Winslet.

One day, I'll explode and tell him the fucking truth.

Eden, Eden, Eden.

How did she fucking know what to ask? How did she pick the one thing I hadn't planned for? Most people leave it alone. They're too scared to pry. Maybe they don't want to know, because then they'd have to have an appropriate response, and they can't plan for the answer. Or maybe they have a fantasy in their head. I'm the boy without a mom, and I need nurturing, and *I'm so broken* and *how can I help him?* "I'll be here for you, Eli. I won't leave you."

I've heard those words from girls before.

I don't think Eden would ever say them.

My stomach churns and I feel sick, too hot, even with the wind biting into my eyes, my cheeks.

I almost don't do it. I almost *don't* look in my rear view to switch lanes at the last minute to make my exit. But when I lift my eyes to the mirror, I see headlights barreling by in the right lane, and if I had gotten over, shooting across the highway to get off at the right place in the nick of time, they wouldn't have been able to stop.

They'd have hit me.

It might be nice.

Mom's fingers are curled around the handle of her suitcase. She pulls at a thin scarf on her neck, her eyes on Dad.

I grip the ledge of the bannister, one foot on the bottom step, another already on the hardwoods of the foyer.

"Mom." My voice is rough from begging.

Mom keeps staring at Dad and she's smiling. It isn't real, because Mom never really *smiled*, but her eyes are watery, and her chin trembles.

"Mom." She still doesn't look at me.

I turn to Dad. "Stop her," I tell him, my voice rising, and I hate that. I hate how I sound scared. But she can't leave me with him. She can't. He doesn't understand me. He's already sent me away once. He'll do it again.

Fight for me, Mom.

Don't leave me.

I'm just like you.

We're the same.

We're the same.

"Dad, don't let her—"

"*Stop, Eli.*" Dad is crying. It's silent; tears tracking down his face, he doesn't look away from Mom. They're just staring at each other, several feet apart, Mom inches from the front door.

But she's wearing a long, wool coat, and she has on tall brown boots I've never seen her wear, which means she's probably leaving.

She's going out.

Without Dad. Without me.

"Mom, you can't—"

"*Eli.*" Dad's voice is angry, and he closes his eyes, his hands clasped in front of him. He's in a dress shirt and slacks. Work clothes. His office door is open, to his left, and I heard them arguing. I heard him chase her out here.

Run her off.

I listened at the top of the stairs.

I begged.

I YANK THE WHEEL, THE TIRES ON THE LEFT SIDE SKIDDING OVER grass as I just barely make it onto the exit, scarcely slide to a stop at the red light right off the highway.

I'm gasping, trying to breathe, warm summer air heavy around me now as I idle, waiting behind a van with a stick figure family. Four kids. A mom. A dad. A goddamn dog.

My heart races.

How did you know, Eden?

And what do you think you're going to do about it, huh?

You can't fucking fix me.

You can't.

You. Can't.

How did she know? Does she see me so well?

I bring up my contacts from my steering wheel, watching the center console's screen as I scroll through them.

I stop at her name.

I bite my lip, looking at those four letters.

Eden.

I dial her number before I can take it back, and I promise

myself I won't let it ring more than once. I glance at the light. Still red. Someone is fighting someone in the back of the stick figure van, hands slapping in the air, maybe over a car seat, I don't know.

"*What?*" Her voice fills the cabin of my car, angry but low. Hushed, like I'm a secret.

I don't care. I can be that. I can be anything for her.

I roll up all of my windows, not wanting to let her words slip away. "Do you know what your name means in Greek?" I ask, flexing my fingers on the wheel, my palm sweating on my gearshift as I think of where Mom went when she left me.

There's a pause. Then, "No." Dead even, she's pissed. But she's still right here. *Right here.*

"A state of innocence." I lick my lips, thinking of her eyes. Her mass of dark hair. Slender fingers. The bow of her lips. How she smells. *Two weeks,* I said.

I'm so full of shit.

We skipped the small talk because two souls know when they're conceived to collide. They don't need an introduction. They just fucking ruin each other without a hello.

"I'm not innocent."

I could've mimicked those words as she said them. Her tone, too, skeptical, haughty. "To me, you are."

"What the fuck do you want, Eli—"

"I'm sorry." I cut off her argument. I think of Mom turning her back to me. To Dad. I think of her walking out the fucking door.

Dad had to hold me back.

He'd never hit me before. We'd fought physically, but he'd never hit me until that night, after Mom walked out, heels clicking on the sidewalk, to the taxi at the bottom of the stairs.

She didn't look back once.

I could see her through the windows of her cab.

She clicked her seatbelt on, and she turned her head away from me.

She didn't look back. She just... left. Like she was... relieved to be away from me and all the problems I cause.

"I... I'm sorry." It's all I can say. *I'm so fucking sorry.* I still see Mom in my head.

There's a pause. Then, "Okay." Her voice is soft, but still lined with annoyance. I'm not entirely sure it's with me. I think I hear someone with her. A man's voice. I grit my teeth, visions of Mom clearing, but before I can ask anything, she says, "I have to go. I'll see you in the morning."

And she ends the call without waiting for my goodbye.

I hit my palm against the steering wheel so hard the entire dashboard seems to jump.

I think of Mom driving away.

I never saw her after that. I still haven't.

I hit my hand again, and again, and again, and later, when I'm in bed, my chest aching from Dad's blows, my knuckles bloody from mine, I stare up at the ceiling, thinking of walking away from Eden in the goddamn library.

I think of Mom never looking back.

She was just like me.

I'm just like her.

A state of innocence.

I can't be that to you, Eden. I can't do what she did.

My phone buzzes under my pillow, and I run my tongue over my bottom lip, swollen. Dad doesn't usually hit me in the face, but I can't blame him for that one. I almost broke his cheekbone, and he was on his back, and I think he was fucking terrified. It felt good, his fear.

I grab my phone and hold it above my head.

My heart lurches in my chest, then a heavy feeling settles in my gut. It's not guilt. No matter what I think about Mom, about Eden, about what I could do to her, I'm not going to stay away. I'm selfish, and nothing will change that.

No, it's the feeling of longing. The pang of wanting to be somewhere that isn't here.

I rub my thumb over the screen, reading the words again and again.

Eden: I'm going to bed. We don't have to talk about your mom. But don't cut me down like that again. And don't fucking walk off either, okay?

I take a breath, and another, smiling as I reply. **Me: You got it, baby girl.**

She takes a minute to respond, and I'm staring at my phone until the screen goes dim, feeling an acute sense of disappointment she might have fallen asleep.

But then she replies.

Her: I should've told you to shut up back there.

Fuck. I shove off my covers, my fan on overhead as I turn and press my nose to the pillow she slept on, inhaling deeply. It smells like her. Like her hair. Violet and goddamn peaches. My hand comes to my dick, and I look up again at my phone, typing with one hand.

Me: Why's that?

She hesitates, dots popping up, disappearing, popping up again. *Come on, baby girl. You said you're not innocent.*

Her: You could've gotten all that misplaced anger out.

I bite my lip, squeezing my erection over my boxers, closing my eyes and thinking of Eden's body, her fat fucking ass. Her letting me hurt her, *begging* me to.

My chest is heavy, and when I open my eyes, my fingers are shaky as I type.

Me: Is that what you wanted me to do?

Her response is faster this time. **Her: Yes.**

Just one word, and I'm aching all over for her. **Me: What if I really did it? What if I really slapped you?**

I push my boxers down, stroking myself, swiping my thumb over the bead of precum on the tip, wishing it was Eden's saliva. I want her pretty fucking mouth all over me.

Her: I'd probably like it.

Goddamn. **Me: Would you get on your knees for me and let me do it again?**

Her: As much as you wanted.

My pulse is loud in my head, thoughts of her kneeling for me in the library infecting my brain.

Me: It would hurt.

Her: I'd want it to.

Fuck. *Fuck.* **Me: I want you. Come here.** I've never meant anything more.

Her: I wish I could. I want to do everything you say, Eli. Even when you're acting like a spoiled fucking brat.

I'm barely breathing, pumping myself faster, biting my swollen lip, tasting iron in my mouth all over again and thinking of Eden beneath me in a bathtub.

In a fucking pool.

Her fingernails digging into my skin. Both of our fantasies come to life as I fuck her in the water, my hand splayed over her face, plugging up her nose as she stares up at me, eyes wide beneath the surface of the pool.

Me: Oh yeah? You always wanna obey me? You always wanna make me happy, baby girl? I kinda like it when you're a bitch.

Cool air from the fan runs over my body, and I think of how fucking hot Eden's body temperature is when she sleeps. It would feel good for her, shoved under cold water as I buried myself inside of her, and she couldn't even moan, or else she might fucking drown, and I know she'd want my cum before she did.

Her: Yes. I'd do anything for you. Anything you told me to.

She ignores my comment about being a bitch, as if she knows what I need right now.

And I know it's only the fantasy she's typing. I know she doesn't mean it. But even still, lust and power and *need* snarl through my veins, and all I want is her face under my hand, her body for me to use.

Me: Touch yourself. Right now.

It takes her a minute to reply, and in my head, I see her fingers trailing down her waist, slipping inside her underwear under the covers of her bed, her family not too far because her house is small, and she's getting so wet and she's thinking of me owning her and she's—

Her: I am. For you, even though you don't deserve it.

Me: No, I don't, but I don't care. Only think about me.

Her: I don't see anyone else.

Fuck, fuck, *fuck*. I'm so close, and imagining her fingers pushing into her tight pussy, and a gasp on her red lips, my name coming from her fucking mouth… I'm almost there. *I'm almost there.* Heat barrels through me, and I just need one more thing.

Just one more fucking thing.

Me: You're all mine, huh?

Her: Only yours, Eli.

I know it's a lie. We haven't even kissed. I know it's part of our game, but I don't fucking care. I'm so fucking close. **Me: Would you let me hold you under? Let me do anything I wanted with you? What if I bruised you? What if I really hurt you, Eden? What if I hit you?**

I feel it coming, my cock swelling, growing harder in my hand. I'm imagining violence, her skin covered in marks from me. But we're not fighting. I'm giving her everything she asked for, and even the things she was too scared to say out loud. She would thank me if she could breathe, but she can't, because I control that too, and I know she doesn't want air back, not yet.

In my head, bubbles come to the surface of the water. Her lungs ache, and she wants to inhale, but I'm not done, and she's not coming up until I am.

Her: I'd beg you to do it. Make my worst thought come true.

Me: You trust me with your body?

I'm almost there, a groan leaving my throat, and I couldn't stop it, no matter her next text, but I see it all the same before I drop my phone, pumping harder, faster, then cum is hot on my fist, over the back of my hand, stinging my bloody knuckles from the fight with dad.

Her messages play in my head as I finish, still groaning, *her* consuming me from the fucking inside out as her name leaves my lips in a jagged whisper and my pulse is too fucking fast, and I remember to breathe only after it's over. After my hand is a mess and I'm fucking spent, and when I turn my head, I read her words again.

You trust me with your body?

Her: All the damage you'd do to it would be worth it. The worst thought won't stop playing in my head, over and over and over, and this time my murderer has a face. It makes it feel more real.

I grab my phone, ignoring the feel of cum on my skin as I text her back, catching my breath.

Me: It better be my fucking face.

Anyone else touching her like that… I think I would fucking kill them. I don't want her to be hurt. I want to *hurt her*, and there's a difference, in my head.

Her: What if it isn't?

This fucking brat. I smile in the dark, exhausted, but I text her anyway.

Me: No one can hurt you but me, Eden.

A few minutes later, my eyes heavy with the need for sleep, she texts me back.

Her: Even though we're talking about you killing me, that sounded sweet.

I roll my eyes, still fucking smiling. **Me: It is sweet. So is the fact you're willing to let me murder you.**

Her: Just not yet. I want to have real sex with you before you suffocate me.

My dick gets hard all over again. It's going to be a long night. **Me: You want to have sex with me?**

She starts typing, then stops, then starts again, and I'm wide awake now. I glance at my desk, knowing I'll probably spend most of the night there. I rarely sleep, and if she hadn't turned me on all over again, or maybe if she was here with me, tonight would be a night I get a few hours in.

But I sit up slowly, staring at my phone, waiting for her answer.

Her: Shut up, Eli. Goodnight.

I tighten my grip on my phone, smirking. **Me: I'm going to pay your ass back for that. Now get some sleep for me.**

Her: Yes, sir.

I fall back on my bed, tossing my phone and letting it land with a *thunk* in my sheets. I slap the palm of my hands over my eyes, wondering how the fuck I'm going to keep my hands off of her until she's *really* ready.

17

Eden

I RUB my fists over my eyes as I pad to the bathroom. The floor is cold beneath the soles of my feet, even through my socks, the thin linoleum creaking underway. The scent of bleach, a long-dead candle and something like weed lingers in the air as I go to shut myself in the darkness, not yet ready for bright lights. It's early, but I want to try a workout before Mom drops me off at school and besides, I didn't really sleep much anyway. Power walking in place, she brought the DVD home for me from one of the housewives' she cleans homes for. If it was from anyone else, it could've been seen as an insult, but Mom once stumbled into my room at the apartment before the crack of dawn to find me doing lunges beside my bed.

It takes me about two seconds too long to realize the door isn't closing. I give it a shove, annoyed, wondering if Sebastian left his clothes on the floor or something. Then the door shoves *back* and I stumble a few steps toward the shower.

In the thin rays of sunlight from the hallway at his back, I see Sebastian's lanky frame in the doorway, his hand evidently holding open the door.

"What are you doing?" The question is automatic as I blink in the darkness, trying to make sense of Sebastian's early rise. He hasn't gotten a new job yet, I heard him in here just after one this morning while I was reading, and as far as I know, he sleeps until noon most days. Reece has been bitching at him about it.

My stepbrother yawns, bringing his hand over his mouth. He's wearing a beige hoodie, track pants, and thick, black shadows beneath his eyes.

They remind me of Eli. I think of last night. Getting off to Eli's texts. My face burns hot, and I lose focus on Sebastian for a second until he drops his hand, slips both into his pockets and leans against the frame of the door.

"Who were you talking to last night?" His voice is throaty, no doubt from whatever party he stumbled in from last night. For a guy who can't find a job, he's very skilled at unearthing numerous places to get high.

"What?" Even as I ask it, I'm thinking of Eli's texts again. Laughing out loud at some of them, imagining myself at his mercy with others. *Baby girl.* I feel sweaty despite my thin sleep shirt and shorts. The knee-high socks might have something to do with it.

I cross my arms over my chest, as if the movement will somehow block Sebastian from reading my mind.

"Probably not Amanda. Eli, huh?" He sounds like he's accusing me of something, and I narrow my eyes at his words.

"Does it surprise you I have friends?" It sounds childish, but I can't resist the bite.

He sighs, loudly, and I watch his chest rise and fall beneath his loose shirt. Everything is loose on him now. He's a little taller than me, average height I guess, and he's never been big, but he just seems so much smaller than he used to. When he was my big brother and I was hanging around the back of our apartment complex, watching him smoke with his friends and pass around stolen bottles of liquor.

When I was fourteen and one of his friends snuck into my room.

"You get any sleep last night?"

"What's it matter to you?"

"I'm just making conversation."

"At five in the morning?"

He rolls his eyes. "Just be careful, all right?"

I grind my teeth so hard my jaw aches, but it still doesn't keep the words in. "You do realize the irony of your warning?"

"I knew you were going to start with this shit," he mutters.

Heat flares through my chest and I drop my arms, gesturing toward him. "Are you kidding me—"

"You were *fourteen*, not a fucking toddler." He scrubs a hand over his tired face. He looks older and harder than he is, and I don't remember when he got that way, it was so gradual. "He made out with you, so what? You've blown this entire thing out of proportion, built it up to be bigger than it was and—"

"You have no fucking idea what he did!" He didn't *make out* with me. He didn't even kiss me. But I remember the feel of his body on mine in the dark, in my *bed*. I remember how he told me Seb wouldn't care, how my brother knew, and he was busy with a girl, and he just let it happen. I remember feeling paranoid after, for years. *Even now.* But as all those thoughts rush through me, I slash my hand through the air like I might break apart the cobwebs of the memory.

Sebastian is momentarily silent as we stare off. I wonder if he remembers the cup we passed around in his room, before. Handing me his cigarette so I could take my first pull. How I coughed but they all cheered. Half a dozen of his friends, guys and girls both, but Richard or Zach or whatever his name was, singled me out. I went to my room, shut the door, but it didn't have a lock.

And Sebastian forgot about me.

"It was more?" he asks, now, quietly, but there's a reluctance in his voice, like he doesn't want to know. We've danced around this for years. He does a better job of looking after me now, like penance. Or so he thought, until Shoreside happened.

"Oh, please." I've got my arms crossed again and I look down. I shouldn't have said anything. It doesn't even matter anymore. I'm mostly over it, but I can't resist testing his words. "Like he didn't brag to you in the morning."

"Eden." He says my name through gritted teeth. *"If he had fucking dared,* I would have killed him."

I keep my eyes on the floor. "Please get out." There's no venom in my voice. I don't care about this shit. I just need to pee, and I think about skipping the workout video to try to go back to sleep, but abruptly, my mind flickers to the sharp, strong points of Eli's collarbones and my resolve strengthens.

Seb shakes his head, closing his eyes a second before he's looking at me again.

"Really. I don't need you looking over my back. I'm fine." The words are petulant. I don't care.

He snorts. "Yeah? History would beg to differ. Besides, I'm your brother. I'm not going to stop."

We stare off for a moment. I want to tell him he needs to look after himself. I want to tell Mom she needs to do something to save him.

But I don't say or do any of that. I stay silent.

Sebastian sighs, then turns, heading to his room. "You really need to get more sleep." He mutters those words beneath his breath. A second later, I hear him snorting, then coughing, and I flick on the bathroom fan to drown out the rest of the noise.

ELI: WHY DO YOU LOOK UPSET?

I read the text under my desk, Ms. Romano's back to the class as she writes the word "occidere" on the board. I had forgotten to turn my phone on silent this morning, eager for any vibrations in the night coming from Eli, really the only person who texts me when I'm home.

Amanda has waned off, and I feel a little guilty I can breathe easier without her frequent check-ins.

I glance at Eli to find him looking back at me, smiling.

Someone kicks his chair—the girl to his left, chewing gum again as she is every morning—and the flash of irritation in his eyes catches me by surprise at how violent it is, like he's thinking about jamming one of the metal chair legs into her esophagus.

Or maybe I'm projecting my own thoughts onto him.

Slowly, he turns his head to face her, and I stare at his onyx hair, ruffled, like he slept on it wet. I want to pull it.

I ignore whatever look he's throwing his neighbor's way and text him back, telling him nothing of Sebastian.

Me: I woke up early to work out. I'm just tired.

I'm not, surprisingly. I've found it increasingly difficult to get any sleep lately, my brain hopped up on thoughts of Eli. But I've taken my heart pills a few times, to help.

I didn't see Eli this morning until he sank into his seat, eyes on me as he did. Now, I watch him turn his attention from the girl who kicked him, to his phone, and I'm thinking of last night all over again while Ms. Romano starts writing out various phrases with the word "murder" in them.

Eli: After last night, you should have rested.

My heart thumps too fast in my chest, my fingers slippery around my phone as I stare at my screen, hot with embarrassment and something else, too, and when Ms. Romano says my name, I startle, the phone clattering to the floor a second later.

Shit.

I don't want to look up, because I can feel everyone's eyes on me, the room eerily silent, sun streaming in through the wall of windows to my right, no doubt illuminating the splash of red on my cheeks.

But before I have to reach for my phone, or answer my teacher who no doubt saw me on it, Eli clears his throat and asks, "I hate to interrupt, but why are we learning about *murder* today, Ms. Romano?"

I look up, leaving my phone at my feet, and see every head slowly swivel to Eli, then Ms. Romano, who has her hands on her hips and probably despite her best effort not to, is fighting a smile as she stares at him.

Jealousy pricks under my skin, even though I know he was doing me a favor. Still, I spend the rest of class both fantasizing about ripping my favorite teacher's nails off and trying to figure out when I became so violent inside my head.

He waits for me.

I feel Ms. Romano's eyes on us, but this time, she doesn't say anything. A class period spent conjugating "to murder" with teenagers has made her quieter than usual, but no less hawk-eyed.

With fingers shaky from adrenaline, I zip up my bag and toss it over my shoulder, sweeping the single braid I put my hair in this morning out of the way as I thread my other arm through my backpack strap, too.

When I look up, my eyes automatically connect with Eli's, like we're magnetized.

He's half-sitting on his desk again, so casual, hands in his pockets as he smiles at me, and for a moment, he just looks… innocent. It does something to my heart, seeing him that way, like I want to protect *him* from the world. Like maybe I'm the corrupt one in this relationship.

Relationship.

I blink, slashing through my delusion. That isn't what this is. *We're just friends.*

And together, as *friends,* we head toward the door.

"I don't think you got enough sleep last night," he says, and I hear the innuendo in his words. "What kept you up?" He feigns blamelessness, and I have to laugh, shaking my head as the familiar blush fans across my face in pinpricks of warmth. I've learned, over the course of years, to ignore it.

"Shut up," I say under my breath, smiling as we walk out

into the hallway, then immediately, hearing his silence, the way he stops short beside me, my entire body tingles with nerves and my smile slips. I look up, my eyes wide as I meet his, and I can only think to say, *"Oh."*

His teeth flash as he grins, his brows lifted. *"Oh* is right." His words are low, and I glance at his hands, but they're still in his pockets. And before I can think through if I'm disappointed or relieved at that, my thoughts feverish, I realize he's no longer looking at me.

He's focused on something behind me.

I frown, turning to follow his gaze.

Then I freeze, tightening my fingers around the straps of my bag, all thoughts of Eli hurting me wiped away by the confusion in my head.

Police officers line the hallway, three of them, shoulder-to-shoulder.

And they're all staring at me and Eli.

For a second, I forget we're at Trafalgar. Cops around the trailer park, the apartment complex back at the beach, all of that makes sense to me, but the three officers with badges and guns and hard eyes turned toward me is strange.

My stomach flips.

Did something happen to Sebastian?

I think of our conversation this morning and feel dizzy, regret ringing in my ears. And because of it, the roar in my head from my elevated pulse, it takes me a moment to understand what it is the cops are saying, and the fact they're saying it to *Eli.*

"Of course," he replies, to the officer in the middle, and I turn my head to face him, my brows pulled together, sweat slick along the back of my neck, blossoming under my arms.

Eli turns his sharp gaze to me, a small smile on his lips as he steps toward the officers, his back to them as they look at me, then him, then back again.

"I'll see you tonight?" he asks, and I don't know what he

means, maybe the library, maybe he wants me to stay after practice.

"What the hell?" I grind the words out, looking again toward the officers. "What do you want with him?" My adrenaline is spiked, and I bite my nails into the fabric of my straps to keep from reaching for Eli when he takes another step away from me and toward the police. I shake my head. "Where are you taking him—"

"It's okay, baby girl." Eli says the words loud enough for the officers to hear. I cut my eyes to him. He shrugs, winking at me. "I'll see you later."

And I don't get another explanation before he walks past me, down the hall with the three officers right behind him like bodyguards, only I don't know if they're guarding Eli or everyone else.

I have no choice but to move my feet to English, amidst the hushed whispers and eyes on Eli as he strides down the hallway without a care in the world.

It's only halfway through English, my mind still whirring, my phone on vibrate and clutched in my clammy palm under my desk, when I realize Dominic isn't in class.

SEBASTIAN: WHEN DO YOU NEED ME TO PICK YOU UP?

I tap my pen against my notebook, sitting up straighter in the shadowy library, my eyes heavy as I scan the room again, seeing nothing but empty aisles and tables, the quiet unnerving. I kept my earbuds in my backpack, set in the seat next to me, so Eli couldn't sneak up on me.

But Eli isn't here, and he hasn't replied to my texts, either.

I check the time. His practice should be over. It's almost eight. I called him once, an hour and a half ago when I thought he'd be done, but he didn't answer, the phone just rang and rang.

My stomach twists into knots as I stare at Sebastian's text. I told Mom I was studying, and she said Seb offered to pick me up. I didn't dispute the fact I'd need a ride, because... well, *where are you, Eli?*

Definitely not here.

I sigh, then open up Sebastian's contact info and call him. I hold my breath, still expecting Eli to appear out of the shadows and explain everything to me, but the only thing that happens is Sebastian answers, and I can tell he's high by the raucous laughter on the other end of the line.

I roll my eyes in irritation, gritting my teeth with his lazy, *"Hello?"*

"You were supposed to be sober." I grip my pen hard enough to hear the plastic crack, but I don't let go as a jagged edge digs into the web of my fingers.

Sebastian laughs again. "I ammmm," he drawls out, and I hear music in the background, bass beats and giggles from a girl.

"Where are you?"

"Don't worry about that."

I close my eyes, dropping my pen and bringing my hand to my temple, elbow on the table.

"Just let me know when you need me—" His words die off with a girl's shriek, and a loud clatter follows. Judging by Sebastian's faraway voice as he says, "Hey, hey!" I'm assuming someone knocked the phone out of his hand.

I don't bother saying anything else. I just hang up and send him a text not to worry about it, although it's not as if I'm counting on him to worry at all.

I set my phone on the table and bury my head in my hands, thinking of walking back in the dark. I'm not scared of the dark, or even of Raleigh, really. I should be safe, there's sidewalks, and if I start getting freaked out, I'll call Mom as a last resort and deal with Reece's lecture when we get back.

But part of me wants to wait, thinking Eli will show up if I just hold out a little longer.

And part of me feels stupid, being on his leash.

I take a breath, then shove away from the table, snapping my eyes open and deciding to take a lap around the library before I go. *One last chance, Eli.*

I glance at my phone, checking he hasn't texted me, then I snatch it up and push it into my pocket, ensuring it's on vibrate before I start to roam.

I glide my fingers over the shelves of Greek mythology first, eyes pausing on a text dissecting Adonis. My heart skips a beat in my chest, but I force myself not to grab the golden spine of the book. I keep moving, further away from my table, down aisle after aisle of heavy research volumes, until I get to the far side of the library, a fireplace never used as far as I can see at my back, and school records of Trafalgar on the shelves in front of me, climbing so high I'd need a stool to get to the top.

I scan the rows and rows of cloth bound, blue texts, realizing most of them are yearbooks. There's a thick volume called *Trafalgar, The History*, with silver letters threaded on the spine. But below that, it's yearbooks by date, and smiling to myself, I reach for the one from three years ago.

It's not very heavy, the school small and elitist (expensive) as it is. I take a few steps back to lean against the exposed brick, beside the fireplace, tracing my finger over the cloth covering. It's made to look ancient. This could be a yearbook from 1909 if it wasn't for the school year printed across the cover.

I flip open the pages, hearing the creak of the spine. I don't think anyone has ever looked through this book, which feels sad in some way, like students are just forgotten. Money taken, donations levied, then they're thrust out into the world of their parents, padded with cash and lawyers and trapped into gilded cages.

But at least they're gilded, right?

The first half of the yearbook is full of photos from sports teams.

I bypass football, swimming, and lacrosse, heading straight for wrestling.

Glossy, black and white photos stare back at me with tiny

captions printed beneath each one, but it's the picture in the center that stands out above the rest.

Eli, a champion in his weight class. A freshman in this picture, I suppose he's used to winning.

His hand is lifted high by the ref at the end of the match, he's a little less muscular than he is now, a little shorter, his hair is, too, his edges not so sharp yet.

But even here, three years ago, there's nothing exuberant on his face, though, veins stark against his skin along his forearms, his headgear dangling from the fingers of his other hand.

He looks bored, and I'm not even sure what he's looking at, like he's just staring through the crowd. He would've been fourteen.

Was his mom there, then?

His dad?

He's just... stoic. Or *empty*, maybe.

Everyone around him, his coach and team on the sidelines, they're wild with happiness, fists lifted in cheers, lips curled up into smiles and shouts of joy. It didn't seem to reach him, though. It's like he couldn't feel it. It's like he's not even there, the look in his eyes blank.

I snap the book closed and push it back along with the rest on the shelf in front of me, marveling over just how many there are here. Scanning the dates along the spine, straining my eyes in the dark as I look up at the higher, faded numbers, I realize this school is over one hundred years old.

It seems like some kind of private school record, particularly in a state always building new schools to accommodate more students, then promptly filling them and bursting at the seams again.

It's kind of startling, knowing in my quest to get into Trafalgar—after Reece's brother mentioned it casually when he realized how good my grades were, when I saw the castle as we drove by to inspect the trailer before we moved in, when I knew my record wouldn't endear me to many places—I didn't really do my research. I went straight to the financial aid section on their website, ensuring this wasn't a pipe dream, and knowing the first thing Reece would ask about would be tuition. Costs. What it would take from him.

But I didn't look at how long Trafalgar had been around. I didn't look at class sizes either, although I did glance at where students filtered to when they left. Ivy leagues, mainly. A few renowned universities in Europe. Those have never been in reach for me, but it was fun to scroll through and imagine being there anyway.

Still, I know this castle isn't *ancient*, the United States lacking the lengthy history other countries do, but it's older than I thought. I glance around the library, at the fireplace beside me, with brand new awe, wondering if the rich kids ever feel that way.

I face the shelves again, my fingers gliding over the cloth spines, and I find last year's book.

Smiling, I pinch it from the two volumes around it, one dating back the year before this one, and a thin paperback entitled, *Theatrics at Trafalgar*.

I retract it from the shelf, and realize I'm holding Eli's junior year in my hand.

Again, I step back to lean against the wall as I flip it open.

I flick to the front, finding the sports section once more, noting this time, it's etched in silver filigree, something that must have cost a fortune for these glossy, heavy pages. I wonder if all private schools take their extracurriculars so seriously. The guidance counselor had tried to sign me up for something —the paper, or yearbook—but I wasn't sure I could count on rides when they were needed on demand, and with no parking spot and no hope of forking out a grand for one anytime soon, I declined, knowing it would look bad on my transcripts, but my grades would have to be enough for Bloor.

Focusing on the silky pages unfolded to me, I realize I've been scanning the group wrestling photo for several minutes, my attention not once snagged on Eli's face.

Smiling to myself at my runaway brain, I hold the book in

one hand, fingers splayed underneath the cloth binding, and drag my index finger over every single face in the huddle, Coach Pensky squatting in the center with a grimace I think is supposed to be his smile.

But there's no Eli.

I straighten from the wall, my own smile slipping. He's not there.

He could've been sick or absent or… anything at all when they took this photo. I missed picture day for fourth grade because I had chicken pox. For the second time. It left a scar over my lip, just above my Cupid's bow.

I turn the page and flick my gaze down to the list of names on the team, divided by junior varsity and varsity.

Up. Down. Over and over again until I could recite a few. Darrel Johnson. Lucas Miller. Kam Harris. Johnny Baca, the guy I met at the party.

No Eli. No other E names at all. Only one Addison. *Jasper.* He looks vaguely familiar, but he's definitely not Eli.

It could be a misprint.

I flip to the junior class, each square photo listed alphabetically by last name.

Again, I drag my finger, my head bent over the page, neck aching in my concentration, but it's all background noise.

The photos skip from Jasper Addison to a girl with dark hair, Emily Adeline, to a boy with no hair, Fernando Alvarez.

I glance over the entire page, rows and rows of smiling faces staring up at me.

Eli's is not one of them.

I flip to the index, every student, teacher, and coach's name listed in alphabetical order. I look over the As, row by row.

No other Eli's in that section.

Frowning, I turn once more to the wrestling pages. And as my pulse picks up speed, confusion and frustration gnawing at me in my tunnel vision, I hear a voice at my side.

"What're you looking for, baby girl?"

I jump, whirling around and slamming the book closed,

clutching it close to my chest like a shield as I take a step back, my pulse hammering too fast.

I blink, a flush of adrenaline racing through my body as I stare up at Eli, his hands in his pockets, his dark hair damp and hanging in his eyes. He's wearing a black shirt, his wrestling shirt. Trafalgar Dragons.

Even from here, the distance I put between us, I can smell the soap on his skin, mingling with the beachy scent of *him*.

He has one brow cocked, a soft smile pulling on his beautiful lips.

My chest is heaving, moving the book I have cradled to it.

"Where were you?" I blurt the words out, glancing past him, like I might spot the cops there, waiting in the shadows. "What happened this morning?"

He stares at me a moment, then steps forward, closing the space between us. I have the urge to back up, but I fight back against the instinct. I'm not scared of him. I'm nervous around him, but there's a difference.

He reaches for the yearbook, his fingertips grazing my wrist as he does, and the hairs on the back of my neck lift with his touch. I can't stop my slight flinch, more a seizing of my limbs than anything else, but it's still there.

He pulls the book from my arms, and I let him, dropping my hands by my sides as he looks down, studying the cover. I take in the slight curve at the tip of his nose, the pale violet shadows like bruises under his eyes as he grips the yearbook in both hands, pulling his bottom lip between his white, straight teeth.

I dig my nails into my palms, waiting for him to explain, and I don't know what I want an explanation for first. The yearbook could be easily explained. The cops, though... that seems like a more sinister story.

After several seconds, he looks up through his lashes at me, his chin still tilted down. "I had practice," he says.

I frown, glancing past him. I can't see any windows from

here, but I know it's well after dark. Past eight by now. "This late?" I ask, bringing my gaze back to him.

"Bleacher runs."

I realize for the first time, his chest is rising and falling faster than usual beneath his wrestling shirt, and his cheekbones are tinged with pink. I know better than to think it's from embarrassment. I don't think Eli ever feels an emotion like that.

"The whole team?" I don't know why I ask it, but I see by the smile pulling at his mouth, it's a good question.

"No." He turns from me, then carefully places the yearbook he's not in back on the shelf, where it belongs. He lets his finger linger against the spine, sliding down it almost sensually, and a shiver crawls down my own spine. I drink in his side profile, his parted lips, defined jawline, the way I can see his pulse jumping in his throat from bleacher runs, which sound like a very low circle of hell.

"Where were you last year?"

He shakes his head once, like he can't listen to my question, like he's trying to focus on something. His finger is still on the spine of the book, and he's staring at it, like it'll give him the answers to his own absence. Then he just says, "I missed picture day."

I narrow my eyes, even though he doesn't look at me. "Bullshit. You weren't in wrestling pictures either."

"Missed that, too." A smirk accompanies his words, and I know he's being a smart ass.

I try my first question again. "Okay, if you want to be an asshole… What happened this morning? Or are you going to tell me I'm delusional there, too?"

"Might be for the best." His voice is low and even, and my temper rises because of it.

"What the hell, Eli? What if I got escorted by cops down the hallway and you didn't hear from me all day and—"

"That's the real problem, isn't it?" He arches a brow, but he's still not looking at me. "It's not what happened. It's not the cops, Eden. You don't care about the fucking cops, do you?" His smile widens, gaze focused on the yearbook. "You don't care what I did. Just like you don't care I'm not in here." He taps his finger once against the spine of the book. "You're just upset because I didn't inform you about my absence last year, and I didn't answer your texts, or your call, which, by the way…" He finally turns to look at me, still smiling.

My heart flutters in my chest.

"I really like when you call me."

I bet you do.

"I was a little busy getting out of a chokehold when you did, or I would have answered."

The image of Eli getting choked is strangely appealing, and I press my thighs together, something he notices, because his eyes dart down before slowly dragging back up the length of my body. Still, I force myself to *focus*. "And my texts? Why couldn't you answer any of those?"

"Are you worried that sometimes, I'm not thinking of you?" He whispers those words.

My face flushes hot for the first time since his arrival here. I bite the inside of my cheek, but I don't look away from him, even as he pulls apart my worst fear, like tearing stitches from a wound. It's what *I* do. I forget about people when they no longer serve their purpose to me. Amanda, for example. A girl I should've been lifelong friends with, because I've known her since I was a kid, and we've had sleepovers, and I know her family, and she knows mine, and she stood up for me after Nic, but I move and I just… don't care anymore. I rarely think of her.

I need Eli to keep thinking of me, until we graduate. Whatever this is can end then, but I need a person until it's over. Someone to stick close to.

He drops his hand from the shelf, then slowly stalks toward me.

I back up, until I can't anymore, the brick wall at my back, the grooves and mortar digging into my shoulder blades. My pulse is pounding in my ears, so loud I'm worried I won't be able to hear him when he speaks.

He doesn't touch me, his hands by his sides, but he leans in close, and I can feel his body heat, and this time, he *does* feel hot, his icy coolness swallowed from his workout.

"I'm always thinking of you," he says, his eyes darting to my mouth, then back up.

I lick my lips, and he tracks the movement, smiling as he does.

"*Always,* Eden. You've done something to me because you're stuck in my fucking head." He sounds suddenly irritated, but not angry. "Last night…"

My face is on fire, the flush spreading down my neck, across my chest, and I'm grateful I'm still in the dark blue polo I wore today, buttoned up to my throat. I have the urge to run, my palms finding the cold bricks at my back, pressing against them and enjoying the prick on my skin, grounding me.

"Yeah?" I manage to whisper, my voice cracking, wanting him to keep talking. Keep telling me these sickly sweet things.

"Yeah?" he mocks me, and there's something sensual in the word, the way he smiles with it. His hands are still by his sides, and I want them all over me just as much as I don't. "Did you mean it? Everything you said to me?"

I kind of want to die. The things we talked about last night, the words I gave him, the ones I think he needed in the moment like I did before, they're so much easier to say in texts. Now, I don't know where to look or how to talk or even really, when to breathe. He has the ability to crumble all of my sharpened defenses.

"It's okay, you know." His words skate over my mouth as he leans down closer, his nose level with mine. "I meant all of it, too."

My entire body is tingling, an ache between my thighs, and I want him. *I want you.* But I'm not stupid. I haven't forgotten. "What happened with the cops?" I ask. "Winslet, you said you fucked her. The vigil, the yearbook—"

"Shh," he says, his breath on my mouth, the scent of cotton candy sweet as I inhale. His eyes search mine and he leans in closer, just an inch, but it's enough, his lips on my own, my heart beating so hard it aches in my chest.

"Shh," he says again, even though I haven't said another word. I think I've forgotten how to speak. "I'll tell you everything, just… let me."

I want to. *I want to.* He's so fucking hot, and charming, and he's so close I can't breathe, but first I want to know. I *need* to know. "No. You tell me *now*. What happened with the cops, Eli? I've been waiting here for hours for you. *Tell me now.*"

He's staring at me, his chest heaving, and mine reflects the movement. "Eden." My name sounds like a plea on his lips. "Just shut up and let me fucking kiss you."

Shut up.

His eyes spark. I know he said it on purpose. For some reason… he wants this.

Before I can back down, I lift my hand, and I… *slap him.* I'm shocked at my own actions, a small gasp leaving my lips, my palm tingling. But in some way, it felt easier than what we're about to do. Things I've never done before.

He smiles at me, turning his head back my way as I drop my hand, his face flushed where I hit him. A second passes. A pause.

He's asking for permission, in a very Eli way, and I hope he understands I can't give it. *I just want him to take it.*

And a heartbeat later, *he does.*

His tongue flicks against the seam of my mouth, my lips part for him, and he's kissing me so hard I can't breathe. I'm frozen, my mind spinning, some distant part of my brain reminding me I need to kiss him back, I need to move, I just slapped him, shit, *fuck*, and… and…

His hand comes to my hip.

I jump, but I step forward all the same, and my palms are on his chest, and I'm standing on my tiptoes and finally kissing him back, and I feel clumsy and I'm not sure I'm doing this right, but I don't stop, and he doesn't stop me.

Not like an explosion. Not a bomb. No fireworks.

Instead, I'm waking up from a dreamless sleep, and reality is better than anything I could've fantasized about. I've watched people fucking on my phone screen for years. I learned how to orgasm when I was much younger. But this… *this is all new to me.*

My fingers dig into his shirt, and I feel the flex of hard muscle underneath as his other hand comes to my ass and squeezes, and I moan into his mouth, a light, breathless sound as I buck my hips.

He smiles but he doesn't pull away, our teeth clashing, tongues circling one another, my face wet with my saliva, his. It's messy, like we're fighting for dominance, but I secretly want him to win. I push him, almost like I'm pushing him away. I'm not sure why I do it, it's like my brain is short-circuiting, and my movements are nervous and erratic. His body jolts from surprise, and he concedes a step, toward the bookshelves.

There's a pause in his mouth over mine, even as I keep kissing him, keep digging my nails into his shirt. Then he smiles, the shape on my lips.

"Careful, baby girl."

It's the only warning he gives before he shoves me forcefully against the wall with his hand gripping onto my hip. I move willingly, his body pressed up against mine, our height difference stupid, but it makes me feel safe, like I'm something he wants to protect even as he devours me. His fingers knead my ass, his other hand sliding up my hip, my waist, his palm pressing against my breast before he rests his hand over my throat, his fingers curling softly, and—

My phone vibrates in my pocket, causing me to jump and pull back, his teeth digging into my bottom lip hard enough to hurt, to sting, trying to keep me with him. But I knock my head against the wall, and he lets go as I run my tongue over my lip, tasting the faintest hint of iron, feeling how swollen my mouth is from our kiss.

I'm breathing hard, and he still has one hand on my ass, the other around my throat. When I lift my eyes to his, my phone continuing to vibrate in my pocket, I see he looks a little off balance, which surprises me. His eyes are glassy, his lips parted as he draws in ragged breaths, and when I sink down to the soles of my feet, he presses into me, like he needs me to hold him up.

I feel how hard he is against my stomach, and all rational thought leaves my head, but at the same time, my phone keeps ringing, and I blink, trying to focus.

I intend to grab my phone, but instead, I bring my fingers up to my mouth, my wrist grazing the back of his hand, still around my neck.

I can feel the lingering touch of him on me, how soft his lips were, the sweet taste of him still on my tongue.

He tightens his fingers on my throat, just enough to get my attention. "You should get that," he says, recovering from his lust-filled haze. It's like he snaps back into place, his eyes focused, the cocky smirk again on his swollen mouth as he drops his hands both from my throat and my ass, and steps back, letting me breathe.

I miss his heat instantly, but as he watches me, my eyes dropping to his sweats, seeing the outline of his erection, enough to make me crave him all over again, I reach with shaky fingers for my phone.

It's Mom.

He must read the name on my screen, too, because he says, "You're riding with me."

18

Eden

HE DRIVES AGGRESSIVELY, made more noticeable by the fact there are no other cars on the road. He accelerates through yellow lights, passes underneath a red one I'm sure the traffic cameras will send him a ticket for, and he goes well over the limit. So fast, I don't want to try and read his speedometer as I squeeze my thighs with my hands in his passenger seat.

"Come Here" by Dominic Fike plays through the speakers, the windows down, a late summer breeze ripping through the strands of my hair that've come loose from my braid. I answered Mom's call and told her I had a ride from Eli.

All she said was, *"Be safe, Eden."*

Either way, it's good I mentioned Eli, since the first thing he asks me in the car is, "Are you still good for Friday?" He doesn't look at me, and I settle on staring at his hand as he shifts gears while we come to a stoplight he decides to obey.

I loop my hair behind my ears, thinking of asking Mom to let me spend the day with a boy she hasn't met yet. But I'm eighteen, I remind myself. I have a car. I don't work at the gym that day. I should be able to do whatever I want.

"Yes," I answer his question. I'll make it work. I lean my head back against his seat as the light turns green and he takes off, engine revving. I marvel over the fact I slapped him, and he seemed to like it. It makes me feel a little high. So does the faint tingle from his lips on mine. It's really hard to stop touching my fingers to my mouth.

"Tell me about the police." I say it quietly, so quiet I'm not sure he heard me, except for the fact I see him spare a single glance my way.

I expect he won't answer. I know the kiss was a ruse, but then again, I think of how dazed he looked afterward. Like it had an effect on him too; just like me, or at least, close enough.

Pride swells in my chest, thinking of it, imagining having power over him. I link my fingers together in my lap and turn my head to watch the darkness flying by as I hide my smile.

"You know all about Winslet, since you wandered away from me at the party, huh?"

My smile falters. I don't trust myself to look at him. Pinpricks of unease run across my shoulder blades as I sit in his passenger seat.

I think of the missing posters, edges curled. *Dominic's sister.*

In my head, Eli's words from the second night he took me home. *"A girl I used to fuck."*

My mouth feels like it's full of sand, and I can think of nothing to say, but mercifully, maybe, Eli keeps talking.

"They had a few questions about her."

I wait for the rest of that statement. For him to explain why it has nothing to do with him, but why they thought it did.

Nothing comes.

Just music, wind, the purr of his car. We're getting closer to my house, and further from any reasonable explanation. I have more questions than before, but I can't bring myself to face him.

I clear my throat, running my tongue over my lips. "Why?"

A beat of silence. Then, "I fucked her, remember?"

"How could I forget?" I turn my head to look at him.

He turns onto the second-to-last road to my house. "So jealous," he whispers. "It turns me on."

"Eli." I snap his name, not giving into his distractions. "Why were they questioning you—"

He laughs abruptly, cutting me off. I rarely hear his laugh, but this is a sound I don't want to experience again. It's cold and clipped, and the look he gives me as he comes to a stop sign isn't any better. His lip curls as he stares at me, like he's disgusted, and I resist the urge to squirm in my seat, reminding myself I didn't do anything wrong.

"Let me guess," he says, and I'm surprised at the venom in his words. "You think I had something to do with it?"

"I never said that." I feel my blood pressure rising, and I long for my medicine, in the bag at my feet, but I don't move, watching Eli, refusing to avert my gaze. "But why don't *you* tell *me. Did you* have something to do with it?"

His eyes narrow into emerald slits, the shadows cast on his face by the dash lights rendering him an eerie, almost mannequin-like expression. "You actually think I'm capable of murder?"

The answer is so obvious, I don't understand why he asked. *Of course you are.* Isn't everyone if the timing is right? The emotions? The circumstances?

But I don't say that. Because I suddenly realize… neither he nor I ever said anything about homicide.

Winslet is reported *missing.* Not *dead.*

It feels as if someone dumped ice cold water over my head. Dizziness passes in a wave. I take deep breaths, quiet, trying not to let him see I'm freaking out. And I keep my voice calm and controlled when I ask, *"Murder?"*

He doesn't backtrack. He doesn't even flinch. His tone is cold when he simply responds with, "You avoided the question."

At the darkened intersection, it is eerily sinister, only Eli's blue-tinted lights spearing through the night. I see bugs in the beam of them, something that looks like a pair of eyes in the woods, just across the street. Probably a deer, but it unnerves me all the same. "You said *murder.*" I speak quietly as I stare straight ahead. "You avoid *all* of my questions, so stop fucking with me, Eli. You. Said. *Murder.*"

Silence fills the car.

He doesn't drive. We idle at the stop sign, and I start to wonder how many bodies could be hidden in these woods.

Goosebumps trail down my arms.

I force myself to stay, instead of run. But I need him to *say something.*

Seconds pass. Minutes.

Slowly, I turn my head.

Our eyes connect in the dark.

His expression is blank, and I wonder if he's intentionally trying to scare me.

I don't move. It seems to be what he needs, to break his silence.

"She's been missing a year," he finally says, his voice low. "They're starting to think… she's not coming back. Not alive, anyway."

It feels like spiders crawling down my spine, a shiver ghosting over my entire body with his words.

Immediately, I think of the yearbook. Like he'd vanished from Trafalgar for a year.

I try to think of a way those two things aren't connected. Dominic's sister, and no record of Eli in school. There are so many explanations, but he won't give me any, and he says nothing else as he turns at the intersection, heading toward my house.

He gives me nothing at all to hold onto, like he wants me to consider the worst-case scenario. Then what? Does he expect me to still choose him, knowing he could've… done something to this girl?

He pulls up in front of the trailer, and I see something is off immediately, dragging me out of my thoughts about Eli and Dominic's sister for the moment.

The door of my house is open, only the screen door separating the living room from outside. Lights flash along the wall, and I know the TV is on. Sebastian's Mazda isn't here, meaning either Reece or Mom or both of them are in the living room, and as I hold my breath, I see a shadow move toward the glass of the screen door.

Fuck.

"It looks like your mom wants to meet me." Eli's words are syrupy sweet, a reminder he is still a smartass and maybe, also, a murderer. *But I don't really believe that.*

I glare at him as I unbuckle my seatbelt, Mom still hovering by the door, her arms crossed. I don't think she can see us in here, as dark as Eli's windows are tinted, but I still feel like we're ants trapped under a glass jar, and now I won't get any answers.

I almost consider it a mercy.

"Stay here," I tell him, grabbing my bag from the floorboard. "You don't need to meet the parents." I reach for the cool handle of the door, knowing I'll have to ask the rest of my questions tonight, under my covers, through my phone. But Eli grabs my wrist, fingers tightening around my bones as the smallest gasp leaves my lips.

I can feel him staring at the back of my head.

He's not holding onto me hard enough to hurt, but it's aggressive, his grip.

"I do," he says coldly. "Because you're going to be swimming half-naked in my pool by the end of the week and your mom is going to want to know where her precious daughter is all day and night, *don't you think?*"

I grit my teeth, casting a glance at Mom's anxious shadow. "If I tell my mom her *precious daughter* is in a car with a guy who is under suspicion from police about a girl's disappearance, I don't think she's going to let me go anywhere with him."

He laughs, slicing through my pseudo-threat and releasing my wrist, only to run his fingers over the bracelets there, tugging on one like he wants to break it.

I'm grateful he's not touching the inside of my wrist. He hasn't noticed the scars, and if I can help it, he never will.

Despite my annoyance, when he breaks free one of the black bracelets, ripping it off against my skin hard enough to cause a sting, lust drives through my veins, a runaway train.

I hear the softest sound as he drops the bracelet in the cupholder of his car, then circles my wrist again. Once more, I'm struck with a jarring thought.

His fingers belong here, around me.

"Shut up, baby girl." His tone is soft. He doesn't sound as cruel as he did before, and something about those four words strung together in one sentence makes me feel like putty in his hands. "I wonder if your mom knows her *precious daughter* is slapping boys in dark corners of the library?" He squeezes me harder as my breath catches. "Put on your lying face and smile. I know you do it so well."

Then he releases me, and before I can think to move, he's shutting his door, rounding the hood of the car and opening mine.

I get out with one less bracelet than I got in with.

I'm grateful it's only Mom who steps out onto the porch as we approach. I don't see Reece in the living room, and I hope he's in bed with no inclination to come out here and make an ass out of himself, and me.

Mom is in soft pants, a light pink T-shirt which doesn't quite hide the jagged scar on her arm that sewed up the rods and plates beneath her skin. Her smile is polite as I watch her tuck a strand of short, curly brown hair behind her ear, and I realize maybe that's where I got the habit from.

The scent of baked goods and Windex seems to have trailed out after Mom, and I glance at Eli, wondering if she can smell the beach on him.

I cross my arms as Eli's already got a polite smile fixed on his handsome face, looking into Mom's eyes, having to angle his head down because she's taller than me, but he towers over both of us. I find myself fighting back a laugh, imagining him looking down on Reece too.

"Um, Mom, this is Eli." I gesture toward him vaguely, wanting to get this over with. "Eli, Mom. I mean, I don't know what you want him to call you…"

"Lucy is fine," Mom says, her Southern accent in full force as she takes Eli's offered hand.

I cringe a little, but Eli seems totally at ease. He's clearly not thinking of cops or missing girls or cornering me in the library for a kiss or breaking off one of my sex bracelets and keeping it in his car.

I'm thinking of *all* of those things, and I'm grateful Mom forgot to turn on the porch light. Eli's headlights aren't directed at us, and the glow from the TV inside is soft, leaving little to illuminate the three of us and the blush on my cheeks.

"Nice to meet you, ma'am."

I want to kick him.

"Eden has told me so many good things about you."

I'm going to strangle him.

They drop hands, Mom shifting from foot to foot, looking down like she's flattered, and I'm annoyed my mom, strong as she is, is succumbing so easily to a few pretty words from a pretty, lying mouth.

But… I can't even blame her.

"Oh, I'm sure they're not all good." Mom laughs a little, finally looking up again and glancing at me, probably trying to read my expression. I try to keep it blank. I don't want her to read too much into how I act around Eli, because then she might think twice about letting me go to his house Friday, which I do not bring up.

"Well, she said you're a good cook, you're the reason she got that car." He nods toward the old white Sentra, seeming to glow beneath the moonlight as Eli makes shit up, except for the fact it's all true. "And—"

"I'm tired." I blurt the words out as Mom narrows her eyes at me, glancing at Eli apologetically. I smile up at him, faking it just like he told me to. I adjust my backpack on my shoulder and say, "Thank you for the ride." I'm showing teeth with my smile, so wide my cheeks ache.

He smiles back, much more real than mine, although I know he's full of shit, too. He slips his hands into his pockets. "Anytime," he says, his gaze lingering on my mouth a moment before he turns back to my mom. "And it was very nice to meet you, Lucy."

Mom beams at him. "Nice to meet you, too, Eli. Drive careful."

"Thank you," he says, then, winking at me as he turns in a way Mom won't see, he jogs down the steps and strides over to his car.

I can't grab the handle of the screen door fast enough, and Mom follows me inside while we hear Eli's engine start up.

"He seems nice," she says, almost dreamily.

I roll my eyes, staring down the hallway to my room, knowing she won't see me do it. "I told you, he is." It's only half a lie.

"There's food for you in the fridge—"

"We ate," I call over my shoulder, meeting Mom's gaze as she shuts and locks the door, but leaves the chain off, because Sebastian isn't in yet. "Thanks, though. I'll have it for lunch."

"You sure?" Mom asks, frowning as I get to my bedroom door, turning to face her. "You should eat—"

"I'm sure." I try to keep the polite smile on my face and take one step into my bedroom. Then I'm stopping, like I've just thought of something when I say, "Oh. Friday is a teacher workday."

"Yeah, I got an email." Mom laughs a little as she rakes her fingers through her hair.

"Eli invited me to his house for the day." *And night*, but I don't add that part in. "Do you mind if I go? I'm off work until Sunday."

Mom studies me a moment. "Are you two… official?" A smile pulls at her lips, but I see the concern in her eyes.

I shake my head, dismissing the idea. "No, just friends." My cheeks flame and I'm grateful the lights are off. I think it would be impossible for me to be *just friends* with Eli, but I cannot explain that to my mother.

Mom still looks like she knows better, but she shrugs. "I don't see why not. But bring your phone and call me if you need to come home."

"I'm driving over," I correct her, even though Eli and I didn't discuss it. I want my car there, in case I need to make a quick getaway.

Mom nods once. "Good idea, but still… just be smart."

I want to tell her it's probably too late for that, but instead I say, "Thanks, Mom. Love you."

"Love you, too, Eden. Goodnight."

After I've changed into my pajamas, brushed my teeth and washed my face—Sebastian still not home—I pull out the notebook I've kept hidden from every single person in my life, my family and Amanda included.

It's black with a glossy cover, dinged and smeared with fingerprints, the pages worn, and back cover creased from hastily stuffing it under a textbook in the spring when Mom unexpectedly walked into my room one night, to talk about *Shoreside*.

Pushing those memories aside, I sit cross legged in my bed, the notebook curled open, front cover touching the back. I lean over to my nightstand and pluck out a pen, straightening once more as I squint in the darkness of my room. Only the moonlight trails in from my open blinds, and I can barely see as I begin to write, the side of my palm smearing over the page because I don't lift my pen. My scrawl is messy, a strange blend of cursive and print I don't hate, despite the fact it's nearly illegible. Or perhaps that's why I like it.

I already looked up Winslet Landers again. Reviewed the facts—vanished from her home—and found a few more. Police have no suspects. There was one article referencing Dominic, a distraught brother, too upset about his sister's disappearance to grant an interview or respond to reporters.

It seems the family has refused any press at all. It seems, then, the only place I'm getting answers is from Eli, and he needs a little coercion.

My heart beats fast in my chest when I finish writing and sit back, blinking in the dark, trying not to find shadows along the wall in the midst of my anxiety. Taking a breath as I glance at the door—if Mom caught me, she'd probably drag me to church for an anointing—I extract all the repeating letters in my sentence. Then the vowels.

Eli trusts me with his secrets.

The line becomes, **LTRSMWHC**.

I compile all of those letters into a shape. It looks a little like a tower, clumsy and awkward because drawing is not where my talent lies. There's an L hooked through the loop of the R. A C capped over the H. S and M are intertwined, all the letters connecting in some form.

My pulse thuds so loud in my ears, I have to close my eyes a second, just breathing. Mom dragged me to church every Sunday on the weekends when I was a kid. Forced me into Sunday school with the same regularity I dove into a pool while she worked during the week.

I loathed every second of it, surrounded by devout Christian kids, screaming and cheering for every popsicle stick activity, every memorized Bible verse we got candy for reciting. I had too many questions. God sent his only begotten son to die for my sins, but I never asked him to. And if he's so powerful, why not *kill* Satan? Seems like a more permanent solution. *Unless God would lose to Satan, every time.* Would be quite the embarrassment.

The more Mom forced me into it, the greater my loathing for religion grew. I was *repelled* to the opposite end of the spectrum. Luckily, she gave up church around the time I went to high school, because Reece didn't like to go. He always grumbled about it, his dad had schizophrenia and when he was alive, he alternated between dragging his sons to church every time the doors were open and ranting about demons infecting the building. Seb never set foot in a church, and Reece never made him.

It's been years since I've sat in a pew, but even now, as I learn about Satan and Lucifer and mythology from all over the world, a part of me feels the sharp sting of guilt that I'm going to hell for doing this.

Still… it seems like a place full of people I'd have more fun with in eternity anyway.

I drop my pen into the drawer of my nightstand, grab the lime green lighter I've had since I stole it from Sebastian purely for the color, and circle my fingers over a fat, white candle in my drawer, too, little more than a stump now. I hold my breath as I light the candle, unable to resist darting glances to the locked door again every step of the way.

I've done sigil magic for a couple of years now, since I read about it in a book at the library back in Wilmington that I didn't dare bring home.

I've made sigils for all sorts of things. Money. Getting into Trafalgar. Numerous ones for college and writing and publishing books.

This is the second one I've ever done for a boy. Not even Sebastian have I tried to save.

The flame flickers in the darkness of my room, the plain, sharp scent of the white candle swirling around me as I tilt the stick, letting a drop of translucent wax drip onto the sigil I've created.

It splatters, spreading over the crudely drawn shape.

Quickly, I blow out the candle, breathing again as I toss the lighter into my drawer. I lick my thumb and forefinger, and ensure the warm wick is cooled before I put the candle back too.

Then I smear my thumb over the wax, distorting the inky lines of my sigil.

Closing my eyes, resting my finger over the wax and the page, I think about my intention.

I think about *Eli*.

It occurs to me perhaps I should feel silly for being enamored with a boy I've known such little time. Perhaps I should be worried this is like what happened with Nic. That I'm obsessing over nothing.

But it's like a connection sparked in my soul at the mere sight of Eli, the very first day I watched him in class. Even that didn't happen with Nic, not immediately.

Maybe I should be more afraid, like I felt in Eli's car.

But I'm not, and I can't figure out why that is.

My chest tightens.

I snap open my eyes, my cheeks flushing as I close my book too, but before I do, I see the stacked letters from the last sigil magic I did.

LWGMYFRSTK.

A convoluted mountain of a sigil born from a silly sentence.

Eli will give me my first kiss.

My face heats as I hug my notebook close my chest. He doesn't even know.

I think about my second boy sigil.

Trust me, Eli. I think I may be the only person in the world he ever would, and it's a heady feeling.

I'm still not embarrassed, thinking of it.

I'm simply... *struck.*

I get out of bed slowly, crossing the room to my green dresser and burying my book among my underwear, pushing it to the very back of the drawer.

And just as I'm settled into bed with thoughts of Eli and his lips on mine drifting through my head, I feel my phone vibrate under my pillow.

Secretly, I've been waiting for it for the past hour. I wanted to know when he got home. I wanted to know he was okay.

I wanted him to think of me again, like he said he always does.

But I didn't dare text him first. I just did some black magic shit to get inside his head. *Whatever.*

Now, I slip my fingers under the cool side of my pillow and roll onto my side, unlocking my screen and reading his message, a smile tugging on my lips before I even get through the words.

Eli: Your mom is nice. Nicer than you, I think.

I bite my lip to stop from laughing. I want to power my phone off and go to sleep. Make him wait, but even with magic on my side, I'm not that strong.

Me: If she knew you were a murderer…

He responds immediately, and I imagine him lying on his side, too, head propped on his arm, his shirt off, his shorts low on his hips, showing off the skull and crossbones tattoo.

I don't see his bruises in my head.

I pretend he doesn't have them.

I pretend no one wants to hurt us. And in my head, as he texts me back, he laughs out loud, freely. He's happy, despite our mini argument.

Him: Do you feel safe with me?

My stomach lurches. I think of slapping him, my veins full of nerves and anticipation. I think of him pressing me against the wall in the library after I shoved him first. I'm not skinny, but even still, I'm so much smaller than him. He could've done anything to me.

I would have let him.

You trust me with your body?

Me: Yes.

Butterflies swarm my gut as my heart pounds, and I wait for him to reply. *Trust me with your secrets.* The sigil is burned into my brain, alongside my intention.

But the three dots don't pop up on my screen, and I think of the shadows beneath his eyes, half-hoping he's sleeping, and selfishly wishing he isn't. Not yet.

I put down my phone and roll out of my queen bed, heading toward my backpack on the opposite wall. I squat down and pull out my medicine, shaking out one pill. I toss it down dry, pushing the bottle inside my bag and zipping it up. I tiptoe back to bed in the darkness, swallowing my meds. Only the faintest hint of moonlight splays through my closed blinds at the head of my bed.

I dive under my covers again, grabbing my phone and feeling a jolt of pure happiness when I see he's texted me again.

Him: Good. I'd never let anything happen to you. I'm not a fucking murderer.

I laugh at the "fucking" but I think it's just to stop from trembling all over at the other part. The second sentence.

Me: I want to know this whole story.

I start to grow hot under my blankets, but I don't throw them off, like this kind of conversation is meant to be in secret, hidden away from the rest of the world.

Him: Wow, just skip right over all the sweet shit I said.

I laugh out loud, unable to hold it in any longer. **Me: Stop trying to distract me. I see through your bullshit.**

Him: I know. It's why I like you, baby girl. Get some sleep for me. We have an entire day together coming up soon. You can ask me whatever you want then.

Then he sends another message, before I can recover from the last one.

Him: How many people have you kissed, before me?

My face grows so hot, it feels scorching. Inside my head, my pulse taps out a loud drumbeat. He'd only ask if I wasn't good. If he knew he was the first. He'd only even think to question it if I sucked at it and oh my God, I can't text him back, not tonight, *shit*, what did I do wrong, maybe I used too much tongue or—

Him: It was the best kiss of my fucking life.

I think I'm going to pass out. My fingers are shaky, and I

want to turn my phone off and flip over and go to bed and wake up in the morning hoping he never asks this question ever again.

But I don't. Because another part of me, falling in love with him too fast, wants him to know the truth.

Me: None. Before you.

I close my eyes tight as I sit up, unable to keep lying down, my heart galloping as hard as it is inside my chest.

My phone vibrates.

I squeeze my eyes tighter. Take a deep breath. In, out, in, out, just like Shoreside's nurse told me to do after the incident.

I look at my screen.

Another text comes through.

Eli: Are you fucking with me?

I can't stop my smile as I bite my bottom lip, laughing out loud in the darkness of my room.

Him: I'm never going to let you go now.

I'm soaring. I can't even sit still anymore. I stand, tucking my hair behind my ear, shaking my head as I do a little dance alone in my room.

I start to type, but he sends another message before I can.

Him: God. That shit turns me on.

I'm trying to breathe evenly, and I somehow manage to text him despite the butterflies in my stomach.

Me: I'm not fucking with you. Keep me.

Him: Always.

Then another text.

It's just an emoji.

A green heart.

I fall backward onto my bed, then lift my arms and rest them above my head as I close my eyes, unable to keep the stupid smile off of my face, despite the apprehension I felt in his car at that intersection.

I am so fucked.

19

Eli

WINSLET'S blue eyes are darker than her brother's. Longer lashes, blonde hair tied up with a bow on her head.

I glance away from her, at the front door, down the foyer of Dominic's mansion, similar to mine, in an adjoining neighborhood. Luna is at summer camp for lacrosse, and Dominic is on his way with the weed. But Winslet is restless. She's been that way a lot lately. Anxious and jittery. I wonder if she's on drugs.

I drape an arm around the plush, white leather of the less formal living room's couch, turning my gaze to her beside me as she sighs, loudly. There's a book in her hands, her nails painted a vivid pink, the same color highlighter pressed between her palm and the pages of the book, splayed open and wrapped around the back, exposing only one.

The Picture of Dorian Gray.

I remember a line from reading it junior year, which is what Winslet will be starting at Trafalgar soon while me and Dom move up as seniors.

It was something about the only way to banish temptation is to give in to it.

Winslet licks her pink lips and gazes up at me, sidling closer. Her face *is shaped just like Dom's. Only ten months apart, they're close in the strangest way. They hate each other, and it looks something like love.*

I retract my arm from the back of the couch, tucking my elbow close to my body. I know she notices, the way her ocean eyes narrow.

"Tell me what this means, Eli," she says, tapping her highlighter against a sentence. Impossibly, the one I just thought of, about temptation.

Irritation pricks under my skin as Winslet slides even closer, her off-white dress rising up and hitting mid-thigh.

You can't use me to get to him.

I don't say it, but I want to.

I glance at the door again, waiting for Dominic's dumb ass.

"It means Lord Henry is fucking stupid," I say, tilting my head back on the couch and glancing up at the vaulted ceilings edged in gold. "Some things you just can't do, or they'll ruin you for life. You get that, right?"

Winslet is quiet a moment, and I close my eyes, annoyed.

Then she says, "Not really, no."

"You have mail." Dad tosses it onto the island of the kitchen, flicking on a light over the stove and loosening his tie, his back to me as he heads to the fridge.

It's almost midnight, and my phone is face up, notifications turned on, one from Eden on my screen. Last night I may have met her mom but imagining ever introducing her to my dad makes me want to hurl this phone across the fucking room. *You aren't going to mess this up for me, Dad.*

I read her message, blinking away thoughts of Winslet, of the questions the cops had yesterday. *At school.*

I think of Eden's questions too. The way she looked at me. I feel sick and kind of annoyed as I try to focus on her words, but then I think about what she told me last night.

Her first kiss.

Which probably means…

I cough, adjusting myself with Dad's back still to me as I read her text, feeling like I won the fucking lottery.

Her: What if I told you I can't swim?

I'm sure she can, but I smile anyway at her playing coy, trying to make up bullshit excuses to not come over tomorrow.

I glance at the envelope Dad threw on the table as my screen goes dim. The letter or whatever it is is flipped over, so I can only see the seam of it. A big, white envelope. I don't reach for it.

"Did you eat?" Dad asks absently, still staring into the fridge. He just got home.

"Are you working tomorrow? At the office?" I don't answer his question. Of course I ate. I had another shitty day of preseason practice, and my body is fucking exhausted, shoveling macaroni and cheese with a protein shake down my throat was the first thing on my mind when I got home after hanging out with Eden at the library again.

She pried about the cops, but I had nothing to tell her she doesn't already know.

Dominic wasn't back today, and Luna texted me telling me he probably won't be in the rest of the week.

"Have you reached out to Dom?" Dad counters my question with a question, since I didn't answer his. He knows Dominic hasn't been in class all week because I casually mentioned it.

Some days, I'm not sure which one of us is the bigger asshole.

I swipe up my phone, typing under the island.

Me: Try again, Eden.

I hear the fridge slam closed, condiments clinking against the door of it.

I look up slowly, a smile pulling on my lips as I meet Dad's eye.

"You haven't, have you?" He sounds disgusted with me, which is par for the course. Just wait until I tell him I'm not going to my psychiatrist appointment rescheduled for tomorrow, because I'm spending every second I can with Eden. *I'm pushing it, huh, Dad?*

He runs a hand through his hair, blowing out a breath as he closes his eyes a minute, and I almost feel sorry for him.

Almost.

"Dammit, Eli," he swears, dropping his hand and leaning against the counter by the sink, palms on the marble as he stares out the glass doors leading to the pool, illuminated by tiki torches and underwater lights.

"Did you know the police came to Trafalgar?"

He looks alarmed as his gaze comes to me, his brows knitted together. *"What?"*

I smile, knowing Ms. Corbin kept her word, not alerting Dad after I told her I'd rather break the news to him myself. She doesn't think I had anything to do with Winslet's disappearance, of course. Might have something to do with the fact I fucked her a few times since my sophomore year in the financial aid office, but if she used her brain, she might realize that makes me *more* likely to be a criminal.

I rub my thumb over my phone screen as I feel it vibrate, but I don't look away from Dad as I slide my feet up on the lower rung of my stool, smiling at him.

"Yeah. Yesterday. They wanted to ask me a few more questions. I think I know why Dominic has been skipping." My stomach flips even as I keep my voice calm. "They didn't tell me, but I think they found something—"

"Yeah," Dad cuts me off, voice low. "There's talk this is shifting from a missing persons investigation to homicide." He scrubs a hand over his face. "Who questioned you?" He demands it, like he'll burn down the entire police precinct if he just gets a name. He steps toward me, thrusting his arm my way. "Why didn't you tell me this yesterday—"

"You weren't home," I remind him, my tone icy.

He drops his hand, shaking his head. *"Who questioned you?"* he asks again. "Did you get their badge numbers? What did they ask? Where did they even *interrogate* you at Trafalgar?" A vein throbs in his temple, and I know he's about two seconds away from calling the headmaster of Trafalgar and waking his ass up.

I don't want that. It's what an innocent person would do, sure, be pissed off, but I dealt with the cops. I have nothing to hide.

"They didn't interrogate me," I explain, holding his gaze, my fingers still wrapped tight around my phone. "They just asked me a few questions about where I was and what I did that night, again." I shrug one shoulder. "Trust me. My story was consistent."

Dad stares at me a long moment, then he says, "Eli, they had no right to drag you out of class—"

"Oh, don't worry. They waited until I was between classes, Dad." I smile at him and his jaw jumps.

"Next time something like that happens, you call me, *immediately*, okay?" He sounds so sincere, for just a second, I want to take it. The olive branch. I want to stop hating him, which is something I do so easily.

I know he feels the same about me, doesn't he?

He's the reason Mom left. But so am I.

If he could just get rid of me, I think he'd start a new family. A *real* family. But I'm still fucking here, so he's still left with a haunting reminder of all the ways he went wrong with Mom.

And I'm stuck knowing I couldn't be normal enough for either of them.

"Sure thing, Dad." I slide off the barstool, glancing at the letter he dropped my way. "You still think I should open that?" I ask him, speaking past the lump in my throat.

He has his hands on his hips, but with my question, he drops them, and his gaze. "No," he finally answers me, his voice hoarse. "Leave it. Have a good night, okay, son?"

I bristle with his words, but I nod all the same, glad this conversation is over, but I'm sure he'll have more questions in the morning. He knows, though, how I can't sleep well. I think he's scared of me when I'm sleep deprived, more than he is when I'm rested.

Sometimes, exhausted with delirium, I even scare myself.

"Yeah. You, too." Then I head up the stairs, reading Eden's text as I do.

Her: What if I told you I'm on my period so I can't swim?

I snort at that, shaking my head as I pad down the hallway, toward my room, shutting my door behind me. But just before it catches, I hear a crash downstairs, like shattered glass.

I know enough about breaking things to understand it's nothing serious.

Just pain.

20

Eden

APPREHENSION MOVES through me as I head out the glass door to Eli's pool. The stones are hot beneath my bare feet, the sun bright overhead even through Mom's cheap plastic sunglasses, and I feel as if I'm immediately drenched in sweat.

Worse than that, with the glaring sun, I know my every flaw is visible to a boy who has none.

I've spent the week getting up early to do the silly workout DVDs, and I've tried to affect confidence in myself all week. Heavy eyeshadow, lots of eyeliner, matching underwear and bra, I've held onto the occult and New Age principles of using your mind to conquer your body.

I'm hot.

I'm fucking hot.

I repeat it in my head like if I say it enough times, the magic will work, and I'll believe it.

But I still have my arms wrapped around my body, my fingers splayed along the warm fabric of my ripped-up, icy gray one piece, my necklaces all on because they look cool, I think.

Once upon a time, this swimsuit wasn't sexy. Just two simple straps, a low-dipped back—not too low, only to the middle of my spine—a lot of my body was covered when Mom brought this home for me last year after my other swimsuits had been picked to hell.

I took a pair of scissors to this one immediately, shredding the sides, the material just over my hips at the back. Now I kind of regret that, even if I felt untouchable on the waves the day after Mom first gave this to me. The ocean can hide your insecurities, and I was only ever swimming with Amanda.

When I glance down, seeing my thighs touch, I have the urge to run back inside, into the cool, air-conditioned mansion, and hide under one of the fluffy blankets in one of the living rooms.

Who needs two fucking living rooms?

But then I remind myself Manda was always jealous of my ass, and even Nic—as stuck up and straightlaced as he turned out to be—could never keep his eyes off of it.

This makes me feel marginally better.

I hear the trickling of the waterfall, somehow spilling from near the hot tub into the kidney shaped pool, which seems to stretch the entire length of the forested backyard. It doesn't, because there's the glass pool house, a garden lining the stone at the far edge of the pool, umbrellas in the center of glass top tables, a bar at the pool house.

As I take another step on the hot, beige stones, I see sleek beige sun chairs, enough to host our entire Latin class, it seems, but I force my gaze to the vibrant blue water.

This, I can do.

There's no diving board, as if such a thing would be offensive in this luxury, but there are stone benches beneath the water at the shallow end, so I head for where it's deeper, arms still crossed over myself.

But when I reach the smooth curve of the deep end, my royal blue painted toes at the very edge of the water, ready to cover myself in chlorine, I hear him speak from somewhere behind me, near the pool house.

"Turn around, Eden."

My throat feels tight, especially with the metal choker around it, which I am now acutely aware of, and I keep my eyes trained on the water. I could just jump in. It's not like his words alone can keep me here. In fact, I'd like to spite him by pretending I didn't hear a word he said. I was changing in the bathroom downstairs, and he said he was going to get towels and set them out here, so I've yet to see him in a swimsuit either.

It's not like it matters. It's not like he hasn't traced every inch of my body with his eyes over the past few weeks, maybe longer. I know because I've done the same to him. Definitely for longer.

I close my eyes, taking a deep breath and telling myself to stop being insecure.

But when I open them again, I see a shadow thrown over the rippling surface of the pool, far taller than my own, and this one is real.

A second later, his hands come to my hips. My entire body seizes up with his cool touch. I can feel him through the homemade rips in my swimsuit, especially when he tightens his grip, the rest of his body not quite touching mine, but if I took the smallest step back, we'd be melded together.

I can hear my pulse in my ears, and it roars louder than the ocean when he presses his lips to the base of my neck, my hair done again just last night in crown braids from the neighbor.

I suck in a breath, my mouth curving into a smile despite my nerves.

His fingers come over mine, wrapped around my body, and he gently pushes my hands down.

"Just let go," he says, and I do, dropping my arms by my sides, my bracelets, minus one, drifting over the top of my hands. He splays his fingers along my waist, and his breath skates over my skin. "Do you want a drink?"

No. Yes. I think of the coke at Dominic's party, how it surprised Eli so much I did it. It surprised me too, truthfully, and I might not have been able to if I hadn't had a few drinks in my system.

But it's only nine in the morning.

If I start drinking now, who knows where I'll be when it gets to be nine at night? I told Mom I'd be back at that time. I think I meant it.

But I have twelve hours until then.

I need to relax, or I won't get any answers from this boy, and I'm still counting on the sigil to kick in. Magic helps those who help themselves, probably not too different than God, I guess. I might as well make the most of all my time here. He said the cops just questioned him because he's Dom's friend and Winslet is Dom's sister and they slept together. But something just… doesn't make much sense there. Eli, I know, is not above lying to get his way.

"Yes," I answer him. "Make it strong too."

He smiles over my skin, wrapping his arms around me and pulling me back against his hard body. I don't feel like throwing up. I don't want to crawl out of my own skin. There's an irritation in the way every inch of my exposed flesh is against his, and a reflex of wanting to pull away, but I can handle it.

Even better, as he locks his hands over his forearms, keeping me close, I realize I'm more than handling it. After a few seconds of adjusting… *I like it.*

He feels safe and thrilling all at once. Danger wrapped in my shelter, I don't understand how he can be both something I want to run from, and to.

"You got it," he says, this time against the side of my face before he kisses me softly, then releases me. "Get in. I'll be back."

I feel a little unsteady without his touch, but instead of turning around to take in every inch of him, to see if those bruises he had are still there, if new ones have appeared, I jump into the deep end, needing to breathe.

. . .

"How long have you lived here?" I sip from the straw in my clear plastic cup, a little blue umbrella stuck in among the ice and coconut rum with pineapple juice. It's my second drink, and my head feels loose, my body too. I smile as I finish it, hitting ice and slurping up every drop of syrupy goodness I can. Straightening, I shift a little on the smooth stone bench, the water up to my waist. Eli is beside me, turned the opposite way, his back leaning against the stone table built into the pool.

He has a joint between his fingers, and there's an ashtray a few inches from my empty drink.

I watch as he brings the weed to his lips, inhaling with his eyes on me. They're brighter, his irises, more blazing emerald, and less forest green. We've been out here an hour, and I see the faintest hint of freckles under his eyes, along his cheekbones. His skin is already tan, the olive complexion giving way to a color I probably won't ever achieve, but I spent years in pools, jumping the waves in the ocean, and I've got a good base, at least the parts of myself the sun touches, stark tan lines along the rest of me I'm not quite ready to let him see yet.

Eli smiles as he exhales, half a foot between us, and I watch the smoke pour through his teeth, sensual in a wicked way.

He props his elbows against the table, and I can't help it. I drop my gaze to the flex of his triceps, the veins in his forearms, the sculpted muscles of his shoulders, even the way his shoulder blades shift with the movement.

Eli has a sexy back, but then again, everything about him is just so damn attractive to me, I'm not sure I could pick out a flaw even if it was screaming at me.

As it is, I don't dare look at his chest, his abs, the tattoo near the V of his hips, or his white swimming trunks. I can't focus when I do, especially with the way the fading bruises lend him some kind of violent sex appeal he doesn't need.

There doesn't appear to be any fresh bruises, and it felt like relief, noting it, even though I think he can take care of himself.

Physically, at least.

"My whole life."

My smile feels lazy as he reflects the same expression back. "What a charmed life."

He tilts his head. "It is right now."

I pedal my feet in the water, my toes skimming over the cement bottom. "Is it?"

His eyes rake over my frame, and I lock one ankle over the other in an effort to keep my thighs together because this *look* he's giving me makes me feel more exposed than I really am. "Yes."

"And why is that?"

His joint is pinched between his thumb and index finger, dangling there with his elbows still propped on the table, the water much lower on his body, giving me a glimpse of the thick, heavy tattoo, and… *eyes up.*

I flex my fingers around the thin plastic of my empty cup, hearing it crinkle.

"If I didn't live here, I might have never met you, and I might have never gotten you to come over."

I drop my mouth open, feigning offense. "You think I'm here because you have a nice house?"

He shrugs, and I see the sweat slick on his skin from the sun beating down over both of us, the day hot for late September. But it is North Carolina. These things happen with the weather.

"Aren't you?"

I roll my eyes, and the words are there. Right on the tip of my tongue, I'm not sure if I've always said them so much or if subconsciously, I want what he promised me. *What I gave him.* "Shut…" I drag it out, but promptly take my own half-worded advice and snap my mouth closed, pressing my lips together and squeezing my cup so hard I feel the plastic give way, the sharpness of the edge pressing into the underside of my finger, melted ice trickling out against my skin.

He studies me a moment, eyes sparking with amusement, then leans in toward me. I catch the scent of marijuana and damn cotton candy. His eyes lock on mine, and I trace the circle of black around his irises with my own gaze.

"What was that?" he asks quietly, barely audible over the rush of the manmade waterfall and the hum of the pool pump.

I see perspiration grazing his sharp cheekbones. Water clinging to his thick lashes from where he jumped in, too. I'm worried I look like a seal with my hair up, wet and piled on top of my head, but his inky black hair is smoothed back from his face, and he just looks even more beautiful. Like a god.

But Adonis is a mortal. And he fell for Aphrodite.

Goddess of sex and love. Even thinking it, I feel bolder as lift my chin, cock my head, and sit up a little straighter. He's into me as much as I'm into him. I *should* be confident.

"Nothing." I barely whisper the word, my voice raspy from the alcohol and the low tone, but it sounds sexy right now.

More melted ice is trickling through my fingers, and I should probably get my broken cup out of the pool, but I currently can barely manage to breathe while affecting poise, so I cut myself some slack.

"Did you want to tell me to *shut up?*" His nose is so close to mine, I feel his breath in my mouth.

I lick my lips, already slightly blistered from the sun. There's a distant nagging in my head, my mom's reminder about sunscreen, which she threw in my backpack, currently on the floor of one of Eli's guest bathrooms, and I smeared it on my face, the tops of my shoulders, but nowhere else, and I need some for my chest but...

"No."

"No?" he questions, leaning closer, so our noses touch, his brow pressed to mine.

I hold his gaze, swaying my feet in the water, ankles still

locked over each other. "Eli." His name comes out sharp and jagged from my mouth.

He looks momentarily surprised I said it, but he recovers quickly. "Yeah, baby girl?"

I feel like I'm melting in my seat. I can't keep up this sensual charade much longer. "Can I have another drink?"

The surprise flits across his face again, but he smiles, too, straightening, putting a little space between us, until I realize he's sliding over closer, his hip touching mine.

"Sure, but here." He holds up the joint between us. "Try this first."

I glance at it, the rolled white paper, the burnt end. I don't really have good experiences when I get high. I think of the walls moving, Amanda coddling me at that one party. But it's just me and Eli. He wouldn't make fun of me, I don't think.

So, all I say is, "Okay."

Instead of offering me the joint, he brings it up to his own mouth, inhales, the tip glowing bright, then reaches for the back of my neck, fingers splayed along my skin as I startle, my pulse picking up pace, and I'm not sure if it's his touch that does it, or the fact the lit end of the joint is so close to my hair.

I want to duck out of his grip and grab him instead, but he tightens his hold, fingers looped around the back of one of my necklaces, and pulls me toward him at the same time I lean closer, giving in.

He cocks his head, and I mirror the action, until our lips are touching, his thumb pressing into the side of my throat, his free hand coming to my bare thigh and squeezing.

I release my ankles, widening my legs at the same time I open my mouth, and he exhales, the earthy-sweet taste of marijuana on my tongue as he blows smoke down my throat. I get the point, inhaling as my lips make a suction around his and I breathe it all in.

His hand shifts higher up my thigh as the smoke trails down into my lungs, and he pulls back slightly, but he doesn't release his hold on the back of my neck, or my thigh.

I cough, closing my eyes a second, trying to catch my breath as I turn my head, but he keeps us pressed close together, his fingers dancing even higher, until he's at the edge of the cutout of my swimsuit over my thigh. I'm too busy coughing up smoke to protest, and I don't want to, anyway.

"Good girl," he whispers against my cheek, and my stomach muscles tighten with the lazy way he says the words, his thumb stroking the inside of my thigh in the same manner.

I take a deep breath. Another. Then one more, relieved I'm no longer choking through my first inhale. It's only as my breathing returns to normal, my heart thumping hard in my chest, that I feel the heat from the lit end of the joint in his fingers, still clamped possessively on the back of my neck.

I raise my eyes to his, our lips close again.

"How do you feel?"

"Don't fucking burn me." I bite out the words, born from nervousness.

His expression is neutral as he stares at me, then slowly, he nudges his nose against mine, almost like a kiss.

I don't move, but I love how it feels.

He angles his head so his lips brush mine when he speaks again. "I'd never hurt you."

I don't know if I believe him as he pulls away, still keeping a grip on my thigh, but... I know I want to.

It's noon when I bring up the police again, and Dominic's sister.

And it's only the thick haze of alcohol in my bloodstream that gives me the courage to do it. We both had more to drink, and I slathered sunscreen everywhere over my body in the bathroom, watching myself in the mirror. I enjoyed the way the sun coaxed out my freckles, and I began to feel more confident as the hours passed and Eli ensured we stayed hydrated with bottles of water he has in a cooler atop one of the tables with an umbrella.

I didn't smoke any more weed. The walls don't move.

I want everything to stay normal.

Now, I tip back my fourth or fifth drink, the hot, muggy day only background noise as I sit on the bench beside Eli, a drink in his hand, his other arm brushing my shoulder. I'm leaned into him, this time we're both facing the waterfall, and I watch the clear and blue of the water spill over the stones and into the beautiful pool.

"Why do they think you had something to do with her disappearance? The truth this time." It comes on the tails of talking about Ms. Romano, her fascination with morbid Latin words, and it just seemed like the best segue to me. Like maybe he was leaving it there to see if I'd bite.

He doesn't even tense beside me. He just rests his hand on my thigh and a jolt runs through my body as he squeezes softly, taking a drink before he answers me. Neither of us look at the other, but I'm staring at his hand, olive brown with green veins snaking beneath his skin, against my paler thigh, the fat and muscle splayed wide from sitting.

I should be self-conscious, I think, but maybe it's the thin layer of water rising up over my legs or the alcohol or the fact we look pretty hot like this, I just feel good about it.

"I was one of the last people to see her alive."

I don't react to his newfound bluntness. It's not the worst thing he could've said, until… he keeps talking.

"*The* last person who came forward." He doesn't give an explanation for why he didn't say that first, and he doesn't sound sorry about it. He takes another drink, though, shifting his hand higher up my thigh, then back down, like he's trying to comfort me in some way, his fingers dancing over my skin.

"Tell me about it. The day she went missing." I try to keep fear from my words.

"Night," he corrects me, propping his elbow up on the table, cup dangling from his fingers as we both keep watching the waterfall, but I notice everything he does out of the corner of my eye.

"Tell me about the night."

I'm still leaned against his body, my empty cup behind me, and I wind one arm under his, hooking onto him.

He glances down at me, smiling softly. "I like that," he says.

I smile, too, but keep staring straight ahead. "Tell me."

He sighs. "It was Dominic's birthday."

I think of the party. *Dominic's birthday then too.* No wonder he wanted to get fucked up.

"His parents never really monitored... anything." His tone is full of annoyance, which is funny, because we're here drinking underage from bottles of rum and beer he'd taken from brown paper bags beneath the awning of the pool house, bottles he'd gotten from some guy in the neighborhood in his twenties, a disappointment to his too-rich parents, apparently Eli scores from him often. "Winslet got drunk."

I keep my eyes on the waterfall, something mesmerizing and peaceful about the steady stream even as Eli keeps talking about the girl I've seen on that missing poster all semester. It's still jarring, the fact he knew her. Not unusual, just... interesting, their tie. "We were all sleeping in the living room. I guess it wasn't really night," he corrects his earlier statement. "Three in the morning or something?" He takes another drink and I hear the ice hit his teeth, feel the muscles in his arm contract as I press closer to him.

"Devil's hour." I say the words without thinking.

He laughs a little. "You'd probably know all about that, huh?"

I smile, still looking into the distance. "I like magic." I shake my head, the sleepy haze of the alcohol distracting me. "Keep telling me the story."

He turns his head, his lips, cold from his drink, coming to my shoulder. I suck in a sharp breath, but a moment later, he's talking again. "Anyway, Dom kept yelling at her to go upstairs. There were, like, six of us in the living room, and Winslet."

I don't ask if Luna was there. In my head, she isn't.

"Dom's parents never came down. Her and Dom fought all

the time. Winslet got up, but she fell into the coffee table and skinned her knee. She was crying, and Dom told everyone to go up to the game room. So, they did."

They.

"I was tired. I wanted to sleep. I curled up on the couch, under a blanket, listening to Winslet cry. It was soft noises." He sounds like he's there again, remembering all of it. Like he's said it before, too, and I suppose he has. Maybe even as recently as this past week, with the police. "The next thing I knew, it was morning. It was like I blinked, and opened my eyes, and sunlight was streaming in through the blinds, the ones facing the lake." He grabs me harder, digging his fingertips into my skin, and I let him. "There was blood on the coffee table. It was like, gold or something stupid, mixed with stone edging. The blood had seeped into the stone. Dominic was throwing shit around, like he was looking for a wallet, the way he tossed pillows and throw rugs to the floor, upturning cushions, like she might fucking be there." He laughs a little, shaking his head. "He asked me where Winslet was. I told him I didn't know."

There's a pause, and I fill it. "Did you?"

He turns to look at me, and this time, leaning against his arm, I meet his gaze, tipping my chin up. "No."

"Then…"

"Her dress was in the yard, between the house and the lake."

I hold my breath, waiting.

"But they didn't find her. They dragged the entire lake. There were so many cops there, in minutes, it seemed like. Dogs too." He shrugs. "There was nothing. They spread out. Checked all her recent messages. Nothing." He's still staring into my eyes, as if he's daring me. *Ask it. Come closer. Do you want to know the truth?*

Did you do it? Do you know who did? "Why don't they believe you? Why did they question you again?"

"I told you," he says, his voice edged with bitterness. "They probably don't think they're looking for a person anymore." He doesn't once look away. "They're looking for a corpse."

I don't let those words unnerve me. He skipped a question. "So, *why don't they believe you?*" I enunciate each word slowly.

I swear the slightest smile pulls at his lips. But he glances at where the waterfall spills into the pool, like he's tracking the path.

My stomach flips.

"No one said they didn't believe me, Eden. But new investigation, more questions, right?" His tone is even, but a chill runs under my skin. I can't tell if he's lying.

I sit up straighter, and he turns to look at me. "Did you sleep with her? That night?"

A smile curves his lips. "So, so jealous."

I narrow my eyes, but I don't speak.

The word is soft, almost innocent, leaving his mouth. "No."

I feel relief warm my chest, but I'm not done with the questions. "Did you do it?"

All he said was he didn't know where she was at the time Dominic was looking for her. It could be a lie by omission. It could be an outright lie. But even if it's the truth, it doesn't absolve him completely because he never said he didn't.

Despite the heat, the way my body has adjusted to the temperature of the pool, I grow cold with his silence.

I feel his fingers press hard into my skin.

I don't dare move.

"I told you." He narrows his eyes. "I'm not a fucking murderer."

※

"I'm really good at it."

I rub my thumb over the little rectangular screen of the stopwatch, the black cord damp and curled over my wrist. "How good?"

Eli smiles, smoothing his hair back from his face, water

dripping down the sharp planes of his cheekbones, over the tip of his nose. "You'll see." He inhales, his chest expanding, and I see one of the faded yellow bruises move with the breath, but I shake my head, holding out a hand to stop him from going under.

"Wait, wait." My tongue feels heavy, my words a little slurred, and I know Eli feels the same. We had more drinks, and his eyes are glassy and red, he's gone through several more joints. We haven't eaten a thing, even though Eli has asked if I want food.

I don't though.

I want to stay right here, soaking up every ounce of his undivided attention.

"How long? A minute? Two? No more than that, right?"

He drops his hands to the water, and I watch his six-pack flex as he does. It's unreal, how fit he is. "You'll see," he says again. Then, without waiting, he sinks under the water, right in front of me, on his knees, his hands coming to the back of my thighs.

I suck in a breath at his touch, barely remembering to start the timer on the stopwatch with the feel of his fingers on my body, his head level with my low belly, the water up to my chest here.

He presses his head to my core, his teeth plucking at the fabric of my swimsuit, and I try to breathe. To not squirm away.

His hands run up and down the backs of my thighs, dangerously close to my ass, his fingertips brushing the underside, but he always stops short, like he's teasing the hell out of both of us. I dart my gaze from the numbers spinning upward on the stopwatch screen, to his wavy black hair, fanning out in the water. I see the coil of muscles in his shoulders, the lines on the underside of his biceps from gripping my thighs. His forehead is pressed to me as he bites my stomach, and I can't see his face because of it as my core contracts, my hips arching backward, pressing further into his hands.

I place a hand on his head, weaving my fingers through the thick strands of his hair, unable to stop myself.

He bites me again, this time on my thigh as he lowers his head, and I jump, heat coursing under my skin. He licks a line up my leg, only to tug at the cutout of my swimsuit with his teeth.

I tighten my fingers in his hair, my nipples hardening into sharp points, I'm barely able to stay standing. I want to sink down into the water with him. *Jesus Christ.*

But after a second, he presses his lips to the crease of my thigh, making my belly jump, then rests his head once more on my stomach.

I feel like I can breathe a little easier, but I keep my hand fisted in his hair.

It's intimate in a tender way, how he rests against me. Heat swells in my chest, and I massage his scalp, feeling somehow like I'm taking care of him.

His touch doesn't tighten against my thighs. If anything, as the time passes, he only seems to relax, like he lives for this. And being this close to him, watching him giddily show me how long he can hold his breath underwater, I almost feel it too.

Because I have no memories of being afraid of the water. I was in it at such a young age, all I experience now—whether in a pool, like this, or tumbling along the harsh waves of the Atlantic—is a strangled mix of excitement and peace. Two contradicting emotions, but the water has always inspired people in the strangest ways. Poems, essays, books, and movies. The sea, the water, it coaxes forth awe and wonder and maybe, in some people, terror.

It can hold everything. Sirens and ships alike.

I tear my eyes from Eli's broad shoulders, my grip in his hair, and look at the number on the screen.

My breath hitches as I widen my eyes. Nervousness nips at the edges of my mind.

If something happened to him… I can't see his neighbors

from here, but I know I could run, and I could call the police, but I'm too tipsy to be *useful*.

I promise myself I'll give him ten more seconds.

Just ten, and if he doesn't come up then, I'll drag him to the surface.

The seconds pass. We're at two minutes. It ticks by, but I feel Eli still holding onto me, and even though I said I would bring him up, I know he's okay, right? He's on his knees, leaning into me, but he's still holding on, which means he didn't pass out or something…

Nerves gnaw at my fingers, wrapped tight around the watch, other hand digging into his hair.

Come up, Eli. I get it. You're good at everything.

But even my annoyance can't combat my fear. I think of what he said, about Winslet. The dress, draped between the house and the lake.

I think about his missing photos in the yearbook. I bypassed any questions about those. It was hard enough to hold onto talking about the police. Being around Eli doesn't make me stupid, but he's a lot to focus on. He requires all of my attention, or else… I'll miss something. I think I already have.

Almost three minutes.

I release the stopwatch, letting it dangle from my wrist as something like real fear, maybe for the first time ever with him, shoots through me when I reach for his arms. I have to squat down a little, and I drag my nails across his shoulders when I realize he isn't moving, not even looking up. I dig deep, blistering his skin all the way past the crook of his elbow, the water lapping at my chest now, and I curl my fingers around his forearms and pull. His own hands come away from my thighs easily, and for a split second, I think he might be dead.

I know it's irrational. I assume when someone drowns… Well, this close to him, I would know, wouldn't I?

But I've never seen anyone drown.

And in the moment before he comes up, on his own, his

head less than an inch from the surface, I remember his fantasy. About the bathtub. And the razorblade.

And I remember something else too. I told him drowning someone sounded easy. His words echo in my head as the sun beats down on my back. *"Because you haven't seen someone drown."*

He breaks the surface then with a splash, standing on his own two feet, and I release him, grabbing the watch as it swings from my arm. It's black and boring and waterproof, but I need something to hold onto. I clench my fist around it, and he takes a deep breath in, but it doesn't sound a thing like gasping.

Water streams down his face, hair falling into his eyes. It takes me a moment to understand him, what he's feeling. But when he slashes his hand through the water, spraying me with it, droplets flecking along the timer—two minutes, fifty-five seconds, still ticking upward—I realize he's... pissed off.

For some reason, the violence of his temper, even just in the spray of water, it makes it hard to look at him.

I stare at the watch instead.

"Don't do that." His voice is quiet. Quieter than usual, hard to hear over the pouring of the waterfall, at his back. "Don't ever bring me up again."

I frown, my eyes still on the numbers, but in my head, I see him on his knees in the pool, temple pressed to my stomach. "You could've died." I'm not sure how long people should be able to hold their breath. Maybe it's three minutes. Maybe this is nothing, and it's why he's angry, because he didn't get to show off enough.

He dips his chin as I look up at him, his brows raised. His collarbones shift, every muscle in his body hard with veins thrumming beneath his skin like livewires.

But his jaw relaxes, and I watch his hands uncurl in the water, splaying wide.

"I won't die, Eden." It's like a reassurance. A promise to me.

I let my eyes drop, to the faded bruises on his chest. Then

up, to the black choker around his throat. For some reason, I'm not sure I believe him. He isn't immortal, even my drunk mind knows that, but what he really means is, *I won't die soon.*

And all I can think is, *you'll leave me.*

I'm not sure they're the same things.

He takes a deep breath, his chest rising, then falling, and he steps toward me, moving fluidly in the water, like he belongs here.

"Do you want to try?" he asks softly. He isn't smiling as he blocks out the sun, towering over me and making it easy to see the soft freckles on his cheekbones, the thin skin beneath his eyes, full of pale violet bruises from not getting enough sleep. Is that my fault? Do we talk too much? "Maybe you can beat me," he adds.

"Will you save me?" I mock myself, not bothering to hide my smile, even though I don't quite feel it. The tense moment between us is still there, and it's not sexual tension. It's the residue of his flash of anger.

It reminds me of the spark of violence I saw in his eyes in Latin when that girl kicked his chair. It was reflected inside my own thoughts.

He grabs the watch from my hand, slowly pulling the string off of my wrist, and I'm thankful my other, with the bracelets, is ducked into the water. He uncurls the string, places it over his neck where it hangs at his sternum. Without looking, he presses the button on the side, stopping the time, then the button above it, resetting it. He didn't even bother checking the numbers, and I guess it wouldn't have mattered since he was already out. It would be like cheating to him.

Useless.

He takes another step closer. "Do you want me to? Save you?"

I shake my head, smiling. "Let's do this." I don't want to think about a deeper meaning to his words.

. . .

I'M NOT VERY GOOD AT THIS GAME.

I last thirty seconds the first time, and this time, when I pop above the surface, ready to give up and drink again, he announces I was under thirty-three seconds.

My footing is unsure in the pool and I stumble against him, my hands on his chest, a smile on my lips and the beginnings of a sunburn, despite my best efforts, across my shoulder blades. He grips my upper arms, laughing a little as I catch my breath, tilting my head back to look up at him, chlorine water dripping down my eyelashes, over the tip of my nose. I have to blink my eyes to clear my vision, but I'm still stuck on the number he told me, the stopwatch swaying against his chest.

"Multiple threes are angel numbers."

His smile widens, a dimple flashing in his cheek. "Well you are a little angel, aren't you, baby girl? So fucking *holy.*"

My face feels hot and I dip my chin, glancing at the blue water lapping between us, against his abs, my lower ribs. "I think I want another drink." I mutter the words, still staring at the surface of the pool, his fingers indented in my upper arms.

Then his grip changes, sliding down my skin, wrapping around my waist as he pulls me close.

My heart leaps to my throat, and I don't look up, my brow pressed to his chest, an out of place laugh coming from my mouth.

"Yeah?" he asks me, his words against my ear, the little hairs all over my body standing on end. "What if you tried it just one more time, huh?" His lips ghost over my skin. "For me?"

The laughter dies from my lips, but my chest is still heaving when I pick my head up to meet his eye. I feel warm but free, loopy, a little giddy, and with his smooth skin beneath my fingertips, his arms locked around me, I think I mean what I said to him before, all over again. *I'd do anything you told me to.*

I sigh, the sound exaggerated. "Okay."

"Don't give me that attitude." He leaves one arm around me, but grabs my chin with his fingers, lifting my head as my pulse skitters with his touch on my face. "Do you want me to help you?" There's something dangerous in his offer, and I can't name it. I'm still pressed against his chest, my palms between us, and I feel the sure and steadiness of his pulse.

But there's just… something off. If I hadn't been drinking all morning into noon, I might be able to name it. But I have been drinking, *a lot*, and so has he, really. Or maybe not… but he's smoked a lot. Still, his movements aren't unsure like mine.

I think I'm drunker than he is, and I don't know if I feel elated with the revelation or terrified. It's easier to let him touch me like this, and it's easier for me to return it. It's almost as if we're a couple, the number of times we've brushed into each other, but we haven't kissed. Not since the library, our first time.

"What is it you want to do to me?"

He runs his thumb over my bottom lip, a hunger in his gaze like he wants to eat me alive. He doesn't speak for a moment, and I wonder what it is he's really thinking, because I know he'll say something different from that, won't he? "I want to hold you under."

I tense with his words, flexing my nails into his chest, realizing as the faintest wince pulls down on his mouth I'm pressing into his bruises.

I don't stop, and he doesn't move away. It feels like control, hurting him. But I'd never let anyone else do it.

"Hold me under…" I echo the question as if I'm not asking it. My voice sounds far away. It's odd, how the day is so bright and nice and *sunny*, but everything feels a little cold.

Even my nipples tighten into sharp points all over again, and I squeeze my elbows closer to my chest to hide it, but I needn't have bothered. Eli's eyes haven't left mine.

I have to look away for a second, and when I do, I think I see a warning of storm clouds. No thunder, no rain, but the skies past his neighborhood have darkened. I didn't check the weather for the day. It didn't matter to me. We've already ran in the rain, haven't we?

"You trust me, don't you?"

No. "I trust you," the lie comes easy, "but I'm nervous."

He lifts his brows, letting his fingers drift past my chin, over my throat, along my necklaces. I wonder if he can feel my pulse flying beneath his hand as he curls it around my neck, softly. A warning, maybe. Painless, but I suck in air through my nose all the same, like maybe soon, I'll need all I can get.

"Remember your fantasy?"

I shift from one foot to the other, squirming as he confronts me with it. Swallowing, I can only nod.

"I wouldn't hurt you like that."

What if I wanted you to?

"But we could…" He trails off, shaking his head, like he's breaking free from a trance. "No, never mind. No."

"No," I tell him, in a different tone than he said it in, as I reach up to grab his face. I turn his head toward me, tipping his chin down. "Say it." I splay my fingers along his jaw, realizing this is the first time I'm touching him here. My fingers are close to his mouth, and I feel the faintest hint of stubble along his jawline, like he shaves every day, and I don't know why, but I like that.

He looks amused I'm touching him, his hand sliding down to grab my ass under the water as he yanks me even closer. Our bodies press together, my hand slips down to his hip, and our torsos are touching, my breasts crushed against his abs. It feels so good, I just want to please him. Do whatever he wants. I want him to own me, but I'm scared he doesn't treat his things very well.

"You want me to say it?" He's smiling.

I let my fingers drift over the softness of his mouth, just touching. "Yes," I whisper, my body growing warmer, but my face doesn't feel hot. I'm not embarrassed. Tentativeness has no room in my veins alongside the alcohol.

I'm Aphrodite.

His fingers dig into the sides of my neck, but I can still breathe. I'm on my tiptoes, though, and I'm not sure if he's making me stand this way, or if I want to be as close to his level as I can be.

"I can never give you your fantasy, for obvious reasons." He leans closer, my fingers still on his lips. "You deserve better. And I would miss you."

I want to laugh, but for some reason, neither of us do. I trace my thumb over his bottom lip, and he nips at it, biting me gently.

My heart thunders, and this time, so does the sky. It *was* storm clouds, and apparently, they're approaching.

He releases my thumb from between his teeth, but he keeps talking, tightening his hold on me, lifting my chin higher, until the angle makes my neck ache.

"But we can play on the edge."

I feel delirious, and I no longer know if it's the alcohol or the weed or… him. *But we've only kissed once. We haven't even touched each other, not really. What are we doing? Is this stupid? What is this? Why is it impossible for us to slow down?*

And I know it is. Impossible.

We can't.

Our souls don't know how to crawl closer. We run head on, seeing the impact up ahead, but we can't stop. Or maybe we just don't want to. We know the wreck will be worth it.

"I won't let you get hurt."

I don't believe you. *I want to believe you.*

We stare at each other, the crunch in my neck, the ache along my jaw, with the angle he's lifting my head, it hurts, and so does the bruising grip he has on my ass, but I don't care.

There's only one thing to say, so I say it. *"Okay."*

He grabs me then, yanking me closer by my throat, and he tilts his head. His lips come over mine, his tongue sweeping along the seam of them, and I'm parting for him, my palms splayed along his chest, his heart finally, *finally* beating faster, like it should. His teeth hit mine, his thumb presses against my windpipe, and I'm still on my tiptoes. He's grabbing a handful of my ass, crushing me against him, and I can feel him growing hard between us.

"God, *you're fun.*" He says the words as I gasp, and I think maybe it wasn't a compliment, like I'm a toy, but I suddenly want to be only that for him as he keeps kissing me, opening his mouth wide, biting down on my lip, then opening again, tongue entwining with mine.

And all at once, when my heart is flying and before I can take a breath, he's sinking to his knees, still kissing me, coaxing me down, too, his fingers pulling on my neck. "Let me push you under," he says, his words breathy, his chest rising and falling so fast beneath my palms. I squat lower, and he's tipping my chin up to keep me above water as he kisses me one last time, biting hard on my bottom lip.

Then he moves back, and before I can blink, he pushes his palm on my face, slipping his hand up over my braids to get better access and shove me down.

But I sink to my knees willingly for him, his hand gentle on my crown of braids as I kneel, going under.

I wrap my arms around his legs, resting my head on his thigh like he did with me as he stands back up. My eyes open as I stare at the cement of the pool, rendered bright blue from the clear water, my mind spinning, and all I can think is I hope he started the fucking timer.

I can still feel his teeth on my lips. His mouth devouring mine. I didn't really get a breath, the way he kissed the life out of me.

I try to relax.

Under here, the sounds are *fuller.*

I think I hear the waterfall careening into the pool, but I can't really tell where the sound is coming from, so I'm not sure. Noises in general are strange under the water, something I've known since I was a kid. Everything is distorted. Sight, sound, the lack of breath in my lungs.

I feel Eli's hand press gently against my head and I shift on my knees, the cement hard beneath bone, but I don't want to come up. Not yet.

I'm growing calm, like he digs peace out of me with his aggression.

I squeeze him tighter, and his fingertips push through the coil of my braids to graze my scalp, like a reassurance. His other hand must have the stopwatch.

I let my eyes flutter closed, soaking in the calm of the water.

"We can play on the edge."

The beginnings of panic edges in, and I'm not sure if it's because I need to breathe, or because of those words in my head. *How far will we go? What did you mean?*

I should've asked, I realize too late.

We should have talked about this.

But I stupidly trusted him. *I'm a fuck up.*

I know better. Boys like Eli don't really care about girls like me. I should've learned that lesson at Shoreside. It's a thought that's been simmering in the back of my mind, only now it's turned up to a boil, and I think it's this position, on my knees, underwater, his hand heavy on my head.

Aphrodite, Aphrodite, Aphrodite.

The way I try to console myself is obliterated with pesky logic.

Rich boys with rich cars and rich parents going to rich schools with their rich friends… Boys interrogated by police, suspects in disappearances, then, maybe, murders…

Drowning, Eden. *Winslet could have… drowned.*

My heart picks up speed, slamming fast against my ribcage, and I really do need to breathe. I need to get up. My mind is doing things to me down here, and all I can hear is his words in my head, and all I can think is I don't know what they mean.

"God, you're fun."

I try to stand up, positioning one foot flat against the bottom of the pool and pushing.

His hand pushes back.

Fear claws at me, and I can't open my eyes, because if I do, I might have to watch it. Him hurt me, just like he said he wouldn't.

I try again, pushing up, raking my nails down his thighs, feeling the firm muscle beneath, I think I've drawn blood, but I don't try to look for the clouds of it in the water. I'm straining as hard as I can against his hand.

Then my world flips.

For a second, his palm lifts, and I rise a few inches, happiness and something I hate to call relief bursting in my chest. But as the clock ticks, the moment passes, and both of his hands come to my shoulders as he pushes me down, down, *down.*

My eyes fly open, I'm unable to stop it, and I see his blurry, beautiful figure over me, his knees on either side of my hips, his body pinning mine down, his hands ensuring my back is pushed against the bottom of the pool. His height combined with the fact we're in the shallow end makes it possible for his head to stay above water. I just barely see the stopwatch around his neck, resting on his sternum, I can't make out the numbers speeding by.

He has his knees so close to my hips, jammed against my bones, I can't move them, and I can't get free. My knees are bent, and I push with the soles of my feet against cement, eerily similar to the way I watched him throw off an opponent at his wrestling match, when it looked like he'd lose.

But his body isn't even jostled with my movements.

My fingers leave the bottom of the pool and come to his forearms, winding around muscle as I scratch at him, trying to get him off of me.

I push, and dig, and I can feel my pulse hit everywhere in my body.

I can feel something else too, as he pivots his hips, so he's almost lying on top of me, but keeping his head above water.

I freeze, nails latched into his skin and the sinewy frame of his arms.

The fact he's so turned on, his erection pressing just above my pubic bone as he squeezes his fingers around my throat, overlapping against my neck, it does something to me.

It makes the fantasy real.

I'm still terrified. I'm still worried he won't let me up, and my head feels dizzy and the pressure against my lungs, the desperate urge to *breathe* is eating at me. Panic is tight around my chest, a burning sensation flowing toward the base of my throat, a pain pounding above my eyes, but… there's something else, too.

He rolls his hips, pressing himself into me, our swimsuits separating us, and yet it still feels sickeningly *good*.

Yet even beneath something like pleasure, I realize I might pass out. I try again to shove him off and for a split second, I think I've won.

But he only releases his hold on my throat with one hand, the other still around it, his thumb pressing into my windpipe, almost as if he wants to trick me to breathe. To *drown*.

His hand trails over my body, squeezing my breast on the way down like it's nothing, like he's done this to me a thousand times, like I'm just a toy for him to play with.

I can't see his eyes, the surface choppy, but I watch the blurred vision of his hand gliding over my stomach, the flare of my hip, then he hooks his fingers into the side of my bikini, shifting the fabric and… staring at me as he shifts back, so he can see. Maybe. Possibly.

He uses his knee to press against the side of my thigh, stretching me, exposing more of me to him, but he doesn't touch me.

No one has seen me like this.

Panic thumps a rhythm in my head.

My ears.

But I'm frozen.

And finally, just as black spots start to pop in front of my eyes, and I think I'm going to get a lungful of water, and I'm going to die right here, he releases my swimsuit, shifts his body, and hauls me up by my fucking throat.

But he doesn't bring me above the surface.

He spins me, wraps his arms around me, my back to his chest, keeping me *under*.

No, no, no, Eli.

Let go.

Let go.

Let go.

My mouth opens. I'm about to suck down water, and I won't be able to stop it. It's an instinct I can't overrule. I'm going to either faint, or I'm going to inhale in this pool, and it only takes a few teaspoons to kill you, doesn't it?

Let me fucking go.

You said you would miss me, you fucking liar.

And just when panic causes tears to spring to my eyes, even here… he releases me.

And the sickest part, I realize like a bolt of lightning to my chest in that second he lets me free, isn't what he did to me.

It's the twisted feeling I have right now, *in this moment before I draw in air.*

Gratitude.

I'm grateful to him.

I find my feet, just barely, bursting through the surface of the pool into the hot September air, and I realize the sky is darker than I left it, and his hand is still on me, wrapped around my upper arm.

I jerk out of his grip, spinning around, not trusting my back to him.

And when I'm finally, *finally* free, heaving in air with such force I forget to be mad—I survived, didn't I?—my pulse is erratic. I can feel it butterfly in my chest, loopy movements, dropping and rising. No hummingbird pulse. Those beats are constant. This isn't.

But I'm still breathing, and as I take a few life-preserving steps backward, away from Eli, it's all I can focus on.

Breathe. Breathe. *Breathe.*

I smooth the hairs come free from my braids back, nervous, fluttery movements like my weak pulse. I feel a few strands of hair along my shoulder blades, stuck lower to my spine, and I don't know why I'm focused on it.

Thunder rumbles overhead but I don't react to that.

I almost died without the storm.

Blinking chlorine from my eyes, lips still parted, abs contracting with every exhale, I realize that isn't quite true.

Dark green irises are locked on mine.

Eli is worse than thunder. Than lightning. He's spread out like rain, but more volatile, like wind. Hard hitting like hail. He damages all of me. A fucking hurricane, impossible to ignore.

"Eden…" His voice is rough.

I keep my hands resting on my head, elbows bent. "I wanted it." The words are jagged. For a moment under there, I thought I might never speak again.

He has one hand just under the surface of the water, clenched into a fist, the other by his side. He looks as if he's desperate to get to me, but he's frozen. So unlike him, I'm not sure if it's true.

I feel a little dizzy, off balance, but my pulse is slowing.

I can feel his skin under my fingernails, what I raked off when I fought him. I don't look to see if he's bleeding, and I'm not sure what I'd hope for more.

He comes closer, and it's hard to breathe, because my pulse is just so erratic, so messy, it's like the electrical rhythm of my heart is short-circuiting.

He doesn't know about that. I can't blame him for what he doesn't know.

"I'm sorry."

"I wanted it." I snarl those words again, which make them sound like a lie.

Another step, and his shadow eclipses me.

Slowly, I drag my fingertips down past my hair, around to

my shoulders, until I cross my arms and my nails are digging into my biceps.

I stare up at him, my heartbeat still too quick.

He reaches his hand toward me, dripping water, unfurling his fingers.

Something in his face asks for permission. He just had his hands all over me. His arms banded around me, his chest to my back as he held me under as long as he could, as long as he still had the nerve to kill me. But for this lighter touch? He wants me to consent.

I don't nod or speak or smile. But he must see it in my eyes, what I'm screaming in my head.

Come. Fucking. Closer.

His fingertips are cold, colder than usual, thanks to the heat of the water warmed by the sun, he feels icy as clouds gather thicker overhead.

I clench my teeth, so they don't chatter with his touch.

He rests his palm over my chest. A little lower. It's sensual, but not sexual, the way his index finger grazes my tight nipple over my swimsuit.

After a moment of my chest heaving beneath his hand, he looks suddenly shocked.

Then... upset.

His eyes lift from my heart to my face.

"Your heartbeat..." The eye of the storm. This is it.

I can't do anything except stare as water drips from his lashes, rendering them thicker than usual, a few clumped together.

He steps closer.

His hand is perfectly still against my skin.

"You know those things we text about, we don't really have to do them. If you want to keep them a fantasy, it's okay, Eden, just tell me you're not ready for—"

"Stop. Stop this shit you're doing. Stop trying to make me backtrack. *I did want it.*" Petulant, childish; Reece would smile at the way I lose this, and it is a loss. Everything between me and Eli is a competition even as we pretend to be on the same team. I'm not sure what we'll win at the end. Maybe we'll carry one of those fucking fantasies through before this is all over. Maybe we'll make it real. Maybe he won't miss me at all.

"Eden. Are you... Are you scared of me?"

"No." It's the truth right now. I'm scared of my feelings for him. But him? Now I can breathe again? No. *I'm sickeningly grateful for you and I don't know why.*

"How long?" I ask him, and he looks momentarily confused. It's endearing, the draw of his brows, the pucker of his lips.

I glance at the stopwatch, flipped so the screen is away from me, dangling from his chest.

He follows my gaze and reaches for it quickly, righting it. He shows me the time, stopping it.

Close to three minutes, but we've been above the surface for long seconds now.

"Are you mad at me?"

I can't resist poking at how unsure of himself he sounds when he drops the watch and his hand from my chest, my arms still crossed over myself. "It was just a game, Eli." I roll my eyes, scoffing, but it doesn't come out with the bite I want it to.

Lightning heats the clouds overhead.

I know we should get out of the pool, but neither of us move.

"Oh yeah?" He loses his skittishness, if he ever really had it to begin with. He doesn't move, but somehow, he feels closer.

I look up at the gray and blue and purple sky.

"Yeah." I repeat his word back.

"Do you want to keep playing?" It sounds like a challenge.

I think of my heart. I don't look at him. I remember his hands all over me. Forcing me down. Panic in my veins. I replay it over and over on a loop, so I don't lose the memory anytime soon. And I know exactly what I'm saying when I say my next words. This time, it isn't a slip.

"*Shut up.*" It comes out through clenched teeth, mainly to stop my lips from trembling.

Silence stretches between us.

Even the thunder waits.

A second passes. Another. Anticipation nearly makes my knees tremble. That out of control feeling in the water, I didn't know what to expect. It was scary, in the moment. *But I want the moment back.*

His hands find my chest, and I shrink back, gasping, hating myself for the fear and the flinch as he pushes me against the rocky ledge of the pool, the stones warm on my flesh.

I instinctively reach for his forearms, but I know there's no way I could fight him off, and he doesn't let go as I stare at him, my chest heaving.

Maybe I need to leave. We're both edging up against danger here, with all these drinks in our system; unsupervised, fucked up kids.

I need to leave.

"Don't run," he says, his lips over mine as his grip shifts and he loops his fingers through the metal of my choker. "When you're free, *don't run.*"

"I wasn't going to—"

"You were going to go home. I saw it. You were scared. You can pretend you're above it all, above fear, you can pretend these nasty things don't eat you alive, Eden, but we all get scared."

I glare at him, fingers still wrapped tight around his forearm. "I'm not scared of you."

"You can lie to your mom, and you can lie to yourself, but you can't fucking lie to me, baby girl."

"You don't know me." Panic makes me feel sick, and I'm not even sure why I'm panicking. "You don't even—"

"I know you more than you think."

"Shut up, Eli. Just shut. *Up.*"

He tilts my chin up, forcing me to look at him.

I know we're both thinking the same thing.

Are you going to cross the line?

"I'm going to pretend those words were an accident."

I'm barely breathing as his nose touches mine.

"You don't *really* want me to hit you, do you?"

I feel dizzy. He's not gripping me too hard. If anything, his touch is light. But his words, what I want…

"Shut up." I ignore the feel of his hand tightening around my jaw. I hold his gaze instead, adrenaline pumping, pulse flying, I even drop my hands and press them to the wall of the pool at my back. Total surrender. "Shut up, shut up, shut. Up—"

He lets me go.

Confusion cuts off my words.

"I'm not going to do what you want." He narrows his eyes. "You keep trying to bypass connection, reaching for pain." He shakes his head, and it could be my drunkenness, or the shadows thrown from the clouds overhead, but I think I see hurt flash in his eyes.

I slam my fist into the water, splashing it up over both of us.

He stares at me, unmoving.

"What the hell are you talking about?" Anger is heat through my limbs as I crash my fist into the water again, stepping toward him. "What the *fuck* are you talking about? You just held me under, you *hurt me*, and now you don't want to do it anymore? What the hell is wrong with you?"

There it is. He snaps back into place again, donning his mask. His smile is twisted, and I have to remember how to breathe. "We shouldn't drink together, huh?"

I roll my eyes, fed up. "Fuck you." I turn away from him.

"I told you you'd run," he says, as I make my way to the steps, wrapping my fingers around the metal pole bisecting them.

I stop, annoyed with him. With myself. General irritation clings to me, and I don't get it. Everything was fine. *Until you thought he might kill you.*

Yeah, I guess that could *dampen* the mood.

"I'm not running," I say.

"Promise?" His voice sounds small.

I swallow a lump in my throat, staring down at my feet below the surface of the water. But I don't say anything except, "I can't figure out what you want with me."

I feel the water move as he steps closer. I see his shadow over mine again, but he doesn't touch me. "I want to be nice to you."

"Why?" I spit the word out, like the concept is unfathomable. I've had plenty of nice people in my life. Only a couple who were less than. I don't know why I can't believe his words. But his actions... they just don't line up sometimes.

"I don't know, Eden, it seems like a thing people do when they like each other."

I ignore the way my stomach jumps with those words buried in his sarcasm. *When they like each other.* I'm just a way to kill time to him, like he is to me, right?

"Maybe I'm wrong, though, maybe they just punch each other in bathtubs or—"

"You held me down in a pool." I cling to that.

His breath is over my ear when he says, "Remember what you said? *You wanted it.* I got these ideas from *you.*"

It's only a half-truth, about wanting it. He asked. I agreed. I didn't exactly know what I was signing up for, but it seems pedantic to argue the point.

"Let's start this over." He presses his mouth to my shoulder in something that isn't quite a kiss because there's teeth. His hands come to my hips, and I can never stay perfectly still when he, or anyone, touches me, but I try really, really hard.

He hugs me close to his body, and for a split second, I imagine him shoving me down again. I imagine him drowning me. I think of what he said, about Winslet's clothes.

Do I only assume the worst about him? Why? Because it'll be easier when it ends?

"Stay the night with me." His teeth hit my skin again, and I keep my hands down by my sides as he makes me feel too many things, all at once. "Stay the night with me and forget about this shit and let me treat you better. *I want to, Eden. I want you.*

"This will never work." My worst fear, out loud. It feels good to say it, though, because I know it's true. Some fears are not far-fetched, anxious thoughts. Some are just inevitable.

"Oh, it won't?" His breath is warm on my skin, but his tone is too agreeable.

"No."

He kisses my shoulder again, open mouthed, and my entire body shivers in his arms. "Okay," he says simply. "But you can make it work for tonight."

21

Eli

WATCHING her perched on the edge of the kitchen island, flipping through a business magazine of Dad's while I drop frozen pineapple juice into the blender, it's like I can still feel her claw marks down my legs. The scratches still burn, and it makes me smile a little.

She has her ankles crossed, and I splash juice on my white shirt when a giant lump of pineapple plops into the swirl of coconut rum and ice.

Because I'm not paying attention.

Because I'm staring at her feet.

She has pretty feet, and I'm not even a foot person. But they're small, blocky kind of, nothing delicate about them. Her toenails are painted, a blue color, and as I set down the empty juice can and inspect the damage on my shirt, I wonder what it is about her that makes me notice things as trivial as her fucking toenail polish.

Except I don't really have to wonder for long.

"Shut up." Those words echo in my head. She said it to me nearly a dozen times. She fought me in the water, but when she

got back up, when I let her go, she said nothing about all the inappropriate things I did to her while I held her down. She was mad, and a little scared, but not mad enough to leave and not scared enough to *not* be sitting her fine ass on my kitchen counter right now.

I wonder if anything happened, to make her this way. What her life was like before me. Or maybe she was just born on the dark side.

"Are you going to keep staring at your shirt or are you gonna make me my drink?"

I can't stop smiling, but I don't look up, white cotton still pinched between my fingers as I take in the droplets of juice splashed yellow on the fabric. "You're supposed to sit there and look pretty, not run your mouth."

A stunned silence fills the room and I finally release my shirt, looking over at her.

Her feet are resting on one of the stools, pointed and arched, and she's wearing my T-shirt, a Trafalgar one that hits her just past mid-thigh.

Seeing her looking at me with her lips parted, the magazine still between her fingers, splayed open against her lap, and shock in her wide eyes, I can't help but think she looks so goddamn innocent.

I know she isn't, despite what she said about me being her first kiss. Her mind is twisted, and she doesn't just keep it all in there. She's told me some pretty dark shit most people wouldn't dare say out loud.

But I meant what I told her before.

She's innocent to me.

I don't know if it's just my male brain talking, like I need her to be pure or something, but I don't think so. I just… know the things I've done. And I know as wicked as she might have been, she hasn't done those things.

It scares me, imagining her having all of my secrets and choosing to turn around and run with them clenched between her fists.

She's temporary, for that reason.

No one stays.

No one smart, anyway.

"Pardon me?" she says, her voice rising at the ends.

"Oh, don't start with your manners now." I grab the top to the blender, still smiling as I fasten it on, locking it in place. I snag the juice cup between my fingers, a napkin with my other hand. I wipe up the mess, and toss it all in the trash can, hidden in a drawer beneath the counter I push back closed with my hip. "I know you're a filthy little…"

I stop, my chest tight.

The words get choked in my mouth, and to avoid having to fill in the gap, I put one hand on the top of the blender, press the button with the other, the loud whirring of crushed ice and rum slinging through syrupy sweetness cutting off any chance of conversation.

I don't know why I couldn't say it.

Filthy little…*whore? Slut?* Shit, I mean, I could have just gone with "girl." It's not like I haven't called girls all of those words before. A guy once, too, at Montford.

But it didn't feel right with Eden. I want to have nasty fucking sex with her. I want to go to the verge of all the things we said we wanted in our wildest, darkest thoughts. I want to *almost* cross the line, but be able to bring her back, because I meant what I said.

I'd miss her if I accidentally went too far.

But maybe it's the innocence thing. Seeing her as someone different from everyone else, different from *me*, but still pure in her own way.

I don't know. She wants me to slap her. She slapped *me*.

I'm probably just dreaming up all the rest in my head. She could even be lying about the first kiss. She was a little clumsy at first, I guess, a lot of teeth, but… I liked it. Maybe she does too. Maybe she's done it dozens of times and she just said I was the first to make me feel good or something. It's something I would do.

When I turn the blender off, the makeshift piña colada (no coconut cream) thoroughly blended, I realize Eden is standing right behind me. I didn't hear her get off the stool with the roar of the blender in my ears, and I didn't see her, because I was too busy imagining bending her over a counter to fuck her while I called her something polite.

My heart picks up speed in my chest with her nearness, which is an interesting feeling for me.

I don't look at her as I unlock the top to the blender, grab two glasses from the cabinet, and start pouring our drinks. But I do speak, because I know she probably won't go first.

"Can I help you, Eden Rain?" I use the nasally teacher voice from before because that was the loudest I'd ever heard her laugh at something I said.

This time she just gives the softest of giggles, but I know she's trying to hold it in. "Filthy little *what?*" she finally manages to say, choking through her muffled laughter.

I almost slosh the drink over the side of one cup, but I correct myself just in time, finishing pouring both and turning to put the blender in the sink. I pop off the lid, rinse the base and top, and flip them upside down to dry on the rack beside the sink. Shaking out my wet fingers, I turn to face her, finding her hands on her hips and her eyes locked on mine.

She's drunk. Not completely obliterated, maybe closer to tipsy than actually intoxicated. Some part of me doesn't want to give her the drink I just made. It's only five in the afternoon, she lied to her mom and said she was going to Luna's for the night—she shot me a glare when she typed out the words while I watched over her shoulder to check for typos, and her mom wanted Luna's address in case something happened; Eden was pissed I knew it—and she could sober up by nine, or ten, when I take her to the entertainment room, and we watch a movie together on the couch.

But I know alcohol lets her loosen up. I just wish she could do that around me without a drink.

"Come here."

She seems to relax a little with my words, but she doesn't step closer. Instead, her fingers drift to her hair, tucking the free strands behind her ear, gliding over all of her piercings. I see the black bracelets around her wrist slip down her arm and she drops her hands, clasping her fingers together. She fixed her hair in the bathroom after our argument in the pool, and her crown of braids is straight again.

I want to remove all the pins in her hair, run my fingers through it.

Tonight. It's a promise I make to myself. If I can't touch her how I want to because she's too drunk, I can at least play with her hair.

And just like *that*, a memory punches me in the gut.

MOM SITTING AT THE VANITY TABLE IN HER AND DAD'S WALK-IN *closet. Her fingers to one side of her head, hair wrapping around one as she pins it back.*

I see my reflection in the glass mirror over her vanity. She sees me, too, though I don't think she wants to.

"I'll be down soon, Eli. Mommy is busy."

"I just want to watch." My voice is hoarse, and I clutch the car in my hand, sleek metal, the real, shiny mirrors. A Trans Am. White. Mom shoved this into my hands a few years back when we went to the store together, and we got separated. I was frantic searching for her, sure someone had hurt her.

A store employee had to help me find her.

She was in the bathroom.

It was by the rear exit of the store.

Sometimes, I wonder how hard she fought herself not to run away.

Mom sighs, her shoulders tightening with tension. She drops her fingers to her lap and meets my gaze in the mirror, her eyes cold. "Go downstairs. I'll be there soon."

I bite my teeth together, wanting to tell her I won't make a sound. She won't even know I'm here.

But she doesn't stop staring at me.

I go downstairs and wait on the couch.

Eventually, I drag a stool to the pantry, grab the box of cereal, move the stool to the fridge to get the milk. I eat breakfast alone with the toy car.

I stare at the pool.

I see a rabbit with a white tail.

Mom doesn't come down until the sun is high in the sky. By then, I've already stripped out of my clothes, changed into my swimming trunks, and the blood is gone from my hands.

When I blink, Eden is right in front of me, her eyes focused on mine. "What are you thinking about right now?" she asks quietly, and I shake my head, stepping back and pressing my palms to the counter, curling shaky fingers over the edge, trying to steady myself.

"Nothing," I lie to her. The word comes out wrong. Too broken. I clear my throat and smile at her, but I know she can see it's a lie. I reach for a diversion. "And you're a filthy little *angel.*" I take a breath. And another, hoping the lightness of my words reaches her.

A smirk pulls on her cherry red lips, but there's still something of concern in her eyes, the way they're narrowed just slightly.

I reach out and grab her by the collar of my shirt on her body, used to the way she cringes every time I touch her. Maybe one day I'll give her a fucking reason to flinch.

But she's not ready for that yet.

This time, my knuckles graze her collarbone, just above one of her necklaces, and I yank her close to me, letting her catch herself on her palms against my chest, her breath leaving her in a sweet little rush.

"Kiss me, Eden."

I don't think she's going to listen, but she stands on her tiptoes, clawing at my shirt. She tilts her head, her eyes on my mouth, trailing up to my nose, then my eyes.

Come closer, baby girl. I won't bite you.

I hold my breath, waiting.

Her grip tightens on my shirt, her body pressing toward mine as I keep my knuckles just over her clavicle, her shirt fisted in my grip.

She's just staring up at me, like she might find something in my eyes if she looks long enough. It's almost hard to hold her gaze. I want to look away. It's uncomfortable, thinking my thoughts might be transparent, even if it's just with her.

Especially if it's just with her.

She has to believe I am who I say I am.

She has to believe I can do *good* things.

"You want me to kiss you?" she whispers, never looking away.

My body is hot, something worse than longing in my veins. "Yes." I jerk her closer, her breasts against me, my thigh between hers. "Yes, I want you to fucking kiss me."

She smiles, and despite this moment, when I want her, everywhere, every part of her, every fucking inch invaded by *me*, it's still there.

The innocence.

And I realize what it is.

It's not about her at all. It's about *me*. She looks at me without wariness in this moment. Her guard is down, it has to be, because I can see a reflection of me in her eyes, what she sees when she looks at me, and she thinks, for right now, *I'm good.*

Then she… kisses me first.

Her lips are sweet like rum, and my hands come to cup her face, smooth beneath my fingers. She keeps her own tightly tangled in my shirt and I want them everywhere, but despite what good she might try to see in me, I think she's still getting used to this. To me.

I know I'm still adjusting to her. Everything she does feels louder than anyone else, even though she's not a loud person. It's just her actions echo, and I can feel her even when she isn't here.

I run my tongue over hers, and she smiles into my mouth. My teeth catch on her lips as she does, and she presses herself tight against me, knocking my back into the counter.

I don't think about it. I just grab her by the waist and lift her up, her legs wrapping around me as I spin us both, setting her on the counter beside our drinks. I'm between her thighs, and she rocks her hips, whimpering into my mouth. I turn my head, my lips over her cheeks, her jaw, hers on mine, her fingers finally off of my shirt and running through my hair. She pulls and I like how it stings.

My hands squeeze the sides of her thighs as she trails sloppy kisses down my face, over my jawline, toward my throat.

"You are unreal." I couldn't have stopped those breathy words even if I'd wanted.

She licks a line up my throat as my fingers slip beneath the hem of her shirt. My shirt. What's the difference anymore? We're the same.

"I'm very real," she says over my mouth, her fingers wrapping around my neck. She hooks her ankles behind my back, ensuring there's no space between us. Her eyes are glassy as they lock on mine, my fingers reaching the hem of the shorts she pulled on in the bathroom after our swim. "Keep going," she says, glancing between us. "Why won't you touch me?" There's a shyness to her voice that makes me want to fuck it out of her.

I don't want her to be shy with me. The irony though, is I am with her. Tentative, at the very least.

"What do you want?" I need a boundary. I have to know when to stop, or I won't. It's something they talked about at Montford. Clear lines, far ahead of danger zones. Dad needed concrete rules. I had to have a curfew and mealtimes and all the things he gave up on within three weeks of me coming back.

That was in the spring. He thinks I'm fine now. Or maybe he just didn't want to put in the work when he realized I wasn't.

Eden looks down between us. "Touch me."

I'm already touching her, but when she widens her thighs, there's no room for misunderstanding. Except... "You don't like when I touch you."

Her fingers are still curled around the back of my neck, and I feel them flex when I speak. Slowly, she drags her gaze from my hands on her body, to my eyes.

"Do I look like I don't like it right now?"

Fuck. "I don't know. Take off your shirt. I can't see all of you."

She leans back, her head tapping the cabinet door, arms extended as she keeps her grip on my neck. For a second, I think she might do it. I think she might release me, pull her shirt off, and let me see her. *Everywhere.*

But then she shakes her head, grinning. "Maybe when I'm a little drunker."

My stomach sinks with those words and my dick kind of hurts, too. I think of Montford and razor blades and closets that smelled like bleach.

Eden glances at the drinks I made us, eyeing them like I want her to look at me, and I lift her chin with my fingers, steering her gaze back to mine.

"I want you to have fun." I mean it. "But..."

She pulls her brows together, confused. "But...?"

"I want you to remember it."

There's something in her face I can't understand. She averts her gaze, her lips pressed together, and she doesn't speak for a moment. But finally, she says, "Okay," and it sounds like a promise.

I glide my hands up her thighs, over her hips, her waist, until I'm cupping her face again, her own fingers still laced behind my neck as I stare at her, taking in her swollen lips, the fullness of her cheeks, even the thickness of her hair at the crown of her forehead, she's just fucking beautiful.

"I'm sorry about the pool," I tell her, and I mean it, mostly.

She doesn't look away, so I keep talking.

"I didn't mean to hurt you or scare you. I just wanted us to do all those things we talked about, as close as we can."

She squeezes her legs around my waist, a smile creeping on her face when I least expected it. "It's okay," she tells me, like she means it, and it loosens something tight in my chest. A ball of nerves, maybe. Fear, possibly. "It's supposed to be a little terrifying, isn't it?" She leans in toward me, pressing her brow to mine. Her breath is so sweet, and I let my eyes flutter closed, inhaling all of her, still tasting her on my tongue. "If it wasn't, you would've been doing it wrong."

For long minutes, we stay like that, pressed together, my thumbs playing at the line of her lips, my eyes still closed. I don't know if she's watching me. All I know is I feel content, right here, just like this, doing nothing at all but standing in my kitchen.

I don't think I've ever felt this good in my own house.

"You said you've lived here all your life." She fumbles with the wrapper of the vegan peanut butter cups I bought and kept in the fridge, just for her, and I bring my beer to my lips, watching her over the cup holders between us set in the theater seats in the entertainment room. "Why do you talk funny?"

I curve a brow, smiling despite the offense I'm trying to feign. "Talk funny?" I mimic her own Southern accent. "I ain't the one who talks funny."

Her eyes widen, gleaming from the lights of the projector across the room, *Harry Potter and the Order of the Phoenix*. She said it was her favorite. I've never watched or read Harry Potter. I don't like make-believe.

She pauses, mid-bite of her food, teeth dug into the chocolate as she cups her hand around it so it doesn't crumble on her shirt.

"Excuse me?" she says, and I hear her try to tone down her accent. "I do *not* sound like that!"

"Hey." I shake my head and lean back in my seat, feet on the floor. "Don't try to hide that shit from me." I wink at her, and she rolls her eyes, but chews her food, setting down the candy wrapper in the console between us and reaching for her red plastic cup. "I like the way you talk."

She sips from her straw, her knees to her chest, a beige throw over her legs, and she's still in my shirt. The surround sound hums, the bass loud for a second as she drinks, and her eyes flicker to the projector screen, giving me a view of her side profile.

Her nose might be considered "big" by some standards, but it's perfect for her face—for those round, lifted cheeks, her swollen fucking lips.

I count the piercings in her ear. Six, just on this side.

I bite the inside of my cheek and force myself not to reach for my dick even though I really need to adjust myself, but I'm in jogging pants, I can deal, I tell myself. I don't want her to feel pressured, because if she does, she'll be uncomfortable, and she'll close up. Then she'll leave.

Stay.

"I like the way you talk too," she finally says, dragging her eyes from the screen to look at me, taking another drink. I hear the straw suction air and ice, and she rattles it in her hand, looking confused at the way it's empty. She's had a lot of drinks, and there's a pink flush to her cheeks now that's fucking adorable but means she's probably on the verge of having too much. I imagine what it would be like, getting her completely fucked up and fucking with her.

But we're not there. Not yet.

She just clutches the drink to her chest, though, instead of asking for more, which is good.

"I just don't get why you don't talk like me. Is it a rich boy thing?" She waggles her brows, like she just told a clever joke. She is so much softer when she's drunk.

I lift my middle finger from around my beer, subtly flipping her off, but she just laughs, tilting her head back, chin up, flashing her teeth. Her canines are big, and while her bottom teeth are straight, her top ones aren't exactly in a perfect line.

It makes my dick swell more.

Jesus Christ.

I tip my drink back, swallowing, before I rest the bottle on my thigh, tucking my opposite hand behind my head as I turn to look at her. "A rich boy thing?"

"You sound like you're from another country."

I've heard those words before. A lot. "I think it's just Raleigh."

She shakes her head vehemently, like I couldn't be more wrong. "My neighbors are from Raleigh. They sound like they were born in a toolshed, like me."

My abs contract as I try to hold in my laughter, but it doesn't work. "Oh my God." I don't stop laughing, and it feels weird as I close my eyes a second.

"I like when you laugh," she tells me. "You hardly ever do." She sounds so serious, wrapping both hands around her cup as she stares at me.

My laughter dies off.

Dad used to say that to Mom in the shadows, when he thought I wasn't listening. *"He never laughs or smiles."*

"Or cries," Mom adds, like it's a bonus. *"He never cries either."*

I glance up from my spot on my bed, music in hand, my headphones on, but the volume is turned down, the song paused.

Mom doesn't fake a smile.

Dad crosses his arms, turning away from my bedroom door. "Yes, even when his friend got a concussion from falling at the playground. He didn't react at all." Dad sighs, and I think of Carter's blood flecked on the cement below where I stood. He's not my friend. *"I just think maybe we're missing something here, Ari."*

Mom stiffens, her dark brows drawn together, lips pursed. She doesn't say anything about it, but I know she hates when he doesn't use her full name.

"Arianna," she once told me before. *"It means holy one."* She had laughed, and I didn't know why. But then she added, *"And Eli…"* She

smiled, lifting up the bucket to rinse my hair in the tub. "Eli means defender of man." It seemed like a joke to me. Something I could never be.
Now, in the doorway, she just stares at Dad for several seconds.
Then she walks off.
I look down as Dad gazes after her, and I pretend to keep listening to music that isn't playing. Dad gives me one last glance before he pulls my door to, but I see his shadow beneath the crack under it.
He doesn't walk away for a long time.

I clear my throat, the memories too, and I say, "You don't sound like you were born in a fucking toolshed." I'm trying really hard not to smile, and it doesn't help she is, too, her bottom lip pulled between her teeth, cherry red blanching white. "I love your voice." She blushes, glancing down again at her empty cup, and I add, for her benefit, "My mom was from Greece." My mouth goes dry, just saying those words, and I have to turn away from her to look up at the screen, even though I'm not really seeing anything of the movie. I tighten my hold on my beer, digging my fingers into my scalp with my other hand, pulling my hair. "My dad taught himself to speak without an accent, something my grandpa passed on to him and my uncle."

Eden says nothing, and I wonder if she's thinking about Mom. I feel raw, just imagining what's going through her head, and yet… I'm grateful she doesn't ask questions.

"Uncle Edison, he owns an autobody shop, and trust me," I glance at her, "his drawl is worse than yours." I imagine my uncle wiping his hands on a faded blue rag, oil and grease smearing over both him and it, talking to one of his customers about *"that rattlin' noise under the hood."*

Dad and my uncle are worlds apart. Dad took my grandfather's ambition and abuse to heart, growing up to try and conquer the world, which in his mind meant accumulating as much money as he could. Uncle Edison… he hated suits and lawyers and most people.

We get along great, and we don't say more words than necessary to each other when we're together.

"Worse?" Eden feigns offense. "See!" She points a finger at me, over the console as she sets her empty drink in the cupholder. "You think my accent is awful!"

I take another pull from my beer, place it beside her cup, and snatch her fingers, yanking on her arm so she's leaned against the console.

Her body goes rigid, an automatic reflex I want to know more about, but I know I can't ask her directly. No one likes to suddenly unearth all the pain they've spent a lifetime burying. For all I know, maybe she was just born with a dislike of touch. I know I was born wrong. Sometimes there's not a reason why.

Still, I don't let go of her fingers, laced now through mine, as I move closer to her, only the console between us as my eyes lock on hers. "I don't think it's awful. I think it's sexy as fuck."

She doesn't laugh, or shy away, or smile. She just stares at me, and the scene goes dark from the movie, dimming the light in the room.

Her breaths come in quick pants as she holds my gaze, her lips parted.

"Yeah?" she asks quietly.

I feel my entire body growing with heat. "Yeah. Everything about you…" I flick my gaze down what I can see of her body. "It's insane."

For long seconds, she doesn't move.

Neither do I.

I feel like I'm on the edge of something. She's going to push me away, ignoring my compliments, or she's going to come closer, and fucking devour me.

Another second passes.

Another.

Then she's reaching for me with her free hand, pushing on my shoulder. She shifts onto her knees, then crawls across the console to straddle me, her knees on either side of my hips.

Her hands rest on my shoulders, and she looks a little unsure of what to do from here.

I don't know what she's thinking, but the weight of her, solid and real in my lap, is making it very hard for me to think with anything other than my dick.

She shifts her hips and I have to bite my lip to stop from groaning as I stare up at her.

"Touch me," she says, her voice a whisper. "Help me." Her eyes are searching mine, and I don't move my hands from my sides.

I close my eyes a second, my heart racing in my chest. In my head, I can still see her. Her bangs around her eyes, a few strands free from her braids. I feel her fat fucking ass on my thighs, the heat from her body in my lap, and her slender fingers on my shoulders, I could easily overpower her. Manipulate her. Push her back on the couch and fuck her.

But I calculate how many drinks she's had in my head.

At least six, probably more.

Still… she isn't acting like she's wasted. Not at all.

I open my eyes, and before I can talk us out of this, I grab her hips, my fingers splayed over her curves.

"Don't fuck with me, baby girl," I warn her, my eyes holding hers, my pulse roaring in my head.

She's breathing so hard, I can hear every short inhale, each sharp exhale.

I grip her harder. "You want this?"

She swallows, hard, then nods.

"I'm not going to do anything you don't want to do," I promise her. "But I want you to be sure." My erection is uncomfortable beneath her, my pulse knocking hard against my ribcage. I need her consent, because with the drinks in her system and the way she likes to play games, I want to ensure this isn't one. If I had known her longer, this wouldn't matter. It could be fun. But she's not that comfortable with me. Not yet.

After a moment, she says, "I'm sure, Eli."

When she says my fucking name, I feel like I'm going to combust.

I keep my eyes on her as I let go of her hips altogether and trail my fingers up her thighs, stopping when my thumbs slip beneath the cotton. I don't ask, but she knows what I want.

Permission. Every step of the way. Then she'll think I'll always ask.

She takes a deep breath, her chest heaving beneath her shirt, then she's kneading my shoulders, steadying herself. "Yeah," she says, leaning in toward me, our noses touching. This time, she nudges mine, her lips skimming over my own. *"Yes, Eli."*

I try to breathe as I pull back the loose cuff of her shorts, exposing her black underwear to me. She digs her nails into my muscles, but she doesn't pull back, her nose aligned with mine.

I hold the cotton of her shorts back with one hand, using my opposite thumb to rub against her center, over her underwear. I can feel her heat, and as I keep going, up and down, her knees parting wider on my lap, her entire body seemingly held up by her hands on my shoulders and her head pressed to mine, I feel how wet she is, too.

And I can smell her.

Earthy and sweet, I'm fucking dying to devour her.

But I don't.

Instead, I slide my thumb beneath her underwear, touching her for the first time, and she feels so fucking *good*.

A whimper leaves her lips, her breath on my mouth, and I love the feel of her slickness against my skin. So fucking hot and wet and she's adjusting her stance again, wider, like she wants to expose all of herself to me. She's *giving in,* and I remember her slapping me and shoving me in the library during our kiss. How good it felt then, for her to fight me, when I knew nothing bad could happen in there.

Now, she's pliant. It feels special, knowing she doesn't give in so easily. *I* feel fucking special. The same I felt when she demanded to know in the hallway what the cops wanted with me.

Goddamn, that was fucking hot.

I can't see much in the dark, and her shorts are in the way, but fuck, her clit is swollen beneath my finger, and the little noises she makes, the way she wraps her arms around my neck, closing her eyes and breathing against my lips, it's all just so. Fucking. *Good.*

Fuck.

I jerk the material of her clothes further away from her, allowing my middle and index finger to dip underneath her, pushing until I find her entrance, and I stare at her closed eyes, waiting to see if she'll pull back. Jerk away.

Flinch.

But it's like once we're already touching, she doesn't mind so much. Once she knows I'm not going to hurt her, she's okay, and maybe *her* being on top of *me* helps her, too.

I push into her tight hole, and she parts her lips, sucking in air, her eyes fluttering open as she stares at me, cupping my neck in her hands, running her fingers over the choker on my throat, then underneath it, and that touch feels fucking good.

"You are so. Fucking. *Tight.*" It's not just something I'm saying. I can feel her walls around my finger like a vise grip, her clit expanding under my thumb as I finger fuck her and circle her, trying to figure out the best way to make her come. I wonder if she'd tighten more if I choked her. If I did what she wanted, what she practically begged me for, in the pool.

I keep that thought inside my head.

She grabs onto my neck, fingers beneath the choker, which in turn is almost choking *me*, but I don't care. She starts to shift her hips. Then she tilts her head and kisses me, her tongue clashing with mine, her teeth pulling on my bottom lip, then my top, her saliva all over my fucking face.

"Yes," I tell her, the words pouring into her mouth as I hear the slick sounds of her on my fingers. "Fuck me, baby girl. Fuck my hand."

She does, pivoting her hips, her knees pressed into the couch as she fucks my fingers and keeps kissing me. She pulls at the choker on my neck too, by keeping her fingers looped under the material and yanking away, stretching it to the point I think she might either rip the leather or choke me out. Either one would be okay with me.

Our kisses grow sloppier, tongues over teeth, heavy breathing, her excited pants as she gets closer. In my mind, I shove down my pants, I take her just like this. I don't care what she wants. I don't care about making it special. I hit her, too, because she'll like it after I do it a few times.

But in reality, I can't. I won't.

Still… "I want to try something," I say over her mouth.

She stops moving, her eyes on mine.

Slowly, I pull my fingers from her, and she gulps down air, gasping a little. Then I reach in my pants, my fingers damp with *her* as I angle my dick so she can dry fuck me easier. I stroke myself once to get her wetness all fucking over me, then I pull my hand out. I push aside the layers of her shorts and underwear.

One arm wrapped around her waist, I pull her closer, so she's over my dick.

"*Fuck me,*" I tell her, our noses touching as I release her shorts. "Move your hips."

She whimpers as she does, her hands coming to my hair, raking through to my scalp, her brow pressed against mine.

I bring my fingers up between us, sucking on them as she watches me, her eyes on my mouth. She tastes so fucking good, I groan, my other hand gripping her ass, more than I could possibly hold onto with one fucking hand and it drives me insane.

She keeps rocking against me, breathing harder, louder, holding onto me as she does. I reach my hand to her throat, squeezing her softly.

"You're so good, baby girl." There're only my boxers and

sweatpants between us, and I want nothing to separate us, I would fuck her right here, but for now… this is enough.

She's enough.

I look down between us as I angle my fingers upward, grabbing hold of her jaw and keeping her head tilted up, my index and middle finger on her lips. She licks me, *her,* and I take a heavy breath in at the sensation against my skin. At watching her rock back and forth over my cock. It's hard to see everything, her shorts still on, but they're shoved to the side, and I catch a glimpse of her, then the wet spot she's left behind on my white pants.

Fuck, fuck, fuck.

I drop my head back against the couch, feeling my core flex, every muscle compacted rigid and taut, my lungs heavy as I try to breathe, to *last.*

But I think she's getting closer, too, the way her lips drag over my jawline, toward my ear.

"Tighter," she says, her voice hoarse, a shyness to the word.

I don't need to ask what she wants. I'd do so much worse. I'd do anything.

But for now, I squeeze her jaw, her throat. She takes one last breath, then she's silent. I open my eyes and pull her by her neck so she's facing me.

Her eyes are wide, lips parted, but nothing comes out.

She can't breathe.

Her face starts to turn the slightest shade of pink as she keeps dry fucking me, and seeing her beautiful fucking eyes hold mine, her mouth open, the slightest frown on her lips as she gets closer, using me, it's enough for me to come undone.

I try to hold back, but with her ass in my hand and *her* all around me, her scent, and her eyes and her lips and her hips rocking in my lap, I can't.

I bite my lip, my abs contracting as the friction and heat of her takes me over the edge.

"Fuck, Eden." I didn't even mean to say it, and it's nothing but a jagged whisper as I tilt my head, my mouth over hers, even though she's still not breathing. I squeeze her tighter as her fingers dig into my scalp, but she doesn't stop moving, hopefully getting closer, too.

Then she grabs my choker, twisting, the pressure tight around my throat, and as warm cum seeps onto my skin, she's digging her nails into my neck with one hand, yanking my hair with the other.

It's violent, her orgasm, and I release her enough so I can hear her against my lips, my dick still pumping out cum, jerking in my fucking pants like this is my first orgasm, but I don't care.

"Eli," she whispers into my mouth, and I lift my eyes to meet hers. They're glassy, but focused, and I'm biting down on her lip as her grip loosens on my choker, giving me enough room to breathe. "Eli, *baby*."

My heart flips in my chest with those last two words.

Our mouths collide as she slows her movements, and I feel heat between us, and I know when she gets up, she's going to have left a spot big enough to rival mine.

Fuck.

She's still panting, but after her body trembles, she's dropping her hands to my torso, her head to my shoulder, twisted away from me, and it's like she just goes limp in my arms. There's a mess between us, but I don't believe either of us think of it as something bad. I wouldn't even care if I was coated in her fucking blood.

Reluctantly, I slide my hand up her hips, release my grip on her neck, and hug her back, holding her in my lap as we just breathe together.

I can smell her, the sweet softness of violets, the musky scent of her between us, even *my* cum, currently stuck to my skin and all over my boxers. It's a heady mix, enough to make my blood heat with lust all over again, but comforting, too, like I could fall asleep just like this, with her head on my shoulder, her arms holding me close. I feel the rise and fall of her chest against me, and I close my eyes, my head knocking back against the couch.

I don't know how long we stay that way, just holding onto each other, but when I blink my eyes open again, heavy with something that feels like peace, I realize the movie isn't playing, just the opening screen again for me to watch it once more or put on something else.

I don't move, my arms still wrapped around Eden's waist.

Quietly, she says, "That was so good." It's almost as if I wasn't meant to hear it, with how low she speaks.

But I did, and I smile, unseen by her, my eyes on the projector in the ceiling overhead. "It was fucking amazing."

Slowly, she picks her head up, shifting back on my lap so she can see me better, her fingers grazing my ribs over my shirt.

I keep my hands around her hips as I look up at her, seeing the same smile on my lips reflected on hers. My mouth feels dry, my muscles a little weak. Like… I thought maybe she'd regret it or something. It's relief, what I'm feeling, and I don't know what to do with that.

"Sorry for the mess." She doesn't look sorry as she reaches between us, readjusting her shorts. Neither of us look down, but I'm just grateful she puts her hand back on my side when she's done.

"There may be a few things I'll want you to be sorry for in the future." I squeeze her sides and smile wider when she laughs. "But please note, a *mess* like that is not one of them."

She runs her tongue over her teeth, flashing them at me, her eyes lighting up, her cheeks pulled high. "Oh yeah? Name something you'd want me to be sorry for."

In this moment, I can't think of a single thing she'd ever do wrong. *She's perfect.* Her dark hair hanging around her face, a few strands stuck to her forehead with sweat, her cheeks pink, those fucking lips looking swollen, maybe sunburned, or maybe from my mouth.

Her, here, in my lap.

"I don't want to think about it," I tell her, finally answering her question.

Of course, it only makes her more interested. She shifts on my lap, dangerously close to my dick, and I want to warn her if she gets me hard again, right now, I'm going to want to fuck her, but she must see something in my eyes, because she stays back. "Come on." She gives me a playful smile. "Tell me something you'd hate for me to do."

I roll my eyes, squeezing her sides and watching as she jerks again, obviously ticklish. But I look up at the ceiling, focused on the light of the projector. "Okay, first of all, I wouldn't hate you." I think that's true. It's hard for me to feel too deeply *anything*, and hate is really just on the opposite side of the same coin of love. But sometimes I get laser focused. Tunnel vision. That's the nice term for it.

Obsession is what it really is.

Sometimes I get *obsessed*.

And with Eden, it's like I'm standing on the edge of a cliff, and obsession is just right there, in the river running beneath my feet.

I could jump. Or I could turn around and walk away.

But I've never been one to shy away from water.

"Just, I don't know…" I swallow hard, still staring at the ceiling, knowing she's watching my every move. *Don't cheat on me?* We aren't even dating. *Don't leave me?* We aren't together. *Don't go to school on Monday and act like nothing happened between us?* We already speak most of the day. It's not like I ever let her get too far out of my sight.

I think about Winslet for a second. Mom. I think about water over my head. In too deep. A hand on my chest.

It's enough to snap me out of my wandering thoughts.

I pick my head up and squeeze her, not to tickle her, but to anchor her right here.

"Be exactly who you are. If something happens between us, something bad…"

I see her eyes narrow slightly, but she doesn't speak.

"Don't do something to hurt me, because I would never intentionally hurt you."

"Sounds ominous." Her tone is laced with suspicion. "Why would something bad happen between us?"

I shrug. "Life is unpredictable."

"So, if you fuck me over, in other words, you want me to keep being nice to you?"

I shake my head, reaching up and tucking a lock of hair behind her ear, trailing my finger softly over her piercings and feeling her tense on my lap. I wonder if she thinks I'm actually going to hit her or something. If someone has done that to her before. I'll find out one day, and if anyone in her house has hurt her, I'll burn them alive.

"No," I say, dropping my hand down to her arm, kneading her flesh. "I'm not going to fuck you over. But *you* seem to think this will never work. And if you happen to be right, if we get pulled apart, just don't sabotage yourself to get at me, okay?" I'm not sure what I'm saying is reaching her. I don't even know what I'm saying. Maybe it's just everything falls apart around me. Anyone who knows me at all—mainly Dad, Dominic, Luna, Janelle—knows that. I am a catalyst for destruction, and the people closest to me feel the deepest shockwaves.

I don't.

They leap under my feet and rise up to meet the few who, for reasons unknown to me, decide to stay close enough to get hurt.

I don't want that for Eden, and she so clearly enjoys hurting, I think she'd dig the knife in deeper and twist if being close to me endangered her heart.

I think it's sadness in her eyes I see now. Big and round, her lips pursed, like maybe she's trying not to tell me to fuck off, or maybe she's trying to stop herself from crying. But in the end, all she says is, "Okay."

I reach in the console, play the movie over again just for background noise. Then I wrap my arms around her, pick her up, and lean over, depositing her at the end of the couch.

Before she can say anything, I stretch out, my head in her lap, a mess still all over my stomach and my pants, but it can wait.

I rest one hand on her thigh, the other under my head.

Her fingers come to my hair without missing a beat, massaging my scalp, and my eyes flutter closed as the movie starts up again. "You wanted me to choke you." I say the words quietly, and her fingers pause in my hair, but a moment later, they start again. *Strangle.* I've been doing some reading. That's the correct word, but choking has a violent sex appeal *strangulation* doesn't.

She doesn't speak. I know better than to talk about my recent education right now.

I squeeze her thigh, her skin hot beneath my fingers. "Have you ever done anything like that before?"

When she answers, her voice is small, like she's shy. "To myself."

I smile, my eyes still closed, imagining her getting herself off with one hand around her throat. "Yeah?"

"Yeah. I've seen it a lot. In porn."

I draw circles on her thigh as she does the same in my hair. "Did you like it? When I did it?"

She glides her fingers down to my neck, massaging me. It feels like I'm having an out of body experience, my soul is fucking lifting through my scalp, she's so good. "Yes."

A hum of contentment leaves my lips.

"Did you?" she asks, her voice rough. "Like it?" She keeps kneading her fingers over the bones of my neck, down to my shoulders, working out all the kinks.

"I loved it. Everything."

Silence fills the space between us, not awkward, it's enjoyable.

But I have to know. Or… I just… *want to know.* "Have you ever had sex before?"

She pauses our massage, but unlike she did through texts, she can't run from me this time. I feel her shift a little underneath me, and I don't say anything, waiting for her answer.

Finally, she just says it. "No." It's barely a breath, like she doesn't want it to be true.

I turn over, then, looking up at her, her hand now on my chest, one still in my hair. Her eyes are on mine, and I can see her flushing from the lights of the movie. I reach my fingers to her side, sliding them under her T-shirt. Her muscles jump with the movement.

My heart is hammering hard inside my chest, just imagining it. Fucking her, for her first time.

"You're going to," I tell her, my eyes locked on hers. "With me. Whenever you're ready. I promise, I'll make it good for you."

SHE STANDS AT THE BALCONY OF MY ROOM, STORMS STILL lingering from earlier today. It's hot, and in the distance, more heat lightning, and heavy clouds over the moon promise rain. It seems, with us together, it's always raining. I don't believe in signs or superstitions, not really and not like she does, but I kind of like most of our time together is spent with water.

I lean back in the outdoor chair, my feet propped on the stool as I reach for the rolled joint on the glass table beside me, snagging the green lighter at the same time. I hold both up, joint in my mouth as I flick the lighter, inhaling and watching the tip grow orange in the darkness.

The wind blows, sailing the gray smoke toward Eden, standing on the bottom rung of the deck, her arms crossed over the railing.

She must catch the scent of marijuana, because she turns her head to me, my shirt on her body rippling with the weather, hugging her small breasts. I can barely see her shorts, but as she twists around to smile at me, I see the shape of her ass, and I wonder if I'll ever get over it.

Like, how is it even fucking real?

"It's going to rain again," she says as I take another pull

from the joint, grateful for the college dropout in my neighborhood whose parents are too ashamed to kick him out, lest he be found wandering the streets and a banker or a lawyer or a mayor recognizes him as the King's son.

I turn my head to exhale, eyes on the darkening clouds. Thunder rumbles, and the air feels thick. Charged. The sweet taste of weed lingers on my tongue, eclipsing the taste of Eden, and I'll just have to kiss more of her before we go to bed, whenever that'll be.

"Good," I tell her, facing her again, the joint between my fingers like a cigarette. "I like to sleep to the sound of rain."

She studies me a moment, feet still stuck between the railings, her eyes on my own. In my bedroom, behind the sliding glass door, pale blue lights strung up along my ceiling are the only glow around us, save for the lit end of my joint.

So, I know she can't see the circles under my eyes, but she still says, "You don't look like you sleep much." There's something of concern threaded through her voice.

It softens my immediate reaction, which is annoyance. I don't want to talk about why I don't sleep, mainly because I don't know why. My brain is always jumping to the next thing, spinning wildness and violence and thoughts I can't have come true. When I lie down, it rushes at me, too fast, boredom creeping into my skin, under my nails like a splinter.

I have to get up and move or the yearning for self-destruction is nearly enough to make me tremble. At Montford, they gave me drugs.

They helped, sometimes.

But they made me let my guard down.

Again, I think of bleach, closets, and razorblades. If I could describe Montford in three words, it would be those, but they'd make sense to no one but the other patients. Maybe one of the staff, too.

I don't think about that because there's no point.

"Does it bother you?" I ask Eden, instead of explaining any of this. It wouldn't make sense to her because it doesn't make fucking sense to me. And maybe worse than confusion, she might feel compelled to stay up all night on the phone with me, texting back and forth, supplying me with entertainment when we're apart. There are a thousand reasons I don't want that, not least of all, my surprising concern for her well-being.

Sleep is essential to health.

Those who don't get enough know it very well.

It's a vicious cycle, compounding and whipping up my problems into a tornado instead of a strong wind.

"No," she whispers, "but I wish you could."

I take another inhale from the joint, wanting the light feeling in my head. It doesn't help me sleep. It doesn't really help me with much, except quieting some of the frantic brutality in my brain. "Maybe tonight I will."

She half smiles. I can't really read the expression in her eyes, but if I had to guess, it might be something like hesitancy. "Maybe so," she says.

"Come closer to me," I tell her, "you're too far away."

Three feet, it's too much.

Another crackle of thunder. This time, a cloud-to-ground strike of lightning in the distance, brightening the sky in violet, just for a moment.

Eden doesn't even startle. She just hops off the railing of the balcony, her hips swaying as she walks toward me. I widen my knees, giving her room, but she doesn't sit.

She only watches me get high, and as I exhale through my nose, I extend the joint to her. "You want some?"

She reaches for a few loose strands of her hair, pushing them behind her ear. I can't tell if it's a nervous habit, or just a habit. But she shakes her head, so I grab her wrist, expecting the flinch in her arm, and I'm not disappointed. But I ignore it, yanking her down into my lap.

She comes down clumsily, and I drop the joint into the ashtray at my side, so I can use both arms to wrap around her, tugging her closer as I kiss her forehead. She smiles, the smallest laugh accompanying it, and her arms thread behind my neck. She's so short, even in this position, her legs over my thighs, underneath the arm of my chair and dangling off, she fits perfectly.

"What do you usually do on the weekends?" she asks as I keep my lips against her forehead, her shoulder pressing beside my sternum.

I look out over the dark sky, and a few seconds later, the welcome patter of rain starts up.

"Wrestling tournaments," I answer Eden, every word I speak fluttering onto her skin. "Swimming." I think of the pool. Of going under again and again and again until I feel dizzy. Tomorrow, I'll show her, and she won't be scared. Not after today. "Sometimes I help my uncle at his shop with my cousin."

"You love cars," she says, satisfied amusement coating her words.

I kiss her again, holding her tighter. "Yeah, I do." The rain is louder now, and I see it streaking down in the faintest white. Some drops bounce off of the railing from the balcony, and I feel them against my skin. Eden probably does, too, but we don't complain. "What do you love?" I pull back so I can see her eyes, her arms still around my neck. "What do you do on the weekends?"

"Well," she says, shrugging, and I already know from the sly smile on her lips she's going to say something smart. "Like most teenagers who aren't Trafalgar blessed, I usually work."

I roll my eyes. "Don't make me toss you off of this balcony."

She tightens her grip, her chest pressing closer to me. "You wouldn't." Her eyes find my mouth. "You'd miss me too much."

I don't dispute her words, an echo of the truth I gave her earlier, but I can't say anything either.

After a moment, she cuts her gaze back to mine. "When I'm not working, I like to drive with the windows down, especially if it's hot."

"In your slow baby Sentra?"

"I swear to God, I really *will* toss you off of this balcony, Eli Addison."

I smile at my first and last name from her mouth. "It's okay. We all have to start somewhere."

She rolls her eyes. "Yes, in my *slow, baby Sentra.*" She parrots my comment with false venom. "I like to go for hikes. Sometimes just in the backyard. I like…" She trails off, but then simply shrugs, as if she doesn't care. "Well… I like occultism. *Magic.*"

I think of one of the books she had at her table the first night. *The Kybalion.* "You like magic," I repeat, savoring the words in my mouth. I think of her reference to the devil's hour, when Winslet went missing. *"Dark* magic."

She tilts her head, frowning.

I shrug. "I pay attention," I whisper over her mouth. *My little angel, built for sin.*

She ignores me, save for the way her lips tip upward. "Mostly, I like to read." She clears her throat, averting her gaze. "And write."

I arch a brow, but I'm not surprised. *The Elements of Style.* The other book she had, beside her Kindle. "And write?" I press, ducking my chin, hoping to catch her eye again.

She stares resolutely at the tops of her thighs. "Yes."

"Write what?"

"Stories."

"Eden."

She must hear the low warning in my voice because she smiles, but she still doesn't look at me. "I write a lot of things."

I'm about to tell her that's a non-answer, but she keeps going, maybe knowing I won't let her get away with her bullshit.

"Women's fiction." She says the words like they taste bad, and I'm not sure why. But after a minute, she just sighs, shaking her head and looking up at me. "I write romance, basically."

Romance." It's like she expects me to be disgusted or something, but instead, I'm just surprised.

"You?" I slide my hand up from her waist to her wrist, circling her bracelets. "You write romance?"

She ducks her head, trying to pull away from me and swing her legs off as thunder rolls overhead, the awning protecting us from most of the storm, but rain is slanting sideways, flecking more frequently across my face. "Look, it's not like it's going to get published. Just, let's go inside—"

I keep my hold on her wrist, but I jerk her body closer, so she's forced to face me again, her legs halfway down mine in her lame attempt at a getaway.

"Why wouldn't it get published?" I search her face for answers. "That's the stupidest thing I've ever heard."

She gapes at me. "What? What the hell do you know about publishing?"

"I know anyone with a computer and a single brain cell can upload a book on the internet, Eden, come on."

She stares at me like I'm a monster. "Yeah, but that doesn't mean anyone *reads* it."

"Okay, so, no one is reading it now in your journal, or on your laptop, or whatever." I shrug. "What's the difference? At least they'd have a chance if you put it out there, right?"

She hasn't lost that look on her face, like she thinks I'm foolish. "I want to be a professor. Professors can't self-publish books."

I consider that a moment, then ask, "What do you want to be more? Professor or writer?"

"Professors write."

"Not romance novels."

"They *can*," she insists, and I guess she sees from my smile she's now the one fighting for her dream. This time, I let her clamber down from my lap, turning her back to the storm as she presses the heels of her hands to her eyes and sighs. I'm not sure why she's so bent out of shape about this, but it's like I've exposed a nerve or something.

I mean, imagining Eden as a professor is hot as hell, but so is thinking of her hunched over a desk, scribbling down plot ideas and chugging coffee, something I've caught the scent of on her breath in the mornings after Latin when we walk together in the hallway.

She could do anything she wanted.

She just doesn't know it yet.

She drops her hands, sighing. "Whatever," she says. "Can we just go inside?" She gestures toward the storm, then my room. "I don't want to talk about my writing."

"I don't see what the big deal—"

"Do you want to talk about your mom?" she snaps.

I curl my fingers over the arms of my chair, the slick, cool wood grounding me.

I feel a hand on my chest.

I see my mom's eyes.

I don't panic for long seconds, until my lungs ache. Until fear like I rarely experience creeps in.

She loves me, though. I'm nothing like Dad, but I'm just like her.

We're the same, Mom, can't you see?

My pulse pounds in my ears.

I squirm, my spine hitting the porcelain bottom of the bathtub. My bladder feels suddenly so full.

She just doesn't know. She doesn't realize I'm uncomfortable. That my lungs are burning. I need to take a breath, but she doesn't know and I'm not sure how to tell her and—

Thunder cracks across the sky loud enough to make me jump.

When I blink, Eden is pressed against the railing, like she's scared of me. I check I'm still sitting. I am. My hands are still lodged over the wood, my knuckles white with my grip, my palms aching. My chest is heaving.

I slowly look up, confused. *Why did you run?*

She's still staring at me, her arms crossed over her chest. *What did I do?* But I couldn't have *done* anything. I'm sitting. I'm still. I'm not close to her. Nothing is thrown, the ashtray still on the glass table.

I swallow the tightness in my throat.

Eden keeps staring for long seconds.

Then, startling me, she comes closer, stopping right in front of me.

She extends her hand, keeping one arm crossed over her chest like a shield. "Come on," she says softly, but not weakly. "Let's go inside, okay?"

I want to ask her if I did something or said something. I don't usually. It was just a memory. Unbidden and unwanted, but still. Just a memory. It's not as if they cripple me. I don't even remember caring anymore. I don't remember fear, or pain.

But when I reach for her outstretched hand, my own is trembling.

I grab her fast, like I can hide it, or stop it.

She jerks in my grip, like an instinct, but I just come to my feet, wrap my arm around her hunched shoulders, and lead her inside my room.

When she first stepped in here, she was transfixed by the lights strung overhead. She asked if I did it. I told her no, my dad did. A gift of sorts, I think. Or a peace offering from a morning fight. One afternoon I came home from practice, and they were up.

Now, though, as we stand in my bathroom, one light on and dimmed, she's transfixed by her checkered backpack, set on my counter as I brush my teeth. I glance at my reflection, seeing my skin has gotten browner from the sun, and Eden's lips are redder from the same thing.

But she's frowning into her bag, a comb in one hand, the other rooting through a small pile of clothes. I spit into my sink, turning on the tap to rinse it away as I set the electric toothbrush beside my toothpaste, glancing at Eden's sink and grateful I have two, because she's the type of girl who likes some space.

I don't dare look in the mirror and see the claw-footed tub behind the open door, or the glass shower adjacent the tub. I might not be able to resist dragging her into one or the other.

"What's wrong?" I ask her, leaning against the gray marble countertop.

She shakes her head. "I forgot my toothbrush." She says this like it's a huge failure. Like she crashed a commercial plane or poisoned a well meant to quench the thirst of small children.

"Okay," I say, seeing her long, straight lashes as she keeps staring into her bag. I grab my toothbrush without looking away from her and offer it her way. "Use mine."

She pulls her brows together, snapping her head up like I touched her. "What?" She glances at my toothbrush, impeccably clean, even along the black handle, because I hate when toothpaste gets flecked across it. "I can't—"

"Shh," I tell her, stepping closer, so she has to tilt her head back to meet my gaze. "I licked you from my fingers." I nod toward the toothbrush as her cheeks heat, the alcohol no longer shielding her nervousness. "You can use my toothbrush."

After a moment, assessing me, as if I'm bluffing—as if I fucking care—she says, "Who else has used this brush?" Her nose wrinkles as her eyes narrow.

"Who the fuck else would have used my toothbrush?"

I see her lips part, a name on the tip of her tongue, but she swallows it down at the last minute and instead, asks, "Who else do you let spend the night?"

"No one." I shrug, dropping my hand and resting the brush on the counter. "Not really. Dominic before, I guess, a few people from a few parties." I angle my head toward the brush. "But, if you're really interested in the history of this particular toothbrush, since I got it, *no one* has spent the night here aside from my dad. And rest assured, he has his own brush."

She doesn't look like she believes me, skepticism in her narrowed eyes, but finally, she swipes the brush from my fingers. "I'll be out soon." Then she waits until I walk out and close the door softly behind me. A few seconds later, I hear the hum of my electric toothbrush.

I lean against the closed door, resting my head on it as I close my eyes, smiling.

It was awkward for her, at first.

Her body is pressed up against mine, my arm around her front, tugging her close, my elbow on the bed, chin propped in my hand. Initially, her body was stiff without the alcohol in her system, a distraction from her discomfort. But as the rain has clattered harder, louder against the door of my balcony, she's relaxed into me.

I wonder if she's going to fall asleep soon.

We're at an angle, my body curved against the pillows pushed into the dark wooden headboard behind me. The fan is on, for her, and the white sheets are up over her shoulders, the dark blue comforter pulled down a little.

I try to watch the movie from the TV mounted on my wall across from my bed, but all I can focus on is the pins in her hair, gleaming with every flash of the screen. I want to pull each pin free, one by one.

"Sit up for me, baby," I whisper against the top of her head.

She glances at me over her shoulder, her lips close to mine. "Why?"

I'm glad she doesn't just do anything I say. Even Luna and Dominic, they take my statements as commands. I don't know how I emerged as the leader when I was the one in and out of psych wards, but I could snap my fingers and they'd jump.

Eden… not a fucking chance.

"I want to play with your hair."

She stares at me a long moment, like she doesn't believe

me. I roll my eyes, tapping her hip as I sit up, disturbing her comfortable position against me.

"What are you scared of?" I ask her. "There's no water in my room. I promise I won't hold you under."

She flips me off, which makes me laugh, but she sits up, and I widen my knees, pushing back against the headboard.

"Scoot back," I tell her, and she does, until her ass is against my dick and it's going to take it about three seconds to get fully hard again.

Her arms drape over my thighs, hands resting on my knees as she focuses on the TV.

"Can I take out your braids?"

"Yes." It's permission, but I feel her fingers tense against my kneecaps, beneath the hem of my gym shorts.

I run my hands up her arms, starting at the bracelets on her wrists. She has a scar beneath them. Maybe several. I can feel a slight bump in her skin underneath my thumb. A few of them. I've never been able to look closely, and in the dark, only the glow of the screen lighting the room, I wouldn't be able to make out any detail. I let it go as her body grows rigid while I rub her arms.

"Relax." I know it's easier said than done. "You're safe here, okay?"

She doesn't believe me; her guard is always up even when she wants to obey me. It's dancing on the line of submission and self-protection and defiance.

She nods once, and I feel her make an effort to rest as I reach her biceps, pushing up the sleeves of her shirt. I knead her shoulder caps, then let the sleeves fall again as I come to her neck, careful not to circle my fingers around her. In my head, I choke the shit out of her as I fuck her, and she loves every second of it, but I've been working on curbing my impulses for years. Turns out, if I can just keep sight of the reward at the end, I'm pretty good at it most of the time.

She has a lot of tension in her neck, and as I start working through all the delicate muscles and bones there, she twists her head one way and the other, giving me better access.

A contented sigh leaves her mouth, and my dick jumps at the sound, but I ignore that feeling. Nothing more is going to happen tonight. I think we pushed each other far enough for now.

Finally, when she feels completely relaxed, her body leaning into mine, her hands no longer fastened around my knees, I move my fingers up to her hair, going by feel rather than sight when it comes to the bobby pins. They're black and her hair is just one shade lighter, and she's got so much of it, coarse and heavy, it's easier to pluck the pins out as I touch them, no light from the TV reaching back here.

I place each pin beside my thigh, on top of the pure white of my sheets so I don't lose any for her. Her hair starts to tumble down, uneven, not like in the movies where it all floods down at once, bouncy and whipping around an actress's shoulders.

This is more work.

I add the tenth pin to the pile, running my fingers over her scalp as she sighs, slouching down a little more. I don't feel any more pins, so I start to work on undoing her braids. It's not easy, her strands thick and coarse, some a little damp from the pool and the rain.

It takes time, running my fingers everywhere, unlooping the three braids, unwrapping the crown on her head. Her breathing sounds even, a little louder as I finally get the last of the braids unwound, dragging my fingertips through them and pulling them apart, then scooping up the entire mass of her hair and running my hands beneath, away from her neck.

She's against me, and I don't want to move her, so I can't see exactly how long her hair is, and some of the strands are caught between my chest and her back. For long moments, I bring my fingers back up and massage her scalp softly, letting the TV flick off automatically.

When I hear the lightest of snores from her, I force myself

to stop, snag all the pins and deposit them on my nightstand, then wrap my arms around her warm chest. Slowly, carefully, I shift my hips, moving us both so I'm lying on my hip, and I turn a little, so she's on her side, tucked up against me.

I rest my head on the pillow, inhaling the scent of her hair, peaches and soft flowers.

I close my eyes, and I don't sleep, but there's nothing but emptiness in my mind.

Despite the storm raging outside, she quiets the one inside of me.

22

Eden

I'M awake when Mom's good morning text comes in. The light is thin, pinpricks spearing through the heavy curtains.

Eli is asleep, curled on his side, his back exposed to me, olive skin pulled over taut muscles.

I can't stop my smile. It hurts my face, and I have to clench my teeth to stifle a squeal. But I keep quiet, ignoring Mom's text as I open up my Notes on my phone, continuing to type for my story. An idea came to me in the middle of the night, I think I've been up… three hours? It's just now six, but I couldn't sleep, the thoughts knocking against my brain for the story I'm working on.

I was surprised Eli wasn't awake, but grateful he was finally getting rest.

In the relative darkness, I keep typing, trying to make my movements small, only flexing my fingers over my keyboard. I fill up page after page of brainstorming, and I don't know why everything hits me this way sometimes, disturbing my rest, forcing me up, almost like I'm… frantic.

I want to get out of bed, truthfully, but another glance at

Eli, so relaxed, his hair curling over the nape of his tanned neck...

I don't get up.

I just type as another hour passes, and when I feel as if I'm running out of steam, and maybe I should try one more time to get more rest, I set my phone on the nightstand and roll onto my side, closing my eyes, plot ideas still scrolling behind my lids, but I try to keep still.

I realize I like it when Eli is so at ease. He rarely ever is.

I PUSH UP, TURNING MY HEAD AND SWEEPING MY GAZE AROUND the room which is brighter now. Dark wooden floors, black paneled walls, there's a leather bench at the end of Eli's enormous bed, and I battle down the cool, fluffy, blue comforter, searching for him. The sun is higher in the sky than it was. I catch the glimpse of it over the horizon, the pool down below the balcony, curtains parted.

I twist around and glance at the square black alarm clock, plain but elegant, like rich stuff tends to be. It's just after nine in the morning. *Shit, I slept for three more hours.*

The bathroom door is open, exposing dark marble and light tile. Frowning, I rub a fist over my eye, mentally cataloging everything we did yesterday. It's through a tipsy haze, mingled with writing on my phone all night. I did that, didn't I?

I frown, glancing at my phone face down on the nightstand.

I know I didn't drink *too much* last night. I can still recall, for example, the moment I admitted to him I was a virgin.

My face heats with the memory, and I realize I should take this opportunity to brush my teeth.

With his brush.

The flush extends to my neck, and when I run a hand through my hair, I see all of my bobby pins in a neat pile beside the alarm clock, something I missed initially.

How can a boy as alarmingly captivating as Eli be so *careful* about things? His room is neat, aside from the unmade bed. The TV is mounted on the wall, an electric fireplace built in beneath it. He has heavy, dark curtains, nothing on his nightstand aside from the alarm clock and my hair pins. No clothes on the floor. The door to his walk-in closet, a beige break in the black panel of his walls, is pulled shut. The dresser adjacent it has every drawer closed; nothing even sits on top of it.

I drag my hands down my face, thankful wherever he went, he closed the bedroom door after him. I snatch up my phone, flipping it over, wondering if I just dreamt all those notes I wrote.

I open up my texts and find one from Mom. A good morning message, sent a while ago, because she's an early riser. I can't remember if I saw it before. I send her a quick one back, check my notes, and scroll through a bunch of shit I presumably wrote in the middle of the night. *Damn.* Kind of proud of myself for that one.

I set my phone down, then swing my legs over the bed. I'm grateful I'm in shorts and Eli's shirt, and I bring the fabric to my nose and inhale, catching the scent of coconut and the sea.

Smiling, I stand, about to take a step along the cold hardwood floors to his bathroom, when I hear a raised voice.

I freeze, my teeth clenched as I turn my head toward the door, trying not to breathe so I can listen.

It's a low murmur, and I know someone is here when I catch a muffled response. My heart thunders in my chest and I see my bag on the sink in the bathroom and think about downing a pill. I'm not much for eavesdropping. I think the things people don't want you to know should stay hidden, but... *who is it?*

He said his dad was away for work or whatever. Something. *Right.*

It can't be his dad.

But then again... it could be.

Just as I'm about to make a break for the bathroom, flip on

the fan to drown out the noise so I can calm down, I hear something shatter.

I flinch, my pulse skipping beats. For one split second, I wonder if I imagined it. But no. *No.*

In my head, I see Eli's chest. His faded bruises. And while I don't think it's his dad who does it to him, the possibility I could let him get hurt in this house is something I couldn't live with.

I cross the floor on tiptoes, reaching for the sleek silver handle of his door and pulling down slowly. I can't tell if the voices are on this floor or not, but I'm careful when I open up the door. It doesn't creak like mine at the trailer, which I guess is a rich boy perk.

I try not to be bitter about it, more important things at hand here.

I stick my head out into the hallway, feeling as if I'm a bad actress in a shitty thriller, but I don't see anyone. Just a set of doors closed at the opposite end of the hallway.

And for a moment, I don't hear anything either.

I start to think maybe it wasn't an argument. Maybe one of his friends came over, because unlike me, he does have those. Maybe they dropped something and it broke.

But just as I'm about to turn back and brush my teeth, make sure I don't look like a complete wreck, I hear someone speak again.

Someone I don't know. A deep, male voice, full of irritation. *Similar to the one I heard in his car after the wrestling tournament.*

His dad. *Shit.*

"Do her parents know where she is right now?"

Oh no.

I clamp my hand over my mouth, so I don't accidentally breathe too heavily or something stupid. *No, sir, my parents definitely do not know where I am right now.*

Eli doesn't respond, or if he does, I can't hear it.

The voices are coming from down the spiral staircase. Maybe at the foyer if I had to guess.

"Are you two dating?"

Not this. I almost want to turn around, because I'm not sure I want to hear what Eli says to that. But he doesn't say anything at all. Again.

I can hear his dad's irritation climbing when he says, voice ragged, "I want to meet her."

Nope. No. I glance down at my legs, Eli's shirt. I think about all the rum I drank yesterday. Thankfully, I had the sense to hang up my swimsuit over the shower door in Eli's bathroom, and none of my things are downstairs. Eli cleaned up the kitchen before we came up. But I'm sure his dad knows I'm here. In his son's room.

He's going to think I'm a whore, and I haven't even met him yet. Now I have to fix a bad impression and—

My runaway thoughts are cut off by Eli's laugh. It's cold, drifting a shiver down my spine. I drop my hand from the doorknob to cross my arms over my chest as I lean against the doorframe, listening and not sure I want to hear what he's going to say.

"Don't you have a meeting with your secretary to run along to, Dad?" The question is rude, innuendo dripping from every word. I imagine speaking to Reece like that.

I have, many times before. It always ends in us screaming at each other. But Eli's dad must have a little more patience because he says, "Go upstairs, let her know I'm here, and bring her down so I can introduce myself."

No, no, no. Briefly, as my knees tremble and I turn my head, looking at the balcony door, I think about climbing out and running away. It's possible, if not ideal, but I *could* do it. I think I'd rather, than meet his dad under these circumstances, with me stowed up here in his bedroom where he probably thinks we had sex and… *Shit.* I think about the "entertainment room," a combination of words which only exist for a certain tax bracket.

Did we get anything on the couch? I feel like I want to faint just thinking about it. I mean, Eli had to change his pants afterward. There could be something we missed.

I wait for Eli to push back again. He says nothing, and I wonder how often he gets away with his deafening silence.

I hear his dad sigh, and he says, "I'm leaving soon. Let me meet her, okay? Just this one thing, do it for me." There's an earnestness in his words. He's not begging, really, but he's sincere, and it doesn't sound like he has ulterior motives. Then again, neither does Eli, even when I'm sure he does.

I don't know what I want Eli to say. My heart hammering in my chest, part of me wants him to argue. A lot of me wants his dad to leave so I can breathe a little easier. A tiny, small sliver wants him to think I'm important enough to meet his family.

But only a miniscule part.

After another tense moment of silence, I hear footsteps on the stairs.

I think it's Eli's silent "yes."

Fuck.

I slip back into his room, closing the door as quietly as I can before I bound to the bathroom. I dig my medicine from my backpack and take two pills, swallowing them dry before I zip up the bag and start brushing my teeth, glancing at my reflection in the mirror.

I don't look terrible.

Leftover eyeliner smudged under my eyes, a pinched, tired look on my face, but my hair looks good, at least. It's wavy from the braids, and the chlorine must have somehow helped style it, because as I fluff it up with my fingers, turning to examine it hanging down my back, I realize it looks better than if I had actually put any effort into it. Like mermaid hair. Kinda hot, grazing my waist.

Aphrodite. But maybe his dad wants to meet, like, Snow White or something?

I roll my eyes and spit in the sink, rinse Eli's brush, and wipe my hand over the back of my mouth, waiting for the pills to kick in as I stare at myself in the mirror, thinking of all the things his dad might ask me. How am I supposed to act? What am I supposed to talk about? How long will he interrogate me?

Shit, and I need to change too.

I grab my bag, leaving it propped on the counter as I pull out a pair of oversized, pleated pants Mom had hemmed for me. I leave my necklaces at the bottom of the bag, snatch up a plain white shirt to tuck into the pants, except, *surprise*, it's actually cropped with slits in the side, another homemade craft from yours truly. *Shit.*

At least I have a belt somewhere in here. Belts are fancy.

"My dad came home early."

I jump, a gasp leaving my lips as I spin around, my fingers closing around the brown belt at the bottom of my bag. "Fuck." It leaves my mouth before I can stop myself, trying to calm the adrenaline in my body. "I didn't even hear you come up here."

Eli is leaning against the doorframe of the bathroom, hands in the pockets of his shorts, and he doesn't have a shirt on. Just the choker. The one beneath my fingers last night when I almost made him pass out while I dry fucked him on his dad's couch.

My eyes linger on the tattoo just visible over the waistband of his shorts. Of course, my gaze wanders to the V of his hips, up his lower abs, and—

"Pay attention, baby girl."

I feel heat creep up my neck, into my cheeks as I bring my eyes up to focus. "I am paying attention." My mouth feels dry, and I swallow, hard. "It's just, you know…" I gesture toward him, the belt still in my hand.

His eyes flick to it but come back to me quickly. "Just what?" he asks, but there's the hint of a smile on his lips. His voice is kind of throaty, I realize, and I wonder how long he's been up. I can still recall the feel of him curled around me when I woke in the night the first time, before I made those notes.

It felt… good.

"Nothing." I shake my head, gripping the edge of the counter with my free hand to steady myself.

He just looks at me a moment, a knowing sort of expression on his face, but then he says, "I'm guessing you heard." He must see my surprise. "Well, I heard *you* running to my bathroom when I was heading up the stairs, so…" He shrugs, sighing. "He's leaving soon. You don't have to meet him. If you don't want to, just say the word."

Well, I definitely don't want to. I wasn't really any good at meeting his friends at Dom's, now I'm expected to look presentable for his dad in this mansion, all while Mr. Addison knows I spent the night here, without his permission.

I suck at small talk, and I never really make a great impression on parents. I mean, I'm certain Nic's mom would not recommend me for dating anyone's son.

Plus, there's this fucking distressed crop top.

Still, how can I really say no?

"It's okay," I lie, glancing at the belt in my hands, remembering to breathe. "I just need to change." I think about Eli's half-naked body. "And maybe you could too."

"My dad has seen me without a shirt on plenty."

I shake my head, still focused on the brown leather belt clutched in my fingers. "Right, but I don't want to be thinking about his son promising to take my virginity because I'm so distracted by all your…" I thrust my hand toward him again, not daring to look up. "You know. Muscles."

There's a beat of silence as I wish I could take back every word that just came out of my mouth. But the pills must be kicking in because I don't feel any warmer than I usually do, and I haven't started to sweat again.

At that moment, when I think I'm going to be steady and calm for meeting the parent, the floor shifts and Eli is standing right beside me. I can see his abs in my peripheral, but I keep my eyes trained on the belt.

"Personally," he says, his voice low, hands still in his pockets, those green veins snaking up his arms, "the only thing I ever want you to think about is me taking your virginity."

I can't breathe.

He leans down close, and I catch his cotton candy breath. He has to eat mints for this or something. No one's breath can naturally smell so good, not even rich boys. "Don't stress about this. It'll be over soon and besides, he's going to love you."

I turn my head, finally, meeting his dark green gaze, my mouth inches from his. "How do you know that?"

His lips pull into a lopsided smile. "You're good for me. He likes those kinds of things." Then without another word, he straightens and walks out, closing the door behind him, giving me space to change.

I do, pulling on the pants, tugging down my white shirt, but it only reaches just above the flare of my hips, clinging to my ribcage, showing off slivers of my torso, tanned from the sun.

Sighing, trying not to think about it, I cinch the belt around my waist before I rake my fingers through my hair one more time, and I can feel the ends grazing my low back.

But out of nowhere, all I can think about is Eli's words, and the look in his eyes last night on the balcony, when I snapped at him, asking snidely if he wanted to talk about his mom, so I wouldn't have to discuss my writing.

Some looks are angry, and some are livid, and others are wounded. I've seen them all, from Mom, Reece, Sebastian. *Nic.*

But the look Eli had for several long seconds was none of those things.

It was just… empty. It kind of terrified me.

"You're good for me."

I meet my gaze in the mirror, focusing on the slivers of green in my irises.

I really hope so.

"You two are matching." Eli's dad glances at our clothes. I smile politely, and it doesn't quite feel like I'm faking it. We *are* matching, and I know Eli had to see the clothes I was planning to wear before he walked out of the bathroom.

Now, we both have on beige pants, although mine are high-waisted and his are definitely not, and we're both wearing white shirts. Mine reveals a lot more than his T-shirt, but even our shoes are nearly the same. He has white Chucks and I have white Keds. Which I may or may not have packed specifically because of his obsession with the color white.

"Yes, Dad, we are." Eli's words sound bored, and I almost laugh at the lack of respect in them, but I don't, because it's not the right thing to do. "Eden, this is my dad, Eric." He gestures toward him, and I take the last step down from the spiral staircase, offering my hand and glancing at my black bracelets, careful they stay close to my wrist. "And Dad, this is Eden."

I don't think it escapes either mine or Eric's notice Eli didn't give me a title, but Eric doesn't seem to care as he takes my hand, his own warm in both temperature and sentiment, squeezing my fingers gently.

"Nice to meet you," I say, keeping the smile on my face as I study Eric's eyes. They're similar to Eli's, but more hazel than pure green. He has a few lines around his face, but he's still a good-looking man, with a head of thick, dark hair, only the faintest streaks of gray.

I see where Eli gets his looks from, although I wonder about his mom.

I glance at Eric's hand as we let each other go and notice a pale patch of skin on his ring finger, no doubt where a wedding band was. *When did he stop wearing it?*

My heart beats steadily thanks to my medicine, and my knees don't shake and sweat doesn't blossom under my arms, but the pills do nothing for my mind. The anxiety is still there, and I have to slide my hands into my pockets to keep from fidgeting.

"You, too," Eric says, and he sounds like he means it. He glances at Eli, standing at my side, saying nothing. Out of the corner of my eye, I see he has his arms crossed casually as he leans against the railing of the stairs.

I try and reach for something to say, but I'm kind of focused on Eric's clothes. He's in an olive dress shirt and gray pants, clearly work clothes. I don't know what he does, but if I had to guess, I'd say lawyer or doctor or CEO of some tech company. Then again, maybe I'm just prejudiced against the rich. I'm absolutely positive he doesn't clean houses, at the very least.

I grind my teeth together, thinking of my trailer, and wonder if Eric would be smiling at me if he knew my address. *Stop judging him if you don't want him to judge you.* I try to hold onto that, but then all I can think about is maybe I should apologize for sleeping in his house when I didn't ask him, and maybe I should assure him I didn't have sex with his son—not technically—and we're not going to wreck his house and—

"How long have you been at Trafalgar?"

I have to blink a few times to realize he's asked me a question, and Eli must have told him we met at school. I wonder if he's talked about me to his dad before, and the idea is so unfathomable, I almost laugh out loud at myself and how blindly optimistic I am when it comes to Eli.

Sometimes.

"I just started," I tell him. "Well, with this school year."

"How are you liking it?"

I feel Eli's eyes on us. It's hard to explain, but his entire presence just feels… cold.

"I like it," I say slowly. "It's interesting. The building, and my classes."

Eric offers a small smile. "It is interesting," he concedes. "Where are you applying to school for college?"

Oh, fuck. I resist the very strong urge to look toward Eli, which would be an appeal to get me out of this situation, but also a show of weakness, like I can't hold my own with his dad.

It's just... I'm not applying to any Ivy League, and I'm not applying to Duke, the holy grail of rich kids in North Carolina. It's just too much. I could get loans, and grants, and scholarships, yes, all those things well-off people like to suggest to not-so-well-off people.

But then I graduate, and I'm buried in debt, and I have no guarantee I can work it off. I don't have family money to fall back on, and I want to move out and I don't want to have to come back. I want to make it on my own, and that means, even at eighteen, I have to make smart financial decisions.

How do I explain this in a few sentences to a man who clearly doesn't have to ever worry about money, not anytime soon?

But I have dreams. I have a goal. That'll have to count for something with him.

"I uh, I'm going to Bloor." I hold his gaze as I say the words. "Maybe applying to UNC-W, as a backup school. But Bloor has the Classics program I want."

I wish Eli would say something, maybe even drag me out of his house and take me home so I can think about the awkwardness of this conversation in private, but Eric has much better conversational skills than I do, so he says, "That's great. Bloor is a good school, and Wilmington is a great city." It doesn't escape me he used "great" twice, which makes it less believable. "I have a house on the coast." He nods toward Eli, his smile pulling higher, and I can't tell if it's more fake or less that way. "Eli should take you some time."

I glance at the high ceilings in the foyer, the chandelier overhead, and wonder what the beach house looks like. I might not want to know.

"I was actually thinking about bringing her in October. Less tourists then."

I whip my head to Eli, eyes wide. I'm not sure what surprises me more, the fact he's agreeing with something his dad suggested, when he seems so antagonistic toward him in general, or the fact he thinks we'll still be... whatever this is in

October. I mean, it's not very far away. But I know this is temporary. I've caught Eli's attention for the moment, but it won't last. Even though I want to keep him until graduation, I know hanging on so long will take effort.

"God, you're fun." How long will I entertain him?

"That would be great." Eric's agreement stuns me, too. That parents can just not care their kids are spending the night with people willy-nilly is shocking to me. I've done it before, but always through lies. Eli and Eric seem open, and given what I've seen of their relationship, it comes as a surprise. "Maybe I can stop by for a night?" Eric flashes me a conspiratorial grin, apparently very aware of the fact his son would *not* want him to spend the night.

But Eli says, "Sure, Dad." Although the words drip with venom, like the way someone else might say, *"Go fuck yourself."*

Eric rolls his eyes, but the grin is still on his face. Then he holds up his wrist, checking the time on the golden watch that's so big with so many intricate details, I don't see how he can feel comfortable with it on. "I hate to cut this short," he says, dropping his hand and pushing it into his pocket as he looks at me again, "but I've got a plane to catch." He smiles apologetically. "Though, you know, Eli has his first match of the season in two weeks, a Thursday, in Roanoke? We could ride together if—"

"She's riding with me." The quiet anger in Eli's words makes me want to elbow him in the ribs, but I try to remember my own volatile relationship with Reece. He's a stepparent, but a parent all the same, and I don't bother hiding my disrespect of him most days, which leaves me with little room to scold Eli. Still, his dad has been nothing but nice which is certainly not how Reece would be, and I feel a little bad for Eric. He's trying, I think.

"But you're taking the bus," he says. "With the team." His brows are furrowed as he waits for his son's explanation.

I glance at him, kind of annoyed Eli didn't check with *me* about going to his first match in *Roanoke*.

"She's riding with me." Eli repeats himself but offers no explanation.

His dad clenches his jaw, and he looks like he's going to argue further, but instead he just says, shifting his gaze to me, "I hope I see you before then, but if not, I'll see you there. We could sit together."

I suddenly do not want to go to the match at all. It's not that Eric is unpleasant. In fact, he's the opposite. It makes me want to try harder to get him to like me, which stresses me out. Imagining sitting beside him for the duration of the night on some date two weeks into the future makes me feel dizzy.

But I just say, "Sounds great," because I was raised with a semblance of manners.

And after goodbyes are exchanged and Eric has gone through the garage to get to his car—the pretentious Tesla—I see what it is that broke. The shattering glass I heard upstairs.

There's a picture frame, empty, lying face down in the kitchen, by the island. Glittering shards of glass are scattered over the floor, and Eli's fingers wind around my wrist, yanking me away from it so I don't step on it, even though I'm in my shoes, on our way back from seeing Eric off.

My heart doesn't jump but I do, instinctively yanking my arm from Eli's grip as I spin to face him. He's staring at me, not at the glass on the floor.

"What happened?" I ask, cradling my arm, the one he grabbed. It didn't hurt. Just a reflex, probably made sharper by the sight of something like violence on the ground.

Eli's hair is just over his left eye, it seems wavier than usual, maybe from swimming yesterday, the chlorine styling his like it did mine. "Dad dropped it on his way in."

And no one cleaned it up? I guess it was probably forgotten whenever Eli told his dad there was a girl upstairs in his room at nine in the morning on a Saturday.

I turn toward it, intending to help pick up the mess. "What was the picture?" I ask, but before I can squat down to reach for the frame, Eli is grabbing me again.

This time, his grip is tighter, and he's more forceful when he yanks me away from the shattered frame, toward him. I try to pull out of his hold once more, angrier now, but he doesn't let me go.

"I'll deal with it," he says. "Then we can go get food."

"What the hell?" I shake my head, taking in the annoyance etched into the hard edges of his face. "What's wrong with you?"

His fingers are circled so tight around my wrist, it starts to ache. I don't try to yank away again though, and I'm not even sure why. We just glare at each other in silence.

Then, after a moment, Eli smiles. It's chilling, the abrupt shift in his facial expressions. "Nothing," he lies to me. "I just don't want you to get cut." He releases me all at once, so fast I don't immediately pull my arm away, and it just hangs there between us.

"You're lying." I know it's true. I tuck my arms by my sides, but don't look away from him. I don't like the way he grew so irritated with the frame, I don't like the things he's hiding from me. I know I do the same, so I'm trying to tolerate it, but these mood swings throw me off.

He studies me a long moment, glancing once at the glass on the floor, behind me. I have the urge to snatch up the frame and examine its contents, but I don't move, in case I miss something in his face.

"You were up for hours last night." He says the words softly.

I feel thrown off. For a second, I don't respond. Then… "You saw me?"

"I always see you."

I shake my head, my skin tingling. This is what he does. He changes the subject. He drops these quiet bombs, trying to turn the tables. I gesture toward the glass. "Stop deflecting. What the hell happened this morning?" I'm still thinking of his words, about watching me, but I don't want him to always get away with shit so easily.

Sighing, he lifts his gaze to mine. "I'm sorry," he says. "It's not you. It's Dad. We…" He trails off, and it feels practiced. I'm beginning to pick up on these things, better even than the first night. The way he forces pauses, has half-formed thoughts he lets drift, to make them seem real. Shaking his head once, slipping his hands into his pockets, he lifts one shoulder in a shrug. "We don't get along well." He swallows, then smiles, and the entire sequence of events feels rehearsed. "Let's go eat?"

I tip my chin, my eyes searching his. *You don't have to lie to me.*

His smile is still there, fixed to his face. Nothing wavers in his gaze, but it's like I hear his thoughts inside my head. *It's better if I do.*

I think of my own secrets, how fiercely I want to guard them while I steal all of his. Human nature isn't drenched in fairness. But I also know when to push, and when to let things go. Eli wasn't the only one born with an uncanny ability to *read* people. He's just far better at manipulation.

But I can try.

I smile, too. We're both full of shit. "Let's go eat," I agree.

"How long have you two known each other?" It sounds like a polite question meant only to take up space.

I look up from my drink, the melted ice and rum sloshing with Diet Coke, and into the dark eyes of Eli's cousin, Jasper. The guy I saw in the yearbook and thought looked familiar. I must've seen him at the tournament.

It seemed odd to me Eli and I would enjoy a drive with the windows down in his G35 all the way into Cary, the next city over, to grab doughnuts at a specialty shop—vegan included—and return to find half a dozen people here at barely eleven in the morning. The cars were parked in the circular driveway, and Dominic, Luna, Janelle, another girl, and Baca, the wrestler, were sitting on the back of their luxury vehicles when we pulled up. Jasper was still behind the wheel of his older model Jeep.

But then I realized what had happened as Eli's carefree mood of sharing sugar breakfast and knowing glances shifted as he aggressively backed into his garage.

He'd ripped off his seatbelt, yanked his phone from the center console, and called his dad.

I couldn't hear Eric's end of the conversation when Eli demanded to know what the hell he did, but the gist I got was Eric thought it would be "great" if he invited some of Eli's friends and his cousin over to hang out while Eric is away for work.

And here I thought I might like Eric.

Now, I take another drink, then one more, finishing the whole thing, only melting ice left as I set my plastic cup down at one of the tables surrounding the pool. There's a portable speaker on the table to our left, some song I don't know playing loud enough to drown out the sound of Luna laughing at something Eli says, the two of them in the shallow end of the pool with drinks in hand. The same place he almost drowned me. It feels like they're desecrating holy fucking ground there.

I squeeze the cup in my hand, noting Luna's white bikini at the same time I think of Eli's taste for white clothes.

He's wearing bright green swimming trunks, low on his hips, his skull and crossbones tattoo visible, and he's got his elbows propped behind him on the ledge of the pool, his gaze fixed on Luna, shielding her eyes from the sun with one hand, giant sunglasses pushed back on her head, holding her auburn hair in place.

There's not enough space between them.

I am irrationally annoyed.

Dominic disappeared inside a few minutes ago. He looked hungover or something, his eyes bloodshot, grunting a few words in greeting to all of us.

"Not long," I finally answer Jasper, dragging my gaze back to him. He's not as tall as Eli, but still far taller than me, especially now with the way he's standing under the umbrella spread over us, instead of sitting in a chair around the table like I am.

Jasper is the only guy outside with his shirt on, and it says Jackal's in pastel purple, a tire wheel meant to be spinning, kicking up dust after the "L". In white print beneath it are the words "Raleigh, NC," and I assume Jackal's is the garage Eli works at with his uncle sometimes.

Jasper runs his fingers through his hair, dark strands slick with sweat from the sun overhead. Despite the fact it's not even noon, it's almost uncomfortably hot. It probably wouldn't be so bad if I got in the pool, but Luna is in there, along with Baca, Janelle, and some other girl whose name I don't remember. They're both on the lacrosse team with Luna, but neither of them have really spoken to her much.

On the steps of the shallow end, they're drinking from bottles of water and in animated discussions with each other. Baca stands off awkwardly a few feet in front of them, his phone in hand. I'm not sure why Eric wrangled him here. Maybe he thinks the more people around, the better behaved his son will be.

I'm not so sure that's true.

"I just moved here, back in August," I continue with Jasper. His brown skin glistens in the sun, arms not quite fully hidden by the umbrella. I heard him speaking Spanish on his phone a few minutes ago, to his mom, based on my very terrible level of Spanish skills. I glance at him as he drags his gaze away from his cousin. I can't really tell if they get along well or not. They were cordial to each other when Eli introduced me, but he's since drifted away after we changed upstairs in his room, me in the bathroom and him in his bedroom.

He seemed annoyed and we didn't really speak. Still haven't since he hung up on his dad, aside from reluctant introductions to the people here I didn't know.

"You know Janelle?" Jasper asks, glancing at the label on his beer.

"Not really," I admit.

I dart a look at Janelle in the pool, and I see her eyes drifting from Jasper, who is oblivious.

"Janelle Nichols. She's nice. Easier to be friends with than Luna, trust me."

I smile. *I think they're crushing on each other.*

I glance at Eli, finding him still smiling at Luna who has pulled her sunglasses down. My eyes drift over her body. I know I shouldn't hate her because I'm jealous, and I keep trying to tell myself she could just be a really nice person, and she's dating Dom, but memories of her on top of Eli from Dominic's party come into my head, and I'm glancing at the glass doors leading inside, curious if Dominic has any more coke.

I could use a dose of happiness right now, but I'm not sure what to say to Dominic. If it's true, if investigators are starting to think his sister might be dead instead of missing, well… I can't imagine what's going on in his house right now, or inside his head.

"You're a senior?" I ask Jasper, dragging my gaze from the doors and taking a drink of the melted, rum-flavored ice from my cup.

"Yeah," he says, smiling at me. He drinks from his beer, and I notice he and Eli have the same eyebrows. Dark and perfectly arched, it's a crime girls don't usually get things like that. "You, too?"

I nod once, grateful I took my medication this morning. Otherwise, I'd be bouncing my leg and pacing, my heart racing with envy the longer Eli and Luna speak together easily in the pool. I clear my throat when I can think of nothing else to say to Jasper and stand, nodding toward the door. "I'm gonna get another one." I glance at the beer in his hand. "You want anything?"

Jasper shakes his head. "I'm good with this one." He lifts the bottle a little.

I force a smile and stalk off, head held high, knowing Eli

has a perfect view of my ass. I've got on my white cropped top, my one-piece underneath. Despite the shredded material, it's got a lot of coverage, but it's kind of hard to hide this ass, and I've seen Eli gawking at it more than once.

Keep your hands off of Luna, baby boy.

I close the door at my back, kicking off my Keds. I only put them on to protect the soles of my feet from the hot cement outside, and I take a deep breath in the cool air of Eli's house. I don't dare look over my shoulder, not wanting to see him sidled up close to Luna again, and instead, I head for the island where bottles of liquor are lined up. I saw Jasper bring in the six-pack of beer, Janelle the rum and vodka, and Dominic, surprisingly, brought the plastic case of water bottles.

I wonder if Eric knew the reinforcements he called in for me and his son would bring so much alcohol, or if he just doesn't care. But on some level, he has to, doesn't he? He cared we were alone here, and I don't know if he doesn't trust me or his son or neither of us, but he had a motive for inviting them all over.

I push it aside and grab a water bottle after I set my cup down. I twist off the cap, breaking the seal, and drink, sweat trickling down my back, little hairs stuck to my neck. I need to put my hair up, because it's way too damn hot to leave it all down, but my pins are upstairs.

Using a rubber band is out of the question, if the Addisons even have something so mundane lying around. It'll rip out too much of my hair when I take it out.

I drink half the water bottle, set it down, and reach for the rum. At the exact same time, I sense someone in the hallway, leading to the foyer.

I look up, and my eyes lock on Dominic's. I curl my fingers around the half-empty bottle of rum and pull it toward me, but I don't look away from Eli's childhood friend.

He's got his hands shoved into the pockets of his tan jacket, the collar up around his face. The jacket seems out of place, considering it's in the high eighties today, a real feel temperature probably closer to a hundred. But he's wearing black swimming trunks, and his feet are pushed into beige boat shoes. His entire outfit could be a mess, but somehow, maybe with his height or his lanky frame or even his bleached white, buzzed hair, he pulls it off.

The bloodshot look to his eyes, though, that's a little harder to make fit.

"Hi," I say, seeing a little of Sebastian as I look at him. Maybe it's why I soften toward him.

"You don't wanna break up the sexual tension between your boy and Luna?" he asks, jerking his chin toward the pool at my back.

Well. There goes my soft feelings. I break eye contact with him and screw off the lid to the bottle of rum, dumping it into my cup until it fills up a third of it. Too much, definitely, but the medicine will wear off soon, and in its wake, I'll have to feign calmness when I don't feel it. I twist the cap back on, and I take a big drink from the rum, wincing as it burns down my throat.

"You're dating her. Why don't *you* break it up?"

"We broke up." He says it like it's nothing, like they do it all the time. Then he steps further down the hall, coming to a stop across the gleaming white island from me. I place my palm on the marble, feel it's hot beneath my fingers from the sun streaming in. "You're just going to get fucking smashed, and it won't matter he's eye-fucking her, huh?"

I take another drink, not wanting to meet Dominic's bleary, blue gaze. The burn reaches into my stomach, and I realize the single doughnut I had in the car with Eli is not nearly enough to soak up the alcohol if that's even a real thing.

Finally, I can't force myself to have any more, not without getting sick, so I lower the cup, circling my hands around it and staring at what's left. "Is that what you're doing?" I keep my voice low, but the first drink I had is already hitting me, and these gulps won't be far behind. I feel a little bolder, and a lot curious, so I lift my gaze to Dominic, finding his nostrils flaring as I stare at him.

He shakes his head once, and I watch his throat roll when he swallows. "You don't know shit about me." I guess the comradery we built at his party is gone.

"Because you're so fucking open, right? Easy to get to know and all?"

Surprising me, after a tense moment, he smiles, rolling his eyes. "God, you are mean."

I press my fingertips into the plastic, feeling it flex beneath my touch. "I can be meaner." I flick my gaze up and down his body. "Rough night last night?"

He looks down his nose at me a moment, and I see the beginning of a pimple along his jawline. Somehow, it makes him more appealing. Human, maybe, or perhaps just rougher around the edges than his boat shoes might indicate. He seems to come to some sort of conclusion, because he grabs a beer, twists off the cap, and with a trembling hand, he brings the bottle to his lips, swallowing as he closes his eyes. Like he's found relief.

He slams the bottle down roughly and grips the ledge of the island with his free hand, staring at me. "Yeah. I went out."

I arch a brow. "Good for you."

He smiles, noting my condescending tone. "Fuck, Eden. I think you need to get laid." He lifts his beer, gesturing outside as his smile turns crueler, and I know what he's looking at. I refuse to turn around and see Luna and Eli in the pool. "Looks like he's about to."

I roll my eyes, throwing back more of my drink. "You aren't jealous? Not even a little?" I crunch ice between my teeth as I lower my cup.

Dominic snorts. "I've gotten used to it." He takes another drink, his eyes on me.

I think about Winslet. I want to bring it up. Her up. I'm sure that's why he's all fucked up. But I don't know what to say.

Before I have to grasp for anything, he steers us there all on his own. "Watching him flirt with my sister was far fucking worse."

My heart thumps hard in my chest. I think about how mad he was when I assumed Winslet and Eli had dated. I take a deep breath, trying not to appear too eager as I ask, "How's the investigation going?"

Dominic stares at the counter for a long moment. I'm worried I crossed a line, but he brought her up, right? I think. "What has he told you?" He finally counters my question with a question, his eyes cutting to mine.

"Not much," I say truthfully. I think of Eli's word in the car. *Murder.* Was it a slip? What am I missing? "You can talk about it, you know... if you want."

He nods once as he swallows, his throat rolling. "Appreciate it. I—"

His words are cut off by a giggle. A girl's laughter.

I clench my teeth, turning my head as flip-flops slap against the marble flooring, and Eli and Luna both appear around the corner, their arms tangled together. There's a bright smile on Luna's face even as her and Eli stop short, by the fridge, staring at us as if they didn't expect to find us here.

Eli isn't smiling. It's the only solace I take as Luna's smile hitches higher, her eyes darting from me to Dom.

"Oh, no, please," Eli says, wrapping his fingers around Luna's wrist as my gut twists. "Don't let me interrupt, Dom." His words are surprisingly cold, and my skin crawls. Out of the corner of my eye, I see Dom's gaze is fixed on both of his friends, too.

Eli leans against the doorway leading into the second living room, pulling Luna up against his side, a smile etched onto his handsome face, water dripping from both of them. His skin is gleaming brown from the sun, his hair wet and pushed back. There's an unlit joint between the fingers of his free hand.

I refuse to think about the fact so much of Luna's bare skin is touching his.

Instead, I twist around, looking over my shoulder, and I see

Jasper talking to the other girls, and Baca is off to the side, looking out of place.

"How did you—"

"There's more than one way in, Eden," Eli interrupts me, speaking in the same cold, detached voice. "But I'm really interested to hear what you two were chatting about."

Luna laughs a little but says nothing.

I turn back, my gaze darting between Dominic and Eli, staring at each other.

"I was really interested to see where *you two* were headed out there," Dom finally says, winking, forcing playfulness over his grief.

Irritation rushes through me. "Why don't you go back outside and fuck with Luna?" I snap, turning to focus on Eli, ignoring the girl he's clutching the wrist of.

"Don't talk about me like I'm not here—"

"Oh, I've done that enough this morning, don't you think, baby girl?" He smoothly talks over her, and she makes a noise of annoyance, clucking her tongue, but says nothing else. Does he always control them this way? Is it what he's trying to do to *me?*

The blood drains from my face. I feel unsteady, and I step closer to the island, gripping my cup so tightly I'm afraid the plastic is going to crack. If it does, I decide, maybe I'll cut him with it.

"You are such an asshole," Dominic mutters, his voice low.

"Says the asshole himself," Luna snaps back.

"And you're such a bitch." Dom growls those words, and it almost makes me feel a little better, the tension clearly still between him and Luna.

"I'm going to go," I say, trying to breathe. I don't want to be in this fucked up triangle.

Eli is still smiling at me. "You're not going anywhere."

Indignation has me feeling dizzy, and the rum probably doesn't help. "Excuse me?" I narrow my eyes, shaking my head, glancing at his tan fingers on Luna's pale skin. "Who the fuck do you think you are?"

Dominic laughs and I whip my head toward him, my annoyance growing. "Don't take it personally, Eden. Eli thinks the world bows at his feet. I'm surprised we're able to fit in this room together with his fucking ego and Luna's goddamn drama." He snarls the last words. "Anyway, come on, let's go back out. If you can't leave, I can at least help you get through the day until you sober up. Fuck these two." He doesn't wait for Eli to react, which is a good thing, because Eli doesn't.

"Fuck you, too," Luna snaps, but I think I hear hurt in her words.

Eli just keeps staring at me, impassive, as Dominic drains his beer, leaves the bottle on the island, then walks around it, toward me, and loops his arm through mine, spinning me around, toward the door.

It's only then, when Dominic touches me, I see the faintest flicker of emotion on Eli's face.

His jaw tightens, his eyes narrow, and the slightest frown pulls on the corner of his lips as he drops his hand from Luna's wrist.

But he doesn't say anything, and together, me and Dominic head outside into the heat.

Doing lines in the pool house is probably not at all what Eric Addison had in mind when he invited Dom and his friends over to keep Eli company. But I wipe the back of my hand over my nose, tasting battery acid in my throat, and glance at Dominic's bent head as he cleans up the table beside me, the coke disappearing into his nose.

He leans back, a smile on his flushed face, and offers me his fist.

I bump it, laughing as I drop my hand and my shoulder

brushes Dom's arm. Music is blaring from a speaker by Dominic's hand, controlled by his phone, something sexy I don't know, and I sway a little on the bench seat behind the table, glancing around the pool house. It's a long, narrow building made mainly of glass windows. The walls are white, the ceiling fan overhead black, and the table a dark wood, big enough to seat six or so people. There's a small day bed along the opposite wall, a soft gray with throw rugs and pillows, a beige rug on the floor.

At my back, there's a door that leads to the bathroom, and a wall just to my left with a door cut in it which apparently gives way to an actual bedroom, according to Dominic, but I haven't been in there.

"God, I needed that," Dom says, speaking faster than he was. He snorts, brushing his hand over his nose and swallowing as he leans back, grabbing one of the bottles of water in front of us.

I smile up at him, my phone face down and under my palm, I just texted Mom and let her know I'd be home later tonight.

I'm not sure I meant it.

"It was a long night."

I glance at the windows, noon sun high in the sky, hotter, too, it feels like. Maybe that's just my temper, because Eli is surrounded by the girls and his cousin, all of them still drinking, Baca sitting under an umbrella, still on his phone.

I don't know if Eli can feel my gaze on him or what, but he turns his head, his hair just over his eyes, and I know he's looking at me.

Dominic keeps talking at my side, clearly oblivious, probably because he's too busy smoking a cigarette, the scent of nicotine strong between us, smoke drifting into my vision, but I keep staring at Eli as Luna puts a hand on his chest, laughing. I wonder if she's trying to piss Dom off, or if she's in love with Eli.

"I don't even know why the fuck I'm here."

I can't resist latching onto that one. "Makes two of us," I say, eyes still on Eli. "You look like you should sleep."

There's a loaded silence between us, my pulse is hammering hard in my ears, the music is blaring, too.

Eli keeps his eyes on me as he wraps his arm around Luna's shoulders.

Jasper glances toward the pool house, the smile slipping from his face.

"Probably," Dom agrees with a short laugh. "Definitely shouldn't be here, my parents hate that shit."

"Why's that?"

Beneath the table, Dominic's knee knocks against my thigh. I vaguely register the touch. With the alcohol and blow, I feel fine at his nearness. It's just everything else that pisses me off.

"You're not going anywhere." Eli's words echo in my head. Why did he even want me to stay if he's just going to flirt with Luna all day? And did he purposefully bring her inside, around back, to piss me off? He should've let me leave. I know I was drunk, and maybe he didn't want me to drive home, but I could've gotten a ride or called Sebastian or something.

But no. Eli wanted me here.

I don't stop staring at him even as he finally turns his head, focusing on the girl whose name I forgot, telling some kind of crazy story, judging by the way she makes grand gestures with her hands, a cup in one.

"They think Eli knows what happened to Winslet," Dominic is saying, and I realize his voice is closer.

I suck in a breath, turning my head, elbows on the table and fingers clasped together in front of me, when I realize Dominic's mouth is only inches from mine, his eyes locked on my own. His thigh is pressed tight against mine beneath the table, and I smell tobacco and cologne with his nearness.

But I don't feel uncomfortable. I feel eager for information.

"His footprints were in the mud, by the lake, you know? Different tracks than the shoes he was helping search for her in."

"No. I don't know." I keep my voice low, and my gaze drops to Dom's mouth. *I can play these games.*

He smiles, his eyes on my mouth, too, then dragging back up. "Ask him about it sometime."

"Why don't you tell me?" I counter.

His grin widens as he shakes his head. "See what he says." His gaze is on my lips again. "It's interesting, checking out all the sides of Eli. Comparing notes. Stories." He glances through the glass windows, and I know what he sees when he adds, "He'd fuck Luna right in front of you and not think twice about it. Not to piss you off, or hurt you, you understand?"

No. No, I do not.

"But because when Eli wants something, he just takes it. The normal rules of human behavior don't apply to him. My parents are more than a little suspicious, to say the least." Dom swallows, licking his lips, the cigarette smoke curling between us, the stick between his fingers, his wrist resting against the table. "I don't know if he was born that way, but his mom really fucked him up, you know?" His arm comes around my back, parking on my opposite thigh, his fingers rough.

I shiver with his touch, sidling closer, and not because I want him. But I want the knowledge he has about the boy who refuses to tell me anything important about himself. Maybe I'm not so bad at manipulation, either. "No," I say honestly. "I don't know." *Tell me everything.*

Dominic's eyes look a little glassy, and he dips his head, pressing his lips to my shoulder.

I bite the inside of my cheek, resisting the urge to pull away. It feels good, on some base level, but despite the fact Eli is being a little shit, I don't actually want to hurt him.

Dominic doesn't bite my shoulder like Eli did. Instead, he runs his top lip over my skin, leaving a trail of cold air in the wake of his mouth.

I press my thighs together as his fingers squeeze my flesh. "That feels good," I murmur, licking my lips and smiling softly.

He leans in closer, tilting his head, his mouth inches from mine. "Does it?"

I glance at his mouth, my entire body alive. *Of course. But I just want to use you, Dom.* Not a shred of guilt burns through me. "Yeah," I whisper, leaning in toward him. We could kiss just like this. *"You* feel good."

Dominic grins, and I catch the scent of tobacco on his breath. It smells good, but not like cotton candy. *No one is like Eli.*

Instead of kissing me though, Dominic picks our conversation about Eli's mom back up, almost like he's stuck on him, too.

"You know she left him? Went halfway around the world and started a whole new family without him." Dominic sounds pissed about it. I see it, their friendship, in the strangest ways. Protective of each other, but willing to piss one another off without a second thought.

"How did she die?" I ask, guessing it was after she left, my voice rough as Dominic turns his head and keeps kissing his way up my shoulder, closer to my neck. I tilt it, giving him access, and it *does* feel good. But I focus on the information. *Secrets.* "His mom?"

I don't dare look at Eli. He's probably not looking at me, anyway, so I know it doesn't matter. I can get the answers I need, and I can get away from Dominic.

But with my question, he stops inching closer to my throat, and instead picks his head up, his lake blue eyes locked on mine, his pupils wide and dilated. "Die?" His dark brows dip together, and he pulls me closer by my hip, shifting me on the bench so my body is against his.

I feel as if the floor is tilting beneath my feet, just grazing the hardwoods. Dizziness makes the room spin a little, and I rest my head on my clasped fingers, not daring myself to speak.

"His mom isn't dead, Eden. She's remarried, living in Athens."

. . .

I don't remember getting up. I don't know if I said anything to Dominic or not, and I don't remember flinging open the door of the pool house and stepping outside, cement hot beneath my bare feet. I don't recall seeing Eli leave the pool, either, but he's dripping wet, meeting me right at the entrance to the pool house, blocking my view of everyone else in the water, shielding me from the sun, his shadow thrown over my body.

He smells like chlorine and coconuts and something fruity I hate to think is Luna, but I don't mention any of that.

"You lied to me." My words are quick and low, and I see the beer bottle dangling from his fingertips, spinning in his hand as he stares at me, his expression unreadable. Water cuts down his nose, dripping off the slope of it. It snakes in rivulets across his hard chest, down the lines of his abs. I ignore how good he looks, and smells, and the chips of emerald in the dark green of his eyes, his lashes long and wet. "You *lied* to me."

I hear someone at my back, but neither Eli nor I look at Dominic.

"Your mom isn't dead." I sound like I'm pleading, even to my own ears.

Eli says nothing, his beautiful lips pressed together as he stares at me.

"Why did you lie to me?" I try to keep my voice calm, but my heartbeat is everywhere, and I want to shove him. I settle for digging my nails into my palms, swallowing down the bitter taste still lingering from the coke in my veins.

Eli finally lifts his gaze from mine, to look at Dominic at my back.

Dominic speaks first. "You made this easy for me," he says, sounding a little amused. "We really should keep track of what secrets we're sharing. Maybe which girls too." I feel him step closer, and a second later, his hand comes to my hip.

This time, unlike the last times he's touched me, I do flinch, mainly because I'm surprised.

But Eli registers the movement, and a smile pulls on his lips.

It makes me feel sick. And in the split second it takes for me to realize why, Eli is already moving. He pushes past me, and I spin around, unsteady as I stumble back a few steps. Eli drops the bottle in his hand, and it shatters on the concrete, amber glass scattering into pieces.

Eli launches his fist into Dominic's face, and I hear the horrifying crunch of bone the second before blood explodes from Dom's nostrils, pouring over his lips, down his chin. The force of the blow sends Dominic backward, his head smacking against the glass door of the pool house hard enough it seems to shake the entire structure.

Someone cries out, maybe Luna, but there's a stranger silence in the backyard as everyone watches Eli's violence.

Dominic's hands are over his nose, trying to stop the flow of blood, and my pulse screams in my ears. I think I need to do something, but I don't know what. It doesn't seem like anyone else is going to do anything. I think they're all still in the pool, but I'm too stunned to look away as Eli snatches Dominic's wrist, twisting it as he yanks it away from his face.

Dominic cries out in pain, blood all over his face, Eli's back muscles pulled taut as his fingers curl around Dom's throat. He tilts his head up, knocking it back against the glass again, Dominic's blood dripping over Eli's hand.

He presses his body close to Dominic's, almost in an intimate way as he stares down at him. Dom is pinned to the glass, and Eli's shoulders heave as he breathes, snatching both of Dom's wrists in his free hand and holding him down between them, even as Dominic struggles to get free.

With the pinch Eli has on his jaw, under his chin, he stops fighting after a moment. I think he knows Eli could make him lose consciousness with that hold.

"You feelin' good, Dom?" Eli asks, his voice quiet.

I realize someone has turned down the music out here, and

only the thud of bass sounds from inside the pool house, a distant noise that doesn't drown out Eli's words.

I take a step toward them, but not another.

Dominic doesn't answer, his eyes closed.

Eli shoves his head against the door again, loud enough I swear it sounds like something cracks. Dominic's eyes fly open as he swallows.

"I asked you a question." I can only see Eli's side profile, but I know his lips are pulled into a smile.

It's chilling, seeing him so alarmingly aggressive with a psychotic smile on his face as Dom bleeds on him. And the way no one steps in... it's almost like they've done this dance before.

"No," Dominic finally says, the word quiet and forced.

Eli smiles, leaning down closer, until his mouth is inches from Dom's, close to the sticky blood on his face. "If you ever touch her again, you're gonna be feeling a lot worse than this, okay?" He asks the question as if he's speaking to a small child.

Dominic swallows, and I can almost taste the iron in sympathy. He glances at me, but Eli jerks his chin toward him, capturing Dom's attention again. "Nah. Eyes on me, all right?"

Dominic nods slowly, as much as he can with Eli's death grip.

"And if you ever give her coke again." Eli's smile widens, and he steps even closer, no space between the two of them, and I know Dominic can feel Eli's breath against his lips. "I promise I'll kill you."

Dominic doesn't make the mistake of looking at me again.

I realize I'm digging my nails so hard into my palms I think I'm bleeding, a sharp pain in my hands, but I don't look.

"Now, you think you're ready to get on your knees and fucking apologize to me?"

"*Eli.*" It's a hiss of a word, from someone in the pool. It's not Luna, I don't think, but it was a feminine voice.

Eli doesn't respond.

Dominic's nostrils flare, and I swear I see tears in his eyes.

My throat feels tight, and I know I *should* stop him, or *someone* should do *something*, but I don't move.

There's a part of me waiting to see how deep Eli has his claws in Dominic. How far his friends would be willing to go for him, to stay on his good side. The fact no one physically tries to stop him seems to mean something about Eli's influence.

The fact *I* don't stop him seems to mean I'm caught in his web too.

Dominic tries to pull his hand from Eli's grip on his wrists, but Eli just smiles, and it looks as if he exerts minimal effort to keep Dom in his grasp.

Knocking his head back against the glass door of the pool house, blood crusted over his lip, flecked on his chin, Dom closes his eyes. "Fuck you," he says, but the words are shaky and hoarse, and they lack any punch at all.

I take a step closer to them, and Eli doesn't look at me, but I know his words are for my ears when he says, "It's okay, baby girl. He's a big boy."

I narrow my eyes into slits, glaring at the side of Eli's head, but I don't say anything.

Dominic's throat rolls beneath Eli's hand, Eli's fingertips digging into his flesh. Dom's eyes are squeezed shut, his face red and wet with tears.

"You had no problem being all over Eden, but now you can't even look at me?" Eli's words are so strangely sweet, if I heard them through a phone, I might think he was genuinely forlorn.

But I know better, and the contrast between how he speaks and what he means is eerie. I can feel everyone watching us, but still, no one moves or says another word, and it's unnerving, too.

In class, Eli is so polite. So mild-mannered. I've noticed the flash of violence in his eyes when that girl kicks his chair, but he doesn't ever scold her, or cut his eyes to her, or anything at all. He's so... fucking charming to the world.

Now, he's *this*.

And no one is surprised at the abrupt shift in his demeanor. It must not be the first time he's switched from calm to carnage in the blink of an eye.

Once more, Dominic tries to shrug out of Eli's grip, his eyes flashing open, but this time, Eli releases his throat and bars his forearm against it, driving Dominic further back against the glass with a *thud*. Eli lifts his arm, marginally, forcing Dom's chin up, his throat to arch, and he's looking up at Eli.

"Don't touch her again," Eli whispers, a smile pulling on the corners of his mouth as he croons the words. "Don't give her fucking drugs again. Don't even look at her too long, ever again. This is different. *Okay?*"

Dominic presses his lips together, crimson crusted on the corners, over the cupid's bow. I see Eli's hand, curled into a fist and grazing Dom's shoulder. Blood coats Eli's knuckles.

"I'm sorry," Dom whispers, and the words are croaked. His face turns a violent shade of red. He closes his eyes, then opens them again, looking at Eli. "I'm sorry, I…" He must see something in Eli's expression, because he doesn't offer an excuse, instead letting it trail off. He dips his chin, looking at the ground. "I'm just sorry."

For a second, Eli just looks at him, smirking, basking in the satisfaction of Dom's submission.

Then he lowers his arm from Dom's throat, and I watch Dominic take a deep breath as Eli pulls back.

Something like relief floods through me, warm and light.

Until Eli leans in close, whispering in Dom's ear, his voice low, but loud enough I can hear him. "Good boy," he says softly. "Now get on your fucking knees."

"No." Dom shakes his head, his eyes still on the ground, but he doesn't kneel. "No, man. Fuck that. This is fucking… *You were fucking with my girlfriend!*" He snaps his head up, the fight back in his eyes, and I see his jaw clench as he searches his friend's gaze for… something. "You were fucking with my girlfriend and—"

"I don't think you should argue with me, Dom." The way Eli says the words, so pleasantly, it's like he's taunting Dominic with some sort of strange threat I don't understand.

Dom's chest is heaving, rising and falling so fucking fast as he glares at his so-called friend.

And then, I don't know if it's because he's drugged up, or because he's *fucked* up, dealing with Winslet's disappearance and his parents and everything that comes with it, or because the threat worked, but shocking me, in what feels like slow motion, Dominic, hanging his head and without more arguing, as if he's compelled by every word Eli speaks, sinks to one knee, pressed against the concrete, then the other.

And Eli still doesn't release his wrists, forcing Dom's arms up with the position he's taken, kneeling.

Secondhand humiliation thrums through me, and I take one more step closer.

This time, Eli doesn't say anything to me.

He just takes Dominic's wrists in both hands, and presses Dom's palms to his lower abs, Dominic's fingers splayed, covering part of Eli's tattoo.

Dom hangs his head, and I realize the heel of his hands are dangerously close to something of Eli's I don't want him to touch.

I swallow the lump in my throat and find my voice. "You wanna dick measuring contest now?" I ask, my words sharp as I stare at Eli, still smiling down at Dominic as blood drips from the latter's nose, splattering on the cement. "I could get the ruler and count the inches."

There's a small laugh behind me, from one of the girls, Janelle, I think, and I'm grateful for it. This moment is sick, and I want to get Eli alone.

His mom is alive and he's fucking deflecting with torturing Dom.

Eli turns his gaze to me, and I'm struck by the intensity in his eyes.

Frozen to the spot, all my snappy remarks get stuck in my throat.

"You're not touching anyone's dick but mine." He speaks coldly, and more than what he said, I'm shocked about *where* he said it.

Here. In front of his friends and his cousin.

Dom's shoulders shake and I blink, realizing in the midst of my fight with Eli, he's crying. He's still staring at the ground as he says, "I'm sorry, please just let me go." It sounds like a plea, broken and hoarse, and I know he wants to get out of here as much as I want to get Eli alone. "Just let me fucking go."

Eli keeps staring at me. He doesn't say a word.

"Let me fucking go, man," Dom sobs, lifting his head. I notice it out of the corner of my eye, see the way Dom presses his fingertips into Eli's lower abs, but he doesn't dare scratch him. "I'm fucking sorry, okay? Please let me go."

Let him go, let him go, let him go.

You made me drag this out. I swear I can *hear* Eli say those words inside his head, that cocky fucking smirk on his face, his full lips curved upward. *You did this to him.*

He stretches it out. Longer, and longer, and before I can figure out what to say to make him stop, he finally hauls Dom to his feet, only to shove him against the glass door again. Dom snaps his head up, his gaze wary as he stares at Eli.

Eli presses his temple to Dom's. "You look pretty on your knees," he says softly, and I hold my breath, waiting for him to say something about his sister.

Don't, don't, don't.

But I realize, maybe, that was all in my own twisted head, because all Eli asks is, "And now you're going to go home, right?"

Dominic looks defiant for one second. Two. But after a long, long moment, in which I want to scream at him to just agree, he nods.

Eli does, too, and he says, cheerfully, "Good talk." Then, all at once, he releases Dom, who sags against the door. But Eli doesn't wait for him to leave like I thought he would.

Instead, his eyes cut to mine as he spins around, and he closes the space between us in seconds, grabbing my wrist.

When I recoil, he narrows his eyes. "Get over yourself, baby girl." He yanks me close to him and puts his arm around me, pulling me close to his side, and I'm amazed his skin is so fucking cold. I'm too stunned to even look and see if everyone is still in the pool, and no one says a word as Eli walks me toward his house, pulling open the door with an ease that confuses me, especially when he shoves me through it, slamming the door behind us and flipping the lock.

My stomach hurts.

I turn to look at him, but his hand plants at the base of my spine and he's pushing me into the kitchen island, sliding his palm up until it rests at the base of my neck. He presses down, hard, my body bent over as he comes to stand behind me, his fingers rising higher and knotting painfully in my hair.

"Didn't you want me to hurt you, Eden?"

My palms are splayed on the cool marble counter, my elbows bent, and I try to push back, against his grip in my hair, but his other hand comes to my hip and squeezes, his body pressing into me, his dick hard against my ass.

I still, frozen as he grinds his hips against me.

"Answer my goddamn question."

I stare at the bottles of alcohol littered over the countertop, and in my head, I see him with Luna. I find my voice again. "You lied to me, and all day you've been flirting with *her.*"

He leans over me, his weight causing the edge of the countertop to dig sharply into my hips. His breath is over my ear, sending shivers down my spine as he twists his fingers in my hair, jerking my neck back. "I'm not sure I see the problem here."

"Fuck you." The words leave my lips before I can think of anything else to say. I shove off from the counter again, or try to, but he doesn't let me.

"I'd love to, but you're so jumpy every time I reach for you, I'm not sure you'd live through me *fucking* you—"

"Shut the fuck up." My voice breaks and I squeeze my eyes closed, humiliation burning through my face. I think of last night, and how stupid he probably thought it was. How he's probably been fucking Luna even since we've met, and how I didn't go far enough for him. "You're such an asshole. Just shut. *Up.*"

It's only a second later I realize my mistake.

He pulls me away from the counter, spins me around, and lifts me up so I'm sitting on the island before I can even blink. He's between my thighs, his hand gripping my jaw just like he held Dominic, his other pinning my arm down. I can feel his chest heaving between us, and I mean to grab his arm and force his hand off of my throat, but instead, my palm finds his heart, and I feel the steady rhythm beneath my fingers, his cool skin hard under my touch.

"Are we still playing the same game?" he asks quietly, his lips moving over my mouth as his fingers tighten along my jaw. "Because if we are, tell me to shut up again. This time, I think I can give you exactly what it is you've been begging me for."

I feel like I'm suspended in time. My breaths come in heavy pants, our lips touching. He digs his fingertips tighter, just on the underside of my bones. His eyes are blank and empty, and in this moment, it's like I don't know who he is anymore.

I like to think I'm the only person in the world he wouldn't hurt. But now I'm not so sure. Play with fire long enough, and no matter how skilled you are, you'll end up getting burned. But the problem is, I think I like how it feels.

And maybe I shouldn't keep stoking it, but I can't stop myself. My own emotions are too loud inside of me, and in some strange way, it feels good to *feel*. "You have the guts to do it now?" I glance at his mouth, pressing my lips even closer to his, so he feels every word as I snarl, "Took you long enough."

He's still gripping my face but doesn't react to my words. Not immediately. I don't know what I'm waiting for. Is he going to hit me? Is it what I want? I glance at his fingers, wrapped around my jawline, and try to imagine him intentionally hurting me with that hand. I see flecks of crimson on his knuckles, from Dom.

What if it was *my* blood? How would he feel then?

When he finally speaks, he drags my attention back up, to his face.

"You're going to hate it," he says, like he's reading my mind. His words are a vicious whisper, as if he's fighting with someone besides me.

Himself.

"The only thing I hate," I say through clenched teeth, my body like a livewire beneath his hands, "is when you act like a person I don't know."

He stares at me, his eyes locked on mine, his fingers no less tight around my jaw and my wrist, but as he studies me, it's like the touch becomes less angry and more desperate. Like he's holding on.

Even outside, amidst the bullshit and lies and choking levels of testosterone between him and Dom, he had my back in his own twisted way. I know that.

"If you ever give her coke again, I promise I'll kill you."

"You're upset about something." I press harder against his heart. "I want you to be a big boy and tell me what it is."

His twisted smile makes another appearance as he cocks his head, running his mouth over mine, his breath so sweet. "A big boy, huh?" He drags his lips up my jawline, over my ear. I feel the faintest pinprick of pain as he bites down on one of the piercings in my lobe, tugging softly.

The little hairs over my entire body stand on end as I suck in a breath, holding it.

"Is that what you want?" He licks his way up the line of my piercings, and I tense, the one in my cartilage still sore. But he doesn't bite it, like he knows. Instead, his tongue flicks along the metal softly, making me squirm.

"Eli." It's half a whisper, half a moan.

"Yeah?" He kisses the tip of my ear, sending shivers shooting through my core. "You want me to be good for you?"

I widen my thighs, letting him step closer, flush against me, no space between us. He still doesn't release my arm, though, and I know I'm in no position to physically fight back, if I wanted to.

As it is, I just want him to give into me. I want him to *open. Up.*

"I want you to be honest," I tell him, my mouth against his cheekbone. "They don't have to be the same thing."

He smiles, and I feel the shape of it on my skin. "They usually aren't."

I press my lips to his face in a soft kiss, even as my heart is like a jackhammer in my chest. "Be bad, baby boy." I hear his breath hitch. "But don't lie to me."

A moment passes between us. Quiet but full of loud tension, tight enough I feel the string of it wrapped around my heart, tugging sadistically, making it hard for me to even remember *how* to breathe, let alone actually do it.

I think he's forgotten, too, and when I realize my words matter again to him, I remember the boy from last night. The one who played with my hair. Who nudged his nose with mine. The boy who promised not to hurt me.

And a second later, when I feel dizzy and nervous and *eager*, he releases my wrist, reaching for my ass, pulling me even closer to him on the island.

He picks his head up, and before I can blink, his mouth is over mine. He releases his grip on my throat, grabbing my thigh hard enough to bruise. I'm overwhelmed, my fingers trembling and clumsy and aching, but I grab at his dick, over his swimsuit, unsure of what exactly to do, but I stroke my hand over how hard he is. How thick and long beneath my hand, the wet material of his swim trunks cold in contrast to his heat here.

I want this. I want him. The rest we can figure out later, can't we? I want his attention on me. I want to be his focus.

He moans against my mouth as I stroke him. I know I'm

probably doing it fucking wrong, but I don't care. I don't care about the glass doors, either. The people watching.

I don't care.

It doesn't matter.

I let him go and reach for the strings of his swim trunks, fumbling with them with both hands. It takes me a moment as he kisses me, our mouths opening and closing in unison, but I get them loose enough to push my hand in. My fingers are around him, soft and hard all at once, and I'm taken aback at how big he feels in my hand, but I'm not sure if I should squeeze it tight or loose or—

He snatches my wrist before I can decide, prying me off of him as he yanks my arm behind my back. I have to shoot my other palm out to the warm marble of the island to steady myself.

I look up, surprised, and he smiles.

It's deranged, wicked, just like the smile he gave Dom when he was threatening him. The boy from last night is gone all over again.

"You want me to be bad?" There's a warning in his words.

I swallow, hard, rethinking my own. *Do I?* Yes. *Yes.* I want to *feel* something. I want to feel him, everywhere. But…

But…

The angle he twists my wrist behind my back brings a gasp up my throat, but I swallow it down, not letting him know the way it hurts, sharp and aching. I don't try to pull away and I don't tell him to stop. It reminds me of the three letters I carved into my skin. The *feeling*.

Euphoria tinged with hurt. *I crave this.*

His hand comes to the cutout of my swimsuit, fingers yanking, pulling at the fabric, exposing me between us. He drops his gaze, and I bite my lip, my face hot from being uncovered and the pain lancing up my hand. But I don't want him to know he's hurting me. *I don't want him to stop.*

"Yes," I whisper, answering his question as he drinks me in. *"Be bad for me."*

He smiles, shaking his head, but not meeting my eye. My heart does somersaults in my chest.

"You're everything I've ever dreamed of," he says quietly, like he means it. His tongue is between his teeth as he stares at me, my chest heaving as I try to keep breathing. His swimsuit is pulled down just enough to expose the head of his dick, and I see white stuff beaded on the tip. *Precum.* I know the word, at least.

I shift my thighs, spreading myself wider to him, trying to not think about the way he can see almost everything even as I give it to him readily.

His eyes drag up the length of my body, resting on mine. His chin is tilted down, his lips parted. "I didn't think anyone like you ever... existed."

I feel power soar in my veins, like I'm on top of the world. Holding his attention, claiming it, using it... *it feels good.* "I'm not a dream," I tell him, keeping the soreness throbbing through my wrist from edging into my voice. "I'm a nightmare, *just for you.*"

His smile pulls wider, and it feels a little like he's mocking me. "You want it right here? Just like this, nightmare girl?" He steps closer, and my hips arch off the counter. The tip of his cock is pressing against me, our bare flesh connected.

I whimper at the feel, aching for him. I don't let my gaze drift over his shoulder, through the glass doors.

My heart drums too fast in my chest even as I feel spent. For a second, I think it's from the fight. From the longing. The fucking *agony.* It could be all of that, but as I inhale, trying to think clearly to answer his question, the bitter taste in the back of my throat reminds me what I'm really feeling.

It's the coke. I already want more.

I try to shield Eli from that truth as the silence stretches between us, and he waits for an answer, rocking his hips softly, making me want him more, too. Eli and coke, they're both dangerous drugs.

"Right here," I repeat his words back to him, my wrist still bent from the grip of his hand, but I don't tell him it hurts. "Like this." I don't care about the concept of *virginity*. There's just never been a time and a place before, never someone I wanted, until Nic, and he was an uptight asshole. *Or I was an insane, crazy girl.*

But Eli is crazy too.

His breath is ragged, and he doesn't stop moving over me, making me moan, the softest sound. His eyes darken as he smiles, like he's proud of himself for getting me to make that noise. He presses his thumb into my inner thigh and his fingers wrap around my flesh.

But I know something is wrong, the way he twists my wrist even more, wringing me out like a crumpled washcloth.

I bite my tongue, refusing to concede to him. Instead, I reach up for his arm, unstable on the counter, I have to wrap my legs around him to keep myself steady.

"Eli, no more." The words are torn unwilling from my mouth, because I *don't* want him to stop, but he clearly wants me to. He wants to make it hurt more than I can stand.

"No more?" he mimics me, his voice cold. "Why?" He moves his hand from holding back the fabric of my swimsuit by my thigh, wrapping his fingers around his cock instead, using the bottom of his hand to push down his swimming trunks enough to free himself.

He guides his erection to me, slapping between my thighs with it. My swimsuit is in the way again, but he's so fucking close, my heart pounds painfully in my chest.

"You want me to fuck you just like this, don't you? That's what you just said. This is how you want it to be. Your very first time, and you don't care all of my fucking friends are watching."

Confusion and anger build a knot in my throat. My forearm is turned at an awkward angle, still behind my back. He brings the tip of himself against the edge of my swimsuit, shifting it. Our bare skin touches, the precum smearing against me. *So close.* I can only stare down at us with horror as he guides the head of his cock up and down me. Warmth flushes in my core, I'm glistening wet, but this isn't how I imagined it'd be. Rough and dangerous, maybe, but with the blunted edge of sweetness.

There's nothing sweet in his cruelty now.

He's hurting me, intentionally, after he promised me he wouldn't.

I try to pull my hand from his grip, but he only tightens his hold, driving my knuckles down into the marble, amplifying my discomfort. I look up as he pushes further against me, shaking my head, unable to speak.

"I thought you wanted me to show you the bad?" he asks, and his psychotic smile is back. "You're so fucking wet, it wouldn't take much, virgin or not." He angles his hips again, pushing downward, and I gasp at the feel of him starting to stretch me.

I drop my legs from around him, trying to inch back, but he winds his fingers in my hair again, no longer needing to hold back the fabric of my swimsuit.

His mouth comes over mine.

"Tell me to stop. Tell me again."

I close my eyes, feeling my pulse points along my wrist at my back. "You don't need me to tell you. You're not stupid, baby boy. Use your context clues."

"Tell me to fucking stop, Eden." He sounds so angry.

I don't want to give in though. "What happened?" I gasp out the words. "This morning, with your dad, what happened? Why are you acting out? You're trying so hard to push me away. What. *Happened?*"

He drags his mouth over mine, in something not quite a kiss. "You sound so smart when you talk like that."

My stomach cramps, waiting for his verbal blow.

"You *are* so smart." He pushes his hips further against me, causing heat to flood my core, wanting him, hating him, feeling both things so sharply all at once. "I just don't understand why you haven't figured it out by now."

"Figured *what* out, Eli?" I hold his gaze, his nose aligned with my own.

He looks like he's searching for an answer I don't have. And before I can say anything else, before I can bring him back to the boy he was, he's releasing me. Completely. He pulls up his swimsuit, tying the string with steady fingers as he takes a step back, glancing at me, still exposed for him.

It takes me a moment to blink through what he's done, how I'm left, the feeling returning to my fingers, which had grown numb from his hold.

I take a breath, sitting up straighter, slowly bringing my arm back around to my front, adjusting my one piece with my other hand, swallowing down my humiliation.

"You want to know what's wrong with me?"

I don't speak, knowing he isn't done.

"You are." He takes another step back, his chest heaving. "Because I *always* behave this way." He seems to have lost some of his arrogance. I think about Dom's comment about his ego. I would have agreed with him then. But now, Eli's words seem raw, real. The problem is I can't tell when he's performing and when he's himself. I don't know if there's ever actually a difference. "Dominic tried to warn you, didn't he? My dad, too. It's why he invited everyone here. No one wants me to be alone with you, because everyone knows you're too good for me."

I don't argue with him, even though a denial is on the tip of my tongue. I cradle my hand to my chest and remind myself he just hurt me.

He glances down at my wrist, and I see a flicker of something in his eyes. Regret? Anger? Surprise? Grief? I don't know, and he doesn't apologize.

"I think you should go," he says quietly, still staring at my hand.

I'm speechless, a flood of emotions dumping down on me at once.

There's a knock on the door, a pounding, urgent, but

neither of us look. He's gazing at my hand and I'm staring at him, unable to break away.

"Eli." It's the only thing I can say.

"No." The word is cold. Finally, he drags his gaze up to meet mine. He smiles again, and I realize how much I hate this version of him. "You need to leave."

I have to look away, I have to breathe. My eyes find the floor, and I think of the shattered frame this morning. "What changed?" My words are hoarse, and I squeeze my wrist, relishing in the pain. "From last night, when we fell asleep, even this morning in the bathroom, to… to the picture frame—"

"Let's not talk about that."

There's another knock on the door. Frantic. A man's voice. "Eli! Open up!"

We both ignore his cousin.

"No," I say, still staring at the floor. "We're going to talk about it." I slide down from the counter, onto my feet, but I don't turn toward him. I piece together Dom's words about his mom. The pale band of skin on his dad's ring finger. "She left you, didn't she?" I know I shouldn't poke, and not right now, like this, but I need to know. If his mother is between us in this way, even when she's in a country across the sea, I need to understand what I'm dealing with. "When did she leave? Why didn't you tell me?"

"Eden…" His words are a whisper.

"You can talk to me about these things, you know. You can tell me the truth. I'm not going to wield it as a weapon against you later—"

"Eden. Please just let this go—"

"Did she leave without saying goodbye?" I force myself to meet his eyes, and I see his are closed. It stabs at my heart. Has no one ever fought for him before? Has no one ever pried? "Did she hurt you? Have you seen her since she—"

"Stop."

"—left? Do you talk to her—"

"I'm asking you nicely to shut the fuck up, baby girl." His eyes fly open, locked on me. I'm vaguely aware the knocking on the door has ceased, but I don't break eye contact with Eli.

"I don't need a confession of undying love here, but I need you to communicate with me about important things like your mom being very much *alive*—"

He closes the space between us and puts his hand over my mouth, not painful, but enough to jolt me into silence. I blink, jerking my head back, but his grip tightens. "Stop. Talking."

I'm still clutching my hand, but I try to turn my head to get free.

He presses his fingers softly into the side of my jaw. "Shh, okay?"

I glare at him, breathing loudly through my nose.

"Let this go. *I'm not giving you this.*" He studies me for a moment, and like everything else he does, it feels practiced. "Anything else is yours. The world if you want it. *But not this.*"

With a violent twist, a crick in my neck enough to zip bolts of lightning down my spine, I jerk my head free of him. "No." I nod toward him, still reluctant to let go of my hand. "That's not how this is going to go."

"I think I told you it is." His words are measured, calm and cold. "I don't want to hurt your feelings." He doesn't sound at all like he means it. "I need you to get away from me." His chest rises and falls steadily, there's not even a muscle in his jaw clenched.

Maybe it's what makes me keep pushing. "You're not shutting me out like this." I step closer, and he steps back, his spine against the glass door. "You're going to talk to me and you're going to tell me—"

Without a word, he grabs my throbbing arm again, higher up over my elbow, dragging me to him, but I clamp my teeth together, refusing to show him how much he hurt me.

"Eden. *Get out of my house.*"

Shame knots in my stomach. Rejection stings, and right now, it's over every inch of my skin. I want to say something else. Run my mouth a little more. But the urge to duck and leave and never look back seems stronger.

He releases me and I stumble back even though he doesn't shove me away. That's all me.

I'm about to turn and go. I see the actions in my head. Turn around. Go upstairs. Grab my bag. Head out the front door. Hop in my car. Drive home. The sequence of events is in order.

But instead of doing what I should, I spin around to the counter closest Eli, and yank off the first breakable thing I can find. The fucking coffee pot.

I hurl it at him, and he sidesteps it, so it crashes into the door, shattering into pieces, the sharp sound ringing in my ears.

Eli turns to stare at it, slowly, watching the glittering shards litter the floor. The second time today such a mess has graced this house.

My chest is heaving, and I feel a little better, seeing Eli appraise the broken glass.

I back up a step.

Then one more.

And just as I'm really ready to go, my dramatic exit secured, Eli looks at me.

His lip curls, and a second later, *he lunges for me.*

My heart almost leaps right out of my chest, but before I can move or defend myself, before he even connects with me, hands grab my shoulders and yank me backward, and three bodies meet Eli, shoving him against the wall beside the patio doors.

"What the fuck are you doing?" Dominic's voice in my ear doesn't break my eye contact with Eli.

We're locked on each other even as Janelle, Jasper and Baca all keep Eli pinned to the wall. I see a vein in his neck pulsing, his clavicle straining beneath his skin as he stares at me.

"I had to pick the lock to the garage door," Dom keeps

talking, sounding breathless. "There used to be a spare key under the mat, but some asshole moved it."

I'm still staring at the asshole. Janelle is nearly as tall as he is, and she looks over her shoulder at me, momentarily obstructing my view. Her eyes are on me. "I think you should go."

Those words hurt, and I'm not sure why. Like *I'm* the problem here. Like *I'm* the one making Eli into *this*.

Dominic drags me backward, grabbing my injured hand so hard a scream *finally* leaves my mouth.

Eli's eyes widen, a raw vulnerability etched in his face. It catches me off guard, stealing my breath, as if when *I* hurt, *he* hurt. He lunges forward again, nearly throwing all three bodies off of him, Jasper saying his cousin's name, Baca telling him to chill out.

"Dominic," Eli says, sounding far calmer than he is. "Let go of her hand or I'll fucking ruin yours."

Dom releases me at once, and I snatch my hand toward my body, but I don't look away from Eli, and he's doing the same to me, no longer fighting to get free now Dominic isn't hurting me anymore.

I don't understand you. I want to scream it at the top of my lungs.

No one does. I swear I see the whisper of just those words in his eyes.

"Let's go," Dom says quietly.

"Where's Luna?" I still hold Eli's gaze. His lips pull into a smile with my question, and it makes my stomach drop. Shaking my head, I turn away from him, pushing past Dom. "Never mind." I mutter it under my breath before I head up the stairs, grab my things, and get in my car. Dominic is at my driver's side door, my window down as I put the Sentra in reverse.

"Do you need me to follow you home?"

I consider him a moment, blue eyes glittering from the sun even as he shields them with his hand, his brow furrowed.

I think about how good it would feel to hurt Eli back.

But that's the thing. The difference between us.

It wouldn't feel good for me at all.

"No." I reverse, then throw my car in drive, and leave without a glance back, my fingers trembling on the wheel. But when I turn out of his driveway, I see it.

Luna's car is still there, and I don't have to think too hard about what they might do tonight.

23

Eli

I SHOULD TELL HER, and I know that. But when I pick up my phone from underneath Luna's elbow, tangled in the sheets of my bed, I decide I won't. Nothing good will come of it, because I've found honesty is rarely *ever* the best policy.

I slowly get up, glancing over my shoulder to see Luna's face buried in my pillows, her back rising and falling softly, her swimsuit on the floor of my bedroom.

I clench my fingers tight around my phone and think about waking her up, getting her out of my house, but I don't want to deal with the talking that would require, so I head to the balcony, slipping outside into the hot summer night and sinking down into a chair, staring at my phone as I do.

"You are incredibly fucked up."

I pick my head up, finding Janelle standing in the shadows, leaning against the wall of the balcony, her arms crossed.

Adrenaline doesn't spike in my body; my pulse doesn't even pick up.

I just ask, "How long have you been out here?" My screen dims in my hand and Janelle turns her dark eyes toward me, arching a brow, a slit down the middle of it. She rolls her eyes, tossing her dreads over one shoulder before she sighs and sits in the chair at the far end of the porch, staring back out at the night sky.

The moon is only a sliver, the pool lights glowing below us far brighter.

Propping her elbows on her thighs, covered with burnt orange shorts, a loose muscle tank on over her bikini, Janelle cups her chin in her hands. "I came to get your lighter."

I see it still on the table between us, next to the ashtray, and imagine she was planning to smoke a joint downstairs or something.

"But then I got stuck out here after you and Luna…" She trails off, sounding disgusted. "And I kind of liked the *outdoor view*."

I smile a little and lean back in my chair, propping my feet on the ottoman, crossing one ankle over the other as I tuck a hand behind my head, the bottom of my phone resting against my sternum. I open up a message to Eden. She's sent me nothing since she left.

Dominic, Jasper, and Baca were gone shortly after Eden.

Janelle stayed. She lives two houses down, and home is not a place she loves to be. Probably why Dad called her, knowing she'd come on a dime, just for an excuse to leave. She's adopted, and her parents are like every other in this neighborhood. More interested in appearances than what's lurking beneath the filthy rich exterior.

Janelle had a little sister. Her family took them in as a packaged deal.

She doesn't have a sister anymore.

"What happened?" She doesn't look at me as she asks, but I know she isn't afraid of me. Same reason she helped pin me to the wall, and probably did more of the heavy lifting than Jasper or Baca. Even here, I see the cut of her arms, lean and feminine, but Janelle spends all of her free time playing lacrosse or training for lacrosse or running at Trafalgar, sometimes even in the dead of night. I assume she thinks it's better than being forced to speak to her adoptive parents.

"Nothing." I type out a message to Eden, regretting I let her drive away. She had been drinking, and she'd done a line.

I watched her through the glass of the pool house. I saw Dominic kiss her shoulder too, and I couldn't stand it, her attention on him, even as I spent the morning with Luna, trying to get Dad out of my head. I didn't want to hurt Eden. It's just, with her, everything is so… *much*. I feel too deeply, and she asks questions no one else will.

It's unnerving.

Janelle says nothing but she laughs; a light, tinkling sound, but she is definitely not amused. "Is every word that comes out of your mouth a lie?"

Me: You good, baby? I send the message and don't expect a response. I click off my screen after I ensure my phone is on vibrate, then I rest it on my chest, both hands coming behind my head as I close my eyes.

"Depends on the day of the week," I answer Janelle.

"Did you hurt her?" This question is lower than her other. I think of her little sister, Jean, and marvel at the fact there were once two unhinged children on this street. What are the chances? The diagnosis isn't given lightly, and usually, for kids, it's unofficial, or called something a little less heavy.

Conduct disorder.

The label I was saddled with until Montford.

"Would you believe me if I said no?"

Janelle is quiet a moment, then she says, "Are you saying no?"

I smile, eyes still closed, but I don't say anything. We all heard her scream when Dominic grabbed her.

A jolt of something unpleasant rises in my chest at the thought, my pulse speeding up marginally.

I feel sick, and I grit my teeth, swallowing rising bile at the back of my throat as her scream echoes inside my head.

I didn't know I hurt her. She didn't show it, until after Dominic grabbed her.

Why do you always have to pretend to be so goddamn tough? Break a little, just for me. Guilt is unfamiliar to me, regret is another planet. But if I could go back, I'd have paid better attention.

I hear the creak of Janelle's chair as she shifts in her seat, and I wonder if she'll leave, but the door doesn't open, and I don't sense her standing. She's just getting comfortable, maybe, and I don't mind. Janelle doesn't care if I answer her questions, and she's okay in silences, too. We aren't extremely close, but after Jean was gone, Janelle wanted to know things, and I was the only person she could ask who knew what it was like to be stuck with a brain like her sister's.

"Why Luna?" Another thing I like about Janelle. There's no judgment in her question. I don't care what people think, which means I don't care enough to argue my morality with them. Janelle doesn't make me.

"Why not?" I counter, rotating my neck, keeping my eyes closed. "She was there, and she's trying to piss Dom off. It worked out."

"Okay," Janelle says slowly, and I can tell another question is lurking. She doesn't make me wait for it long. "Then why *not* Eden?"

I open my eyes, staring at the awning of the balcony, but in my head, I see Eden's thighs spread for me on the island, feel her hand over my heart. *"Be bad, baby boy."*

My abs flex, involuntarily, like hearing her words in my mind is a punch to the gut. "I don't know." It's partly true.

I can feel Janelle looking at me, trying to find the lie. It's there, too. "What's your best guess?"

My phone buzzes on my chest, and I sit up straighter, swinging my feet from the ottoman, planting them on the hot wooden planks of the balcony. I pick up my phone, flipping it over and holding it with both hands.

Eden: I'm fine.

I smile at her lie, biting the inside of my cheek as I text her back. **Me: Try again, but with the truth this time.**

I send the message and turn my head to find Janelle's eyes locked on mine. Her knees to her chest, ropey muscles of her arms flexed, wrapped around her shins.

She really wants to know, because she thinks of her sister every time she tries to get into my psyche. The reality is I don't know why Jean was playing with her dad's big game rifle. I don't know if she intentionally pressed the barrel under her chin. I don't know if she knew it was loaded. If she intended to kill herself when she pulled the trigger with her toe.

I can't give Janelle the answers she's looking for.

I don't want to kill myself. Not for hurting Eden, not for fucking around with Luna after she left, and not for anything that happened the night Winslet went missing.

But sometimes, I do wonder what it would be like to feel content. Less restless.

I got a taste of it last night, with Eden in my arms.

And that's the answer to Janelle's question. *"Then why* not *Eden?"*

One day, even she wouldn't be enough to silence the noise. And just like with Jean and the gun, maybe I wouldn't intend to pull the trigger, perhaps it would be a twisted little accident. But either way, I don't want to be the one who breaks Eden's mind into pieces.

She deserves far better than me. *That's why.*

But all I tell Janelle is, "Luna knows what this is and what it won't ever be."

Janelle doesn't back down, though. "Why can't Eden know that too?"

But that's the thing, isn't it?

I look down at Eden's text, surprised she responded so fast.

Her: I don't want to talk to you right now.

I stare at my screen a long time, rubbing my thumb over it, like I could reach her through the phone. I think of her scream. I never want to hear that sound again in my life.

Me: Are you hurt?

I keep looking at my screen, like she'll reply immediately, even though I have a feeling she won't. Only when the message goes dim do I answer Janelle her final question of the night.

"She does know. The difference is we both want to imagine it might be different for us."

Janelle doesn't speak for long seconds, until she says, Jean probably dancing through her mind, "But it won't be."

And I know my own history better than anyone, so it takes nothing to repeat those words back to her, like a nail in the coffin. *"But it won't be."*

"You will always be fond of me. I represent to you all the sins you never had the courage to commit."

- The Picture of Dorian Gray, Oscar Wilde

Act II

24

Eden

"WHAT HAPPENED?"

I jump at the sound of Sebastian's voice, snatching my hand to my chest and flipping off the cold water, my wrist still swollen since Eli twisted it yesterday. "Why didn't you knock?" I counter, turning to watch as he leans against the doorjamb, hands in his khaki pants.

His eyes drop to my hand, and I shove both of mine into the pocket of my black hoodie, pulled on over my bra and pajama shorts. He's shirtless, and his chest is birdlike, as thin as he is. I feel something deep in my own chest, looking at his. A pull, a tightening. It's like being at the top of a rollercoaster ride, I imagine, knowing there's nowhere to go but down. I feel a little sick, looking at his ruin.

"The door was open."

I glance at it, then the hallway beyond, the orange light spilling over the thin carpet. He's right, I guess. It's late, Mom and Reece are both asleep, I just forgot to close it all the way.

"Why are you still here?" It sounds like an accusation. I'm

glad he is, I just don't want him to circle back to his original question.

He rolls his eyes. "I stay in sometimes."

"Have you applied for a job yet?" I smile nastily at him, propping my hip against the sink.

He lifts his middle finger but he's smiling too, before he slips his hand back into his pocket. He jerks his chin toward me, glancing down, and my heart sinks, knowing he isn't going to let it go. "What happened, E?"

My mind goes over every option in what feels like a nanosecond. Lie, and pretend I don't know what he's talking about. Tell him the truth. Or fake a different accident. I go with the latter, but blend it in with a little truth. "Slammed my hand in my car door."

Seb blows his wispy blond strands out of his eyes, raising his brows as he does. "Sounds bad."

"It was fantastic."

He grins, flashing yellowed teeth. "You're such a little smart ass, you know that?"

I shrug, my heart thumping hard. "Can you leave me alone now?"

"You didn't eat dinner last night."

"I wasn't hungry."

"Uh huh." Seb keeps staring at me, and I feel like he can see right through me.

I kind of wish I could tell him the truth. About the fight with Eli yesterday. How I'm worried he hooked up with Luna. The way I feel like I'm drowning with him, and I can't really keep my head above water. But I know I can't tell him because I know this is all fucked up.

I haven't spoken to Eli though, not since yesterday when he texted to ask if I was okay. I've been writing, and yesterday I ran on the treadmill at the gym during a lull in my shift. Anything for a distraction.

"Your light has been on pretty late the past few days." Seb

keeps going with his assessment of me, and I shift from one foot to the other, grinding my teeth.

"You literally get high in your room. I don't think you can judge my bedtime choices."

He pulls his lip ring between his teeth, glancing up at the ceiling. "I never knew having a sister was going to wreak such havoc on my ego."

I smile despite myself. "Shut up and let me go to bed."

"Seriously, E…" He trails off, scrubbing a hand over the side of his face before he drops it, looking down at the white linoleum between us. "You were like this before, you know? With that one dude."

That one dude. Like Nic didn't fuck up my whole junior year. My face flushes hot, and I want to say something to cut Sebastian down, tell him to mind his own fucking life, but he keeps talking, and I stay quiet.

"Staying up all night, skipping meals, going out to parties. I just… I don't know if *Eli* has you all twisted like that dude did, but I just don't want you to—"

"It's not like that." I'm whispering the words, but I feel every black rubber bracelet against my skin with Seb's judgment. "It's not like that at all. I…" I swallow a lump in my throat as Sebastian brings his eyes back to mine. "I'm done with him anyway." I don't know if I mean it, but I haven't answered his last text. "We're done."

Sebastian narrows his eyes. "You're done." He repeats the words with cynicism.

I shrug, rocking back and forth on my heels. Sebastian tracks the movement with his gaze, but he doesn't comment. "I'm done."

I can tell he doesn't believe me, especially when he says, "You think you're gonna take your mom up on the offer?"

Therapy. *The offer for therapy.* She mentioned it again just this morning over breakfast. I sat in the living room and read the paper before I took a walk outside. When I got back, she asked about it. *Fucking. Therapy.*

I shake my head, annoyed. "No." Then I step past Seb, and he lets me go, but once I'm out into the hallway, he speaks.

"Let me find out he hurt you, E, I'll fucking kill him."

His words make me bristle. "Why don't you worry about applying for jobs before you get involved in homicide, all right?" Then I slam my door after I walk into my room.

I WRITE UNTIL MY PEN RUNS OUT OF INK. THEN I SWIPE A NEW one from my nightstand and keep going.

My inner world has always been louder than anything I could say on the outside. When I don't get enough time to focus on my imagination, everything in reality seems too much. Like my make-believe characters need tending to or else my internal garden wilts and I alongside it.

Maybe that's how I lost myself in Eli so quickly.

I've been wilting.

My phone vibrates but I don't look at it. I've texted Manda today a little about classes back at Shoreside, some chick who found out she was pregnant, a teacher who quit, and she's sent me photos of the beach. She never mentions Nic, and I'm grateful for it, but every time I communicate with her, it's like I can feel *him* and *it* just there below the surface of our conversations.

I keep writing in my notebook, the blue lava lamp the only thing on. I can barely see with it, but it means I can't go back and correct any spelling mistakes or grammatical errors. I write until my wrist is throbbing, but I push past even that.

Inside my head, my morally gray characters dance along, like a movie playing behind my eyes, and I just have to transcribe it. It's like getting lost, except I never want to be found. It's like living in a daydream, where everything is possible, and anything could happen. And sometimes, when I get to the touchy subjects, the hard parts, it's like expelling every negative emotion I've ever had but never had the chance to scream about. It's like living that day again, the day I got suspended.

I'm in the bathroom and I'm screaming at Nic and everything is black and fuzzy and it's a little hard to piece it together, and I have a knife in my hand, one I took from Sebastian's room, and Nic's fair skin is flushed pink and he has his arms up, and his wide eyes keep darting to the blade and he's telling me he's sorry and he's telling me he'll do it too, and he's telling me he loves it and me and—

I drop my pen, my fingers shaky.

I can feel my pulse in my wrist. I close my notebook, swipe it and my pen onto my bedroom floor and bury my head in my hands.

I got too far in again. Eli lied to me, right to my face, about his mom, then he spent all day yesterday flirting with his best friend's girl, or ex-girlfriend, whatever the fuck mind games they play.

I got it all confused inside my head again. I fell too fast again.

But there's a reason he lied to me about his mom, isn't there? There's a reason I cover my scars. Sometimes we don't want to go backwards. Sometimes it hurts looking in the rearview mirror.

I snatch up my phone from my nightstand and lie on my back.

Eli has sent me a few texts, asking about my day.

I want to text him back, but I kind of enjoy his suffering a little. *Let him wait.*

I open up my web browser, and with the volume on mute, I slide my fingers under my pajama shorts and even as my wrist stings, I get myself off watching porn that looks like it would hurt, imagining Eli inside my head.

Afterward, just as I've turned my phone on silent, rolled over to go to sleep near three in the morning, I hear something inside the house.

I suck in a breath, burying further under my covers as I strain my ears, trying to hear beyond my own thudding heartbeat.

It sounds like… moaning.

The A/C is running, and I've never heard Mom and Reece… *doing anything* inside this house. I know it can't be them, and Seb never brings girls over. I don't even know if he likes girls anymore. I don't know if he likes *anyone*.

But as I hold my breath, eyes closed, I hear it again.

A whimper, a moan, and I can't tell if it's from pleasure or pain.

It could be Sebastian watching porn, I guess, but I think he, like me, would turn down the volume or else use headphones. You know, common courtesy.

After a second of being a chicken, I bat down the covers and sit up slowly, turning my head toward the door.

Then a *thud* hits a wall, and I jump, clamping my hand over my mouth.

What the fuck?

I grab my phone from my nightstand and yank it off the charger, diving down under my covers as I open up a text to Sebastian, ignoring all of Eli's.

Me: Are you okay?

The moans keep going, getting louder, and I squeeze my eyes tight shut, wanting to go out into the hall to check on my brother but being too much of a coward to actually do it.

A cold sweat breaks out over the back of my neck.

I take shallow breaths, in and out, in and out, my chest heaving. I'm going to have to take my fucking medicine, and there better not be someone breaking into this trailer right now or I'm going to be pissed off. There's nothing here to even steal.

But the noise gets louder, and it doesn't sound like a robbery.

There's a crescendo of moans, then another *thud*, then… silence.

I open my eyes and stare at my text with Sebastian. He isn't typing. Nothing is coming through.

I clench my fingers tighter around my phone.

My screen goes dim until it suddenly flares to life again. Sebastian is typing. *Maybe he heard it too.*

But when his text comes in, all it says is, **Yeah, why?**

I immediately text him back, ignoring the ache in my wrist, adrenaline spiking over the pain.

Me: Did you hear that noise?

His reply comes a second later. **Him: What noise?**

And all I can think about is Shoreside, and forgetting everything, and an adrenaline high with a knife to my skin.

I don't text my brother back, and I don't let myself read Eli's texts.

Sometimes, I'm scared to live inside my own head. Sometimes, I think things would be scarier if he lived in there too.

25

Eli

THREE DAYS PASS. Eden doesn't look at me. She doesn't speak to me. And it's pissing me off. It gets under my skin, and no one does that. Not Dom, even though he tries his best. Not Luna, even though I know she's in love with me and uses Dom to try and drive the point home, much like Winslet did, except it wasn't me she loved. Not even Dad, and he annoys me by sheer virtue of the fact he's breathing.

I follow her in the halls. I even showed up at the gym last night and was happy when that hulking asshole who stalked her wasn't there the entire three hours I was. She checked me in, scanned my keycard, and asked if I wanted a towel, like I didn't mean anything to her.

That's it.

That's all.

I'm not even sure what part she's pissed about most because she won't talk to me. Does she know I did something with Luna? Luna wouldn't tell her because her and Dom are still a thing, broken up or not. But maybe she just assumed? She'd be right, of course. But if I'd have known fucking around with Luna would've cost me this much, I never would have done it.

I'm going out of my mind thinking about her. I've texted her dozens of times. I've called. I've sent memes. I've stopped by her house, but I never seem to catch her without her parents or her brother there and I haven't wanted to knock on the door unannounced just yet, in case I fuck things up there too.

This fight is real.

Probably the most time anyone has ignored me in my life, aside from my goddamn mother. I should let it go. Her go. I should count my losses. It doesn't matter, anyway. She was right all along. This would never work.

I'm eighteen. I know, logically, we won't end up together. It's not how life is. We're adolescents. Babies. We have entire lives. I'm not against dating so long as it serves its purpose. Sex, mainly. But I've never been under any illusion relationships last. Mine never have. I've never quite wanted them to.

But Tuesday night, I'm lying on my bed and texting her, wanting impossible things.

Me: I'm sorry. It was stupid. I was stupid. Forgive me.

As usual, no three dots. Nothing. But I stare and stare because tonight is the first full moon of October and it means fuck all to me, but it means something to her.

My screen dims. Annoyance and rage both twist in my gut.

Until… my phone brightens.

She's typing. *Finally.*

I clench my phone tight in my hand, waiting.

And waiting.

And waiting.

The dots disappear. Then reappear.

Then… vanish.

Me: I know you have some things to say to me. Get them out, nightmare girl.

That doesn't even warrant the *hint* of a response.

No dots. Nothing. I wait five minutes.

Then I throw my phone across the room. It hits the wall and clatters to the fucking floor.

Yesterday and today I've had to watch her prance around Trafalgar like she doesn't even know who the fuck I am. I've listened to Dom's bullshit about it, felt Janelle's weighted stares, and Luna laughs like it's the funniest thing.

I sit up, raking my hands through my hair as I let my eyes flutter closed, a smile forming on my lips. It's okay.

Tomorrow, *I'll make sure she can't ignore me.*

26

Eden

ELI: **Don't ignore me today. Please.**

I smile at his pleading. It's been four days since he told me to leave his house. I managed to ignore him when he came to the gym, Monday, and yesterday, inventing questions to ask Ms. Romano after Latin to stall for time. I crept through the hallways like a ghost, I haven't responded to any of his increasingly frequent texts, and something about it all... gets me a little high.

I click my phone screen off and push it into the front pocket of my backpack, heading for my bedroom door. *How long will you chase me?* Do you feel this dizzying, all-consuming *need* for me like I do you? I've kept it in check with writing and poring over Bloor's course catalog and reading *The Book of the Law* and working on my Chaucer paper.

With thoughts of Nic, and spiraling, and embarrassment.

Those little reminders help me strengthen my resolve.

Keep begging.

I brush my hair behind my ear, pulled into a low, messy

bun, then flip my wrist, sliding the dozens of black jelly bracelets down my inner forearm.

Tracing the three letters carved into my skin, pale white and faded, I feel my face grow hot with the memory.

This time, I want someone to bleed for me.

I glance at my other hand, trailing my eyes over the back of my wrist. It's no longer swollen, no bruise, no discoloration, *but I remember.*

My heart picks up speed.

I feel a sick thrill, knowing he could hurt me if I made him.

Dangerous, getting high off of his violence.

I reach for my door, trying to forget my scars and Eli grabbing my wrist, and I flip the lock, pulling it open and stepping out into the narrow hallway.

Sebastian is walking by, surprisingly since it's still so early, and he turns to face me, looking over his shoulder, a hand cupped over his mouth as he coughs. It's a hoarse sound, his eyes red-rimmed, his golden hair oily and hanging in his face. His lip ring is gone.

He glances over my Trafalgar uniform—the pleated, plaid skirt over my black boots and silver, calf-high socks. The black polo, buttoned all the way up. It's another hot day, and I've got my gray sweater stuffed into my backpack, but I know I'd just sweat right through it, so I didn't put it on.

And the skirt… it's the first time I've worn it. I know Eli is obsessed with my thighs and my ass. *I want him to see me, as I ignore the fuck out of him.*

"Did you invite him here?" Sebastian asks, his voice cracked as he drops his hand from his mouth. His fingernails are stained yellow from nicotine.

I frown, confused. "What? Who?"

His brows knit together and he shakes his head. "You want me to tell him to leave?" There's something vaguely threatening in his tone.

I glance down the hallway, seeing nothing. Paranoia lights through me, my heart racing. "What are you talking about?"

Sebastian narrows his eyes. "Your little boyfriend is here to give you a ride. He was knocking on the door at seven this morning, when you were in the shower."

Are you fucking kidding me?

"I'm gonna tell him to get the fuck out." Sebastian turns from me with my silence, but I reach for him, grabbing his clammy skin.

He stills, spinning around to face me as I drop my hand, his face expectant, lips pressed together.

"Eli." I say the word like I never have before. "You're telling me *Eli* is *here?*"

A voice carries from down the hall. *Reece.* I can't hear any response, but I know that's because Eli keeps his words quiet.

"Yeah," Seb says. "But I can change that."

I shake my head quickly, annoyance pushing through me. "No." I keep my tone firm. "I'll deal with him."

My brother studies me for a long moment, but I think his desire for sleep wins out and he just nods once, then stalks down the hall to his room, closing his door behind him.

What. The. Fuck.

My bag slung over one shoulder, I head to the front door, catching the scent and sound of bacon frying, popping over the stove in the kitchen, just past the living room.

"You gonna bring her home too?" Irritation makes Reece's voice gruff, and I lift my eyes as my fingers tighten around the strap of my bag.

The front door is closed, and Mom is the first person I see.

She's in her work clothes. A loose, oversized shirt, gray, stretchy pants, and her white tennis shoes. Her hair is pulled up in a clip, and her eyes are on mine, a small smile on her lips as she flips the bacon she usually only makes on the weekends for her, Sebastian, and Reece.

"Yes, sir." I hear Eli's quiet, lilting voice.

I turn my head, finding Eli and Reece facing off in the living room, in front of the worn, striped couch him and Mom strapped down in Reece's truck and brought with them from Wilmington.

I think there's still sand from the beach in that couch.

I drag my gaze from the picked threads up to meet Eli's eyes, now on mine as he turns a little away from Reece to welcome me into their *conversation*.

"Hi," he says, just like he did the first night we spoke in the library. Immediately, his gaze drops to my bare thighs. Something in his composed demeanor seems to falter. He clears his throat, and I relish in his momentary discomfort as he takes in the fact I'm wearing a skirt.

But a second later, he's back in place. Ever the actor as he looks away from my legs.

With his composure returned, he seems surreal in here. Too good for this place. After so long of me giving him the cold shoulder, being this close to him, forced to interact, his presence is overwhelming. His thick, dark hair is beautiful, just over his eyes, a smile on his sensual lips, far too sexual to be making an appearance *here*. In my living room. With my stepdad.

Unlike me, Eli *is* wearing the gray, V-neck sweater, overtop the white dress shirt of our uniform, and the collar looks hot as hell over his black, leather choker.

"Next time someone is gonna give you a ride to school, why don't you let me or your mother know so we can adjust our schedules accordingly?" Reece's Southern accent slices through my sinful thoughts. Reluctantly, my cheeks growing warm, I face Reece.

He's an unattractive man.

Next to Eli, the ugliness is jarring.

Average height, with a few bits of beige-blond hair around the sides of his head, his bald spot pink and gleaming from the sun streaming in the windows by the TV, and beady blue eyes. He's dressed in a mustard-yellow shirt and khaki pants, and I honestly can't tell if I find him so hideous objectively, because of how he looks, or simply because we never get along.

"Yes, sir." I bite the words out. Out of the corner of my eye, I can see one of Eli's dark brows lift at my words, or maybe my venom. I'm not sure which.

"Bacon is almost done," Mom calls out, as she always does, trying to interfere before there's interference really required. She's seen the fights play out so frequently she knows exactly when to divert one before it ever begins.

Reece has turned his gaze back to Eli, a furrow in his light brows, his thick arms crossed over his chest.

"Actually, this is my fault." Eli doesn't smile, and he looks genuinely contrite, hands in his pockets, eyes on the muddled gray of the carpet. "I... I just thought it would help." He glances up at my mom, then back down, swallowing hard. "I knew what time you two usually left, and I thought if I could save you a trip..." He trails off, lifting his gaze slowly. He towers over Reece, but somehow manages to give the impression he's looking up at him with his pious performance.

It's unsettling, watching it.

He looks like he believes what he's saying, and while it could be true—because I certainly didn't agree to let him pick me up for school—his submissive act is bullshit.

Eli doesn't bow for anyone, and certainly not a man in a mustard shirt inside a trailer.

"Eden didn't know." He clears his throat, and I see Reece's eyes twitch over to me for a second. "I apologize."

Mom gives a polite laugh, flipping off the element and bringing the bacon pan to the sink. In this moment, I'm glad I never told her we were ever fighting. "Please, don't apologize," she says, grabbing the plate lined with paper towels and stacked with an entire pack of cooked bacon. She turns to the rickety, pale wooden table pushed against the wall opposite the stove. "Thank you for picking her up. Reece was just startled to see a car in the driveway, that's all." She sets the plate down and turns to grab more from the cabinets.

"I wasn't *startled.*" Reece speaks through thin lips, glaring at the back of Mom's head. "I just didn't *expect* to see a shiny new sports car in my driveway when I stepped outside this morning." He rolls his eyes, sighing, then turns back to me.

His target, always.

I'm not even sure why we hate each other so much. I've known him since I was five years old, and yet over the course of thirteen years, the loathing between us hasn't waned even marginally.

"When were you going to ask us about your plans for next Thursday? That's a school night." His face is red, because his face is always red, and his jowls shake as he barks out his question. Over a week away, I have plenty of fucking time to ask, but right now, that's not what I focus on.

Anger zips through me despite the fact I have tried very hard to play into Eli's submission. If I can keep myself calm, this entire thing will pass over, but this is entirely *Eli's* fault, and it only took me a second to put together Reece's question and the *plans* I allegedly have for next Thursday.

He doesn't think I'll call him out on it. *It's almost like he doesn't know me.*

I smile a little as I blink at my stepdad. "What plans?"

Quiet seems to echo in the house. Reece looks from me, to Eli, then back again.

Eli, of course, breaks the silence. He laughs, an unsure sound. "You said you wanted to ride with me to my match, remember?" Sighing, as I drag my gaze to his, he keeps talking, glancing at the floor, ducking his smirk. "But you haven't been sleeping well, you were probably tired when you said it—"

"You haven't been sleeping well?" Mom's voice is full of alarm as she carefully sets down plates on the table, staring at me with raised brows.

My heart thumps too fast in my chest. I think of the last time I *wasn't sleeping well.*

Blood on my wrists. The confrontation with Nic.

Mom's face is pale.

Are you afraid of me, Mom?

"Anyway, if you don't want to go," Eli continues, maintaining his mask of politeness as I have a violent flashback of him twisting my hand behind my back. "It's okay, I just thought I'd ask permission to pick you up while I'm here…" He trails off, lifting his eyes to smile at me, throwing this back in my face.

Say you want it. I can hear his voice in my head. *Embarrass yourself a little, just for me.*

Seconds pass. Reece is still staring at me, and for once, he seems perplexed.

Eli arches one dark brow. *Give in.*

Fuck you.

Before I have to say anything at all, Mom speaks, pulling back a chair and motioning to us all. "What time do you think you'd be back? Next Thursday?" she asks, and I want to tell her I don't want to sit at the table, but I already see she made oatmeal topped with berries for me, in a bowl at my usual seat.

I glance at Eli as Reece heads to the table, sitting down and grabbing the orange juice to pour into his glass, a little more aggressive than orange juice really requires.

"No later than ten, Lucy." The utmost respect is in Eli's words even as he calls Mom by her first name, which is what she told him to do when they met on the porch. He gestures toward the table to me, wanting me to go first. I don't want to move.

But Mom is seated, Reece is crunching his bacon, and both of them are watching us.

I take a deep breath and stride across the living room, but it's too small not to pass close by Eli. I can smell him, and it's enough to make my knees feel weak, made worse by the fact his fingers graze the back of my arm, so subtle I'm sure my parents didn't see, before he follows me and takes a seat, too.

I spend the rest of the time we're in my house slopping the oatmeal around and pretending to eat, but all I can think about is my heart racing in my chest and Eli's elbow brushing mine every time he makes an excuse to reach for something in the center of the table, the orange juice more than once.

Despite my annoyance with him, I can't help hold onto his preference for it.

Huh. Eli Addison enjoys orange juice. It's endearing, even as I want to stab him with my fork.

"What the hell was that?" I don't wait for him to pull out of my driveway to ask.

He has his hand wrapped around the shifter, A/C mercifully blowing cold in his car, but before he puts the Infiniti in gear, he turns to look at me, leans in close, and just as I'm about to push him away, I realize he's grabbing my seatbelt.

His mouth is too near mine, his arm brushing my chest, and I don't breathe. I don't want to smell cotton candy or the beach or any of his rich boy scents. I want him to give me room so I can think. With his body so close to mine, his eyes locked on my own, that is impossible.

After a moment, he slides the belt around me and clicks it into place.

Then he's back on his side of the car, and while I stare at the veins of his hand, clenched around the steering wheel while he drives us out of my neighborhood, I can at least use my brain again.

"Good morning to you, too, baby girl."

"Stop calling me that."

He doesn't even look at me as we come to a stop at the exit to the trailer park, but I see his stupid smirk. "You like it." He doesn't say it accusingly. It's just a fact, rolling off of his tongue, like the sky is blue and the grass is green.

He's wrong though. I don't *like it*. I'm obsessed with it. No one has ever called me that before. Not a single person has given me a term of endearment like it, no nicknames aside from the first initial of my birth name. And even "E" is just lazy shorthand, something with no thought. Boys have said "babe" in exasperation, and Amanda would call me "dude" every other sentence, a habit I almost didn't even hear, it was so ingrained into her vocabulary, much like nobody bothers to track their friends' breaths.

But I am not foolish enough to think I'm the first girl he's ever said it to, and as immature as it may be, right now, with my fading anger, I don't want to be to him what anyone has ever been before.

"I don't," I insist. *Lie.* "I don't want a throwaway term you've used on all of your other girlfriends."

This time, *he looks at me.*

And it isn't until the *look* I realize what I've said.

His smile has pulled higher and my heart sinks as he leaves my neighborhood, shifting gears with ease, as if I didn't just almost ruin this.

"I didn't mean *I* was your girlfriend." I nearly choke on the word, sweat slimy beneath my arms even with the full blast of A/C. I want to open the door and hop out of the car, but he's going over the speed limit, I'm sure, based on the purr of the engine and the fact he's *always* going above the speed limit. Even the backs of my thighs are sweaty, though, uncomfortable beneath my skirt and—

"You didn't?"

"No," I manage to say, keeping a forced, cool detachment in my voice. "It was just a passing remark, a slip of the tongue."

There's a pause between us. Silence, save for music playing low and the hum of his car.

Even though I don't want to, I watch his hand as he downshifts, the engine kicking back, and I jolt forward in my seat a little.

Then he's turning, and I look up, realizing we didn't head toward Trafalgar.

We're entering the state park a couple of miles from my house.

My stomach twists into knots. "I can't skip class." It's the first thing I think to say, and as irritated as I am about the detour, I'm grateful my transgression is being neatly avoided. "What are we doing here?"

He keeps driving, down a dirt road, thick forest on either side of us, blotting out the sun. He swerves around divots in the path, slowing and maneuvering deftly over holes and big rocks. Despite the fact I really can't miss class, I'm momentarily silenced enough to take in the tall trees, shielding the warm day, a coolness even from the interior of his car as he pulls onto a gravel lot, backing up by glancing over his shoulder, his taillights reflecting on glass over a map of the park.

I see a lot of blue, and something relaxes in my chest.

He puts the car in park but doesn't turn it off as he looks at me.

"A slip of the tongue?" he repeats my words back to me, and I feel as if I'm *drenched* in perspiration.

"Yes." I don't think twice about sticking to my defense.

But with my answer to him, I didn't expect him to look so *angry*. A muscle in his jaw moves as he stares at me, and his fingers curl tighter around the wheel.

"You're saying you're *not* my girlfriend?"

"What the fuck do you want?" I bypass his question, the way he does with all of mine. I'm still angry. I still want him to beg me. He doesn't get to do this... this *deflection* shit all the time. "Why did you come to my house?"

"Why did you let Dom kiss you?"

For a second, I'm shocked into a disbelieving silence. And then, "You're joking, right?"

He shakes his head once, never looking away from me. "Do I look like I'm joking?"

I throw up my hands. He is unbelievable. "You were ignoring me. You were mad about what the hell ever, with your dad, and you were all over *her* in the pool and—"

"Were you hurt by that?" There's a quietness to his question, but I can't place his tone.

I drop my hands back to my thighs. *Are you stupid?* But if he wants to play this game... "I distracted myself with Dom."

His eyes narrow, and here, shielded by the trees, the emerald in his irises is all gone, only forest green around his pupils, contained in the black lines ringing his eyes. "Do you do that often?" He raises his brows. "Distract yourself?"

"Why were you even mad at me?" I ask instead of answering. "It's why we fought," I remind him, not gently. "It's the entire reason I didn't want to speak to you Sunday, and Monday, and yesterday, and I didn't want to speak to you today, either, but of course, you're a spoiled brat who always has to get his way, so you don't respect boundaries and—"

He grabs my face, causing me to jump in my seat as he jerks me closer to him, my hands going to the console between us to steady myself. We're nose-to-nose. I let him touch me this way for one second. Two.

Then I grab his wrist, pulling his arm down as I back away and release him. "Don't touch me like that. Don't fucking grab me again."

He smiles, his hand on the console. But he says nothing about my words. He just asks, once more, "Why did you let him kiss you?"

I remember his fist against Dom's nose. His threats to hurt him. *Kill him.* "Why did you pretend I didn't exist and throw your arm around Luna and ignore me all fucking day?"

His eyes trace my mouth, and I see his dark lashes, fanned just over his cheekbones. He doesn't look up as he speaks. "Me and her are friends. Nothing more."

"But you didn't even *look* at me the entire morning—"

"I wanted you to myself." His eyes slowly drag up my face, to meet my gaze. "You're right, you know. I *am* a spoiled brat, and I'm trying very hard not to be when it comes to you. Because I'm also selfish, and you are more than I have ever deserved, and maybe I'm playing it safe by trying to ruin this before it can really begin."

His words stun me, but I cannot make this so easy for him. He'll leave me faster, if I do.

"When I left, did you fuck her?" I try to find the answer in his eyes before he speaks. But he's already too good. Eighteen, and he could act in a Broadway play.

You good, baby?

His text from that night. What had he done before? Why did he wait so long to check in with me? Does he care, or does he only pretend to, because it gets him what he wants?

I don't know.

I can't figure him out, and I'm not sure he has himself figured out, either.

He stares at me for long seconds before he asks, "Are you going to hold it against me?"

I inhale against the sharpness of the knife. *At least it's not in my back.*

"I'm sorry." He must see it in my eyes, how it hurts, and I wish I could hide it, but I already failed.

"You've said that before." I feel as if I'm stumbling over those words, reminding him of what he told me at Dominic's, the two of us drenched in rain. I haven't forgotten his promise then.

"I'll say it again," he says, barely above a whisper. "I'll always mess up."

"And you expect me to always accept your apology?"

He doesn't answer.

I squeeze my thighs together, grateful he hasn't said anything about me wearing this stupid skirt.

"What exactly did you do with her?" I don't look away, but he straightens, putting more distance between us.

He doesn't answer as he grabs the shifter, then closes his eyes, like he's trying to steady himself. He beats out a silent rhythm with his fingers to the music I can barely hear.

"Built for Sin," Framing Hanley, one of my favorites, I wonder how many more we share. How many things we've never discussed because surface conversations don't seem to exist for us. It should be special. In this moment, hearing this song I love playing in his car, I wonder what we're missing out on with one another.

I take a deep breath. "Let's go."

He stills his fingers but doesn't open his eyes and doesn't respond.

"I can't miss class. Unlike you, I have an attendance record to maintain in order to keep my financial aid."

He smiles, and I smooth down my skirt to keep from punching him in the middle of his chest, right over the bruises he already has.

"You haven't been absent once yet," he finally says.

I clench my teeth, staring at my broken, black bracelet in the cupholder between us. He never moved it. He's kept track of every day I've been in class—all of them. I don't know why this matters, except as a reminder even when I thought he didn't notice me, he was always paying attention.

Spoiled and loathsome and rich and able to get away with everything just short of murder, it's another way he can manipulate everyone around him.

"What did you do with her, Eli?"

I see his knuckles blanch as he squeezes the life out of the shifter, green veins stark against his skin. "Eden."

I don't look away from his hand. "Tell me."

Long seconds of silence.

"What kind of details do you want?" he suddenly snaps, and when I look up, his eyes are on mine. Still leaning back in his seat with a careless sort of posture, arrogant and right now, with his tight jaw and pursed lips, mean. "I answered your question. Isn't that enough for you? Would you have rather I lied—"

"You didn't answer me." I push the button on my seatbelt, twisting in the seat to face him. His gaze leaves mine for one second, going down to my thighs, and I press my knees together, trying to ignore the sweat slick on my skin. "Did you… make out?"

He scoffs, rolling his eyes, and a knot of anger, almost tight enough to choke on, forms in my throat.

"Did you have sex?" I can barely get the words out.

He loses his nasty little smirk.

My heart leaps to my throat, and in my head, I see them. Her on top of him, his fingers in her short hair, over her breasts, grabbing her ass.

"No," he says, too late, the memory already imbedded in my brain. And is it even false? I hear what he's saying. I just don't know why he's saying it. Because it's true, or because it's the best truth for him right now? "I don't understand why this part matters to you."

I want to hit something, but there's a sincerity in his words I can't quite fault.

"If I fucked her or kissed her shoulder," he gives me a knowing glance, and the urge to strike out at something grows stronger, "either way, it's crossing a line to you, right?"

"Stop dancing around the truth. Just tell me what you did."

He shakes his head, as if I exhaust him.

"*You* came to my house this morning. *You* weaseled your way into getting my parents to let me come with you next week. *You* dragged me out to this damn park. If you didn't want to talk about any of this, you should have stayed away." My chest is heaving, every muscle in my body tense. "So, tell me *what the fuck you did.*"

He chews the inside of his cheek, dropping his gaze over my body, and despite the fact I know he's trying to make me squirm, and I know I should resist, I can't. Especially as his eyes linger over my bare thighs, the skirt's hem resting three inches from my knees.

"We kissed."

My body temperature skyrockets, already dangerously high, at the same time I clench my abs, waiting to hear it hurt worse, because I know he isn't finished.

He brings a finger to his choker, running it along the underside, stretching it a little away from his neck. "I wrapped my fingers around her throat."

I can't look away from his pulse beating at his own, just underneath the leather band.

"I think I bit her hard enough to make her bleed."

I want to scream. To tell him to shut up. But I can't look away. I can't stop listening. It's impossible to tear my eyes from the stark white collar of his shirt, the contrast of the strip of leather, his finger beneath it all.

"She kissed her way down my chest."

Shut up, shut up, shut up. I don't realize I'm squeezing my thighs with my fingers until I feel a sharp sting, like my nails have broken through my flesh.

I still don't stop.

"I grabbed her hair. She doesn't have nearly as much of it as you do, you know." I hear the softest laugh. The innuendo.

I keep my eyes on the base of his throat, imagining digging my teeth into his skin, hearing him whimper in my ear.

"She grabbed my dick, put her mouth on it, and… Oh, do you want to hear how it ended? You look a little angry, baby girl."

Reluctantly, as if I'm fighting myself with every second of it, I drag my gaze to his. His eyes are dark, but he has that half-smile on his face, cocky and spiteful.

I force myself to smile back.

There's only a second of surprise in his eyes. Just a blink, then it's gone.

"She doesn't like to swallow," he continues, pushing me by keeping his tone light, as if we're talking about homework or Latin or his wrestling schedule. "Did you know that? I guess I can see it. She's a bit of a princess, don't you think?" He sighs, as if this is a fatal flaw, then he turns his head from me and looks out the windshield, into the trees, as if he's not ripping me apart with his words. "After that, well, this is the part you might hate the most."

I don't let my goddamn smile slip.

"She fell asleep in my bed."

I take a deep breath, in through my nose, out through it, too.

Seconds pass, but I wait him out.

And it's only when he slowly turns to look at me, more of the confusion from a moment earlier knitted between his brows, that I respond.

"Thank you for telling me." I keep my words syrupy-sweet, as if I'm not rattling off dark magic sigils in my head to gut him and Luna both.

But even with my act, mimicking his, I can't stop myself from getting out of his car. I don't even remember it, I just know I did, the door slamming echoing in my head as I walk away, as fast I can without running, my arms crossed over my chest. Leaves crunch beneath my feet, dead in the summer heat. I bow my head, I hear his door opening, closing, and I speed up, staring at the ground, but not seeing anything at all. I follow a dirt path past the map he reversed in front of, and somewhere in the distance, I hear rushing water.

I see his shadow fall across mine.

I keep moving, fire in my limbs, begging to spring free from my veins. I want to hurt him, but I think, truthfully, I want to hurt myself more. Maybe because I know it's *that* he'll dislike the most.

I dig my nails into my biceps, my pulse pounding a painful rhythm in my head.

And when he grabs me without a warning, I'm not entirely surprised. But I still jump as his arms band around my chest, yanking me toward him, rendering my upper body completely motionless.

"Let me go, Eli." The words are harsh. They don't even sound like they're coming from me. I try to twist in his grip, using my feet for leverage, but my boots slide against the dirt, and I have to rely on him to keep me upright.

"Shh," he says in my ear, his hold almost tight enough to steal my breath. "I can't let you go; you know that."

I know his words have a deeper meaning but I'm not in the mood for his games. I close my eyes tight, my arms still squeezed around my chest by his over my own, and I just start talking. "I should've fucked Dom."

His body tenses at my back, and I can't help the softest smile pulling at the corners of my mouth.

I feel his breath over my ear, sending shivers down my spine, but I keep talking.

"He offered to follow me home. To make sure I was okay enough to drive." *And you waited until hours later to check in on me.* I don't say it, but I don't need to. "I could've done anything I wanted with him. I can play with him just like you can. Like Luna. I think he's desperate, you know?"

I feel his erection against my back, growing harder with every word I speak. I don't know if it's the quiet anger or imagining me with someone else. I'm not sure if I want to know.

"But I didn't," I keep going, eyes still closed. "Do you know why?"

"Because you don't *like* when people touch you." His words are soft but full of a calm sort of aggression, as if he's daring me to tell him his statement is incorrect.

I shake my head, even though it's a half-truth. "Because I don't want to intentionally hurt you."

He doesn't speak for a moment, his mouth still by my ear, but then he says, "That's exactly what I said."

I frown, confused as I blink my eyes open, taking in the sun stabbing through the canopy of the forest, but before I can say anything, he grabs my face, turning my head so our lips are touching.

"I told you not to grab me—"

"You don't like when anyone touches you," he interrupts me, his words ragged. *"Except me."*

Before I can respond to that, or think it through, he releases my face, then shoves me forward, towards a thick tree. He grabs my arm, spinning me around, handling me like a ragdoll, his palm pressing into my chest, pinning me to the rough bark at my back.

Everything feels out of control, all at once. Inside my head, I see them. Luna on her knees, his fingers around her throat, maybe his palm over her nose.

It's like black blurs my vision and my actions just *happen*.

I dart out my hand, slipping my fingers into his pocket, the one he always keeps his phone in. I snatch it out at the same time I shove my free hand against his chest. He doesn't budge, of course, but I bring his phone up to my face, the screen lighting up as I do.

A black background, the time, no notifications. I stare at it as I speak. "That's a shitty excuse," I say, my voice low. "Because you think I don't like when people touch me, that gives you permission to touch whoever the fuck you want?"

His hand is over my chest, fingertips splayed right atop my heart. "I'll give you my passcode." His words are quiet, addressing nothing of what I said.

I swipe my thumb over the screen, the keypad opening up for me. "Yeah? Give it to me then." *Let me see everything.*

He curls his fingers over the fabric of my shirt. He lifts his other hand, pressing it beside my head, trapping me to this tree. "3, 3, 3, 3."

I raise my eyes to his. He's smirking down at me as he tilts his head. "My secrets are inside my head," he says in a whisper. "But you can look, if it makes you feel better."

I don't believe him, about the passcode. With shaky fingers, I enter it in.

My breath hitches when it opens.

I scan the apps quickly. Only four on the initial home screen. His emails and calls and messages are at the bottom, alongside music. No emails. No missed calls. No texts either.

It feels... bizarre.

"Go ahead." He leans down closer, his eyes inches from mine. *"Look."*

I grit my teeth, feeling a little sick. Eli is... known. Popular isn't really the right word. He's not always with his friends, not constantly surrounded by a crowd in the hallway. Dominic and Luna and Janelle seem closest to him, and they speak to him more than everyone else. But... people know him, don't they?

Everyone seems to. Who does he text? Who does he talk to? *It can't just be me.*

The thought is disorienting. That maybe all those texts to get me to forgive him for Saturday weren't because he wanted me, but because he… doesn't have anyone else.

I decide I don't want to do this anymore.

Without thought, I throw his phone over his shoulder, thinking he'll fetch it. We hear it drop to the leaves, a gentle thud, but he doesn't react. He just keeps staring at me.

"Get off of me." I bring my palms behind me, grasping onto the tree, like I'm surrendering even though my words aren't submission.

Slowly, holding my gaze, both hands coming to my chest and shifting with his movement, *he drops to his fucking knees.*

I suck in hot, early-fall air, dipping my head to watch him bow at my feet. His hands come to my thighs, his fingers splayed wide, possessive even as he kneels.

He turns his head, biting the inside of my thigh softly, the strip of my flesh exposed just beneath the edge of my skirt. "You wore the skirt." His voice is hoarse, and my head spins from his change of subject.

But we're not done, I want to say.

We are for now. He doesn't say it, but I'm sure he would.

This stupid skirt is *for you, for you, for you.* I want to speak those words out loud, I want to tell him I *want* to drive him insane, just like he's doing to me.

But I don't like the way he hurts me. It's not a prick of pain. Not a tease. It's a knife in my gut. But his obsession is almost like a bandage.

"Get *up.*" I say the words as cold as I can. "Get your fucking phone."

He licks along my inner thigh, his nose brushing up the hem of my skirt.

I dig my nails into the bark of the tree, my spine arched against it as my belly jumps.

"I like it," he says, ignoring me. He slides his hands down

my thighs, over my knees, his fingers grazing the top of my silver socks. "I like these, too." He lifts his head, his eyes on mine, his lips parted as his chest heaves, like just being here, at my feet, turns him on, too. "I like *you.*"

"Then why did you—"

He turns his head, biting my other thigh, hard enough a whimper bubbles up my throat, but I bite my lip and swallow it down. I see teeth marks this time when he releases me, saliva glistening in the sun, against my skin. "Because I am an idiot."

Yes.

"It won't happen again."

I don't believe you.

He pushes his hands down, crumpling my socks in his wake, the air cool on my exposed flesh. His fingertips massage my calves, a weakness in my knees trembling with his touch. "Eden."

I hold my breath.

"I can't get enough of you. I can't stop thinking about you, dreaming about you. I have nightmares where you run away from me, and you never look back."

Stop.

"None of these shitty things I do… they don't mean anything to me."

"But they do to me." I inject ice in my words even as I feel as if I'm on fire.

He kisses the inside of my knee, then pulls back, sitting on his heel as he slowly glides one sock back up, his fingers drifting over my skin, then the other. He places his hands on his thighs as he looks up at me when he's done.

"I know. I'm sorry."

In the distance, I hear a car's tires crunching over gravel. He doesn't look over his shoulder, but I know he hears it too, because he sighs, like he didn't want this to end here, even though he's already righted my clothes. Maybe he heard the car before me. It's not impossible. When he's on his knees below me, it's hard to pay attention to anything else.

"Forgive me. Don't hold this against me."

I think about his phone. I see it, just over his shoulder, face down. *Are you only lonely, Eli?* The realization I might be the single person on this planet to understand him is staggering. It obliterates thoughts of Luna and him from my mind. It… scares me.

I straighten from the tree as we hear voices from the parking lot, and I see a stroller being unfolded from the back of an SUV.

Slowly, I offer him my hand.

He doesn't take long to grab it, jerking me forward until he can flip my palm and nuzzle his face against it. The hairs along the back of my arms stand on end, then he's getting to his feet, yanking me into him, wrapping his arms around my body as I grab his own, peering up into his face.

He tilts his head and kisses me, but I don't kiss him back.

"I'm sorry," he says again, pulling away, nudging his nose to mine.

"I know." He's as sorry as he could be, I think.

He smiles a little, kissing me again, and this is the softest our lips have ever touched one another, even though I don't reciprocate, testing my willpower, flexing my restraint.

He groans, but he doesn't say a word about it. Instead, he asks, "You're going to stop ignoring me now at school?"

"It was two days." I squeeze the hard muscles of his arms, my eyes locked on his, my thoughts a million miles away.

"It was torture." He smiles, but I don't return it.

I want to say something. Demand he won't do this anymore.

I think of his phone. His passcode. Him on his knees.

All I manage to get out is, "Don't fuck with me again." It's half-hearted. My voice is even distant. I'm barely here.

He studies me a long moment. Then he says, like he means it, "Okay."

"Don't forget your stupid phone."

He smiles, shaking his head, then he drops his hands from me, turning to grab his phone and push it into his pocket.

My mind jumps to Dominic and deviousness as he turns to face me again. If Eli is lonely, how far could I push him? Could I make him... *need* me?

As we walk to his car, hand in hand, the family going for a stroll in the park giving us shallow head nods, the man glancing at my skirt and Eli parking his hand on my hip and pulling me into his side, I can't help but agree with him, about the torture of ignoring him.

No matter what we do to each other, hearing about everything he let Luna do, it's all preferable to not speaking to him at all.

It makes the thought of the future hurt that much more. I think I'd let him get away with anything at all, stabbing me over and over and over, if only he would beg me to come back, over and over again, just like this.

The torture kind of makes life worth living. The power makes me feel loved.

It's why we won't make it.

You can only survive so many knife wounds before you simply... bleed out.

27

Eden

I SKETCH OUT, in words, the backstory to my main character of the book I'm working on. Sitting alone in the darkness of the library, earbuds in and my phone face down and on silent, I think about my heroine's trauma. We put so much emphasis on it. The worst things that ever happened to us. Like an ugly, red wax stamp sealed over our foreheads, marking it for life. My heroine has a past, sure, but much like my own, she doesn't spend every waking moment thinking about it.

After I finish up the two sentences it takes to sum up the low point of her childhood, I drop my pen to my notebook and my head into my hands. Spreading my elbows, knocking into *The Light of Egypt*, the black tome sliding across the table, I massage my temples as BANKS plays in my ear.

But inside my head, I hear Eli's words from yesterday morning, in the park. Touching on my own trauma. *"You don't like anyone to touch you, except me."*

He hasn't asked, but Nic did. Another of my exes too. I always stumbled over the truth. *"I just don't like to be touched."*

It's true. Fingers on my skin make me feel trapped. Stuck. Sweaty. It's not painful or emotionally loaded. It's just... I like to be in control, and with a hand on my body, I don't feel that way.

Is there trauma?

I press my thumbs over my eyelids. Who cares? We all have it.

Sighing, I sit up, snatching up my phone and curling up in my chair. I'm wearing ripped leggings, the destroyed jean jacket I keep hidden from Mom over a tied white tee I think used to belong to Sebastian.

Eli has texted me.

I don't even read it, despite the fact I want to. I know what I told him yesterday morning in the woods. I know he thought when he got on his knees for me, he absolved himself of his sins.

But the more I've imagined his dick in someone else's mouth, the more I've distanced myself from him. *And the more he's chased me.*

I open up a message from Manda.

Her: Maybe we can get together soon?

A pang of guilt courses through me. Even after what happened, she was on my side. I was escorted down the hall, and she walked beside me, stride for stride. I remember wishing she hadn't. I remember hating the pity rolling off of her in waves, even as she glared at people snickering on the sidelines, crowded around lockers, discreetly snapping photos with their phones.

I've left Amanda on read for a few days now, and in that time, she's sent three messages. I don't know why the fuck I'm like this.

I blow out a breath and respond before I try to put this off, too, and never get around to it.

Me: That would be great.

Truthfully, I wouldn't mind a drive down to the beach. I could stay at her house. Free food and a place to sleep, in exchange for the charade of socializing.

Her: Wow, didn't expect to get a response.
Me: Didn't expect to send one, honestly.

Shit. Not what I should've said. Sighing, I close out that message and open up Sebastian's.

Him: I'm dropping your car off at 9. You good with that?
Me: Huh?

How the hell is he getting anywhere then? Of course I'm good with that. I rarely get to drive my car during the week unless I'm going to work, but then how is he getting home?

Him: A buddy is following me, going to his place afterward. Won't be able to take you home like I said I would.

I frown, thinking I should say something. *Do* something. It's Thursday night, though. I guess for a guy with no job, it's basically the start of the weekend, right?

I sigh, sending off a text with no argument, no questions.

Me: Cool, thanks.

I put down my phone, skip to "37 Stitches", and turn it up loud.

I glance at the book on the table, briefly think about diving into Egyptian mythology and magic, but instead, music in my ears, I close my eyes in the darkness and try to… tap into the spirit realm, something I do when I have time alone in the dark. So far, to no avail.

But one day.

On the one hand, I feel kind of silly. Kind of nervous, too. On the other hand, I think of the sigils scrawled in my notebook in my underwear drawer, and if I believe any of that came true, it's not entirely out of the realm of possibility magic exists, is it?

I've heard rumors of sects channeling darkness, even in North Carolina. There's a heavy, underground occult scene in this state which has a cult-like following. Mom thinks her sister was taken by a cult. My aunt and Mom haven't spoken since I was a toddler. But then again, Mom also thought Pastor Griffin down at the coast was a saint, and Amanda and I heard rumors about what he did with the older teen boys who went to Sunday school.

Wrinkling my nose, I try to relax.

The song plays on repeat, and the repetitiveness helps me zone out. When I'm writing, when I'm running, sometimes when I swam laps, the wireless speaker on the edge of the pool near the end of after-school care when Mom was a little late. Not enough to pay extra but enough to make me the last person there for pick up. Maybe it's there I found comfort in solitude.

I wrap my arms around my shins, my boots slipped off and socked feet on the chair. I press my temple to my knees, closing my eyes in my cocoon.

This castle is old. If death lingers anywhere, if spirits wander places with pasts, maybe it would be here.

Chills skitter down my spine. I feel a pinch of fear, the same feeling I always get when I'm crossing lines I was conditioned to stay safely within. Lines that say this kind of thing will send me to hell. My soul is corrupted. I'm going to burn for eternity. But it's confusing because I prayed the Sinner's Prayer like one thousand times growing up, and allegedly, that single act will send me to heaven. Multiply it by a thousand, and what do I have to fear?

I settle in deeper in my chair, relaxing a little at my own caustic thoughts. I can hear nothing beyond the music, and that includes my heartbeat.

I just breathe, knowing Seb will be here soon and he doesn't know where the library is and I'll need to go meet him in the parking lot. But for now, it all falls away.

Then cold graces my shoulder blades, despite the fact they aren't exposed. My throat feels a little tight, and I think maybe I should get up, and go wait outside, but I force myself to stay. To fight against my nerves. *Nothing is going to get me.*

I just breathe. Being with Eli feels a little like this. A thrill mixed with paranoia.

There's no one here. Nothing here. Trafalgar has a lot of after school activities but very few take place outside of a sports arena and even fewer in the darkened corners of a library. Language has their own wing of the castle, math and chess are on the business hall, marketing and design in one of the smaller brick buildings dotting campus.

No one is here.

Breathe.

Then I hear it. A thud. A loud crash.

I spring open my eyes, ripping my earphones out and tossing them to the table, staring in the darkness, my chest heaving. The music from my ear buds plays softly in the background, and as I scan the aisles, I see nothing flickering in the pale orange light.

My chest heaves.

Am I hearing things?

I close my eyes shut tight, my fingers gripping the table as I try to combat the terror.

I shouldn't have done this, play with my mind when it's already so fragile sometimes. But I'm okay. *I'm okay.*

If I didn't have an overactive imagination, I'd probably be a shitty writer.

I'm fine.

Until… someone grabs me.

I jump up, eyes flying open, blinking in the darkness. I don't really think, I just throw an elbow into a body behind me as my chair clatters to the polished floor. But hands grab my upper arms from behind, squeezing painfully, and I'm jerked backward into a hard chest, my socks sliding against the floor.

I twist in a strong grip, opening my mouth to scream, seeing no one ahead of me, only rows and rows of silent books. No ghosts have come to save me, either.

Before a sound leaves my mouth, a hand comes over it, and the release of my arm gives me more leverage. I thrust my hand behind me, searching for a weak point, eyes, a mouth, anything, at the same time I open my own mouth to bite my attacker. My canines sink into their palm, and I hear a loud hiss as my heart thuds painfully in my chest.

Whoever it is shoves me forward, yanking their hand from my teeth.

I spin around, my hips colliding with the table.

Dominic is holding a hand over his eye, glowering at me.

I don't speak, my chest heaving as silence is pulled tight between us. He has no books, dressed in a black track jacket and fitted sweats, I caught the scent of chlorine on my mouth, now that I can think, I remember it. He must've come from the pool.

"A seance? Summoning demons?" He drops his hand and glances at the black book on the table, and at the same time his eyes move to the notebook behind me, I shift on my feet. Just a little, enough to get his attention and block my scrawl from view as I catch my breath.

If you act like your secrets matter, anyone who steals one has power over you.

If I close the book, he'll know I don't want him to read it.

I refuse to do it. I act more subtle. I don't show him how freaked out I am right now, either. And how, some strange part of me is relieved it's someone actually here. *I wasn't hallucinating.*

I have to swallow a few times to ensure my voice won't shake, then I say, "Yeah, looks like the summons worked." I eye him from head to toe and see how he tries to fight his smile as I cross my arms, waiting for his move. I think of Sebastian, and if Dom doesn't start talking in three seconds, I'm getting my ass out of here.

"God, you're such a bitch." He laughs as he says it, and it doesn't bother me at all. I don't mind being a bitch. If it means I put down boundaries and, occasionally, as long as Eli isn't around, respect myself, then so be it. "If I want his attention, I should just be a little meaner to him, huh?"

Speaking of the devil. I roll my eyes, thinking of Eli's texts on my phone. The way he looked as if he'd tear Dom's throat out when Dom made me scream.

My pulse starts to fly again.

"I gotta go." I turn my back to Dominic and carefully close my notebook, taking my time so it doesn't seem important to me. I snatch up my checkered bag from the floor, drop in my writing, book, pens, then I scoop up my earbuds from the table and put those away, too. I push my feet into my boots, then zip up my backpack, sling it over my shoulder, and grab my phone, glancing at my texts.

Another from Eli. One from Amanda. Two from Seb, but he hasn't called, so he must not be here yet. The preview isn't visible on any of my texts because I never want anyone in my family to read them over my shoulder.

I hear the floor creak behind me as I swipe up to unlock my phone, and before I can read more than one line of Eli's most recent text—of course the thing displayed first, **Baby girl, I'm coming for you**—Dom speaks in my ear, causing a shiver to slide down my spine.

I ignore Eli's words, dismiss them as empty, even though a part of me knows he doesn't say things like that for shits and giggles.

"Did you know we used to come down here with Winslet sometimes, in the night?" Dom's breath is warm, coasting over my piercings, and I smell alcohol. My stomach flips.

Is he drunk at school? What is he doing here? Waiting for her?

I take in the high ceilings, dim orange lighting. Anything to distract myself from his nearness, but I want to hear his words. Just like Saturday, I play into how close he is to me.

I back up into him.

His hand comes to my hip, curling around my flesh, just over my leggings.

My mouth goes dry, but I don't say anything at all.

"It was our favorite place to hang out." The scent of chlorine and alcohol dissipates the smell of old books and decades of history. "Sometimes, I think she's just waiting behind one of these aisles." He laughs and I flex my jaw, scared despite the fact I don't want to be.

"What do you think happened to her?" I ask quietly, seizing the moment.

Dom's lips graze the skin of my neck, exposed from my hair, pulled up in a crown of braids again, done just last night.

Goosebumps erupt on my flesh.

I close my eyes. I see Eli's text in my head. *Baby girl, I'm coming for you.*

"Maybe she just ran away from us."

My mouth goes dry. *Us.*

I want Eli's secrets. He won't give them. But Dominic...

Heart racing, I take another step back into him.

I feel how turned on he is and cringe a little, but he doesn't notice. I hear his sharp intake of breath.

"Why would she run?" I ask quietly.

Dom's hand glides over my hip, around to my belly, his thumb slipping under the hem of my shirt. On my skin.

It feels like cheating. Like a wave of guilt I'm going to drown in.

"Don't you want to, sometimes? Being around him?"

I tilt my head back, resting it against his chest, my phone gripped tight in one hand, other still flexed around a single strap of my bag. "Yeah," I say. "Sometimes."

Dominic laughs, the rumble against my back. "He hurt you, didn't he, at his house?" My stomach drops as Dom's mouth moves over my neck.

"Has he ever hurt you?" My voice is hoarse.

"Sure." He kisses the tip of my ear and I grind my teeth. "And I think you're the only one who could hurt him back."

I open my eyes, staring at the ceiling, but I don't move away from him. "Dominic." I say his name very slowly, then turn around, and his hand slips from my hip. I can breathe a little easier this way, facing him, not touching him. With my flat tone, I see the same surprise I saw in Eli's eyes when I didn't immediately react to his description of getting head from Luna is deeper on Dom's face. Boys always seem to underestimate me. "You're drunk." *But I can use you, can't I?* "You don't really want me to hurt him."

He only smiles at me, and it looks like something he learned from Eli.

I see my phone light up in my hand. Sebastian is calling, and I don't want him to drive off with my car or lock my keys in or something stupid. And part of me… part of me wants to get away from Dom. I shouldn't bait him, I know, it just seems so easy to do sometimes.

Still holding Dom's gaze, I bring my phone to my ear and answer the call. "Hello?"

Dom's smile falters.

"Yo, I'm out here. In the visitor lot."

"Be there in two minutes." I end the call. "Move," I tell Dominic. "Or I'll summon Satan this time, instead."

Dom steps back, and I refuse to show the relief I feel. Phone in one hand, the strap of my bag in my other, I veer around him and head for the exit.

Naturally, he follows, and my boots clomp along the wooden floors while at one point, his sneakers squeak, maybe from pool water or perhaps the cleaning crew.

I'm content to walk in silence, even knowing his dick is nice and hard because of me. I don't feel guilty for *that*, and nothing in me wants to break the quiet. But as we head down the narrow, dark hallway of the library that'll lead to the visitor lot, Dom must not feel the same way.

He brushes his shoulder against me, and I stiffen before discreetly moving away. I focus on the sliver of lamp light from the rectangular pane in the door leading outside, straight ahead.

"Why do you do that?" he asks quietly. I'm surprised he doesn't appear to be mocking me, but I still don't look at him.

"Do what?" I feign ignorance even as my palm grows sweaty over my phone and I walk a little faster, trying to outpace Dom's long-legged stride.

"I mean, do I stink or something?" Dom pulls at his jacket, like he's fanning himself.

I roll my eyes but a smile forms anyway on my lips. "I like my space."

Dom drops his hand and scoffs. "Didn't seem like it in there."

I ignore his quip.

He keeps pushing. "And Eli doesn't give you any. You already made up, huh?"

We reach the narrow door and I turn to the side, pushing it open with my elbow, cool air giving me a much-needed breeze as I look at Dom, following behind. "Stay out of my relationship with Eli." I don't move from the doorway as we lock eyes.

He narrows his. "Relationship? That's what you're doing now?"

"Oh, no. With the shit you have going on with Luna." I shake my head. "Don't talk." I want to tell him what Eli told me, but I'm worried he already knows, and if he doesn't, I'm not really sure I want to be the one to cause more tension between him and Luna. Besides, it'll just make *me* look bad.

He rolls his eyes. "Luna and I don't really *date.*" He shrugs, glancing at the ground. "I don't know, we just fuck around because we've been friends so long, I guess."

Kinda like what you do with Eli?

I study him a moment, then, wanting to change the subject far away from *Luna*, I jerk my chin toward the lot, see Sebastian opening the door to my *slow, baby Sentra*, a truck idling beside it. "You wanna meet my brother or you want to stop stalking me?" I glance back at him and watch as he cocks his head, bottom lip pulled between his teeth. He doesn't look at all like I've pissed him off with those words.

He looks… like he wants me.

Cool. Exactly what I wasn't going for this time.

"I don't need to meet your brother," he finally says, stepping closer to the doorway and knocking it further open with his shoulder, jostling me so I concede a step. He cuts his eyes over my head a second, in the direction of my car. "I already know him."

Sebastian drops the keys into my upturned palm, but he's not looking at me. His friend in the truck is listening to something twangy, window rolled down and a vape cloud pouring out the driver's side window. He's got a hat pulled down low, so I can't see his face as we stand in front of my car, but I can feel his eyes on us.

Or, maybe like Seb's, just on Dom.

I curl my fingers around my keys, holding them by my side but discreetly slipping my house key between my index and middle finger in case I need a weapon.

Dom is far taller than Seb, but my brother is used to being one of the shortest people in the room, and it doesn't seem to bother him at all. In an off-white muscle tank, a cigarette tucked behind his ear, almost hidden by his wispy blond hair, he stares right up at Dom without backing down.

"You dealing to my sister?"

I roll my eyes. "Your sister can speak for herself and—"

"I don't deal. I buy. Some of us have the money," Dom puts a hand over his heart, "and some of us just wish we did." He drops his hand but not his smirk.

His words make me bristle. Seb and I live in the same fucking house.

"Fuck off, Dom," I snarl, and Seb glances at me with surprise, like he can't believe I'm sticking up for him.

I ignore the flush of heat rising up my chest as I turn toward Dom, so my shoulder is next to my brother's.

Without taking his eyes off of Seb, Dom smiles lazily. "I'm just curious how you even have the money for dope. Or do you just suck King's dick?"

King. The name sounds a little familiar.

"I'm just curious how no one has snapped your neck yet, or

did you just share your sister every time you pissed someone off—"

I step in front of Dom as he lunges, shoving him back, digging my key into his chest as I put myself between him and my brother. He has his fist cocked, his eyes on Seb, who definitely crossed a line.

"Get the fuck out of my way, E." Dom grabs my upper arm with his free hand, my skin crawling beneath his touch, and he tugs me closer to him, pushing me up against my car with a thud.

Sebastian steps up, standing on his tiptoes to get in Dom's face. I let my bag slide down my arm, grabbing the strap when I can and hurling it toward Dominic, whacking him in the side to get him away from my brother.

Dominic ignores me, pointing in Seb's face. "Fuck you, you piece of shit. Don't ever talk about my sister—"

I hit him again, and this time he grabs my bag, jerking me and it toward him. My boots scuff on the pavement and Sebastian is reaching for Dominic's throat but he's too fucking short and—

"Eden?" I hear a feminine voice at my back.

Everyone stills, and I realize the guy in the truck hasn't moved an inch, but I see something over his shoulder in the dark.

A fucking rifle. These are the people my brother is hanging out with. Including *Dom*, apparently.

My stomach flips as I meet Dom's eye, then turn to see a tall figure striding toward me in the dark.

It takes me a second to realize who it is, but when I do, I feel relief.

"Let go of her," Janelle says to Dom, a growl in her words. Her dreads are pulled in a high ponytail, and she's wearing a fitted white shirt with capped sleeves, like for running. Judging by the glow of perspiration on her cheekbones under the lamplight, that's exactly what she was doing.

She doesn't touch me as she gets closer, but her eyes search mine, then dart to Seb, and finally, his friend in the truck.

I know she spots the rifle.

I see her freeze.

It's over in a second, two heartbeats, but it was there. Slowly, she turns back to me, coming between the truck and the car as Dom releases my backpack and I stumble toward her from the force.

She glances at my Sentra. "This yours?" She doesn't ask a thing about Dom, or Seb, or the gun.

I nod once, keys still in hand as I sling my backpack on my shoulder again, trying to pretend I'm fine.

"Give me a ride?"

I arch a brow, but Janelle turns a knowing look on me. I want to get the hell out of this parking lot and she's offering me an exit.

I nod once and clear my throat. "Sure."

Dominic laughs bitterly. "I hope the two of you have a great night." When I glance over my shoulder, he's looking at me, then Janelle, and neither of us speak as he spins around, walking off. I wonder for a split second if I should offer him a ride, too. I assume he drove to school, drank after practice. He probably shouldn't be driving.

Before I can say anything, Seb calls after him. "Sorry to embarrass you, man."

I roll my eyes at Janelle, not facing my brother. Now's not the time to discuss it, but I heard Dom's words. *Dope.* I feel like I was pushed into ice cold water. I mean, maybe he was referring to weed, but I'm starting to think it's more than that. More, even, than a few pills on the weekends at parties.

I don't know what to do. I don't know what the fuck to say.

Feeling uneasy, I pull open the back door of my Sentra and toss my bag in, shut the door, and open up the driver's one.

I nod toward Janelle. "You got anything you need to bring?"

She smiles. "Nope."

Taking a breath as Janelle walks over to the passenger side, I turn to Sebastian. He's still glaring in the direction of Dom's retreating form.

"I know he's a dick but why'd you have to bring up his sister?"

Seb doesn't look at me. A cool breeze blows through the night, rattling the trees in the dark lot. "He was messing with *mine*. Besides," he lowers his voice a little, "I've heard he was fucking weird about her."

"Well, she *is* missing," I point out, knowing he knows, because he brought it up. The first time he tried to warn me away from Eli. *This is how he knew of him.*

Seb nods once, then trains his gaze on me. "Yeah," he says, "she is."

Janelle hasn't closed her door, I realize, as I hover outside of mine, looking up at Seb over the top of it. Like she wants to be ready to help me.

Gratitude surges through me even though I know we're safe with my brother. Then again, judging by the company he keeps... maybe not.

"Be careful around him." Sebastian's words are quiet, and he's lost some of his testosterone fueled bravado.

I nod once. "Be careful tonight," I counter, glancing at his friend with the gun.

Seb doesn't smile, but he says, "Drive safe." Then he turns around and heads to the passenger side of the truck.

I slip behind the wheel of my car, turn over the engine and fiddle with the frayed cord to connect my phone to the stereo, blasting "37 Stitches" again, so many questions dancing in my mind.

My phone lights up in my hand before I drop it in the console.

Glancing up at Janelle, who is turned to look out her window and seems in no rush to get out of here, I unlock my phone.

There's the text I read from Eli in the library.

Him: Baby girl, I'm coming for you. I thought we were over this shit.

And a new one.

Him: I wouldn't trust my friends if I were you. And next time you want to get some other guy hard for you, consider the fact I might actually kill him.

A lump forms in my throat.

I look up at Janelle again.

She's still staring out the window.

Another text comes through from Eli. This time, it's a photo.

It's dark and blurry, but thanks to his bleached blond hair and the trees edging the sidewalk, I don't need to zoom in to know *who* it is.

Dominic.

And *where.*

Here.

My heart races as I stare at the screen, but it isn't fear I feel. Not exactly.

It's intrigue. *Where are you hiding?*

This time, I text him back.

Me: You should've done something about it.

I drop my phone, slip on my seatbelt, and I sweep my eyes over the dark campus one final time before I drive Janelle and I toward the iron gates. I think I see a looming shadow by the fountain in front of the library. I tap the brakes, but when I look up in the rear-view mirror, the shadow is gone.

"Thank you," I tell Janelle. "For your diversion back there." I've been following the directions to her place, and she warned me she lives in Eli's neighborhood. I try not to think too much about it. Apparently, given the fact he's stalking Dominic, he's not home.

I like Janelle. There's something a little distant about her and I like it because it's a reflection of myself.

She shrugs, waving off my thanks. Rain starts to spatter on my windshield, and I flick on my brights and my wipers as we take a winding back road.

"I was going to Uber home," she says, which surprises me.

I glance at her but keep my eyes mostly on the road, taking a curve a lot slower than Eli would. Then I remember him mocking my car.

I press down a little more on the gas. The RPMs rev up, but he's right. My Sentra is slow.

"Really?" I ask Janelle. "I thought you had a car?"

"Oh, I do," she says quickly, with the smallest, tinkling laugh. "But my *mother* backed into our mailbox the other night after she wanted it for a girl's night out." She rubs her arms, crossed over her chest. "Better than her coupe. She would have lost it over that. Anyway, it's just getting a fresh paint job."

I wonder about her mom, and if she was drunk, or it was intentional. But maybe none of those things are true. Just shit that would happen with Sebastian.

So, all I say is, "I'm glad I could give you a ride."

Janelle smiles. "Keep going straight 'til the stop sign, then take a left." She clears her throat as I nod, grateful for her directions because I suck at them, even though I've been to Eli's before. For a moment, we ride in silence, but I have too many questions to keep quiet. I don't know why I never thought of it before, getting closer to Eli's female friends. Maybe because they didn't particularly seem to want to get close to me. Or maybe that was all in my head. Janelle was always nice to me. I just seem to constantly believe everyone is against me.

I take the most obvious lead, considering where we just left. "Is Dominic always an asshole?" My heart beats fast, and I grip my wheel tight in the split second after I ask, but relief spreads through me as Janelle just laughs.

"Oh, boy," she says, and I see her turn to look out her own window. "Well, yeah, but he was less so when Winslet was around." Her tone grows more serious, and I wonder how close she was to Dom's sister.

I clear my throat, staring at the dark road as I drive. "They were close?"

Janelle sighs, still turned away from me. "Yeah. Really close."

I keep pushing, pulse racing as I do. "My brother back there, Sebastian… Did you hear him? What he said about Dom being weird about Winslet?"

I tighten my grip on the wheel. Lightning forks in the sky and the rain comes down harder, clattering loudly over the roof. I increase the wiper's speed and take a few deep breaths as the stretch of silence grows.

I glance at the dark woods my headlights jump over as I drive. I remember Eli's words.

I wouldn't trust my friends.

Was Janelle good timing? Does she know he was there? *Does he want me to question everything?*

"I'm not as close with Dom," Janelle finally says.

It sounds like half of the truth.

"Him, Winslet, Luna, Eli… They were like a whole… group. I was friends with Eli, because we live in the same neighborhood, you know." She turns to glance at me in the dark, smiling a little, but it seems off. Like she's keeping his secrets.

"Eli was close to Winslet, too?" I try not to let my fascination show, but I can't stop the way my voice rises. I see a sign cautioning of a stop up ahead and I slow down, my tires jumping over puddles.

Janelle is staring straight ahead, too. "As close as he is to anyone."

The hairs on the back of my neck stand on end.

"It seems a little different," she keeps going, voice soft. "With you."

I come to a complete stop and meet her gaze in the dark.

"When he talks about you..." This time, her smile is genuine. "It's like he's at some kind of peace."

I think of his texts. I wonder what Janelle would say about those.

On some level, I know he's scary. Maybe going too far. Evil instead of eccentric.

But on another level, well... *I like it.*

"Is he usually not so... peaceful?" The word seems strange, to describe him that way.

Janelle laughs, and I love the sound. It's light and beautiful. Nothing like Eli's cold bite of laughter, or my own caustic huffs of amusement. "Eli is..." Janelle trails off, and I realize I'm gripping my steering wheel so tight my hands start to ache as I wait for her to finish her sentence. *Tell me everything.* "He's like the ocean, you know. The surface always looks so calm, most nights," I don't miss the fact she uses *night* instead of *day,* "but underneath, it could be hell, and no one would ever know, unless they dive in deep."

My pulse is rabid in my throat. "And have you? Dived deep?" I slow my speed, knowing Eli and Janelle's subdivision is coming up, and I don't want to finish this conversation just yet.

"No," she answers without hesitation. There's no amusement now in her words, only a solemn sort of wonder, and I can feel her eyes on me as the looming mansions high up on the hill come into view. "You have to hold your breath a long time to go that far under."

I think about Eli keeping me pinned down inside of his pool, my stomach twisting into knots.

My fingers are shaky as I flick on my turn signal. I press the brakes, dragging out the turn.

"Eli likes to pretend he doesn't give a fuck about anything," Janelle continues.

I hold my breath, taking the turn into her neighborhood. The clink of the turn signal cuts off, but the same song still plays in the background, on a loop. Janelle hasn't once complained.

"Sharks shed blood in the ocean all the time, and we sit on the beach watching the waves without thinking twice about it. It's only when they get too close we panic."

Come closer.

Tell me when to stop.

I keep driving on the dark street, and I'm no longer pulled in by the opulence, the shimmering pools visible as I drive, the luxury vehicles, the four car garages. I don't even know where I'm going, but I don't care. I just want Janelle to keep talking about my boy.

"I think he knows what goes on inside his head…" Janelle drifts off and I tense, my shoulders hunched around my ears as I drive. "It isn't exactly normal. And he doesn't want anyone to panic."

My mouth goes dry, and I come to a stop sign in the neighborhood. It's a four-way stop, and she doesn't give me a direction, so I press the gas, shooting straight across the intersection, not wanting to break this moment to talk.

"Or maybe he's just learned how to mimic everything, and he shows us what we want to see." Janelle is whispering, but her voice has a far-off quality, like she's sitting right beside me, but she's not really *here*. Like she's talking about someone else.

I don't dare look at her. I'm a little nervous about what I might see.

Then she just laughs, like it's all a joke. "Anyway, he's really into you."

I feel her eyes on me and I can't help but ask, "Has he been like this? Before? He never talks about exes." I want to ask about Winslet specifically, but it feels a little too much.

Janelle is quiet a moment, then she says, "No one can keep that boy's interest for long."

Somehow, I get roped into going inside Janelle's house after we exchanged numbers in my car. She had something for me, she said. I sent Mom a quick text I'd be a little late, and she told me to be home within the hour, so I don't get far inside Janelle's mansion. It's dark, and kind of dreary, with a gray chandelier hanging in the foyer. But she sprinted upstairs when I told her I couldn't stay and came back with a stack of books, thick, well-worn volumes she thrusts into my hands now.

I take them, glancing down, thanks on the tip of my tongue, when I catch the title of the one on top.

An Introduction to Teleportation.

Shocked, but smiling, I lift my eyes to hers as she adjusts her ponytail, then places her hands on her hips, shrugging. "Eli said you liked magic."

My chest warms, and I think of his texts, meant to make me nervous. But now, this. He's talking about me, and not about my body, or how he wants to fuck me—although maybe he's talking about that, too, in which case, great—but about *me*.

"Wow," I say, shaking my head, feeling a little off balance as I take a step back, toward the towering double doors behind me. "Thank you. Are you sure you want to part with—"

"Yes, definitely." Janelle nods once, but I see the crease between her brows. She pulls her lower lip between her teeth, staring at the books in my hands, my palms on the bottom and top of the stack, five tomes in total. "They're just collecting dust. You'll enjoy them more than I would." She brings her dark gaze to mine. "I have trouble believing."

I accept that without argument. You can't talk people into belief. "Well, thank you," I say again. "I really appreciate it."

She smiles, and we hear thunder rumble outside, shaking her entire house, which is a feat. She glances over my head, at the panes of glass above the doors as rain slams into them, making me jump. "You could stay the night here, you know." She glances around her silent house. "It's nasty outside—"

"I'll be okay." I don't have any of my things, and I know she's just being nice. I'd feel like an inconvenience, and she's already done a lot for me tonight. I turn from her, swiping at my bangs, tucking them behind my ear. "Thank you again, and I'll see you tomorrow."

She darts in front of me, opening up the door to the onslaught of the storm.

After I reassure her I'm more than okay to drive, I tuck the books close to my chest and sprint down her steps, past the fountain in the circular driveway, and to my car, parked behind a freaking limo.

I yank open my back door, dump in my books, close the door, and slip in behind the wheel, slamming my own door closed and wiping water from my temple with the back of my hand as I take a breath, adrenaline coursing through me.

The rain is *loud*, and I can't see shit through my windshield. But my car isn't on yet, and the wipers are stationery, so I know once I get that taken care of and my lights flicked on, I'll be okay.

I turn the key I left in the ignition, and the dash lights fill the cabin of my Sentra as my yellow headlights shine on the rear of the limo.

"Fifty Shades" by s0cliché starts playing loudly as I blindly reach for my seatbelt, watching lightning streak across the sky in a bright, vivid shade of blue. When I drop my gaze to click my belt in place, *I almost fucking scream.*

My heart leaps to my throat, the belt slides from my fingers, and my pulse ricochets inside my head. I don't even have words for a long moment, they're stuck inside my open mouth as I blink, taking in *Eli Addison* in my back fucking seat, opposite the books I hurriedly tossed in.

He has his elbows on his knees, his hands pressed together, resting just under his chin as he watches me, dressed all in black, the skull ring on his middle finger glinting from the dash lights. There's the slightest smile on his face, and he is perfectly still.

I press a hand to my chest, feeling my heart racing beneath

my shirt, my jacket pushed back on my shoulders as I tighten my other hand around the wheel.

"Hi," he says softly, and I still haven't yet caught my breath. I can't speak, so he keeps going. "If you don't mind…" He nods toward the front seat, and without waiting for my response, he gets out, shuts the door, and gracefully gets into the front, closing the door and quieting the storm raging outside.

I inhale, great gulping breaths, heart hammering hard. "What the *fuck* are you doing?"

He swipes his hand over his dark hair, rain flecking from his strands as he looks at me, dropping his palm to his lap, fingers splayed.

I think about his texts.

The photo of Dom.

"I could ask the same of you. You like playing with Dom in the library?"

Every limb in my body is tense and shaky all at once. I want to smash his head against the window. I want to kiss him so hard he bleeds. "You're stalking me."

He rolls his eyes, a smirk pulling at his lips. "Who has whose passcode to their phone?"

My pulse is loud inside my head. The music seems louder, still, as I stare off with him.

"Let me see yours." The request is said like an afterthought, like he's asking for spare change. His eyes drop down to my phone in the console.

"See it?" I taunt him.

His smile is eerie as lightning illuminates just this side of his face. "What has Dom been whispering to you in the dark?"

"What happened to Winslet?"

His eyes lift to mine. "Unlock your phone for me."

"Get out of my car." The cold rain is wicking away from the back of my neck, causing chills to course through my body. My leg starts to tremble, my foot on the brake even though I haven't put the car in drive yet.

He stays silent. I wonder what he thinks about in these moments, when he's watching, taking everything in, but refusing to give a piece of himself. He wants all the cards. He makes all the calculations. He writes the rules of the game before anyone makes a play.

"Unlock your phone." He repeats the words.

I grind my teeth, turning to stare out at the storm.

I sense him as he leans in close. He's an icy darkness, far more terrifying than the lightning and thunder and downpour happening all around us. He's frozen in my veins, he could stop my heart. He could take my life, and I'm not sure I'd mind. *That* is what scares me. Not him. *Never him.*

"Unlock. Your. *Fucking.* Phone."

I close my eyes as if I can turn off my feelings.

His finger trails over one of the rips in my leggings, and pinpricks of pleasure and nerves swirl beneath my skin. Slowly, he curls every finger of his hand around my thigh, sliding it up, and up, and up, until his smallest finger is between my legs, and I feel the cold ring of his middle finger on another tear in my pants.

"Show me." He runs his mouth over the top of my ear, and I feel my nipples tighten, an ache between my thighs, his finger teasing me, barely touching me. "Show me how you hurt me when I can't see."

"He doesn't have my number." I grit the words out, my eyes still closed. "You fucking psycho, *he doesn't have my fucking number.*"

Another round of silence. It's a weapon, the way he wields it. But then he says, "I'm sorry. For what I did. I know you're trying to punish me. But if you ever grind against Dominic like you did tonight in the library again," my heart skips a beat and I'm craving my pills, in the front pouch of my backpack on the floorboard behind me. "I'm going to kill him, and you'll help me bury his body, okay, Eden?"

My eyes snap open and I watch lightning heat the dark clouds overhead.

I twist around in my seat, grabbing his wrist, digging my nails into his skin as I face him, my eyes locking on his as he straightens.

"Next time you see him corner me in the dark," I say, my words low, hopefully as cold as his were, "don't just watch. *Do something about it.*"

I release him, shoving his hand off me as I try to catch my breath.

He smiles, and I'm not afraid, but my anger rises to the surface faster with the expression. "Take your own advice when it comes to any other girl talking to me, or touching me, or dry *fucking* me, *okay, baby girl?*" He undoes his seatbelt, reaching for the door.

I have the urge to tell him to stop. To stay. To let me drive him home, at the least. But I keep all those words inside my mouth.

"I want you to want me all to yourself." He opens the door, the sound of spattering rain a roar in my ears. "It's exactly how I want *you.*" He still doesn't get out, and cold rain flecks across my chest, bouncing inside from the open door. "I'm taking you out tomorrow night, so if you made plans with Dom, cancel them. Go straight home, and text me when you get there." Without another word, he slips into the night like he belongs, closing my door gently as he does.

It's only then I hang my head.

Only then I close my eyes, gasping in the quiet interior of my car as I try to fucking *breathe.*

ME: HOME. IN BED.

I text him when I'm buried in my covers at home, face washed, and teeth brushed. I hold my phone over my head, watching him type, giddiness leaping in my heart. Our relationship is strange, and the warning signs are screaming at me, but I like the way they sound. And when I'm around him, when I'm talking to him, no matter what he did, or what he's going to do, *I can't get enough.*

Some fucked-up part of me is glad he stalked me at the library. Grateful he followed Dominic. Pleased he slipped inside my car at Janelle's. High off the nerves that had me shaking the entire drive home.

Some logical part of me knows it's wrong. *On so many levels.*

But I glance at my black bracelets, and though I can't see it in the night, I have the shape of the scars there memorized.

Him: Good girl.

My stomach clenches. He sends another text before I can reply.

Him: You're going out with me tomorrow, okay?

Me: Beg me. I'm smiling as I send off the message. I'm ignoring every bad thing we could be. With distance between us, fear gone, *I just don't care.*

He doesn't take long to respond. **Him: My Beautiful, Beautiful Nightmare Girl, please, fucking please, grace me with your presence tomorrow night. Let me take you on our first ever REAL date. I'll open your door and hold your hand and pay for the movie and you'll lie to your mom like a bad little girl and sleep in my bed, right beside me all night.**

Something worse than butterflies knot in my stomach and I bite my lip to keep from laughing.

Me: Are you going to touch me in your bed? My heart hammers hard as I send off the text.

Him: I can never keep my hands off of you.

I feel my face heat, and I'm scared to think too much about what could happen tomorrow night.

Me: You can't keep them off other girls either, apparently. I know I sent it as deflection, but… I'm still hurt. I'm not holding a grudge, I just don't like how I can't release the pain.

Him: I fucked up, Eden. I'm sorry. I know it hurt. I wish I could take it back.

I don't think I believe him, not really. But it's the best I'm going to get from him. So I just give him a little truth. **Me: You make me a jealous person.** I clutch my phone to my chest a second, unsure if I should have sent that or not.

Then he responds, but I wait until the vibrations die off to look at the screen.

Him: You have no idea how hot that is to me. And you have no idea how jealous I feel when it comes to anyone too close to you. But I promise, no one compares to you, Nightmare Girl.

I ignore the way those words make me feel dizzy. *Don't hurt me, Eli.* But I let it go, and what I say is, **Are you going to be able to sleep tonight?**

Him: Yeah. Finally.

And I know, without him saying it, he's talking about the past few nights, when things haven't been quite right between us.

After we say our goodnights, I roll onto my side and open up the photo I took of him in the rain at Dom's. He's sexy, and dark, and beautiful and free, and wanting to keep him just like this—content, at ease, belonging—it suddenly feels very, very heavy.

Icarus.

But I can't see his wings in this photo, and in this moment, I can't feel mine either.

28

Eden

"WHO ALL IS GOING?" Mom glances at me over her shoulder as she rubs down a spot of grease on the table in the kitchen.

I shake out my bracelets, shifting from foot to foot. I only got a few hours' sleep last night, and it's embarrassing, how many times I got myself off to that picture of Eli, long after he'd gone to bed.

"Janelle," I lie to Mom, "Luna," I almost choke on her name, "Eli, and maybe his cousin, I don't know." My hair is down for once, I rake my hands through it, for something to do as I stand under Mom's scrutiny. Does she know I'm lying? Does she feel sorry for me? Does she think I'm falling too hard and a boy like Eli would never, ever stick around to catch me?

But she just keeps wiping down the table, her soft arms jiggling a little, the thick, red and pink raised ridge of her scar visible beneath the sleeves of her soft shirt. Reece is gone to work, which is why I waited until now to ask, and Sebastian is presumably where he went last night.

He never came home.

Mom sighs, blowing a strand of her brown hair from over her eye. "And you're staying the night with Luna this time?" She glances at me once more, then straightens, walking over to the sink to rinse out the kitchen towel.

I chew the inside of my cheek and nod, then realize I need to speak out loud because she's turned the faucet on and is studying the towel as she rinses it. "Yep."

"Are you coming home after school?" Another glance toward me.

"I don't think so."

"Who are you going home with afterward?"

My body temperature grows hot. No one ever asks Sebastian any of these questions. I know he's older, and not in school, but he's literally getting high every other day it seems, and no one does anything about it. "I don't know, Mom, probably Eli." I clench my fingers around the straps of my bag, full of clothes to change into for the movie tonight, to wear at his house, and for tomorrow morning.

My swimsuit is presumably still in his bathroom, and it almost calms me, imagining it hanging over his shower.

"Lose your attitude." Mom flips off the sink and drapes the kitchen towel over the ledge, then runs her hands through her hair, leaning back against the counter. "You can go," she finally says. "Just be safe."

I can't hide my smile. "Thanks, Mom." I glance at the front door, the sun streaming through the little glass pane near the top. Eli isn't here yet, or I would've heard his car pull up. I'm thinking of going back to my room to triple check I've got everything I need for tonight, but Mom speaks before I can move.

"How do you think Seb is doing? With the move?"

I freeze, holding my breath as I take in the fact she isn't looking at me while she waits for my answer. My mouth feels dry, and I have to swallow a few times before I get the words out, glancing over my shoulder, down the hall, as if Sebastian might walk out from his closed bedroom door any second, even though I know he isn't here.

"Um, I don't know." I'm stammering, Mom has her arms crossed, staring at the linoleum floor, and I know this is the time. This is where I can say something, *do something to help him.* Mom is the adult. Reece. They're the parents. If I tell them the truth, maybe things will change. "I just… He goes out a lot, right? And it's not like he's working or anything." I laugh a little because I'm nervous.

I see Mom's shallow nod, like she's agreeing with that point.

"I think he's getting high in his room too."

Mom turns to look at me, but she doesn't seem shocked. "You can smell it?"

I nod once, still feeling as if I'm betraying my brother in some way. He's always been there for me, except that one time, but it wasn't even his fault. Really, it was mine. I never said anything. I could've screamed, I think. I mean, his friend had a hand over my mouth, but I could've screamed for him, couldn't I? And this is more important anyway.

This could be life or death, couldn't it?

"I'm so sorry, Eden." Mom's apology is strange. I blink, confused, but she keeps talking. "You shouldn't have to deal with that. Is it… every night?" Her brows are furrowed as she looks at me.

"I mean, I'm asleep usually by the time he comes in." That's not true, but I don't want to talk about my lack of sleep with her. I don't even want to hint at it. She'll bring it up again. *Therapy.* "I think he needs a job though. Something to do, you know?"

Mom hums softly in agreement, and she's still looking at me, but it's like she's looking through me. I wonder what she's thinking. I wonder what there is to do. I think of last night, the guy in Seb's truck, with the rifle. *Dope.* But I've thought of that word, a lot. It could've just been weed Dom meant. He's an asshole, he was just baiting my brother. What does he really know about him?

"Yeah," Mom says at last, exhaling and straightening away from the counter.

Down the street, I hear the purr of Eli's engine, and butterflies and nerves both tumble around in my stomach. I'm tucking my hair behind my ear, pulling at my shirt, running my fingers over the pleats of my skirt.

"Do you know… Has he been sleeping okay?" Mom asks quietly as I turn toward the front door. "Have you heard him sleepwalking or anything like that?"

Sleepwalking. My blood runs cold as I think of the noise I heard the other night. The sirens he said he couldn't hear. I remember a whispered conversation once, one I overheard between Mom and Reece. About Reece's dad and the drugs he used to silence the things he wasn't supposed to see. Wasn't supposed to hear. Because they… weren't there.

But I've always been good at fabricating things that aren't real, building castles inside my head on foundations of sand. Am I really trustworthy in this? What if I imagined the sirens? What if *I'm the one seeing things?*

"No," I lie to Mom as Eli's engine cuts off, and I hear him close his door a second later. I reach for the lock on the door, flipping it off. "No, I think he sleeps okay." I open up the door, rays of sunlight spilling in, shooting from behind Eli—a dark angel in the morning light—and I tell my mom bye as I let Sebastian down and leave with my Adonis.

29

Eli

SHE REACHES for the popcorn in my lap, but her eyes never leave the screen. We're alone in the back row; this theater will probably close down soon. It plays movies that have left most theaters, and the tickets are cheaper because of it. But it was her idea. She wanted to watch *this* movie, so here we are, being relegated with an attempt to keep the Harry Potter franchise alive.

I couldn't care less about Harry fucking Potter, but what I care a lot about is my arm around her shoulders, the way the cupholder between us is flipped up, and she's leaning into my side, her legs bouncing, her attention wholly stolen by magic.

She chews with her mouth closed, but I still hear the crunch of popcorn between her teeth. My eyes are fixed on her mouth, the curve of her cheekbones when the screen flashes bright.

And the fact she's wearing the school uniform skirt, but she's rolled it up so high, I almost wanted to tug it down as soon as we got out of my car in the parking lot and some old fuck's eyes went to her ass.

I bite my bottom lip, dropping my gaze down to her thick thighs, spread wide from the fact she's sitting. I catch the slivers of stretch marks in her skin as the screen goes white, filling the darkened room with light.

My erection is uncomfortable under this tub of popcorn, and I shift in my seat, trying to relieve some of the pressure.

When I move, her hand is in the bucket, fingers poised to grab a handful, and my eyes meet hers, and in the light from the screen, I see her cheeks flush pink.

"What?" she asks, a sheepish smile pulling on her lips.

I want to touch her thigh. I want to slip my hand under her skirt. I want to push her underwear aside and feel her again, pushing two fingers into her tight cunt as her walls contract around me. I want to get on my knees and go down on her, right here in the aisles of this shitty theater.

I want to taste her, everywhere. I want to pull her onto my lap, and she'll dry fuck me, and maybe it'll be an accident but maybe my cock will push aside her underwear and I'll crown her, and she'll freeze with her hands at my neck. Then she'll tell me to keep going. To fuck her for the first time just like that and—

"Nothing." I return her smile, dancing my fingers along her upper arm. I lean down and press a kiss to the tip of her nose, then nudge my own with hers. My mouth is over her lips when I speak again. "I just love watching you watch something you love."

She smiles and I feel it on my lips. Then, with one hand still in the popcorn tub, she's kissing me, no tongue, just a sweet, soft kiss.

And even though it tests every ounce of patience and resolve I have, I don't let myself grab her thigh. Not one time.

SHE SITS ON THE FLOOR WHILE I SCROLL THROUGH MY EMAIL, trying to find one from a guy about a Supra. I told her to sit in my lap, but she's texting Janelle. I know because I read the message over her shoulder when she didn't know I was.

Dad is away, I'm not sure for how long, but I told Eden he wouldn't be back tonight. Even if he comes, it's not like he'd care she's here.

I click open the email, see the guy is trying to get a grand more than his shit is worth. I'm typing out my final offer, rolling my eyes at his idiocy, when I realize Eden is no longer sitting on the floor. She's standing behind me, and she leans in to rest her chin on my shoulder, her phone abandoned on the floor.

Inhaling, I catch her scent. Peaches and violets, soft and beautiful. I smile to myself, and I think my email is a little nicer by the time I finish and send it off because she's standing right here.

"Thank you for taking me to the movies," she says, her breath against my ear.

I turn my head, my hand still over my mouse as I brush my lips against hers, my eyes holding her own. "Thank you for coming with me."

She shifts her head a little to nudge her nose with mine. "You're buying another car?"

I smile at her question. Her spying. I don't even care. "Come sit in my lap and you can help me pick one out."

She laughs, but straightens, walking around my chair and sinking down into my lap as I roll the chair back to give her room. Her ass is warm and soft in my lap, and I wrap one arm around her waist. She moves a little to the side so we can both see my computer screen. I feel her toes against the top of my feet. Her own don't even reach the ground.

"Why do you want another car?" She settles back against my chest, focused on the screen as I scroll through more listings after I close out my email.

I slide my palm down to her skirt, then a few more inches, squeezing her tight, warm skin. She shifts just slightly, and I feel the muscles in her leg flex, but she doesn't tell me to get off of her.

"Why not?" I counter her question with a question.

"Because they're expensive." She turns to look at me with narrowed eyes but a playful smile. "You can't drive two at a time anyway."

"Yeah but maybe I want to get an automatic so *you* can drive one of mine. You know, a fast car? Have you heard of those?"

She rolls her eyes, and I squeeze her thigh tighter. Tilting her head, she's staring up at me as I glide my hand up higher, under her skirt, and I know she's got to feel how hard I am for her, but neither of us say a word about it.

This is about cars.

She turns back to the monitor, and my finger slips, accidentally clicking and closing the car tab.

Another screen comes up.

I'm barely breathing as my eyes scan the text on the website, and after two seconds, I know Eden has read over it, too.

I see her hands fist in her lap, just at the hem of her skirt. Feel the muscles in her thigh tighten under my palm.

I feel her shallow breathing, her back rising and falling against my chest. For a long, long moment, no one speaks, soft music playing from the speakers of my computer. *My Soul*, by Thrice.

My throat feels tight, my finger hovering over my mouse, thinking maybe I should close this tab. Thinking maybe I shouldn't have let her seen. *But isn't it what she wants?*

"What is this?" she finally asks, the words barely more than a breath.

There're no images. No video. What would she think if she saw those?

I read the words inside my head, but all I say, leaning in close to her, my mouth over her ear, is, *"What do you think?"*

I hear her swallow. I see her knuckles blanch white, her hands still fisted in her lap. *"Eli."*

All the blood has rushed down to my dick, and when she shifts back, just the slightest, I have to bite my lip to stop from groaning. Images rush through my head. Things I could do to Eden. Things she'd *let me* do. Violent, borderline fucking murderous.

With her, I don't think I'd ever get bored.

"Yeah, Nightmare Girl?" I let my bottom lip run up the side of her lobe, and I feel every piercing hit against my mouth.

Her back rises and falls faster. "How do you pronounce the word?"

I flick my tongue along the tip of her ear, and she shivers, brushing against my erection again.

My palm grows clammy over my mouse. My fingers press into her thigh.

"I don't know," I admit. "But it's what you want, isn't it? It's what turns you on? Do you imagine it, safe and sound in your bed? My hands around your throat? Your head under water? Do you think about a knife to your skin? All the fucked up things you'd let me do to you?"

I dip my brow to the side of her head, closing my eyes, feeling hot and tight all over my body. *Say yes, say yes, say yes.*

I see the word in my mind. The name for her fucked up fantasy.

It's the risk that gets her off, isn't it?

"Letting me control you? Your breathing, your whole fucking life?"

I swear, in this moment, she stops doing just that. *Breathing.*

Then, my eyes squeezed shut tight, I feel her fingertips dancing over the back of my hand, on her thigh. "Yes," she whispers, the sound rough and broken.

"Yes, *what?*"

"Yes, I think about it. Getting hurt… Getting hit…"

"By anyone?" I dig my short nails into her skin and hear her sharp intake of breath. "You'd let just *anyone* hurt you?"

A moment's pause, my pulse beating so fast inside my ears. Then she says, *"Only ever you."*

"Yeah? You lying to me?" I glide my hand up higher, under her skirt, and she loops her fingers around my wrist, but she doesn't stop me. Instead, she spreads her thighs wider, and I swear I can smell her.

"No."

I bite down on her ear lobe, her body tightening up, probably a lot like her tight little hole, too. "Better not be. Don't ever lie to me."

"But you do it all the time—"

"I can do whatever the fuck I want." My eyes are still closed, my chest so, so tight and raw and aching for her. I speak every word against her skin. "I can do what I want, but *you* listen to *me*. I keep you safe. I make you feel good. I protect you."

"You protect me." She repeats the words, savoring them in her mouth. They sound so good, coming from her lips.

"Yes." I press my forehead harder against the side of her head. *"Always."*

She clears her throat. "Have you always liked…" She trails off, but I know what she's asking as I run circles with my thumb on the inside of her thigh.

"I've always liked violence. But not like this." *I want to fuck you. I need to fuck you.* And it occurs to me, as her chest keeps expanding and shrinking while she struggles to stay sane, coherent, to breathe, that maybe this, everything exploring this *fantasy* on my screen, is far too much for her first time. And maybe, just like with the pool, what she says and what we text about aren't what she'd want right now.

I open my eyes, pulling back. Letting the violence go.

"It doesn't always have to be like that, though." I speak slowly, staring at her little neck. "I can treat you good, too. I can be so, so fucking good for you." I swallow the knot in my throat as silence stretches between us, only the song playing.

And then…

She turns so she's sideways in my lap, her eyes hooded, searching mine. She reaches for my face, cradling it in her hands. And I'm not even thinking of blood or bruises or broken things anymore.

Her lips graze over mine. Once, twice. I glide my hand around to her hip, just over the line of her underwear. Then she's kissing me, her tongue parting my lips, and I can't stop the groan coming from the back of my throat.

But then she pulls back, slowly slipping her hands off of my face and wrapping one arm around me, turning to look at the computer screen again.

A flush of warmth fills my gut, and I dig my fingers into her hip, but I don't tell her how she's driving me fucking insane.

"You're sweet," she says softly. "I like it when you're sweet."

I close my eyes a second, gritting my teeth, but then I'm looking at my monitor again, and I exit out of the browser. I go back to the cars, scrolling through them. But I'm not seeing a single one, because I'm focused on her hair tucked behind her ear. All six of her piercings in one. The fullness of her lips, slightly parted as she stares at my screen. The way her chunky foot shakes, hanging off of my lap. How her fingers are twisting in her skirt.

I clear my throat, trying to focus. To let go of whatever just happened between us. "Maybe when I get this new car, I can take you up to Bloor in it. Have you been?" I remember, she told my dad and Ms. Romano that's where she wants to go. I don't want her to go there. I want her to come to Caven with me, but we'll cross that bridge when we come to it.

She swallows. I hear it and see the column of her throat roll as she does, but she still faces away from me. "Yeah, that would be cool."

I shift a little in my seat, and her fingers grip my hair,

playing with the strands just over my neck. I see her knuckles go white as she tangles her other hand tighter in her skirt.

"Cool?" I echo.

She smiles, the apple of her cheek rising upward as she does. "Yeah. *Cool.*"

"Why do you sound sad about it?" Because she does. She's smiling, and she seems happy, but there's something in her tone. Maybe I missed it at first, because I'm so horny I think I'm going to die of it, but I hear it now.

She shrugs one shoulder and I stare at it, the tan line just visible from the white strap of her tank top slipping down an inch. "I'm not sad."

I squeeze her hip tighter. "Hey. Look at me."

Slowly, she turns her head, then wraps both arms around my neck, tilting her chin as she looks up at me through long lashes. "What?"

I let go of my mouse, holding her close with both hands parked on either side of her hips. "What's wrong?" *Is it the shit she just saw? Did I just go to far?*

She tries to smile it away, but she ducks her eyes when she does. "Nothing."

I tip her chin up with one finger, drawing her gaze back to me. "Don't be lame. Tell me what's wrong."

She rolls her eyes and tries to turn her head out of my grip, but I place my palm on the side of her face and guide her back to me again.

"Bloor is so far away." She finally says it. What she's really thinking, her eyes searching mine. They look greener in this light, even with the blue lights of my room the only thing on. Maybe they're green when she's sad or something. I don't know. Not yet.

"It's four hours. Not far at all."

She frowns. "Four hours is a lot for you."

She's not wrong, but I just shake my head. "Where is this coming from?" I rub my thumb over her bottom lip, and she nuzzles her face into my hand, her fingers still playing with the strands of hair at my neck.

"I just like you a lot, that's all." She laughs a little, to lighten the mood. To make it a joke. She doesn't even look at me when she says it.

I know what she's thinking. This will end when we graduate. Maybe she's right. I can't see any world where she stays. I can't see any version of the future where I do the right thing. I can lie, though. Then. Now. I lie like I breathe. I don't even think about it. I know why I do it, thanks to years of therapy. To get what I want. To *manipulate.* That fucking word, like I just think all day long about how to get the most out of people while hurting them in the greatest capacity. Like I'm just a monster or some shit. A different species.

I don't think that way.

I just… want things. People. Then, I don't. I lose interest. What's wrong with that anyway?

Before I say anything to her, I drop my hand from her face, which causes her to squirm in my lap, turning back to the computer and leaning against my chest, probably hoping I'll drop this entire conversation.

I open up my music app and shuffle it to another song. "All I See" by Lydia starts playing, and I don't think I could've planned a better song. Then I pick her up, easy to do with as small as she is, and turn her around completely in my lap. She makes a noise of protest, but she's grabbing at my shoulders to steady herself, her knees splayed on either side of my hips as she looks down at me through her curtain of hair, a pink blush on her cheeks.

"Eli, what are you—"

"I like you a lot too." I keep my hands parked on her hips as I lean back in my chair, looking up at her. "I like you so, so much." I can't stop my smile, mirrored with hers as she tries to play it off, rolling her eyes and turning her head. "I like your hair, and your eyes, and your smile, and your *poison* necklace, and your body, and your voice, and the way you like to fight because it feels easier than being *sweet*, huh?"

Her face is now the lightest shade of red, and it's fucking adorable, the way she squeezes her eyes shut tight. "Shut up," she mutters.

I squeeze her more, and her eyes come to mine. "Excuse me?"

She arches a brow. "You won't do it."

For several seconds, we just listen to the song as we stare at each other, her body so soft beneath my fingers. So warm in my lap. I think about the fantasy, but there's a time and place for everything. So I just say, "No." It's like a whisper, the words jagged. "I won't."

"Why not?" There's something vulnerable and open in her face when she asks. She licks her lips, a nervous smile pulling at them.

I sit up a little straighter, bringing our mouths closer together, inhaling the scent of her shampoo, her hair all around us. "Because," I say, dropping my eyes to her lips, then back up. "I like you too much." *One day, I will. But not today.* In my head, I hear my own words, and I meant them. *I protect you.*

She looks stunned with that answer. Like she's never really believed anything I've said this past month. Like she still doesn't believe it now. She's completely still.

Then she dips her chin down a few inches. I can smell her breath. Like cotton candy. Like the gum I gave her in my car. She threw it out the window when she was done.

She tilts her head.

A second passes, like she's gathering her nerve.

Then her mouth comes to mine. She kisses me deep, open, our lips parting and closing in unison, her hands gliding up to my neck, circled around my throat, but her grip is loose. She bucks her hips into me, arching her back, pushing her tits to my chest, releasing my throat, looping her arms around my neck. She's whimpering, moaning as her core grinds against my erection.

I run my hands up her skirt, my fingers beneath the cotton fabric of her underwear as I grab her round ass, pulling her closer to me. She widens her thighs, gasping into my mouth as she rubs herself against me.

My mind is spinning.

It's not like I didn't think this might happen. It's not as if I haven't been *dreaming* about fucking her before we ever spoke the first time in the library. But even still… I'm just kind of mesmerized we might go there tonight.

I knead her ass with my fingers, then slip them from her underwear, coming up to the waistband. We're both breathing hard, and I stop kissing her, my brow on hers to look into her eyes.

Neither of us have been drinking. We're completely sober, even though I feel a little high, and it's kind of hard to breathe as I push the elastic waistband of her underwear down, waiting for her to stop me. To tell me not to. To say she doesn't want to go that far.

But she doesn't.

Her lips are parted, her chest is heaving, her shirt low cut, showing the tops of her breasts, and I watch the rise and fall of every inhale, each exhale.

I push her underwear down further, and I can smell her. She's musky and sweet and all the blood in my body feels as if it's rushing to my dick.

Slowly, I keep tugging down the material, and she steadies herself with her arms wrapped around my neck when she lifts one knee, then the other, letting me drop her underwear to the floor.

My eyes don't leave hers. Hers are fixed on mine, and I know she's nervous. I can see it in her face. Feel it in the shakiness of her limbs.

I glide my hands up the back of her thighs, cupping her bare ass under her skirt and squeezing hard. Her skin is firm and soft all at once, there's so much warm flesh to hold onto, it's hard to think about much but my cock straining beneath my pants.

I pull her closer, and this time, when she rubs her bare pussy against my erection, her eyes flutter closed, and she whispers my name.

I can feel how hot she is even with the layers of my clothes between us.

My lips skim her jawline, her cheekbones, under her eyes, over her temple, all while she moans into my ear and grinds herself on my cock.

I drop my hands lower, one gripping her thigh, with the other I bring two fingers underneath her, and she tenses, freezing as she stares at me, our foreheads pressed together again, her arms tight around my neck.

"Let me." I'm so, so close, and her skin is so fucking smooth. She's completely bare, shaved now, and it turns me on more to know she probably did that for me.

She licks her lips but after a moment, she nods slowly.

I take a breath, then push two fingers against her wetness, feeling how hot and soft and needy she is as I enter her, her walls tight around me.

She sinks down a little lower, and I smile at her impatience, as she pushes against my cock and fucks my fingers at the same time.

"You're so beautiful." The words are automatic. I'm not even *trying* to say nice things, I just can't seem to stop. "You're so, so fucking beautiful."

She keeps bouncing on my fingers, staring at me with wide, innocent eyes. "You feel so good," she manages to whisper, her hand sliding down to my chest, gripping the fabric of my shirt.

"I can feel even better." I pull her closer, by her ass, so she knows what I mean.

I see her swallow, her thighs shaking as she pauses grinding on my hand, so I just finger her, slow and deep, all the way up to my last knuckle, in and out, feeling all of her.

"Okay," she says, like she's decided. She sinks lower onto

my hand, a whimper leaving her lips, around another moan of, "Okay, Eli."

"Yeah?" It's the only thing I can manage to get out, but I have to ask. She's so fucking precious. I don't know why I'm apprehensive about this, with all the homicidal fantasies I've had with her. But maybe that's it. I don't deserve her. This. When it all comes crashing down, I'll be okay.

But will she? Will she look back on this moment and regret every single fucking second of it?

She drops her forehead to my shoulder as I finger fuck her. "Yes. *Yes.*" Her words are muffled against my shirt.

I can't wait after that. I slowly pull my fingers out of her, swiping them on her thigh so she feels just how wet she is for me. I wrap my arms around her waist and pick her up, her head still against my shoulder, her legs tangled around my hips.

I carry her to the bed, and I can feel her heartbeat against my chest, our torsos crushed together. It's so fast, her pulse. It's strong and eager and *ready* for me.

I lay her down carefully, planting my hands on either side of her head as she shifts underneath me, getting comfortable, and tugging her skirt down, like she's nervous for me to see all of her. But the only light in the room is the blue ones, my computer screen gone dim. I hope it'll be easier for her, this way.

As I drag my gaze over her body, not for the first time, I'm in love with our height difference. She's just so fucking small, I could eat her alive. I have to force myself to remember to slow down. To be gentle.

I see her chest rise and fall fast, deep.

I think it mirrors my own.

"You sure you want this?" I make myself ask it.

She nods, one arm crossed over her body, like a shield.

I clench my teeth together. My body feels like it's on fucking fire.

"I want to touch every inch of you."

She bites her lip, half-smiling beneath me. "Yeah?"

"Yes." And no longer content to just look, when she doesn't protest, I lift my hand and trail my fingers down her curvy, compact body to the waistband of her skirt. I undo the clasp, but she moves fast, grabbing my wrist.

I lift my eyes to hers.

Her brows are drawn together, anxiety over her beautiful face. "Sorry, I…"

I shake my head. "Don't be sorry. But trust me, okay? I'm going to take care of you." *I protect you.*

I hear her swallow in the dark, and she looks down, at her fingers circled around my wrist, mine over the clasp of her skirt. "I know, I just…"

It's like there's a weight on my chest, spreading warmth through every vein in my body, including to my dick. "You just what, baby?"

She keeps her eyes averted, her cheeks flushed as she traps her knees to my hips, the side of my body, like she's trying to cover herself.

Then it dawns on me. "Has anyone ever seen you naked before?"

Her fingers squeeze my wrist tighter. Slowly, she shakes her head, but doesn't speak.

"Eden."

I wonder if she hears the roughness in my voice. Whatever she hears, she looks up, her eyes searching mine.

"I've seen you. *I see you.*"

Her fingers loosen on my wrist.

"I am obsessed with every part of you."

Her lips are pressed together, and I wonder if she'll change her mind, right here. Right now.

Seconds pass.

The same song plays because I have a habit of putting my shit on repeat and forgetting to undo it.

But finally, *finally*, she releases my wrist.

Then, every movement of mine slow, she lets me pull her skirt off as she forces herself to fist the sheets, staring at me. I toss the plaid skirt to the floor, sink back on my heels, and lift her foot by her ankle, to kiss the bottom of it.

I drag my teeth over the pad of her toes, and she's squirming and bashful beneath me, twisting her head. "You don't have to—"

I bite her toe and she sucks in a breath. "Let me do what I want to."

She smiles, a shy thing, but she stills, staring at my face.

I lower her foot, pick up her other, and touch and kiss and gently scrape my teeth against her skin. Then I release her, so the soles of her feet are on my bed.

Without breaking eye contact with her, so she doesn't get embarrassed and uncomfortable, I slide my hands down her thick thighs, feeling ribbons of stretch marks that cause heat to flush tight and hot through my body. I press my thumb into her imperfections, obsessed with every fucking one.

Then I widen her thighs, shift back, and lower my head.

She tries to close her knees, but I cut my eyes to hers, from between her thighs, holding them open with my hands.

"Eli."

My mouth is inches from her pussy. I can smell her. I can practically taste her. I want to fucking devour her. "Eden." The word is barely more than a groan.

"You don't need to—"

"Pull my hair." I give her the direction for something to distract her. "Right now, okay?" My breath skates over her cunt. I know, the way she trembles underneath me as I speak.

Her slender throat bobs as she swallows, but she does what I say, tangling her fingers tentatively in my strands. It's like she needs my guidance. Like we work well this way—I feel high, telling her what to do, and I think she feels the same listening.

Then I lower my nose to her, inhaling before I lick her, my tongue pressed flat as I drag it up the center of her. Hot and wet and fucking divine, when I glide my tongue over her swollen clit, her fingers tighten in my hair, but she's still so rigid.

I press my nose to her center again, inhaling her musky, clean scent. She's yanking on my strands so hard my eyes water, but she's not telling me to stop. I'll take it.

I meet her gaze as I pick up my head, then lower my eyes. To *her*.

Her pink clit is aching for me, her lips are puffy and fucking beautiful. I widen her thighs more, seeing every part of her, glistening and *needy*, and all fucking mine.

I flick my tongue along her clit and look up, watching as her eyes flutter closed and she's yanking my hair so hard a fucking tear leaves the corner of my eye, but I kinda like it.

I push one finger into her tight cunt, and the way she arcs her hips up, pushing herself further against my mouth, drives me fucking insane. I put another finger inside her, feeling her walls tighten around me. This is exactly what I fantasized about in the theater, except in reality, it's better than anything I could dream up. I have to stretch my legs out as I lie almost flat, just so I can grind my dick into the mattress.

I pull back, to watch myself finger her. To see how tight she is around me. To watch with every thrust as I enter her.

She tries to close her legs again, getting nervous, and on reflex, I gently slap her clit.

She freezes, making a sound between a whimper and a moan, and I smile up at her. "Don't."

Her chest is rising and falling so fucking fast, and I swear it's like the necklace around her little fucking neck is bouncing from her heartbeat. Her fingers are just grazing my hair now, but she just nods in obedience.

It drives me crazy, her listening to me. I lap at her clit with my tongue, soothing the sting. I keep finger fucking her, twirling my tongue over her, then dipping my nose and using it too, to circle her.

She tenses up, and I feel it around my fingers, and I don't know if she's embarrassed I'm getting her close to coming with my nose, or if she's just...

No. *Fuck no.*

She isn't embarrassed. Several moments later, I feel her orgasm as I nudge my nose back and forth against her, and everything gushes over my fingers, and she's pushing with her walls against them as she calls out my name.

"Eli, baby, baby, baby." She's ripping at my hair, and I don't care, and I don't stop until her body goes limp.

Immediately, my face wet with *her*, I climb up her body, and her face is flushed. Her hands slip down to my triceps, squeezing hard, and she's panting as she stares at me with heavy lidded eyes.

"You okay?"

She looks dazed, her eyes glassy. Like she's completely stunned. It makes me feel a little proud of myself.

I dive down to kiss her, and she stills for a moment, like she's not sure of the taste of *her* on her own lips, but then she opens her mouth, and my tongue is twirling around hers. She trails her hands down my arms and over my chest.

I reach behind my head and pull off my shirt, dropping it over the side of the bed and placing my hand down by her head again, both of them bracketing her as slowly we disentangle ourselves from our kiss once more.

Her fingers dance over my muscles, and my abs jump with her touch as she looks at me. Then her thumb is gliding over the waistband of my sweats. She keeps her eyes off of mine as she pulls them down, alongside my boxers. I help her, pushing them to my knees, then kicking them off, my dick breathing a little easier now it's free.

She avoids my eyes when she asks, "Help me."

I guide her hand slowly to my cock, and her breath hitches as I circle her fingers around it between us, and help her stroke me, all while I stare at her face.

"Harder," I tell her as her cheeks flush pink. "Squeeze me harder."

She does, and it feels so fucking good, moving her hand up and down my shaft. Her movements are a little clumsy but knowing she hasn't done this before… it turns me on more.

I close my eyes, guiding her still, groaning at the feel of her. I move her hand faster, squeeze it tighter. In my head, all I'm thinking about is diving into her tight pussy. How it's going to feel so fucking good to be her first and—

We hear a fucking noise downstairs, over the music.

I still.

Her eyes widen as I look at her, and her fingers curl tighter around my cock, but she stops moving her hand. "Eli—"

"I'm not stopping." The words are automatic, but I want her to understand this. "I'm not stopping, baby girl."

"But *your dad*—"

"Isn't going to come into my locked bedroom." I say the words through gritted teeth because I feel like I'm about to explode over here, but I'm not mad. I just… I'm just not fucking stopping for my goddamn dad.

I lean down and kiss her. She turns her face, but she doesn't let go of me.

I lick a line down her throat. "Please don't make me stop." I release my fingers over hers and run my entire hand over her pussy, still so hot and so fucking wet. "Put me inside you. Don't make me stop. *Please,* Eden." Driving my finger inside her, her body at once tightens and relaxes, and she turns her head to stare back up at me.

"Look," I tell her quietly, and she keeps squeezing and stroking me, not fast, way too slow to make me cum, but that's going inside her anyway. "Look down, baby."

Her face is flushed, but she lowers her gaze, coming up on one elbow, other hand still around me.

I glance down, too, seeing my thumb inside of her, and her knees widen. Slowly I pull my finger out and run it between her lips, separating them, so she can see herself, see how turned on she is, everything probably still sensitive from her orgasm.

There's a creak from down the hall. Dad walking up the stairs. She tries to snap her knees together, but I slap the inside of her thigh, and when her eyes cut to mine, I know she liked it.

"You mad?"

She narrows her eyes.

I smile at her and whisper, "Make me hurt, too."

Giving me one last vicious squeeze, she releases my dick and yanks at my choker, twisting her fingers under it. It doesn't cut off my air supply, but it digs into my skin and the pressure feels good.

I wrap my fingers around myself and circle her clit with the head of my cock, glancing down and watching the precum leaking from the tip get all over her.

"Do you want me to use a condom?" I ask at the exact same time I glide myself down to her entrance, butting up against it.

She slowly lowers back on my bed, her hold loosening on my choker.

Somewhere in the house, a door closes.

She shuts her eyes.

I press against her tight little hole, holding out hope she gives me the right answer.

"No," she finally says. "Do it fast."

I lean down over her, and she opens her eyes. "I'm not doing this fast."

She's still gripping my choker, and I cradle her head in both my hands, putting my body weight on her as I press against her, but I'm not in yet.

I run my thumbs up her cheekbones, and she digs her fingers into my hair. "I'm not doing this fucking fast. I'm not messing this up for you, okay?"

She doesn't say anything, but she nods. "No condom," she answers me, "but…"

Her face is so, so flushed. I smooth her hair back, tilting my head. "What? Tell me what." I can feel how warm and wet she is, how she widens her thighs to accommodate me.

"Kiss me a lot."

I don't make her wait for that. I'm devouring her as her fingers wind in my hair. I position my hips over her, reaching with one hand to circle my cock. I stroke myself once, then find her warmth, circling the head of my cock against her opening.

Her fingers come to my face, the movements fluttery. She's a little shaky, and I want her to relax.

"It's okay, baby girl. I've got you, okay?"

She kisses me again, a nervous gesture. Like she doesn't know what to say. I kiss her back, soft and slow as I push against her.

I know it will, logically, but there's a moment inside my head where I think, *I'm not going to fucking fit.*

But I keep kissing her, loving the feel of her fingers all over my face. The way she whimpers into my mouth. I think she's terrified, she doesn't want to slow down, her movements are so frantic. I don't tell her to stop because she's underneath me and I can do this slowly no matter what she has to do with all of her fumbling, nervous energy. I want her shirt off, I want my tongue on her tits. I want to feel all of her, but one thing at a time.

I keep pushing, letting go of myself to place one of my hands over hers, on my face. My other is planted on the bed, and my palm starts to sweat as I push inside of her.

She gasps, her fingers digging into my cheekbones. "I've got you, baby girl." I whisper it over her mouth. "I protect you." I keep pushing, and she's so wet, but she's so, so goddamn tight.

"Eli." It's a whimper, and my eyes lock on hers as I pull back to take in her face. I want to see her, when it happens. I want to watch her.

"Yeah?" I'm pushing, and pushing, and it's like my dick is in a fucking vise grip.

Her cheeks are flushed, her hands still around my face. "Is it okay?"

I almost laugh at her question. At her, thinking of me. But I don't. "Perfect," I tell her. "Everything is perfect." Even as I say it, it's painful, how tight she is. "Lift up your shirt, baby girl."

She drops her free hand, the one not under mine, and

slowly drags her shirt up to her chin, shifting her back to get the fabric to glide all the way up. I glance down and see her round tits spilling out of her green bra. Her skin is so smooth and beautiful and there's a blue vein I want to kiss and lick and bite.

But I'm almost there.

So fucking close.

I lift my eyes to hers. She can be so tough, but beneath it all, she's full of so much fucking goodness. It's overwhelming, seeing the way she trusts me. The ways she shouldn't.

And when I push through the barrier between us, when I can finally get all the way in, I almost regret it, this moment in time. I almost wish it had been anyone but me to do this with her.

But her eyes flutter closed and her lips part and her back arches, bringing me further into her wet cunt, and I know I don't. If anyone else had seen this, if anyone had done this… god, I'd feel like I'd been robbed.

I move more freely now. Slow, still, as I shift my hips and her eyes open, seeking mine out, her chest heaving.

"Are you okay?" *She* asks *me* that. Her voice shakes, but she fucking asks me. As if this is *my* first time. The thought is kind of hilarious.

I press my hips further into her and her chin lifts, a whimper leaving her lips. I drop my mouth to hers to feel it inside mine. "I'm more than okay." I pull out of her, slowly, then push back in, my stomach tightening at how good she feels around me. Then I lick a line down her throat, over her collarbone, biting the top of her breast, finally. I slip my tongue beneath the cup of her bra and feel her pebbled nipple. Using my chin to shift the material down, I suck her into my mouth. She says my name, and I can't stop the smile on my face as she fists my hair in her hand.

Then she's dragging my head up as I fuck her, the headboard of my bed hitting the wall, and I'm sure my dad can hear us, but I couldn't care less.

She wraps her legs around me, and a moan leaves my mouth, the way the movement draws me in deeper.

"Harder," she says, kind of shyly. The same way she told me to choke her tighter the first time she spent the night.

I smile at her trust, then I grab her hand from my face and lift her arm over her head, her hand pinned to the mattress by my hold on her wrist. "Harder?"

She nods, unafraid.

"How hard? What do you want me to do?"

She lifts her chin, exposing her throat.

I smile, then keeping myself up by my hold on her wrist, I bar my forearm over her throat. Her eyes widen, and her legs untangle from my waist. But I don't put a lot of pressure on her neck.

I dip my head down, though, sucking her other tit, leaving marks I know will bruise, biting at her skin, then her nipple, so hard and tight between my teeth. She shivers beneath me, her sounds little cries from my forearm over her throat.

I fuck her faster, licking a line between her tits, burying my head in the valley of them, wanting to bite this fucking bra off.

I move faster, now she's all fucking mine and more relaxed, the hardest part over for her. She feels so fucking good, and the sounds of me entering her are better than any song I could've played.

I'm so close, and her thighs are shaking, and she's calling my name, over and over on top of her little breathy noises.

And when I tilt my head and rest my ear over her heart, listening to how frantically it beats for me, I realize I love that, too. Her pulse thudding loud and clear beneath me.

"Baby, I'm going to come," I say, my lips sticking to her skin, my arm still over her throat, one holding down her hand. Her other is in my hair and she pulls, hard.

"Inside me." It's like a plea, and we've never talked about birth control aside from that second she said she didn't want a condom but right now, I can't imagine a time I'd ever come inside of her with anything between us, or ever pull out of her. It would feel like a fucking waste. *"Please."*

My entire body tenses with her begging, sweat damp in my hair, and I push into her softness one more time, two, then faster, and faster, and I'm coming so hard it feels as if my entire body is vibrating and I see white spots in my vision. I feel her heart thumping harder, faster, with my release, and it pushes me over the fucking edge.

I pick my head up, wrapping my arms around her, lifting her shoulders so she's staring at me as I come, my eyes wide and my mouth open.

"Eden, baby. Eden, Eden, *Eden."* I can't stop saying her name. I can't stop falling further. I can't stop feeling something like love for her. "God, you're so perfect." I'm shaking and I don't even know why. "You're so fucking perfect for me."

Her arms are around my back, cradling me close to her chest. She looks proud of herself, and I'm still inside her, everything in her. It turns me on all over again, knowing my cum will drip down between her thighs later.

I'm breathing hard and coming down, but it's like my dick is still pulsing inside of her, and in this moment, I never want to fucking move.

She's smiling shyly, and I huff the smallest laugh and she says, "That was…" Then she trails off.

I drop my head, kissing her nose, closing my eyes.

"Does it hurt?" I ask her, kissing her temple, her eyelids, holding her close, shifting my hips a little. "Are you sore?" I don't open my eyes.

"Perfect," she finishes her sentence. "It was all perfect."

I want to ask how she really feels, but I can't argue with her. It was. She is. We are. *Fucking perfect.*

And later in the night, when she's curled up next to me and she made me promise I'd sneak her out in the morning so she doesn't have to face my dad, and I can't sleep but I don't mind, not with her by my side, I think about that word.

Perfect.

I don't believe in it. But this... this is the closest I've ever gotten in my entire life.

When I checked my phone, after she'd fallen asleep, I saw Dad texted me, and despite the fact he probably doesn't enjoy coming home to hearing his son fucking his girlfriend, I know even he knows she's too good for me because all his text said was, **Be careful with her.**

30

Eli

"ELI, get your ass on the bus."

I shake my head, my bag slung over my shoulder as I pull my sunglasses down to cover my eyes from the bright afternoon sun. Coach Pensky has his hands parked on his hips, the rest of my teammates filing into the dark blue bus owned by Trafalgar, a castle topped with a disproportionate dragonfly painted along the side of it.

"I'm taking my car." I glance over my shoulder, seeing Eden dancing in my passenger seat, the rest of the lot nearly empty save for the wrestler's vehicles and Ms. Pensky's minivan.

Coach Pensky narrows his eyes when I turn back to face him. I know he's seen Eden, heard the hum of my car as it runs because the heat out here is stifling, even in the middle of October. I'll roll the windows down when we drive, but for now, while I inform Coach I'm not taking the damn bus, I didn't want Eden to overheat. She seems excited to go to this shit. She's been talking a lot more than usual, and like this dancing, it's... another side of her.

I like it.

"She was at the tournament."

I don't answer Coach's words because it wasn't a question. Just an observation, like he's piecing things together.

He shakes his head after a moment, running his fingers through his thin brown hair, and I wonder if he's thinking about his own wife on the bus right now, in the front seat, going over our unofficial weigh-ins from a few moments ago.

"Don't let this distract you from tonight. And don't get pulled over." He drops his hands, turning his back to me, and without another word, he strides to the bus. I can hear him yelling at everyone to shut the fuck up when he climbs up the stairs, the doors closing after him.

Smiling to myself, I walk back to my car, toss my bag in the trunk, and slide into the driver's seat.

"You good with the windows down?"

Eden is pulling her hair into a low bun, teasing some strands around her face as she smiles, not looking at me. When she's done, she nods. "Yep."

I turn off the A/C, roll down the windows, and steal a glance at her thick thighs beneath the gray and blue and black plaid of her skirt. Every time I see her in it, I think about last Friday, when I fucked her. *For the very first time.* We've exchanged notes in the hallways since then, I haven't been able to keep my hands off of her, and we haven't had the chance to fuck again, but it's all I can think about.

And all. Damn. Day. *All over again,* I've watched her in this goddamn skirt. She reached behind her after Latin when we parted ways in the commons and swatted the fabric up, just enough for me to see where her wide, round ass meets her fucking thighs.

I grind my steering wheel hard, wishing I was fisting my dick instead. It *aches* in my pants, but there's nothing I can do about that right now. I settle for passing the bus as soon as we leave the gates of Trafalgar. In my head, I can hear Coach screaming.

"Is your dad coming?" Eden asks, glancing out the window as we merge onto the highway, and I pull off my sunglasses, tossing them in the pocket of the driver's door.

Her words are fast, and she bounces her leg. I think she's nervous.

"Can I connect my phone to your car?" She doesn't wait for my first answer.

I roll up the windows just enough to stop the wind from ripping through every word I say as cars get over for me in the fast lane. "Yeah." I scroll through the settings on my steering wheel. "Do it now."

She plucks her phone from the console and is focused on it, like she's tuning me out.

"Unfortunately, yes, Dad will be there."

"Unfortunately?" Eden turns to look at me as music fills the speakers.

Some white guy rapping about a girl getting punished. *I'll punish the fuck out of you, baby girl.*

I try to focus on what we're talking about. "Well, the first time you met him, he ruined our weekend, so I can't imagine you're too happy with him right now." Besides that, I can feel the ache in my chest from mine and Dad's fight the night before last. It had been my fault, really. A ripped-up photograph, a dig at his work, a threat to expose him for being a child abuser, even though I know he isn't. The accusations would ruin his career all the same, and I would never do it because of the disruption to my own life, but it's fun to watch him squirm.

I feel slightly bad about it now, what I did and said to Dad. He has a bruise blossoming along his throat he might need to wear makeup to cover up at the office.

I smile to myself, thinking of it. Guess what I'm feeling isn't remorse after all.

"He seems nice," Eden says beside me, and my smile widens, knowing she wasn't saying that when I snuck us out of the house last Saturday morning to get breakfast so she didn't have to see him after he heard us fucking.

"Does he?"

"Is that your cryptic way of saying he isn't?"

"*Et facient ea.*" Be careful. We went over it this morning with Ms. Romano, and I didn't miss the look she gave me as we did, like a silent warning. She was my teacher last year, too, the only one at Trafalgar who teaches upperclassmen Latin. She has a basic working knowledge of Greek as well, something I found out when I muttered a swear word in the language the week before everything happened with Winslet. Sometimes I see my mother when I look at Ms. Romano, and I don't know why, but it gives her a strange appeal for me.

I think she senses my fascination, and it repulses her. I think she wants me to stay away from Eden.

Unlike what Eden may want to believe, I cannot charm every person I meet. I usually don't even realize I'm trying, but Eden has made it abundantly clear what she thinks about my "rich boy" persona.

"Is that a threat?" she asks me, amused.

I glance at her thighs again, one leg still moving up and down. I imagine the taste of her skin on my lips last Friday. Slightly salty because Eden is always sweating. It's fucking hot. "My dad is fine," I say. "Your sassy attitude is not."

She giggles, a pure sound. I can't help myself when I reach for her, grabbing her leg between my fingers. Her muscles still beneath my touch, her skin hot, but she doesn't pull away. She presses her hand on top of mine, like she wants me to stay.

I bite my lip, my eyes trained on the road, one hand on the wheel.

"You like my attitude." Her words are low but fast, and I slide my hand up her thigh, her skirt gliding back as I do.

"Yeah. I do like your attitude."

Her fingernails dig into the back of my hand.

"I like everything about you." It's the truth. I'm fucking *aching* for her, and I think if I fucked her *before* I wrestled, it might be ideal, but then again, I could just be depleted. Maybe after. That could work. I keep dragging my hand up her leg, until I feel the material of her underwear. Cotton, soft, I want to slip my fingers beneath the elastic and finger-fuck her while I drive, but I think the feeling of her wet cunt around any part of me would cause me to wreck this fucking car.

I stop myself, the tightness in my chest enough to choke me.

She clears her throat, but the way she's gripping my hand so tightly can't hide the lust in her own bloodstream. "Is he going to ask me questions?"

For a second, I forget what the hell we're talking about, then I realize she just bypassed my compliment, and she's back to nervously thinking about my dad. Eden is dark and soft and full of nerves. I wonder what she'll be like as she gets older. I hope to God I get to watch her come into her own.

"Probably," I admit, "but he gets really into matches. You can ignore him if you want—"

"That would be rude." She doesn't let me finish. "I don't know if you noticed, but I'm actually very polite, Eli Addison." Her fingers press further overtop my hand, and she's grinning at me as she sits up straighter. "Unlike you, I have manners."

You sure fucking do. "Ignore my dad. It'll be hot."

"You want me to tempt your dad?"

I widen my eyes. *"Eden."*

She ignores me completely. "You wouldn't even know anyway until he came home tonight and told you to stop dating me."

Dating. She didn't even trip over the word. I'm not sure if our talk last week made it official despite the fact she ignored me for a day afterward, but she doesn't backtrack like she did then when she said the word "girlfriend." Warmth spreads through my chest, thinking of her as mine. I've always assumed it, since the first night we spoke in the library. The tension between us is something that can't be neatly labeled but calling her "mine" is the closest I can get.

"He would never say that." I squeeze her thigh.

"Remember what I said?" I turn to her again, and see she's smiling. It's blinding, her smile. I like it almost as much as her anger from last week. The stormy look in her beautiful eyes like she wanted to hit me in the darkness of her car. It made me want to *get hit*. "You are probably the best thing that's ever happened to me."

"Probably?" She shakes her head, none of her nerves in her retort. "What the hell do you mean, *probably?*"

"Well, I mean..." I shrug, grinning. "I *did* get this car, so, you know... you're a close second."

With that, she releases my hand, and smacking my chest with the back of her own. I laugh and hear her do the same, and it feels good, in this moment, *to feel good.*

※

I KNOW EDEN IS BEAUTIFUL. SHE'S FUCKING STUNNING, actually, from the thickness of her hair, to her *ass*, to her strong nose and big lips and the colors in her eyes. Her slender arms and the curve of her hips, even the way she walks like she's the most confident girl in the world.

It's not up for debate how attractive she is, and I know I'm not the only person with eyes.

But despite the fact I know all of this, watching nearly every eye turn to gaze up at her as she strolls through the gymnasium of Roanoke High with her chin lifted and her shoulders rolled back, her hips swaying and her phone clutched in one hand, makes me wish everyone here was blind, save for me.

Even the parents quiet as she passes by, headed toward the far end of the bleachers where the away team is seated, Dad in the stands. He's fixated on his phone for now, and I roll my eyes, breaking away from the laps we were running around the mat to head toward Coach and his wife.

"Water," I say, and Coach pinches the bridge of his nose between his fingers, bumping his glasses as he does. Ms.

Pensky's eyes are on Eden, a smile on the former's lips, and I know they both know I don't need water, besides which we have an entire cooler full of bottles beside Coach's chair.

But the match hasn't officially started, nothing but warmups for the away team now, the Rhinos not even out of their locker rooms yet.

I have a Trafalgar hoodie on because one of my shiny new bruises from Dad is just above the edges of my black singlet. Easily explainable, not least of all because news of my fight with Dominic spread when he showed back up at school with his nose taped up last week, but still, I'd rather not have eyes on the blooming red fist print if I can help it. The less I give people to talk about, the better. They already have enough as it is.

But when I intercept Eden at the bottom of the stairs, her eyes widening when she sees me before she darts a look to my dad, who is now, finally, paying attention and offering us both a wave, his eyes lingering a second too fucking long on Eden, I strip off my hoodie before she can say a word.

Then I thrust it into her hands. She takes it on instinct after offering my dad a polite smile that makes me want to yank her out of this gym and into a bathroom stall so I can fuck her with my hand clamped over her pretty little mouth.

"What's this for—"

"You'll be sitting on the bleachers," I answer her, my hand circled loosely around her wrist, her fingers clenched in the soft fabric of my hoodie. Her eyes stay on mine, never once drifting from my face. If she just looked eye level, she'd see Dad's handiwork, but she doesn't. I release her wrist and drop my hand to her thigh, just grazing it, a touch that to anyone else's eye might look accidental.

The flush on her cheeks tells me she knows it wasn't.

"I don't need to be distracted, and neither does the rest of my team." I smile with the words, although I mean them.

"You sound like a boy right now." She narrows her eyes, but there's nothing but playfulness in her expression. Then, surprising me with so many people watching us, my dad included, she steps closer, standing on her tiptoes with one hand on my chest, the other holding my hoodie. She tilts her head and presses a deep kiss to my lips. "But I promise not to distract you if you promise not to lose." She starts to pull away, the feel of her mouth nearly enough to snap all my self-control. But I grab her hand, still on my chest, and lean down, kissing her *harder*, my mouth fucking owning hers, our tongues clashing, teeth too.

I hear Coach Pensky clear his throat somewhere behind me, and I'm sure Dad's lips are pressed together in a tight line.

When we've become a spectacle for everyone in this gym, and I know I've claimed her in front of all these fuckers, Dad included, I pull back, breathless just like she is.

"I never lose, Eden." Then I gently pull her hand from my chest and turn away from her, rejoining Coach and my teammates, all of them staring at me, some in awe, some with knowing smirks, and a few who take this sport a little too seriously with narrowed eyes.

Coach is one of the latter, but as his gaze flicks to Eden, then back to me, even he doesn't say anything about it.

Eden

At first, I don't notice it. There's something there, scratching beneath the surface of my awareness, but my thoughts are racing from the size of Eli's opponent—he's huge, with a shaved head—to the smell of Eric Addison's cologne—peppery and dark—to something not quite right on Eli's dad's skin.

"Did he tell you he's been wrestling since he was twelve years old?" Mr. Addison turns to look at me with pride in his eyes, his hands clasped together, his elbows on his thighs as he sits hunched over, ready for his son to win, like he always does.

It's the angle, I think. The way Eric is twisted toward me,

the fabric of his pale gray collar bunching up just slightly, enough to make a single wrinkle in the material of his dress shirt.

A fresh bruise, blooming red in spots, darker and nearly purple in others. It's thin, layered against his throat in such a way I can tell immediately what it is, and I know, instinctively, where it came from.

Fingers wrapped around his neck.

It only makes sense while he continues talking about how Eli was really into swimming, until he suddenly wasn't, then went into martial arts before settling on wrestling, everything would click into place inside my head. Like speaking of Eli's aggression, his love for physical activity, at the same time I see the wound, makes it all come together for me.

"Yeah, he's really good too." The words come automatically. It's like I can't fucking shut up even as my mind jumps over the wounds, clicking with Eli's bruises. *They fight. They fucking fight.* "Do you think it helps him? You know, like an outlet?"

His dad claps his hands together once, eyes wholly focused on the sparring stance Eli and the other guy are in.

I'm bouncing my legs, playing with the collar of my shirt, my pulse elevated and I'm not even sure why. I hope his dad isn't thinking about the sounds I made in his son's bedroom when I lost my fucking virginity. *Jesus.*

"I think so," Eric says with a smile. "He's got a lot going on inside that mind of his."

"Yeah," I say, turning to look down. Eli twists his head to look up at me as he tugs on his headgear. I open my mouth, ready to say something, words vomiting out of me tonight, but I see it then. The bleachers aren't very high up, and with all of his smooth, olive skin, I can't believe I didn't notice before now.

A semi-circle of red and purple, just visible above his singlet.

He smiles at me, and I force myself to return it as I knot my fingers in his hoodie, draped across my lap.

All I can think about the entire sixty seconds of the match, in which Eli pins the guy by cradling him to his chest but ensuring his shoulders are on the mat, is what his house must look like when no one else is home. Does Eric start it? I want to blame him entirely. He's the parent. It's... his fault. But I cannot block out the facts of everything it means to be Eli Addison.

My stomach cramps as the ref lifts Eli's arm, and Eli's gaze is locked on mine. Eric is standing up, cheering beside me, along with most of the parents on Trafalgar's side. I'm on my feet, too. I couldn't stay seated if I tried, but my movements are mechanical as my thoughts loop.

Everyone loves Eli. He's *adored*.

But adoration isn't enough for him, is it? He wants to feel the sting of life too, just like I do. Still, images of Eric's violent hands on this boy who I think I could fall in love with flash inside my head. I only manage to last until Eli walks out of the circle of the mat and accepts his coach's congratulations and slap on the back before I stand, excusing myself to Eric and walking down the steps and out of the gym without another word, Eli's hoodie clutched close to my chest.

"Why did you run off?"

I tense, turning in the darkness of his car to meet Eli's gaze. Trafalgar won, his dad was still beaming when we parted ways with him out here in the parking lot, Eli's car at the very back of the lot, forests behind us that line Roanoke High's property. There were a lot of sweaty boys, frosty congratulations between the two teams, then Eli took a quick shower, his hair still wet now, and we walked out here together with his dad.

Everyone, it seems, has left, the bus long gone, the cars from parents and students too.

Eli has the Infiniti running, windows rolled up, even though the night outside actually felt really good, having cooled off from the humid, hot day. But as clammy as I get, I'm not complaining about the cold air from the vents.

"I had to pee," I lie.

His hand is on the wheel, one on his thigh. He's in sweatpants and a white T-shirt, and even from here I can smell the plain soap he must have showered with.

I glance at the time on the console. I have another three hours before Mom expects me to be home.

It'll take an hour and a half to drive back, maybe less with Eli behind the wheel, which means we have plenty of time to sit here. But in my head, I'm thinking of the bruises, and Eli's dad, and the shattered picture frame from the weekend before last that seemed to ruin Eli's entire mood.

"You did good tonight," I keep talking. "Watching you wrestle is kind of surreal. You move so fast and you—"

He unclicks his seatbelt, reaching for the button on the side of the seat to move it back.

"Come here." His words are gravelly.

I look up, my arms crossed over my chest, a way to try and ease some of the discomfort running through me, the way I feel fidgety in my seat. "What?"

He drops his hand from the wheel, to his lap. "Here," he says, nodding toward his thighs. "Come sit with me."

I feel feverish, tingling aches flooding through my body, physicality overriding everything in my head for a moment. I glance through the windshield at the empty parking lot of the school, and he must know what I'm thinking.

"No one is here. My windows have five percent tint. No one can see us."

"Your windshield isn't—"

"No one is here." He repeats the words, more urgent.

I turn to look at him, my fingertips pressing into my upper arms. When I still don't move, he leans over toward me, unclicking my own seatbelt, letting it slide across my chest before he reaches for me, underneath my arms, hauling me over the console even as my knees bang against it, and I have to duck my head. My fingers scramble for purchase against his shirt as he pulls me onto his lap, my knees on either side of his hips, depressing the leather of his seat.

My spine is touching the steering wheel, but as short as I am, once I'm on top of him, I don't have to duck much. It's not uncomfortable, even with his hands planted along my hips, squeezing hard as he stares up at me, my bangs hanging around my eyes.

He reaches up with one hand, gently releasing the clip in my hair and dropping it into the console alongside my bracelet without looking away from me. His fingers tangle through my strands as he pulls me down to him, so our noses are aligned.

"You looked so fucking hot sitting in those bleachers." His throat sounds sore, his words gruff.

My fingers are splayed over his shirt, feeling the hardness of his chest, the shallow, sharp rises and falls as he breathes. "Yeah?" *God, I want to fuck you again.* I haven't gotten it out of my head since last Friday. I don't know if I did anything right. I don't know that I did anything *at all,* but it felt so good, and *he* was so good. I've imagined it in my head all week, I haven't even watched porn to get off. I haven't even imagined all those violent things he said, all that shit he was studying on his computer.

He still has his hand fisted in my hair, and he pulls me even closer as he tilts his head, his lips brushing mine. "Yes." He gives me just the ghost of a kiss, not lending me the time to kiss him back before he's speaking again. "I want you there all the time. Every match."

My pulse feels fluttery in my chest. I don't really believe him. I don't know if it's because I intuitively understand Eli will only ever be temporary, for *anyone,* or if it's my own personal block. There are two possibilities, and neither make me feel good. Either I'm too damaged to see his authenticity, or else I am able to see it *exactly,* because of my damage. Just like when he stalked me from the library. I shouldn't have got high on it, the power of having him follow me. *But I did. I do.*

"Not just this season," he continues, his eyes gleaming in the dark. Only the dash lights in his car give us anything to see by, but it's enough. "Next year too."

The longing is deep enough to feel in my bones. I push my fingers so hard against his chest, I expect his sternum to snap. I remember his bruise, and I know I've touched it, the way the softest wince flits across his features, his brows pulled together.

But he doesn't stop me.

"Okay." I say the word anyway, giving in to dreams of us together, even while we're in college, knowing it's all a lie. But what else can I do? I know this will end. When we graduate, I have this gut feeling Eli will do "out of sight, out of mind," far better than anyone ever could. If I'm not around to entertain him—and going to two different schools, I won't be—then he will find a way to ease his boredom elsewhere. *What could I ever do about it?*

"Okay," he repeats, like it's settled, if a little precariously. He drags his mouth along my jawline, causing goosebumps to erupt all over my skin, my nipples tightening as my eyes flutter closed for a second, my fingers still tangled in his shirt. "Okay," he says again, against the base of my throat. He licks a line up it, and I shiver, but before anything else can happen, when I feel everything wound up tight and I want to forget about these broken promises and what our future looks like, he lets go of me and leans back in his seat, staring up at me. "Just like that? *Okay?*" His voice sounds almost… scared.

I blink, my eyes heavy, veins sticky with lust. *I want him right here.* "What else do you want?" I ask quietly. His abrupt shifts in mood throw me off, like he tries to be assertive when he's feeling timid, but it all overwhelms him sometimes, and I imagine putting on an act every day can make you fray a little at the edges.

"I want you to mean it when you say things like that to me."

"I do mean it." And I do. I just know it can't be true.

He runs both hands over my ribcage, his thumbs grazing

the underside of my breasts, my shirt still buttoned to my throat. "Do you?"

"Yes."

"How do you know? How do you know you want this so much?"

It could be a confusing question, but I have the answer all the same. I don't have to reach back far for the memory of *how I know*. "Thinking of you with her..." I don't need to say who. But I shake my head, the words trailing off as he glides his hands up higher, over my arms, to the back of my neck, my hair spilling down my back. He presses his fingers to the side of my throat, and I hold his gaze even as I falter.

"Tell me, baby."

"Makes me feel physically ill. And not just her. If it was anyone..."

He studies me a moment, his thumb tracing circles at the base of my skull. Then he nods. "I felt the same way when I saw Dominic's mouth on you." His words are cold, enough to make my body feel tense with something almost like fear. "At my house. In the library."

I smile, ignoring how that night in my car, he turned his inaction against me by throwing Luna in my face. "So next time Luna touches you, I can break her nose?"

He leans his head back against the seat, still holding on tight to me. "I would fuck you right there if you did."

My smile falters. It's a joke, but it's not.

It's like he needs someone to fight for him. *It's like he wants my jealousy because it makes him feel loved.*

I think of his bruises, the matching ones on his dad. *Love.*

I decide right here, now, in this moment, if this is all we have, I don't want an *almost* relationship.

If this is all we have, if this is going to break my heart into fucking pieces, if I'm going to cry over this boy when he inevitably leaves me and I, him, then *I want all of it.* More than the one time, I want to keep doing this, over and over and fucking over until he's sick of me.

I shift forward, bringing my center closer to the bulge in his pants, my skirt hiked up dangerously close to the tops of my thighs, barely concealing my underwear.

His gaze becomes guarded, and surprising me, he drops his hands from me, clenching them into fists at his sides.

When he speaks, I hear the hoarseness in his words. "Eden." It's like a warning. "I don't think I should fuck you in my car—"

I dig my fingertips into his shirt as I look into his eyes. "Stop."

I hear his breath hitch.

"I know I'm safe." *I protect you.* I hear the words inside my mind. "Be in control," I tell him. "Do anything you want." *Touch me, touch me, touch me.* I drag my fingers down the length of his hard body, feeling the ridges of muscle in his skin, stopping at the hem of his shirt and twisting it in my hands, wanting it off of him. I think again of his dad, and their fights, and the complicated relationship Eli probably has with everyone around him. How scared he is I'll run because I'm sure everyone has at some point in time. Even his dad is barely hanging on by a thread. How must that feel, to be unwanted by your own parents?

I think of what Dom said about his mom leaving him.

Even Reece has never suggested Mom abandon me. We hate each other and he's never once tried to kick me out or said I should live with my dad.

My heart aches for this boy beneath me.

"Anything, Eli. Do anything. It's not the first time anymore." *Touch me now.*

Slowly, like he might scare me or himself if he goes any faster, his strong fingers come to my thighs, his middle ones just under the hem of my skirt. My muscles twitch with his touch.

"Anything?"

I look up, finding his head tilted back against the seat as he gazes at me, his bottom lip between his teeth.

His hands slide up higher, under my skirt, around to my

ass. He dips his chin, groaning as he nudges his nose with mine, and I hold in my head the shape of his affection as I sign myself over to his aggression.

But I meant what I said. "Anything, baby boy." I drop my hands by my sides, leaning against his steering wheel, letting him shove my skirt up between us, his thumbs close to the cut out of my underwear. "I'd do anything, I'd let you do anything." Inside my head, the violence I've seen through my phone screen plays, the words on his computer screen, and I want that for us. I want him to be that awfulness to *me*.

He's staring at my thighs, his fingers tracing circles on my skin as I wait, barely breathing, trying not to think of what it is he might actually do to me. In this car, there isn't room for much. But to put his hand over my mouth, cover my nose, that wouldn't take much room at all, would it?

It's enough to make me want to beg him for it.

"Eden." The word sounds choked. He still doesn't meet my gaze. "I don't want you to ever regret me."

I'm already opening my mouth to protest until I realize what he's said. I thought the last word would be "it." Whatever he's going to do next in this car. I thought I would tell him nothing he hurt me with could scare me. I'd remind him of my fantasies, the way I liked how he barred his arm over my throat last time. How he slapped my thigh. How my brain isn't so different from his. And despite his dark thoughts and chaotic impulses, I know he isn't going to kill me.

But I don't speak, stopping short. My lungs ache as I inhale, exhale, think of his words.

"I don't want you to ever regret me."

Slowly, his eyes come up to mine.

He goes very, very still, no longer running his fingers over my thighs.

"Why would I regret you?" My voice is small, trying to save room for how loud his answer may be.

"When you're caught up in the moment, you say things to forge closeness." He dips his head and presses a kiss to my sternum, over my clothes, like a gesture that comes before a blow, nothing sexual about it. "You *do* things to fake it. It's like your logical brain shuts off." Before I can agree or argue, he lifts his head and snatches up my wrist, flipping it between us and brushing my bracelets out of the way with his thumb.

I try to jerk back, surprise jolting me into a new awareness, but he tightens his hold, pressing into my bones. "Eli. *Let me go.*"

"Anything, you said." His eyes hold mine, brows lifted in stern admonishment. "You said *anything.*"

My face burns with humiliation, and I try again to get free.

His hold tightens, and it hurts a little, the pressure from the other weekend lingering in my muscles. I still, trying to breathe, refusing to show him I'm in pain. If I did, I'm afraid he'd stop. *Maybe I don't ever want him to.*

For a second, we stare at one another.

Then he says, "Did you think you could hide it from me forever?"

Don't look down. I plead it, over and over in my head. *Please don't.* "We don't have forever." I say those words to hurt us both, to make us remember. To distract him.

But he only smiles, tracing the three letters with his thumb. "Is it a name, or initials?"

No, no, no.

I know he sees the mortification in my face, hears my shallow breaths, but he just holds my gaze, his smile thinning out into tightly held ire. "Tell me, Eden."

"I don't want to talk about—"

"If you can't talk about *this,* then you have no business crawling into my lap and offering yourself up to me so goddamn easily."

I feel as if he slapped me, wincing as I try again to jerk my wrist free. His grip is too tight, and he yanks me closer to his chest, my palm stopping me from falling into him. "You pulled me to your fucking lap." It's the only thing I can think to say. "*You did that—*"

"You let me choke you. You want me to hurt you. You want me to *slap you*. Hit you. You want me to place my hand over your mouth, stop you from breathing?" He brings my wrist up to his mouth, closing it over the pearly scars, sucking my flesh with his lips until he pulls away, teeth pricking me. "Before we get there, why don't you tell me this secret, baby girl."

Then his gaze lowers, long lashes along with it, and the burn of humiliation in my stomach is painful. I close my eyes, so I don't have to see him examine me.

"I know the answer already." He kisses the inside of my wrist again as I try to stay very, very still, coldness flushing out the fervor of my embarrassment. We've never talked about this.

He can't possibly know.

"Nic." He whispers the name, and my eyes fly open, my pulse crashing in my chest, nausea swirling in my gut. "Nic Penn. Tell me I'm wrong."

I feel as if someone threw ice water over my head, waking me up from a dream.

I glance out the dark driver's side window, part of me foolishly hoping other cars will be here. Other people.

I try to back up, but my shoulders hit the horn of the car, and it beeps, causing me to jump, my gasp coming out strangled.

Eli smiles, but he doesn't even look up.

"You didn't love him, did you?" He asks like he knows, not like he's insecure about what my answer may be. His teeth catch my skin. I feel his breath along my flesh, but I'm still staring out the back window, at the stretch of forest that seems to go on for eternity. It's Thursday night. At a day school.

We're alone here. I was counting on it when I gave him permission to hurt me. Now, I'd be grateful even for Reece or Sebastian's surly appearance.

"How did you know that?" Anger heats my entire body. Like he waited for this moment to humiliate me. Did he know the first time we fucked? And he just let it go then because he was so ready to take my virginity? "How the fuck did you know that?"

He licks the veins on my wrist, then pulls back, one hand still under my skirt. "I want to know everything about you, Eden."

I inhale, holding the air in my lungs.

"Look at me." He says the words softly, but I don't mistake the command in them.

I shake my head. "No, that's not… You shouldn't fucking know that."

"Eden." His voice is lower, the warning clear. "I want to see your eyes on mine."

I give him what he wants. Dark green. A ring of black. I'm not sure what it is he's feeling. His lips are parted, no smile pulling on them, no amusement in his eyes. If he's proud of making me nervous, he doesn't show it.

"How did you know that?"

He rolls his eyes. "It's beside the point."

"How, Eli? How the fuck did you know?" I want to back away. I want to get out. I want to move.

"Calm down," he says, like one might say to *turn left* or *good morning*.

I try again to pull my wrist from him, but I can't get free.

"Did he do this to you?" His tone is cold, but his face betrays nothing.

"Eli—"

"I'm not answering your question until you answer some of mine."

The words seem to explode out of me. "No, he didn't fucking do it to me! I did it!" I swallow past the dryness in my throat, try to get ahead of my racing heart. "How did you know? I told you something, now tell me, Eli. How the hell did you find that out?"

I think of the texts from Amanda I haven't yet read. Theoretical plans she's making for us now that I've agreed to see her.

I have a wild urge to reach for my phone, in my bag in the backseat, but I'm fidgeting here, in his lap.

"The internet is a valuable resource."

My breath rattles in my lungs. My records would be sealed, wouldn't they? He wouldn't find that on the damn internet.

"Are you scared of me?" It's an honest question, not meant to taunt me. He runs his thumb over the scars again, each shaky letter.

I feel completely undone, in the worst way, like he's pulled apart my stitching and now he's examining all the ways I'm wired wrong.

It pisses me off. He shouldn't have looked so far. "Scared? I'm not fucking *scared.*" I try to think, but being so close to him, it's hard. I need space. *I need air.* "Tell me right now, *right fucking now,* how you know. Don't lie to me."

"I saw the name. I… have a connection. In the office?"

Trafalgar. Financial aid. Ms. Corbin. For fuck's sake.

He closes his eyes a second, but he speaks fast, like he's scared I'm going to walk away. "I'm sorry, I know, it's too much. It's a lot. But he plays baseball, doesn't he? And I saw your yearbook, digitally, it's online. Very high-tech." He's looking at me again as I hold onto his words. "There were some photos of the two of you, in the *Students Having Fun* section." He can't hide his smile with that phrase because the title falls short.

My mind races. I grind my teeth together as I watch him try to explain, even knowing, where Eli is concerned, I'd give a free pass for anything.

"He didn't deserve this from you," he says, pressing another kiss to my wrist.

My heart seizes and I feel emotionally exposed.

Closing my eyes, I try to clear my head for a moment, even as I shift on Eli's lap and desire burns through me, maybe more so since this obsessive revelation.

I remember Nic's face when he saw what I did.

A baseball game.

I was at his baseball game. He looked so good in his uniform. Blond curls, pale, flushed skin. Bat in hand. We said we'd get matching tattoos one day, but we never even kissed. I just… I just assumed, him walking me to class, holding my hand… I just assumed it meant something more. I built it all up inside my head. I… imagined it.

I wanted to… *I wanted to feel something. I wanted to belong to someone.*

But when I'd shoved up my sleeve, out of place in Wilmington's heat, he'd looked as if he might be sick. Then he'd spun around, checking no one was near us. And he said, *"What the fuck did you do, Eden?"*

When I open my eyes, I think I'm still waiting for the same revulsion in Eli's face.

I wait for his lip to curl, his eyes to narrow. For him to shove me off of his lap. Maybe make me get out of his car and walk home.

"I want to carve over it," he says instead, like one might say they're hungry, or they need a rest, or a drink of water. "I have a box cutter. At home."

I try to remember I need air to live. That I can't just hold my breath every time he makes me feel things I want to run to and squirm away from all at once.

"Do you still speak to him?" He tilts his head as he asks, his fingers now pressing tight over the scars, like he no longer wants to see it. But not because he's disgusted, I realize.

Because he wants his name there instead.

Something akin to elation bursts in my chest. It knots up with anger and I couldn't exactly name how I feel, right now, in this moment.

"No," I tell him, like a promise. "Never."

He squeezes my thigh tighter. Harder. "Good," he whispers. He leans in closer to me, pinning my wrist behind my back, but not in a painful way like he did before. "Don't ever talk to him again. He hasn't earned any more of your fucking time." And before I can respond, before I can formulate words, or work through my emotions, he's kissing me.

His mouth fucking devours me, bruising and biting, teeth hitting together, his tongue fighting mine. I reach for the string of his joggers, arching my neck as we break our mouths away from one another and he bites a line down my throat, his fingers spread out over my ass, one hand still pinning my wrist behind my back.

"Baby girl," he says, like a warning against my throat. "What're you doing?"

I untie the string, pulling down the waistband of his pants. I push my hand down his boxers, wrapping my fingers around him, hard and heavy and *aching* for me.

"Fuck me." I remember our words from the kitchen as I pump him, unsure if I'm doing it right, because last time we had sex, he guided my movements. *"Right here. Like this."* He's already peeled back some of my worst secrets and I think, maybe, I want him to prove he still likes me, after learning about these scars.

A groan leaves his throat, the sound against mine. Slowly, as I stroke him, my wrist cramping from the angle, he pulls back, looking up at me, hand still gripping my ass, his chest heaving. "Yeah?"

Lust catches fire inside of me, and all I can feel is relief at the fact he's not going to stop me. *Oh, thank God.* "Yes," I tell him. "Yes."

His eyes search mine, as if trying to find how I really feel. My true consent.

Whatever he sees, it must be enough, because when I tug on his pants after I reluctantly give up the feel of his cock, he obliges, shifting his hips. And as a startled little sigh leaves my lips and all I can think about is sinking down onto his dick, filling myself up with *him*, he's turning us.

It's one fluid motion from him, but I'm awkwardly pressed against the seat, and he's reaching for another button which lowers the top half down, down, *down*, until he's over me, his hand jerking my thigh to the side, fingers pulling down my underwear. I help him, both of my hands free now, and when the fabric is between my ankles, I kick it off with my shoes.

He shoves up my skirt, exposing me to him, and I have the urge to clamp my thighs together, just like the first time, but he must sense it, crouched down in his car over top of me, because he kneels on the edge of his seat and uses both hands circled around the crease of my thighs to hold me open, exactly like he did before.

I'm grateful for it.

I dig my fingers into the side of his leather seats, fighting the urge to push him away because I'm under his scrutiny. A toy for him to examine.

His chest is rising and falling sharply beneath his shirt, his cock thick and heavy, balls tight and aching. I want to touch him. I want to taste him. I like how every muscle in his body seems tense as he examines me.

He slides his hands up higher, his thumbs peeling me apart, exposing me to him, how wet I am for him, my slick, pink clit throbbing for his touch.

"You want me here?" he asks quietly, lifting his eyes to mine.

I'm leaned so far back, I somehow feel dizzy, my world turned upside down like my position in his car. I nod, scared to speak.

"What if someone sees us?" He doesn't sound at all concerned. It's like a test.

"I don't care," I finally manage to say.

He smiles. "I do, Eden." He leans close, kissing me deep. "I want to be the only one." His words are against my lips, then, before I can speak, he slides his knees from his seat, his head bowed, and his mouth comes to my pussy, tongue flicking along my clit.

I gasp, my back arching upward, his thumbs still pulling me apart, exposing every inch of me to him, more than he did the first time. I've never been seen so intimately, save for by myself, one time when I took a mirror into the bathroom and learned all the parts of my body after reading about it in a book Mom tossed my way. This is far more private than that. I want to twist away, to buck my hips, clamp my legs shut, but I can't, and I don't.

He sucks on my clit, causing me to whimper, his eyes cutting to mine, a smile on his lips that I can feel between mine. He moves his hand possessively over my inner thigh, twisting his wrist, then curling two fingers inside of me, pulling back from me just enough to groan, like fingering me feels good to him, too.

"You have the tightest little hole," he says, eyes focusing back on mine.

I reach for him, wanting to grab his hair and yank, but he pushes roughly inside of me, all the way to his last knuckle as he shakes his head, his breath still against my clit, index finger and thumb of his other hand still spreading me for him.

"No," he says. "Put your hands over your head, on my seat."

I know he sees me freeze. Sees my indecision, because he licks me, all the way from the tip of where his fingers are seated inside me, to the top of my pussy, his bottom lip catching on the sensitive spot.

"Now, Eden, or I'll stop, and we'll leave."

But I want to touch you. I can't stay still. I can't, I can't, I can't.

My chest heaves, my breasts ache, I want to rip free every button on my shirt. I want him to have all of me at the same time I want to hide everything.

"I'm done." He says the words flatly as he pulls back, and I know he's bluffing, but I don't want to test him on it.

"Okay, okay, okay," I say quickly, my body wound tight. I raise my arms over my head. I bend my elbows, clasping my wrists behind the headrest so I can try and stop the temptation to move building higher inside of me.

He smiles again, licking me once more as he fingers me,

twisting and pushing and hooking his fingers in a way that makes me cry out.

"I love when you do what I say, baby girl." He looks down, right at me, and I've never been so grateful for illegally tinted windows as I am right now, blocking even the moonlight from outside of his car. Shielding me from the intensity of his gaze, in the smallest of ways.

Inhaling, I catch my own scent, and I have to dig my nails into the tops of my hands to keep from reaching for him, from wanting to bury my head in his chest, too far away.

Sensing my discomfort, he looks up again, his mouth glistening with *me*. He attempts to add another finger inside of me, and I tighten up, whimpering.

"Shh," he whispers, turning his head to softly bite the inside of my thigh. "Breathe for me, baby girl. Let go. I've got you. *I look out for you.*"

You've got me. He said those words to me before, and I adore them. *You have no idea how much you've got me.*

He licks where he bit me, then bites harder, causing me to arch up, and he quickly kisses the bite. "I've got you," he says again, still trying to coax another finger inside of me. "You're so, so fucking mine, Nightmare Girl." He pushes, the pressure and fullness feeling so *good,* and so does the look he gives me, like admiration, even as he controls everything about this situation.

I try to relax.

I try to breathe.

He groans as he finally gets three fingers inside of me, and I can feel my walls tensing around his fingers. "You are just *so fucking tight."*

I blush with his words, dragging my nails so deep against the veins on my hands, I know I'm peeling my own skin off.

He turns his head again, his nose nudging my clit, then he's kissing me, open mouthed, then sucking, lapping his tongue against me, over and over as he finger-fucks me so hard my back jolts against the seats, the car no doubt rocking from the outside.

I close my eyes, so fucking close, *so close*, my stomach twisted into knots, my core hot, the pulsing need beneath his mouth, his tongue, around his fingers consuming me from the inside out.

I feel myself cresting, so close, my hips arched off the seat, pushing harder against his mouth, wanting all of him, everything. I lift one foot, propping it on the console, at the far end, exposing myself more, my knee dropping open, inner muscles of my thigh pulled taut.

"Look at me when you come," he whispers over me, and I know I'm there with his words, like a command. I open my eyes, locking on his, and I feel myself tighten once more around him before the strongest release I've ever felt rocks me.

I'm saying his name, moaning, keeping my arms over my head, but it's taking everything in me not to touch him, scratch him, hurt him, as I watch him watching me, something I mistake for love in his eyes as I come, gushing all over his fingers, exploding into pieces for him.

I'm shifting my hips, fucking his hand, wanting to drag it out, and he lifts his head, pushing his palm against my clit instead, letting me have the friction, and I grind against him. He looks down at his fingers inside of me, and he bites his lip so fucking hard I swear he's got to be bleeding.

When I'm completely undone, spent, my body relaxing as much as it can, he slowly pulls his fingers out, but he doesn't move his palm.

He runs his fingers up my slickness, and I hear the sounds of how wet I am.

Lifting his hand to his mouth, his eyes on me, he tastes me from his middle finger, licking all the way up his knuckles.

Then he's climbing on top of me, dragging his hand up my body, his knees on either side of my hips, his cock free, and before I can think, or move, or speak, he's covering my mouth, my nose, with the same hand he had inside of me, wetness over my face.

He uses that hand to hold up his weight, fisting his cock with his other, and without a word, he pushes himself into me, groaning against my ear as he does, nothing slow about it. Not like the first time, this is so much rougher.

I'm gasping beneath his hand, and he tightens the seal of it, ensuring my nostrils are covered with just the edge of his palm, the rest over my mouth.

He feels so good inside of me, my flesh sensitive from my orgasm, slick from *him*, and even as he fills me up far better than three of his fingers ever could, even though I feel him hitting deep, even though I'm sore in so many ways, stretched tight around him, it only makes it all feel that much better.

Especially, maybe, because I can barely breathe.

"Fuck," he says, the word jagged, one hand now on the seat beside my head as he drives his hips into me, grinding against mine with every thrust. "You… you are perfect."

I start to unwind my arms from the back of the headrest, but he nudges my face with his nose, exposing my neck and biting, *hard*.

"No." He brings a hand down to my knee, pushing it almost painfully out to the side so he can hit as deep as possible inside of me, driving me into the seat. "Don't let go. This isn't your first time." My face grows hot. "You're for me to play with right now."

I melt with his words, sickly sweet in the most twisted way.

"Nod your head if you understand."

It's only then, in that moment, *right now*, when I realize… I can't breathe.

"Eden." He almost chokes on my name as he fucks me, my gasps silent even as my lips part beneath his hand smashed over my mouth. "Nod your head."

I do, I manage to nod just as my vision swims, black and gray obscuring my view of his shoulder, jammed close to my face, his lips still at my throat.

He kisses me, so soft, reassuring. "Good, baby. I've got you. *Fuck*, I've got you." His thrusts become wilder, more violent, almost painful, my body jostled with every single one, pinned beneath him in the car. I turn my head as he moves his hand from my knee, and I see his fingers warping the leather of his seats, knuckles white. There's nothing soft about this, and yet, the way he kisses me, the side of my neck, my jaw, my face not covered by his hand, my brow… *it is*.

I can't breathe.

I don't want to. I don't want him to stop. *I want all of this. I want everything he can give me.*

But I still release my own hold over my wrists, my arms aching as I finally bring them forward, digging at his biceps, solid beneath my fingers. Stronger muscle than I could ever hope to have, to push away, but my head is full of pressure, my lungs are aching with his chest pressed to mine and the fact I haven't had oxygen in… how long?

"Just a little longer." He seems to be begging me, his words at my ear. "I'm so close, baby girl."

I want to give in for him. I want to let him use me any way he wants. He feels so good, the depth of him coaxing me to the edge again, the pain in my thigh, in my sore pussy, a gift.

I want to do this for him. *I want to. I want to.*

He goes faster, painfully so, the sound of our hips colliding adding to the hurt, my clit swollen, opening my lips to the point I can feel his hips graze against it with every thrust.

I grab his arms, but I don't try to push him off anymore.

Don't stop.

"I'm almost there, baby. I'm almost… almost…" His voice cracks, then he's whimpering into my ear, panting, groaning my name. Coming completely undone. It sounds so beautiful, it's enough to break my heart.

"Eden, fuck. Eden, Eden, Eden."

Just like the first time, it's like a song inside my head as his body tenses and releases over mine, his cum inside of me, claiming me, *marking me*.

I always want to be yours. I only ever want you to say my *name.* It's the last thought I have before my vision goes black.

I can still feel him, his palm pressed painfully over my face, stealing my air, *killing me.*

And I can still hear him, something he should never say. "I need you." It's strangled words, I don't know if I'm conscious, or dreaming them. *"I need you so much."*

Then I blink.

I suck in air, feeling his hand cupping my face, gentle.

My vision is blurry, but as I keep blinking, keep breathing, it clears.

I don't know how much time has passed. A minute? A second? Hours? I glance out the window, noting nothing has changed. It's still dark.

Eli jerks my chin toward him.

His eyes aren't wide. He doesn't look alarmed. Just… tired. Spent. Satiated. *I passed out, and did he panic?*

No.

"There you are." He whispers the words, his knee against the seat, his back hunched as he gives me space to breathe, his thumb over my bottom lip.

I realize my hands are limp by my sides.

I realize, too, I'm empty. I'm all wet and used and satisfied, but empty.

His pants are pulled up, his boxers sticking up out of the top.

Glancing down, my skirt is still hiked around my waist, my underwear on the floorboard.

"How do you feel, baby?" He has the softest smile on his face.

My own throbs, and I flex my jaw.

He frowns, tracing two fingers along my jawline. "Talk to me."

"I…" I trail off, unsure of what to say, feeling disoriented, strangely high, but subdued. "I'm sorry." I don't know why I say it. Maybe because of the look of concern on his face. The way he now seems troubled.

But with my words, he's moving too fast for me to comprehend.

He's spinning us again, one arm scooping around my back as he drops into the seat, and I'm in his lap, knees around his hips. I'm a little dizzy, the interior of the car spinning, and he's putting the seat up, then he's hugging me to his chest, his lips to the crown of my head.

I huddle against him, my fingers clasped together, tucked under my chin as I just breathe and close my eyes.

"You're okay," he says, his strong body capturing mine to him. "I'm here." He kisses me again, hugging me tighter. "Just relax. We can stay like this. We don't have anywhere to be." All things I didn't know I needed him to say until he says them.

And I… go limp in his arms, confused on what to think, how to feel. There's a mess between my thighs, and I should really pee, but I don't have the energy to fight him.

I just give in.

Heaviness and contentment settle over me, and I drift off.

BY THE TIME I REALIZE I SHOULD GET UP AND GET OFF OF HIM, there's drool at the corner of my mouth. I try to wipe it off, but before I can, he grabs my chin, lifting my head so my eyes are on his. He dips his head, licking off the drool from my face, his eyes closed, a low, soft hum of serenity against my skin when he's done.

Then he pulls back, eyes on mine again, and I see he looks dazed. Like he's high, but I know we're both sober. "You're always so good," he says, tracing my lips with his finger. "That was so fucking good."

Pleasure from his approval flushes through me, feelings of pride and awe tangled tight under my skin. I slide my hands up his chest, cupping his face. Then I lean in, planting a soft kiss on the upturned tip of his nose.

His smile is real, or, if it isn't, his mask in this moment is flawless.

I pull back and he drops his hand to my hip. My skirt is still hiked up around my waist, my underwear still by the gas pedal. He notices me glancing over my shoulder to look at it, and keeping a hold on my hip, he leans down past me, snatching up my black bikini briefs.

It takes work, but with his help, I manage to get them on over my shoes, up my legs, lifting one knee, then the other as I'm still kneeling in his lap.

Then, feeling clumsy and awkward, I plant my hand against his chest and move one knee to the passenger seat, knowing I'll need to adjust my skirt, still rumpled up over the waistband of my underwear, but I'd rather move off him first and get some space between us.

And yet, when he reaches for my wrists, gently, helping balance me, I gasp, and it's not from his touch.

Looking down, I see my underwear, tangled from being put on so quickly, is caught on the gearshift, pulling enough to expose me.

My fingers wrinkle the cotton of his shirt as I hold on to him tighter, and I don't know why I don't just move, until I realize he's only circling one of my wrists now, and his other hand is on the outside of my thigh, furthest from him, my knee pressed into the base of the passenger seat.

I'm straddling the hot leather of the gearshift, my pussy grazing it. My abs are tense, my breath caught in my chest, and even though I should just keep going, the way his fingertips dig into my skin won't let me.

Slowly, I drag my gaze up to his, and find he's biting his bottom lip, wholly focused on the shifter he spends so much time with his hand on.

It's like two of his favorite things, come together.

My cheeks are hot, one hand on his chest, another coming to my heart.

I try to remember to breathe, but he has this look in his eyes that steals the air from my lungs.

"*Fuck.*" Every time he says that word, I feel this need to please him. But this time, it's worse. Maybe because of what we just did. Maybe because I've never seen him look so enraptured before. Maybe since I've already let him steal the air from my lungs enough for me to black out, this feels like nothing.

I want to keep his attention.

And I'm still so fucking horny.

Before I can think through it, I lower myself down, just enough to rub myself over the shifter. Enough to tease the ache building all over again between my thighs, a whimper on my mouth.

I look down, feeling *his cum* seeping from me, the smallest drop of pale white on the shift knob. Heat like I've never known sears through me.

His eyes snap up to mine, lust in his gaze, I'm not even sure he's breathing until he says, "Get your ass back in your seat."

I drag my nails over the fabric of his shirt, shifting my hips, the warmth of the shifter knob against my clit, knowing more of my wetness and his cum are smearing all over it. My words are strangled when I speak. "I like how you're looking at me too much to move."

He stares at me, my fingers pressing hard over my own heart to try and calm my pulse, one hand still on his chest to keep myself steady.

I grind myself against the gear again, dirty thoughts racing through my brain, ways to hold his attention just like this, to get his dick fully hard all over again, because I can see it straining once more in his pants. But before I can even dare consider it, he's grabbing my upper arms and hauling me back into my seat, pinning me against the leather as he leans over me, his face inches from mine.

"Don't do that." He sounds angry, or tortured. I keep my palms pressed against the warm seatback, my skirt falling over my lap, having come loose from the waistband of my underwear because of his sudden movement. There's a messy wetness between my thighs from me and him and I squeeze them together, wanting him to fill me all over again.

"Why not?" My voice is rough.

He doesn't answer with words. Instead, he's kissing me so deep, there's no chance I can take a breath. My fingers find his hair, his palm plants against my chest, then he's undoing the buttons I have up to my throat on my shirt. His short nails are clawing at me as he undoes each one. I think he wants to feel me up, but he scratches against the skin over my heart instead, deep enough I might bleed. His tongue wraps around mine, then he's biting my lips, every inch of my mouth, sharp, quick bites, pinpricks of pain, possession, he's holding himself up with his hand beside my head. I yank his hair, relishing in the smallest of whimpers coming from his lips into mine. I moan in his mouth, then he's pulling back, dragging out my bottom lip as he nudges his nose against mine. I squeeze my thighs together, wanting him so much it hurts, but when he releases my mouth, he says, "You'll regret it. You're high tonight, but you might wake up and regret it."

I'm breathing hard, my pulse so loud, I'm not sure if I really heard him correctly. *High? Am I high?*

"I'm not… I'm not on drugs," I gasp out. "What are you talking about?"

He closes his eyes tight. I wonder what he sees there, inside his head. He doesn't open them, but he nudges his nose against mine, so soft. He takes a shaky breath. "Nothing. I just… don't want you to regret anything, okay?" Slowly, he opens his eyes. "I fucking want to see it. Trust me, I do. But when you're thinking clearly, all right?" He kisses me again, like he knows maybe I don't understand. Then he pulls back, letting go of my heart last as he settles back into his seat, adjusting his pants and his erection, tying up the string on his sweats, like it'll keep his self-control strong.

I right myself, too, trying to breathe as I glance at the time.

"We should go." I say it only to have something to say. In

my head, I'm repeating his words about thinking clearly. It doesn't fit with who I suspect he really is. I don't want to let my guard down and think his sweet nothings mean more than they do, but it's so hard when he's so good to me.

"Okay," he says. He starts the car, hand on the shifter, and this time we're both staring at it. Slowly, we look up at the same time. *I still want it.* But he doesn't mention it again. All he asks is, "You're my girlfriend, okay?"

I raise my brows, not a calculated move. "What?"

"Do I need to spell it out for you? Don't let Dominic, or anyone else, kiss you. Don't let him touch you again like he did before. Don't fuck anyone else. And I'm only fucking you." He doesn't quantify our time. When this agreement ends.

But it's all I'm thinking about.

This can't last forever. I know I should just enjoy him being mine while I can, but jealousy for when he's not anymore is already stabbing my gut.

It's like a lease and I want to own him.

I don't say that, though. Instead, I say, "What about kissing? You only kissing me too?"

He smiles, dropping his gaze as he shakes his head. He puts the car in drive, and it's only when he's glancing in his rear view as we pull out, his eyes just barely jumping over mine, that he answers me. "Possessive."

I don't deny it.

"I like that."

"I'd like if you answered me."

He glances at me with a smirk. "Yes, Nightmare Girl. Just you."

31

Eden

I DON'T SLEEP.

I replay it all, over and over in my head, just like I did last weekend.

Sex with Eli. The feel of his hand over my mouth. His words in my ear. The way he held me. I get off to it, three times in a row. Then, sometime around two in the morning, I get up.

I do a workout video, careful with my steps so I don't wake anyone up. I read through *The Kybalion*. I finish *The Picture of Dorian Gray*, highlighting a passage over and over and over, so often I tear through the thin, yellow paper.

The only way to get rid of a temptation is to yield to it. Resist it, and your soul grows sick with longing for the things it has forbidden to itself, with desire for what its monstrous laws have made monstrous and unlawful.

I think I hear words coming from my fan, turned on high.

I stop, tilting my head up and watching the blades spin as I strain my ears.

Then there's the creak of a door.

My heart races as I freeze, my breath hitching as I drop my gaze to my bedroom door. Oscar Wilde's book is in my hand, clenched tight in my fingers.

Sebastian walks in.

He slowly shuts the door behind him, his phone clutched in his hand.

I frown, glancing over my shoulder. Thin trails of light seep through my closed blinds. I drop my gaze to my phone, buried around my sheets. I snatch it up and toss down the book. Before I say a word to Sebastian, I check the time, and my messages.

It's six in the morning. *Shit.* It's six in the fucking morning.

But for some reason, I'm not exactly perturbed by Sebastian's unwelcome, early morning entrance.

Despite the early hour, I'm smiling as I read the texts I ignored all night, busy and involved in other things, thinking after Eli let me know he got home, he'd be going to sleep.

Him: I didn't shower. I still smell like you.

Him: It's driving me fucking crazy.

Him: You must be asleep baby girl. I hope you sleep so well. Text me when you get up.

"Read it." Sebastian drags me out of my bliss, shoving his bright phone screen my way. Reluctantly, I tear my eyes from my own, clicking the screen off as I take Seb's phone instead, the metallic case cold beneath my fingers, and sink down onto the bed. "Why the hell are you up?"

"Why are you reading the fucking news?" I mutter under my breath, ignoring his question.

And it *is* the news, the headline bold and in red letters. Just as I'm about to ask Sebastian why the hell he came in here so early over a news article, I actually read the title. Above the photo of a blonde girl wearing a dress and jelly sandals, standing in front of a lake.

I swallow the knot in my throat. It's the same photo on the missing posters. The same one I saw in Dom's room.

I force myself to read the headline again, not really believing it.

Missing Trafalgar Student's Remains Found

I drop my gaze to the tiny text of the article but in the near darkness of my room, my eyes strain against the dimness of his screen. "Turn on the light."

Sebastian, still standing, pulls the dongle by the fan. Pale orange light floods the room.

I blink, my head spinning as I scan the text, scrolling down with my thumb.

Remains found by police in Lake Wisteria has been confirmed as that of Winslet Landers. My throat feels dry. I force myself to keep reading. 17-year-old declared missing last September. Vanished from her home. No suspects. Still... none. No cause of death released. No information on the state of the body. Family has been notified.

"Wisteria is behind her house." Sebastian's voice drags me away from his screen.

I want to throw the phone across the room, and I don't know why. I settle with dropping it like it bit me. Like it's physically painful to hold.

Unease settles in my bones, and I think of Dominic, and when he found this out. Was it last night? Will he come to school today? We haven't really spoken since the library, last week.

I create a stack of pillows behind me, my movements frantic even as I lean back on them, pulling the covers on my body, resting one hand on my torso, and gripping my phone in my other hand, my fingers sweaty.

Sebastian plucks up his own phone, pockets it, then lies horizontal on my bed, his legs hanging off, a forearm over his brow, his fingers drumming a rhythm only he can hear against my comforter. He's in pajama pants and a baggy T-shirt.

"What the *fuck.*" It's not a question. I didn't even know the girl, but... is Eli upset? Does he know yet?

I click on my screen, hoping Eli is awake at the same time I want him to be sleeping.

Me: I miss you. I almost don't send the message, my thumb hovering over the button as I pull my bottom lip between my teeth, despite the somber news.

Then I smile hard enough to make my face ache and send it with a little thrill skipping in my heart.

"Dom's dealer is my friend," Sebastian says with groggy words.

I frown, lowering my phone to my sternum, the screen up so I can see if Eli texts me back. Then I laugh a little, to hide my nerves. Seb and I haven't spoken about the parking lot bullshit. It's still surprising, thinking of Dominic getting coke from a guy who knows my brother. He probably lives in a trailer too. I assumed Dom's dealer would be in a penthouse somewhere, wearing silk robes and smoking cigars. Maybe flying in private jets from Colombia to deliver lines to Dom personally.

I don't know much about drug dealers, I suppose.

"He's a dick." Sebastian clears his throat. "Dominic, I mean. You should stay the fuck away from him."

I roll my eyes, looking up at the ceiling. "What does that have to do with any of this?"

There's an edge to my brother's words when he speaks. "Why's he following you out from the school in the middle of the night anyway?"

My face heats when I think about grinding up on Dom. *Answers.* I let him bother me because I want *answers*. "He's Eli's friend." I don't feel comfortable talking about Eli with Sebastian, but he asked.

"Yeah? And why do you think that is?" Sebastian asks the question like he knows the answer.

I drop my gaze to meet his, his blue eyes on mine. "Spit it out," I snap.

Sebastian grins, but it's lacking warmth. "I've heard your boy's name mentioned a few times."

I bristle, rolling my eyes. "Here we go again," I mutter under my breath.

"Yeah, keep talkin' shit, E, you know, some people think he killed the chick."

Why would Eli kill Dominic's sister? That doesn't make any sense.

I wonder again how Dom is taking the news, but my thoughts, as always, circle back around to Eli. "What did you mean? About why they're friends? They've been friends for a while."

Sebastian shrugs, his eyes drifting closed. "If I killed someone, I'd want to stay as close as possible to the murder investigation, know if anyone was gonna question me about shit. Besides…" He pauses. "King said the three of them were together a lot. The chick, Dominic, Eli."

I want to immediately dismiss all of this. Sebastian barely got a high school diploma, has no jobs and no prospects. But if he knows anything about anything, it's crime. Maybe not homicide, exactly, but even so…

"I knew they were friends." It's all I can say.

"Yeah, I mean…" Sebastian trails off, eyes still closed. "I told you before. King said Dom was always weird about Winslet. They couldn't seem to stand each other, he said, but he brought her along sometimes for pickups. Eli too."

"What're you saying?" I ask anyway.

"Maybe they did it together."

I roll my eyes, but it feels like it's for show. Unease twists in my stomach. "Was this posted today?" I change the subject, veering off track a little.

"This morning," Sebastian confirms. "King told me about before I left, and I read it on my way in."

His way in. Jesus. "You were out until… now?"

Sebastian laughs, and it turns into a cough. He puts his fist over his mouth to muffle it, then says, "Yeah. Just like you, I was wide awake."

I don't know what to say to that, so I stay quiet, my eyes

drifting over the flooring of my room, but it's Winslet's face peering back up at me in my mind. Then I see Eli's, in my head.

Why was he absent so much of last year?

He has to have a limit to his evil. *But does evil have a limit? Am I just making excuses because… because I'm falling in love with him?*

But no. The police would have him in custody if there was any connection. He didn't do it.

I close my eyes for a second, and I feel his hand over my face. I feel myself spinning in his car, my mind growing black.

But I liked all of it.

Chills run down my spine, and I pull the covers up higher, to my chin. In the tunnel of darkness under my blankets though, I see a glow, and it doesn't seem to matter what I did or didn't think about Eli. My body warms anyway, knowing it's probably a text from him on my screen.

I snatch my phone up as Sebastian starts talking again.

"Just be careful, E." His words are soft, and he sounds contemplative. I wonder if this is the moment, when I should talk to him about the ways he's throwing his life in the trash.

My throat feels tight, and I take a deep breath, but I don't know what the hell to say, and I don't think Mom has talked to him, about everything I told her last Friday.

All I manage to get out is, "I will," as I stare at my phone.

Eli: Good morning, baby. Can I pick you up?

"I'm serious. I don't trust them."

I grit my teeth, but Seb isn't being an asshole. He's being protective. "Okay, okay, I get it." I clear my throat. "I'll be *careful.*" I want to remind him *I'm* the one who got suspended from my last school, but I don't waste my breath.

"You have a future," Sebastian continues, and there's an edge to his words that causes me to lift my gaze to his, meeting his bleary eyes in the watery light streaming in through my blinds. He glances at the phone in my hand. "Don't throw it away."

I roll my eyes, annoyed. "Neither Eli nor Dominic are

going to…" *Make me like* you. "Throw me off my path, all right?"

Sebastian's eyes search mine. "King told me some other weird shit about Eli."

I still, holding my breath. And I remember, the name. King lives in Eli's subdivision. It's where he got alcohol from. Not a trailer park dealer after all.

"He's been in trouble a lot, all right? He sounds a little… fucked up."

"Fucked up *how?*" My pulse races in my ears as I try to keep my voice calm.

Sebastian shakes his head. "Just watch yourself. I wouldn't be surprised if your boy knows exactly what happened to that girl."

I narrow my eyes, my blood pressure rising. "If you're trying to tell me you think Eli had something to do with this because you've got a drugged-up conspiracy theory floating around in your empty head, then—"

"Cool it with the insults, asshole."

I do, only because Eli has text me again, and if Sebastian had heard anything substantial from King, he'd have told me. They're just getting high talking shit about people because they've got nothing else to do. That's how rumors start. Jealousy, or fucking boredom.

Eli: Do you like it when I beg you?

I bite my tongue, typing out a reply, momentarily forgetting my brother completely, just like that. Eli has that effect on me. Sometimes, even as I hold onto my future of college and moving and writing and teaching like I told Seb I will, Eli has the ability to make it all fade into background noise. Like nothing else might matter in life but him. It's dangerous, which also makes it thrilling.

I read his question again and think of his whispers in my ear from last night.

"I'm almost there, baby."

His hand over my mouth, the way I tried to breathe only to be stopped by his flesh.

Me: I really like it when you beg me while I can't breathe.

I squeeze my thighs together, wishing Sebastian would get the hell out of my room, but he's talking, still going on about Winslet.

"I just don't want you to end up the story one day."

"It wasn't *him, okay?*" I don't bother hiding my anger this time.

Sebastian lifts his hand in the air, toward the ceiling, before he drops it back over his face, softly smacking himself and shaking his head. "Jesus." He blows out a breath of defeat. "Eli was the last person to see her alive, E."

I marvel at the fact *he* knows this and wonder just how many people have discussed Eli's possible involvement with Winslet's death. The theories seem to have worked their way through various socioeconomic planes and occupations. Even the unemployed, as in Sebastian's case.

"If he was involved, the police would have him in custody."

Sebastian laughs, unkindly. "Shit doesn't work like it does on TV. Besides, I saw him when he came to pick you up. He's just… He's got weird fucking eyes. Like no one is in there."

Eli's text comes through as my blood boils over Sebastian's words. **Him: Don't say things like that unless you mean it. I got a high from suffocating you.**

Warmth and cold both work in unison beneath my skin. I'm shivering and sweating because Eli has a habit of making me feverish.

"I'm telling you, E, I think he's like, a psychopath or something. King spent some time in prison. He said you could always tell." Sebastian coughs, and I hear the phlegm rattle around in his chest. "It's in the eyes. They're dead. His are dead."

I stiffen as my thumbs hover over my phone screen. He couldn't be more wrong. When I look into Eli's eyes, I see intensity. It startles me, sometimes, how *much* I see. Never how little.

But then I think of the balcony when I asked him about his mom, the first time I stayed the night. My scalp prickles.

"Get out of my room."

Sebastian cracks a soft laugh but doesn't move.

Me: I mean it. I want you to do it again. Fear is linked with lust in my head, and I'm not sure if it's supposed to be that way, but while I know logically things could go wrong with the stuff we play around with, it's exactly the risk that gets me off.

Sebastian sits up then, sighing as he cradles his head in his hands, his back hunched over. I take in the spiky points of his shoulder blades, the knobs of his spine visible underneath his T-shirt.

I think he's falling apart, and I think no one is going to do anything about it.

This conversation is so oddly normal, despite the subject matter and maybe because of Seb's needling, that I almost want to put my phone away and hold onto it.

Almost.

Eli: Risky words, baby girl. Like a permission slip for me to do whatever I want with you?

I smile at his question mark. He wants me to sign the slip.

"Fuck his eyes, then. Let's talk about the facts. If he saw her last, did he watch her go?" Sebastian picks his head up, stretching as he does, arms veering away from each other in the air while he twists one way, then the other. Finally, he drops his hands to his knees and stands, exhaustion in his posture, drooping like a wilted, strung out flower. "Being complicit is still evil, E." He doesn't wait for me to respond, and instead, he crosses my room, opens the door, and closes it softly behind him. A few seconds later, I hear his own door close and imagine him collapsing into his dirty sheets.

I look back at my phone, and I don't think Sebastian meant to really leave an impression with his last comment, but the words seem to ring in my head as I text Eli back before I know I need to get up and shower for the day.

Me: Permission granted. Do whatever you want to me.

WHEN I SPRING OUT THE FRONT DOOR AN HOUR LATER, calling goodbyes to Mom over my shoulder, closing and locking up behind me, I'm focused on Winslet again.

Eli opens the passenger door for me, but he grabs me by my collar before I can slip into his car and kisses me deep. I'm wondering if he knows. If he's seen the news, or if someone told him. Maybe his dad? Maybe he found out before I did.

He seems to be in an unusually good mood, though. As I watch his hand on the shifter, I hope it's from what we did in this car last night, which still smells faintly of sex beneath the usual scent of leather and coconut.

I talk a lot. About books and the weather—gray skies—and how I want a Maserati one day—he laughs and says he'll help me get one. He asks what time I went to bed. I lie and say early.

I don't say anything about Winslet. I'm not sure I could say why. It's not fear, is it?

He doesn't even bat an eye when we pull up to Trafalgar and see camera crews strewn about the lawn, a police presence, too.

He grabs my hand tight in his as we walk toward the red front door, and I don't know if anyone looks at us funny, with suspicion or not, as we head down the halls together, hand-in-hand.

But I'm not really focused, as he gives head nods to people in the hallway, verbal greetings to others.

Finally, I can't hold it in anymore, and I look at Eli before we walk into Latin. "Did you hear?" I ask him, my voice low. "About Winslet?"

His eyes study mine. *Dead eyes,* my brother said, but it's not true. Right now, they're not dead. But they're not other things either. Sad, surprised, shocked.

He just lifts a brow, tilting his head. "Yeah," he says, no emotion in his words. "I heard."

After we find our seats, Eli twisted in his to look at me, I'm still thinking about Sebastian's words, and I wish I could scrub them from my brain.

"Being complicit is still evil, E."

32

Eli

"INVITE DOM OVER TONIGHT," Dad says before he smacks his palm over his mouth, swallowing vitamins from his hand. He grabs his glass of orange juice, chasing it all down with a pinched expression on his face. "You guys can watch a movie or something."

I peel the skin from my orange, the scent of citrus bright in the kitchen, unlike the sun hidden by clouds beyond all the glass in this house. "He just found out last Friday his sister is dead." I don't look up at Dad as I speak. "Besides, if he wants to come over, he'll show up."

I see Dad's fingers tapping against the island, across from me.

I wonder what he'd think if he knew I almost fucked Eden right there, where his hand is.

My gaze catches on the pale strip of skin on his ring finger.

I go back to peeling my orange, juice dripping down my hands onto the plate beneath them.

"Why do you say that?" Dad asks, keeping his tone even.

"Are you having a party? Tomorrow is another teacher workday, isn't it?"

I think about the rumors rushing through the halls of Trafalgar. Eden asking me if I'm okay. If Winslet's death bothers me. I've felt her lingering looks when I told her I'm fine, no, it doesn't bother me. It's been a year. I think we all expected it. Even if we didn't… it still wouldn't bother me.

I haven't seen her outside of school since last Friday night, when the news broke about Winslet's remains. It's Wednesday now, and she's had work, while I've had wrestling. We've spoken on the phone a few nights. She seems to stay up later than I do. I wake up to a thousand texts from her. I fucking love it.

Every time I close my fucking eyes, she's got her thighs spread in my seat, her skirt hiked up around her waist. Her cunt over my gearshift.

Juice shoots out from one of my orange slices, spraying droplets across the white marble, stopping at the tip of Dad's trimmed nails.

My heart drums strong and fast in my chest and I try to swallow back the fantasy of Eden *fucking* my shifter.

I pop the orange into my mouth as I meet Dad's gaze. He's waiting patiently for me to answer his question. The marks on his throat have faded away, like the ones on my chest.

I smile at him, and watch his fingers tighten almost imperceptibly around his cup. "Yes and yes." I grab another slice of fruit. "If that's okay." It's not really a party, exactly. But Janelle wanted to come over, and I want Eden over, and I'm sure Luna will show up, and I kind of hope Eden punches her in the face. A few guys from the team might stop by, according to the group chat Janelle roped me into that I didn't say a word in. I hate group chats.

It seems everyone at Trafalgar is a little spooked about Winslet. Luna hates being alone, and they all feel the need to huddle together, I guess, so they don't die next.

I'm not spooked, but I can admit I don't particularly want

to be alone. Last night I dreamed about Winslet. In my dream, I shoved on my white Chucks—identical to the ones I'm wearing now, but I have three pairs—and followed her out the back door. She was running, and laughing, and telling me to keep a secret.

My phone lights up beside my plate, and I glance at the screen. The message preview is hidden, but it's a step up from the fact I usually keep all of my notifications from popping up at all.

I grab the phone after I lick the orange juice from my fingers.

Eden: I just thought you should know...

I smile, holding my breath.

Dad is saying something about keeping things in check tonight, no cops, but I'm barely listening, thinking Eden is going to tease me or something.

My heart almost leaps to my throat when I see a photo has come through.

I tighten my fingers around my phone, tilting the screen down so there's no chance Dad can see whatever it is.

But it's not at all what I was expecting.

A white towel, carelessly dropped onto a carpeted floor.

Dark crimson drops against the white, contrasting boldly. It takes about a second for me to register what it is, even though I've seen a lot of it in my life.

Blood.

My stomach tightens, and I feel at once turned on *and* concerned. It's not *a lot* of blood, but I think of Eden's brother, and her stupid fucking stepdad and—

Her: I started my period this morning.

I blink at her message.

Then I almost laugh out loud.

Fuck. My dick gets hard all over again as I marvel over the fact she just sent me a picture of period blood. Holy fuck.

Me: Thank you for informing me. That's a hot photo.

Her response comes through right after. **Her: Yeah… do you still want me to come over tonight?**

I frown at those words. The question. *What?*

Dad is saying my name, so I look up, brows pulled together. "I asked if Eden would be here."

I glance back at my screen, starting to dim. "Yes," I answer him. "Why?"

Dad swallows, his throat bobbing over the collar of his dress shirt. He averts his gaze a second, then says, "I really like her." His words are soft, but they feel like a blow.

There's a tightness in my chest I don't like. "Good."

We don't look away from each other for long seconds, his palms pressed to the counter, his shoulders curved. Then he releases a breath and straightens. "I'll be home tomorrow evening. Since you're off this weekend, we can do dinner Friday night?" He doesn't give me a chance to answer. "Invite Eden. We can go out somewhere." He adjusts his cuffs, and in my head, I hear his unspoken words.

I really like her.

So don't fuck her up.

I bite the inside of my cheek, and with those thoughts in my brain, I realize why Eden might think I wouldn't want her over.

I respond to her before I say anything to Dad.

Me: 1. I can still fuck you on your period. Blood doesn't bother me. Especially not yours. 2. Even if I couldn't, you have a working mouth. 3. That was just a joke. You're coming.

Then I flip my phone over as Dad carries his glass to the sink. "Sure," I tell him. "That sounds great."

He stiffens, his shoulders snapped tight with tension as he pauses on his way to open the dishwasher.

Twisting to look over his shoulder at me, he offers a rare, genuine smile. "Great." He puts the cup away, closes the dishwasher, then gazes out the window over the sink. "Have you thought any more about…" He trails off.

I clench my hand into a fist, willing him to shut the fuck up. But he doesn't. "About your mom's request?"

I think of shattered glass. Glancing at the floor, I imagine the picture frame broken across it, glittering in the sun from that day.

I hop off the stool, snatch my phone from the counter, and leave my plate and half the orange behind as I turn my back to Dad and head up the stairs, not bothering to answer his question.

He knows my answer.

***

"You sure I'm allowed over?" Luna pushes her sunglasses up over her head, wispy auburn hairs falling into her red, swollen eyes. She leans against her white Mercedes, arms crossed over her chest. "Since you and Eden are practically fucking in the hallways every time I see you, I thought I'd been banned." There's a bitterness to her words, and I know it's because she's upset about Winslet, for Dom's sake, and she's taking it out on everyone else.

I roll my eyes, tossing my gym bag into the trunk of my car, over top the bottles of liquor I managed to snag from the King kid in my subdivision on my way out this morning. I sent him a text while I got ready, took the money from my wallet and we did a quick transaction when I drove by his house. King stared at me a long time, then counted my money twice, which is unlike him, but I waited it out in my car, and he finally gave me a head nod in dismissal.

Eden would've mocked me, probably. Something about rich boy drug deals.

I scrub a hand over my hair, still damp from the shower after practice. I close my trunk and pull my phone from my pocket. Eden got a ride home with her mom and I want to make sure she's still good for me to pick her up now.

I ignore Luna.

Me: You ready?

Luna scoffs. I look up at her through my lashes, the sun still beating down overhead. The weather shows no signs of cooling off anytime soon. I'm grateful. Means I have more time in the pool.

"How long do you think it's going to last?"

Eden: Yeah. I'm driving over.

But I want to pick you up.

I glance up at Luna. She's now chewing on the end of her sunglasses, her eyes on my phone.

Me: Hurry.

I pocket my phone and grab my keys, clenching my fingers around them. I don't speak as I stare down Luna.

She narrows her eyes. There's a dot of mascara just below her brows, no doubt from the fact the sun is practically melting us both. Maybe from crying too.

I don't point it out.

"You and Eden," she adds impatiently, as if I didn't know what she was referring to.

I walk around to my door, resting my hand over the hot roof of my car, relishing in the feel of it, just looking at Luna.

She smiles. "Am I touching a nerve, Eli? Talking about your girl?"

I tap my fingers against the black paint of my car but don't answer her as her smile falters. Our practices got out at the same time. It's the only reason we're currently occupying the same space.

She lifts her brows. "What're you going to do when she fucks Dom too? I know you want her all to yourself, but I'm not so sure that's how she's made. She might be a little like Winslet, you know?" I hear a note of bitterness in her voice, and not for the first time, I wonder what, exactly, she knows about Winslet and Dominic.

But then the thought is obliterated, driven from my mind, when I imagine sharing Eden. I grind my teeth together. I'm startled by my own possessiveness. Glancing at my dark windows, I imagine her again, beneath me in the driver's seat. Her eyes locked on mine. Her mouth under my hand. Stealing her breath. The way she fainted, just for a few seconds. How innocent she looked when she came back to.

I arch my hips a little, undetectable by Luna because of the car between us, but my erection grinds against the side of my door.

Fuck.

"I actually like her." Luna shrugs, and I keep my eyes on her, but my mind isn't there. She's attractive and fucking her was fun, but it's not her I'm thinking of right now. "Janelle is in love with her. I think Dom is too." She rolls her eyes, crossing her arms as she tilts her head. "But I miss you, Eli. Dom needs you. We could all play with her—"

"Luna." My voice is rough, my cock still hard, thinking about Eden's breathless whimpers, the way she collapsed in my arms, how she trusted me. How I don't want to break her faith in me. I don't think any girl has ever felt safe with me before. Not like she does. Not even Luna, who I don't look away from when I say, *"Don't fuck with me about this."*

Luna blinks at me, frowning. But after a moment, she must get the hint, because she straightens from her car, putting her sunglasses back on as she rakes her fingers through her hair, and it all falls neatly back into place when she's done. She reaches for the handle of her door. "Have you checked in with Dom?" Her back is to me when she asks.

"No. I have not. Have you?" I don't bother hiding the boredom in my voice.

Luna whips her head around to glare at me. "You could pretend you have a heart, Eli."

I open up my door, the heat and scent of leather and sex nearly overwhelming as I do. "I could."

Her mouth presses into a thin line.

I smile at her, and keep my voice low as I ask, "Do you know how many times he checked on me when I was at Montford?" Even Luna sent letters.

At the mention of it, *Montford*, her gaze falls.

Yeah. Everyone wants to pretend they're sympathetic to people with mental illnesses until they start showing signs of being mentally fucking ill.

"Sometimes I think he's in love with you," Luna says quietly. "And he doesn't know how to explain it."

I don't have anything to say to that. It happens. People thinking they love me. They rarely truly do because they're only in love with what I reflect back to them. Who I try to be, for them, so they become someone *for me*. I gave Dominic a level of popularity he wouldn't have had otherwise. In turn, just like Luna, he was my... puppet. Things haven't really been the same though since I got back from Montford. He's grieving. It makes him a little boring. *"Most people are boring and stupid."* An Oscar Wilde quote, from *The Picture of Dorian Gray.* For a split second, I see Winslet reading that book in my head.

"You're scarier when you don't talk, you know," Luna breaks the silence after a moment, a note of apprehension in her words. "Make sure you're getting enough sleep."

I blink at her.

When she realizes I'm not going to respond, she shakes her head, ducking down into her car, long legs exposed from the way she's rolled up her skirt a few times. She grips the armrest of her door but doesn't yank it closed. "I'll send Dom a text and let him know he can come over. He's just hurting." She slams the door then, but a second later, her engine starts, and she rolls down the window. "Try to remember what that's like." With one last lingering look at me, she drives off.

I get in my car, start it up, rolling down the windows and turning on the A/C because my shirt is sticking to my back with sweat.

Creed starts playing from my phone, and I don't change it as I see Eden has texted me back.

Her: Drive safe.

I don't, but all the same, on my way to the house, the smile doesn't leave my fucking face.

33

Eden

MOM: **Text me if you need me. Be safe. Stay smart.**

I smile at Mom's text at the same time a knot of guilt tightens in my stomach. Eli wanted to pick me up, but I have to keep up pretenses I'm spending the night with Luna or Janelle. Especially now Mom has heard the news too, about Winslet. She casually mentioned her before I left, told me to be very careful.

Sebastian must have kept his mouth shut about how close Winslet's ghost is to my new friends.

"You want a drink?"

I jump, startled as I drag my eyes up from Mom's text. I didn't even hear anyone come in, which has been happening to me a lot lately. Spacing out, totally engrossed in my own head, and forgetting the world exists.

Forgetting the world, with the exception of Eli.

My eyes meet Janelle's dark ones. She doesn't seem to care I haven't yet answered her question despite the long pause between us. She pours rum in both of the red plastic cups on the counter, turning her back to me. Her dreads are pulled up on top of her head, and I tentatively reach a hand to my crown of braids, ensuring they're in place. Glancing out the back door, I see a few guys Eli introduced me to, wrestlers, jumping into the pool at the same time, different variations of a cannon ball—some tightly wound, others… not so much—and Luna beside another girl in two of the chairs pulled close to the edge of the deep end, drinks in hand.

Bass is thudding through the door, but I can't tell what the song is.

Eli is smoking a joint closer to the shallow end, his cousin, Jasper, sitting beside him under one of the tables with the umbrellas over it, flared open in the blazing afternoon sun.

"Here." Janelle has closed the space between us, offering me a drink. I glance at the counter behind her full of bottles of liquor, and see soda, juice, and carbonated water as potential mixers.

I take the cup, her fingers grazing mine when I look down, seeing pale yellow in my drink. I want to down the entire thing.

"Pineapple juice," she confirms.

I look up as I take a sip. It's really damn good. "Thanks," I tell her, drinking more, the ice in it she got from the fridge door making it the perfect temperature. I finish the entire thing too fast, but it's like I need something to do with my hands.

She doesn't seem to notice.

She doesn't drink from her own cup as she turns her gaze to the pool, one arm crossed over her body, her elbow propped in the opposite hand. I glance at her swimsuit. White, contrasting with her dark skin, and one piece, like my gray suit. But I've got shorts pulled over the bottom half of mine, and I'm annoyed I started my period this morning. The first few days are always heavy for me, to the point I'm wearing a pad and a tampon right now, which means I won't be getting in the water unless or until I take it off.

And with *Luna* here, I don't want any… accidents.

I take another sip of the dregs of my cup, crunching the ice. "You okay?" I ask Janelle. We've been texting a little, but not since last Friday. When we all found out about Winslet. I know Janelle wasn't as close with her, but I'm sure it's still a little harrowing. "About the news?" I sink down onto one of the stools of the island, feeling a little dizzy already, from lack of sleep this week and the drink.

Janelle swallows, but she doesn't look at me. I've pored through a few of the books she gave me, we talk a little in the hallways. I think we're becoming friends, and I know I should be there for her if she's upset or whatever. Besides, I really am curious how she feels about this. Everyone else pretends nothing even happened. Aside from the police presence that first day when the news broke, and the flyers being ripped down from the entrance of Trafalgar, nothing has changed.

"I'm okay," she finally answers me, her voice low. "I didn't know her that well. But... *he* seems okay too, huh?" She smiles as she says the words, but she doesn't look at me. She's staring at Eli, I realize, as he brings the joint to his lips, inhaling before exhaling smoke through his nose while he listens to something Jasper is telling him, leaned in toward his cousin and speaking with his hands.

"Yep." I stare down into my cup. "Seems like it." Looking at Eli without his shirt on, the hint of his tattoo visible beneath his white swim trunks, his abs glistening in the heat from the sun, it's enough to make me ache for him. But even though I know he said blood doesn't bother him, some part of me has no inclination to have period sex with him, not as heavily as I bleed.

I cross one leg over the other under the overhang of the kitchen island.

Janelle clears her throat, but she isn't shy with her next words. "Did anything happen with you two?"

I feel my face growing hot, and don't lift my eyes from my cup, mainly empty, ice cubes clustered together between thin rivulets of pineapple juice and rum.

I take another drink of melted ice, just for something to do with my hands, and a way to mask my silence.

"It's not really my business," she continues, but in a way that makes it seem as if she doesn't really care if it isn't her business or not because she's going to make it her business, "but… I've seen you two in the halls."

The room seems to spin a little, a pleasant buzzing in my ears. *I guess we kind of have been all over each other.* I haven't had much time to hang out with him because of his practice, and my work, and I've been reading and writing a lot. I've almost finished a rough draft of a story I'll probably never let anyone read. I've been working out every morning, too.

I tip my cup back and suck in an ice cube so I can crunch it between my teeth as I lower my cup down, my other hand balled into a fist on my thigh as I finally look at Janelle.

She's watching me with the softest smile on her face.

I relish in the burn of alcohol down my throat, into my belly as I swallow the remnants of the ice cube. "Something might've happened." My face grows hotter, and Janelle's smile widens before she laughs a little. Quickly, I ask, "How long have you two been friends?"

Janelle cocks her head, thinking. After a while, she just shrugs. "A long time," she says. "Since I was a kid." She shifts her focus back to me. "He was friends with my little sister too. Jean." There's a heavy sadness in her tone when she says her sister's name.

I think of Winslet, then Sebastian.

The look in Janelle's eyes is faraway. It's clear something bad happened to Jean, and before I have to wonder what it was, she keeps talking.

"Jean and Eli were a lot alike."

There's that word. *Were.*

Janelle breathes the smallest laugh. "My parents were so confused about Jean." She meets my gaze a second, remembering I'm still here. "We're adopted. They didn't really know what to do with her. Then one day, Eli and his dad came over, they were introduced, and Jean cracked a toy car on top of Eli's head. He was probably… eleven?" She guesses, still smiling. "Eli didn't cry or scream, my parents and Mr. Addison watching in the living room, their mouths were hanging open while I hid in the kitchen, waiting for him to react. He just calmly snatched the car from Jean's little hands and broke every single wheel off it, set it down on the hardwood floor, and crushed it beneath his shoe with one vicious little stomp."

I'm not sure if I should laugh or not, but I do, and Janelle, thankfully, joins in.

"After that," she says, "they were friendly with one another." She takes another drink and turns her gaze back to Eli. He's leaned back in the chair at the patio, one arm resting on the armrest, joint still dangling between his fingers, his other hand curled around a beer bottle while Jasper keeps talking.

There's the slightest smile on Eli's face, and I take in his sharp jawline, those pouty lips, his black hair flopped over his eyes, and the choker around his neck.

My stomach flips as I imagine him befriending a mean little girl.

Seems like a very Eli thing to do.

"How old is your brother?" Janelle asks, but she doesn't take her eyes off Eli.

I shift on the stool, glancing at the back of my phone and flexing my fingers around my cup, warping the plastic. "Twenty-one."

She nods once and takes another sip of her drink. "Has he met Eli?"

I roll my eyes, unseen by her. They have met, but I missed the introduction, and clearly Sebastian doesn't like Eli. "Yeah. Sebastian is kind of difficult to get along with though."

Janelle laughs at this. "Even with Eli? He's entirely too charming, don't you think?" Janelle shakes her head, tearing her eyes away from the boy who has his fist wrapped too tight around my entire soul.

"Yeah," I say. "He is." And I'm not sure why it is of all the people he could charm, he chose me to focus his magic on.

Janelle doesn't seem to share my confusion. She sighs, then

walks to the sink, dumping her ice out and pouring water in her cup from the fridge. She glances over her shoulder at me. "I'm headed out there, do you want to come?"

I appreciate the offer. But I don't feel like sweating out there with all those people just yet, nearly a dozen total. I'll probably make another drink after I take my medicine, then see if I have the liquid courage to socialize.

"I'm good for now, thanks," I tell Janelle and she nods, taking her cup to the back door and heading outside with a small smile over her shoulder, directed toward me.

I watch her after she closes the door behind her, and see Eli look up, brows pulled together in silent question. He glances past his friend, and I'm not sure if he can see me or not, but his gaze lingers, and Janelle just offers him a wave, like she's dismissing him, before she walks to the pool house and lets herself in, where I see a few people huddled around the same table I did coke with Dom at. Jasper is staring after her.

I smile at that, then slide down from the stool, a little dizzy as I do. My fingers feel jittery, inexplicable anxiety in my veins. I leave my cup and phone, and hurry down the foyer in bare feet, grabbing the railing for the stairs and heading up, the single drink already infecting my bloodstream. It hadn't tasted strong, but the burn is still in my stomach.

I head down the hallway toward Eli's room, where I left my bag, and push my way inside. It's nice and neat, as it probably always is. I unzip the side compartment on my bag, tossed onto his made bed. I grab my medication, twist off the cap, swallow back a pill dry, and put the lid back on the bottle, then zip up my bag.

I glance in the mirror beside Eli's desk, smiling at my reflection. There's sun on my cheeks. I tuck my bangs behind my ears, running my finger over my piercings as I do. Then I turn, checking out my ass, making sure the pad I'm wearing isn't too visible. My shorts are black, so I'm good. I think about changing the pad or taking it off entirely to get in the pool, but decide I'll wait until I have one more drink. I can't shake this feeling of nerves or *something* under my skin. I think, maybe, I need sleep. But now isn't the time.

I head down the stairs, and when I'm halfway to the foyer, I see a shadow appear outside of the frosted glass of the front double doors. The light on the porch is flicked on, the sun is setting, and I pause, waiting to see if the person is going to knock. I think Eli said something about ordering food before he followed Jasper outside so he could smoke.

I keep walking down the steps, and finally, after what seems like an unusually long time, there's a loud, thudding knock against the door. I hit the landing, noting no one in the kitchen, everyone still out by the pool. I decide to get the door and if Eli hasn't paid for the food, I'll just go grab him.

I flip the lock on the door and pull it open, the heat hitting me in an uncomfortable wave.

My discomfort only increases as I tilt my head back and find Dominic standing on the porch, twirling his keys around one finger, his placid blue eyes still and cold, locked on mine.

He's not wearing a shirt, black swim trunks on, and I can't exactly ignore his abs, his broad shoulders, or the fact there's dried blood under his nose, and his pupils are round, black orbs almost blotting out the blue of his irises.

The softest breeze rustles through the shrubs around the porch at his back, and I inhale the scent of his cologne. He cocks his head, and I see the start of his dark roots showing through the bleached blond of his hair.

My heart thuds fast in my chest, my medicine clearly not kicking in yet.

I swallow, hard, thinking of Winslet. The news. The fact Dom hasn't been at school.

I'm still gripping the ledge of the door, and as Dom's eyes slant to my bracelets, I follow his gaze and see the thin black bands have fallen down my forearm, and my scars are visible.

Nic.

All at once, the memory of Eli's words come rushing back to me from the night in his car.

"I want to carve over it. I have a box cutter. At home."

"Nice," Dominic says, and when I look back at him, sweat damp on the little hairs at the back of my neck, his sharp smile indicates he read the letters, and he's made an assumption about what they mean.

I ignore his bullshit and try to force politeness. "Are you okay—"

"Just let me in." His voice is hoarse, and the taunting edge is gone from his words. He sounds more… desperate, or exhausted.

I step back, and he walks through, closing the door at his back and flipping the lock. He squeezes his eyes shut a second. I think I smell alcohol. I can't stand still, shifting from foot to foot.

"Do you… want a drink? Do you want me to get Eli? Do you—"

"I'm good." His voice is soft. He doesn't open his eyes.

I feel too hot. A little dizzy. I'm still moving on my feet, weight in one foot, then the other. The silence is thick between us, and I'm wondering if I should grab Eli, when Dom starts to talk again, eyes still closed.

"My dad beat the shit out of my mom, when he found out Winslet was dead."

There's a ringing in my ears. I lick my lips, and I don't even realize I have until I see Dom's eyes snap open, tracking the movement.

I glance at his half-naked body, over the dips and curve of his muscles, the indentation of his triceps, his collarbones jutting up over his defined chest. I don't see marks on him, and I'm relieved.

"I'm sorry," I say. "Come on. Why don't we get a drink—"

He runs his hand over his head, groaning. "I don't want a fucking drink." He drops his hand, leaning against the door, like it's the only thing holding him up. He tips his head up, staring at the ceiling. "Did you know my sister wanted to fuck Eli once upon a time?"

I feel a little nauseous when he says those words, knowing she *did* fuck him, but I keep quiet.

"You know, it's funny…" He blows out a breath, eyes still on the ceiling, the whites of them infected with red. "After she disappeared, Eli got himself pulled out of school."

I don't know why he's telling me all of this. If he's drunk, or high, or both. Or just… delirious in his grief. But I'm not going to let this opportunity go to waste.

"How?" I ask, trying not to sound too eager, but I still can't stop moving. It's like my pulse is alive in my head, jolting through my entire body. I'm swaying a little as I cross my arms over my chest. "Where did he go?"

Dominic pockets his keys in his swim trunks. I hear them clanking. But his eyes stay focused on the ceiling even as he speaks quickly, his pace the same way I feel. "One day, a week after she goes missing, dogs and cops and helicopters still looking for her, Eli, unconcerned as always, he walks down the aisle of his Latin class, a pencil in hand." He presses his lips together, pausing. I glance at the crust of blood under his nose.

My stomach is hard, full of tension, but I just wait for him to finish speaking.

"There was a sharpener fastened to the wall. Kind of old-fashioned bullshit since most people use pens or their tablets."

I step closer to him. My fingers curl over my biceps. I want to touch him, to keep him talking. I want to know.

Tell me, tell me, tell me.

"And Eli, out of nowhere, smashes the head of some poor, unsuspecting kid against the desk, and breaks his goddamn nose." Dom sniffs, his eyes dropping to lock on mine, and my heart thuds violently in my chest. "Then he takes his pencil, right, and jams it into the back of the guy's neck." He laughs then, suddenly, a twisted little sound, and I don't think I'm breathing. "Turns out, he really did need to sharpen the damn thing. It was dull, so the kid probably has a scar, but he doesn't have a hole in his neck."

I picture the cruelty in my head. It isn't hard to imagine.

And for some reason… it isn't hard for me to accept it as part of who Eli is.

"Why are you telling me this?" I ask, even though I know. We're so close, I see his chest rise and fall. I glance at the base of his throat, and I think it's his pulse there, moving violently beneath his skin, not so different than mine.

"Of course, Eli, being Eli, isn't a criminal, you know." Dom's smile widens, and he looks unhinged. "He's a poor little rich boy, and he doesn't get charged with anything. No, Eli gets flown first class to Idaho."

Idaho?

"He gets admitted to a psychiatric hospital, and he stays there while people volunteer to look for my sister's fucking *corpse.*" He's angry with the last word, and I'm almost relieved. Anger is a more appropriate emotion than the creepy smile he had on his face a moment ago.

"You think he's hiding something," I say, because it would explain all of this anger. "You've been thinking about this all week, and you think… you think he murdered her. Do they have a cause of death? Do they know… if there were injuries?" I can't seem to stop talking, even though I know I'm crossing the lines of societal expectations on grief here. I lift my shoulders in a shrug, eyes darting from the ground to Dom's face, to the door at his back. "What happened to her, why do you think—"

"Once upon a time, Eli told me he'd squished three white mice between his fingers when he was a kid, just to watch them bleed."

I think about his text this morning. About blood not bothering him, but I'm still jumping from one thought to the next.

"So yeah," he says, "I think he's fucking hiding something."

"But you were all there, weren't you?" My mind darts to Eli telling me about the fact he was the last person, presumably, to see her before she disappeared. Maybe the last to see her alive. "If he'd done something, wouldn't you—"

He closes the small space between us, his hand going to my

bicep, fingers splayed over my skin. His touch is hot, like a brand, and bordering on painful, the way he squeezes.

My instinct is to jerk away, but I override it. I want to know.

"You ask him about those footprints?" His words are a whisper. I vaguely remember this, from the last time Dom and I were here together. *Footprints.* "It was *chaos* that morning," he keeps going, leaning down into my face. The scent of alcohol is stronger, the closer he is. "He said those prints were from when he was helping look for her. The problem with that was his shoes. When he was helping search, he was in sliders, what he usually wore to the lake. But the footprints, they were his Converse. You know, the white ones he always wears? There was mud on them too."

I don't know what to say. I never did ask. I forgot, after our fight in that kitchen. It just... never came up again. Or maybe I don't want to know. Maybe a part of me wants to keep Eli innocent inside my head. But if there was proof of anything, the investigators would know. If there was evidence, they'd—

"Do me a favor," Eli's cold voice startles us both. "And back the fuck up off my girl. I really don't want to ever have to tell you that again."

I yank away from Dom, and he drops his hands from me as I spin around.

Eli has a chef's knife dangling between his fingers carelessly, and I don't know if it's to use as a weapon, or... if he was going to cut up fruit, which is what I'd like to believe, but the look in his eyes is a little empty, and it unnerves me.

I take a step back, into Dom.

Eli smiles.

"Hi," I say.

His lips curve higher.

Dominic says nothing at my back. The dying light streaming in through the front doors glints off of the silver blade, and Eli's grip is so loose around the handle, I wouldn't be surprised if it slipped from his hand and clattered to the floor.

I kind of hope it does because I remember what he said to me. About killing Dom, if I ever let him touch me again. *Fuck, fuck, fuck.*

"I need another drink." I blurt out those words. It's probably true, considering the situation I find myself in between these two boys, but I just say it to corrode the tension.

I can feel Dom's heat at my back. Wisely, he keeps silent.

Eli's eyes come to mine, and while he's smiling, I can tell there's nothing good natured about it. "Do you?" he asks softly.

"Yep." I play with my bracelets, and the movement catches Eli's attention. My eyes flick between his, and the knife in his hand. I can almost feel the blade against my wrist again, like I did when I carved Nic's name.

"Come here," Eli says, lifting his gaze to mine. "I'll make you one." He glances at Dom. "You want anything?" There's something in his tone I don't like. I've never truly trusted him, but my doubt has faded to the background the past few weeks, at least when it comes to present moments. Now, mistrust and unease come roaring back in full force.

Dominic sniffs. Then he must nod, because Eli points the blade absentmindedly toward the kitchen.

I make myself move, one bare foot in front of the other, and after a couple of steps, I hear the shift of the floor as Dominic follows.

Eli still has the knife, but there's no tension in his shoulders, turned brown from the sun. His jaw isn't clenched, and the handle is still loose between his fingers.

I keep coming closer.

Behave yourself, Eli.

His eyes don't leave mine. But this time, I can't imagine what he's thinking. As I step by him, I have the urge to grab his choker and yank him into the kitchen after me. But I think he needs to deal with Dom.

Preferably without the knife. I stop short, lifting my head to hold his gaze. Reaching for his wrist, I circle the bones there gently. "Were you making something?"

He bites his bottom lip. Lust seems to heat his eyes as they drag along the length of my body, then slowly back up.

I relax a little, seeing a true emotion in his face.

"Yes," he says. Without elaborating, he carefully twists his wrist out of my grip. "I'll be right there."

I drop my hand by my side, wanting to reach for him again, but knowing I shouldn't.

I look to Dom, only to find him staring at his friend. I consider a moment, then decide there's not much I can do.

They'll work this out.

Still, I think about Dom's story of what Eli told him, about the mice. I think of the footprints. I glance at the blade again. In my head, Eli's threats ring.

Dom arches a brow my way, and I take it to mean he can handle himself. I smile at Eli, then head into the kitchen, holding my breath as I come around the island, so I can see them. There're several feet between us. If something happened, Dominic could be dead before I'd get there, but...

Relax. Stop being ridiculous.

I take a deep breath, willing my heart medicine to kick in as I reach blindly for a cup full of something on the counter. I don't know whose or what it is, but I tip it back and swallow down what I think is straight vodka. I wince as Dom approaches Eli.

Eli doesn't move. I can see only a little of his face, but the smile is still there.

Dominic swallows. He doesn't look down at the knife. "Luna said I could come."

I take another gulp of vodka. Even when I'm done, I keep the cup to my lips. It's like a drinking game. Every time they speak, I'll drink. The way it's going, it'll take a while for me to get completely wasted.

Because Eli maintains that eerie, empty smile, saying nothing.

Behind the door at my back, I hear a splash. A few claps

and cheers. Music turned up louder. Everyone outside is blissfully unaware something ominous is unfolding here.

"Thanks for calling." Dominic doesn't look so nervous now, and his tone takes on a hard edge. "Or, you know, texting." He snorts, shaking his head as he runs a hand under his nose. I see a fleck of blood against his pale skin as he drops his arm and curls his fingers into a loose fist. "I really appreciate you being there for me." He clenches his jaw. "I'm sure even *you* heard the news. Always got an eye for the creepy shit, huh, man?" His voice breaks. "But they didn't publish everything. You still keeping my secrets, or are you giving all those away?" He steps closer to Eli, getting in his face.

I've quickly discarded my drinking game in favor of keeping an eye on the knife in Eli's hand.

"There's hardly anything left of her. They're not going to find a fucking cause of death." Dominic sniffs again, his voice gravelly but rising in pitch. "It's like… bone broth, being left out there so long."

Pins and needles crawl beneath my skin.

He steps even closer, and plants a hand beside Eli's head.

Eli doesn't move.

I do, taking a small step to the right, so the path toward them is clear, the island no longer in my way.

Dominic brings a fist to his eye, bowing his head as his shoulders hunch, but he's still got one hand by Eli's head. "She was barely a person when they found her." He slams his fist into the wall, groaning as he does. He immediately drops both hands, seemingly oblivious to the pain, or numb, maybe, and stares at Eli, Dom's chest heaving, snot running from his nose. "Did you know something?" He rubs his face with both hands, up and down, fast, like he might scrub free the viewing of Winslet's remains. "Can you just tell me? She was right behind me, all this time. *She was fucking right there.* I don't wanna play this game anymore. Did you know something, man? I just need to know if you… if you saw anything or… or remember it. Even if you didn't then, maybe something clicked," he snaps his fingers beside his own head, "in that *fucked up* brain of yours—"

"Hey."

Slowly, Dom turns to stare at me. I lower my cup down, setting it on the island. I take one step, and notice Eli is fixated on Dom's neck. Or maybe he's not even here. He could be a million miles away in that head of his. He certainly doesn't react to anything Dom has said.

"I know you're upset, but you don't need to insult—"

"You need to back off, Eden." Dom holds a finger up and points it my way. "This isn't any of your fucking business."

I take another step. "I understand. But I really think you should head home. Be there for your family."

Dominic's eyes narrow. "You have no idea what's going on here, do you?" He's still got that finger pointed at me.

Eli continues to be zoned out. Or in. I can't tell.

"Dom." My tone is clear, my words even. I keep my hands by my side, and some distance between us. "Nothing good is going to come from you being here." I glance at Eli. He's motionless. "Go home, comfort your mom. If Eli knew something, he'd have told the police."

Dom doesn't drop his finger. He takes a small step toward me. I thought Eli wasn't here anymore, maybe reliving the last night he had with Winslet over again, or perhaps simply drowning out Dom's words with his own thoughts. But when Dom moves, Eli's eyes move with him. His feet, however, pushed into his white Chucks, stay firmly planted in the same spot.

"Is that what you think?" Dom asks, a snarl pulling at his lips. "You really think if *he* knew something," he talks about Eli as if he isn't right here, and I feel my temper spike, "he'd fucking tell the *cops?*" He throws up his hands, then drops them by his side, the muscles in his biceps flexing with the movement as his abs contract. "He's really got you fucked up, huh?"

I smile at Dom. My body hums with energy but I fight it,

staying still. "You should go." I nod toward the door at his back, down the hallway. "I can see you out."

Dom presses his lips together. He takes another step. I glance at Eli. He's keeping up with Dom's every move while making none of his own.

"Who the *fuck* do you think you are?" Dominic's fists are clenched at his side, blood on his hand from where he wiped his nose. "I guess if you're anything like your brother, you think you're something, huh?" He laughs at that, a raspy sound. "Fucking pill head, did you know I stopped by the night he did H for the first time?"

I tense, my heart knocking hard against my chest. I feel unsteady on my feet.

Dom must see my confusion, and he chooses to pick at it. "Yeah, bet you didn't know that. My buddy thought he was gonna have to drag his sorry fucking ass to a dumpster because he was fucking comatose. Skin got blue." Dom drags his fingers over his forearm as he shivers, like my brother is disgusting. "You aren't shit, Eden." He jerks his thumb to Eli, still behind him, still just watching. "You aren't shit, and he's gonna realize it sooner or later. Your brother is trash, you're fucking trash, you don't get to tell me to fucking leave, you get it?"

I'm imagining a needle in Sebastian's arm. Him stumbling home near dawn every weekend. How does he always find his way home? Why doesn't he just get fucked up in his room? Is he trying to respect our parents? Does he want to die in his bed if he goes?

Heroin?

I never brought it up with him, after Dom and Seb confronted one another outside of the library. Now, it's thrown in my face, and I can't run from it. The thought makes me feel queasy, but it's not that reaction I show Dom. It's anger.

Trash. One of my worst fears when I started Trafalgar. That I'd be found out, and here Dom is, having already discovered me.

I step forward but leave a healthy distance between us.

I'm not trash, and I'm not stupid.

"Get the hell out." I keep my voice low, but I don't whisper. I nod again toward the door. "Get the hell out of here, and don't come back until you're *invited* back by someone who actually *lives* here."

"Fuck you." Dominic closes the space between us.

Eli doesn't move.

My heart thunders in my chest.

"Fuck." He points his finger to me but doesn't touch me. "*You.*"

I slap him, a vicious thing, my adrenaline spiked, my temper even higher. My palm stings, and I know Dom's face does too, because his head is slanted to the side, his mouth open, like he didn't expect it. A red handprint easily blooms on his pale face, his skin tone a shade above pure white.

My chest is heaving, and I want to hit him again, but I settle with shoving him back. He stumbles a step, and it makes me feel good. "Get out." I whisper the words, but I don't back down. "Now."

Slowly, Dom twists his head once more toward me. His eyes are full of malice, his nostrils flaring, a vein ticking in his temple.

My palm still itches, and I dig my nails into it.

Do something else. I fucking dare you.

And I think he's going to. I think he's going to lunge at me, or hit me back, or keep running his mouth. But after a tense moment of silence between us, his shoulders sink down.

He takes a step back and sniffs once more, running the back of his hand over his nose, and swallowing hard. Then he nods.

"All right," he says, my handprint still on his cheek. "All right." He brings his own hand to his chest, over his heart, then he looks at the floor. "Okay." He sounds defeated, and before I have to say another word, he turns from me.

He walks by Eli, his steps cautious. "Sorry," he mutters. "I... Sorry." Then he keeps walking, shoving his hands into the pockets of his swim trunks. I see the muscles in his shoulders bunch up, and I start to breathe a little easier.

But right at the moment he's *almost* out of reach, *almost* free, Eli moves violently fast. He grabs Dom's wrist, shoves him against the wall, and holds the tip of the knife just above Dominic's heart.

Dom's palms press back against the wall, as if he knows there's no use in fighting Eli.

I see spots in my line of sight, my muscles frozen, the hand that struck Dom clenched into a tight fist at my side.

Eli's face is still strangely devoid of emotion, and it makes this threat—the heavy tip of the blade against Dom's ribcage, right where the organ of his heart is beneath—all the more unsettling.

"I'm sorry," Dominic is whispering. "Please." I'm not sure what he's pleading for, and I'm not sure what he's apologizing for, but everything he says fades into the background of Eli's fingers now wound tight around the handle of the blade, his other hand pressed flat to the wall, his triceps flexed, veins snaking up his hand. "You just don't know what it was like. It wasn't even her. *It wasn't even her.*" Dom's voice is ragged, pricking at my conscience.

Eli, though, doesn't really have much of one.

He doesn't appear to be at all affected by his friend's pleas. Still, he doesn't speak.

Dominic squeezes his eyes tight shut, his face still red from my hand, but now splotchy all over from his grief, the twist of anger probably wrapped up in it all.

I feel for him, but I think it's best for him to leave, now, before he doesn't get the chance to.

I try to think of how best to word this to Eli without risking that knife gutting Dominic's flesh, but before I can decide the appropriate tactic, an anguished wail leaving Dom's lips, Eli speaks.

"You're never going to speak to Eden that way, ever again."

All the blood seems to leave my head.

I sway a little, reaching out to the counter to grip the ledge, keeping myself upright. I don't know what I expected, but it wasn't any of that. I feel compelled to tell Eli I'm okay, I handled my own, he doesn't need to threaten Dominic for me, but I decide the best course of action is for me to be quiet.

Dom slowly blinks his eyes open, and I can tell he's confused too.

He darts a glance to me, which is apparently the wrong move, because swiftly, Eli brings the knife up to the underside of his chin, and Dominic starts to tremble as Eli directs Dom's gaze back toward him.

The blade looks wicked sharp, and considering this is a house of wealth, I'm sure the Addisons do not let their knives grow dull.

The chances of Dominic walking out of here without at least one cut are very, very small. The best he can hope for is to walk out at all.

The silver of the blade seems to disappear on the underside of his chin, but I can tell Eli hasn't yet broken Dom's flesh.

"Do you understand?"

Dominic is shaking all over. Even his fingers are unsteady against the wall. He glances at the handle of the knife, pressing his lips together like he might lift his chin up, and avoid getting sliced just above his neck.

Eli's lips curve into a smile all over again, and I push the pads of my fingers harder against the counter. Someone splashes into the pool at my back, beyond the doors, and while it might make sense to get other people involved, to help me diffuse this situation, there's no part of me that wants anyone else to see Eli this way.

"Eli..." Dom slowly shifts his gaze back up, to Eli's eyes. He must see emptiness there, because Dominic visibly blanches, a feat considering his complexion. "You just don't understand. You don't understand what she *looked* like—"

"I don't care." Eli's words ring true. He really doesn't. "I'm not going to repeat myself. Do you understand what I said?" *About Eden,* he doesn't add, but I hear it ringing in my head.

Dominic looks as if he might nod, his nose arching upward a fraction of an inch, but he seems to realize if he completes the motion, he'll impale himself on the knife.

He settles with, "Yes." A whispered, tangled word. "I understand." I see tears stream down the side of his face.

I want to tell Eli it's enough. *Let him go.*

But Eli doesn't move.

I hold my breath, waiting.

Dom seems to be doing the same.

Then Eli steps back, lowering his hand by his side, and Dominic almost crumples, his hands on his knees as his body deflates, a ragged exhale leaving his lips.

I don't celebrate just yet.

Eli still has the knife, after all, and the blankness of his expression causes the hairs to rise on the back of my neck. He hasn't turned away from Dominic.

And when Dom picks his head up, straightening and taking the smallest of steps to the side, toward the front door, I see Eli's fingers grip the handle of the knife tighter.

"I don't understand you," Dominic says, shaking his head, his body still shaky, his fingers twitching at his side. "You loved her too." He tries to sound brave, but his voice cracks, like he's unsure. "I really hope you didn't… I really hope you didn't see anything, okay? I just hope you didn't." With a parting glance toward me, Dominic turns fully toward the door.

I am not relaxed.

And a second later, I understand why.

Eli lifts his arm, flicks his wrist, and Dominic's jagged cry pierces the air, causing me to startle, even though I watched it happen. Dom backs up against the wall edging the spiral staircase, cradling his arm close to his body, his back sliding against the wall as he swears under his breath, a sound laced with pain.

Eli simply watches him, and I see blood against the blade, just a thin sheen of it, but as Dominic sinks down to sit on the marble floor, his head bowed, shoulders shaking as he cries, I know Eli cut him, and I know too, Dominic cannot leave this house yet, not in this condition. Not because he's severely injured, but because in his state, he's likely to call the police and press charges, if only to get his sister some sort of misguided justice.

Dominic breathes in deep, picking his head up as he glares at Eli, and my suspicions are confirmed when he speaks. "You're insane," he says, his brows furrowed, lips trembling. "You're fucking insane. You did it, didn't you? You knew?" He doesn't wait for an answer, but he releases his hand from his forearm, and I see a lot of blood, bright crimson against his pale skin. Dominic smacks his wound, crying out as he does, but he repeats the motion, violently hitting and hurting himself over and over and over, veins in his neck bulging, his skin turning a dangerous shade of red. "I fucking hate you," he says, but he's still staring at his arm. "I fucking hate you, I hate you, I hate you, I *hate. You.*"

I don't know if he's talking to Eli or himself anymore, but when he bashes his head against the wall, over and over and over, thrusting his neck back more sadistically with each hit, I release my hold on the counter and come closer.

Eli is just watching him, the knife still in his hand, dangling by his side.

The sounds of Dom's head plastered against the wall are loud, and I'm worried he'll draw attention from someone outside, and I don't know who would do what. It's only a matter of time before someone comes inside anyway.

But what propels me to move quicker is Dominic struggling to his feet, swiping his hand over his bleeding arm, the cut thin but long down the inside of his forearm, blood snaking around his skin and dripping from the tip of his elbow. He looks dizzy as he stands, staggering sideways, and I don't think it's from blood loss or anything, but from his headspace. He's having a breakdown of sorts.

He grins at Eli and steps again toward the door. "I don't

need you to keep my secrets anymore. You're going to spend the rest of your life in prison," he says, laughing as he shakes his head and takes another step back. "I can make it happen for you, you fucking psychotic—"

I push past Eli, who doesn't move, and I gently grab Dominic's wrist.

He cannot leave, not right now, because he cannot tell anyone about this.

Slicing someone with a knife is a crime, no matter how shallow the wound, and I think Dominic was waiting for something exactly like this to happen. It's not enough to cause Eli to spend the rest of his life in prison, but it's something. Violence, and with Eli's history, with the place in Idaho he allegedly went after supposedly slamming a kid's head against his desk, it would not look very good for Eli.

Dominic tries to snatch his wrist from my grip, but I hold tighter, unfortunately sliding toward him with his movement, my bare feet skidding along the floor.

"Let me see." I speak softly, glancing at Dominic's other arm, behind his back, like he thinks I might finish what Eli started and just slice the entire thing off.

"No," Dom says, shaking his head. "No." He's still trembling, and I feel it beneath my fingers around his wrist. "No, Eden. You need to get away from him. *You need to get the fuck away from him.*" His nose is snotty, and I watch bloody mucus trail down his Cupid's bow, to his top lip. "I don't understand him." His breakdown is nowhere near over. "I don't fucking *understand him.*" He's crying again, but with the tears and the confusion come a physical weakness, and I gingerly reach for his shoulder cap, twisting a little.

He knows what I want, and in this moment, he gives in, bringing his arm forward. I take his fingers, dropping his other wrist, and I turn over his hand. Like I thought, the wound is shallow, but it spans from the crease of his elbow to the inside of his wrist, blood smeared across his skin, down onto his palm.

"I think we should clean this," I say quietly. I glance over my shoulder, not at Eli, but at the back door to the pool. No one is approaching, but I don't want to give them time to. "Right?" I look back at Dom's bleary eyes, staring at his arm like he's never seen it before. "I'll take you upstairs and we can take care of this, and you, okay?" I speak quietly, and I think it's my medicine and the drinks I've had, because I'm calm, now that I didn't let Dominic leave after all, and I feel in charge.

I don't look at Eli and I don't speak to him, but his gaze on me is like a burn.

Dominic sniffs. "Okay," he mutters, defeated. The adrenaline that had been in his system when he confronted Eli, then me, is probably fading fast in the wake of him beating the shit out of his own head against the wall. I slowly lower his hand and link my fingers through his other, tugging him toward the staircase, just a few feet from us.

"Come on," I say, but he's already shuffling forward without my prompting.

It's only when we're on the stairs, moving upward, my free hand gliding along the railing to propel me up, that I look to Eli.

His eyes lock on mine, and for a second, I pause, even as Dominic continues on, his hand pulling mine.

Eli has one arm crossed over his bare chest, his opposite elbow in hand, the knife's blade tapping against his lips. He smiles beneath the blade.

You are so smart and so, so in trouble, nightmare girl.

It's that kind of look.

I return his smile, then I continue escorting Dom up the stairs.

34

Eden

I CREEP out of one of the guest rooms in the Addison house, sparing one last glance at Dominic. He's snoring softly, courtesy of the shots he knocked back while I cleaned his cut in the sink, then dried it with a towel, poured antiseptic over it, and used medical tape and a long, white bandage—of which there was plenty in the hall closet—to cover it. Really, probably all unnecessary things, but after I retrieved the vodka from downstairs and saw Eli was outside, the chef's knife back in place in the knife block, I only wanted to kill time.

To calm Eli, and Dominic.

There's a soft glow in the room from all the lights around the pool outside, no curtains in here, only wood shutters. Dominic is curled up on his side in the bed, and I'd watched him text his mom to let him know he was at a friend's. He didn't specify he was at Eli's, and I'm grateful for it.

I pull the door closed softly, exhaling the smallest sigh of relief, but it's short lived.

As soon as the door is closed, quiet echoing in the dim hallway, *I sense him right behind me.*

"That was awfully sweet of you." His words are a whisper, and my heart ricochets in my chest, only rising faster as Eli comes closer, the barest amount of space between us.

But he doesn't touch me.

I press my temple to the door, closing my eyes. "Was it?"

I feel his breath along my jawline as he leans in close to me. "The way you took care of him… You're good, baby girl."

Downstairs, I hear people laughing. Some of them, then, have come inside. I feel a flush of pleasure, knowing they're all down there, and we're… up here. Separated. I'm sure they're imagining what we might be doing. The pleasure turns to smugness, and something else, thinking of Luna getting off to the thought of me and Eli fucking.

I try to push the lust aside enough to speak. "After you sliced him up, it really seemed like the least I could do."

His mouth trails along the side of my throat, and my limbs feel heavy, craving his touch to make me weightless. I curl my fingers against the door, arching into him, wanting to feel him.

And I do. His erection presses against my low back, but he still doesn't touch me with his hands.

"Did it?" he asks, his words rough.

I squeeze my thighs together, knowing I need to change my pad, maybe take out my tampon, all unsexy things that can't be ignored much longer, but I try for now. "Yes," I answer him. "I think I'll spend a long time cleaning up your messes." A smile pulls on my lips with the words, but I think I mean them.

There's a moment of silence between us.

Then he asks, quietly, "Can I touch you?"

Warmth grows in my low belly at his *asking*. I keep my eyes closed as I whisper, "Yes."

Slowly, as if I'm something he's trying to be careful with, his cold fingers come to the front of my throat, slowly tilting my chin up. A shiver runs through me, a flinch, but I don't want him to let go.

"You've been avoiding me tonight," he says against my ear. "I don't like it."

"I'm here," I tell him, the anxiety flaring under my skin again.

His index finger taps against the column of my throat, and he wraps his arm around my waist, tugging me back into him. "What's wrong?" He shifts his hips against me, and I feel how much he wants me.

I don't want to talk about Winslet. All the things I learned tonight in Dom's breakdown. I don't want to face what Eli could be capable of. Instead, I say, "Remember… I'm on my period." My cheeks are warm, and the medicine wasn't enough. It leaves plenty of room for my heart to beat too fast in my chest.

Eli smiles against my skin, just under my ear. "Remember, I don't fucking care."

"I do." I don't want to care, not right now, but I still do.

He splays his fingers over my hip. My breath hitches, and he kisses the sensitive spot between my ear and my neck, an open-mouthed kiss. I shiver beneath him, my throat pulled taut because of the hold he has on me.

"What are you afraid of?"

"I'm not afraid." He kisses me again, and my next words are shakier than the last. "I just don't want to do it."

"You don't trust me?"

I roll my eyes, looking up at the dark ceiling. "It has nothing to do with trust. You wouldn't understand. You're a boy."

"A *boy*, huh?"

"Shut up."

His grip around my throat tightens in a warning.

I freeze, holding my breath.

"Those *fucking* words," he says. "Do you want me to slap you, like you slapped Dom?" He bites my ear lobe, hard, tugging at my piercings as he does, the little hairs all over my body standing on end. "It was hot. But it'd be hotter if I did it to you."

The physical manifestation of his desire for me, hot and

hard against my back, makes me feel weak, and his words unfurl some sort of sick need in me to please him. To say yes to his question.

I can't.

I've never been slapped before. I've watched it in porn, I've circled my fingers around my own throat trying to hurt myself when I get off alone, but I've never actually done what *we're* discussing.

My body trembles, and I don't know if it's from fear or want. I wonder if something was broken in my brain that day Sebastian's friend got into my room, or if I would have always craved dangerous things. I want them in spurts, I want to let go at different times. Like, maybe… now.

Eli bites my neck, bringing me back here, to the most dangerous thing of all. And it isn't him. It's how I feel about him. How, if he had decided to sink that knife into Dominic's heart, I would have done everything I could to cover for him.

Dangerous.

"Answer me."

My throat feels tight, and not from his hand wrapped around it. "What if I said no?"

He bites me again, a pinprick of pain among a promise of pleasure. "You'd want me to hit the shit out of you anyway, wouldn't you? You wouldn't want me to respect you, would you?"

You'd want me to force you to do anything I want.

"Eli, seriously." I try to think logically, which is very hard to do when he's behind me, asking if I want him to hurt me, to fuck me, to punish me. "I don't… It'll be a mess, okay?"

"You think I care about a mess?"

I take a deep breath. From downstairs, we hear someone laughing again, high-pitched, followed by a playful scream. "Are they staying here all night?"

"Whatever you want, I'll do it for you. If you want them to leave, I'll make them leave."

My body seems to turn to putty with those words. I lean

back into him, and he releases my throat, pulls his hand from my hips, and wraps both arms around me instead. He kisses the top of my crown of braids. "Really?" I ask, closing my eyes.

"You seem to think I wouldn't do anything for you. Anything *to* you. Whatever you want from me… *I'm yours.*"

This is getting very hard to view as something temporary, when we speak like this, which is all the time. "Did you really go to Idaho last year?" It comes out before I can stop it, like a buffer between us, or a reminder to me.

He doesn't let me go, but instead, he squeezes me tighter, then he starts to walk us forward, taking a step that prompts mine, my eyes opening. We walk this way, together, to his room, and he kicks the door closed behind him, removing one arm from around me to lock it.

Guess we're going to leave everyone downstairs after all.

He leans against the door, me still nestled in his arms. "You really want to talk about that right now?"

No. Yes. I don't know. "I'm just tired of everyone knowing these things about you I don't know."

"They don't fucking know me. *You do.* No one knows me like you." I wouldn't believe him, because I don't trust him, but his tone isn't sweet or charming or even sensual. He just sounds exhausted. I think about him being unresponsive downstairs, when Dominic was advancing on me. I think about the emptiness in his eyes when I asked about his mom. Then Sebastian's words, about Eli being a psychopath.

What were you thinking in those moments, baby boy?

I don't ask. Maybe I don't want to know.

We stand there a moment, me leaning into him, him propped against the door, arms banded around my own, holding me up. The sounds of everyone downstairs are minimal, and I wonder if he's worried about them breaking things, or doing anything stupid, but I guess, since it's Eli, he's probably not worried about much.

"Why did you cut him?" I decide to veer away from Idaho

for a moment, and work on simpler truths. Things I witnessed myself.

"I didn't like the way he spoke to you."

A thrill zips through my veins, and I smile in the darkness of his room, only those blue fairy lights strung around his ceiling giving any glow to see by. "Heroic."

He holds me tight enough to momentarily steal my breath. "That might be pushing it."

My smile widens, but when I press back into him, I feel blood between my thighs, like a small clot has seeped through the tampon, hopefully against my pad. *Fuck.*

"I have to use the bathroom," I say, mortification replacing any good feelings. I try to pull away from him, but he holds fast. "Eli. Seriously." I don't want to bleed all over his floor. I don't care if blood doesn't bother him. Blood from my vagina, on my boyfriend's hardwoods, would bother *me.*

"Stop being skittish about natural things."

"Look, I understand you are a boy ascended above the mortal planes of most teenage boys, but I still would rather handle this privately, okay?"

He laughs a little, which feels like a win, then he releases me, and I get away from him as fast as I can, making a beeline to my backpack on his bed. I reach inside the main compartment and pull out a smaller bag stuffed full of all the things I need, then I cross the room to his marble, rich boy bathroom.

"Don't take too long or I'll pick the lock," he says at my back.

I don't reply as I shut and lock the door behind me.

Thankfully, there's no leak, although I curse myself for not bringing my entire bag in here. I could've changed out of this swimsuit and into my pajamas and a baggy shirt. Too late now without walking back out. After I've done what I need to, leaving the tampon out and going with just a pad, I wash my hands, zip up the bag of my supplies, and unlock and open the door.

Eli is sitting on his bed, his shoes pushed off into a neat

row by his nightstand, and he's got something I don't recognize in his hand, not at first. Not until I get closer and put my little bag into the backpack, zipping it up and moving it to the end of his bed and taking a seat beside him, my feet dangling off the edge as I look at what he's studying, a frown pulling on his lips.

An orange bottle.

He spins it around, my name on the label. *Eden Arella Rain.*

My heart skips a beat and I grab for it, trying to snatch my medicine from his hands, but his grip is strong, and he doesn't let go. I don't either.

"Give that back."

He looks up through his lashes at me, his eyes dark in the glow of blue lights. "What is this?"

"Give it back." I yank again, the pills rattling around but he doesn't release his hold on the bottle.

"Sure," he says calmly. "After you tell me what it is."

"Jesus, Eli, just give me the fucking bottle." I drop my hand all the same, rolling my eyes as I cross one leg over the other, wrapping my arms around myself. I don't like explaining my heart problem, because it's not really a big deal, but as soon as you say, "heart defect," people freak out. Still, considering Eli has spent time in a psychiatric facility, according to Dominic anyway, this should be nothing.

I just don't really want to talk about it. It's frustrating, him holding so many of my secrets while I have none of his.

"I'm going to look it up," Eli says, pulling his phone from his pocket. "So, you might as well say it yourself."

"Since you're so great at talking about your problems," I mutter.

He smiles, shrugging as he clicks on his phone screen.

I snatch it from his hand and toss it behind us on the bed.

He looks amused, but he doesn't release my pills.

"It's heart medication," I say, staring at the floor, my feet propped on the bottom railing of the bed, arms still crossed tight over my chest. "I have a valve problem. It's not fatal, it won't kill me. It just causes my heart to race sometimes, and I take those pills to get my pulse under control."

He looks from me, to the pills, and back again. I'm not sure what he's thinking. This entire night, I haven't quite been sure what he's thinking.

"What happens," he says, giving the bottle the slightest shake, "if you take too many of these?"

I tighten my arms around my chest and feel this quick heart of mine do what it does best and beat so loud I would be surprised if he couldn't hear it.

"I don't know," I answer him, holding his gaze, irritated. "I've never taken more than two at a time, usually just one."

His eyes gleam, brows raised, like he's just discovered a well-kept secret. "Do they help you relax?"

I run my tongue over my teeth, trying to get ahead of his train of thought. I drop my gaze to the bottle of powder blue pills. "Physically," I answer him. "Mentally, no."

He smiles. "I have something to help with the mental anxiety." He taps his fingers over the label. "Arella," he says, reading my middle name. I know he must have known it, because he knew I had financial aid, he accessed my file from my old school.

Which means...

Fuck.

I sit up straighter, my face scorching hot, my pulse erratic and no longer simply quick. There could have been other things in that file. The real reason for our move. For my application to Trafalgar.

Does he know?

Did he see?

But I swallow down the questions at the tip of my tongue. If he knew, he'd have said something. He would have wanted to be connected in that way.

He must not have seen it. I decide not to bring it up. If I ask, and he doesn't know, he'll pry the answers out of me anyway.

"I love your name," he continues, still gazing at the bottle, apparently unaware of my mental distress.

I can't believe I didn't think of it before.

I try to let it go. It doesn't matter.

He places his palm flat on the lid of the medication, then twists, popping the top free. He jostles the pills around, examining them, then taps out two into his free hand.

His eyes raise to mine. I try to force thoughts of my student record from my mind, worried he'll be able to see into my brain and extract just what it is I'm thinking about.

I look at his outstretched palm, the two little blue pills in the center. Before I can tell him I already took one earlier, he seems to change his mind.

He shakes out three more.

My stomach tenses. I reach for the bottle, circling my fingers over his as I try to yank it back.

He doesn't let go, his eyes on mine, a smile playing around his mouth.

"Let go, Eli." I grab onto the prescription with both hands, shifting my hips so I can yank more forcefully.

He curls his fingers around the pills in his palm, then jerks the bottle suddenly. I pull back, and all at once, it slips from both of our hands, little blue tablets scattering all over the bed, his hardwood floors, one rolling to the crack just under his door as the orange bottle hits the floor with a soft clatter.

I curl my hands into fists, shooting up to my feet, staring at the last of the pills to cease moving, by his nightstand. My chest heaves.

He says nothing.

"You're going to pick all of these up," I tell him without looking his way. "You're going to pick every *fucking* one of these up." My words are fast and low, irritation twisting and turning in my brain, under my skin.

"You're the one who ripped it from my hand," he says mildly. "Besides, I'd like to see you crawl on your knees and pick up every one of them with your teeth."

I put my hands to my head, spinning to face him. "Pick them up right now." It's like a tornado in my mind. The medication I took earlier seems to have faded, the alcohol maybe ramping me up *more*. *"Right. Now."*

His eyes darken as he tilts his head. He observes me, like I'm his patient. "Have you been sleeping okay?"

There's a tingling in my limbs, a prickle along my scalp, like I've been found out, even though I don't know what, exactly, he's found out. I think of all the writing I've been doing. The books. Staying up late, needing little sleep at all. I feel fine. I mean, now, I'm pissed, but considering everything that's happened, I think it's normal, and—

"You haven't, have you?"

My mouth goes dry as he interrupts my racing thoughts, my fingers digging into my scalp.

"I just want you to *chill out*, Eden." He runs his tongue over his teeth. "You've been so… excited."

The word rings true. *Excited.* Something like a scream and a groan leaves my mouth and before I can think through anything, I'm closing the space between us. I'm shoving him backward, on the bed. He goes willingly, the pills still in his hand, his arm banded around my back. I spread my thighs as I straddle him, my fingers on his face, pushing roughly into his hair. My pulse is fast and I'm no longer thinking about my period or Dominic's bullshit or anything but this, this, *this*.

How dare you see me so well? How dare you find all the fucking secrets I don't even know I'm keeping from myself?

He grabs my face, squeezing my mouth open.

Our lips collide, and I taste marijuana and cotton candy on his tongue as his teeth nip my bottom lip.

I shift my hips and he groans into my mouth. I yank his hair, feeling a flush of warmth in my core.

We have to pull apart to breathe, but my eyes are still locked on his, his hand still gripping my jaw, one arm around my back.

"You want me to take those fucking pills for you?"

His lips are swollen, and he doesn't smile or laugh.

"You wanna fuck me up after you drug me?"

The green in his irises turns to something darker. "I don't want to damage what's mine."

A thrill of lust dances in my low belly with those words.

"But there are so many fucking things I want to do to you."

I pull his hair harder, watching as his eyes flutter closed. I lean down close, my mouth over his as I speak. "Like what?"

He doesn't look at me. "You don't trust me, but I promise I won't let anything bad happen to you. I can't… I don't want to do this without you."

This.

I don't want to ask what he means. Like if I do, and he doesn't say what I want, it'll break my heart.

He shifts his arm up, around the back of my neck, and pulls me close, turning his head so his mouth is against my ear. "Are you afraid?"

There's a tingling in my chest.

"No," I say honestly.

"You told me being terrified is what made it real for you. In the water."

It's suddenly hard to breathe, even though his hold is loose. *"Eli."* My face is pressed against the crook of his neck. I feel his body tremble with my breath ghosting over his skin.

"You said if you weren't afraid," he dips his head and nudges his nose to my throat, dropping his hand from my face and wrapping this arm around me, too, "I would've been doing it wrong." He enunciates the last three words very, very clearly.

"This is about period sex." I laugh a little because I mean to ease the tension as my eyes flutter closed.

I don't even think he smiles. "No. This is about the fact you have only once asked if anything Dominic told you was true, and only about one of his revelations. You didn't care I cut him. You didn't get angry for him, or at me. You led him upstairs and took care of him, so he wouldn't get me in trouble." He smiles now. I feel the crescent on my skin. "Am I close?"

I don't say anything. Truthfully, I meant to ask him about Dominic's accusations, and I tried, with Idaho. But I let it go too easily. It didn't seem the time to bring it up again, and timing is everything with Eli.

He runs his nose over my jawline, and I inhale his scent. Coconut and marijuana and citrus. Sweet and peppery and dangerous.

He arches his hips into me, and I push back against him. He groans the softest sound at my ear, like he couldn't keep it in if he tried. "Did you mean it? I could do anything?"

I close my eyes a second, chin resting on his shoulder. I meant it. *I mean it.* "Yes," I whisper, wondering what I'm getting myself into. But it's not the first time I said it. I gave him a permission slip.

He pulls back and I do, too, our noses touching as we stare at one another.

"No one has ever understood me," he says quietly. "And no one has ever really wanted to." He licks my mouth, right in the center, flicking his tongue over the scar above my top lip.

My hips arch more, and I'm not thinking about the blood in this moment. The mess we could make of his white sheets.

All I can think about is how much I want him. How much I crave these words.

"Until you," he finishes against my lips. "Open your mouth for me, Eden. This is just another level, right? I drug you, maybe you pass out. Maybe I fuck you. Maybe I take care of you. I mean, I'll never stop doing that. Like I said, *I protect you.* Just trust me." He turns his head, nose caressing mine. "Show me you won't run."

I think it over. What he wants to do. The mess of my medication on his floor. Another, bloodier mess.

I could give him a blowjob. I would love to try, actually. I lick my lips just thinking about him stretching them, secured tight around his cock, hitting at the back of my throat. I even have images of him pinching my nose closed while he fucks my mouth, saying mean things about not fainting and swallowing every last drop of him.

But I have a feeling if I suggested that, with the plan he has forming inside his beautiful, messed up brain right now, he would refuse.

He wants me to swallow all five pills. He wants to slow my heart and take advantage of the ensuing lethargy. And despite the left side of my brain screaming at me to get away from him, to talk myself out from under him, and run far, far out of his reach... I don't.

Because the right side wants all the danger. The right side sees the romance in the darkness. And the right side believes if he lets us get this twisted, then *he* won't run from *me*.

I reach behind me, one hand still gripped in his hair, but I grab his arm.

I bring it slowly between us, clutching his wrist as he unfurls his fingers. I see all five pills there, and they won't kill me, but my heart still thumps fast, like it knows it's about to be stifled. The dose is low, though. It shouldn't do too much to me. Likely, I'll fall asleep. I say just that to Eli.

"Would you even care? If I fucked you while you're unconscious?" The words are filthy, and I'm embarrassed, heat flooding my cheeks, but I still want it.

"No." I whisper my consent, staring at the pills.

"Because you know I will *always* look after you, even when you're too fucked up to know I am."

My throat grows tight. Being used like that, it turns me on, and I don't hate that it does. I can get this nasty, with Eli.

"And afterward, I'll sleep with you," he says, as if it's simple.

"Everyone downstairs..." It makes me feel uneasy, thinking of strangers down there while I'm knocked out on heart medication up here. Eli might take care of me, but I wouldn't trust anyone else to.

"If you think I'd let anyone touch you, under any circumstance..." He leans up and licks a line up my throat, then bites. *Hard.* It sends a flush of heat between my thighs.

My mind flicks to Dominic, in the room just down the hall. "Really?" I remember Dom's words about the threesome as Eli unclenches his teeth on my skin, the pinch of pain still throbbing. "You wouldn't want to watch anyone else fuck me—"

"Stop talking and open your mouth." There's no malevolence in his words, but there is the thread of something like it. Jealousy, I think.

I smile at him, dropping my gaze to the pills in his palm, my fingers still wrapped around his wrist. "Don't let anyone else in here."

"I promise."

"And don't..."

He is very still. "Give me a line, and I won't cross it."

I don't believe him, but I try anyway. "Don't leave me in here alone."

A slight frown graces his lips.

For a second, I wonder if he thought he'd just knock me out, then creep downstairs and fuck Luna. Was that his plan? I lift my eyes to his. He holds me closer, with his arm around my back.

"I never planned to," he says softly. "You thought I'd fuck around with someone else?"

"You did," I remind him, and this time, I'm the jealous one. Thinking of Luna's mouth around him.

"You said you wouldn't hold a grudge." He sounds almost offended.

But he's right. I did say it. It's just, now she's so close, and I might become incapacitated in the next few minutes. I don't care what he does with me. I just don't want him to do anything with anyone else. I take a deep breath. "I'm letting it go. Just stay with me, okay?" *I won't run, but you can't leave.*

I don't wait for an answer. I sit up on top of him, one hand resting against his chest. I feel his pulse pick up, and it emboldens me. Slowly, I bring his palm to my mouth and dip my head.

Then I lick up all five pills from his palm.

A low noise leaves his throat.

I close my eyes, and each tablet sticks to my tongue with my saliva. Guiding his wet hand, I glide it down my throat. I work up saliva, then I swallow beneath his fingers along my throat as I shift his hand down lower, over my chest.

My heart.

When I open my eyes, he's smiling up at me.

I smile back.

"Before we do anything," I tell him, clawing my fingers against his chest. "You're picking those fucking pills up."

35

Eli

HOW CAN I want to do so much damage to someone I crave every second of every day? I glance at the bottle of pills on my nightstand, every single one I picked up, save for the five she swallowed down all on her own. Now, she's far calmer. I know the pills are to blame.

"Do you want to take a bath with me?" I ask her, thinking of laying her down in the jacuzzi tub, her legs draped over the side, her hips flush with the base of the tub, thighs spread wide as the water from the faucet gushes down over her clit.

I think of water rising, up to her ears, then over them. Her mouth. Her nose. Her eyes wide and staring up at me in fear, excitement, lust.

Faith I won't let her drown.

If Dominic had touched her downstairs, I would have twisted the knife in my hand through his shoulder blades. I would have punctured his heart from the back.

As it was, even just hearing him talk down to her... if I hadn't zoned out, I would have seriously injured him. I still might.

I don't know how I can feel so possessive over her well-being around other people but put her in danger with my own hands.

Maybe because I know I'd never *truly* hurt her. As it is, I think *she* has the most power to hurt me. I'm just not sure she recognizes it yet.

Her big eyes meet mine, and in the glow of blue lights around my room, her irises take on the color, too. She is the most interesting person in the world to look at.

I grab her hand and snatch it up, bringing the back of it to my lips. My thumb caresses her bracelets, and I know *Nic's* name is beneath. I have never wanted to own another person until her. And it's not that I don't think she should have autonomy.

She should.

But I never want her to leave.

It conflicts with what I know to be true. *People always leave.*

But she can't, which contradicts my belief she should be in control of her choices.

She just… can't make that one. The one to run.

If I had to chase after her… I think I would rather her be dead than someone else's.

"We can't take a bath," she says, smiling. "Remember?"

I bite her hand playfully, turning my face into her palm, my head propped up in my own, elbow bent on the bed. "You're on your period. How could I forget? You've only told me half a dozen times."

She rolls her eyes, her head dropping to the pillow. "Means we can't have a bath."

"And we can't have sex, yeah, I got it." I massage her fingers with mine, gazing down at her as her eyes flutter closed. "But isn't a bath, like, I don't know… good for washing away the blood?" I've been around enough girls to understand menstrual cycles. I can appreciate their hesitancy, I guess, and maybe how they don't feel comfortable when their bodies are doing all the other things that accompany periods. But I've never seen it as a turnoff. I have never seen *much* as a turnoff, truth be told, and since I'm obsessed with Eden, I'm obsessed with *everything* about her.

She laughs, keeping her eyes closed. "It can be a mess."

"I don't care about a mess."

She looks at me then, snatching her hand back from my grip, leaving mine to rest against the sheets. "Do you think you'll ever respect a single boundary of mine?"

"What boundary haven't I respected? We haven't done anything you didn't want to." *What boundaries do you even have? What would you ever hold back from me?*

She glances at her hand. I know she's thinking about the fight downstairs we had those weeks ago. I hurt her, but I didn't realize it. We never talked about it.

"Hey," I say quietly.

Her eyes come to mine, but she doesn't say anything. There's only a hesitancy in her gaze, like she already doesn't trust what's about to come out of my mouth.

I reach for her, feeling her jump as my fingers glide over the inside of her wrist. "This," I tell her, tracing over a blue vein, "I didn't know." I hear her scream inside my head, when Dominic grabbed her. I run circles over her skin now, warm and soft, and she just stares at me. "I don't ever want to see you hurt. Not even by me." *Not* truly, *anyway.*

She bites her bottom lip, and my body tenses with want, but I don't say anything, letting her decide if she should trust me.

But she must decide, instead, to drop this conversation, because the next thing she says is, "I don't want to take a bath, and have you float in… you know." Her face doesn't flush, probably because of the pills, but I can see her discomfort in the way her canine teeth dig into her red lip, blanching it.

It makes my dick fucking *ache.*

"I'll give *you* a bath. There's a difference." I tug her hand toward me. "Come on. All you have to do is relax."

She frowns, staring at the sliver of sheets between us. I

wanted to give her space to make the decision. The pills won't make her high, per se, but she's going to get very sleepy, very soon. I can't have her fall asleep in the bathtub. Even if I'm right there, it doesn't take much to drown.

"Why do you want to do this right now?"

Because I'm horny. Because I want to push you. Because I want you to push yourself. I crave these things, with you. Adrenaline highs, and taking care of you, and needing you to rely on me.

I don't say any of it. It's too much.

Sometimes I forget how young we are. When we're around our peers, it's easy to feel older, and wiser, more mature. They don't care about things I care about. Maybe before Eden, I didn't care about much at all, but now she's all I'm fixated on. She is my entire focus.

And I want to play these games with her. They make everything... fun. *She's* fun.

"Do you like baths?" I ask her, sidestepping her question. I trace my fingers over the sheets, a meaningless pattern, but she tracks the movement, and I think she's obsessed with my hands.

I'm infatuated with every inch of her, so our mutual rapture is a little unbalanced, but whatever.

"Yes," she says slowly. "I don't take them often at home."

I stop drawing patterns, pressing my index and middle finger harder into the mattress. "Why is that?"

She shakes her head, and I know she's not focused on my fingers anymore. "Sebastian is always in there, and he's messy."

I clench my teeth together, but I don't speak. I heard what Dominic said about her brother. She's not the only one who didn't ask questions. Why do we dance around these things? For me, I don't want to talk about them because I don't want the pity. I don't want to be psychoanalyzed. It's boring for me, and sympathy makes my skin crawl.

But Eden isn't like me, in some ways.

Then again... I think of her with Dom. How she handled him so completely. It was like looking into a mirror, seeing the way she was unaffected when he started to hit his head, when I cut him, when she walked him up the stairs to save me from potential punishment.

But what are the things she doesn't speak of? What are the things she hides even from me? The medication, for one. The heart defect. The way, lately, she's been so giddy. *Excited.* I'm not sure she even recognizes the abrupt change in her moods.

"I just don't feel like the bathroom is my own," she finishes, looking up at me through her long, thick lashes, straight instead of curved, now I know it, I can't stop seeing it. She's beautiful.

She smiles at me, but I don't think she means to.

A mask, just like my own. I wonder what it would take to pry it off. Would it be like removing mine, bits of my own flesh stuck in places, the disguise tearing out my skin, blood along the coverup? I wonder if, right now, she's thinking of horrors from her brother, or maybe what the future holds for him, or things she's witnessed or experienced or seen, and yet her little smile is still firmly in place, isn't it?

Does the medicine hide her anxiety so well? How often does she take it with me?

She said it helps with physical symptoms of anxiety. But nothing else. Nothing of the mind. She could potentially break down, and no one would know because her body would keep it hidden inside.

It's like those pills are a metaphor for my entire fucking life.

How much do you hide from me, too, Eden? How much of your life has been a lie?

I glance at the bed again. My white sheets, the mattress which hasn't seen me sleep nearly as much as it should.

There used to be a crib in this room.

Mom said I slept a lot, then. I didn't cry much, she told me. Only when I was hungry. I wonder how many hours I cried for a bottle in here. Did Mom ever shut her door and head to her bathroom, flip on the fan, and get in her tub, the sound of the faucet filling the basin drowning out any of my infant screams?

Unlike Eden, I felt like everything in this house was my own.

I've grown to love solitude, but I think, once upon a time, I craved Mom more than anything. I wanted to share this place with someone, but no one seemed to want to share it with me.

"Good news." I push up, climbing atop Eden, my palms on either side of her head, her body beneath my own, a slight smile on her parted lips. She presses her palms to my bare chest, and I love the way her breath hitches when she touches my skin. "Everything that's mine here is yours." I lower my face to hers and kiss her nose. "Let me bathe you. No sex. You can change by yourself, get in alone, and if you decide you don't want to do this, you tell me, and I won't come in."

"You're a liar," she says, correctly, her fingers splaying wide on my chest as she looks down, her smile widening. "You will *definitely* come in."

I nudge my nose to hers. "Trust me, okay?"

She drags her gaze so, so slowly to mine, and it's maddening to see the reality in her eyes. She doesn't trust me. Not even a little.

She's skeptical, and cautious, and as much as she likes me, maybe even loves me, she doesn't trust me at all.

But she still says, like a good little liar, *"Okay."*

"You can come in." Her words are strong and clear, and I press my temple to the door, exhaling a sigh of relief. I would've gone in anyway, but now, at least, we can pretend she should always take me at my word.

The lights are dim when I enter, only the one above the glass shower on, but it's enough to see by, so I don't make her more uncomfortable by flicking on the others. I close the door behind me and lean against the counter, between both sinks, arms crossed over my chest.

She's sitting up, the water full of bubbles from my body wash, on the ledge of the tub, and she has her knees pulled to her chest, arms draped over them. The air is sticky, and when I glance over my shoulder, I see the mirror is fogged with steam. Her clothes are folded neatly on the floor by the tub, and I see the yellow edge of a pad tucked discreetly beneath her sleep shirt. But not completely hidden, like a reminder. *For me.*

The fan is on, nice background noise over the gush of the faucet in the tub.

"What lines are you going to cross now?"

I can only smile at her. There are no lines between us, I don't think. Not anymore.

"I'm going to fall asleep soon." Her words are thick with exhaustion, a little sluggish.

"I think we already discussed that wouldn't stop me?" Truthfully, I don't think I'd enjoy fucking with her if she wasn't awake to enjoy it, too. But there's only one way to find out, right?

She ducks her head, shyly. "Yeah," she whispers. "We did."

I walk to the tub, sitting on the edge of one corner, gazing at the water dripping over her kneecaps, down her shins, her calves soft and curved. Her legs hide her breasts from view, but not the slender column of her throat. The fullness of her cherry red lips.

The suds cover everything else though, and the tingly tang of minty body wash overrides her own natural scent. But she's doing this how she wants, the way she feels most secure, and I can appreciate that.

It's just... not how it's going to go.

"Give me your foot."

She gives me a *look;* her eyes narrowed and lips pressed together. "Eli."

I reach for one of her hands, wound around her shins. Pressing my fingertips against her inner forearm, working my way up to her wrist, then her hand, trying to relax her with my touch, I don't look away from her. "I do not give a *fuck* about your period, Eden. I just don't, okay? It doesn't bother me, and I've already seen you naked—"

"Mostly naked."

"—so I know that's what this is about. Give me your foot. Let me do this for you."

She studies me, unblinking, but she doesn't pull her hand away either. The slightest flinch when I reached for her, but otherwise, no resistance. I wonder what it is she's looking for, then she says, the running water by my ear almost drowning out the words, "Why does everything always feel so heavy between us?"

It takes me by surprise, her question. But it gets under my skin, too, because there's nothing about it that isn't true. "Because it's the only way we can feel," I answer her, my nails biting into her palm. "Deeply, or not at all."

Her eyes drop to my abs. "Maybe not always deeply," she says, a smirk on her lips.

I sit up straighter, glancing down at the tattoo on my hip, half-hidden from my swim trunks. I've always been in shape because of sports, and tan from staying outdoors and Mom's genes. I'm accustomed to people ogling me, and I use it to my advantage. But when Eden looks at me that way, well…

"Baby girl, give me your goddamn foot." I drop her arm, and this time, she doesn't hesitate or ask questions that make me think more than I want to right now. Things have been *deep* between us from the moment we first spoke in the library.

If they had been shallow, she would be a one-night stand. Maybe like Dominic or Luna. A pawn. She is none of those things.

But I still want to enjoy her all the same.

She shifts in the tub, and lifts one perfect, chunky foot for me to take hold of, my fingers around the base of her ankle.

I reach into the water, scalding hot—a temperature she chose—and press the slippery, silver button to the drain. A moment later, it starts gurgling and the levels of the bubbles sink down slowly.

Eden jerks in the tub, splashing water over the sides as she twists around. "What the hell—"

I pull her close to me, her bent knee crashing into the porcelain, her arms slapping into the water, palms seeking purchase to stop me from yanking her close.

But all I can focus on for a second is her tits.

It's the first time I've seen them without anything in my way. Her nipples are dusky pink, drawn up tight, the tiniest hairs standing up along her skin. Her breasts are small and firm, a light orange freckle grazes the underside of one, and I want to run my thumb along it, pinch her and bruise the paleness of her skin here, untouched by the sun.

"Eli, what are you doing?" She starts to shiver, propped up on her hands, the water winding its way down the drain.

I can't stop myself from touching more than her fucking ankle, perfect as it is.

I lean over from my seat on the edge of the tub and place my hand over her chest. I feel the curve of her breast beneath my palm, her nipple sharpened into a tight point.

Her pulse I can feel too, slow and steady like a soft knock against my hand.

Her body is still coiled tight with tension, even as her eyes are sleepy, but they hold mine.

"What do I need to do?" she whispers, staring up at me with what I choose to believe is adoration but could just as easily be terror. I think, maybe, they're the same thing.

I push against her sternum. She resists for only a moment, then, probably realizing if she goes down like I want, the dwindling supply of water will cover her for a little longer, she lies down on her back.

"You need to chill. Let me do everything." I crawl my fingers up over her throat as water pools around her halo of braids, then arcs down the drain, causing no harm to her. My hand grazes her throat, and she tucks her arms close to her body, like she might cover herself, but she settles with her clenched fists grazing her shoulders, her elbows bent.

I don't examine her again until my hand is pressed gently over her eyes, which close as if on command. Like she'd been waiting for me to let her look away from this.

And I've been waiting to take in every fucking inch of her.

"I don't know what you want me to do, Eli—"

"Nothing at all. If I need you to do something, I'll tell you, understand?" I keep my voice authoritative, but my throat feels raw as I drag my gaze over her body. The curve of her breasts, the palest hairs along her chest, standing on end as she shivers in the tub, arms still tucked tight to her body. Her pale skin contrasting with the tan line from her swimsuit, the starkness of those black bracelets on her wrist.

I look lower, the impressions of her ribcage, substantial for such a short girl. I could place my fingers in between each one on sight alone. I bite my lip as I see the flat, soft plane of her tummy, small divot of her belly button.

But I almost lose every ounce of self-control I possess when my eyes trail over the crease of her thick thighs, her ass pressed against the base of the tub, her knees wide with the underside resting on the ledge of the tub, warm water gushing from the faucet onto her pretty little cunt, hitting just to the right of her lips, so she's not getting any direct pleasure.

Not yet.

"Eli." She sounds uncomfortable, and it pulls at my heart.

I force myself to look at her face, her mouth turned down into a frown as her eyes struggle to stay closed beneath my fingers. "I'm right here, Eden."

She slides her fingers over her tits, and pulls her legs slightly in, her knees going together as she tries to hide herself from me. There's the faintest trickle of pink in the shallow water that collects at the end of the tub. I say nothing to her about it.

"Widen your knees, okay?" I don't tell her to move her hands from her tits. Not yet.

"I don't think we should do this."

I close my eyes and clench my jaw. But I'm not going to force her, even though that would be fun, too. It's unfair, the playing field tilted as is. My strange little experiment is likely only working because her adrenaline crashed from caring for Dom, and the pills she took, and the alcohol I watched her drink earlier.

Don't push your luck, Eli. "Do you want to stop?" I try my very best to keep my tone even, but with all the blood rushing to my cock, it's hard to do that.

She's quiet a moment. Then she says, in a small voice I wonder if I should believe, "No." And taking a deep breath, she widens her knees, scooting closer to the base of the tub.

And she whimpers before I can direct her on what to do next.

I tense, slowly, so slowly, opening my eyes as I slide my hand up to her knee.

And I see it. The water pulsing over her pussy, her pink lips parted, her clit growing redder as her blood rushes to it, the feel of the water stimulating her.

I dig my fingers into her kneecap, watching.

Her eyes are closed, her fingers still covering her breasts, and she's trembling.

"Does it feel good, baby girl?" I ask her, the water arcing around her beautiful body, her bottom lip pulled between her teeth. She doesn't answer me for a long moment, her eyes squeezing tighter, the faintest creases forming around the edges.

Finally, she says, "Yes." It's a moan more than a word, and I bring my free hand to my cock, palming myself over my swim trunks, watching her thighs widen more, falling out to the side, the soles of her feet brushing one another, the silver of the faucet between her ankles.

I bite my lip, rubbing myself, watching the small muscles in her abs clench, the ones in her thighs pull taut as she opens herself up more, as wide as she can.

It's beautiful, seeing her pink flesh beneath the gleaming water, watching it pound against her, making her feel good.

I release myself, holding onto her knee still, and reach in to stopper the water.

Her eyes open, and I'm inches from her, my palm flat over the silver drain. "What're you doing?" Her words are hushed, and pink splotches form on her cheeks, even with the pills in her system.

"Trust me." I know she doesn't, and every time I say it, I see it in her eyes. It enrages me at the same time I convince myself I don't deserve her trust. Eventually, given enough time, I'll break it, and she'll have been right to have kept her guard up all along.

The water begins to fill up, but it's not even to her ears, not yet.

"It's like a… game," I explain quietly, bringing my hand to her shoulder, massaging her knotted muscles, full of tension. "I want you to come."

"You want to act out *your* fantasy this time." It sounds like an accusation, which seems unfair, because we did most of hers in my car without judgement.

I guess, though, she's the victim in both cases. She has more to lose.

"I won't let you get hurt," I promise her. I smile, crawling my fingertips to her throat, grazing it with my index and middle finger and watching her swallow with nerves. "Dominic is here, and I don't want to spend the rest of my life in prison."

It's supposed to be a joke, but she glares at me, unamused.

I lean down closer, brushing my mouth over hers. Her lips part for me, despite her annoyance, and I feel her resistance soften. She's as gone for me as I am for her, despite our walls.

"I want to make you feel good. That's all." I speak against her mouth, and she reaches for me, threading her fingers through my hair and pulling me closer. Her tongue brushes the seam of my lips and I open for her, our mouths gentle, soft, a different speed for us.

I feel her relax as I hold her throat, my thumb against the hollow of it. I don't squeeze her as the water fills higher. Both of her hands are now wound in my hair as we kiss, and she moans against me, shivering, the water still pulsing on her.

I want to see.

I want to see.

But I'm worried if I pull away, she'll grow anxious again.

Still, as she moans again into my mouth, I can't help it.

I pull back, shifting my palm possessively down the center of her chest, thumb and pinkie finger over the curve of her breasts as I watch her get closer to her climax, my mouth going dry with lust.

Her eyes close, the water climbing higher, over the piercings in her ears, the metal glistening beneath the suds, but she just grabs the outside of her thighs, digging her nails in.

I slide my palm down her sternum, over her belly, grazing her clit with my fingers, then circling her hole as she gasps, still keeping her eyes closed. I want her to look at me. I want to see her come, but I know she's probably feeling a little awkward and exposed like this, and she's already done so much of what I want, I don't want to make her more uncomfortable.

I push my index and middle finger into her, her thighs stretching even wider, her back arching up. Soap bubbles cling to the edge of the tub, but with my hand and the stream of water, they don't obstruct my view of her. I push in and out, finger fucking her, feeling the tightness of her walls close around me, the ache in my cock growing deeper.

The water rises higher, over her ears completely, but she doesn't let go of her thighs, straining to find her release.

Her knees are shaking, her entire body trembling.

But I see the moment her eyes open, and the bubble bursts.

She starts to panic at the rising levels of water.

She grabs the ledge of the tub, fingers curling over the sides as she intends to pull herself up, but I turn fully, one knee on the ledge, the other pressed against the outside of the basin, and I shove her down, my hand over her chest.

She gasps, still seeking purchase against the white porcelain ledge, but I shove harder, my fingers still inside of her, and this time, her head reaches the bottom of the claw-footed tub. Her eyes close and her face is submerged, even the tip of her nose, her lips, bubbly water swirling over her face.

Her knuckles grow white against the ledge, but she doesn't move her lower body.

She wants this as much as I do.

I keep fingering her, water squelching up from the force of my fingers inside her tight hole, and I know she's close. So fucking close, the way her clit is swollen, pummeled by water as she arcs her hips to ensure the force of it is still felt.

I bite my lip, watching, pressing her down with one hand, fingering her with the other.

But she's getting scared.

Her body tenses. I see her eyes open under the sudsy water. She doesn't move at all for a second, as if trying to wait out the panic, then she's pushing back from the base of the tub, sliding as she wiggles her hips, and she's clamped so tight around my fingers from fear, attempting to get away from me, from this.

I told her to trust me.

The thought slams into me like a fucking freight train. So is the knowledge she's not fighting as hard as she could because her body is probably weakened from the pills I told her to take.

I release her immediately, bringing both hands up, like in surrender.

She gets her calves off the ledge of the tub, pulling up, gasping in air as she breaks the surface. I bring my fingers to my mouth, sucking her off of me, the taste of iron and water and *her* causing my chest to tighten. I carefully get in, straddling her as much as I can as my knees sink to the base, the hot water making me flinch when my thighs are submerged.

I bring both hands to the back of her head, her hair wet as I lean down and pull her to me, kissing her as she gasps for air, her fingers still splayed along the edges of the tub.

I grind myself against her pelvis.

I release one hand from her head to let the water go down the drain, the gurgling sound rivaling her heaving breaths. Then I sink back on my heels in the tub, grab her arm and flip her body, slippery beneath me from all of the bubbles. Her palms splash in the water, her knees knock against the base of the tub, then she's clawing at the far end of it, but she's not trying to pull herself up as she hisses my name.

Her back muscles shift as she holds on tight, and I trail my palm down her spine, until I'm grabbing her round fucking ass with both hands. She has white stretchmarks, and I lower my head, biting them, hard.

She's on her knees, and I'm between her feet.

She whimpers with my teeth, still trying to catch her breath, and I don't know what she's thinking, or feeling, or if she hates me or loves me or hates this or loves it.

"Do you want me to stop?" I force myself to ask.

"Like you would." Her words are angry, but she isn't trying to get away, even as she gasps for breath.

The lines between fantasy and reality blur, and I'm not sure either one of us can tell what side we're on right now. *Give me a fucking line.*

"Eden."

Her spine stiffens. I see it move, and it's fucking sexy. Seconds tick by. A minute. My heart feels like it's going to explode in my chest. Finally, *finally,* she says, "You protect me, but you always get what you want." She laughs a little, a bitter sound, throwing those words in my face. "Why stop now?"

All right.

I lift my head, shoving down my swimsuit, shuffling my knees so I can pull it down to my ankles. I grab my cock, still keeping one hand on her ass, then I'm lining up with her entrance, her knees spread as wide as they can be in the tub, both of us dripping wet.

I push down on her spine, her ass arching up, and I nudge myself against her, just at her tight entrance.

She sucks in a loud, sexy breath.

I wait, to see if even now, she'll protest. If she really does want to stop. If she wants to go home. Her fingers tighten along the ledge of the tub. She turns to look at me over her shoulder, her eyes narrowed.

"I want it, Eli. Fuck me. I'm all yours," she says, her words jagged, like this is a dare. *How far will you go? You almost killed me.*

I smile at her, then I'm pushing inside of her. *I'll always go too far.*

I drop my gaze and see a crimson drop of blood as the last of the water gushes down the drain. I groan, low in my throat, sliding my palm back to her ass, gripping her hard enough to hear her soft moan as she bows her head against the side of the tub, her slender shoulders hunched.

I circle her throat with one hand, forcing her head up. I don't want her to bow for me. Not right now.

"You are…" I thrust hard into her, her blood lubing her cunt, cancelling out any dryness the water might have caused her, "everything." I mean every word as I grind my teeth, fucking her hard, her throat crushed into my hand.

I slap her ass, just to watch it bounce, to see the red print of my hand against her. I do it again, and again, until she's moaning, and she might be crying, but I know she doesn't want me to stop.

I grab her hard, hoping my fingerprints will bloom into bruises on her skin, and it makes me fuck her harder, wanting to possess her, to own her, to cross over every line she's ever fucking had until they're nothing but faraway memories and she can't believe she ever put any kind of boundary between us.

She moans again as I shift up the flesh of her ass, hitting her deeper, and I'm so fucking close, and I want her to be there, too, but she gave it up.

She fucking gave it up.

Anger courses through me, that she didn't trust me, and something on its heels, like longing. *I want you to, I want you to, I want you to.*

In my head, I can hear her mind screaming for mine. *I want to, I want to, I want to.*

I haul her up by her throat, her arms extended, fingers still gripping the tub.

I press my chest to her back, reluctantly letting go of her ass as I wrap an arm around her waist, my thrusts shorter, but with her pussy even tighter at this angle, it's not going to take much.

"Are you mine?" I whisper against her ear, my hand still fixed around her neck. I want to hear it again. I kiss her cheek, my mouth running up the side of her face as I fuck her. "Tell me you are. Tell me you love—... Tell me you're mine." I almost said something else, because she makes me stupid, but we can't go there. Not yet.

She's still holding onto the ledge, her slippery body so warm in my arms. "Yours, I'm yours," she breathes, her belly rising, falling as she tries to keep breathing. "I'm *yours*, Eli."

I'm so close. I just... I just want to do something bad. I want to do something terrible to her to drive me over the edge. The misinformed think sociopaths can't be sadists because we can't *feel* things. They have no fucking idea. "Can I hurt you?" It's a gasp, the question, and I don't think I can wait long for an answer.

She doesn't make me. *"Always."*

I shove her down, releasing her so she collapses, her fingers slipping from the edge of the tub to the base of it, and I push her head against the porcelain, her face twisting to the side as she lies there, her ass still in the air.

I see her eyes close, her lips parted as she whimpers.

I want her beneath me, *always*. I feel good like this. She feels good like this. But I know too, as my own release seems to catch fire beneath my skin, and I collapse over her, holding her to me as my elbows crunch against the hard bottom of the tub and I come inside of her, moaning her name in her ear, I'd gladly bow to her too. I'd lie down at her feet, I'd do anything she asked me to, I'd let her hurt me and punish me if she wanted, and just because she's beneath me, just because I obliterate all of her boundaries, it doesn't mean that, eventually, I won't let her do the same to mine.

36

Eli

I FEEL something warm beneath my hip. At first, even with the fan spinning overhead, the A/C on high in this house, I think it's my sweat. Coming awake happens slowly, and I know I only slept because Eden insisted *I* try her pills. It was a suggestion I could have easily forgone, but truth be told, after fucking her in the bathtub, bruises over both of us, I could use the rest.

It was probably the best sleep I'd had in years.

Now, my mouth is dry, I feel *heavy*, and I wonder if this is how people usually feel when they have a full night's rest. It isn't a great feeling, like chunks of uncontrolled time have passed without me.

I roll onto my hip, sliding my hands from under the cool side of my pillow. The first thing I see through bleary eyes is Eden's braids, still coiled on top of her head, a few strands of dark hair at the nape of her neck, my shirt on her body, an old Trafalgar wrestling one with the dragonfly on the back.

My sheets are pulled only to her hips, covering her ass, and I want to run my fingers over her bruises, I want to *see them*.

But instead, I look for the damp spot that is very clearly not sweat, because I'm actually cold.

Dropping my gaze a little reluctantly from Eden, the faintest tendrils of morning light filtering in through my curtains pulled closed from the patio, I see the spot of crimson.

I swipe my hand under the white sheets, lifting them marginally, not enough to disturb my girl.

The stain is right by her round ass, her black shorts hiked up enough to expose one fingerprint of mine, blooming purple and red. A smile curves my lips at the quarter-sized spot of blood beside her. I drop my hand and cover it. It's still warm, and when I lift up my palm to examine it, the ridges of my hand are coated with red.

I shift over closer to Eden, picking my head up just to see the time on my alarm clock. Ten minutes after nine in the morning. I hear nothing in the house and assume Dominic is still sleeping. But right as I reach for Eden, wanting to pull her to me, uncaring about the blood that soaked through her shorts, I hear my phone buzz on the nightstand beside me.

Rolling my eyes, not wanting the vibration to wake Eden, I slowly turn over and snatch the phone, yanking it off the charger. Propping myself up on one elbow, I see the text from Dad.

Him: Dinner tonight instead, I'm coming home early. I'm having it delivered, my flight is delayed.

I don't respond, and instead drop my phone on the nightstand, turning it to silent before I do. Then I flip over, pull a still-sleeping, warm Eden into my arms and hold her close, my chin resting on her head.

I think about last night. The bathtub. Her willingness to indulge me.

I don't want to ever go without that. *Her.*

I just need her to feel the same way about me. I need her not to run when she asks me all those questions she's put in the back of her mind, born from Dominic's big mouth.

I'll give her the answers if she'll give me some too.

I drop my head, nudging my nose against her neck.

You've come too close, now you can't ever leave.

THIS TIME, WHEN I WAKE UP, IT'S ABRUPTLY.

It's like I sense she's gone before I really see it's true.

I jerk upright, shoving the covers down to my hips, shocked I even managed more sleep. A quick glance at the alarm clock and it's after ten o'clock. An hour. I was out another whole fucking hour, and Eden isn't in here.

The stain of her blood is, but she's gone, the bathroom door pushed ajar, and I know she would've closed it if she was in there.

I glance at my phone, clicking it on, but I have no more messages. I swing my legs off the bed, bare feet hitting the hardwoods. Slipping them into my black sliders, I don't bother going to the bathroom to brush my teeth first.

I open my bedroom door and peer down the hall, to the guest room.

The door is open.

I hear the softest laugh from downstairs, like it's muffled between fingers over Eden's pretty mouth. A second later, and Dominic's hushed voice says something I can't quite make out.

I don't really think about it. I just head to the stairs, taking the steps two at a time, my hand gliding along the railing.

When I walk toward the kitchen, I see them both twisted around to look at me over their shoulders, their heads near one another. They're on the bar stools, Eden's feet on the lower rungs, toes curled around it. She's still in my shirt, but she changed into sweats, probably because she bled through her shorts. Her hair is down, wavy and rumpled to her low back, and she looks fucking stunning with sleepy eyes and a soft smile.

Her phone is face down on the counter in front of her, the sun is streaming in through the doors leading to the pool, and Dominic has a protein bar half-eaten beside her phone, his mouth full as he chews, bleary eyes on me.

He isn't wearing a shirt.

He's in low slung shorts and sliders, flat on the floor, the muscles in his back flexed as he keeps looking at me. There are circles under his eyes, even though I know he got more sleep than I did, and I slowly walk down the hall leading from the foyer, coming to stand in the archway of the kitchen.

I fold my arms over my chest and lean against the wall, smiling from one to the other. I feel as if I interrupted something, and I don't like the feeling.

"Hi," I say, my eyes on Eden.

A smile curves her red lips. She has her arms crossed, elbows on the island. "Hi." Her voice is still thick with sleep, and I hope they haven't been down here long together. I still can't believe I slept so long. "How did you sleep?" she asks, as if reading my mind.

I keep my gaze on her, but out of the corner of my eye, I see Dom's hand along his thigh, the unnecessary bandage still taped to his skin. I want to rip it off and make him really deserve it.

"Good," I answer Eden honestly.

"That's a first," Dom mutters. "Maybe you should attack me with a knife every night before you go to bed. Sleep like a fucking baby."

I raise a brow as I meet his blue eyes, but he looks down first, like he can't hold my gaze. "Maybe I should," I agree quietly.

A bone in his jaw moves, and Eden clears her throat. I wait for either one of them to bring up Winslet.

But Dominic just slides from his stool, his sliders clacking as he does, and he shoves his hands into the pockets of his shorts. "I'm going outside." He walks past me, stopping at the patio door. Lowly, he mumbles, "I'm sorry about last night." Then he heads out, closing the door behind him. He walks to the shallow end of the pool, kicks off his shoes, and puts his feet in, sitting down by the metal railing.

"What were you two talking about?" I ask, keeping my eyes on Dominic even as I feel Eden's on me.

"Are you *jealous?*" She picks at me, humor in her words, that bubbly undercurrent of new energy back in her voice. A small laugh leaves her when I don't respond, and I still don't look at her. "I have bruises, I want you to know."

My throat feels a little tight, and slowly, I drag my gaze to her. She's fully facing me, one leg crossed over the other. She's leaning back against the counter now, her elbows propped behind her.

"Oh yeah?"

"Yes. Thank you for those."

"You're very welcome."

I step toward her, and without me saying a word, she uncrosses her legs, spreading her knees apart. I come between them, my hands on her thighs as her muscles tighten beneath my touch, but she tips her chin up to hold my gaze, still smiling, her throat exposed, her hair falling over one shoulder in knotted waves.

"One day," I tell her, bringing my hands to either side of her neck, holding her gently as I run my thumbs up the column of her throat. "You won't jump when I touch you."

Something passes through her eyes. Something I can't quite puzzle out. Darkness, maybe, blurring the colors of green, brown, and blue, morphing them into a secret I don't know.

Why are you skittish?

It's on the tip of my tongue to ask. But I say something else. "Tell me about this heart problem of yours."

The darkness is gone, and she raises her thick brows, her knees closing against my hips. I step closer, and she pushes up from her elbows, wrapping her arms around me, having to look up even higher. I slide my hands over the curve of her jaw, back toward her ears, then thread my fingers through her hair, smoothing it back from her face.

"It's not a problem," she says, a little defensively.

"You have a prescription for it. When were you diagnosed?" All things I wanted to know last night, but I was thinking with my dick instead of my brain, and now I realize I need to understand the severity of her problem. I'm not sure why, my long-term outlook into the future has never been great. But with her… I want her there beside me.

Her fingers press into my back, hot against my cold.

Her chin comes to my sternum as she pins me with big, beautiful eyes. "When I was fourteen." There it is again. The *thing* that makes her eyes go from multi-colored to darkness, all in a blink.

"Tell me what happened."

She looks down, her long lashes grazing her cheeks as she presses the softest kiss to my abs. Longing for her has me taking deep breaths, but I know this trick. I'm not going to let her distract me. "There's nothing to tell."

I reach for her chin, keeping one hand in her hair. I tip her face up, so her eyes are on mine again. "Don't be a little liar," I tell her. "Tell me the story."

"You've told me none of yours."

I feel a tightness in my chest, and I glance at Dominic, still sitting with his feet in the water, now scrolling through his phone, probably looking for a distraction. Was that what our fight was last night? Is it what he's using Eden for?

"I will," I tell her.

"When?" Her tone is edged with impatience.

I meet her gaze, tracing her bottom lip with my thumb, searching for a distraction of my own. "My dad invited you to dinner tonight. Here."

She pales, her body tense as her thighs squeeze around me. "Really?" She sounds so unsure of herself, like she doesn't understand why my dad would be interested in having her around.

"Really." I lean down and press a kiss to her mouth, not opening my own, because I still haven't brushed my teeth. I pull back, keeping a grip on her chin. "Tell me about your diagnosis."

"I will." A shitty little smirk tugs on her lips as she repeats my words back to me.

I grip her jaw harder, not enough to hurt, but to get her attention. "Tell me now."

She shakes her head, brings her hands to my abs and pushes me away slowly. I step back, allowing it, and she twists her face out of my hold. "No." She slides down from the stool, raking a hand through her thick mass of hair. "I'm going to go change." Then she starts to walk off.

I grab her wrist, but don't pull her to me.

She stills, and I feel her pulse rise in her veins just beneath the base of her hand.

"If I had a heart problem, I would *want* to tell you all about—"

She yanks her arm from my grip and spins around, her eyes flashing. "Don't start," she says, her voice low. "Dominic said you were in a psych ward last year." She steps closer, anger making the vein in her neck stand stark under her skin. "I asked you about it. You said *nothing.*" She jerks her thumb toward Dom, still sitting in the water. "What happened with his sister? Why does he think you had something to do with her death? What is he talking about, all these secrets you're keeping together?" She drops her hand, curling it into a fist. *"Did you have something to do with what happened? Why don't you care at all?"*

I don't say anything.

We stare at one another in silence for long, long moments.

Then she laughs, a callous sound. "That's what I thought. When you decide you want to tell me something about *you,* then you earn the right to ask me questions." She turns her back to me again, intending to stalk off.

I think of the blood on my bed. Her in the bathtub. Letting me fuck her, after she said no.

I think of how she could twist Dominic's pain into anger toward me. She has a heart. She would feel for him, and if she somehow found out, from anyone else, about what happened that night…

"I saw her leave."

Eden stops, her spine stiffening. She doesn't turn around.

I glance at Dominic again, and marvel over the fact he'll miss the truth because he's a dozen feet away. That's it. It's the only thing separating him from answers. Strange, the way life works.

"It's blurry. I drank a lot that night." I wait for her to ask why, but she doesn't, so I keep going. It's better this way, anyway. Some things I'm not ready to discuss, and probably never will be. "I don't remember everything. But she had been on her phone. She was talking to someone inside. She told me she was going out. The lake. It was dark. I think I followed her."

Eden still doesn't look at me.

I remember the rain. It was cold, unusually so. I pushed my feet into my shoes, by the door, and I followed her out, because of the night. The lake. She could swim, but she wasn't very good at it.

"She ran around the lake. She was laughing. And drunk. Very, very drunk." I remember her golden hair. Her high-pitched squeal. "She said she was going somewhere. A man was picking her up." I clear my throat, but I don't look away from Eden's crown of braids. "I followed her, my shoes were sinking into the mud, I told her to come back, that I was done with this game, and she was going to drown out there. The weeds were thick around the lake, but on the other side, I could see a car at the bridge that borders the neighborhood. I asked who was picking her up. She asked if I was jealous."

Eden asks, "Were you?" It feels like a shot to the heart.

I don't say a fucking word. That question doesn't deserve an answer.

Eden turns to face me, tilting her head. "Answer me, Eli." There's ice around her words.

I don't.

Her beautiful eyes narrow into slits. Then she pushes me. My spine jars into the counter at my back as I stumble. *"Were. You. Fucking. Jealous?"*

I smile at her.

She looks more pissed, and her gaze slides to Dominic, just for half a second.

My smile widens, cold coursing through my veins. "Are you going to tell him? Is it *him* you're in love with, Eden? If I really hurt him last night, would you have been the first to call the police?" I step closer, until we're toe-to-toe.

"Are you stupid?" she asks flatly.

"Are *you?* Playing games with me would really hurt my fucking feelings." I keep a smile on my face as I say the words.

She smiles back. "I could say the same to you."

I lift a brow. "Oh? And what is it you would do if I played games with you, *nightmare girl?* Would you have me arrested? An accessory? Would you make your brother's shitty friends rob me at gunpoint or—"

"Don't."

I stop talking.

We take a minute to rein in our tempers, so close to breaking the more time we spend around each other. It feels like an omen, but I'm drawn to those.

"Tell me the rest of the story." Eden's tone is laced with a hint of hostility.

"I let her go." That's all there is to say.

Eden stares at me blankly, and I have no idea what she's thinking. It's unnerving. Like when she strolled up the staircase last night with Dom's hand in hers and smiled back at me while I held the knife to my lips.

Then she whispers, "You let her go?"

I don't repeat myself. Instead, I say, "Tell me about your heart problem." I glance at where the organ beats beneath my shirt on her body. It feels odd, knowing a weakness of hers. Understanding she isn't invincible. I don't like the feeling because I can't be with her all the time. I can't insulate her from the world. That would make me… my dad.

She doesn't speak for a second, and I know she's still thinking about Winslet. I don't feel relief having told her. I don't feel anything. It wasn't my fault. I did nothing wrong. Winslet could make her own decisions, and she had been doing so for a very, very long time.

I wasn't her keeper.

But Eden's lips curve up again, and I feel as if she thinks, maybe, I should've been.

"I was diagnosed when I was fourteen. I had a panic attack." She shrugs, as if that alone is nothing. "I woke up in the middle of the night with a racing heart. I'd had a bad dream. I dreamed about the time someone snuck into my room and… they used me. It wasn't so far-fetched, the nightmare." Her words are steady. "He was my brother's friend, and he spent the night often enough at my house."

I feel my blood run cold. I'm not sure what I expected her to say, but it was none of this. I dig the tips of my nails into my palms. I bite the inside of my cheek so hard I taste blood. "Used you? Used you *how?*"

She shrugs, so flippant. "Don't worry. Nothing actually *happened* to me. I was still your little virgin. But I told him he could when he kept begging me. When he said I just had to lay there. I didn't have to do anything. And maybe I liked it, in the end. Maybe I wanted to feel wanted."

The pressure in my chest rises.

"I wanted *someone* to want me. Maybe what Winslet wanted that night."

I try my very best not to outwardly react to her comparison. She wasn't there. She doesn't know anything about it. What Winslet wanted.

"It's what *you* want, too, isn't it?" Her smile is cruel. Her tone is condescending, but the truth is louder than all of it. "You want someone to know all of your bullshit, and want you anyway, because you're so tired of pretending, aren't you? It must be exhausting, wearing your perfect, shiny, rich boy mask all the time."

I clench my teeth together, but there is nothing I can honestly say to refute her statement.

I'm terrified she's going to leave. This is the part where she's figured me out, just like Mom. Just like Dad. Just like the meeting they had in the white room with the doctors in white coats, and they found out their son wasn't just temperamental. He wasn't simply sporadically violent in fits like children sometimes have. He wasn't moody or only six and volatile and prone to temper tantrums.

He was fucked up.

There was no fixing him.

Me. There is no fixing me.

Cold slithers under my skin. I glance at Dom again, and he is still so oblivious. I feel raw, exposed. I don't believe I did anything wrong, but with Eden's story, that won't mean she doesn't. And I never told the police what I saw. Now, she could fuck me up.

"You're not leaving me." I blurt it out because I can't stop it. And I couldn't let her leave right now if she tried. I'd rather not have to hurt her to make her stay, though. I want her to choose it. *Choose me. Stay with me.*

"Eden, you're not leaving—"

"I never said I was." She smiles at me, though, and it doesn't seem to match her words. She takes a step back, and I want to grab her, but I force myself to remain motionless. Sighing, she rakes her fingers through her mass of hair, and she turns from me, to look at Dom, staring at him in contemplation as she crosses her arms over her chest. "I won't leave you. We all want someone to want all the fucked-up parts of us, don't we?" She glances at me. "Yours just happen to be a little more fucked than the rest of us. But what, exactly, does that say about me?" She doesn't pause for an answer, and I wouldn't have been able to give her one, anyway. "I'm not going to tell him, or anyone, if you're wondering."

I was.

"So, whenever you start thinking you're the worst person in the world, Eli, just remember, *I'm the one keeping your secrets.*"

37

Eden

"DID YOU HAPPEN TO SEE DOMINIC?"

I look up from carrying dishes to the sink, trails of golden butter swirling around the white plate, shells of lobster I didn't eat, probably from Eli's meal.

I set the stack of plates down quickly, but soft enough they don't clink together, and I discreetly wipe my hands on the back of my shirt as I turn around.

It isn't Eli's shirt, because I changed into one of my favorites, a light, oversized sweater, emerald green and slightly cropped, showing a sliver of skin over my high-rise black jeans, fishnet stockings beneath them. I tug down my shirt, not wanting Eli's dad to see all of that, but since I didn't know I was having dinner with him until I was already here, I didn't have much to choose from.

"I'm sorry, what?" I ask Eric Addison as he wipes down the kitchen island, and I think about Eli and Dominic talking at the pool, the way I only watched them before Dom left, seemingly far calmer than when he arrived. They've made up.

I blink, focusing on the now. There are still white Styrofoam takeout trays spread along the island, but they're closed, lids flipped into latches, the scent of shrimp and grits and mussels and lobster heavy in the air.

But he had veggie "salmon" patties delivered for me too.

It was thoughtful, and I wondered when Eli told him I was a bad vegan.

Eric straightens, the dark gray tea towel in his hand as he clears his throat. "Sorry, I know it's… a lot. But I just wondered if Dominic came over last night?" He averts his gaze as he asks, and I take in the way his white dress shirt is rolled up over his forearms, the tension in his shoulders and the frown marring his lips. He's as anxious as I am, for whatever reason. And stupidly good-looking, which makes me *more* nervous around him.

Stop thinking about his dad being hot, Eden.

My heart picks up speed in my chest, and I'm grateful for the medicine I took before he arrived with our food a couple of hours ago. Now I'm short quite a few pills, thanks to Eli, and I'll need a refill early, but I had enough for tonight. And last night, I slept like the fucking dead with all the medication in my system.

Eli is outside, walking around the edge of the pool, his phone to his ear. His coach had called him. Something about wrestling down a weight class, he'd explained before he walked outside, leaving me with his dad. I might kill him when he gets back in, wrap the choker around my fist until he faints.

I plaster on a polite smile and refuse to think of his hand over my mouth and nose as I meet his dad's gaze, my palms growing clammy by my sides.

"Yes, I saw him." I clear my throat, wondering if I should keep talking, or let him pry the information out of me.

"You heard about… Winslet?" Eric leans against the island, trying to be casual, but he's got that dish towel clenched tight in his fist, one hand in the pocket of his dress pants.

"Yeah, I did." I nod once. *Do not think about Eli's confession.*

Do not. Do. Not. "It's… awful." I feel heat bloom along my chest, but don't look away.

Eric nods, his brows creased together as he glances at the stone flooring. "Was Dom okay? I know he's had a tough year, and I think he's messing around with drugs, his parents were telling me, before all of this." He coughs, unnecessarily. "I just hope he's all right." He peers up at me, almost skittishly. I imagine he doesn't get many answers from his son, and I feel a little pang of guilt because fuck, neither do I.

"He seemed okay," I lie carefully. "A little quiet…" *Not really. At all. Until he got sliced up by your spawn.* "But okay."

Eric sighs. "I'm not sure how he could be, after the news, and there were camera crews at his house, but the gate is closed, at the end of the neighborhood, across from ours. The first time in probably…" He trails off, then says, "Probably five years."

Five years. Eli would have been thirteen then.

"Oh?" I keep my tone only politely interested. "What happened then?"

Eric's gaze lifts to mine. Something crosses his face, a shadow of sorts, the way he frowns, little lines creasing around his eyes. "Well, you know… Eli's mom… she moved away then. He kind of… Well, he had a hard time."

I try not to betray my spinning brain. I knew she left because Dom told me. But I didn't know when. I don't know anything else, still. And "moved away" and "left" are very different terms. I don't know what to say for a long moment. Eli's dad releases his death grip on the kitchen towel, pressing his fingers between his brows and closing his eyes a second.

I, who rarely initiates physical contact of any kind, have an urge to hug him. I'm not sure why. It's not this moment of weakness, exactly. Not this *present* moment. It's thinking of our futures with this boy we love, and how holding onto him is a slippery thing, never guaranteed.

I take a single step, my heart racing in my ears, and I don't know what to do. But before I have to do anything at all, the patio door opens up and Eli walks in, a smile on his handsome face, phone held loosely between his fingers, at his side.

He closes the door behind him, the heat rolling in despite the fact it's fall.

He rakes a hand through his onyx hair, the same one holding his phone, and I see his biceps flex beneath the sleeve of his white shirt.

"Wow, who died?" he asks cheerfully, cutting his eyes from me to his dad and back again, his hand still wrapped around the silver knob of the back door.

Eric forces his own smile, but he doesn't do it with the same practiced ease his son does. He grabs the dishtowel, likely for something to do with his hands. "What did Coach P want?"

Eli lifts a dark brow, his smile slowly faltering, a haughty look replacing it, lips pressed together, expectancy in his eyes. He drops his hand from the door, gripping his phone tighter. "Baca is going to be out next weekend," he says, but his eyes are on mine. "He wants me to take his place."

"You'll have to cut, what, how many pounds…" His dad trails off.

Eli shrugs. "I'm not worried about it." He's still looking at me.

I turn around, flipping on the faucet and rinsing the dishes in the sink before I begin to stack them in the dishwasher.

"No, Eden, really, that's okay," his dad says behind me.

Jesus, just let me do this so I can pretend I'm too busy to talk.

But I screw on a polite smile and say, "It's okay, I've got it."

"Absolutely not." Eric's voice is a little sterner this time. "You two go hang out at the pool or something." *Or something.* Like he doesn't want to be alone with his son just yet, after all.

I straighten from putting silverware into the little basket for it in the dishwasher and turn to see him striding toward me and gesturing toward the back door.

Eli is smiling at me, but it isn't a nice smile.

It's a *we need to talk* smile.

I nod toward his dad, then say, "If you're sure…"

"I'm more than sure," Eric replies warmly, and his arm almost brushes my shoulder as he walks past, but it doesn't. It's just enough for me to feel the heat from his body.

I release a quiet breath. I don't particularly want to be alone with his son right now either.

But together, without a word between us, Eli and I step outside under the darkening sky, the heat enveloping me as I wrap my arms around myself.

Neither of us dressed for the pool, we walk around it, the sharp scent of chlorine familiar to me, but not enough to ward off the cold in my stomach, knowing Eli is going to ask what his dad and I discussed, and I'm not going to lie.

Probably.

We stroll to the pool house where Eli opens the door and gestures for me to enter first. I do, catching the scent of laundry detergent, wondering if the housekeeper cleans this place too, and saying a small prayer of gratitude this neighborhood isn't on my mom's list of clients.

Eli doesn't turn on any lights, and only a sliver of orange sun streams through the wall of windows.

I hear the lock flip behind me as I head toward the daybed, sitting on the edge of it with my arms crossed over my stomach as Eli looks at me in the dimness of the small house. I remember doing coke with Dom here, and it was only a few weeks ago, but it feels like a lifetime.

I've learned so many secrets, some earned, some stolen, I'm a different person now than I was then. Is this what it means to meet your soulmate? You grow by leaps and bounds instead of tiny increments? You age years instead of days?

But I don't think that's a soulmate exactly.

Something darker. Something worse. The opposite, perhaps. What is the term for it? *Something terrible.* In Greek mythology, we were created with four of each limb, two faces. Zeus cut mortals in half, fearing their power.

But there is no power between me and Eli.

There's only ruin. Perhaps there's more to the myth.

Maybe Zeus spared our split, because he always knew we'd self-destruct alone. He had nothing to fear from us. We burn out before we can rise.

Eli reaches into the pocket of his slate gray pants, and surprising me, he pulls out a joint, a lighter right after, bright green. He inhales, the cherry glowing bright before he pushes the lighter back into his pocket. I glance past him, toward the house, but he scoffs at my concern.

"It's the least bad thing I do," he says quietly.

The least bad. I press my knees together, thinking I need to leave soon. Mom will have questions for me, I have a feeling. If not tonight, tomorrow morning on the way to school.

I've barely responded to her messages, I've been spending so much time with him I haven't kept up my lies very well, I don't think. We took showers, separately, after Dominic left. I brought one of the books Janelle gave me and read it on the back porch, and after a while, Eli jumped in the pool, timing himself as he dunked his head under again and again. We had frozen lasagna for lunch, and we've spoken little. But he never suggested I go home. I never asked if he wanted me to. Even in our stormy silences, we don't want to be apart, do we?

"What did my dad want?"

There it is. "He wanted to know if I saw Dom, and how he was doing."

Eli doesn't react. "And what did you tell him?" He inhales from the joint, and I turn my head, putting my fingers close to my mouth as I stare at the wall. I want to move, to pace, but I try to stay still, the medicine doing its best to keep me this way.

"I said yes, I saw him, and he was doing... fine."

"Fine, huh?"

I don't look at him. "What did you want me to say? That you cut him? He banged his head against the wall and had a breakdown in your dad's house?" I rip a nail off with my teeth, no longer caring if Eli sees.

"Well, Eden Rain, I didn't think you were the kinda girl to

lie to your boyfriend's parents." He uses the teacher voice, but this time... I don't smile.

I mentally trip over the word "boyfriend." It feels juvenile, but I don't say anything about that either. If we're talking about this, then we're talking about it.

I turn to face him again, dropping my fingers from my mouth to my lap. "Is there more to the story?" I ask him cautiously as he gets high, pressed against the door to the pool house, like he's blocking my exit, even though I haven't got up from the daybed, soft beneath me as I bounce my leg. "About Winslet?"

He says nothing, his eyes glittering in the dimness, the burning end of the joint glowing in his irises.

"Tell me the truth. You know I'm not going to judge you for it."

He gives me a rude, half smile, and I already know he isn't going to answer me. "Tell me how you learned to talk like us." He brings the joint to his lips again, and he's holding it like a cigarette. It throws me off and I can only stare as he pulls from it, then exhales through his teeth, his eyes never leaving mine. "I've been to a different type of school." He doesn't say "public." My stomach twists into knots and I'm grateful I didn't eat much at dinner. "There's a certain way we speak, private schools. In Idaho," my breath catches with his words, the confirmation he was there, "their slang is different, but so are their voices, in general."

The way he uses the present tense pricks at my skin. Like he expects to go back. Just like I expect to leave him when I graduate. I think we're smart enough to have expectations which ring true.

"I don't talk like you." He speaks like music. I speak like I'm from the South.

He smiles, smoke unfurling from his nostrils. It's hot, and I sit up straighter, watching him. "No," he agrees. "Your voice is sexy. But your mannerisms, it's like you... copy things. You become what people expect you to be."

Expectations. Such weighty things between us.

"Do you think I'm what *you* expected?"

He looks down at his joint, still between his index and middle finger, like a cigarette. "Yes." He glances up at me through his thick lashes. "And more."

I let the compliment pass through me. Meeting Eli's expectations is an achievement enough in itself.

I think of studying his hands in class. My silent crush, my heavy gaze. He felt it all, didn't he? "Do you think it's an act?" I ask.

He strides across the open room, stubbing the joint in an ashtray on the coffee table, then he turns to me, closer now. "I think you tell me what I want to hear."

I can't hide my flinch because it's true. I do.

"About never leaving. About trusting me." He comes even closer, and I have to tilt my head to look up at him. The tension between us, as always, is stretched almost beyond the breaking point. "You're going to, aren't you?" His eyes pierce mine, his lashes black in the dying sun, shadows under his cheekbones, in the hollows. "You'll never trust me." He says it all like facts.

Indisputable.

He's right.

I don't want him to be.

"What happened with your mom, Eli?"

He doesn't react. I can never surprise him, can I? "So many questions tonight." And before I can respond, he moves, and he's on me. I'm pushed back against the bed, his hips between my thighs, his cock hard on my stomach. He grabs my wrists, jerking them over my head, pressed hard against the mattress, his other hand clamping over my mouth. He gets up to his knees, so he has more leverage over me as he stares down at me.

I think of his dad watching, but know he probably isn't.

He doesn't want to know all of the things his son does in the dark, does he?

"I know what you're thinking," Eli whispers, his temple to mine. His breath is cotton candy again, laced with marijuana. Sweet and soft and everything he rarely is.

I take a deep breath, unafraid. I don't speak.

"About Winslet. Tell me," he says, turning his head, his lips over mine. "Tell me I should've done something." He runs his nose over my jawline, up to my ear. His next words are just little breaths along my skin, his hand still pressing tight against my mouth. "Tell me how much you hate me. Tell me how sick I am. Tell me I should've fucking *done something.* Get it over with, Eden." He says my name like it's a curse.

"You should've stopped her." My voice is muffled, an animal caught in a trap. I'm straining against his hold on my wrists, but I don't want him off. It's just what I'm supposed to do in this game we play. "You should have done—"

He peels his hand away and slaps me lightly. I wince, and this time, as I struggle beneath him, it's real.

His eyes swallow mine, and he grinds his cock against me. "Tell me again." His thumb runs over my bottom lip.

My face still tingles with his hit. It wasn't hard, and it didn't *hurt,* but I didn't use our word. I didn't want it, and I didn't expect it.

These fucking expectations.

"Get off of me, Eli."

"Tell me all the terrible things you think about me. Are you wishing I was Dominic now?"

"*You* have the hang up about Dom, not me. Maybe because you know he deserves me, and you don't—"

"Yes, Eden, giving you coke and getting you high so you end up just like your brother certainly means he *deserves* you." He presses his thumb into my bottom lip, hard.

I pull against his hold on me, arching my hips to give me leverage, but he just smiles, unaffected.

"When something happens to me, you'll run to him, won't you?"

I still.

His smile pulls higher. It's blank, and eerie, and right now, I kind of hate him. *Not soulmates. Something terrible. Far more tangled.* "We both know I won't behave forever."

"That's your choice."

He cups my face, squeezing. "Is it?"

"Yes. Whatever is… is *wrong* with you, your actions are *your choice.*"

The smile leaves his face. He pulls down my bottom lip, glaring at me. He nudges his nose to mine, but it's rougher than usual. "It's like," he says through gritted teeth, words on my mouth, "you don't know me at all."

"Maybe I don't." I want to hurt him with my words because he hurt me first. "I don't know you because you won't let me. Get off of me. I'm going home."

"I'm not letting you leave me."

"I'm not fucking asking."

"Good. The answer would still be no."

"You slapped me."

He pulls back then, space between our mouths, but he doesn't let me go. "You're mad about that? I thought I could do whatever I wanted to you. Hit you? Almost fucking *kill you*, and you're mad I touched your face? It's like you don't want these fantasies at all. Like you're just trying to be a tough girl, edgy and fucking hardcore, but you're so fucking fragile—"

"You don't respect me. You don't respect anything though, so I'm not sure why I thought I'd be the exception." My heart hurts with his words. Throwing my insecurities in my face.

His eyes narrow into dark green slits, ringed by black. He looks as if he doesn't understand me in this moment.

The feeling is mutual. I think back to before I knew him, sitting at the desk a few rows in front of me, the girl beside him who always kicked his chair, his easy smile, polite, correct answers in class, but the feeling something was *off* about him.

I wanted it, his strangeness.

It drew me to him.

But I never expected to get so close. I never thought, if I

did, he'd try to hide his sinister side from me. I naively believed, in my fantasies and my daydreams, if we ever met, he would be the wild animal only I could understand.

I never believed I could tame him. I just assumed he wouldn't bite me.

"You *are* an exception. To *everything.*" He releases me all at once, standing and backing away. I'm too stunned to sit up immediately.

I blink, looking up at the ceiling.

What will we be?

Something terrible. Tangled. I grip my necklace for something to do with my hand. I hold on tight to the *ouroboros*.

Is that what we are?

"Why haven't you figured that out by now? That there is *no one* like you for me on this whole fucking planet."

Slowly, my head reeling, I sit up. I feel off balance. I feel exhausted. Two days with Eli and I'm worn down. What does a lifetime look like?

Short.

That's what.

I get to my feet, looking to the door. "I'm leaving."

He doesn't say a word.

I wait another minute. Still, nothing.

So, I walk out, I gather up my shit, and not for the first time, I leave Eli Addison behind.

THERE'S A SOFT KNOCK ON MY DOOR. I FLINCH, PICKING MY head up from my notebook, my fingers clenched tight around my pen.

Slowly, blinking rapidly, I come back to reality, homing in on my bedroom door.

Mom won't wait to push it open, and I didn't lock it, for that reason. I saw the look she gave me when I let myself into the trailer. Even Sebastian was, shockingly, home before me.

He'd sent me a bleary glare over the top of the fruity cereal he was eating at the kitchen table.

Reece barely gave me a grunt and a glance, but from the awkward hush that fell over the living room, some sitcom with a laugh track set to run every ten seconds the only audible sound, I knew they'd been discussing me.

Mom steps inside my room without me saying a word, and softly closes the door behind her. I don't want to talk. I don't want to do this. I clutch my notebook to my chest, full of scrawls and theories about Winslet and Dominic and Eli. I feel a little like a detective.

My knees are bent and covers pulled to my waist, and I hope Mom has no idea what the hell I was doing, but I feel a sense of paranoia maybe she does.

"How was your day off?" Mom starts, a smile plastered on her face. She turns from me and starts to straighten the books stacked on top of my small bookshelf against the wall beside the door. It's nervous energy with an outlet. When Mom is cleaning, she's in her zone.

Luckily, I stuffed the books Janelle gave me in the same drawer as my sigil notebook.

I watch Mom work, irritation under my skin, but I know I need to put my all into this conversation. It could impact future plans I make with Eli, whom I haven't spoken to since I left his house two hours ago. Because I haven't checked my phone.

"It was great," I lie to Mom. I pick a stray thread on my comforter, my book still pressed to my chest with one hand "Went swimming. Watched movies." I mean, theoretically, these things happened. Maybe not to me. But I was around them. Osmosis, right? "I'm pretty tired though." It's a lie. I'm wide awake now, but I still stifle a fake yawn with the back of my hand, abandoning the loose thread.

Mom keeps tidying stacks of books, although she's really doing nothing at all save for knocking the spines tighter together. "Did you see Eli?"

He role played his murder fantasy with me in his bathtub and told me about another murder he just let happen.

"Yeah, he came over to Luna's." I clear my throat. "But her mom wouldn't let him spend the night or anything." *Little liar,* he called me. If only he could hear me now.

The sleeve of Mom's loose T-shirt slides up as she reaches for a non-existent cobweb in the corner of my room with a book in hand to knock it away. If it wasn't a particularly dull biography I think she got me from a garage sale, I might be annoyed. As it is, I'm focused more on her skin, and I see the scar on her arm, lumpy and pink.

I avert my gaze, clutching the notebook in my lap with both hands.

"That's good," Mom says softly, staring up at the corner of my room with the biography held by her side now the ghost cobweb is gone. She pauses, but I don't rush to fill the silence. This is the part where she's going to say something I don't like, and I cannot react, because it'll only make it worse.

I take a steadying breath, staring at the back of her curly brown head.

Her shoulders stiffen, as if she's preparing for me to talk back, then she finally gets on with it. "You know, I think maybe you and Eli need a little time apart."

My pulse slips into overdrive, despite the fact I expected this. I stare at my sheets, pulling my knees closer to my chest, tops of my thighs pressing into the soft cover of the book. "Why do you say that?" I keep my retorts tucked close but let them filter through my brain.

I'm eighteen. You don't even know how much time we've spent together. If you did, you'd never let me out of this house again.

Mom clears her throat. She still doesn't turn to face me. "Well, you know, you're wanting to get a scholarship, so you really need this semester to count, right? It's the last one to show on your transcripts?"

I don't speak. I'm not sure I trust my own voice to carry me through this. It was one thing to leave Eli willingly. It would be another thing entirely if I was forced apart from him. Panic claws beneath my skin.

"And..."

I hold my breath, keeping perfectly still, waiting for her to say what it is she's really thinking.

"I don't know."

I don't exhale yet.

"I've just... Eli is a nice boy," *no he's not,* "but Sebastian mentioned some of his friends hang around shady people Seb knows, and Eli was involved in that poor girl's disappearance and—"

"Mom." I've found my words again because anger bursts through my fear. "Sebastian *is* shady people. And Eli was *not* involved."

Mom sighs, dropping her head for a moment before she turns to face me. I grab my covers as her mouth twists, her eyes down on the floor, the book held to her chest, almost mirroring my own.

I pull the sheets up high, over my knees, my bracelets, my wrist, my notebook.

I think about Eli going through my student file. The truth I think I'd rather he never get his hands on. I know Mom is going to go for it now.

"Eden." Her words are soft. "With everything that happened, back at Shoreside..." My wrist feels as if it burns with her words, although the wound is long gone. The nurse didn't see it. The principal when he separated us. Nic didn't tell anyone or I would've done more than just sit in the nurse's office. He was too much of a pussy. But Mom saw later. The day I got suspended. "And you've been avoiding Amanda," her big eyes meet mine. "She said she tried to make plans, but you never got back to her about them. She just wants to make sure you're... doing okay."

I feel a flash of hatred toward Amanda whereas before, I'd only had a lazy sort of indifference. Clearly, though, she's reached out to my mom since I'm not responding to her texts again.

"This isn't like that." I hate the way I sound like a child to my own ears, my voice whiny. But Eli and I aren't children. It's different. "We're taking it slow," I say, keeping my tone even as I fucking lie. "It's not anything crazy, Mom." I scoff, to add truth to my bullshit.

Mom seems to sense it. She tucks an errant curl behind her ear and smiles politely at me. I hate polite smiles. "I don't think you've been sleeping well, you know. And if something happens at Trafalgar…"

I want to throw this notebook across the room. Shame is hot around my ears, and worse than that, I feel Eli being snatched away from me far too soon. "Nothing is going to happen." I grit those words out between my teeth.

"I know, honey. I know you needed space and a fresh start, but I'm just reminding you. If something *does* happen, it's not going to look good on your applications. You have plans, Eden, don't ruin them for a boy." She sighs, her features softening from fake civility to pity, and the latter makes my skin crawl. She doesn't see it, or else doesn't take it as a warning, because a moment later, she's sitting on the edge of my bed and locking her calloused hands around my ankle, my sheets between our touch. "I want the best for you. Eli is very nice. But there's a life beyond this one… if you want it."

My mouth feels dry, but I don't look away from her as I bite the inside of my cheek before I speak, trying to steady myself.

"You don't think I know that?" *You think I don't want to get the fuck out of here? Away from you, so I never end up like you or Reece? Away from Sebastian before I become him exactly?* I want to rip my ankle from her grip. Tell her she's blind and she should've had this talk with Sebastian, and she shouldn't have made him my babysitter when I was too young to hang out with him and his friends while she worked the job she had to because she barely graduated high school because she was too wrapped up in my fucking dad.

"Of course, but our heads can be distracted by our hearts, Eden."

Get out. Get out. Get out. Mom is kind and sweet and soft, and no one has ever misjudged me more than her. Even Reece sees my defiance. It's why we constantly butt heads.

"I'm going to college." I fist the sheets in my hand. "Nothing will change that."

Her eyes search mine for a long moment and I wonder if she believes me. But I can't tell, and eventually she nods and stands, retracting her hand from my ankle, dragging her fingers along the length of my bed like she doesn't quite want to let me go yet. As if she ever had me at all. Maybe before Reece, I guess, but even as a child, I was in *gifted* programs, and we couldn't relate, and I've never seen her read a book a day in my life. She just… doesn't get me. She doesn't understand how much I won't fuck this up, my dreams, even if it means breaking my own heart to pieces.

"Maybe just stay home this weekend, except for work? Spend some time at home next week, too?" She turns her back on me as she says it, a sign I can't talk my way out of this one. "Text Manda back and if you want, I can drive you down to see her next Saturday morning."

Get. Out.

But if I'm not smart about this, she'll forbid me from Eli for far longer than a week, and he had mentioned his beach house later this month, but maybe he doesn't mean it anymore, after our fight. Still, I think I could talk him into most anything, because he can do the same to me.

And while I could lie to Mom and sneak around, it's unnecessary trouble I don't want to cause. Just for this weekend, I'll keep my distance outside of school hours. That's it.

I don't say it, though. It's hard for me to give in so easily.

"Goodnight, honey."

I mutter a low, "Goodnight," and as soon as Mom walks out and closes my door behind her, I grab my phone from my nightstand, flicking off my lamp as I do, shoving my notebook free from the covers and to the ground as I lie on my side. It's all bullshit anyway. Stuff I made up inside my mind. It's worthless.

Eli has texted me three times. If it had been anything less, it wouldn't drown out Mom's words in my head. *"You have plans, Eden, don't ruin them for a boy."*

But he did. And his words wash everything else away. I forget why I was mad at him. Why I cared he slapped my face. It doesn't matter anymore. Nothing does for now, except him.

Eli: I didn't mean to hurt you.

Him: I was nervous because you could probably send me to prison now, and after I told you, and what you told me... I'm sorry.

Him: Text me back, Nightmare Girl.

Smiling, silencing Mom's words, I reply an hour after his last text.

Me: You don't trust me?

It takes two minutes for his response, and I stare at my screen the entire time, hoping he hasn't pulled another impossible feat and fallen asleep.

But the three dots pop up and my breath hitches, even as thoughts of washing my face and changing my pad prick at the back of my mind.

Him: I trust you when you love me, not when you're angry with me.

My heart jolts at the L word, despite the fact I've thought it too. It feels like a thing with a future, or something that'll hurt more without one.

I ignore it.

Me: Which means you don't trust me.

Him: We're not mad, are we?

I smile, grateful we've passed over "love," and yet yearning to retrace my steps. Go back to it just for a second to clarify. Bittersweet, that's how it feels glossing over it.

But I don't bring it up again.

Me: I think I'm mad for you. My finger hovers over

the send button. It's silly, childish, beneath him. Something I might write in a book some day or read inside one.

I send it anyway.

I'm not mad at him. I am confused by him, and sometimes, I don't understand him.

Except, maybe, I understand him perfectly. I just wish him to be something else sometimes because it would be easier on my heart. For all of our intensity when we're together, the day we let go, my world will feel like it's burning down around me.

But that day is not today.

He takes so long to reply, my screen goes dim. My stomach twists into knots, and I begin rethinking what I said. It was too much, too lame, too… soft.

But he said "love." He said that word first. And when the text comes through, my phone brightening up again, my mood switches like a flip of the lights.

I'm grateful I said it.

Him: I have been mad for you since I first saw you staring at my hands in class.

My face flushes warm and I'm grateful I didn't take any more pills this evening, as I sometimes do to help calm myself enough to sleep. Right now, I want the constant thrum of my pulse, the skipped beats of my heart. The way my entire body is hot, and I start to sweat even beneath the fan.

Me: Don't lie to me. I bite my tongue to stifle my laughter even as I send the message.

Him: I would never. I watched you too, you know. I wish you were here.

Me: Me too.

Him: I didn't even wash my sheets.

I tense, rubbing my thumb over the screen to blot out his words. When I got up this morning, I had a leak through my shorts, but I hadn't seen anything on the bed. I thought I caught it just in time. But maybe he meant my scent. *Yes, my scent.* Or even just the fact I was in his bed.

I'm about to go with that assumption when another text comes in.

A photo.

My heart leaps to my throat.

It's of him, lying on his back, a cocky smirk on his full lips, the green of his eyes visible even with his arm outstretched to show off his abs, the top of his skull and crossbones tattoo. I see the veins in his forearms, the line of his biceps, the muscles of his neck straining against his choker.

And because of how ridiculously hot he is, I almost miss the point of the photo.

When I see it, I kinda wish I had.

Fuck, fuck, fuck.

With his free hand, he's got his thumb aimed at a spot on his sheets. Unmistakably, blood. It's the size of a quarter with a jagged border, and I know it's mine.

I feel lightheaded as I swallow, neck growing hot with my flush.

Shit. How did I not notice?

Before I can throw my phone across the room and bury my head under my pillow, another text comes through.

Him: I hope this never washes out.

My God, I hope to hell it does.

My fingers feel shaky, and I want to get up and run to the bathroom just to put distance between myself and my phone.

Deep breaths, Eden. It's not that serious.

It is, though. It is. My nervous brain is screaming in my ears about being so careless, but another part, the logical part, asks what the hell I could have done about it anyway? I would have just known the entire day and thought about it constantly.

It's good I didn't know until now.

Shit.

Before I can decide if I want to feign sleep or get this over with and respond with something vaguely witty and revealing nothing of my mortification, he texts me again.

Eli: I know you're over there being very uncomfortable. Don't be.

I laugh out loud. It's a shallow sound, more for my benefit than anything else, because obviously he can't hear me, but laughing when embarrassed seems to be a universal, human thing.

I blow out a breath, shaking my head as I roll to my back and hold my phone over my face.

Me: This is awkward.

Him: No, that's not what you're supposed to say, Eden. You're supposed to say, "Yes, sir."

Despite my lingering feelings of humiliation, I feel a bolt of something else. I squeeze my thighs together and vividly imagine me calling Eli "sir." I don't think I could stomach it, but it's a nice fantasy.

Me: I never do what I'm supposed to.

Him: If I had you pinned against the wall with my hand over your mouth and my knee between your thighs, I think you might consider it.

My heart flutters, and thankfully, the stain I left on his bedsheets fades away into the dark corners of my mind, probably for some future year when I'll stay up late overthinking every horrible and awkward thing I ever did in my life, and that will be front and center.

I leave it for future me.

Tonight, I give in to this little game.

Me: Pin me against the wall? You've almost drowned me twice. You'll have to escalate your fantasies accordingly.

I smile, pretty proud of myself for that one, but a minute passes. Another. Five more. Nothing comes through.

I toss and turn, phone clutched in my hand, but I get nothing, and I fling off my covers, leave my phone, and head to the bathroom to get ready for bed. With freshly brushed teeth and my pores still tight from washing my face, I dive into bed after I close and lock my door behind me.

I grab my phone, nervous there will still be nothing.

But he's texted me again. Twice.

With greedy fingers, I unlock my screen and open his messages.

The words are first.

Eli: Is this far enough?

The photo is next.

His chin is tilted up, he's lying in bed again. I can only see from his swollen lips, down, but it's enough. Because his shorts are pulled low and I see the V of his hips, his defined abs, the broad muscles in his chest and shoulders.

And the knife he has in his hand, the same one he used to cut Dominic.

The sharp edge is against his throat, slid underneath his choker. There's an indentation in his skin, and I can't breathe for a moment. I have no idea how he could do that without cutting himself.

Another photo comes through before I can respond, tingling aches flooding my core.

This time, the blade is against his mouth, like it was when I walked Dom upstairs.

But there's the slightest trace of blood against it, his tongue lapping at the flat side of the blade, and crimson streaked over top of his choker.

Him: Do you want to hold the knife this time?

This time.

I pull my bottom lip between my teeth, rubbing my thighs together. I reach for the apex of them, letting my knees fall to the side. I have to work over the pad, the crinkly noise loud, but not loud enough to drown out the sound of my pulse in my ears.

I type with one shaky hand.

Me: Don't hurt yourself.
Him: Hurt me yourself.
Me: You want me to?
Him: Yes.

Me: I thought you liked to be in control.

I circle myself faster, over my underwear, under my shorts. I'm panting, and I scroll back up to look at his photos before he sends me another text, shifting the messages down.

Him: I do, of you. But sometimes, I want you to feel what it's like.

I'm breathing in through my nose, out through my mouth, shallow gasps.

Me: What?

Him: Almost killing you. It's a rush.

Feelings of pleasure and nerves and fear run through me at once, and so does another feeling. Something I don't really have the name for. Like I'd bow at his feet. Throw myself on my hands and knees to please him. Do anything he wanted. Anything at all.

I'd degrade myself for him if he wanted it.

In this moment, *I adore him with everything I am.*

And it's what makes me type out my next words.

Me: I could never kill you.

Him: I feel the same. But it's the best part, isn't it? When I bring you back to life and let you live.

I circle myself faster, tipping my head back, arching my neck. I close my eyes, but it isn't enough, my imagination. I want to see the knife to his throat. The blood on his skin.

I hold my phone up higher as I buck my hips against my hand.

I see the tendons in his neck. The stark ridges of his clavicle and the shadows beneath.

Then he sends more texts, and they're enough to drive me over the edge.

Him: I'm hard just thinking about it. Your wide eyes, the way you fight me, but we both know I could murder you if I really wanted to. And that's just it. I don't. You're precious enough for only me to hurt, so I can kiss you all better and have you thank me for every part of it.

Him: If you're not touching yourself, you need to start.

But I don't, because I'm gasping, my legs splayed to the side, my aching wrist over my brow, eyes closed as I imagine being held down in the water, his hand over my mouth and my nose, I've already finished. It never takes me long with him.

38

Eli

I SEE MOM.

She's sitting on the edge of the tub in her nightgown, the water running, but it's just slipping through the drain.

Her shoulders are shaking, her long, dark hair pulled into a single braid.

I can't see her face, but I know she's crying. Even with the hum of the bathroom fan and the sound of the water pouring from the faucet... I can hear it.

Swallowing hard, I step inside the warm room. She keeps a heater by the tub.

Dad told her it's dangerous.

Mom seems to like dangerous things.

I once watched her hold a kitchen knife to her arm, but when I walked in, her head snapped up and she dropped it. Pretended it was all an accident as she kissed me on the head.

"Mama?" I call softly, one hand still on the silver handle of her bathroom.

For a moment, I'm not sure she's heard me, but then I realize her entire body has gone rigid.

She drops her hands to her lap, smoothing down the silk of her black nightgown.

Then she looks over her shoulder and rearranges her features into something that's trying to be nice.

It's how she always looks at everyone else.

Nicely.

But I'm not sure she quite understands what I can see in her eyes.

Emptiness.

Blue and green orbs of... nothing.

When she looks at Dad. At me. Sometimes, I think she'd love to run away and leave us. But she can't, because Dad doesn't know me at all. The things I've done in the backyard with the mice and one time, a rabbit... he wouldn't let me do that.

Mom caught me once.

I'd stared up at her with blood on my hands. She'd sighed and scooped up the vivisected little animals before tossing them into a plastic bag, then the trash.

She gets me.

Dad doesn't understand us.

Sometimes, I wish he'd disappear and just leave me and Mom here alone. I think we'd be happier, being able to be ourselves without his constant watch.

"Do you need something, baby boy?" she asks me quietly, the pained smile still on her face. Her skin is olive. Far darker than Dad's.

I love it.

I glance at the bath water going down the drain. "Why are you not keeping it all?" I whisper, meeting her gaze. My heart pumps hard in my chest, and my palms are sweaty. Next week, in June, I'll be eleven. Maybe I won't be so nervous around Mom then. Maybe she'll like me when I'm older. When she sees how alike we are, and how I can do so many things by myself, like get my food and brush my teeth and put on my clothes and ride my bike and even swim.

But for now, I always feel like I'm walking on eggshells around her. Like I'm not enough for her. As much as I admire her, I don't think she feels the same about me.

I think she thinks I'm like Dad.

I'm nothing like him.

She turns from me, cocking her head, her braid shifting slightly down her back as she stares at the water. "Sometimes I like it to keep running." Her narrow shoulders shrug and she adds, "I like the noise. It's... nice." Looking at me again, she tucks a lock of dark hair that came free from her braid behind her ear. "Does that make sense, Eli?"

I listen to the sounds in the bathroom. The fan. The water. It muffles the noise of my own pulse. My heavy breathing, because I never know what to say to Mom to get her to keep talking to me.

It drowns out the feel of unease in my body.

I nod once. "It makes sense."

She smiles again, and this time... it almost seems real.

It's been five days since we spent time together outside of Trafalgar's walls.

I shove on my wrestling hoodie because Castle Hall turns chilly once the sun has sunk down, and it's late October. The heat hasn't been turned on yet, the days still warm, but after practice, fresh out of the shower with my hair damp, I'm cold.

I rake my fingers through my waves, tousling them, and grab my bag from the rickety bench in the locker room, walking out into the hallway parallel to the wrestling room.

"You sure you're okay for this weekend?"

I glance to my left, seeing Coach Pensky in the doorway, a clipboard tucked under his arm, one hand splayed against the doorjamb. He adjusts the little glasses on his face, sweat blooming under his gray T-shirt, matching his sweats. Coach isn't fashionable, yet he still exudes a feverish sort of confidence which serves us well. Beyond him, inside the room we had practice in, I see Ms. Pensky on her hands and knees, scrubbing at the mats with a bottle of spray and paper towels.

I wonder if she ever wanted to do something else, or if she fell in love with the sport before she fell for her husband.

I grip my bag, pushing my other hand into my pocket and grabbing my phone, itching to text Eden. She's had a lot of homework, she's said, but I know she's avoiding me for some reason. At least, she's avoiding being alone with me, after school hours.

"Yep," I tell Coach, and I mean it. I've cut five pounds since we spoke on the phone last week. The tournament is Saturday, I'll be able to drop three more pounds of water weight by then. Not healthy, but it's only temporary so I can wrestle in Baca's place.

Pensky nods. "Is the girl coming?" He barks out the question like he barks out most everything else, but I see a small smile on his thin lips.

Even Ms. Pensky turns to look over her shoulder, curly brown hair down her back shifting as she does. She winks at me, then goes back to cleaning, but I know she's listening.

"Maybe." I smile back, but I'm not feeling so sure right now.

Coach pushes up his glasses again and lets the clipboard dangle from his fingertips at his side when he's done. "Maybe? Already screwed this up?" I know it's a joke, but it takes a little extra patience from me to keep my smile hitched on my lips.

I grip my phone tighter in my pocket and shake my head. "You know me," I say, sighing. "Always messing things up."

I expect Coach to laugh, maybe tap me on the shoulder with the back of his clipboard and send me on my way. Everyone else has filed out and left, and darkness is falling beyond the double doors at the end of the hall. But surprising me, Coach's smile slips.

"You know," he says, glancing over his shoulder to his wife, who is pretending not to eavesdrop while obviously doing so, "I've never seen you bring a girl to a match before. I mean, there's the one, with the red hair…" He trails off.

"Luna," I supply. Her hair isn't quite red, but I see why he'd think so.

"Yeah, her, and your little asshole friend who swims and drips water on my mat when he wants to piss me off."

I nod once. "Dominic." He's come in before in the middle

of practice when Coach was busy, just to fuck with me and, as Pensky said, drip water on the damn mats.

He's back at school, and we're okay, except for those times I kinda want him dead like his sister. I'd like to say I'm above jealousy, but clearly that's not the case. Sometimes he walks with me and Eden in the halls, and it seems him and her have some sort of easy bond I could never even attempt with her. Like she said, things are always heavy between us. I refuse to believe it would be our downfall, connecting *too* fiercely. But the thought lingers sometimes in my mind.

"And your dad, good guy." Coach says it like an afterthought as he mentally scrolls through the people who come to my matches, like Dad is someone he's supposed to mention.

I don't have any fresh bruises to speak of, so maybe my dad isn't so bad, I guess.

"Anyway, no chicks. But I've seen her watch you."

I wait, not moving, and I'm not sure what it is I want to hear. Reassurances this isn't all in my head? I'm not getting so wound up in someone who won't tangle themselves in me, too?

That I won't be like Dad?

"It's like…" Coach smiles, flashing crooked teeth as he looks at Ms. Pensky again, and I see her shoulders shake with the softest laugh. "I don't know," he finally says, sighing and leaning against the doorjamb completely as he crosses his arms, eyes back on me. "I just think she's really into you, so bring her to the damn tournament and take your shiny, stupid car too, if it'll get her there."

I don't think Eden cares at all about my *shiny, stupid car*, but I nod anyway. "Will do." Then he finally *does* clap me on the back with his clipboard in a dismissal.

I head toward the parking lot, shoving the doors open and pushing out into the cool air, but I don't go to my car immediately which I moved after school so it'd be right here when I was done.

I pull out my phone and send Eden a text.

Me: Where are you?

I give her one minute exactly. She doesn't answer, so I call her. It goes to an automated voice message which doesn't even say her name.

I glance up at the moon, nearly full but not quite.

Sighing, I spin around and tip my head up, seeing the turrets of the castle, but just barely in the night. I drop my eyes, toward the front of the building. The parking lot with its orange glow of streetlights.

Then I grit my teeth and drop my bag off in my car, locking it behind me as I head toward the library.

It's worth a look, at least.

It's colder in here, down in the basement levels of Trafalgar. The lights are dimmed, orange just like the ones outside. The librarian isn't at the desk when I walk in, the heavy wooden doors creaking closed behind me.

I sweep my eyes over the rows and rows of dark, polished wood, inhaling the scent of old books and leather and buildings built long before I ever stepped foot in them. Eden belongs in a place like this. As much as she likes the water, as much as she seems at ease in the gym, and beside me in my car, *this* is the place for her.

Romance, she told me she wrote.

I looked into it a little, trying to understand the societal views on indie publishing now. It would be an uphill battle for her to be taken seriously as a self-published author attempting to go into academia, just like she said, but not impossible. I saw two professors who had done it, granted one was in Germany and another in Canada, but if anyone could do it, it'd be her.

I meant to bring it up with her at some point, but I rarely think of the future. Besides, she's very reluctant to discuss her art, although that means it's probably worth discussing.

The wrestlers with the biggest mouths have the worst finesse.

The quiet ones are the people I watch out for, the ones second-guessing themselves. They're the type who work the hardest, striving for perfection.

I swirl my key ring over one finger, glancing down at the fob, the key to my house, and the only keychain I own. It's silver, something my dad bought me from a work trip to D.C.

All For Nothing, with the F scratched out. It was a thoughtless gift, a souvenir to bring his kid because he didn't want to show up empty handed.

I close my fingers around it, smiling as I shake my head. I set off down the aisle that leads to the fireplace no longer in use, listening as I walk. I don't really expect her to be here, but practice ran late tonight, and I don't think she'd be at Fit4Ever, either, which means I'd have to show up, unexpectedly, at her house, and I don't think that'd go over well for me.

I take a left turn between bookshelves rising almost to the high ceilings, on each side of the walkway. The scent of old paper is stronger the further in I go, and up ahead, to the right, is the narrow aisle where Eden would be if she was here.

But I prepare myself to see nothing at all.

I slowly step to the aisle, my body half-hidden by the enormous oak shelves.

I stop.

My muscles relax, my face stretching as I smile. I couldn't hide it if I wanted to, but I don't, because I'm still in shadows, and she doesn't see me.

Her hair is only half up, no braids today, and dark strands hang in her eyes as she leans closer to her notebook, pen in hand. Her laptop is open, and I see it's school issued, "Trafalgar" engraved onto the silver casing in the lower, right-hand corner.

I push my hands into my pockets and lean against the bookshelf, one ankle crossed over the other. If she looked up, she would probably spot me. As it is, she's completely engrossed in whatever she's scribbling down onto the page, folded over and halfway filled with her inky scrawls.

I consider it could be homework, but the way she leans in, her forehead inches from the paper, her knuckles white as hard as she's gripping the black pen… I don't think even Eden would be this enamored with something school related.

She doesn't even lift the pen once. It's like cursive, maybe, and I'm too far to read it, but it could be she's just that excited. Or frenetic. Like she can't get the words out fast enough.

And I can't stop watching her.

I become so mesmerized in her fascination that when she finally, *finally*, gets to the bottom of the page, drops her pen with finality and glances over her work almost as if in dismissal before burying her head in her hands, I breathe out. And on the exhale, I'm not sure I was ever inhaling normally, the entire time she wrote.

I lean my head back against the shelf behind me, marginally relaxing as she does, and I realize my muscles were tense as I watched her. Like I could physically *feel* her passion. Like I can only let go when she does. We're more than connected. We're fucking tangled.

Her hair is between her fingers, the pieces which came free from her clip, and the rest of it is down her back. She's still in her Trafalgar uniform, a black polo, as usual, buttoned up to her throat. Today, she wore the skirt again, although it's still very much a rarity.

I couldn't stop stealing glances at her in Latin this morning, her knees pressed together like she knew I was watching her. My dick gets hard, and I have to adjust it with my hand in my pocket.

I like to think when she puts the skirt on, it's an exception for me.

I like to think everything she does is an exception for me, but I know there are parts of her darker than most people, and they were alive long before we met.

It's probably why we fit so perfectly together at the same time we repel one another with stormy emotions and strange jealousies. Magnets, but not always attracted.

I want to go to her, but I like watching too.

I'm not sure how long she stays that way, her head bowed, her work done for now, me against the bookshelf, waiting patiently to approach her.

I have no desire to move. I could stand here all night, looking over as she fell asleep. I want to know why she's been avoiding me outside of class, but when she's in view, there's no urgency to ask anything at all.

Eventually, though, the spell is broken.

She sighs, audibly, and pushes away from the table, her fingertips pressed against the ledge after she drops her hands and looks at her notebook.

I see it, then, the moment she senses someone is here.

Her shoulders tense, her chin lifting slightly even before she looks away from her notepad. Her grip seems to tighten on the ledge of the table, and slowly, she picks her head up.

Her lips part, the smallest of startled gasps escaping her pretty mouth, and I smile at her as I straighten from the shelf, then walk toward her, my hands still in my pockets.

Her eyes track my movements, and I stand on the opposite side of the round table, glancing at her notebook. She abruptly closes it, flipping it over, too, as if it adds an extra layer of protection from me. She keeps her palm flat on the dark green notebook, her other hand still clenching the ledge of the table, big eyes on mine and her red lips pulled into the slightest frown. There's a crease between her brow, and I want to kiss it and smooth it away.

"What're you doing here?" Her voice is low, in accordance with unwritten library protocol. I like it. The quiet makes me feel like we're the only two people in the world.

"I had practice." I lift one shoulder in a shrug, my thighs pressing against the table. I don't sit down or walk around toward her. "I called you."

She glances at her checkered bag on the padded seat next to her chair, and I assume her phone is in there, although I can't see it. "My ringer is off."

"Why have you been avoiding me?"

Her cheeks flush pink in the orange glow of lights overhead from the chandeliers in the library. "I haven't." We both know it's a lie, and I don't bother calling her out on it.

I lift one hand to my choker, grazing the shallow cut beneath it.

She watches, worrying her lower lip between her teeth, and I imagine she's thinking of the photos I sent her last week.

She loops her hair behind her ears and drops both hands in her lap, under the table, leaving her notebook unguarded. "I just needed to catch up on work."

I bring my hand to the back of the chair closest me, curling my fingers over it. "Yeah?"

She nods once. "This weekend I'm going to Wilmington."

I think about Coach Pensky, the tournament, and anger flashes hot through me she has plans without me. "Why?"

"To visit my friend, from my old school."

I think of Nic. The initials under her wrist. I press my fingers further into the seatback as I remember her words about her brother's friend. I don't know if it was him or not. "Who?"

"Amanda."

I feel the slightest measure of relief, but I don't release my grip on the chair. "Amanda." I repeat the name like it's foreign to me because she's never mentioned it.

"Yeah."

"And Nic?"

She rolls her eyes, looking up at the ceiling. "No."

"Who was it, Sebastian's friend, the one you told me about?" My voice sounds cold to my own ears, and I quickly debate the chances of me blowing off my match this weekend. But since Baca is out, and the team needs the win, and I hate to lose... the chances are slim.

But I can convince her to come. Later.

Eden, surprisingly, doesn't visibly react to my question. Her eyes are still on the ceiling. "It wasn't Nic," she says, like she knows that's what I want to know specifically.

"Who was it?"

"I don't remember his name."

I'm not sure if I believe her. "Are you lying?"

She drops her eyes to me, tilting her head and crossing her arms as she sits up straighter in her chair, resting her elbows on the table. "No."

"How many guys have you obsessed over, before me?"

She narrows her eyes. "You tell me first. How many serious relationships, before me?"

I pull out the chair I'm holding onto and slowly sit, mimicking her posture, arms crossed and on the table as we stare off at one another. "You really want to know?"

She doesn't look away. "Yes."

I smile at her, and I see her shoulders tense, a muscle in her neck shifting as she braces herself. "No one."

She waits.

"I've dated," I continue, shrugging. "Casually. I wasn't a virgin when we met. I've fucked someone in administration, here." *It's how I know all about you.*

She has a great poker face, but she can't stop the reddening of her cheeks.

"When I was in Idaho—and I've been a few times, you know—I took what I could get. Often, it came at a price."

"What kind of price?" She says nothing about anything else, and I admire the way she holds back. I'm not sure I could do the same. Not when it comes to her.

"Do you know why people like me are so self-destructive?"

She shakes her head a fraction.

"We're bored. It takes a lot to spike our adrenaline. The price was often some sort of danger, because we seek out thrills, and usually, the most exciting things to us are illegal, or, at the very least, immoral. When you don't care about much, least of all what other people think, you're not held in check by things like laws or the opinions of the masses." I lift my fingers, drumming them once against my bicep. "It can be freeing. But the consequences are always waiting in the wings."

"But you don't care about those either, do you?"

I smile at her. "Not particularly, although I do not want to spend the rest of my life in a cell, whether it be prison or a hospital. I can think of no greater punishment than that. I'd rather be dead."

"I'd rather you live."

There's a lightness in my chest when she says those words. "I could," I tell her honestly. "With you."

She shifts in her seat.

"Like I said, there's been no one like you for me. Fucking, sure; brief, emotional encounters, yeah." I take a breath, glancing at the table between us. "But even when we aren't touching, like now, even when we just text, or when I hold your hand, or you're sitting in my passenger seat… I feel high."

She swallows as I drag my gaze back up to hers.

"I've never felt that way about such little things with anyone, ever before."

"So, I'm like crashing your car, or going over the speed limit, or burning down a house?"

I roll my eyes, smiling despite it. "Yeah, but you're better because I can have sex with you too, and housefires and fucking are never a good idea. Smoke inhalation, you know?"

She snorts, bringing her nails to her mouth, but she drops them quickly as she catches herself in the habit.

"For the record," I continue, "I've never crashed a car or burned down a house."

The corners of her mouth even out, no longer pulled into a smile. "What have you done?" It's a whispered question, each word enunciated clearly, and for some reason, the little hairs on the back of my neck stand on end. I told her about my involvement with Winslet, and even though I don't think it's much, I've never told anyone else that, because it would seem like *something*, when I didn't want to tangle myself further into her. The reason being all the things I did *before* she disappeared.

The things Eden wants to know about now.

But I fix her with a stare because there's no longer any point in holding back. She's going to stay. "I used to draw guns and knives, when I was a kid, and everyone else was drawing their family or animals and sunrises and shit. The teachers were disturbed, had a few conferences with my parents." I run my tongue over my top lip, the choker feeling uncomfortably tight around my neck. *I don't feel uncomfortable, but I know how this sounds, to people who aren't inside my head.* "I pushed a kid from the playground, and he was knocked out. Once upon a time, I peed on a few kids because they were assholes. I made sure to do it outside, around the corner of the school, so no one would see me."

Eden doesn't react.

I keep talking. *"Callous and unemotional traits."* I mimic the language the psychiatrists used with my parents. I overheard Mom and Dad talking about it in low voices on the drive back from one of the local hospital's psychiatric wards. "I had never cried much as a baby, and even less as a kid. I can't tell you the last time I did." It's a lie. I remember the last time. When I was thirteen, but I don't bring it up now. "My parents couldn't beat remorse out of me, not that they tried very often. They couldn't ground me into being sorry or take away toys for me to feel bad." I take a deep breath, moving onto the next thing. "Mom used to throw celery to the rabbits in our backyard. She'd coax them out in the spring, little families of them with brown and white fur." I can see them so clearly in my head, and Mom's excited smile as she spotted them. She never smiled at me that way. "I never liked to feed them."

Eden tightens her fingers around her biceps, but otherwise, doesn't move and she doesn't look away.

"But they came to her with the celery. She'd hold it out, by the pool sometimes when I was swimming, her eyes on them instead of me, and they'd slowly reach her, close enough to touch. Anyway... the first time I went to Montford, it was because I did the same. I coaxed one over, and when it pulled the end of the celery stalk from my fingers, I grabbed it by the back of its neck."

Eden's face goes pale, but she still has her big, beautiful eyes on mine.

I smile at her. "It makes a crunchy sound, and you can *feel* the bones snap, when you twist their necks. I could feel his pulse, too, faster than yours, even."

Her lips are pressed together, and I wonder how quick her heart is beating right now.

"And all that fur, all that skin, it takes more than you'd think to break through it with a rock. But the skull is tiny, and it's not a lot, to crush it." I sigh, glancing at the ceiling. "When Dad found out about it, they took me to Idaho for the first time."

I don't speak for long moments, just staring at my girl, letting it sink in, wondering what she's thinking about me.

Then she asks, "What about the next time?"

I think about Mom holding me under the water. Her telling Dad about it. He didn't let her give me many baths after that, but I'm not sure he took it very seriously. Or maybe he didn't really know what to do about it. Or maybe... maybe he half-hoped she'd kill me.

"The next time." I repeat Eden's words, the smallest smile curving my lips. "I've been half a dozen times, *Nightmare Girl.*"

She blinks.

"Not always long-term stays, because of course, Dad has appearances to maintain, and Mom couldn't be fucked enough to spend that much time away from home, her cocoon of a room. Sometimes there were only check-ins, because sometimes I behaved very well. Dominic and Luna helped. Puppets to play with, you know. I didn't have to resort to violence. They'd do whatever I wanted. We'd steal shit from the mall, once upon a time I got Luna to flirt with some drunk guys on the coast at the beach house, and when they started touching her, Dominic and I jumped all three of the guys. Not because I was jealous, but for something to *do.*"

"What happened with your mom, Eli?"

I lift my brows. "All of that, and you want to ask what the fuck happened with my mom? Were you listening?"

She doesn't back down. "Tell me when she left."

I slide my arms from the table and lean back in my seat, curling my hands into fists in my lap. "I was thirteen." I hate the fact my voice sounds so rough, like it's hard to talk about. It shouldn't be hard. It's been five fucking years. Still, I don't look at Eden. I stare at the fireplace, the lingering of ash from the last time it was used still inside the grate. I start to imagine pushing Eden's face into it.

I start to think terrible things about her.

I hate this part of my brain.

"Why did she go?" Her voice cuts through my violent visions.

I don't want anyone to hurt you, but what if I slip up one day? What if, one day, I can't fucking help myself with you?

I stand, pushing back so hard from the table as I do, my chair tips back, clattering against the polished floors of the library. The sound is loud in such a quiet room, and my pulse roars in my ears as I glare at Eden.

"If I knew that, don't you think I'd have figured out how to *make her stay?*"

Eden stands slowly, but her shoulders are pushed back, her chin lifted high, nose in the air. It's how she walks at Trafalgar, like she owns the fucking place even though everyone's parents in this school make more money in a year than her family will probably see in a goddamn lifetime.

"You couldn't have stopped her." Her voice is low, but even.

"We're not talking about this."

"There's nothing you could have done."

But there is. Dad trapped her, and I could have… well, I could have fucking killed him. Now, what's the point? She's gone, and she's not coming back.

"There is," I correct her, a horrible grin stretching my face.

I can *feel* the disgust from her when she sees it, but she doesn't visibly show it. "I could have stopped her."

"How, Eli? Tie her up in your basement? She was an adult. You were thirteen."

"She was trapped, and depressed, and they fought all the time." I don't need to tell her who *they* are. "And she understood me, but he never understood either of us."

Eden laughs. It shocks me, and I take a step back from the table, putting more distance between us. *"She* understood you?" She shakes her head, closing her eyes a second as if my stupidity astounds her. "She didn't understand you. I don't think anyone has *ever* understood you, Eli. She was in over her head, and she couldn't see your potential. Your greatness."

"I don't need you to feed my fucking ego. It's big enough as is, thanks."

"You're terrible, too," she keeps talking, but in a placating way, like she's conceding a point to what I just said. Her fingertips graze the table, and they don't tremble. "You are *awful*. Everything you just told me, what you watched Winslet do, and you didn't tell *anyone*, when they could have found her *alive*. Even how you speak about people, your disregard for everyone around you, you are a *tragic* human being, Eli."

This is what I want to hear. It's what I need. I need her to see how disgusting I am, and I need her to admit she can't fucking handle it. *Run away, baby girl.* Or, at the very least, *try.*

"But you aren't too far gone."

I laugh. A cold, wicked sound. "You are delusional."

"Maybe," she admits. "But would you ever hurt me?"

I give her a look. *I already have,* it says.

She smiles. "In a way I didn't like?" Her words are seductive as she dips her chin.

"Do you want to know the truth?" *Do you want to know what I was just thinking about doing to you?* I glance at the fireplace, only for a second.

She pauses for a moment, not moving, not speaking. Then she walks around the table, fingertips of one hand still gliding along the wooden surface. She approaches me, but I back up. We do this dance until I'm against a shelf, book spines digging into mine.

Her fingers come to the choker around my throat, her head tilted up to meet my eyes. She splays one hand over my chest, fingers wide. Her index finger slips under the leather band, grazing the shallow cut on my skin.

"Would you ever hurt me, Eli?" she asks again, our bodies so close, I can feel her warmth. I can smell her as well, the peach scent of her shampoo, and her own fragrance, soft like violets, and wild too. She scrapes her nail against the scab of my cut.

My hands are by my sides as I stare at her, thinking about her question. *If you left me, maybe. Because you can't walk out like Mom did. I learned from that mistake. The worst part is knowing Mom is still alive, happy and thriving, somewhere without me.*

I think about ash. The fireplace. *I don't know what I would do to you, sometimes, nightmare girl.*

"No." It's a lie.

She knows, and her bland smile shows it. "Would you try to stop yourself?"

"Not if you walked away from me."

"That isn't love." She doesn't sound angry about it, and she's still touching me, her hand over my heart, the pulse in my throat.

"I don't care. It is for me."

"This is the type of relationship they write books about," she says, glancing at my mouth as she steps between my feet, her breasts grazing my core. "It never ends well."

I clench my hands into fists as she keeps her eyes on my lips. "This isn't a fucking book."

"You can learn a lot from stories."

"Write a different one. Just for us."

"You're so obsessed with the idea of me never leaving you," she lifts her eyes to mine, peering at me through her lashes, "but have you ever stopped to think you'll grow bored of this soon, and leave *me?*"

My mouth goes dry. No. I never have, although it's a possibility, I guess.

"You said I'm a high. But I'm not an adrenaline junkie like you. I like dangerous things, but I cling to people, Eli."

I glance at the bracelets along her wrists. I want her to tell me he was different. I'm not him, because if she's to be believed, she hasn't spoken to him since she moved, which means she easily forgot about him and moved on to me.

Could she do the same with us? Out of sight, out of mind?

"What happens when I become less useful for fulfilling your craving for excitement?"

I don't answer her immediately. Instead, I reach for her wrist, the one at my throat, and watch as she startles, just slightly. One day, she'll tell me the story about her brother's stupid fucking friend, and I'll get a name, and I will murder whoever it is who hurt her.

For now, I wrap my fingers around her wrist and press my thumb to her pulse point, feeling how rapidly her blood pumps through her veins.

I swallow down the dryness in my throat before I start to speak. "My mom used to run the bath water, after a fight with Dad. It gave her some kind of peace, drowning out the noise of her thoughts, maybe." I bring her hand to my mouth, sucking on her index finger, then her middle, her ring. I lick a line down that one, biting the top of her knuckle lightly.

Her eyes are fixed on my mouth, and I keep her fingertips against my bottom lip as I keep talking.

"You're kind of like that, for me."

She steps even closer, only her hand between us, still over my heart. My body grows warm, blood rushing to my cock at her nearness, her scent, her gaze rapt on me.

"It's not just adrenaline, or *excitement.*" I dismiss the word. "You... You're what water was to Mom. Something that soothes. Water can be still, or... or rapid. Calm, or dangerous."

I bring her hand to my chest, so both are against me, then I wrap my arms around her body, jerking her close so she can feel how much I want her.

She smiles, digging her fingers into my shirt.

"You're all of that to me. It's the best part of you. You're so many fucking things, and I don't really know when it happened, kind of like how it's hard to tell when the ocean turns from safe enough to extremely fucking risky, but I'm in love with you. And maybe it's obsession, and maybe you don't believe me, or you think it means less because I'm wired differently."

She tilts her head, her eyes fixed on mine.

"But it feels real to me. If you were to ever leave, I just don't think I could breathe without you."

There's a long stretch of silence. I have no idea what she's thinking. My fingers are against her spine, just over her hips, and my blood is hot in my veins, and I want to kiss her and hurt her and fuck her, but I don't move.

Until she drags one hand down my chest and pulls at the waistband of my pants.

Then she's dropping to her knees, kneeling between my feet, pulling down my sweats and my boxers, circling her fingers over my cock, one hand pressed to my hip, keeping me against the bookshelf.

"Eden." Her name is a groan from my lips. I relax against the shelves, tipping my head up and back, my fingers in her hair, pulling the clip free, letting it drop to the floor.

Her tongue is warm, her hand, too, and she digs her nails into my hip with her other, a sharp sting with the pleasure.

She's just teasing me, though, flicking her tongue along the head of my cock, a soft moan from her throat as she tastes my precum. It occurs to me she probably doesn't know how to do anything *other* than tease me.

I tilt my head down as she licks me like she would a lollipop.

Her eyes find mine, big and sexy and submissive, and her

cheeks are flushed pink as she pulls back, her hand still wrapped around me. She doesn't know what to do.

"Open your mouth," I tell her.

My chest is heaving, waiting for her to do as I say.

"Now, suck it. As much as you can. Move your head back and forth." I tighten my grip in her hair.

She closes her eyes, like she's embarrassed to look at me, and takes me in her mouth. Just the tip, at first, but she's good, now that her lips are a tight seal around me.

I push her head further onto me, and her eyes fly open, looking up at me as I keep going, until she gags around my cock, saliva dripping from her lips.

I pull her quickly off of me.

"Are you okay?" My voice is a jagged whisper.

She drops her hand from my hip and wipes the back of it over her mouth, but she nods. Then she tightens her hold on my dick and deepthroats me again, all on her own. She has a gag reflex, but it's hot, feeling her throat tighten around me.

I help her with the pace, my hand in her hair.

She sucks even without my urging, gagging as she does, but she doesn't stop.

"*Fuck.*" It's a ragged sound I can't hold back.

Her hair is so soft and thick beneath my fingers, strangely, the feel of it only heightens my pleasure, because every inch of her is so fucking perfect.

My eyes flutter closed for a second as she sucks me, then I watch her knees shift on the polished hardwood floors, knowing she'll have bruises tomorrow, and I take pleasure in that, too.

Because they're from doing something for me.

She'd hurt herself, for me, and the perverseness of it drives me faster to my release, my core tightening with the feel of her wet little mouth clamped tight around me, her nails digging into my hips. I guide one of her hands to cup my balls, and groan with the feel of it as I squeeze her fingers tighter over me.

A rush of what must be love warms every muscle in my body, including my heart.

Then I feel her teeth.

A gentle nip, it's enough to catch my attention, and I jerk her back by her hair, saliva connecting the tip of my cock to her swollen, red lips.

"What the fuck do you think you're doing?" I ask her, my voice stern, but I'm not mad.

The look she gives me is innocent, even though she is anything but, down at my feet after everything I just told her.

"Don't be sweet." She says the words as a whisper, a plea, pink filling her cheeks.

Then she's taking me into her mouth again, all the way back, gagging on my cock, her body jolting as she heaves.

I gather her hair into a makeshift ponytail, jerking her head up, her eyes searching mine, begging for what she asked for, and I reach for her nose.

My entire body trembles marginally as I stop her from breathing, my fingers pinching her nostrils.

"Don't stop," I tell her, shoving and pulling and guiding her head with her hair in my hands, like a leash. "I'm not done."

She makes a strangled sound in her throat, and I feel it vibrate against my dick.

I bite my lip, watching the pink of her cheeks turn to a splotchy red along her face, down her neck, those buttons all done up like she's a goddamn angel.

She is anything but. She is a fucking *nightmare*, leading me into temptation instead of trying to guide me out.

I smile at the way she's digging her nails into my thighs now, both of her hands pushing away as she tries to turn her head, because she needs to take a breath.

But she doesn't want me to let it go that easily.

She wouldn't have asked for it if she did.

Besides, now she's grinding herself against my shoe, her cunt rocking back and forth along the top of it like she's a starved, desperate little whore. So many facets to her, she makes my fucking head spin.

When I see a vein in her temple strain against her skin, I release my hold on her nose and cup her face, tracing her lips around my cock with my thumb as she breathes, her chest rising and falling before she starts to suck me harder, faster, her eyes on mine.

"God, you're so fucking good, baby girl." I keep my thumb on her bottom lip, stretched tight around me, and ask, "Do you want me to come?"

She nods, making a sound over my dick.

"Yeah?" The word is barely more than a breath because I'm so fucking close. I glance at the muscles of her thighs flexing as she moves, her poor knees ground into the floor.

She nods again, her cheeks hollow, her eyes wide and full of love.

"I want you to swallow all of it, do you understand?"

She's eager, nodding again.

My body feels like it's on fire, my stomach twisted into a pleasurable knot, pulled lower, tighter, until I'm grabbing her nose again, stopping her breath, and I'm coming inside her warm mouth as she bucks her hips, getting her own pleasure from my fucking shoe.

"Fuck, Eden." I knock my head back against the bookshelf, still coming, still holding her nose as I look down at her through my lashes, watching her come apart on my foot as everything comes out of me, and I can barely fucking breathe myself.

Finally, *finally*, I release her.

She grabs my cock so she can pull her mouth off of me but still stroke me, and as she tips her head up, her mouth parted, gasping, I see my cum on her tongue, saliva dripping from the corners of her mouth.

"Eli," she whimpers, grabbing my thigh, still stroking me, the aftershocks enough to make me tremble. "Eli, *baby.*" Her eyes are closed, but when she calls me "baby" like she did the first time, I feel like I could fall to my fucking knees.

And when she's done, hanging her head, her shoulders moving as she heaves gasping breaths, I slowly uncurl her fingers from my dick, pull up my boxers and my pants, and sink to the floor, pushing her down onto her back as I kneel between her thighs.

I lift up her skirt and see the wetness along her white panties. I reach for it, running my thumb over her slit, and she whimpers, her eyes on me. I slip my thumb beneath the edge of her underwear, and I groan at how fucking wet she is as I push into her with ease.

I bring one hand down beside her head and my body is over hers. Dipping my head, I kiss her, and her lips part for me as she moans, grabbing my damp hair, holding my head to hers. I keep fingering her as her tongue swirls with mine and I taste me on her.

It makes me hard all over again, and I could fuck her right here.

I pull my thumb out, gliding it up to her swollen clit, circling her as she moans, bucking her hips.

Then I just can't take it anymore, and I shove down my pants all over again, move aside her underwear, and fuck her there, on the floor of the goddamn library, her legs tangled around my waist, her nails digging into the back of my neck.

It takes me longer, and I enjoy her more, and when the second orgasm shatters through me, I pull out so I can watch my cum coat her pussy, her thighs spread wide as she snatches up her skirt, to give me a good view. Then I press the heel of my hand against her clit, over my own cum, and shift it in circles until she's coming, too, calling out my name as she falls apart beneath me.

Afterward, I pull up her underwear without cleaning her up, and I help her to her feet.

She's dizzy, leaning against my chest as I hold her, my back supported by the bookcase.

I kiss the top of her head, the smell of sex mingling with the scent of all these old books.

A little laugh escapes her lips.

I speak against her hair. "What is it, baby?"

"The librarian," she says shyly. "What if she saw?"

"She probably watched and fingered herself while she did."

Eden jerks back, a frown marring her swollen lips. "I'll kill her," she says viciously.

I laugh, pleased with her protectiveness. But I thread my fingers through hers, between us. "She can watch," I tell her. "Just, no one can touch."

It's a warning, more than a joke.

Eden smiles, and I know she's going to say something fucking smart. "Unless we agree."

I try to imagine it. Someone else touching her, even with my *agreement*. "All right," I say slowly, keeping my anger in check. "As long as I get to kill whoever touched you immediately afterward."

She licks her lips, and I think about how they felt around my dick. I don't want anyone else to feel that, ever again from her. "Deal," she says, like she means it.

I don't think she realizes though I actually *would* murder someone for touching her.

It's like she didn't pay attention to the story about the rabbit at all.

But I know she did, because later, as I'm walking her to my car, my arm around her shoulders, she looks at me in the darkness of the parking lot and asks, "So, no pets, then?"

I shove her against the side of my car, and it takes a lot of self-control to only kiss her instead of fuck her again.

Eden

I REACH for the handle of Mom's van, glancing at the cloudy day. Two have passed since the library, and I've been grounded both, because I was supposed to call Sebastian for a ride home, or Mom, but I didn't, and she was waiting for me at the front door when Eli dropped me off.

She was polite enough to him, probably because of his ever-present charm towards her, but she snatched my phone from my hand as soon as Eli drove off. Reece had a long-winded lecture to deliver, and this time, I didn't argue or talk back.

I was still buzzing from Eli's high.

"You told Scott you're away this weekend, right?"

I fix my eyes on a cloud, backpack over one shoulder, and I grip the door handle tighter. "Yes, Mom."

She sighs, and I know she isn't done yet. I want to get out and slam the damn door, but I know I'll get my phone back sooner if I don't.

"Eden."

I grind my teeth together, but somehow manage to make my, *"What?"* sound less hostile than I feel.

"Do you know he's texted you sixty-three times?"

I close my eyes tight, resting my temple against the cool glass. I know she hasn't read my texts, because neither her nor Reece know my passcode, and I turned off my notification previews before Eli dropped me off, knowing I would be in trouble.

He doesn't know I got my phone taken away, or that I'm grounded. I told him yesterday my phone died Tuesday night and I fell asleep before I could charge it, even though I've barely slept at all. Today, I'm sure he'll ask me what the hell happened to my phone *last night*. For some reason, I don't want him to know I'm in trouble. I'm not sure why. Maybe I don't want him to hate my parents. Part of me wants to protect him from their suspicions. I know he doesn't have many feelings left to hurt, but if I can spare him any damage, I'll try.

"Probably memes," I lie, because I don't know what else to say. *Dammit, Eli.* I have to tell him now, and I knew I would today before we have to spend the weekend apart. He mentioned his wrestling tournament, telling me to cancel with Amanda, but I told him I already did because I have work, which is a lie. I just didn't want him to think I was choosing someone over him.

Now I'll have to come clean.

Mom says nothing at my back. I know she doesn't believe my bullshit.

"It's... a lot," she says softly.

I curl my fingers tighter around my backpack strap. Yeah, it is. It's Eli. *He's a lot.* He's perfect for me. The thought of sixty-three messages to read doesn't scare me. If anything, I'm excited, but I give none of that away to Mom.

She sighs again, ultimately deciding to drop it. "We'll have fun this weekend, okay? I'll pick you up early tomorrow so we can go then instead of Saturday." She's adopted a tone of false cheer, and I don't believe her, but I really, *really* want to go to

Eli's beach house on Halloween because then we have fall break afterward, and I'll probably lie and say I'm with Luna, but she won't let me go anywhere if I don't behave.

"Yeah," I say, turning to give her a fake smile. "We will."

She reaches for my shoulder, and I bite my tongue, refusing to flinch as I see the jagged scar on her arm. "Have a good day, okay? I'll be right here when school lets out." She drops her hand and I nod, still smiling as I get out of the van, closing the door softly behind me when I really want to break the thing off its hinges.

Immediately, someone falls into step with me, and at first, I think it's Eli. I spin around, looking for Mom's green van, hoping she doesn't see.

But then Dominic speaks, and my attention goes to him as I stop walking, arching a brow up at him.

"Nice van," he says, flashing a smile that doesn't quite meet his tired eyes. I guess him and I are both full of shit today.

I shake my head, hands by my sides as I turn from him and head up the walkway to the propped open red door of Castle Hall.

He walks beside me, hands in his pockets, and I glance at his boat shoes. A different pair from his white ones, these are tan. I give him another quick look and note the circles beneath his eyes, a breakout on his chin, and his roots are freshly bleached. He's squinting from the sun as he looks ahead, a rare break in cloud cover for the day, but I can tell he's a million miles away from here.

I'm surprised he's been back at school. I know Winslet was missing for a year, and the news about her death is a couple weeks old, but still. It seems like a lot to process in such a short amount of time, particularly when there are no answers. Then again, I've never had loss touch me so close before. I know people can die. I like graveyards, and reminders of death. Flirting with it, like when Eli takes my breath away.

But it's never got its hooks in me, not yet.

"Luna wants to be your friend, you know?"

I almost trip over my own two feet, black boots scuffing on the stone walkway. I reach for the metal divider between the small set of stairs we were headed up, balancing myself. "What?" I ask, my mouth dry. Luna and I haven't really spoken much recently, didn't talk at Eli's latest party, and we rarely see each other during the school day.

"You good?" Dom asks, amusement sparking in his eyes as we get up the steps and keep walking, people brushing by us, some guys calling his name. He throws up his hand, and I see one of the people he's waving at has a Trafalgar Swim hoodie on, and it does not say "dragons."

I make a note to ask Eli about the dragonfly wrestling one.

"Shut up," I murmur, a blush grazing my cheeks as I do, but I stare straight ahead. Dominic doesn't know about the code word. I clear my throat. "Why are you telling me this? Has she told you that?"

"Yes. She misses him, and since he's obsessed with *you*, well..." He shrugs.

"I'm a way to get to him, in other words?" I keep my eyes on the mass of students heading through the open door.

"Sure," Dom says. "She's not half bad, really."

I snort in reply.

"What has she ever done to you, though, seriously?" Dominic asks, and I note an edge to his words. He's protective over her, maybe over their bizarre relationship, and the one they had with Eli. He probably believes I stole him away, too.

Thunder rumbles somewhere above the castle.

"She straddled him right in front of me," I answer Dom's question. "And *you.*"

He makes a dismissive noise in the back of his throat. "That's child's play compared to what they used to do."

Used to do. I like those words, but I don't say anything about them. "Well, she's not going to do even *that* now. We're dating."

Dominic nods as I slide a glance his way, gauging his reaction. Eli and I made it official, when he told me I was his girlfriend in the car at the park, but we never *announced* it or anything, so I didn't know if Dominic or Luna knew.

"Yeah, she knows," he confirms.

A burst of glee thrums through my chest. "She does?"

We're a few feet from the entrance, and I can feel the A/C, still running inside the castle. It's chilly, because the weather has cooled off the past couple of days, but I'd rather be cold than hot, since I sweat so much as it is. Still, even knowing the coolness is waiting for me, I stop, turning to look up at Dom. He faces me, too, a furrow between his brows despite the playful half-smile on his lips.

"He told her."

A flush of irritation rolls through me, and I'm not even sure why. I guess I just want to know when he told her, why, how it came up. But then that thought replaces another. The things I've been scribbling in my notebook. The shit I can't let go of. All the things I don't know.

"Dominic."

He stands a little straighter. We're off the walkway, people passing by us, and I know Eli could, too, sometime soon, but I can't wait anymore. It's like a need in my head, no filter for my mouth.

"What motive would Eli have for hurting your sister?"

His eyes widen, and he glances around us, like he's looking for eavesdroppers. But I just don't care. I'm shifting from foot to foot, shaking my head, all the things I've been thinking about coming to the surface.

"I mean, when you came to his house…" I trail off, thinking about my notes. My conclusion. What Eli told me, but I keep that confession wrapped up tight in my head. "You were accusing him, and you said he went to that place, in Idaho—"

"For a long time," Dom confirms, his teeth gritted. "Went there instead of prison. He came back in the spring…" He trails off, his voice breaking as he drops his gaze to the ground. "I don't think he did it though," he finally says, eyes finding mine through his lashes.

I feel a little dizzy. "What? You said—"

"I was drunk." He says the words with finality. "He didn't do it."

"Then what do you think—"

"I don't know." He looks up at the sky, another rumble of thunder closer now. He still doesn't drop his gaze, and I watch lightning reflect from his eyes.

"Did they ever sleep together?" I just blurt it out, my speech rapid, my thoughts too, as Dom's eyes flash on mine. I know they did, but I want Dom's side of the story. It's like he told me, right? It's interesting to see all sides of it. "I mean, I was thinking, if they did, maybe she was trying to make him jealous by disappearing with someone else or—"

Dominic shakes his head, his teeth gritted. "They didn't sleep together." He says it so forcefully, I don't even think *he* thinks it's true.

You're lying, you're lying, you're lying. But why? Is he covering for Eli… or is he covering for himself?

I worked this all out. Eli watched her walk off, but Dom doesn't know, and she was probably in love with Eli like everyone is and she made a wrong choice by getting in someone's car, and maybe they hurt her and dumped her body in the lake and—

"Are you okay?" Dom interrupts my thoughts.

I still. I have no idea what I looked like just then, going over all these things inside my head. I nod once, slowly. "Yes." I force myself to speak slow too.

Dom stares at me.

A bell rings from inside the school, loud and ominous, a low note. My heart thuds in my chest. There's all this *energy* inside of me, and I don't want to go sit in class, but I don't really have much choice. Besides, Eli is in there.

"Look," Dom says quietly, "I know I've been a shit. I'm sorry." He shakes his head. "Eli said you guys were going to the beach house for Halloween. There's a memorial for Winslet because it was her favorite holiday, from my parents, for all

Dad's *co-workers.*" He snarls the last word. "I don't wanna go. Do you think…" He drops his gaze again. To the ground.

Thunder booms around us.

Rain starts to fall, light on my skin.

"You think me and Luna could come, to the beach house? Maybe Janelle? Jasper?" He lifts his gaze to mine. "I know it's a lot to ask. It just might be nice, all of us together. We were close, before."

Before you. What he doesn't say.

I have no inclination to say no. I just nod, stupidly, a few times. Maybe Luna isn't so bad, but even if she is, the idea of a party, right now in this moment, seems appealing. Besides, I'm only half here, thinking about Dom's insistence Eli didn't sleep with Winslet. The aggressiveness in his tone. *Someone is lying.* "Sure, yeah."

Dom smiles, just a half tip of his lips. "Thanks, E."

I nod, turning to the open door, the empty commons inside the school. "We're late, let's go." And surprising myself, I reach for him, grabbing his arm, and he comes willingly, the two of us walking inside together.

I drop his arm and he hurries alongside me as we both head into the cold hallway. Sweat is damp at the nape of my neck and I'm grateful for the A/C as we stroll down the corridor.

I glance at Dom before we get to the second intersection, where we split. "I'm going away this weekend," I tell him. "Keep an eye on him." I don't need to specify who, and I see Dom's slow smile.

He nods once. "You got it." Then he winks at me as he walks backwards a couple of steps before he spins around and heads to his class.

When I duck into Latin, unsure of just how late I am, I *feel* Eli's gaze on me before I see it. I mutter an apology to Ms. Romano who breaks off from her lecture for only half a second before she picks it back up again.

Eli's green eyes lock on mine, his posture casual, a pen in

hand, tapping against his desk, but I see something in his eyes. As I make my way to the back of the class on shaky legs, I puzzle over it. Not anger, or jealousy, even.

Something else, the way he seemed to sag a little in his chair.

Relief.

It was relief.

HE'S WAITING FOR ME AFTER CLASS. WE HAD TO PAIR OFF FOR A major translation project, but we didn't get to choose our partners. Mine—Ansel—smiles at me before he swings his bag over his shoulder, running a hand down his blazer.

I return the smile and watch Ansel's lanky frame pass by Eli, leaning against the wall by the door. He, too, watches Ansel, and he has a strange smile on his face as he does.

I tuck my hair behind my ears and meet Eli at the door, feeling Ms. Romano's eyes on me as we leave together.

"Why're you looking at Ansel like that?" I ask, not wanting to talk about the sixty-three texts and the fact I'm grounded.

Eli's smile curves higher, and my gaze, as always, is drawn to his mouth. His lips are just so pretty and full, and he looks slightly evil when he smiles, like his charm is cracking, especially now as his elbow grazes my shoulder and he says, "Like what?"

I'm sweating all over again with the feigned innocence of his words, even in the coolness of the hallway. "I don't know. You had a creepy little look."

He stops as we approach his locker bank, and I don't realize he's backing me up into it without touching me until my backpack zipper clanks against the metal of the lockers.

He places a palm beside my head, his focus wholly on me. "A creepy little look?" he repeats, his tone teasing.

I find it hard to breathe and when I do manage it, I'm inhaling his scent and I'm thinking of going down on him

Wednesday night and how good he felt coming in my mouth and—

"See, now *you* have a look."

I blink, my chest growing hot. "I don't know what you're talking about."

He tilts his head, nudging his nose to mine. "You look like you want to get on your knees for me all over again, *baby.*"

I suck in a breath, thinking of what I called him that night. I couldn't have stopped myself if I'd tried. "Shut up."

His laugh is soft against my mouth. "I can't hit you here. They wouldn't understand."

I knock my head back against his locker, rolling my eyes. I want to disagree with him. Private schools host strange people, case in point Eli and his posse. But I don't say anything as he pulls back, putting a little space between us.

I dip my chin and see his eyes searching mine.

"You didn't text me last night." All playfulness is gone from his voice.

I slide my hands up and down the straps of my bags, my palms growing clammy. "I know, I…"

He lifts a brow, waiting, and since it's Thursday and starting tomorrow we'll be apart all weekend anyway, I just tell him the truth. "I got my phone taken away. I'm grounded."

He studies me for a second, and I think he's looking for a lie, but he must find the truth instead because he just asks, "Why?"

I don't want to tell him, because it'll make things weird between Eli and Mom and Reece. I don't care about the latter, and I'll be leaving both of the others next year, but until then…

"What's wrong, Eden?" Eli doesn't touch me, but he's very close, and I hate the concern in his gaze. I feel guilty he doesn't ask, *what did you do wrong? How did you get into trouble?*

He doesn't care what I do wrong. He doesn't care if I'm trouble. He only cares about me. I sometimes feel as if I could tell him I murdered my entire family and he wouldn't say a word except to ask if I needed help cleaning up the blood.

It's dangerous. *We're* dangerous. One day, if we kept this course, we'd do something very, very dangerous, together. I'm not sure I'd hate it.

"Mom wanted me to put some distance between us." I blurt it all out, quick and fast. I drop my gaze to his chest, broad and beautiful beneath the dark gray blazer clinging to him. "She probably knows I'm lying about my sleepovers with Luna," I trip over her name, "and Janelle and… yeah." I lick my lips, debating my next words, but I decide to say them, so he doesn't take any of this personally. "She just wants to make sure I'm focused on school. That I'm not… like she was." I keep staring at his chest, waiting for him to speak cruelly of my mom.

But all he says is, "When do you get it back?" I lift my gaze to his and he must see my confusion because he adds, "Your phone?"

I'm a little startled. "I… I don't know."

He looks annoyed by this answer, cutting his eyes to the floor and shaking his head. "What's wrong with your mom?"

I clear my throat as his eyes find mine again. I realize the halls have cleared and we probably have seconds left to get to class, but I don't care. "What do you mean?"

"Why doesn't she want you to be *like she was?*"

Shame is hot in my chest. "Because… well, she cleans houses, you know, and…" I'm stammering over my words, and I just want to go to my next class and talk about this later. I shake my head. This is a thing I don't like discussing. It's easy to stereotype all of his nice things as "rich boy" stuff, but the truth is there are miles between us in class and wealth and along with those miles come opportunities.

And for him, a lack of worry over how he may be perceived because of his parent's job or his home or car. "I have to go."

But before I can turn away from him, he speaks. "Your

mom raised you. There's nothing wrong with cleaning houses. Someone has to do it. My dad, for one, is grateful for someone like your mom."

I stop, but I don't turn to face him.

"I know why she wants to put distance between us. I understand it. She cares and she's worried."

I'm staring down the hallway, unseeing, only listening.

"People won't understand us, Eden."

My throat feels tight, hairs prickling along the back of my neck, every sense heightened in my body. I wonder if Eli wears a choker because the constant pressure keeps him alert. I wonder if he likes it in the same way I enjoy having my breathing restricted.

Dancing with death.

Do you want to hold the knife this time?

"They don't have to. They wouldn't be able to, even if we could explain it."

He's right. My mom would have me committed if I told her how I feel about him. I don't even understand all the ways I'd die for him or bleed for him or let him hurt me because it's the same, for us, as love. Bruises and butterfly kisses, from him, I wouldn't be able to tell them apart.

Sometimes I wonder if this is another incident waiting to happen. Another attachment and obsession like the one I got in trouble for at Shoreside. Sometimes I feel like I'm flying. But there's always a crash, isn't there?

"But I need a way to get a hold of you this weekend. Do you have a home phone? And does the gym have—"

"I'm not working." He gives me so much. I want to give him honesty, for once.

He's quiet a moment and I keep my face turned away from him. "You're going to see *Amanda.*" He says her name like he hates it.

"Mom is coming." Reece, in a shocking turn of events, decided to stay home and let my mom and I have some time together, alone.

"Why did you lie to me?"

Lies are easy. But I decide to tell him the truth, because of how many he gave me Wednesday night. "I didn't want you to worry, about me seeing… anyone else."

There's a moment's silence. Then, "Look at me."

I do, squeezing my backpack straps tighter as I meet his eyes. He still has his hand planted beside my head.

"You're not going to see *him.*"

I don't know if he means Nic or Richard/Zach, but I just nod once. "I'm not," I agree. I won't.

He drops his hand, then grabs mine from my strap, linking our fingers together. My heartbeat quickens at our touch, but I don't pull away. He squeezes softly, running his thumb over the back of my hand. "Don't lie to me again, okay?"

I know I probably will, but I don't argue. I simply say, "Okay."

40

Eden

MOM GAVE me my phone back for the trip, pulled out an aux cord from inside the center console of the green van and thrust it into my hands. *"You control the music, you get your phone, and a beach vacation. What could possibly go wrong this weekend, hmm?"*

There are a few things, I think, but I said nothing.

"Mount Everest" by Labrinth plays for the thirteenth time in thirty minutes, and Mom smiles at me, cutting her gaze my way, but she says nothing. There're two enormous cups of tea in the cupholders between us, one sweet (hers) and one unsweet (mine).

Mom has finished hers off and is already looking for a place to pull off the highway because she has to pee, and I'm texting Eli. Turns out, he *did* send me a lot of memes. Art and literary ones, including one about *The Ecstasy of St. Teresa* by Lorenzo Bernini, in comparison to a drunk celebrity. I had to bite my tongue to stifle my laughter.

He sent photos of his dad's beach house, which looks like a mini mansion tucked away on the sand, questions about what I was doing, then questions about what the *hell* I was doing. A few threats to come over, concerns for my wellbeing, and sexually suggestive texts about what he planned to do with me when he found out why I was blowing him off (every pun intended).

Now, I tell him where we are on the journey and he sends me a photo of his pool, where *he* is. I miss the chlorine scent wrapped in his already.

I cross one leg over the other, slouching down in my seat as I text him.

"Can I have a milkshake?" I ask Mom at the same time I text Eli.

Me: I miss you, what's wrong with me?

His reply is immediate, as they've all been. **Him: Same thing that's wrong with me.**

I smile to myself, and I hope Mom doesn't notice. I'm sure she realizes I'm texting him, but she's just happy I'm going with her to the coast, she wants to see some of our old neighbors, and probably lie in the sand, without worries of scrubbing toilets or polishing countertops. Thankfully, she hasn't brought him up at all.

Mom laughs. "Sure," she says, sounding a little thrown off. "What kind?"

Me: Favorite ice cream?
Him: Moose tracks.

I swallow down my laughter as I repeat the flavor to Mom, in answer to her question.

She laughs herself. "Guess I need to go somewhere fancy for that."

"Guess so." My eyes are still on my phone, my fingers flying over my screen. For no reason at all, I think of my conversation with Dominic this morning.

Me: I need to tell you something, don't be mad.
Him: Okay...

Biting my tongue, I give him a brief summary of how it came to be Dom and everyone else were invited to Eli's beach house. By me.

"You need to pee?" Mom's voice startles me. I glance over at her, sensing the van has slowed, then take in the small rest stop with a slated roof over a brown building, a few families heading down the sidewalk to the restrooms.

"No, I'm good," I tell Mom, meaning it.

"Be right back, then we'll get the milkshakes." She leaves the van running, the A/C on even though it's a little chilly out. It must be a Rain family trait to sweat without reprieve.

Eli: I'm starting to think Dominic has a crush on you.

I laugh a little. **Me: You just figured it out?**

Him: No, but I've just now seriously considered killing him.

☠

AMANDA IS CURLY RED HAIR AND FRECKLES, AND WITH A popsicle clutched in her hand, she looks like a child. Or maybe just younger than I feel.

Mom is in the kitchen with Manda's mom, cackling at something that can't possibly be so funny, or maybe I just feel nothing could ever be amusing in this tiny blue house by the ocean.

Maybe I'm obsessing so much over Eli, I can't find anything positive at all anywhere he isn't. Except the milkshake. I finished that in record time in the van.

"How's the new school?" Amanda licks her cartoon character popsicle with square pants and a yellow body, she said she got it from the ice cream truck which Mom and I saw a couple of barren streets over. The best thing about this house, besides the blue exterior, is the ten-minute walk to the beach, and the five-minute walk to the carwash. Sometimes Amanda and I would go there, back when we didn't have cars, and spray each other down with hoses and pink foam, which, in retrospect, probably wasn't great for our skin or our lungs, but it smelled good, and it was fun.

The *worst* thing about this house is I'm forced to make stilted conversation with someone I've blown off for months now. Someone I used to call my best friend. I think I lied.

I shift on the scratchy, coral-colored couch, staring down at the thin, brown carpet, arms crossed over my chest, feet dangling an inch from the floor. I glance at the fading tan on my legs beneath my cut-off black shorts, made from a pair of jeans with wide legs I didn't love Mom bought me last year. My ripped-up lavender shirt slips off of one shoulder, but it's supposed to be like that anyway, so I let it go.

"It's... a castle." I lift my gaze to Manda, smiling.

She pauses her licking. These are things we never spoke about. Things best friends should've discussed. She knew I was going to a new school, of course, but we never talked about much beyond it.

She blinks wide blue eyes, scooting to the edge of the faded gray chair she's in across from me. She takes a bite out of the yellow cartoon body, lopping off an eye, too. "Really?" she asks between mouthfuls of ice cream.

My phone is in my hand, tucked under my bicep, and I squeeze it tight as I nod. "Really."

"Damn."

"I know."

Our moms laugh again from the kitchen at my back.

"The boys?" Manda's freckly face turns pink when she asks, because we both know it was *the boys* that got me in trouble at Shoreside.

"They're hot. And rich. And some of them are assholes." Well, really only Dominic, and sometimes Eli. Ansel was nice today, a kind smile, soft hair between the color of brown and blond. His Latin pronunciation was phenomenal.

"Of course. People with money are always assholes." Manda takes another chunk out of the sponge character.

It's a lie we were raised to believe, maybe indirectly. People who have money are bad, people without it are treated unfairly, and it's the ones with it doing the maltreatment.

I just nod because I don't want to argue some are nice. Like Eric Addison. A single dad with more money than I'll ever see in my life, and he's as kind as they come.

Except for that one little thing.

Except for the bruises.

I dig my nails into my skin. "You wanna go to Sky Wash?" I want to get moving.

Manda slowly looks up at me from her treat, gripping the wooden stick tightly. A smile spreads on her face. I feel a strange pang of guilt I've ignored so many of her messages, only texting her when I needed a distraction.

"Yeah," she says slowly, like I might take it back. "Yeah, I do."

The walk is warm, and it seems like the temperature rose even as the sun has fallen. Still enough pink and yellow light to see by, it's dim outside, and I like it this way.

Amanda tossed her ice cream stick in the overflowing trashcan of her mom's kitchen, and we told our parents we'd be back before too long. Mom rented a motel room for us for the night, not quite on the ocean, but I'm kind of, finally, excited for it. No Reece. No Sebastian. It should be nice.

"So," Manda says conspiratorially, and she seems to have lost a little of her animosity toward me, "you remember Sebastian's friend?"

We turn a corner, walking over grass-infested sidewalk, green shoots sprouting between sea-worn cracks. I glance at the yellow and blue and white lumpy houses beside me. The scent of the ocean is strong, humidity causes little hairs to stick to the back of my neck, even though I pulled my hair into a braid.

I forgot how much I loved this.

I feel *good* here, despite the fact everything wasn't when I lived in this town.

Up ahead, little kids ride a red and yellow pedal car,

another in only a diaper as he trails behind and a woman sits on the sagging porch, smoking a cigarette. When we pass by, I can smell the tobacco in the air.

"Which friend?" Sebastian has a lot of friends. Drugs do that, oddly enough. Bind you to people living in the gutter alongside you. No one wants to be down and alone.

I glance at my phone and see a text from Eli.

I open it up as Amanda prattles on. I'm half-listening, but I get the gist of what she's saying. Dating one of Sebastian's old friends, which seems like a terrible idea, but who am I to judge?

Eli: Send me a picture.

I roll my eyes and don't reply, crossing my arms again as the scent of bubbles and car soap pick up on the light breeze passing through. Up ahead, tucked on the side of the road not far from a food truck and a trailer, is Sky Wash.

It's crowded, by manual carwash standards. A pickup truck pulled into one of the bays, a yellow Mustang backed into another, but it's the bay at the far end, one empty between it and the Ford, that Amanda flings her hand toward, a tarnished gold bangle jumping on her wrist.

"Oh my God," she says, white teeth flashing in a smile, a tiny hint of yellow sludge from the cartoon ice cream between her front two. She drops her hand and turns to me, suddenly tugging at her tied-off white shirt, pulling up her high-waisted yoga pants. "Do I look okay?" she asks, seeming to blush from head to toe, her entire body a light shade of red.

I frown at her, the sound of vacuums and the swoosh of hoses background noise as we stand by an air-vac a few feet from the bays, the gray, coiled tube not in use. "You look great."

She flicks her curly red hair over one shoulder, a strand or two damp and stuck to her forehead. "Are you sure?" she asks, scrubbing at her teeth, as if she knows the ice cream is clinging to her like the last, shredded remnants of girlhood.

To push it all away, she cups her own breasts while she

yanks at the V in her shirt, trying to expose the freckled tops of her chest.

"What's going on?" I ask, glancing at the older man rinsing his Mustang and staring at us, and the frizzy haired lady at the pickup with pink foam flecked on her cheeks.

My gaze finally rests on the old Cadillac reversed into the last bay, and I assume there's a person in there, judging by the spray of water over top of the pale blue car, but I can't see them.

"It's *him,*" Manda says, gushing like I've never seen her do before.

"Who?" My phone vibrates in my hand, but I don't look at it, arms still crossed as I squint at the last bay, as if squinting will help me see more instead of less.

"Zachary!" Then she's grabbing my hand, unwinding my arms and ignoring my flinch as she hauls us toward the last bay. Her jelly flip-flops slap against the asphalt almost as fast as my heart pounds in my chest, my sweaty hand wrapped tight around my phone, like a lifeline.

Zachary?

My mind buzzes through everything she told me on the walk here, but I was only half paying attention, and I don't feel guilty, but I'm suddenly nervous as we get closer to the last bay, water running in rivulets along the pavement, draining off from the cement stalls.

Sebastian's friend.

Zach or Richard.

I was fourteen then. He was seventeen. Which means he's… twenty or twenty-one now? How did Manda even meet him?

"I wonder if he remembers you," she's saying, and my heart feels like it's literally flipping over in my chest.

I don't fight her, and I don't ask questions. It was a long time ago. But he stayed over for an entire year afterward. One of those nights was when I had my first panic attack. When I got my heart medication.

I know his name.

"Zachary," Manda calls, and I watch my white Keds splash into a shallow puddle, soaking the sides of my shoes, but I don't remember making the decision to get them wet. Water pools all around us, thin ribbons of pink laced through it alongside white bubbles.

"Zachary Richard." She snaps his name then, the spray of water hitting glass almost as loud as my friend's voice.

I'm still staring at the ground. At thin tires.

The smell of cleaners and water is bright in a way scents can be.

"Do you remember Eden?"

I lift my gaze to the car, the leather seats inside. The center console. The steering wheel. I think of fingers threaded through my hair, and how he groaned as he moved over me, frozen in my bed. How he lied to me and said my brother was busy. No one would care.

His hands all over me, the smell of his breath, like nicotine and some sort of meat. Hotdogs.

"Oh, shit," Zach Richard says, and the force of water against a window stops, steadying to a small drip upon the ground.

I glance at my phone, just to remind myself it's still in my hand. Eli's name lights up on the screen, another message coming in after the last unread one.

I smile to myself, and Manda drops my hand. When I pick my head up, she's tucked under Zach Richard's sinewy arm, a gray muscle tank showing off most of it, cargo shorts giving me a view of his knees and the hairs on them, stuck to his skin from sweat or the carwash.

Zach Richard spins the faded black cap on his head backward, tufts of lanky brown visible beneath it. He's only a couple of inches taller than Amanda, and he looks a little like a string bean, but he didn't feel that way, back then.

His hand rests on Manda's ass, but he releases her to move toward me after he drops the black hose in his hand, just letting it fall to the wet cement without a care in the world. Amanda is smiling, her arms crossed as she fingers a strand of her hair, but there's something distrustful in her smile.

It's directed at me.

Zach opens his arms for a hug. "Shit, you're all grown up."

My legs feel weak, like my knees are trembling, but I don't look down to confirm. I just keep my arms by my side. There's a pain in my chest that could be from my racing heart or my bad memories. Instinctively, I press a hand over it, feeling the warmth of my own skin, the too-fast pulse. I didn't think I'd need my medication here. Familiar things don't scare me. Except, apparently... they do.

"How does Sebastian beat the boys off of you, huh?" He's still coming closer, and I glance at his dirty sneakers, the hair along his ankles, over the top of his white socks.

My phone slips from my hand, and I step back, water splashing up my shins, dizziness making me feel unsteady on my feet, my mouth parting open, a gasp ringing in my ears.

I reach for the phone, swiping it up, checking the screen for damages—a small scratch, nothing else, Eli's texts are still there—and wiping the damp corner on my shirt.

Richard's arms close around me.

My face is pressed to his chest. I smell his sweat, and cologne, something choking. I can't think through anything, much less how to push away or speak.

"Don't move. God, you feel so good. Let me fuck you."

I didn't speak. Thankfully, he didn't try.

His fingertips press at the base of my spine. "God, I just can't get over it." He's saying other things, about how I didn't grow much taller, but I look like a woman, and how is Sebastian and how come he never answers his calls.

He finally pushes me away, holding me at arm's length.

I meet his gaze, the color lost on me in this moment, because I'm not really seeing much of anything.

A slight frown graces his lips. "You okay, baby doll?"

Baby doll.

I think I might throw up. I don't speak for fear of it.

I hear Amanda clear her throat. I can't see her because he's too close to me.

Do you remember? Do you? Do you? Do you?

The words are screaming in my brain, clawing beneath my skin, but if he remembers, it's nothing more than the whisper of a thought in his mind. It isn't plagued with anything so trivial as guilt.

I smile at him, coming back to life.

"It's good to see you," I lie. "Sebastian is doing well." I lie some more. "Send him a text, he's not much for phone calls."

Zach grins, the faintest hint of a moustache drooping over his upper lip. He still has his hands on my shoulders, and his thumbs are running circles by the crease of my underarm. I can feel his smooth fingers on my skin, where my shirt has slipped down my arm.

I don't move.

"It's so good to see you," he lies. "Where are you now, anyway?"

"She lives in Raleigh," Amanda says, saying the name of my relocated city like a slur. "She goes to a fancy private school."

Zach arches a thin brow. "No shit?"

"No shit." I repeat his words without the question mark. I'm hot all over, and I want to check my texts, and I want to go home. I don't want to stay at the hotel anymore.

I want my mom.

Zach pulls me in again.

His hands trail lower this time, to my hips. I bite the inside of my cheek as I'm suffocating against his chest.

"Don't forget about us country folk when you make it big," he says into my hair. His fingertips are over the curve of my ass.

I pull away, softly, like I mean him no offense. I take another step back as his hands come to his sides, and I don't miss the disappointment in his gaze.

Amanda comes to stand by him, glancing at me before she loops her arm through his, the bangle of her bracelet slipping up to the crease of her elbow. I wonder if he bought or stole it for her.

He messes with his hat again, slipping it off his head then pushing it back on the way people do when they're too hot.

"Come over," Amanda says, love drunk. There's a slight smile on her lips, and she's hanging off of him more than holding onto him.

He scrubs a hand over his face. "I will, baby," he lies. Liars know liars so well. "Just let me finish up here, all right?" He darts his eyes my way.

I step back again, but I smile at him. He returns it and my skin crawls.

I had bruises on my arms for days afterward. I couldn't sleep for a full night for months. I'd wake up, thinking someone was in my room. I pushed my dresser in front of it every night. I moved it back every morning, so Mom wouldn't know anything was wrong.

I look at my phone, unlocking it and reading Eli's texts.

Him: Do you think it would help if I had dinner at your house? You'll have to invite me, though. Probably wouldn't look so great if I invited myself.

Him: What're you doing, baby girl?

Another one comes through, just now. **I hope you're having fun with your mom. I miss you. Tuesday was fucking amazing. I like when you call me baby.**

I text him back as Amanda and Zach work out when they're going to see each other next, although I have a feeling it won't be tonight, despite what he's saying.

Me: I wish you were here, baby.

I don't have to wait long for his reply.

Him: Me too. Tell me a secret.

I smile, despite where I am, and who I'm with. Amanda's laughter cuts in the background and the sound of wet tires along gravel means someone is leaving Sky Wash. I don't look up from my boy's words as I send him my own.

Me: What do you want to know?

Him: Anything. Right now. Give me a secret. Before you go to sleep, give me three more.

I bite my lip and look up.

Amanda is kissing Zach, and he's picking her up by her ass, his grip shifting her yoga pants so they pull uncomfortably against her, but she doesn't complain.

Just like I didn't. Not after he started.

I drop my eyes to my phone.

Me: I've started writing a story about you.

It must catch Eli's attention, better than anything I could have said about the man standing three feet away from me. He responds so fucking fast. *Thank you, thank you, thank you.*

Him: Who am I, in the story?

I'm smiling so hard I forget to be nervous. I forget the feel of Zach's hands on me, then, or five minutes ago.

Me: The story is nothing without you.

Him: Stop making me feel so good and fall so hard.

Me: I can't. I'm hooked on you. Muse, nightmare, dream.

He's typing, then he's not, then he is, and I'm holding my breath the entire time, even as Zach calls my name, then snaps his fingers, trying and failing to get me to focus.

Finally, Eli's message comes through, and I think I could drown Zach in the puddle of water at my feet without a care in the world as I read Eli's words.

Him: I love you, too.

41

Eli

ME: **Three secrets, Rain.**

I have one hand tucked behind my head, the other gripping my phone, and I hope she hears the teacher voice when she reads my text. It's nearly ten at night, and surprisingly, she's been texting me non-stop since a few hours ago. I hope her mom doesn't mind.

I also hope her mom lets her keep her fucking phone. If she doesn't, I'll buy her one and pay for it myself. *Take that, Lucy.*

Somewhere downstairs, a door closes. Not loudly, not slammed, but even in a house like this one, the air circulates in such a way my own door squelches a little tighter shut.

I wonder what Dad is doing.

He watched me swim for a while, earlier in the evening. He grilled, we ate together on the patio. It was nice, but I know he wanted to ask about Mom. There was another letter with my name on it, stamped from Athens, left on the kitchen counter.

I didn't open it. He didn't either.

I glance at my ceiling fan, always on now because Eden

likes it, and when she comes over, she'll want it on, so I might as well grow used to it.

I close my eyes, my body tense, then I bring the inside of my elbow to my nose as I sneeze, wiping my nose over my forearm.

Fucking fan.

Sighing and sniffling, I look back at my phone.

Eden: Okay, Professor Addison.

I bite my lip, the taste of toothpaste minty on my tongue. Eden tastes fresh that way, nothing overly sweet or clean, just… newness. Like her mouth always lingers with her last brush.

Me: That's "sir" to you.

Eden: I have trouble distinguishing a secret from a regular fact, sir. Help me, please.

I shift on the bed, pulling my knees up, feet flat on the mattress, under the top sheet. I finger my hair, pulling absent-mindedly until it hurts, and I'm focused again.

Me: Questions, then, Ms. Rain?

She's typing immediately, no lag in our conversation, and while I'm not sure her mom is thrilled about it, I'm grateful.

Her: Yes, please, sir.

Jesus Christ.

Me: If you could do anything in the world and get away with it, what would it be? Bank robbing, murder, kidnapping, etc. No career-oriented goals. I know you're going to publish a book and become a professor, so don't waste your answer.

Her: So, things I likely wouldn't otherwise get away with, then?

I smile at her understanding. **Me: Yes.**

She doesn't reply immediately, because she's thinking it through. There's probably something burning, just under the surface of the restraint hardwired into most of us from birth, but it takes a moment to take off the chains. Remember we're free. There are consequences, up to and including death. Imprisonment, for example. But we *can* do anything we want.

Her: I would keep you.

I wait, to see if she's going to say anything else. But she doesn't. She isn't typing anymore. There're so many things *wrong* with the way she answered the question, I'm irritated enough to sit up, flinging off my covers and using both hands to grip my phone now, poised to tell her every way her statement is ridiculous.

But before I can get anything out, there's a soft knock on my door.

I glance up, seeing it's unlocked, and I clear my throat, sniffing again from the fan, annoyance adding fuel to my irritation. I could tell Dad to fuck off, but this will probably be over with faster if I don't.

"Come in."

He waits until I've said the words to open the door. His eyes rake over my body, ensuring I'm clothed, probably, and I am, basically.

I have on gym shorts.

It's enough.

He scrubs a hand over his face, and I catch sight of the pale strip of skin on his index finger. Still wearing his dress shirt, rolled up and unbuttoned, I wonder when he ever just fucking *relaxes*.

"What's up?" I ask, my screen dimming, thumbs still over my keyboard.

Dad's hazel eyes are tired as he glances at the blue lights around my room, the lamp flicked on beside my bed.

"She wants you to read the letter."

I don't say anything. I don't *do* anything except hold my phone.

Dad slides his hands into his pockets like a very exhausted lawyer, then leans against the door frame. He has one ankle crossed over the other, striped socks on, expensive, I know, but almost childish in some ways, with their bright, nonsensical colors. His eyes are on the floor now, and I can see his broad shoulders deflate as he exhales.

"I could read it," he offers. "I could summarize it for you."

I laugh at that. He doesn't look up. Once upon a time, he told Mom my laugh was off. He didn't think I heard him. He said he wished he could make me really laugh. He said one time, he had, when I was younger. He tickled me.

He said he held onto that laugh in his head.

Mom said nothing. She walked away, like she didn't want to talk about it.

I was in the pool. They were in the kitchen, but the screen door was the only barrier between us.

I've always been very good at hearing and seeing and sensing things I shouldn't.

"You think it would hurt me less, coming from you?" I ask Dad when he still doesn't react to my laughter.

He glances at me but doesn't pick his head up. "Does it hurt?"

"You sound like Dr. Langley."

"So, you're not going to answer me, because you don't answer Langley, either, do you?" There's a hint of exasperation in his tone, but he tries his very best to hide it.

I rest my elbows on my bent knees, phone dangling from my fingers between my lap. "I'm not sure how many times I have to tell you, Dad."

He takes a deep breath with my last word.

"I don't want *anything* to do with Mom unless she's coming. *Back.*" Something strange happens to my voice, but I ignore it. I hold Dad's gaze.

"She loved you, you know?" It feels like an insult, the way he says it. "Her leaving had nothing to do with you—"

"And everything to do with *you.*"

His brows pull together, a deep crease between them. "If I could change anything, Eli, you know I would."

I drop my phone and get off my bed, needing to move. To stand. I drag my fingers through my hair and turn my back on Dad. "I don't want to talk about this anymore."

"You need to, because if you don't, son, it's going to keep eating at you."

I glance at the glass of water on my nightstand. I picture my hand swiping through it, sending it crashing and shattering and splintering to the floor like the picture of Mom and the boy, the photo she sent framed, thinking I'd actually *want* it.

How long are we going to do this dance, Mom?

I don't want you anymore.

Not the way I can have you.

I don't want pieces. You know I like everything whole.

I pull at my hair, hands still on my head, and I don't move. "There's nothing more to say." I keep my voice low. "Reading her letter when I will never respond is useless, right?"

Dad grasps at straws. "What if she apologized? What if she explained everything to you—"

I spin around, hands by my sides. "You explained everything to me. Just by watching the both of you, *I saw the explanation*. You're overbearing. She's cold. I'm not right."

Dad shakes his head, pulling a hand from his pocket and gesturing at me, hopelessly. "Don't say that, Eli. You are everything we could've wanted. I daydreamed about becoming a father with Ari—"

"She hated when you called her *Ari*. Did you ever know that?"

He flinches, like I hit him. His mouth closes, I see his throat roll over the unbuttoned collar of his shirt. "I… It was just a habit."

"A habit she hated." It feels good, driving it in a little more.

"Eli." He says my name like someone might say *please* or *I'm sorry*.

"How many other things did you not see, right in front of your fucking face?" I throw my hand up, wanting a fight.

"Eli." It's different this time. *That's enough* or *stop*.

"Was she always so distant?" I ask, and I can tell he thinks it's a genuine question at first. There's a moment of surprise flitting across his face, his brows raised, his expression full of openness instead of the step before anger. But before he can answer me, I keep talking. "Or was it just *you* that made her that way? You kept her locked up in this house and you never wanted to fly her back home and you never wanted her family to visit and—"

"None of that is true."

"I *heard* you, don't bullshit me, Dad. I heard her argue with you about dates and flights and—"

"She wanted to take you. I thought she wouldn't bring you back. She got in these moods sometimes, she was... she was sick and I—"

"You wanted to control her. You wanted to keep her in a cage."

Dad straightens from the doorway, pointing a finger at me, his shirt clinging to his biceps, and I feel like I'm going to get exactly what I want. "You're wrong." It's all he says, but I see the rage in his eyes.

"I'm not." I smile, because I know it infuriates him more. "You wanted to own her, and you couldn't stand the idea she might never come back *to you.*"

He steps closer to me. "I didn't want her to take you from me." His voice is raw. "And she had no idea what to do with you."

"And *you did?*" I laugh, and it's not meant to hurt him this time. It's just amusing, Dad thinking he knew more than Mom about how to handle me. "You're fucking clueless too."

"Then help me." He drops his hand but steps even closer. We're two feet apart, maybe less. I can see his pulse beating at the base of his throat. "Help me, Eli. All I've ever wanted to do is what's best for you, but I'm lost."

"If you think you're going to appeal to my better nature by trying to make me feel sorry for you, then you're stupid." I close the space between us this time, so we're nose-to-nose. I can smell his cologne, something aquatic, and the smoke from the grill. "You should know, Dad. I don't have a *better fucking nature.*"

"Eli." *Shut up.* "Watch your tone."

"I think my tone is just fine. I think what you really want me to do is watch the facts, right? Stop spelling out all the ways your son will never be the golden boy you wanted him to be? Is that what you want, Dad? You want to pretend I didn't break that kid's fucking nose, and I didn't play with those mice and I didn't fuck my babysitter and—"

He clamps his hand over my mouth, like he can't bear to hear it. His fingers are warm. They remind me of Eden, in temperature alone. "Stop," he says, his eyes holding mine, like he can reach me.

If he wanted to reach me, he'd have to understand me. There is only one person in this world who does, and I'm blowing her off right now to fight with my fucking dad.

But I've never been one to back away from violence.

I grab Dad's wrist, holding tight before I jerk his hand down.

He releases his grip on my mouth but tries to shake mine off.

I don't let go.

"You're more than enough," he says, and I hate him for it. "You are *more* than anything I could have ever asked for in a son—"

"I hate when you lie to my face."

He tries again to pull his wrist from my fingers, but I don't let go, and I watch in amazement as his temper rises and rises and *bursts*.

Muscles and veins flex beneath his skin, his lips are pulled back, nostrils flaring. I think he's fighting with himself, so he doesn't fight with me.

But I want it.

I love this.

"Let go of me, Eli." Fear flickers just once when I only tighten my grip, but the violence comes on its heels. Maybe he hits me because he's scared, and he loathes that part of himself.

Because he wants to believe what he says. That I'm *more than enough*.

But moments like these, when he gets his wrist free and his fist connects with the side of my face, haphazard and without aim, like he just needs to hurt any inch of me to feel better, we know the truth.

You don't want this. You don't want me.

Who could?

We wrestle. I wrap my arms around him, dragging him down, down, *down*. My leg sweeps behind his ankle, and he hits the floor of my bedroom with a thud.

My ears are ringing as my fingers find his throat, and he's grabbing at my own, thumbs going over the hollow, and I'm laughing even as I can barely breathe.

He flips us over, and I'm not sure if I let him, if some strange part of me submits to him because no matter what, he *is* my dad, or if he's just stronger than me.

I doubt it, but either way, I don't mind when my head cracks against the floor.

I don't mind when he straddles me, pinning my thighs with his knees, and he grabs my wrists and yanks them over my head and I grin up at his angry, red face and the way he hangs his head a moment after, and his shoulders shake.

And he's crying.

He's crying.

I feel the warmth of a tear on my abs, and I hate him for that.

More than anything else, more than the pounding in my temple, the bruise sure to stay on my face, I hate him for his weakness.

But I don't have to stay underneath it for long.

He says, "I do love you," in a choked, strangled way, then he releases me, gets up, and walks out, not even bothering to slam the door after me.

When I'm up off the floor, the feel of the bruise forming on the side of my face pulsing alongside my heartbeat, I throw myself down on my bed, lying on my back, still smiling, my nose running from the fan all over again.

It feels good, the inconvenience of it.

Eden has texted me.

Three times.

Her: Two more secrets before you can ask more questions you may not like the answers to.

Her: I've thought about following you to college, but I know I'll never get into wherever rich boys go.

The second secret is a photo.

When I see it, I forget the fight with Dad, already a lingering memory as is. I forget Mom's letter. Her photos. All of her mistakes.

My stomach twists into pleasurable knots, the kind of pain I crave.

A straight razorblade, lying on top of Eden's wrist, her bracelets pushed down to her forearm. The silver of the blade sits over the white letters of a boy's name who never deserved to know hers.

I can't breathe as I text her back, phone held over my face.

Me: No.

I hope she waited.

Me: You're going to college with me. Caven U. Apply.

Me: But the second secret. No.

Her response comes thirty seconds later. **Her: Why?**

It should be obvious, baby girl.

Me: I want to do it.

She's typing as my heart pounds hard in my chest, and I wonder if this is what hers feels like, all of the time. Anticipation makes my stomach flutter, and I'm breathless, waiting.

When her message comes through, it's enough to quiet every thought in my mind that isn't about her. Her. *Her.*

Eden: I love you, too.

I think, really… that's all that matters.

But hours later, when she's asleep and we've said our goodnights, and I'm tossing and turning and scrolling through cars on my phone, I remember what she said.

Her answer to my question.

The thing she would want to get away with if she could. A crime.

I would keep you.

And I don't feel so great anymore.

Instead, getting out of bed, stumbling toward the bathroom and flipping on the light, examining the bruise forming beside my eye, the snot dripping down over my lips, I just feel a little lost.

42

Eden

"DID you see anyone we used to know?" Sebastian is crouched by my open window, a cigarette between his fingers, night fallen a few hours after Mom and I got back today after staying another night. He turns his head to blow smoke through the screen, the forest dark and alive beyond it.

I'm leaning against the wall adjacent my bed, legs draped over the mattress horizontally, my phone in my hands. Both of us are in pajamas. Through Sebastian's white T-shirt, I see the knobs of his shoulders and the line of his biceps, not from strength, but the opposite of that.

It's uncomfortable, watching his ruin.

He doesn't want to talk about it.

I don't know what to say.

I glance at my notebook, closed and face down beside me, my green pen thrown atop it. Sebastian is in the story I'm plotting out too, alongside Eli. They have different names, but at the end of my fictional manuscript, the boy who is Sebastian will die.

I bend my knees, drawing them up to my chest under my

sheets. I think about my sigil notebook, tucked away in my drawer. I've still never conjured up magic for any boy but Eli.

Guilt rests heavy on my shoulders.

"Yeah," I tell my brother as I lean my head against the wall, clutching my phone on my thigh. "Amanda."

Sebastian glances at me. Our eyes stay locked for long seconds, and I know he's wondering about anyone else I might have seen. I can see the guilt in his face, illuminated by the cherry of his cigarette and the lamp on my nightstand. *Who else?* It's in the crinkle of his eyes, the way he's unnaturally still.

"Mom had a good time," I continue, dropping the subject, letting him off the hook. "She talked my head off, you know, but we went to that pancake place—"

"Slap Jack's?" Sebastian brings his cigarette to his lips, turning from me, finally.

I nod, thinking of my stomachache from yesterday after so many pancakes. "Yeah." I flip my phone over, but Eli hasn't responded to me yet. "How was Reece?" I can't stand him, but the single second of happiness on his face when Mom walked in earlier was almost enough to make me soften toward him.

"How he always is," Seb says, dismissive. "An asshole."

"Did you two hang out?"

Sebastian cuts his eyes to me, arching a brow as if to say, *are you fucking serious?* "No." He snorts. "He cut the lawn at like, eight in the fucking morning today. Started on my side of the house, so you know, I slept well."

"Might help if you came home before sunrise." I shrug, smiling at his scowl.

"Whatever." He goes back to staring out the window.

Silence stretches on until I can't stand it anymore. "Sebastian." I keep staring at my screen to keep from looking up to meet my brother's eye.

He grunts something, permission to continue, I guess.

I swallow down my nerves. "Are you okay?"

The quiet between us is sharp. *Loud* in the way heavy quiet can be.

"What do you mean?" His tone tells me he knows exactly what I mean, but he has no idea how to talk to me about it, just like words fail me, too.

"Why do you always come home?" I could have started anywhere with Sebastian. Asking him about getting another job, or going back to school, or… avoiding parties. But I know all of those things would come off as a lecture, and he'd tune me out and get up and walk back to his room.

Besides, I really want to know. Why not stay out? Why not *move* out?

I risk a glance at him, only to find smoke curling around his side profile, his eyes fixed on the woods. His shoulders are relaxed, which surprises me, but after a second, I see his grip on his cigarette is tight enough to snap it in half.

The cherry dies out.

The stick is barely held together by a thread as tobacco spills out through the white paper.

"I feel safe here," he finally says. "High or not, I don't feel good anywhere else."

I think of Reece's mask of indifference, Mom tiptoeing around the subject of her stepson's demise. Me, noticing all of it but doing and saying nothing.

I feel safe here.

It's a mix of emotions in my chest, a physical pang of guilt with a touch of something like love. Fondness, at least.

I kind of want to hug him, but I don't think either of us would really appreciate the reality of the gesture.

I stay where I am, and he does, too.

"I'm glad you come back," I tell him, and I mean it.

He turns to face me, and his mouth is lifted in a smile, but his eyes are sad. "Really?"

I nod once, dropping my eyes to my phone. "Really."

43

Eli

I STAY under far longer than I should.

Eden is above the surface, on the coast again, where she was just yesterday with her mom, whom she lied to in order to stay here. Fall break is this week, and I think it helped Janelle picked her up and took her to my house before we started driving.

She's up above the water, sitting beside Dominic. Luna and Jasper and Janelle must have bonded on the drive because they're past the gate of Dad's beach house, down at the ocean, forgoing the pool. Naked, probably.

Eden isn't.

She better not be.

I need to go up, my lungs aching and the urge to *breathe* clawing at my mind. But that's all it is. Psychological panic. I could stay under a little longer.

I splay my fingers along the pool wall, smooth beneath my palm.

We really shouldn't be out here at all.

Thunder and lightning have been our constant companions

since we arrived, retreating to our rooms to drop off our things, Eden in mine, Dom and Jasper beside us.

We watched the rain fall in sheets for a long, long time along the balcony. But eventually, we all did what we came here to do.

Shuck off our clothes, pull on our swimsuits and scatter toward different sources of water.

The rain died off.

The storm remains.

I push up, toes flexing along the bottom of the pool to propel me to the surface.

The first thing I hear after I breathe, and swallow, in that order, is Eden's laugh. Swimming toward the ladder, I pull myself up, blinking through the chlorine, to see her beside Dominic on one of the wicker couches, gray cushions damp from the earlier rain.

Her tan shoulder brushes his, her legs curled underneath her. One of the straps of her silver swimsuit is drooping from her arm, and I see the white line of skin beneath it from her tan. I want to push the strap up. It's like a habit, an instinct, to keep her covered.

Even so, my eyes drop to the fabric along her torso, everything shredded and ripped like most of her clothes outside of school. My gaze roams over her thick thighs, the round curve of her ass just visible beneath the cut-out of her one piece.

She takes something from Dominic.

A joint, I realize.

Their fingers brush, and she doesn't lose her smile, the aftereffect of her laughter.

My fingers tighten around the metal bars of the ladder at the deep end. I'm still on one of the rungs, and I don't get out yet. They haven't noticed me, I don't think. All that time I was under, they didn't notice.

Thunder cracks overhead.

Eden jumps, withdrawing from Dominic at the sound, as if

it brought her back to a reality where she squirms away from the feel of skin on hers.

Dominic has his elbow propped on the arm of the couch, bleached head of hair resting in his palm as he watches my girlfriend.

His knees are spread, dark blue swim trunks rising just over his kneecaps. He's shirtless, and even in the soft orange glow of lights around the pool, his skin is pale enough to mistake him for a cartoon ghost.

Eden inhales from the joint as I get out, water dripping on the cement. I make my way toward her, and she passes the joint back to Dominic as she exhales from her nose, smoke curling up around her pretty face while she watches me. I grab a towel from the opposite end of the couch from Dom, and scrub it over my face, patting my arms and torso dry.

Bottles of vodka, rum, and wine are nearly empty on the glass table to Dominic's right, cups stacked up high, a trashcan Janelle thought to bring out shoved beside the table to keep things relatively clean.

"How was your swim?" Eden grins at me as I sit, then place one foot on the low table in front of the couch, the towel on my lap. Her eyes are red, lids lowered, but she hasn't drunk anything at all, which surprises me.

"Good," I tell her as lightning forks violently down from the sky. I hear a distant scream from the beach, but it's too full of laughter to indicate true distress. "How's the weed?"

Eden laughs, spreading her fingers over her mouth as she does, like she's trying to hold it in.

"You wanna experience it yourself?" Dom asks, leaning across Eden, his ribcage touching her thighs.

I glance at the joint he's offering. "I'm good."

He looks surprised, brows flicking upward, but he just shrugs, then leans back, taking another pull.

None of the three of us are touching, but Dominic is far closer to Eden than I am.

I know what she sees in him. He's hurting, unassuming,

mildly funny, and she isn't intimidated by him like she sometimes seems to be with me.

I've seen his mom's arm, though. The way her fingers tremble as she sets the table in the Lander's household. I've seen Dominic's temper, and Eden has, too, but she writes it off as his grief over Winslet. The reality is he's always been that way.

A bomb.

I don't think children become their parents all the time. I'm nothing like Dad. But Dominic has the same temper as his father. I think he's well on his way to filling his shoes, whether he wants to or not.

I wonder what Eden would think of him then.

"Lollipop" by Lil Wayne is playing from someone's phone, connected to the speakers inside the house and around the pool. Definitely not my fucking phone. I run a hand through my damp hair, then grab the joint and the green lighter from the kitchen island upstairs, all black marble. The house is a contrast, light marble flooring, floor-to-ceiling windows looking out over the ocean, bathed in black now, at nearly midnight.

I changed into white sweats after my swim, but I don't have a shirt on, and I catch a glimpse of the top half of my tattoo as I lean against the counter and light up, facing the windows, heat lightning flickering through the clouds.

I got tattooed because I could. Because I'd turned eighteen and Dad couldn't stop me. It's good enough, but I didn't put a lot of forethought into that or the play on the keychain Dad got me.

The next thing, though… I want it to be meaningful.

As I inhale, I think of Eden with tattoos. It turns me on, just imagining it.

I spark up the lighter to watch the flame jump in the darkness of the kitchen and open plan living room, then I push it in my pocket, inhaling from the joint again.

Aside from the music, I can't hear much of anything. I know it's thundering outside though, and I can see the glint of waves tumbling from the thin stream of moonlight to the east. There's the faintest glow of the blue pool lights two stories below, too.

Eden is down there. With my friends.

It makes me feel good, for some reason. I don't particularly want Dom near her, but I know Janelle and Jasper will watch out for her. And I just wanted another joint, and a second alone. Truthfully, I was half-hoping Eden would follow me, but she was talking with Janelle, their feet in the pool at the deep end, and she must like her.

I close my eyes, listening to the music, the taste of marijuana on my tongue, down my throat. I exhale through my teeth, tipping up my chin, keeping my eyes closed. In my head, I see Eden smoking, clouds of white smoke drifting through her nose.

That was fucking hot to watch, even if it was Dom's fucking joint.

I drop my hand to my dick, over my pants, palming myself and thinking of how I'm going to fuck her tonight.

I inhale again, not high, but I feel loose, and good, and I want to go find her and take her away from everyone else and—

Someone's hand comes over mine.

My eyes fly open, my heart racing as I look down into Luna's eyes.

Confusion and annoyance pound through my temples. *It's very, very hard for anyone to sneak up on me.*

But I was thinking of Eden. She's got me all fucked up.

I stand up straighter, joint pinched between my thumb and forefinger, and I see the orange tip glow bright as I take another pull.

The light reflects in Luna's eyes.

She's in only her white bikini, her hair pulled back into a short ponytail, diamond studded flip-flops on her feet.

I slip my hand from under hers, pushing mine into the pocket of my sweats.

And she just grabs my fucking dick. All right, then.

My body feels hot, and I see her lips pull into a smile, one dimple flashing in her oval face.

"Why are you up here?" she asks, her voice low, palm running up and down me.

I turn my head, exhaling, watching white and gray smoke drift through the darkness of the house, the bass from the speakers jolting beneath my white Chucks. I don't answer Luna.

She keeps running her hand along me, then she presses her other palm over my tattoo, just above the waistband of my sweats as she flicks her eyes along the length of my body.

Sleeping with Luna is easy. Not because *she's* easy, because fuck, so am I, really. But we've done it so many times, she knows what I like, I know what gets her off, it's effortless.

But now, thinking of the same old shit with her—grab her throat, her eyes roll back, she can come without me having to touch her clit, she deep throats like a champ—it feels a little… boring. And I know she's probably fucked Dom recently too, and when I think of him, downstairs with *my girl,* untouched by him, or anyone, I kind of want to snatch her away from the whole fucking world.

She's just for me.

I've never wanted someone just for me. Not since…

I take another pull from my joint, refusing to think of my psychological issues.

Luna drags her gaze up to meet mine as she lifts her chin. She's taller than Eden, and her touch isn't hesitant. But it's not possessive either. It's kinda… bland.

I don't *feel* anything with her hands on me. Maybe all this time, I never really did. Of all the people I've fucked, the only one I got high from before Eden was Ms. Corbin. And that was because it wasn't allowed. Even at Montford, where I should feel the highest, there's a slight concern for my safety that makes the adrenaline spike a little off kilter.

Eden is just... I don't fucking know. *More.*

"I've missed you," Luna says, her lips close to my sternum. She drops her eyes, then leans in, squeezing my dick over my pants, running her mouth over my chest. It feels good on some base level. I can't deny that. I won't fuck her, because I think of Eden running from me in the woods, and I hate the idea of her doing it again. *You can't leave me.*

But I'm not going to stop Luna. Not right this second, anyway. Besides, Eden is currently with Dominic.

I blow smoke over Luna's head, letting her touch me, hand still in my pocket as I stare out the windows at the rolling sea. From what I can tell, it looks a little violent tonight.

The song changes as Luna licks a line up my chest.

"The Hills" by The Weeknd. This must be Dom's fucking playlist.

It's turned up louder from somewhere else, and in my head, I see him getting up from a pool chair. Pushing his phone into his pocket. Heading toward my girl without his fucking shirt on—

"What the fuck are you doing?"

Luna startles, both of us surprised as she jerks back, but she doesn't move her hand from my abs or my dick.

I slowly dip my chin, biting back a smile as I bring the joint to my lips, my girl's words ringing in my head. *What the fuck are you doing?*

I don't have to see her to know she's fucking pissed. And as I turn my head, catching the gleam of her eyes in the dark, I know I'm right.

Her hair is loose, wavy and thick down her back, her hands fisted at her sides. She's wearing one of my shirts, white and contrasting with her tan, it hits at her thighs.

God, I love you.

But she doesn't look like she loves me so much right now. Wearing her white Keds with no socks, she steps back, shoes squeaking on the marble floor as her gaze flicks from me, to Luna, still touching me.

Luna forces a laugh. "What's it look like?"

I bring the joint to my lips, just watching my girl.

Fight for me.

She turns her head to look up at me. *I'm going to fucking murder you.*

I smile, smoke curling around my teeth. *Don't tease me with a good time.*

"Get the fuck away from him." She doesn't move her eyes from mine as she addresses Luna.

I cough, a laugh bubbling up my throat.

Luna's nails dig into my skin. She grabs me harder.

I keep looking at Eden. *Show me what you can do, Nightmare Girl.*

Without a word, she lifts her chin and walks toward me. *Us.* My heart races in my chest. Her hips sway, her black painted nails tapping out the rhythm of the song on her bare thigh, just under my shirt. *Come closer. Come to me. Push her away from me. Show me you love me.*

But then she… passes us.

She doesn't even look at us as she does. She's so close, I can smell chlorine and peaches and violets, and I want to grab her fucking hair and drag her back, but she keeps walking as Luna and I both track her movements.

She steps onto the white tile of the kitchen, headed toward the sleek, black fridge. But instead of opening it up, she passes it, too, until…

Until she pulls a knife from the fucking knife block.

It's sleek and black, sharp, because Dad keeps all of our shit sharp.

Spinning around, Eden turns to face us both again, grinning in the dark as she twirls the knife between her fingers.

"Get. The fuck. *Away from him.*" Her words are aimed at Luna, cold and vicious, and I glance at the bracelets on her wrist.

The blade in her hand.

I think of the name on her wrist. The scars of someone useless. No longer relevant.

My chest feels tight. Full of... her. I told her I had a boxcutter, but this knife... Imagining her blood curling around her wrists, streaking over her arms...

My dick jumps in Luna's hand, but she's already stepping away from me, dropping her arms, giving another fake fucking laugh.

"You're not going to *cut me*, Eden," she says, but we all hear it. The thread of panic in her words. She doesn't know Eden. I don't think anyone is quite sure what she's going to do.

Luna tightens her ponytail for something to do with her nervous energy.

Eden is a shadow in the dark, unmoving, the blue lights from the clock on the stove glinting over the blade in her hand.

Luna takes another step back, scoffing. "You're fucking insane."

Eden comes closer.

My pulse jumps to my throat, staring at her. The knife. I almost forget I've got a joint in my hand until I instinctively bring it to my mouth as I stare at my girlfriend.

"I like you, Luna," Eden says softly, and she doesn't stop walking until she's right beside me.

We're shoulder to shoulder.

I reach for her, intending to wrap my arm around her waist.

She reacts faster than I thought she would, pressing the tip of the blade lightly to my sternum, stopping me from touching her.

A chill slides down my spine as I drop my hand. I feel a little nervous, and it gets me high. I think of the knife emoji she put beside her name in my phone, and I don't move as Luna's mouth drops open and she backs up another step.

"I really do," Eden continues, voice low.

I take one more pull from the joint. My chest expands, and

the blade's cold tip presses against it. There's the dullest pinprick of pain. The warmth of what might be my own blood.

I don't even look.

I just exhale through my nose, watching Eden address Luna.

"But I don't want your hands anywhere near my boyfriend ever again, you got me?" There's a sharp edge to her words, some of that private school prep accent she's adopted crashing away and overtaken by her upbringing.

God, I cannot wait to fuck her.

Luna's eyes flick up to me. The knife over my heart. Then Eden.

She nods once, pursing her lips. "Whatever," she mutters. "You're fucking insane. He'll be done with you too when he gets bored—"

Eden drops the knife, cutting off Luna's words as the blade clatters.

Then Eden closes the space between them and grabs her by the top of her bikini, exposing Luna for a second as Eden yanks her down to her level with another hand twisting her top lip.

I couldn't speak even if I tried.

I don't bother trying. I twist around and drop my joint into the glass ash tray, then cross my arms over my chest and watch, leaning against the island.

"Stop running your stupid fucking mouth." Eden's words are low, I can barely hear her over the music. "Turn On The Lights." "And stop telling Dom to try and fuck me. I don't want to play your sick games." She yanks harder on Luna's lip, and Luna squeals just as my eyes narrow.

For the first time since Eden came up here, I'm something other than turned on.

"I don't want him. *And Eli is fucking mine.*" She releases Luna, stepping back into me. Instinctively, my arms wrap around her chest, and she tilts her head as Luna watches us, her mouth dropped open.

She makes a low noise, like a muffled scream.

I glance at the blade on the floor.

She does too.

And without another word, her hands clenched into fists, she storms off.

For a moment, we wait, then we feel the house shake as Luna slams the door closed.

Neither of us speak, music still playing loudly in the background. "Last Time I Checked," but I'm not exactly focused on the song.

"She told Dom to try and fuck you—"

"Why *the fuck* would you let her touch you like that?" She spins in my arms after Luna is gone, lifting her chin to glare at me, cutting off my words.

I arch a brow, thinking of ripping Dominic's fucking throat out. "Did he touch you?"

She rolls her eyes, and without looking away from me, she reaches a finger up to my chest, pressing against the place she cut me.

My jaw tightens, but I don't speak as the sharp, brief pain lights through me.

Slowly, she flips her hand, and between us, we both see blood on her skin.

Her lips curve into a smile. "You let her do that again," she says softly, bringing her hand to her mouth, then pushing the tip of her finger between her lips and sucking my blood off as she sweeps her eyes up to mine and I feel like I'm going to pass out. She pulls her finger from her mouth, tugging down her bottom lip, eyes still on mine. "It's going to be Dom's blood I taste."

A second passes.

Another.

A third.

Then I'm hauling her up, spinning her around and setting

her on the counter. The glass ashtray hits the floor, splintering to pieces. I don't give a fuck.

I'm grabbing her ass, pulling her to the edge of the counter.

She drags her nails down my chest, over where she cut me. It stings, and I like it.

I push down my sweats and my boxers, circling myself as she widens her thighs, wrapping her legs around me. I knot my fingers in her hair, yanking her head down, her chin lifted as she looks at me, her fingers drifting over my abs, causing my muscles to jump, until she's grabbing my dick, too, pulling me toward her.

"You put your hands on him, I'll fucking cut his off."

"What would you have let her do?" she counters as she moves her hand to pull aside her swimsuit and I push against her tight entrance, a moan at the end of her question, her eyes closing, only for a moment. The single sign of weakness from her in this moment, it feels like a goddamn victory.

I grab her face with both hands, and she shifts on the counter, desperate for me. She's so hot and fucking wet and she grips my biceps, nails in my skin, owning me.

"Nothing," I tell her honestly, mouth over hers, my eyes locked on her own. The scent of chlorine and weed and *her* is strong between us.

"You weren't stopping her—"

I kiss her, biting her bottom lip, my tongue clashing with hers. My fingers are over her throat, and I press into the tendons there, stealing her breath, but she doesn't stop kissing me, attacking me as I push into her, and she moans.

"Eli, don't lie to me, baby." Her words are in my mouth.

She's so fucking tight around me, I swear I've never felt anything this good in my life, especially with her legs latched onto me like she doesn't ever want to let me go.

"You have me," I tell her, pulling back, my brow to hers as she bucks her hips, trying to fuck me herself. I slide my hands lower, circling her neck with both, squeezing her so tight she can't breathe, and she's still shifting on the counter, fucking me, shallow movements, but it feels good all the same. *"I'm all yours, Nightmare Girl."* I bite the side of her face, hard, and her calves tremble, wrapped around my waist. I flex my fingers tighter.

No breath leaves her lungs.

And if you want to keep *breathing, you're all fucking mine.*

I think some things, maybe, are better left unsaid.

44

Eden

LUNA IS on the balcony off the living room, alongside everyone else.

Her eyes snap to mine, and for a moment, Eli's fingers tangled with my own, his scent all over me, we stare at one another as I stand in the doorway, Eli sliding the door closed behind us.

Jasper, Janelle, and Dom—sitting in a row in Adirondack chairs—stop talking, and only the tumultuous ocean waves cut through the silence.

The wind blows, Luna's short, auburn bangs intwining around her eyes. She's got a pack of cigarettes clutched in one hand, a white lighter in the other as she leans against the balcony, her back to the sea.

Eli squeezes my hand.

I ignore him.

Then Luna shrugs, like she's shaking off any animosity between us, and pulls a cigarette from her pack with manicured nails, the lighter in her palm.

Surprising me, she extends the long, white stick toward me. "Want one?"

I glance at her peace offering, my eyes taking in the cream-colored dress she's wearing over her bikini. The way her hand trembles a little, and I have a feeling she doesn't try to stop fights and put aside grudges very often.

Despite what I saw her doing with Eli, I recognize the gesture for what it is.

Dropping Eli's hand, I nod once, taking the cigarette.

"Thank you," I tell Luna, and it feels as if everyone is still holding their breath around us. But when I put the cigarette between my lips and she offers to light it as I cup my hands around it to block out the breeze, the conversations pick up again.

I can feel Eli's eyes on me, and I wonder what he's thinking. I hope this doesn't feel like a betrayal to him, but I know how relationships are tangled in Eli's head. He probably doesn't really feel like anything *bad* happened in the kitchen. Like it's normal for us to move on so quickly.

Maybe it is.

I put up a boundary and I think Luna will respect it, moving forward. Besides, it's been a couple of hours. The clock in the bedroom I'm sharing with Eli—where I went and cleaned up and pressed a damp cloth to his shallow cut—said it was three when we headed out here. It's officially Halloween, and it's the devil's hour.

Anything can happen, and befriending Luna seems like a magic all on its own.

Together, we lean against the balcony and watch the water, a dark blue, glinting under the moonlight. Behind us, conversation between Janelle and Jasper picks up. About cars, of all things. Something about imports being "trash," according to Jasper. I expect Eli to join in, but shockingly, him and Dom are both quiet.

I cough a little on the tobacco, turning my head away from

Luna to blow out smoke, then I twirl the stick between my fingers, looking at the cherry under the moonlight.

"We good?" I ask her, keeping my voice down.

She's got her elbows propped on the sleek metal railing. There's an entire day bed behind us, beside the padded chairs, but no one is on it.

I imagine sweltering summers, lounging with Eli there. Sticky nights spent in bliss. I imagine how this trip would've gone if we'd been alone.

But I like the fact I claimed him. It was an urge I couldn't resist, with the knife. I never would've really cut Luna, I don't think, and I didn't mean to hurt Eli, either, but… I wouldn't take it back. Besides, I wanted him to know I want him. I've come to understand he needs his love drenched with a little blood, wrapped up tight in bruises.

"Yeah," Luna finally says, blowing smoke into the night, the blue-green glow of the pool down below tinting it aquatic colors. "We're good."

I smile in the night, inhaling the scent of the sea over the smell of nicotine. "Tell me what the fuck is up with you and Dom anyway." I ensure I'm whispering, but the conversation between Janelle and Jasper is growing louder, their laughter filling the air, and someone turned on music because it's climbing in volume from a speaker somewhere behind me, or maybe in the awning over our heads. A hip-hop song I don't know, but I sway my hips a little all the same.

Luna snorts. "He's looking for someone to mommy him, and we're always off and on because that is not me." She curls her short bangs behind her ears, pursing her lips as she exhales again.

"And you think it's *me?*" Downstairs, before I walked in on her and Eli, Dominic whispered to me Luna was confident I'd fuck him if he just asked. He said it as a joke, but I knew there was truth behind it.

Luna glances at me, grinning a little, her cigarette between her index and middle finger. "No," she admits. "I just…"

"Wanted to get Eli alone?"

She rolls her eyes. "It's not like that with me and him," she says. "It's just a good time, you know, and... I don't know." Her face turns pink. I can see it even in the dim lights. She ducks her chin, avoiding my gaze. Finally, she shrugs, sighing. "We're all a little messed up." She glances over her shoulder, and I know she's talking about her entire friend group. "Eli most of all," she says quietly, so he can't hear, her eyes on mine again. "It's just attention without strings." There's a vulnerability to her words, and maybe it's the alcohol I can smell on her breath, or the weed, or the nicotine, all of it going to her head, along with our fight, but I appreciate her getting real with me.

I don't think I could reciprocate, but it feels nice, all the same.

"I get it," I say, and I think I mean it. Nic was kind of that. I tap the unlit end of the cigarette over my bracelets, thinking of my scars. From the outside, it'd appear he meant something to me. Mom thought I was *broken* over him. Sebastian wouldn't look me in the eye for a week, and even Reece left me alone out of disgust, maybe, or, I like to think, a little fear.

But I didn't give a fuck about Nic.

I gave a fuck about what he gave me. What Luna wants. Dominic, too.

Attention.

"Anyway," Luna says, sighing. "Guess I'll stay off that if you're gonna be drawing knives and shit." She side-eyes me, and I just laugh, and for once, with someone besides Eli, I think I actually feel it.

I take another inhale, blowing out smoke before I ask, "You guys don't do anything for Halloween?" I didn't bring a costume because Eli never said anything about it, and I can enjoy it without dressing up, but I'm kind of surprised.

Luna grins. "We do." She tips her chin up, exhaling gray smoke into the night sky. "A Halloween Hangover party," she says with a laugh, turning to look at me.

I frown, thinking this is another rich kid thing I don't understand.

"Every year, my parents go out of town two weeks after Halloween, on a cruise. I have a party at my place."

"Wow," I say, shaking my head. "Was no one going to tell me this?"

"I'm telling you now." She winks. "You're invited. Just leave the knives at home, killer."

DOMINIC, ELI, AND I STAY UP LATER THAN ANYONE. LUNA GOES to bed with a grand exit, flicking her tongue between her peace fingers. Janelle and Jasper were much more somber, and I think they were trying to be sneaky, because one minute, they're on the balcony with the rest of us, and the next, they slipped through the door, gliding it closed quietly.

I had a few drinks, Dom a few more, but Eli didn't drink anything.

We all smoke, though, passing the joint and listening to music as the waves roll. And eventually, we end up in mine and Eli's bedroom, the three of us, together.

I lie between them, passing the joint to my left. Eli's fingers graze my own, lingering for a heartbeat before he takes the weed, and I drop my hand by my side, my arm against Dom's.

The lights are on a dimmer switch, a set of three on a horizontal bar attached to the ceiling, and they're at their lowest setting in Eli's room. I thought it was his dad's, when he dropped our stuff in here earlier this afternoon. But no.

Of course, it's his.

A king bed in gray, black walls, a door ajar leading to a bathroom with only one sink instead of two, but the claw foot bathtub is there, just like the one at his house.

There's another balcony, too, and now, only the screen separates the room from the outside, the sound of the ocean turning over against the shore drifting in, heavy curtains pushed apart to let the cool breeze filter through into the room.

It's mainly empty, save for the pair of nightstands, our luggage, the door to what I assume is a walk-in closet, the entrance to the bathroom, and the three of us, on the made-up bed, wearing our pajamas.

Or rather, I'm wearing pajamas—a loose, white tank with a green skull on it, faded and picked from years of use and oversized, black shorts—and the boys are in gym shorts, no shirts.

Bare skin, too close, but I'm high enough not to care.

"You believe in heaven?" Dom asks the question beside me as he chokes on a crackling laugh.

I let my eyes close, bringing my hands to my core, fingers wide and a smile on my face.

The scent of marijuana and the ocean is a salve, the boys like bookends beside me an indulgence. For now, everything is settled. Everything is behind us.

"It's this," Eli says, his voice low.

I feel like I'm spinning. Floating. I keep my eyes closed.

"Remember the first time we got high with Winslet?" Dom's words are so quiet.

"I remember." There's something sexy in Eli's voice. More than usual.

It's... disturbing to me, and I don't know why.

My heartbeat is climbing higher in my chest, and my medicine is in my bag, on the floor, and paranoia seems to seep through my high. I felt it earlier, before this conversation, after I smoked the first shared joint with Dominic and Eli on the living room floor while Jasper and Janelle spoke, sober, on the couch.

The creeping panic then felt like a knowledge of time passing. The clock on the wall—matte black and white, analog—ticking seconds by, contributed. The music was loud then—it's softer now, "Take On the World" by You Me At Six, playing from Eli's phone somewhere—but I could still hear the shift of time.

I started to think I might be high forever.

I chewed all my nails, but Dominic and Eli volleyed conversation back and forth, and I sat propped up against the latter, until he decided we should head to bed, but Dominic came, and no one told him to leave.

I try to swallow down my panic attack.

I try to breathe in. Out. With closed eyes, the room feels like it's spinning faster. I open my eyes, digging my fingers into the thin fabric of my shirt to ground myself.

"She was so happy." Dom sighs the words more than says them.

Eli is quiet. He passes the joint to me, and when I turn my head to tell him no, I'm good, dark green circled with black sucks me in. His face reflects some sort of… tenderness. He never acts as if he hurts, unless he's lashing out. But maybe Winslet meant more to him than he lets on.

I take the joint, nearly finished.

I bring it to my lips, and Eli turns on his side, propping his head up in his hand, watching me as I breathe in, holding smoke in my lungs. I give the joint to Dominic without looking at him.

He takes it.

Eli is still staring down at me.

"Sometimes, you remind me of her." It's Dom who says that, and I know without looking, he's talking to me. "She was smart, and soft, but…" He clears his throat.

I gaze up at Eli.

"She was so fucking dark too."

A second passes. Then, Eli dives down without warning, breathing in some of the smoke I held in my mouth, but his lips are on mine before it all flows through my lungs.

I startle, a reflex, but I reach for him instead of away.

I'm gripping his shoulders, my body pivoted toward him as his tongue demands entry into my mouth, and I give in, melting as I do, closing my eyes, surrendering.

Despite his sudden pounce, this kiss is strangely gentle. *Passionate.* He grabs my wrists, even so, positions them both over my head. He pulls my body down lower with one arm, then climbs on top of me.

"She was so, so dark," he echoes Dom, his voice quiet, and I don't know if he's talking about me, or Winslet. His fingers are gentle around the bones of my wrist. I think of the name there, scarred into my skin.

I think of his text when I sent him the picture of the razorblade.

I want to do it.

He nudges his nose to mine, and I realize Dominic is curiously still beside us.

My pulse is a drumbeat inside my head.

Eli's scent is stronger than that, his mouth is over mine. "You're so much dark and so much light."

"Just like her," Dom adds, his voice ethereal.

I lick my lips, and Eli's tongue laps over both mine and my mouth, warm and soft.

I let my knees fall to the side as he licks me.

I don't know when it happened, how he got so close, but Dominic's mouth presses to my shoulder cap, so similar to the way it did at Eli's pool house. A hushed whimper leaves my lips.

Eli turns his head marginally to train his gaze on Dom, and I trace the curve of Eli's nose in my mind.

I can feel the lingering of Dom's kiss, the cool air from the balcony seeming to drift over my skin. Next comes Dominic's fingers along my arm, and Eli is shifting from his knees to press against me.

He wants this.

He wants me.

He licks my mouth again, all the way to my nose, letting Dominic stay as he cuts his attention away from him.

I glance at Dom to see if he's surprised, too.

Eli grabs my face. *"Me,"* he says. "Look at *me.*" He kisses me softly, squishing my lips together with his hand. "She always looked at him."

My stomach flips. Dom says nothing.

My knees widen.

Dom keeps his fingers dancing over my arms, and I can feel him watching me. So close.

My tongue dances with Eli's, and I want to touch him. I want to reach for him. I want my hands all fucking over him. My boy. *Mine.*

Him.

Him, him, him.

"Eli," I whisper against his mouth when we try to breathe, but we can't, because he's kissing his name from my lips until he answers me, my mouth numb from his.

"What is it, baby girl?" Before I can answer, we're together again. He's licking me and biting me softly, and our saliva isn't contained inside our mouths. It's over my top lip, and on the corner of my face, and he's all over me.

Dominic's fingers drift over my underarm, down lower, along my side.

I think the panic is receding. The weed makes me feel loose instead. Limber. Floating. Dominic's fingertips reach my ribs.

My muscles jump.

"I love you," I say, even as Dominic's lips whisper over the inside of my arm, and Eli's punishes me for it by gripping my jaw harder.

I try to break free of his hold on my wrist, but he only laughs, suddenly cruel, against my mouth. "Oh yeah?" I feel how hard he is, but I think he's angry, too. "You *love* me?"

"She said that to you before, too, didn't she?" Dom's voice sounds faraway.

"But she only ever loved *you.*"

I close my eyes. I don't know what they're talking about.

"I love you, Eli." I whisper it, and I feel as if I'm drifting toward the ceiling.

Our mouths are a collision again. He groans into me. I swallow the sound.

Dominic kisses me so, so softly. His fingers stroke up and

down my ribcage. Sensations overwhelm me, and I want to touch Dominic's hair. I want to grab Eli's throat.

I want them everywhere.

My thigh muscles ache with how far my legs are spread, inviting them in, giving them permission to own me like I own them. My nipples are tight points, my tank top shifts as Eli lets me breathe and dips his head and pulls at the cotton strap with his teeth, exposing me. He sucks on the underside of my breast, a strangled sound in his throat, like he can't get enough of me. I'm tense, my spine curved as I arch into him, tipping my chin up as Dominic's kisses grow more frequent on my skin, but still feather soft.

I'm whimpering, my fingers are curled into fists, wrists still under Eli's bruising grip.

But in my head, as Dominic's fingers drift lower, I'm at Sky Wash.

I never told Eli.

What was the point? So he could hurt over an old wound too?

Now, I think I should have told him.

"Eli," I whisper. "I don't think I want this."

Dominic's lips are so, so soft. But when he speaks, his words don't match. "I think *she* said that before too."

I don't hear Eli. I just feel Dominic shift on the bed, no longer touching me, no longer kissing me. Eli cups my face in his hand, but it's like I can't see anything at all.

ZACHARY'S HANDS ARE ON MY HIPS. HE MISSES ME. HE DOESN'T *remember, or maybe there's a different version in his head, or maybe I dreamed it all. A nightmare come to life, maybe he's innocent. Maybe I'm the problem.*

It's me.
It's me.
It's me.

. . .

I show up at Nic's house after his game. My wrist is throbbing from his initials. He isn't answering the phone. He doesn't come to the door. He doesn't open his window. He's avoiding me.

Sirens wail in the distance.

They're not for me, but I'm running.

Sebastian vouches for me to Mom, when she asks where I was, because Sebastian is high.

It's the next day.

I follow Nic into the bathroom at school. He's scared of me.

He's scared, and I like it.

He's scared, he's scared, he's scared—

I'm in the car wash.

I'm in my bed.

I smell Zach's sweat, and his hand is sticky, fingers in my hair.

I

I

I—

There's a crack. A clatter. Something shatters.

A thud.

"I'm sorry, I'm sorry, I'm sorry." Dominic's words, meant to placate.

Eli says nothing.

I'm on my side, curled into a ball, no one is touching me, my fingers are over my face, and I don't want to move them. I'm trembling, my heart is beating way too fast. So fast, I think I'm going to throw up. The taste of marijuana has my stomach convulsing. I'm rocking back and forth, and I imagine jumping over the railing of the balcony.

I'm going to jump.

If I get off of this bed, *I will jump.*

Another thud.

Dom's words again. "I... *You were right fucking there!*"

I feel something wet on my fingers. Blood?

No, no. It's worse.

It's tears. Salty and hot and hopeless.

I press my fingers harder against my eyes, wanting the pressure to keep me grounded. I don't know how much time passes. The only sound seems to be my own lungs working, too hard, too fast alongside my heart. The streaky tears along my cheeks burn, matching the fire of humiliation and panic and dread in my stomach. I want to be alone.

I hope they left.

I hope they're gone.

I hope I can climb over the balcony by myself when I can stop shaking.

After what feels like an eternity, I hear a voice.

"Eden."

I freeze.

They didn't leave.

I wish I could wake up in my own bed, my own house, because when I move my fingers from my face, I'll have to say something. I'll have to explain something, won't I? I can't. I don't want to. My thoughts feel like they could eat me alive, if my heart doesn't give out first.

I barely remember that word is my name.

"Eden." Again, from his lips.

Despite my quiet panic, it's like a compulsion, giving in to his unspoken request.

Open your eyes. Let me in.

He has too much power over me. I can't do anything about it.

I move my fingers.

I open my eyes.

They feel so heavy, and the room is spinning. The marijuana hasn't slowed my pulse and it's so fierce against my ribcage, I think it could crack my bones.

Eli is kneeling on the bed, leaning in toward me. His face is full of concern, a wrinkle in his brow, his bottom lip between his teeth. It's almost as if, when he saw my eyes, he also saw how bad this is. There're words on the tip of his tongue, but he doesn't get them out immediately.

I'm fucked up too.

I'm just like you.

I wonder if he'll recoil. A monster wants an angel. An Adonis of any gender. Not a reflection of his wrongs. Not Narcissus, a mirror of his tainted beauty.

But he doesn't back away.

He says, "Tell me what you need. Tell me how to help." The plea sounds like an echo. A performance of something he's rehearsed or heard before.

My tongue feels stuck to the roof of my mouth. The taste of marijuana is thick like cotton, edging even around my teeth.

Eli reaches out and brushes a stray hair behind my ear and I'm shivering. But I've stopped rocking.

When I don't answer him, he carefully pulls back the top sheet, knocking off a pillow to the floor as he does. I don't look for Dominic, but I hear him sigh or groan or both.

Eli slides into bed, leaning against two stacked pillows, then he's lifting me from under my arms, pulling me to his chest. I'm on my knees to help him, and after adjusting elbows and hands and thighs, I'm in his lap, my head resting on his shoulder, arms twined around his neck.

I thought I'd hate this. I thought I needed to be alone to breathe.

I don't hate it. I don't want to move.

"I can feel your heart beating through your back." It's not sweet, the tone he uses. I'd like to think it's fear, or worry, but it sounds more reverent than both. "It's so strong," he says, where I might have used "wild" or "dangerous."

I bury my head against his collarbone, his chin rests on my hair. My knees are pulled close to my chest like his arms hold me to him. Me curled in on myself, him curled into me.

I keep seeing it in my head. Not the past. A future action. Getting off the bed. Walking to the balcony. Grabbing the rails. Hauling myself over the side. It's like a call. A summons. A beckoning.

It's like I'm haunted or possessed. Over and over and over, my brain plays out my fear.

There's a noise. Constant and jagged.

It's hard to breathe as is, and I want the sound to stop. I turn my head into Eli's skin, my nose along his clavicle, hoping his familiarity will calm me.

I'm breathing and breathing, and I realize... the noise is me.

"What's wrong with her?" Dominic's words as I hold in air, trying to get the terrible wheezing to cease. "Should we call someone? Do we need to—"

"She's having a panic attack." Eli speaks calmly. Loudly. Like maybe he's talking to me more than Dominic. His fingers brush down my hair, drifting over my skin. He shifts his head and presses cool lips to my temple. "You're having a panic attack," he says, and I know.

I do know. Logically. But it's brought on by the weed and I think it's more like a bad trip or something or...

"How long will this last?" I keep my eyes closed as I speak against his chest. "How long?"

His arm tightens around my back, hand resting over my hip. "Not long, Eden."

I like when he says my name. Better than anything else he could call me, I like when he says my name best.

His lips touch me so softly, it's like the whisper of a breeze. "It's okay. You're okay. I've got you."

My heart doesn't slow. My mind doesn't stop spinning, but it's everything I need to hear. I drop my fingers to his chest, flexing them against firm muscle, my face pressed over his heart.

"Do you want to talk?" he asks softly, still grazing his hand over the back of my neck.

My lips stick to his skin as I speak, my words muffled, but I don't pick my head up. "I… Yes." A distraction. I need a distraction.

"Okay," he says slowly, not stopping the way he touches me, tracing patterns on the nape of my neck, my hair swept to the side. "What do you want to do tomorrow? For Halloween?"

I keep breathing, and my breath echoes back to me as close as I am to him, warm puffs of air along my mouth. "Let's go downtown." I don't want to think, I just speak, throwing something out. "Let's go into the ocean. Maybe after, a road trip. A haunted house."

"I love driving." I hear the smile in his words, and it makes me feel like smiling, too. "We'll do all of that," he promises. "What do you want to do downtown?"

My chest is heaving, my pulse still beats throughout my entire body. But as I think through his question, I'm not on the balcony. I'm not jumping over the side. I'm not splatting on the concrete.

"A bar," I say.

He smiles. I feel his lips curving into the shape of it, high along my forehead. "A bar?" he repeats.

Somewhere in the room, away from the bed, Dominic snorts. *He didn't run either.* "And what would you like to do at a bar? Watch everyone else get drunk?" He tries for teasing, but there's a shakiness to his words betraying his nerves.

I don't open my eyes, but I force a false lightness, too. "You don't have fake IDs? I thought it was a rich boy thing."

"What kind of movies have you been watching?" Dom counters, incredulous.

Eli drops his head and runs the tip of his nose over the back of my neck.

Goosebumps form along my arms.

"She doesn't watch movies," he says, and I think of our failed attempt to watch one on the couch. My face grows hotter. "She reads books." He kisses me again, over my top vertebrae. A shiver runs down my spine, once only damp with sweat. "Don't you, baby girl?"

I nod but don't speak.

"Well, I don't know what books you're reading but fake IDs are hard to come by..." Dom trails off, then adds, with a dawning awareness, "Wait." He snaps his fingers. "There's that place, Eli. The one we went to. Before..."

Eli tightens his hold on me. "Yes. We'll go to a bar. We'll get drinks," he tells me, gently steering the conversation away from what I think is Winslet.

In the silence, I realize my pulse isn't shaking my chest anymore. I don't feel as if my body jolts with every beat.

I relax, marginally, in Eli's arms.

"You can get drunk," he keeps talking. "Do whatever you want. We'll spend all day in the ocean, all night following you around. Driving, if you want."

Dominic laughs again, but he doesn't argue.

Eli's fingers slip through my mass of hair, massaging my scalp. Panic recedes, little by little, with his touch and his words.

"We won't smoke any weed," he promises, and my teeth show this time, when I smile. Another kiss planted on top of my head, almost like a compulsion. Like he couldn't stop himself even if he tried. "We'll jump the waves, you can push Dominic under. I'll hold him there for you until you tell me to stop."

My heart slows, even though I know I should be a little nervous for Dominic with those words. I just don't have room to feel anything or think anything. All I can do is hold onto the sound of his voice.

Then, ten minutes or two or one hour later, everything slips into darkness, and I'm happy in it.

When I slowly come to, eyes fuzzy from being caught in that gray space between waking and sleeping, I realize there's a crick in my neck.

It isn't excruciating, but I feel the precursor to pain. It'll hurt to move.

There's only darkness when I manage to get my eyes pried open, full of what feels like sand as I blink, and blink again, and some more.

My mouth is stuck to something, wetness down the side of my chin that I realize with a sudden surge of embarrassment is drool.

With the realization is another.

I'm stuck to Eli.

I shift slightly, trying to get more comfortable, my fingers pressed against firm, soft skin.

But I nearly jump out of my own when Eli's quiet voice, so close to my ear, says, "Hi."

My pulse ricochets all over, and I wonder when my heart will get a break. If I should simply plan to take my medicine every day I spend around him.

He must feel me jump, because he says, "It's okay, Eden."

I suck in air, resisting the urge to push him away and barricade myself in the bathroom. What a disaster I was, just hours ago. *Was it hours?* The sun isn't up, and I couldn't have slept an entire day away, right?

I lift my head, wipe the back of my hand over my mouth, resettle against his chest, forcing myself to stay.

Stay, stay, stay.

I can hear it in his pulse.

Don't run from me.

I close my eyes, fighting the impulse. "What time is it?"

His arms, already so heavy around me, pull me in tighter. "I don't know. Sun isn't up yet."

My fingers are splayed over his chest, the sliver of a cut I made. I feel the roughness of his skin there. *God, I really did that.*

I brush my thumb across my bottom lip, trying to wipe away the drool completely.

I want to spiral back to sleep.

It would feel just like running away, but more polite.

I know it won't happen, though. My mind is free of the panic, but now comes another type of anxiety. Embarrassment from a moment of weakness.

"Dominic?" I ask, my voice throaty as I try to deflect from my own actions.

"In his room." I can't read anything in Eli's tone. I wonder if he regrets letting Dom touch me.

"Can you tell me what you were thinking, last night?" Eli asks, so quietly.

I don't want to tell him because it'll sound like a weakness. Like I'm a victim. It'll sound like I need him to fix the problem and I don't.

But I remember his truths in the library. So many words spun with blood, and maybe he doesn't experience shame, but he's intelligent enough to know he should. To understand everything he confessed—and it *was* a confession—is something society bristles at. He's dealt with the proof for so long. Doctors, psych wards, a mother walking out.

I keep my head buried against him, aware I should brush my teeth, but I know I can't put this off for that.

"I saw someone I used to know. When I went with my mom to the beach."

Eli doesn't react. He doesn't speak or move or… breathe. His chest doesn't rise and fall beneath my lips.

I guess it is a reaction. Just the quiet kind.

"My brother's friend." I hope he remembers the story, so I don't have to say it all over, out loud. He works very hard not to move a muscle. But he inhales again. Just once.

He remembers.

I want to know what he's thinking at the same time I'd rather move on. Never speak of this again. Three words I gave him, and it feels like three words too many.

He exhales.

"Was your mom there?" If I heard him speak from the distant line of a telephone, I would assume he's disinterested. Bored.

But I feel the tension in his body, shielding mine.

"No."

"Did he hurt you?"

"No."

"Eden."

I tip my head up, my eyes woolen, and the dark edges of the ceiling spin, but I meet his gaze in the cover of what looks like night.

"Baby, please don't lie."

"He didn't." It isn't a lie. I wasn't hurt. Not physically. But I know he wants more. Maybe telling him some of my secrets will help him feel closer with me, like his in the library that night did to us. "He… hugged me." I hear the words. How they sound.

Dull.

They carry no weight as words alone.

But everything is always heavier with us.

"He did, huh?" Not even a touch of anger. Only endless depths of calm.

I am not fooled.

I take a breath. "It's over."

He smiles, the white of his teeth visible in the dark room. "Oh?"

He doesn't have Zachary's name. I won't give him a name. "People have hurt you too. I don't go around smiling creepy little smiles and asking cryptic little questions in order to get back at them." His mom.

Tell me about your mom.

"You attacked Luna last night for touching me. You pulled a knife on her." There's wonder in his tone, even as he reminds me I'm not a saint. I possess him, too.

But I don't want him to get in trouble over someone not

worth a breath. "If you had been there, it would've been one thing—"

"Let's not talk about what would've happened if I had been there."

My temper grows, seeming to burn away some of my high. All of my paranoia. It feels better, to be angry. Better than sad or scared or haunted. *"Eli."*

He lifts a single brow, his face a mask of boyishness. Like we're discussing ice cream or movies or bands or Chaucer. "Hmm?"

"I'm okay."

He sweeps his gaze over me.

I disentangle myself from him, like if he can see me from further away, he'll see how okay I am.

At once I panic over the loss of his warmth while some of my anxiety eases for it, cool air rushing in where our bodies had been joined. I rub a fist over my eye, grateful it's still dim.

I have no idea what I look like.

"Eden."

I drop my fist, glancing at it on my thigh. "I'm sorry I panicked. The weed… I'm sorry I ruined your night."

My shin is parallel to the head of the bed, my kneecap close to his, beneath the covers, and it occurs to me he was sleeping sitting up. With me.

For me.

I don't look at him, only stare at the sheet over his thighs.

"Eden."

He wants me to look at him, I can tell. But I don't. Not until he says, "Eden, don't be like this," and I hear it. Maybe it's the late hour or strange night or maybe even the marijuana lingering in his own system, but there're the wobbly notes of his voice, some of his surety slipping away.

It's so unusual for him, I look up.

"I won't make this a thing," he says earnestly. "But…"

I grit my teeth. It isn't that I don't understand. I just don't ever want him to see me as less than, and he's already so hard to keep up with. If he starts thinking he has to save me at every turn, watch over every move I make, he'll grow bored, faster. He doesn't need any more burdens to carry.

Whether he realizes it or not, I know he already has so many of his own. He needs to chase highs, not swoop down to catch my lows. And I *know* he'd do bad things for me.

Something terrible.

But I need to keep him as long as I can. I don't want him taken from me, too soon.

The silence stretches.

He doesn't finish his sentence.

"What?" I find myself asking, even though I didn't think I wanted to hear it. I run my tongue over my teeth, lips dry. "What is it?"

He brings his hand up, over his mouth, turning his head. Then he drops his hand and says, without looking at me, "I won't make it a thing," he promises again. "But the way I feel about you, sometimes… it's overwhelming."

There's a soreness in my throat. *In my lungs.* Like I've been hit in the chest, and all the air has abandoned me.

I curl my fingers in the sheets for something to hold onto.

"Sometimes I think I'll do something we'll regret just to keep you."

We'll regret.

I'd like to say I don't know what he means. That it's not possible to feel remorse for something I didn't do.

Except those words feel like an omen, and I know with us, nothing is impossible.

And *nothing* can be a nightmare as much as a dream. Besides, he's echoing my own fears back to me.

"I won't let you." It's a promise. A vow. "I wouldn't let you do something… like that."

The silence lingers, and I'm torn between the urge to flee and the desire to never move. We could leave it like this. My word to him, to keep him out of trouble when it comes to me. We could pretend it'll never end, because of it.

But he doesn't let us pretend.

I build castles in the sky. He kicks them down into hell.

Still facing away from me, he smiles before he says, "Even you wouldn't be able to stop me." And I know it isn't words of bravado.

It's only truth.

45

Eli

THE HALLOWEEN MORNING is barely there to greet us.

Shivering beside me, her arm brushing against mine, Eden says, "Maybe they were right."

Probably. Based on the empty coastline, the thin threads of pink and orange not enough to warm us, the waves rough and the sand cool beneath our feet, her sandals and mine dangling from the fingertips of each of my hands, they were likely right. Dominic and Luna, shockingly the only two people up, refused to come outside because they said the water would be too cold.

Janelle's door was closed.

Jasper's was open, and he wasn't in the room beyond.

Dom and Luna trudged downstairs when they heard us heading out, but when they saw us in swimsuits with towels over their shoulders, it was a no from them.

I can't say I'm not glad.

I drop mine and Eden's sandals, then my bright green towel.

Eden's, bright, electric blue, is still wrapped around her body, tucked under her arms as she hugs herself. Her eyes are swollen from lack of sleep, no trace of makeup on her face because she cried it all off last night.

It felt wrong to interrupt that, the tears tracking down her cheeks.

I had to wait.

After I pushed Dom against the wall because I needed to do *something*, I made myself wait for the worst of her silent tears to stop.

I already flushed all of the weed down the toilet. It didn't affect me like it did her, but then again, I let Dominic touch her.

I think it did affect me, after all.

And someone else touched her, too. More crippling. *Just this past weekend. When I wasn't there for her.*

I swallow the knot in my throat as I watch her.

A strand of hair slipped free from her messy braids whips around her face as a cold breeze blows.

She's staring at the Atlantic, and I can see the wildness of the tide in her irises, specifically at the top, above her pupil, where a shard of blue is lodged between brown and green. Her lips are trembling, despite the fact it really isn't *that* cold.

But she hasn't eaten, she's running on fitful starts and bursts of sleep, and I don't know exactly what went through her head last night, but it was hard to watch.

I'm thinking of some words to offer her, something to touch on what happened but to stay away from her confession, because I know she doesn't like to talk about it. Him.

I grind my teeth together.

I think of him climbing into her bed. I think of choking him to death with her sheets wrapped around his fucking throat, whoever he is.

"I'm getting in." Her words erase my thoughts, and so does the way she drops her towel. Without preamble, no teasing, it isn't meant to be seductive. But as she walks away from me, a straight path to the water without looking back, it's just that.

I see the smallest of dimples on the back of her thighs, her wide hips, and in the space between them both, the best ass I've ever seen in the world. For a moment, I'm transfixed by it, and I don't realize she's dived into a shallow wave until her body disappears from view, bringing me back to life, jerking me from my fantasies.

Get it together, Eli.

I know she can swim. I've seen her do it. But something propels me forward anyway. A rush to save her, even though she doesn't need it. It would just make me feel so much better, to know I could. An overabundance of caution, I run toward her, kicking up sand and my pulse as I do, trying to search through my memories for an affection like this one.

Did I ever feel this way about anyone?

My mother's eyes come to mind. They're always so bright in my memories, like they were the day I stared up at them through the bathwater. They shouldn't have been, it seems impossible, human eyes weren't made for seeing underwater, she should've been a blur.

But in the memory version of the event, at least, she was crystal clear.

Did I want to protect her?

Would I have jumped into a freezing cold ocean on the possibility I might save her? Maybe once upon a time. Or maybe I didn't realize the emotion—protectiveness, possession —until she walked out.

Is that the lesson you wanted to teach me, Mom?

Icy water splashes around my ankles, the ocean so much harder to heat than anything else, and with little sunlight, it's not even close to warm.

The sea laps against my shins, the churning noise of white-capped waves almost as loud as my thoughts.

Did you want me to care about something?

Did you not see I always cared about you?

But I didn't look like love. She couldn't see me as that. Maybe because Dad loved her too close, she needed something lighter. Kinder. More gentle.

I dive down into the navy water, the cold sending pins and needles along my limbs. I don't open my eyes, salt seems to burn worse than chlorine, and I have no idea where Eden is, but I know I'll find her. Our souls probably wouldn't ever let us get too far apart. She's close, I know.

I don't think about her being anywhere but close.

Instead, I'm thinking of the type of love Eden wants.

Soft and sweet or hard and dangerous? With her, I feel each of those things, tenfold.

Nothing is shallow. But when will it be too deep?

I push my toes along the bottom of the ocean floor, sand and shells and things I'd rather not name beneath them. Dom is obsessed with sharks. I'd rather never meet one.

Bursting through the surface, gulping down cold air, every hair on my body standing on end between the contrast of cold water and cool air, I tread water, realizing I don't stay touching the bottom.

I shake my hair from my eyes, using one hand to scrub over my face and clear my vision as I turn my head one way, then the other, looking for her. The coast is empty.

A bird caws overhead.

"Eden!" I shout her name as I circle my arms under the surface, keeping myself afloat. *You know how to fucking swim.* Anger over fear, because one makes you move and the other can freeze you.

But what if she was still high? What if she was still messed up from last night, and her mind forgot how to tell her body to fucking move in the water and—

Arms come around my neck, legs winding over my torso, ankles locked against my abs.

"Jesus fucking Christ." The swear is a whisper, even as I close my eyes, relaxing with the feel of her slippery, warm skin against mine while she clings to me. I clamp my fingers over her wrist, using my other arm to keep us both above water.

I feel her laugh against my back, then her mouth on my shoulder.

My entire body grows warm in the cold of the ocean.

"Were you nervous?" she whispers, her breath against my skin.

I glance at her out of the corner of my eye, releasing her wrist and moving us toward the shore, because the waves are choppy, and we're past their breaking point, but I don't want to risk it.

"Shut up," I tell her, and when I can stand in the water, I grab her again, pulling her around my body as she lets out the softest gasp. I wrap my arms around her waist, and her legs do the same to mine, her fingers through my wet hair as she tilts her head and looks up at me, water dripping down her nose, over her lips.

"Do you want me to slap you, Eli Addison?" she whispers, a smirk on her mouth, sleepy eyes crinkled, and thick, wet lashes clumped together.

The ocean jostles us a little, and before I can answer her, she turns her head, and her mouth falls open into an O, her hold on me frantic. "We should move."

I turn to follow her gaze, seeing the big wave curling upward, white foam rising from the rough surface of the sea.

She tries to get down, pushing against my chest, dropping her legs from my waist, but I just move my hands to her ass, keeping her close to me.

Her nails find my chest as she whips her head around, flecks of saltwater splashing the sides of our faces, the roar of the wave coming closer.

"What?" I ask her, biting back my smile. "You don't trust me?"

"Eli, it's fucking enormous!" She's still fighting me, her body slick against mine, and she's right, actually, it's a pretty big wave, but…

"That sounded a lot like 'no'." I pull her close, turning my back to the approaching crash, and a second later, a scream laced with a laugh leaving her mouth, the wave descends on us, sending me to my knees, but I don't let go of her as we're both forced under, abruptly silencing her voice.

The sand burns against my kneecaps, my shins, and the force of the wave spins us both along the bottom of the ocean.

For a second, dull thuds of the power of the sea echoing around me, Eden still in my arms, my eyes closed, and breath cut off, I wonder what it would be like to never come up.

How would it feel to drown?

I really, really don't want her to leave me.

Down here, she couldn't. There's nowhere to run, for two bodies at the bottom of the Atlantic.

But just as the wave leaves us, and I feel the change in the temperature of the water, marginally warmer because it's swept us to the shore, all I have to do is stand on shaky legs to pop above the surface, the depths only to my shins now.

She's gasping for air, still in my arms, which is quite an accomplishment, us clawing onto one another in the turbulence of the sea.

Her nails are lodged into my shoulders, her eyes wide, dark hair slicked back from her face, her cheeks pink.

I take a few steps with her in my arms, getting us out of the danger zone of another wreck.

"You..." She sputters, closing her eyes, a laugh leaving her lips. "You are such a jerk." Her eyes flash open, and for a second, the weak rays of sunlight reflecting off the expansive sea, her irises appear wholly blue, like the ocean, and I don't know why, but I stop breathing, just staring at her.

Joy, and adrenaline, and she even looks less tired. It's all over her beautiful face.

Then she slaps me, out of nowhere, not hard enough to hurt, but I still feel the sting, and her burst of laughter, more a nervous giggle than anything else, has my heart swelling, no ill feelings in my body.

But I still drop to my knees and push her against the sand, the water a receding halo around her body.

I press my palms to the shore, on either side of her head,

my fingertips sinking into the wet sand. Water drips along her body beneath me, her hands gripping my biceps.

"Sorry," she says, but she doesn't mean it.

I dip my head and kiss her, and she pushes against me, tearing her mouth away. I know what she wants, and I roll over, onto my back, and she's on top of me, her thighs splayed, core over my pelvis.

She grabs my wrists and yanks them over my head, and I let her, admiring the view of her overpowering me, even if it's only pretend.

She already has so much power in so many more important ways than the physical.

This position suits us.

She presses her wet palm flat to my cheek, where she hit me. Leaning close to me, so we're heart-to-heart, she says, "I love you, you little brat."

My heart is racing in my chest, and it's a feeling so foreign to me, outside of physical exercise and wrestling matches, I almost forget what it is, the thudding of life inside my veins.

"Are you saying you only hit me because you love me?" It's a joke, but her face falls, and I wish I hadn't said it.

I think of my dad.

I wonder if she knows.

I don't find out, though, not right now. Right now, she releases my wrists, grabs my face in both hands, and presses her lips to mine as my fingers dig into the sides of her hips.

We don't get up for a long, long time, and by the time we break apart, my lips are numb, and my dick is hard, and all I want to do is take her back to the house so I can show her just how much I love her, too.

I ROLL TO A STOP AT A GREEN LIGHT.

Immediately, her attention lasers in on me. Satisfaction achieved. I'm smiling at her when we make eye contact. The glow of dash lights and buttons from the center console illuminate the curve of her cheekbones and the pout of her lips, even with the darkness dropping around us.

"What're you doing?" She has one arm on the ledge of the rolled down window, drumming her fingers to The Plot in You playing too loudly for us to hold a conversation.

I glance in the rear-view mirror.

No one is coming. Jasper, Janelle, Luna and Dom are long gone, because I stalled getting ready. Because the last thing I wanted was to share Eden's attention with Dominic again. I needed her to myself, just these few minutes.

It's October on Grove Beach Island. Or Grove Beach, rather, since we just crossed over the bridge. This is a tourist town. There's a college not too from here, but far enough away that affording even a studio apartment in the city limits is too much for the average college student. A few pumpkins line a few houses, but otherwise, this place is dead.

We run this shit tonight because there's no one else here to do it.

"I'm just looking at you."

A long, dark lock of hair falls from behind her pierced ear, to the front of her face. She has her hair down tonight. A long black skirt that clings to her, ripped up at the ends in a way that's borderline trashy, the boots she always wears, and a white crop top with thin straps, the purity of the color contrasts with the darkness of her hair and the silver of her three necklaces. In my back seat is a ripped-up jean jacket she likes, an inverted cross on the back of it painted in black. I kind of wonder if she made it herself. It's cool, though.

A blush blooms over her face, along her nose. "Stop looking and start driving."

My fingers flex over the shifter. Then, for no reason, I see it in my head. Someone touching her, someone who had fucking hurt her. I can't tell if I'm more jealous or angry, and I don't really care either way. It just doesn't feel good, no matter the emotion.

"Yes ma'am." Then I shift gears, the engine humming as I tighten my grip on the wheel and run through the red light at the intersection.

"Eli!" She squeals out my name in equal parts admonishment and pleasure, and something about it warms my chest.

I don't love that it makes me so happy when she's happy. It means my happiness is tied to hers. And not just happiness, either. Last night, when she was upset, I could feel her pain mirrored in my heart.

I've done this dance before.

It's like running toward a cliff you've already dropped off from once, barely made it out alive after the fall. But I can't stop. She's bewitched me, and even if there was a potion to take it all away, make it all stop, I'd shatter the bottle and let it seep onto the floor before I'd ever drink it.

I am fucking gone for her.

Two hours later, and we're leaving the bar. Skeletons, the same place Dad told me he used to score coke at. I don't know how he became a lawyer, but I'm sure if anyone ever looked into *that* place, he might not be one anymore.

Everyone, save for me and Jasper—who's driving Janelle's car with her and Luna—had shots. But even Jasper, alongside Eden, took the Adderall Dominic passed around after we paid the bill (*"Chill, it's literally just Adderall."*) I didn't think it was a good idea, knowing Eden's condition, and everything with last night. But who am I to control her?

I hate control, personally.

It's hard for me to breathe beneath it. I know on one level society may believe my dad is abusive, but I don't see it that way, because what would feel real to me, what would feel *more* like abuse, would be stifling. Being grounded. Not allowed to wrestle. To come here, alone. He checks in with me, because if I wind up in prison, it doesn't look too good for his law firm. It's not as if he's completely neglectful. But he gives me a long, long leash, and for that, I'd take our fights any day.

So I let Eden do whatever, and when she went to the bathroom with Janelle and Luna, and came back out clutching cigarettes between her fingers, smiling like she won the lottery, I didn't say anything about that either.

Just like I didn't say anything about this allegedly haunted hotel we're driving to now, in the middle of the night. It's in Virginia, just past the border, several hours away, but everyone was down. And Eden was excited.

In the backseat, Dom is, too.

I shift gears over Eden's hand, my fingers splayed between hers as I attempt to pass a neon orange SRT-4 from the right lane.

But as I do, my engine whining, the Dodge revs their own, trying to thwart me.

Eden laughs from the passenger seat and Dom says, "You gonna let them disrespect you like that, man?"

Before I can decide, the Dodge blows their horn once, long and loud.

I glance over at them, my window cracked, and I see their headlights flashing on the empty highway ahead.

We're not quite in Virginia yet, where speeding is a very bad idea, no matter who you are. They catch that shit with planes.

My adrenaline surges, and Eden does a little dance in her seat. The Adderall is obviously kicking in. At least she's not panicking.

She reaches into the pocket of her denim jacket that she shrugged on during the drive, and I see one of the cigarettes between her fingers. She puts it between her teeth as she grins at me, not lighting it yet.

"You're going to race them, aren't you?" she asks, excitement making her words a pitch higher than her usual tone.

I arch a brow her away, neck-and-neck with the Dodge. The air is cool and loud streaming through our windows, and, in the nighttime, the highway looks like a stretch of endless possibilities. A place where this doesn't have to be only a dream, a blip in time.

A place I can keep this girl beside me, her warm hand beneath mine.

"You want me to?"

Dom slaps his palms on either of our seats, sitting in the middle again in the back, and he says, "Fuck yeah she wants you to, don't you, E?"

"Do it," she says, speaking around the unlit cigarette. "You'll win, right?"

I roll my eyes. *Of course I'll fucking win.*

Sighing, gauging our speed—forty over the limit as is—I flash my lights, too.

Together, me and Orange drop down to the limit. We're going from a roll, because even I'm not rebellious enough to stop dead in the middle of a highway and race from a stop.

"Do you need me to move my hand?" Eden whispers, our eyes locking in the dark of the car for a split second. She snatches the cigarette from her mouth, clenched tight in her black painted fingers.

It would be easier, if she moved her hand.

But the feel of it beneath mine, remembering when we had sex in the car… "No," I tell her. "Do not move."

Her lips curve upward as she leans her head back against the seat, reaching for the hem of her skirt and pulling it up, over her calves, above her knees. Just enough to show me the lower half of her thighs, spread wide on my leather seats. It's sexy, with that fucking cigarette between her fingers, too.

My heart flutters, and a flush of warmth coils in my gut, but the Neon is honking its horn, a short sound. Once. Twice.

I'm ready on the third one, knowing they had the advantage because they're the one starting the race.

With my fingers over Eden's, we shift when I redline, once, then again, and even Dominic is quiet as we hear the turbo from the SRT-4 spooling over the growl of the Infiniti's engine, but it doesn't matter.

It's too late.

We're fifty over again, fucking *flying* down the highway, and no shitty American engine, turbo or not, is going to rocket them past me now, at least not for several long seconds.

Eden is laughing her head off, it's a beautiful fucking sound even if it is a little drugged, and she's beaming at me when I finally switch lanes and slow down enough, I won't get my car taken for street racing.

"That was too easy," Dominic says, but I hear the wonder in his voice.

"You try it sometime," I tell him, my eyes on his in the rearview.

He flips me the bird, but he's got a smile on his face, and he doesn't say anything else. I glance at Eden, winking at her. "There's a lighter in the console."

She runs her tongue over the underside of her top teeth, looking at me like she wants to fuck me. But after a moment, she puts the cigarette back in her mouth, grabs the lighter, sparks up, and starts to smoke in my car.

The hotel is in Acid City.

A middle-of-nowhere plot of Virginia probably haunted by sheer virtue of the fact there're very few live humans here. The Gore-Booth Hotel is set upon a hill, a sprawling building of white with a red roof. My engine whines as we head up, and up, and up, no headlights in the rear view, because I'm sure Jasper, as good as he may be with cars, isn't as fast I am.

"What do we think?" Eden asks. Her voice is soft, but I feel the tension of her fingers beneath my hand. She's leaned forward in her seat, taking in the circular driveway, a fountain in the center lit with a yellow glow, but not currently running. It's a little eerie.

She scans the four-story building, and I can see in her eyes she's imagining the two rooms she booked on the way here from her phone. Two, despite the fact I told her to get three.

"Three? That's... that's a waste of money."

I wanted to argue, considering I have a lot of money to waste, but I just shut my mouth and let her do what she wanted. We'll see how she feels about rooming with someone else, when the someone else in question isn't allowed to kiss her shoulder and put their hands on her tonight.

I grind my fingers against the wheel and decide to forgo the archway where the sliding glass doors beckon to the weakly lit lobby. I can't see much but pale yellow lighting beyond the doors, but we already have reservations, so I head to the back of the building, for customer parking.

Eden gasps in the seat beside me, yanking her hand from underneath mine.

"See a ghost?" I ask her, but my eyes are following her gaze, and I know what she sees.

It isn't a ghost.

"Holy fuck," Dom says, leaning closer between our seats, his head between them, and I smell the beer on his breath.

I reverse into a spot closer to the building, with its endless windows and a dingy, incidental aesthetic that probably only came about recently. I imagine this place, back in the day when it was still owned by the Anglo-Irish family it's named after—facts Eden read off to me as we drove—used to be beautiful.

It's like life, isn't it?

Always decaying.

And then... then we slip into death, like someone could slip over the cliffside the hotel is built along, the thing Eden and Dom are fixated by.

I cut the engine after I roll up the windows.

I don't get freaked out easily, but even after I scoop my keys from the console, I rest my hands in my lap, and don't get out of the car, my headlights still on, automatic until I shut my door on the way out.

The view is kind of sinister.

Fog descends over the drop. The darkness of the night and our angle obscure the valley from sight, but judging by the climb we did up this hill, a fall from here would be fatal. Turning my head to look at Eden, I see past her, instead. There's a white gate bisecting the parking lot from a low building I realize is an oblong pool house, and the pool is lit up even tonight, Halloween, a sparkling, clear blue out of place in the whites and grays and red of the building and the night.

"This place is already creepy," Dom murmurs, like he's lost some of his Adderall high.

"Let's go look," Eden says, and she's clicking her seatbelt off, letting it slip across her chest before she grabs the door and flings it open, cold air filtering to the interior of the car.

"How far will she go?" Dom asks in my ear, awe in his words.

He doesn't mean anything nefarious by it, but my skin crawls. I think of my mom's obsession with Greek mythology as I watch Eden cross the parking lot without looking back once, heading into the sliver of grass which separates her from the peril below.

Icarus, flew too close to the sun.

Then he drowned after falling from a great height.

There's no sun now, but as I open the door and get out of the car, too, I hear the rush of water somewhere far below.

I don't know why, but something propels me to jog toward her, keys in hand. She takes another step closer to the edge, her hair blowing behind her.

In her black skirt, the black cross painted on her jacket, with dark hair and sun kissed skin, it's almost hard to see her properly, like she blends in with the wildness of the landscape.

The hair on the back of my neck stands on end as I keep jogging to her, and she takes another step closer to the edge.

"Eden." It's a reflex, a kneejerk instinct to call out her name as my stomach cramps, watching her get so up close and personal with death.

She doesn't look at me, and she doesn't speak.

My heart races in my chest. *What're you thinking, Nightmare Girl?*

She says nothing, only tips her chin, looking *down*.

I'm thinking I want to jump, just to see how it feels.

"This is creepy, and we haven't even gone in yet," Dominic mutters somewhere behind me, but I don't look.

I don't come closer to Eden. I don't leave the pavement of the parking lot, even as her boots are planted over the soil, her fingers fisted in her skirt, raising it over her boots so she doesn't trip. Instead of moving toward her, I try to see what she sees.

My eyes take in the fog, thick with thin stretches of transparency. On the other side of the drop is another slope of a hill, rising up and up into the darkness. If there were people on the other side, I wouldn't see them. Nothing less than a large fire would draw our eyes to it.

The rushing water below the drop is loud, the feel and scent of fall—cool and lush—seems to press on me and Eden, even though I hear Dom's footsteps a few feet behind me, coming closer. I block him out. I block out everything but her.

I know she won't jump, but I wonder why she's thinking of it. Maybe just to experience the adrenaline, the fear, the realization life is finite. We know it to be true, but until you're staring it in the face, knowledge doesn't hold a candle to realization.

I think of Mom.

Sometimes, I feel as if I'm waiting for a letter, not from her, but about her. Telling me she died. Suicide. She couldn't bear the fact she left me.

It's the only way, I think, I could forgive her.

Don't make it that way for us, Eden.

She still doesn't turn around. I think about her fantasies of dying. *She'd rob it from me, if she jumped.*

I feel Dom's presence before I see him out of the corner of my eye. "I'm not getting any closer," he says, his words fast, but his voice low.

Eden doesn't acknowledge either one of us, but she's reaching for something, something inside her boot I realize as she bends down, her skirt long enough to cover her, but I still zero in on the curve of her ass, the fullness of her thighs.

A phone.

She's pulling out her phone.

I breathe a little easier, knowing she's just going to take a picture. She can remember this landscape in that way, without experiencing something more permanent here.

Tension loosens in my chest.

She holds up the phone, still gripping a fistful of her skirt in one hand, and I see the tiny image of the fog, the drop, the hill. It doesn't do it justice, but Eden takes a photo anyway. Then she turns her phone horizontal, wanting another shot, index finger over the capture button.

As I step off the paved lot, just one foot in the dirt, there's a small part of me wanting impossible things. To plant my hand along her spine and push. To let her free fall, but find her safe at the bottom, unharmed. I think of my car. My hand over her mouth and nose. The way she blacked out. *I protect you.*

Where is the line?

Where do I stop?

I freeze, afraid of myself getting close to her. We both stare out into the darkness of the fog, the void. There's a call here, tugging us closer, like a compulsion. Like the way I can never seem to keep my hands off of her.

Photos.

It's only photos.

Beside me, Dom makes a sound between a sigh and a laugh.

Then he's moving toward her, where I wouldn't, and I have this urge to go after them at the same time I simply stand still.

Impulse control.

He walks quietly up behind her, and she still doesn't turn toward us or say anything, taking more pictures, tilting her head this way and that, but never moving from the precarious position she has over the ledge. If she drops her skirt, takes half a step, she could trip. She could *die*.

Dom is closer, a foot from her now, six inches a second later.

He walks strangely, his khaki pants and white boat shoes easy to see his pace in the darkness. It's like he's creeping up on her.

I curl my fingers into fists.

Then he reaches her at the exact same time her name leaves my mouth again. An instinct, a reflex.

He lifts his hands, palms facing her, and plants them square over her shoulder blades.

My heart is pounding too fast in my chest, but… he doesn't shove her.

He only grabs her.

His body eclipses hers, but I hear her startled breath, her gasp of fear. I'm scared to move closer, like if I do, it'll taunt him.

"We used to play games," he says, loud enough for me to hear.

I think of his words last night. His memories about Winslet.

"Me, and my sister, and Eli."

I stare at his hands kneading Eden's shoulders, and over his own, I can see her still holding her phone up, but she isn't taking photos.

"Kind of like truth or dare, but there were never any truths. Winslet thought those were *boring.*" He glances at me over his shoulder. "And you too, didn't you?" He has a smile, and I force myself to return it. Slowly, he faces the cliff edge again, fingers still along Eden's shoulders. "They'd probably dare each other right over the edge of this cliff right now." He dips his head, his mouth over Eden's ear.

I take one silent step closer, in the dirt, away from the parking lot.

Eden says nothing. I wonder what she's thinking. Right

now, I can't hear her voice in my head. The only thing I hear is my fear, pulsing inside my brain.

Let go of her, let go, let go, let go.

I hold my breath.

Headlights sweep the parking lot behind us, casting the cliffside in light, for one split second.

It's a long way down.

Finally, *finally*, as Jasper cuts the engine to Janelle's car, Dominic releases Eden. He steps back, then turns on his heel, facing me.

He walks by, shoulder checking me as Eden turns around.

But I grab his wrist, gripping it so tight, I hear his small gasp of pain.

My mouth is by his ear, and we're facing opposite directions.

"I'll only give you so much allowance, for grief." I twist his wrist, and I can feel the tension in his body. The pain. "Don't touch her again."

46

Eden

I FEEL certain half of us will miss the ghosts.

Jasper and Janelle are sleeping back-to-back in one of the cramped beds of the red room. Red wallpaper, burgundy sheets, even the single lamp built into the wall casts a sickly, reddish glow around the thin gray carpet and tiny square unit.

The chain is on the door, the bathroom is divided by a wall only, with *no* door, and the TV is big and boxy, plopped on a dresser with the drawers glued shut.

Dominic looks as if he dove into the sheets of the bed on the opposite side of the nightstand between him and Jasper and Janelle.

His arms are askew by his side, head twisted toward the divider for the toilet, lips parted as he snores softly, rumpled sheets reaching to the middle of his back, his broad shoulders exposed, shirt on the floor.

He had a few drinks from the nearly empty vodka bottle on the nightstand someone thought to bring. Jasper and Janelle stayed sober, but it's late. Ten minutes until 3:33, when Luna insists we'll see ghosts, if this hotel really has any to offer. I have to agree with her. It's a holy hour.

According to a Google search we all did, the spirits exist on the stairwell and by the pool. It's not open for swimming; the bored check-in clerk told us when I showed her our reservations. I shouldn't have been able to rent a hotel room, but she didn't ask for ID.

I don't think she cared about much of anything except getting back to taking selfies of her long, white hair and shadowy eye makeup.

She had been doing just that when we walked through the doors of this place.

The entire hotel smells a little like the library.

Old.

Luna rakes a hand through her hair, staring at the cracked mirror above the sink that's so close to the toilet, you could brush your teeth while you pee.

"Ready?" she asks, her voice breathy from exhaustion. She partook in a lot of the vodka drinking, along with Dom.

Neither Eli nor I had any vodka from the little clear plastic cups that had been covered with plastic wrap beside the TV, presumably for ice, although we couldn't find the machine and couldn't be fucked enough to use the ancient phone beside the Bible on the nightstand to call for directions.

I turn to Eli, both of us standing by the wall beside the door.

Our arms are crossed, and I see in the red glow of the lamp, Eli's dark circles have darkened. I wonder when he last slept. Last night, he held me. He was sitting up. Did he drift off at all?

I nudge my elbow against his arm, admiring the way the white shirt he's wearing shows off the broadness of his shoulders, the muscles in his chest, and contrasts with his darkened olive skin.

I squeeze my thighs together, still in my skirt. Luna said she'd sleep with Dom, and I'm sure it means nothing more, but

I'm grateful Eli and I have the room next door alone tonight. I should've gotten three like he said, but it seemed like such a waste of money.

"Ready?" I ask him, echoing Luna's question.

He smiles, staring at me from the corner of his eye. "Yes."

"You two are honestly disgusting," Luna says, but there's nothing harmful in her words.

Eli's smile widens. I think of his cool distance from Dominic the past few hours, since we all came up here.

The cold in his demeanor is gone now Dom is asleep.

He drops his arms, offering me his hand.

I glance at it, then take it in mine, my heart jumping in my chest.

Luna unlatches the door, the metallic sound a little eerie in the otherwise quiet room.

The door creaks as she pulls it open, and Eli and I follow her out into the dark, narrow hallway.

It's quiet here, and I have no idea if there *are* other guests. There were a handful of cars in the parking lot besides ours, but they could be staff, or abandoned for all I know. Either way, on the fourth floor, it feels as if the three of us are the only people in the world.

I almost expect it's the end of it as we head toward the door at the end of the corridor. Like the apocalypse has come, and if we ran down to the lobby, the white-haired girl would be gone, Dom and Janelle and Jasper will have disappeared. I'll call home but have no signal, and no one would be there to answer anyway.

My skin feels sensitive, and I feel every hair on the back of my neck stand on end as we follow Luna in the dark. She kicked off her strappy heels for seamless beige slip-ons, and she's in jeans and a beige crop top instead of the dress she was wearing when we first arrived.

I grudgingly realize I like her. Beneath her snappy attitude, I think she really does care about Eli. It's why she accepted me. And maybe the knife ordeal is why she respects me.

Eli squeezes my hand.

Luna is clutching her phone and she glances over her shoulder at us as we get closer to the door. "Don't do anything sneaky," she says, gesturing toward us with one hand, waggling her fingers.

"We won't," I tell her, and I mean it.

I think of Dom scaring me at the drop. The way I scared myself too, long before he approached me.

Luna reaches the door first and waits for us to catch up. Then she presses her ear to it, like she's going to hear the specters beyond.

"Can you hear hell?" I ask her, smiling as she cuts her eyes to mine.

She backs away from the door and wraps her fingers around the silver handle, wrenching it open. It's a fire escape door, probably seeing little foot traffic. Most people are likely content to use the rickety elevators we took up to the fourth floor.

A gush of cold, stale air rushes out as we peer into the darkened stairwell.

There's another door directly opposite us, night sky beyond the pane of glass in it.

The stairwell itself is steep, leading to a landing, then another disappearing out of view.

For a moment, none of us move.

Then Eli says, in a flat voice, "We come in peace."

Luna looks at him, startled, and I wonder how often he made jokes with her and Dominic.

A laugh bubbles from my mouth before I can stop it.

I turn to him, his hand cool in mine.

He raises his brows. "What? I think they should know we don't mean any harm."

I roll my eyes and stand on my tiptoes as I lean into him, planting a kiss on the side of his face. I can feel his cheekbones lift with his smile.

"Disgusting," Luna says again, but there's amusement laced

in her words, too. "Come on. We'll walk down to the pool through here." She stifles a yawn with the back of her hand. "Then I'm going to bed, haunted or not."

Eli and I slip into the stairwell after her.

When the door thuds closed, it's a lot darker than it was, the orange lights flickering and buzzing, a sound I didn't hear in the hallway.

Luna has her arms folded over her chest, phone clutched in one hand as Eli and I follow her down the steps. "I don't like this," she says, although there's nothing much to dislike. I know what she means, though.

There's just a… *feeling.* It reminds me of seeing things. Paranoia twists in my gut, and I don't know if it's the Adderall I took or what, but my nerves feel raw.

"I feel as if we're wading through the Styx." Eli's musical voice is like a duster pilfering cobwebs. He knocks away all the bad, soothing me slightly.

"What?" Luna asks, looking back at him. A lock of auburn hair falls over her eyes, narrowed and confused. "Sticks?"

We keep walking and she turns back around to face the landing and head to the next stairwell as Eli starts speaking again.

"It's a river the Greek believed we crossed, to get to the underworld. The boundary between the living and the dead."

"Shut up, Eli," Luna mutters. "I don't want to see the dead. I've changed my mind."

I exchange a knowing glance with him, his green eyes darkened in here.

"Too late. Once Thanatos sends you along the river, you can't fight the tide."

Luna huffs. "It's all Greek to me."

"Did you just make a joke?" I ask.

Luna flips her middle finger at me over her shoulder without looking. She drops her hand, crossing her arms over her chest again, wobbling as she heads down the stairs, shoulders shifting with every step.

We're on the second floor, indicated by the lettering in black against a white placard over the door on the landing, when we hear something slam closed a few floors up.

Luna and I jump.

She flattens herself against the door of floor two, inching her fingers toward the silver handle as she peers up at the maze of stairs.

I press myself against Eli, who wraps his arms around my waist, my back to his chest. "What the fuck was that?" I whisper.

"It's almost as if this is a hotel," Eli says quietly behind me.

"Shut up," Luna and I both counter at the same time.

Eli's hand slides up my waist, over my chest, to my throat, resting along my cheek.

A shiver glides down my spine.

"What was that?" he whispers in my ear.

I bite my bottom lip, eyes on the stairs above us, but my heart is in my throat, my body growing flushed with heat.

I'm trying to pay attention to any footsteps, anyone heading downstairs like we are, but all I can give attention to is Eli's dick against my back, growing harder the longer we stand here.

"Let's just hurry up," Luna says, her voice tinged with nerves.

Eli brushes his thumb along my bottom lip. His tongue flicks over my piercings, and the cool air wicking against my skin in the aftermath has my knees feeling weak. "Yeah," he says, only for me to hear as Luna scurries down the stairs. "Let's hurry."

"Tell me more. About the underworld." There are no ghosts by the pool. Not exactly. But when I look to Eli, his knees to his chest, arms wrapped loosely around them, eyes on the bright blue water, the lights surrounding throwing shadows on the beautiful planes of his face, I see we were looking for something that was right here all along.

He has a faraway look.

He's not really here with my words, haunted by something long gone.

Luna is asleep.

Draped over a plastic pool chair, ankles crossed, mouth open, head tilted back and aimed toward the sky, phone in her lap.

It's too cold for me to sleep, but I think the vodka in Luna's veins helped her along when we didn't find anything dead come back to earth around the pool or in the pool house, doubling as a gym. We settled here, in our respective spots, and talked about nothing until Luna nodded off.

"I don't know much," Eli answers me.

I don't believe him.

"Why did you take that Adderall?" He changes subjects so fast, I feel as if he dunked me in the cool water.

I tested it with a finger when we first spilled out here, bursting with adrenaline, no more sounds from the stairwell, no phantoms, no devil, despite the hour. It was like pins and needles on my fingerprint.

My skirt is looped over my thighs, to my ankles, legs to my chest. My posture mirrors Eli, but our thoughts are snagging, tangling for dominance.

I tuck a lock of hair behind my ear, brushing my piercings, the metal cold in the night.

The valley of fog and rivers and danger is at our backs, beyond the wrought iron gate. I'm glad I got the photos.

I'm glad I didn't fall. Or jump. *The call of the void.*

I don't want to answer it right now.

"Why not?" I counter his question. "Did your mom teach you about Greek mythology?"

His jaw clenches when he hears the third word of my second question. His eyes don't lift from the pool. I trace the curve of his lips with my gaze, the tilt of his nose. The strong column of his throat, and the choker above the white collar of his shirt.

"Please." It's a prayer to someone who doesn't grant them. I'm a disciple to a god who doesn't believe in his own existence.

He blinks, long lashes fluttering in a boyish way, I don't understand how anyone could walk away from him.

I knock my elbow softly against his.

He doesn't look away from the pool, and I see the blue reflection of it in his eyes.

"Eli."

"I don't know how to talk about her."

The breath leaves my lungs. I wanted the truth. It feels heavier than I thought it would. My mouth is dry, and I think I should say something, to keep him talking, but it turns out, I don't have to.

"Sometimes I forget."

The emptiness of his words shreds at my heart like claws. He knows he's a god, after all. But benevolence is beneath him, and old, dangerous gods speak with quiet voices. If Eli wasn't always so indifferent, keeping his temper mostly in check, who knows what he could do?

"Sometimes I don't think of her at all. Then, sometimes, I do."

"How does it feel?" I ask softly. "When you do?"

His lips are pressed together.

I think, for a moment, he won't answer.

The ghosts are here. The ghosts have always been in you. They just traveled to Virginia with us. This place loses all its terror without you.

"I miss her. I hate her. I want to kill her. I never want to see her again." His tone is flat.

My heart aches. Blood is squeezed out from its chambers. His pain is mine, and I think of leaving next fall. I think of walking away.

I don't want to. Make this work, make this work, make this work.

You can't stay here. Get out. Get out. Get out.

"Do you ever..." I have to clear my throat. He's still as a

statue. A myth. A god. "Have you ever spoken to her? Since she left?"

His eyes darken. I have to force myself to stay exactly where I am. I forget about his strength, sometimes, until the smallest things remind me. "I don't want to talk about this."

It's a brake. Full stop.

A train coming to a screeching halt.

"Eli, I—"

He drags his gaze to me, and it looks wholly black. "Please," he says, but there's nothing pleading in the word. "I don't want to talk about her."

Fear, or something like it, wrapped in reverence and want and *need* forms a knot in my lungs. I don't want to, but I force myself to nod. "Okay," I whisper. *Okay.*

"Why do you flinch when I touch you?"

I don't want to talk about this. It's on the tip of my tongue, but I won't do that to him.

"Is it *him?*" Eli pushes. Giving me an out.

"I don't like the way skin feels on mine." It isn't really a lie.

Eli frowns.

"Suffocating," I try to explain. "I need… space to breathe."

He tilts his head, his gaze focused on me. "It isn't him?"

"Sometimes there isn't an origin story for horror." The words sound colder than I mean them to be.

His expression doesn't change as he watches me without blinking.

"You were killing animals before your mom left you."

He doesn't shy away from his own truths. But he studies me, eyes searching for a hint of something. Fear? Revulsion? A lie in my answer? "It doesn't bother you? The shit I've done?"

I don't look away from him. "No pets, remember?"

Neither of us smile. "Give me another reason," he says quietly.

"For?" I shift on my skirt, knowing the concrete is picking at it, but I couldn't move if I wanted to. My soul is tethered to his.

"For staying. Not running."

I don't need to think it through. I could talk about Shoreside. Nic. I could tell him all these things that don't matter. Obsession, wanting to be wanted, a need for attention, suspension. But they're not true.

There's only one true thing. "You. It's the only reason there is."

I don't really see him move. It's just, one moment we're sitting side by side, and the next, he's over me, his hands on either side of my head, mine dragging up my skirt for him as I let my knees fall to the side.

His mouth is over mine, then my face, my neck, his teeth scraping along my throat. One hand comes to his pants, he's undoing his belt, shoving down his boxers, my eyes are closed with the feel of his mouth everywhere, along my clavicle, back up.

"We're going to figure this out." His words are breathless. Hopeless. Sad, with the weight of them. A god fallen. Never a god at all. "You're not going to leave me." So painfully mortal it hurts. He grabs my knee, shoving it open, the muscles along my inner thigh stretched painfully, the pool just behind me. I inhale the chlorine, the scent of Eli, a cold and haunted fall night.

He lines up with my entrance, and dark green eyes are locked on mine. I don't know if he's waiting for me to speak, if he's waiting for anything at all, but it feels like a pause.

Like he wants a promise.

I circle my fingers around him, thick and hard beneath my hand, for a moment, I don't want to do this here, because I don't want Luna to see him like this, ever again.

But I know she's still sleeping, or she would've said something.

And thinking of her, of them, of his past and my present, something horrible slides under my skin as he stares at me while I stroke him, his bottom lip blanching from his teeth.

"Look at her," I whisper. All he would have to do is look up. *Just look up.*

He narrows his eyes. He knows what I'm telling him to do. "No."

"Look up. Last night, with Dom—"

He grabs my face, his chest pressed to mine as he leans down, his cock so, so close to where I'm aching for him. His lips move over my own when he speaks, his fingers digging into my jaw. "You want me to look up?" he whispers, his tone laced with taunting, possessiveness, something primal that makes my body flush with heat, with *wanting.*

He angles his hips.

I suck in a breath, moving my fingers from him, to me, spreading myself wide, like I could force him that way. "Fuck me, Eli."

"While I look at her?" He smiles, the devil in his eyes.

It doesn't hurt. It doesn't scare me. "Yes. *Yes.*"

A groan leaves his throat as he dips his head to kiss me, pulling my bottom lip hard enough to hurt at the same time he pushes against me, my fingers still there, between us. I moan, feeling him nudging me, and he says my name against my ear, turning my face away from him so he's speaking over my skin.

"This is only for me," he says, like a question.

He pushes and pushes, and he's inside of me, and I'm wrapping my legs around him, but I don't answer him, and it pisses him off.

I like it.

He likes it.

"Eden." He bites my ear, tugging hard. I arch my neck, my eyes flying open, and I can see the pool, upside down. *Right there. Inches below my head.*

I know he knows it, too, the way he moves his hand from my jaw to my throat, his fingers wrapping tight around me.

Fear flickers through my veins, *but I'm not afraid.*

They are not the same thing.

"Eden. Are you mine, or is this just a fucking game you play?" His words are low and throaty.

I move my hands from between us, my fingertips slick with me, and I swipe my fingers over his lips before I thread them through his hair, but my neck is still arched, exposed to him, tendrils of my hair falling into the pool.

I don't speak, taunting him without an answer, and he pulls out slowly, just to the tip, then he's slamming into me, our hips colliding with a sickening sound, my back scraping along the cement of the pool. I relish in the sting. "I know what you want to do." I lower my chin, meeting his dark gaze as his chest heaves between us.

"Yeah? And what do I want to do?" He fucks me softer, slower while he waits for an answer.

I tighten around him, gasping with the feel, then I pull his hair, lifting my head to stare at him. "Push me under." I think of all the shit he studied, on his computer. The words he whispered in my ear. *"Letting me control you? Your breathing, your whole fucking life?"*

His gaze flickers to the pool. The lust in his eyes is heavier than it would ever be looking at Luna, or anyone else. Maybe even me.

For a moment, we don't breathe, or move.

I'm stretched around him, his hips are melded to mine, and it's hard to breathe with the depth of him, with my pulse flickering beneath his hand and my heart held there, too.

But he seems to make a split-second decision. All at once, he's not just holding my throat, he's moving me by it. My jacket scrapes along the cement, my head hangs over the pool, my shoulder blades just off of it.

"You could get hurt," he says, like a question. Like he's torn.

And I don't know why, except I just have this *need* to do something drastic and rash and stupid, I say, *"If it's for you,* I want it. You could kill me, if you wanted."

There's a pause, broken by his jagged laugh.

Then his hand comes to my face, and he leans down close and whispers in my ear, *"Hold your fucking breath."*

Then he shoves me under.

The cold is the biggest shock.

His hand over my nose, my mouth, my eyes, it's the next. If he had held my throat, I could have lifted my head, or at least tried.

But I can't now.

I grip the back of his neck, one hand pressing against his chest as my entire body starts to tremble while he moves inside of me. It's so much worse than I thought it'd be. *Stupid, stupid girl. Playing with fucking fire.* He was right. I'm just... trying to be edgy, aren't I? The reality of death, it's more painful than I realized.

I protect you.

No.

He wants to drown me, so I can never break free. Come above the surface and realize *this isn't good for either of us.*

But I won't let him take the easy way out, showing me how bad it can be. How bad *he* can be.

I can be evil too. *I can hurt you back.*

I reach up with my fingers, straining my arm as I wrap my index and middle finger around his choker. I pull it as tight as I can, my face numb from the cold, my head dizzy without oxygen in my lungs. I bring my other hand to his face, scratching down it, over his eyes, his jawline. My body aches, fear settles in my bones, but I keep scratching, raking my nails over and over, pulling at his lips as I try my best to choke him, his fingers flexing over my face.

My limbs feel heavy, pins and needles, and I lift my hand, taking all the strength I feel I have left, and dragging my nails as deep into the side of his face as I can, feeling his skin curl up beneath my nails.

Something happens then.

His hand on my face slips. The pressure on my chest loosens. He pulls out of me.

I grab his throat with both hands and yank myself up, cold, crisp air freezing me to the bone as my hair drips down my back, soaking my jacket. A chill sets in, and I'm trembling, blinking chlorine from my eyes as I see he has a hand pressed to his face, fingers over his eye. His rings gleam in the lights around the pool. Red, jagged marks curl beneath his fingertips.

"*Fuck.*" He whispers the words. "What the *fuck*, Eden?"

I don't wait to do more than catch my breath for half a second.

Then, my gasps loud as I breathe, I tighten my hold on his neck and shift my body, pushing *him*, so he's on his back on the cement, one hand on my ass, my skirt flipped up over my back, the backs of my thighs freezing, my lips feel numb as cold water drips from my hair.

But I don't think about any of that.

I push on his chest as his fingertips press into my ass. He says nothing more, one eye still covered, but I slide my hands up to his throat, and he shifts willingly, his shoulder blades off the edge of the pool. I slap my hand over his face, and he drops his own hands to the ledge of the pool, gripping it tightly.

I shove him down, my fingertips swallowed by the icy water.

Bubbles pop to the surface, his eyes closed tight under the water, his body tense beneath me.

I can feel him, though, still hard, his cock against my stomach.

I hold him down with both hands.

His knuckles turn white as he grips the ledge.

I circle my fingers along his throat. My pulse roars in my head, power rushing in my veins.

He's completely still.

I feel his lips beneath my palm.

Seconds pass.

I glance up at Luna. She's still asleep.

I shift my hips, my underwear back in place, but I feel him all the same. I dry fuck him, although we're both soaked now.

I wonder if his cuts sting, where I scratched him.

Warmth fills my veins even as my teeth chatter, the more I rock over him, all my weight into my hands, along his throat, his head. *It feels good, owning him.*

I splay my fingers over his face. I see his long lashes. The circles beneath them.

I rock harder.

My breaths come in gasps. I have to move one hand down along his body, right over his chest. I lean into him, wanting to hurt him at the exact same time I want him to feel *good*.

He moves one hand from the ledge of the pool. He grabs my throat, pressing his thumb to the hollow of it. His fingertips are ice cold.

I can't breathe.

He can't either.

We're even.

I slap my palm over his chest, trying to crush him beneath me. Like if I can get him to stay here, stay small, stay beneath me, I can save him from the whole fucking world. We can hold our breath together, and we can live this way, underwater. Isolated.

I bite my lip, eyes fluttering closed, my head spinning from the lack of air, but I don't stop rocking against him. *How long can you stay under there, baby boy?*

He pinches his fingers around the sides of my neck, like he wants me to black out.

It's like fighting, the way we fuck to hurt each other. I want to break his ribs, just to curl against his heart. He wants to snap my neck, so I can't ever walk away.

Breaking me from my trance, he has both hands around my throat. He's using me to pull up, up, up, gasping for breath. My eyes fly open, and I see anger in his. Maybe a little fear, too, the way his entire body trembles.

Time seems to freeze for a moment, standing still as we shake.

His lips are parted as he gulps in air. His hands are still around my throat, mine at his. His face is drained of color. His lips are tinted blue.

He looks, for a blink, *terrified*.

Then his lips curve up.

A dimple flashes in his cheeks.

"Fuck. *You*," he says softly.

And my world is turned upside down as he rolls us over, plunging me into the cold again.

Eli

After this, I'll be good.

After this, I'll stop.

I know I don't mean it, watching her hair float around her in the water, drifting toward the surface, her face just under it, the water to my wrist, the position we're in making it easier for her to float upward.

But I keep her down.

She twists her head in my grip, and my hand is numb from the cold. I can only imagine how she feels.

I claw my nails over her chest, using her sternum to hold myself up. I run my fingers over her breasts, her nipples drawn tight. I squeeze, hard, and I feel her mouth open beneath my hand as I bruise her.

Smiling, I'm putting all my weight against her heart again.

I know it hurts because it hurt when she did it to me.

My face stings with her nails, and those scratches are going to take a few days to disappear. But the feeling of her pushing me under... it'll take a lot longer to shake off.

Anger burns through me. For a second, I was in the bathtub again. For a moment in time, she was Mom, and I was dying.

A snarl leaves my lips as I position myself between her again, pushing in, and it's like a relief. *A balm.*

She's not Mom.

She's mine, she's mine, she's mine. She'll never leave. She won't, she won't, she won't.

Her body is tense, her legs no longer wrapped around me, but her knees are still wide, and despite all of it, despite everything, she's so fucking wet. Her hands are dug into my skull, she's holding on.

For me.

Every time I drive into her, her back is jolted inches over the concrete, and I know it has to hurt.

I know, baby, I know.

This is the last time.

I promise.

I see the slender arch of her throat, her narrow shoulders off the edge of the pool, and she feels so fucking good and so fucking tight around me. A sound of something like need leaves my mouth without permission, and it's wasted, because she can't hear it.

I glance up, seeing Luna, still asleep.

I trail my eyes over her throat, too, the curve of her breasts, her narrow waist. I do exactly what Eden wanted me to, as I use her. Fuck her, drown her, lust after an old friend, all at the same time.

Is this how bad you want me to be, baby girl?

I'll be good, though. After. After. After.

I'm so sorry.

I'm not, though.

I'm not.

My chest aches, swelling and bursting, like I'm scratching an itch, like I'm free. Like I'm slipping off of a leash. Like I'm coming undone with her permission for my recklessness.

She doesn't try to cage me. She doesn't want me to fall in line.

To her detriment, she wants me to be exactly who I am.

My fingers are pressed along the bones of her cheeks, over her temple, her nose is beneath my palm, and if I pushed any harder, I could break it, with all the force over her face.

You wanted this.

You want to hurt for me.

You got me into this shit in the first place.

And it feels so fucking good.

I look down, dropping my head, seeing where we meet.

Watching my cock driving into her tight cunt, how spread open she is for me, the muscles pulled tight along her thick thighs, jostled with every thrust I make into her. I see the pink of her pussy, her lips stretched around my cock, the slickness of her on my skin.

I bite my lip so fucking hard, I split it, iron on my tongue, mingled with the taste of her when she ran her fingers over my face after she touched herself.

Fuck, I love you.

I love you, I love you, I love you.

I'm so close.

Her hands move from my head, to the back of my neck, then she's feeling blindly for my face. Her fingers find my eyes.

No, no, no.

You only need me.

You only need me, baby girl.

But I remember how it felt. *I remember the fucking terror.*

I circle her slender throat, and I lift her head. Just until I hear her gasping out loud, panting, her pulse pounding beneath my thumb over the hollow of her throat, chlorine infecting my senses, I don't look up.

I don't stop staring at where we meet, her body jolting every time our hips connect, my breath coming in shallow pants, sweat beading along my neck, rolling over the muscles around my spine.

"Do you want me to stop?" It's a jagged whisper. There's only one right answer.

And she gives it, swallowing down air. "No," she gasps.

"*No.*" Like she's fighting with herself. Like she hates me for wanting this. *She fucking hates me, doesn't she?* "Push me under. *Do it again. Push me fucking under, Eli.*"

I pause, lifting my eyes to her.

She's gripping the ledge, tendons in her neck flexed as she strains to keep herself above water. Her eyes are dark.

We stare at one another.

"Beg me."

Her lips press together. They're tinted blue. Then she says, "Hurt me like you want to hurt her."

An unwelcome heat infects my veins, my pulse pounding in my temples.

"If it makes you feel better, *since you can't fucking talk about it.*"

She has no idea. She doesn't know what happened to me, but her words are scarily apt. It's like our souls know every secret, no matter how black.

I grab her face. And I do what she said, pushing her back under as she takes a breath before she sinks below the surface.

I flex my fingers, clawing at the material of her clothes, feeling her breastbone under my hand.

I need to be more careful with you.

I know you're not her. You're not. Not even close.

You're so fucking precious.

But I can't be careful.

I don't know how.

I don't want to know.

This is love, this is love, this is love.

Her fingers rake down my face, over the scratches she already put there. I know she doesn't want to come up. She just wants to hurt me back.

Her body moves beneath me, her knees drawing up, closing toward my hips, but the angle makes it feel even better.

I don't stop.

I pick my head up, seeing her twist her face, but I'm latched onto her, and my hand just goes where she goes as bubbles leave her lips.

I feel my release tightening, and the longer I watch her struggle beneath me, not wanting up, just wanting to give me exactly what I want to see, the closer I get. Her fingers rake across my eyes.

They water, but then she dives for my choker. She twists it, and it cuts into my neck.

I don't care. Choke me, Eden. Make me feel it too. I don't care, I don't care, I don't care.

I can't breathe either, but only for a moment.

Her grip loosens.

I'm so close, and she feels so good around me. Everything feels perfect, just like this.

In the distance, I hear something.

I don't care.

It's just her. It's just me.

It's just us.

I haul her up, hearing the gasp of her breath, water dripping down her hair and cascading over her face as I shift us both back, never leaving her, and she's still gulping in air, her chest rising and falling as fast and as high as it can beneath my hand. I brush her wet hair from her eyes, staring into them as her lips are parted and she tries to catch her breath.

I don't stop.

"Fuck, you look so beautiful like this." With my handprint over her face, little halfmoons from my nails along either side of her cheekbones. I know I look much the same. *Like she owns me.*

But something else is in her wide, fearful eyes.

I don't stop.

Not even when I hear the creak of a gate. The thud as it closes.

I keep my hand along the side of her face, the other pressed into her sternum, and she lifts her arms up, resting them along the wet cement, elbows bent as she lets me have all of her without a fight.

"Thank you," I gasp out, dropping my temple to hers,

inhaling the chlorine, feeling the dampness, the cold of her skin, of her lips. "Thank you." A jagged sound leaves my lips and I'm coming, the release tightening every muscle of my body, every thought in my brain.

My eyes flutter closed, our noses together, my lips on hers, but we're not kissing.

"Eden," I whisper. *"Baby."*

I see stars. I see nothing. It's just us.

It's just us.

I stop moving, collapsing on top of her, my arms to either side of her, her chest heaving beneath mine, nearly crushed by the pressure of my hand.

My eyes close.

I feel her heart flying beneath my ear.

She doesn't touch me, still giving in. Whatever I want, whatever I need, she'd give it to me, wouldn't she?

I think of her twisting the choker along my neck.

I'm still buried inside of her.

I think about kids.

I feel sick, especially with the look she gives me now. Bulging eyes, rasping breaths, her lips are trembling. She's a fucking terrified mess.

My lips are parted, the material of her skirt stuck to the edge of them as I try to breathe, to get it out of my head, her shame.

My hands circle into fists.

I want to hit something. The good feeling from fucking her is so fleeting. It's like I need it again, and again, and again.

Her body starts to shake beneath me.

She's freezing, and she almost drowned, and she hurt me, too, she became *me*, and she's… *she's* with *me*. *This is what happens when someone is with me.*

I drag my palms along the concrete, feeling the pricks against my skin as I cup her arms beneath her wet jacket, goosebumps over every inch of her I touch.

Her heart feels as if it's tripping in her chest.

I don't pick my head up. I don't look at her.

"I'm here, Eden."

Her trembling is violent, and I squeeze my eyes shut. She doesn't speak. She doesn't touch me. A sound leaves her lips, between a sob and a scream.

I know. I know what it's like, being with me.

But I don't say that. Instead, what comes out is, *"You hurt me too."*

Her shaking worsens.

I can't keep lying on her.

I sit up, one hand still gripping her arm as I yank up my boxers and my pants with the other, still unbuttoned, belt undone, the skull and crossbones of my tattoo visible.

Her eyes are closed, her lips pressed together, her arms still limp at her sides. Her face is pale, save for my handprint edging along her jaw, her temple, her cheekbones.

Her lashes are clumped with water, thick and beautiful, her hair slicked away from her head.

Another sound leaves her lips, pale and blue.

I roll off of her, pulling her up into my arms, holding her close, her head pressed to my chest, her knees between mine, my legs extended and hers tucked underneath her. She's like a ragdoll, possessed with a vibrating fear.

"Eli." Her voice is muffled against my chest. She's not touching me. She's not reaching for anything. Her arms dangle at her sides.

I won't do it again.

"You wanted it," I say instead, more urgent, angrier. I kiss her head, tasting chlorine, feeling how cold she is. *"You fucking asked for it. Isn't this the shit you dream of? You should be thanking me."*

Her teeth are chattering, but I still hear her weak words. "Fuck you."

I tighten my hold along her back, lips to hair, eyes closed. "Yeah, fuck you too."

She doesn't stop shaking.

I hate this.

I hate me.
I hate her.
"You're not leaving me." She has to know.
I hold her so close, her face dampens my shirt, and it sticks to my skin.
"I don't care if you're scared. Don't leave me."
She laughs. It's jagged and wrong. My anger grows over my fear. I wrap my arm around her neck, forcing her to stay with me, forcing her body still.
"I always come inside of you," I tell her, my voice low. "I can make you stay."
She buries her head further against my chest. "Fuck you," she says again, her voice muffled and wavering.
I smile. I can't help it. Her trembling is growing less violent, less catastrophic. "I'll keep you." *Whether you like or not. I won't let you go.*
She doesn't say anything. Her shaking is still there, but *less*.
Say you'll stay. I'm happy with you, don't you know that? I'm fucking happy.
Nothing.
She says nothing.
I keep my aggressive hold on her, and I realize I'm rocking back and forth, too. I'm shaking too. Nervous energy, it doesn't have an outlet. I can't hurt her, I can't kill her, I can't let her go.
I hate this. It's your fault.
I take a breath, ready to beg if I have to. To say anything at all, anything she wants to hear, even if I don't mean it. But before I can speak, she does.
"Get off of me." Her words are low, still on my skin, against my chest. But she says it again, and it's so much louder, and so much angrier. *"Get. The fuck. Off of me!"* She pulls away, and I grab at her, but she shoves me, hard, then jabs her fingers into my throat.
I'm stunned enough to release her as she stands, backing away, dripping water all over the concrete. Her lips are still

tinted blue, her hair is soaked, dripping onto her shirt, and her teeth chatter, but it doesn't cool down her rage.

"Fuck you." She's pointing at me, her eyes narrowed, her face lined with anger. "You're fucking sick, you know that? *You are fucking sick.*"

Slowly, I get to my feet. This is better. I like she's yelling. *This is better.* I smile at her, and she takes another step back.

"It was *your* idea."

"I hate you." She steps closer this time, her movements frantic. It's like… it's like she's another person entirely. Like all this darkness suddenly came over her without a sound. A sign. Just… this. "*I. Fucking.* Hate you!" She points her finger against my chest, then she's shoving me, hard. There's nothing careful. Nothing gentle.

I don't know what to say. It's almost beautiful, watching her lose her mind.

"Do you want to kill me?" Her voice is ragged, just like her breaths as she balls her hands into fists at her side. "Is that it? *Do you want to fucking kill me, Eli?*"

I reach down, buttoning my pants, because they're about to fall off my hips, and it's not exactly warm out here.

She glances down, then shakes her head. "You only think with your dick. You only care about getting off. What the fuck is wrong with you, huh?"

I still don't speak.

Her eyes flash blue in the night. I don't see any other color. It's beautiful. It's terrifying. It reminds me of someone else. It reminds me of another time.

"DID YOU DO ANYTHING WITH HIM TODAY? DID YOU TAKE HIM *out? Did you let him swim? I mean, fuck, Arianna, what do you do all day?*"

I stop on the stairs, one hand curled against the railing.

My hair is damp from my shower, and it's just so hot *outside this* summer, I can never seem to take enough of them to stay clean enough for Mom.

"He doesn't like to do anything," she snaps, her voice edged with anger.

All day, she's done things. Picked weeds in the garden. Planted more flowers. Yoga outside, by the pool. I came to her mat, she snapped at me to get off. One single toe along it, an accident, and she hated me for it. I'm going to burn all of them tonight, rolled up and kept in the basement gym. Every. Fucking. One.

After that, she was on the phone. She paced the house. She wrote in her journal, and when I tried to ask her if she wanted to go on a walk, she said, "You're ten. Go by yourself."

"And what the fuck have you done, huh? I saw the photos you posted, you and Delilah." Her voice is a sneer.

Delilah. *I frown as I stand frozen on the stairs. It's Dad's secretary. Mom doesn't like her, but I'm not sure why.*

Dad sighs. "It was a work meeting. It wasn't just her and I, we were with—"

"She had her hand on your arm." Mom's voice is rising. "She calls you in the middle of the fucking night—"

"About cases, Arianna, you listen to my phone calls, you're right there *in the bedroom when I take them*—"

"She shouldn't be calling you after work. She shouldn't be fucking calling you, *Eric.*" She swears in Greek, and something shatters.

I flinch on the stairs, my pulse jumping.

There's a brief quiet. Then Dad asks, "Have you taken your medicine today?"

Mom laughs. It's hysterical. It's strange. It doesn't feel right. "Have I taken my medicine?" She parrots his words, like she's making fun of him. "You think we're both just insane, don't you? You think we're both defective? Do you ever think maybe something is wrong with you, too? Do you ever think maybe you're why we're this way, Eric? No, no, of course you don't. Of course you never think you do anything *wrong*—"

"Ari." *Dad is speaking low, trying to soothe her, I think.*

"Don't call me that. Do not call me that."

Something loud clatters on the floor. I hear pacing.

"Stop throwing things." Dad's voice is calm. "Our son is here."

Mom laughs again. So, so loud and bright and mean. She doesn't stop, for a long, long time. Then it sounds like she hits something, maybe her palms on the kitchen island. "Our son is here," she repeats Dad, and my stomach twists into knots, "and he is the worst thing you have ever done to me."

I GRAB HER WRISTS.

She's jerking away from me, screaming at me, I don't even know what she's saying.

I hear Luna, quiet at first, beneath the roar of Eden's words, Eden's eyes closed, her face red, her skin so, so cold.

"Eden, Eden, Eden." Luna gets louder, she comes closer.

I hear someone else, too. Janelle. "Leave her be." *When did she get here? The gate. The creak. Did she hear everything? See all of it?*

"Get off of me, get the fuck off of me." Eden lifts her knee, shoving it into my groin, and I tense up, releasing her as she spins away, raking her hands through her wet hair, messing up her braids. She turns her back on me, on Luna, who is wide eyed and fearful, looking from me, to Eden, and back again. I don't see Janelle. She's behind me, in the shadows.

"What happened?" Luna's voice is thick with sleep.

I take a breath, hunched over, but I don't speak.

"Eden... are you okay?" Janelle whispers the words.

Eden isn't screaming anymore, and I think maybe she's calm, but then she snarls, a vicious sound, and she kicks one of the lounge chairs.

It flips over onto its side.

She screams again, kicks another one. Then she bends down and grabs one, spinning her body as she tosses it into the pool where it makes a weak splash.

"Eden..." Luna sounds nervous. Scared.

But Eden's eyes, bright and so, so blue, like her rage has turned the shade of her irises, is staring at me. "I want to go home. I want to go home *now.*"

I smile at her. Luna's chest is rising and falling fast, and she doesn't know what to do. She's nervous. She's probably thinking of her parents. All of ours seem so fucked.

"We're not going home," I tell Eden.

This enrages her. She closes the space between us so fucking fast, and she's shoving me again, she's hitting at me, my chest, across my face.

Luna squeaks, but she does nothing.

Janelle calls Eden's name, but she doesn't move to help her. She thinks I deserve this, doesn't she?

I feel the sting of Eden's hit, but I don't care. I kind of like it.

"Take me home. *Right now.* You're going to drive me home *right fucking now!*" Her words are so fast and nonsensical, because I'm not taking her home, and it's just after three in the morning, and she's in shock or… or she's having some kind of episode like Mom or—

She slaps me again.

This one hurts.

There's a silence, after it.

Even she's quiet.

My face stings, and slowly, I bring my palm to my cheek, feeling hot skin beneath.

We're a foot apart. I could grab her if I wanted to. I could throw her in this fucking pool.

But I just say, hand still pressed to my face, "Let's go up and lie down, okay?"

Luna looks horrified, just beyond Eden, her arms held by her sides, her lips parted, eyes wide.

Eden is staring at the cement, water still slicing a trail down her shirt, dripping off the back of her denim jacket.

"Eden, baby." I drop my hand to my side and curl it into a fist.

She doesn't look up.

"Let's go up, okay?" I step closer, and Luna sucks in a breath, but I ignore her. My focus is wholly on Eden. "Come on. I'll help you get back to our room, let's lie down together." My face still stings, but I see tiny halfmoons by her eyes, from my hand on hers when I held her under.

We're even.

I watch the slender column of her throat roll as she swallows. Then, slowly, she nods. "Okay," she whispers.

I step closer.

She tips her head up, her blue eyes on mine. "Okay." Her brows pull together, and I think she's going to cry.

I reach for her, pulling her to my chest.

She flinches, but she lets me, and though she doesn't hug me back, she sobs against my heart.

I know what she's thinking. It's the same thing I'm thinking.

We'll probably kill each other before this is all over.

47

Eden

SEBASTIAN'S ROOM IS A MESS, and from the television speakers, the theme song for *Harry Potter* plays.

I kick aside a haphazard pile of laundry—probably dirty, based on the state of things—and he presses play, slunk down in the bean bag chair in the far corner of his room.

It smells faintly of weed in here, but I don't care. He texted me to come watch a movie with him, and twenty-four hours after fighting with Eli in the pool in Virginia, I don't want to be alone.

Janelle dropped me off this morning after a silent, too-long ride. Mom waved at Luna, in the front seat. Luna didn't get out, still hungover, maybe a little afraid of me. But that single wave from Luna back to Mom bought me more time to lie to my parents.

I just don't know if I want to anymore. I can still feel Eli's nail marks in my skin, and I wore makeup to cover them.

"You can take the bed." Seb's smile is wide, and as the TV flickers over his features, I see his eyes kind of look weird. Not red, like he's high. Something else. I don't know.

I cross his room in my Slytherin socks and grab a folded-up blanket from the foot of his bed as I settle against his pillows.

"Damn, it's been a minute since I've watched Potty." He starts laughing at his own joke. As I pull the beige blanket up to my chin, I'm laughing, too, but it doesn't feel real.

The movie starts, from the very beginning, and I'm grateful. The first two Harry Potter books and movies are child's play. Easy watching. Then the rest are like a downward plunge into hell or something, and I don't want anything heavy. It's hard for me to watch scary movies, or emotional ones. Sometimes I even avoid books like that. It seems to trigger my anxiety.

I try to focus on *The Sorcerer's Stone* even though my phone lights up under the blanket with texts from Janelle, Luna, and Amanda every so often. Janelle asked if I was okay and sent me a video I haven't watched, probably something funny. Luna asked if I needed a Xanax. Amanda allegedly wants to see me again.

But I feel exhausted just thinking of trying to open up to them, and Seb has his eyes glued to the screen and out of some sort of respect, I keep mine there, too. It's nice spending time with him like this.

But it doesn't last long.

When Harry's getting put on the spot by Snape in Potions, Sebastian seems to sort of... jump, in his chair. I hear the *swoosh* of the beans, and I startle a little as I turn to face him.

My blood runs cold.

He's staring straight up at the ceiling, the column of his throat exposed, his fingers digging into the sides of his chair.

It takes me a minute to catch my breath, to feel brave enough to speak in the dark. "Seb?"

He doesn't look at me. He's still got his neck elongated, chin up, eyes wide on the ceiling.

I glance upward, too, almost afraid I'll see something. But there's nothing but the flickering of the movie. My throat feels tight, my heart pounding hard in my chest. I grip my phone with clammy fingers as I look at my brother again, motionless.

"Seb?"

"Sometimes I hear shit at night." He turns to look at me, and I bite my cheek, waiting. "Do you hear it too?"

I don't know what to say. I'm worried if I say no, I'll upset him, and besides that, it might even be a lie. *I hear shit, too.* What the hell is wrong with us? Why did I explode in Virginia? Why did I *suggest* he should hold my head under water? What did I think was going to happen when he did? He'd be *nice* about it?

Did he murder Winslet? Did he watch her drown?

Sebastian blinks slowly at me, and fear is icy in my gut. He looks possessed. I'd like to think he's high, but I'm just not sure. I just don't know.

I take a deep breath and I answer with, "Yeah, you know. There's a lot of stuff going on in the trailer park." I laugh a little, to cut the tension.

Sebastian doesn't even smile. "Do you ever see God?"

There's a knot in my throat. *He's high, he's high, he's high… isn't he?*

Despite the words repeating in my head, I feel anxiety, deep in my stomach. Blooming and bleeding black into my veins. I start to think there's no hope for either of us. For Eli. For anyone. I start to spiral, in my thoughts.

I need to get back to my room.

"I'm tired, Seb." My voice shakes, and I worry I'm offending him, but I can't help it. I swing my legs off the bed after I push the blanket aside, and I stand on weak legs. "I think I'm gonna try to sleep. Maybe you should too, right?"

He doesn't even blink at me.

Fear runs its way down my spine.

As fast as I can without running, I go back to my room.

My brain.

My own hell.

Under the safety of my covers, I read another message from Luna.

Her: Seriously, are you okay? It didn't look good… whatever was happening with you two.

My heart races, and I close my eyes tight, not wanting to text her back. I feel strangely defensive of Eli, and I don't even know why.

But I can't stop thinking about it. His grip on my face. The way I felt out of control, and I didn't think he was in it, either.

I don't open my eyes.

"Do you ever see God?"

Sebastian's question echoes inside my head. I know it won't work. I know this can't be. The darkness is coming, and it's so quiet. I don't know why I exploded. I don't know why I came undone.

But I see a god when I close my eyes.

Dark green and hungry.

I see a god when he says my name.

When I speak his.

Do I ever see God?

I think I do.

I think I do.

But sometimes, I wonder if Winslet saw the same god too.

Eli and Eden's story continues in *OMINOUS: BOOK II.*

ACKNOWLEDGEMENTS

First thank you always goes to you, my readers. I've said it over and over, and I mean it. I have the best fucking readers in the world, and I will never take that for granted.

Thank you, too, to my husband. Without you, none of this would be possible. I fall for you more every day, and I have so much gratitude for the ways you let me be *me*. Not once have you tried to change me, and it's the best gift I could ask for: *freedom*.

Thank you to Liza James. Always and forever, until we die, we'll be obsessed. Your friendship is unlike anything I've ever had before. You're the light to my dark, and I don't think I'd be able to see without you.

Ashlee O'Brien, who designed this cover, makes my teasers, and listens to my rants, raves, and spending addictions… *thank you for being grumpy with me.* I like you, or whatever.

Christina. Thank you for reading every single version ever of this book. Thank you for your artistic talent. For being my shoulder to doubt on. For pushing me through to actually *finish this book*. For loving Eli, and Eden, even when I thought maybe this was all garbage. Thank you for believing in me.

Taylor. TAYLOR. Thank you for beta reading, but more than that, thank you for checking in when I really needed someone to. Thanks for always texting me when I'm barely hanging on. You mean more to me than you know.

Thank you to Abby for not only being my PA and beta reader, but encouraging me, listening to my too-long voice messages when I go on a tangent, etc, etc, etc. Thanks for keeping everything on track because my mind is a runaway train.

Thanks to Kandace for beta reading, but also for always coming in clutch with the life advice. I need it, you know that.

You're wise as hell, and I know you're probably just laughing at this, but it's so true.

Thank you to Amy for getting this shit done with me.

To Vanessa Veronica for continually supporting and checking in with me.

To anyone on my street team and ARC team, to CE Ricci, Elijah, LUNA, Jacqueline, Marie Ann, Kae, HM Brooks, Katie, Allegra, Quinn, "Gigi", Amy Jo Wilcox, May, Mia, Sum, Victoria Pauley, April, Sam, Stacey, Kristen, Brandilyn, Bluvsbook, Dani, and more. Everyone who has reached out to me, continually supported me, for *years* now, just… thank you so much. I really cannot express how much it means to me. To all of my newer readers, too, thank you for joining me on this crazy fucking ride.

If I missed you, I swear it's only because my brain is currently fucking mush.

And lastly… shout out to myself for getting through this monster of a book. Some days, I wasn't so sure it'd happen. Shit, some days, I wasn't sure I'd get through the damn day, let alone a book. So good job, K. *We fucking made it.*

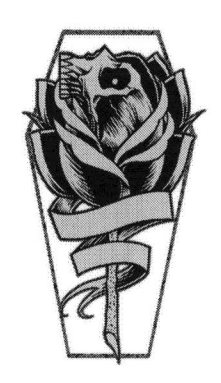

K.V. Rose is an author of dark romance and lover of the profane. You can find her on social media nearly everywhere at AuthorKVRose. She also hates talking about herself in third person, but this is the last sentence so, whatever.

pinterest.com/authorkvrose
instagram.com/authorkvrose
facebook.com/authorkvrose
authorkvrose.com
order of kv
spotify

Also by KV Rose

Ominous: Book II

Ecstasy

Unorthodox

Unsainted Series

These Monstrous Ties

Pray for Scars

The Cruelest Chaos

Boy of Ruin

Like Grim Death

Printed in Great Britain
by Amazon